The Promise Of You

A Small Town,

Lovers-To-Rivals-To-Lovers

Romance

BELLA RIVERS

ebook ISBN: 978-1-962627-02-3
print ISBN (couple cover): 978-1-962627-13-9
print ISBN (discreet cover): 978-1-962627-07-8

v5

Developmental editing: Angela James

Copyediting/Proofreading: Grace Wynter, The Writer's Station

Final Review: Teresa Beeman, Next Chapter Editing

Cover design: Echo Grayce, Wildheart Graphics

Contents

CHAPTER ONE

Chloe

B *reathe in, breathe out.*

    I got this.

I clench and unclench my hand around my leather back-pack-slash-laptop bag, and glance at my reflection in the mirrored walls of the office building. Nothing weird like greasy paper stuck to my four-inch heels or a pigeon dropping on my elegantly understated pantsuit.

I got this.

I deserve it.

I check my phone screen. Thirty minutes early.

My meditation app interrupts its ocean sounds to announce *Fiona wants to connect via video. Answer?* I've been dodging Mom's calls this morning because I don't need another one of her lectures on how I should live my life.

But my sister rarely calls, and when she does, it always brings a smile to my face. And it's always on video. A lightness spreads through me as I accept the call and her feisty face fills my screen.

"Hey, did Mom call you?" she asks point blank.

My chest tightens. "Why?"

"Uncle Kevin died."

I blow air as dull sadness over my uncle's passing replaces the tension I always feel where Mom is concerned. "Oh no." Images of my uncle's big belly trembling with his hearty laughter blur my vision. "How's she doing?"

"Not great. You know how she gets."

Yeah, I can just picture it. Mom sobbing, Dad mumbling, *'Another asshole gone.'*

Another lovely day in the Sullivan household.

"Funeral is next week. Think you can make it?"

"I'll make it." Uncle Kevin was a nice guy, and even if I haven't seen him or my aunt Dawn—or my cousins, for that matter—in what must be now over ten years, they hold a special place in my heart. And not only because summer vacations at their home in Vermont is one of my favorite childhood memories.

They were good people.

"How about you? Can you make it, or will you be touring?" I ask her.

"Nah, couple concerts got canceled." Her eyes shift to the side. "I'll try and make it."

"What's the holdup?" I ask.

"They're kinda behind on payments, and last-minute flights from Europe at this time of year are going to be through the roof. But it's Uncle Kevin. I'll make it work."

"D'you need money?"

"Nah, I said I'll make it work."

"I'll send you money."

"I don't want charity, Clo. It's annoying enough."

"Charity? Who's talking about charity? Consider it a loan. You can repay it by playing at my wedding."

"You have that kind of money sitting around?" She grins. "Damn. I wish I had my shit together the way you do."

"Um, hello? *You* are a rock star. I mean, how many people can actually say that?"

"I'm not a rock star. Just a rock musician. I think a lot of people call themselves that, these days."

"You write your own music, do your own thing."

"And am currently starving doing so."

I lower my voice and glance nervously around me. "Well, I'm up for a promotion," I whisper into the phone. A much-deserved, well-paid promotion that will be handed to me in exactly... twenty-two minutes. "I'm feeling generous. That okay?"

Through the video I can see her blushing. "Did you mention a wedding earlier? Did I miss something? Did he propose?"

I was wondering what took her so long. "Um... no. But I think this *promotion*"—I lower my voice again "is going to speed things along." I step away from the building's entrance and cross the street for more privacy.

Fiona narrows her eyebrows. "That's whacked, Clo. Although I will say, when a man marries a woman for her money, that could mean progress for the rest of us? Maybe?"

I chuckle, seeing where she's coming from. "To be honest, Tucker and me, we're going through a rough patch." I sigh. "Basically, he's saying I'm not spending enough time at home. I work too many weekends and evenings."

She tilts her head. "And this promotion is going to help how?"

"It's a move to a cushier department. More pay, less stress, less hours."

"Really." Doubt seeps from her tone.

It does sound counterintuitive, but there it is. It's a bigger job, one where I would have a large team working for me. After the initial few weeks or months settling in, I'll have more free time. I think.

"What's this job about?"

"It's..." I hesitate on how to best describe it to her in few words. Tucker hasn't asked me about it, and it's the first time I've had to explain it to a lay person. "It's financial analysis on the feasibility of opening new breweries." My new team will do the grunt work that requires travelling, as well as weekend and evening calls and meetings. If I play this right, I'll be able to wind down, put my mark on this department, and fix things with Tucker, all while having a job I think I'll love. A job that will feel more like I'm running my own thing. "Trust me, Fi, I got this."

"I trust you. You're a kick-ass boss woman, even if Tucker doesn't appreciate it."

Not this again. "Fi..."

"You know how I feel about him."

"I do." Fiona has made that clear. She's not a fan of my boyfriend. Moving on.

"And you wanting to marry him gives me anxiety, and the fact that Mom and Dad would be beyond themselves happy is further proof that something's seriously whacked when it comes to him."

I roll my eyes. "I gotta go, Fi. Wish me luck," I say and touch the four-leafed clover at my neck.

"Good luck in the elevator." She chuckles. "Here's to hoping it doesn't break down on you."

"Not funny," I answer, forcing a smile, my stomach clenching. I'm extremely uncomfortable in small, enclosed spaces, and my worst fear is to be stuck in an elevator. Not that it's ever happened to me, but Fiona teases me about that every chance she gets.

"Proud of ya, putting yourself through that shit twice a day for a career," she says before shutting down the connection.

Make that six times a day, what with lunch break or outside appointments, and the ride up and down to the apartment.

I quickly access my banking app to send her money for a flight, put my phone on silent, cross the street, and enter the building feeling awesome about myself.

❧

Thirty minutes later

Assholes.

I can't believe they're doing this to me. The voice sounds tinny, remote. *"New management is shifting our focus, Chloe. The whole department is let go. It's not just you. God, if it were me, we'd keep you."*

Crap. Crapcrapcrapcrapcrap.

"An uber competent, ambitious person like you won't have trouble finding a much better job elsewhere. Your severance package will give you all the time you need..."

I struggle to keep my composure. I remind them my plan could make the company millions in profit over the first three years.

These ignorant assholes don't seem to care.

I bite the inside of my cheeks until I taste blood.

I take no time packing all my stuff in the brand-new moving boxes provided by HR. They also thought of the packing tape. With a whole department let go the same day, they had to prepare. Make it as clean and quick as possible.

I take the emergency staircase down, avoiding the clusters of dejected colleagues all carrying the standard-issue box, lined up at the elevators. All cramming an already suffocating small space.

My fern is heavy. That bugger needs a lot of water. Which means, it's not only heavy, it's humid, and the humidity is seeping through the box. Add to that the fact that HR didn't extend the courtesy to provide bubble wrap, which means my photo frames clink against each other. I set my box on the sidewalk and schedule a car from my phone. I'm not carrying that stuff on the subway.

My next job, I'm not getting too comfortable until I'm the boss and no one can fire me. My next job, I don't want to deal with small spaces.

I haul myself and my belongings into the car; three and half years' worth of work and all I walk out with is this one little box.

On the upside, Tucker should be happy. I'm going to be home the next few days or weeks until I find the right job, not only for me, but for the two of us. I want our relationship to work, I really do, and I know I'm to blame for the dry spell we're in.

I lean over and ask the driver to swing by the mall and confirm that he'll wait outside, meter running.

The upside of being home is, I won't be so tired in the evenings. I wouldn't mind picking up the bedroom action where we left it off a few months ago. I mean, it's not like I'm fending him off. He's not showing any interest either. But with one of us to focus on that, we should be good.

So I charge through the mall and pick up a few necessities at Victoria's Secret. And on the way out, I stop at Whole Foods and grab fresh lobster, onions, and cream. I already have everything else I need to make Tucker's favorite dish. That and a bottle of Chardonnay and

I'm ready to go home. I'm not going to let a setback at work take over my whole life. It's midday. I have literally hours to prep a romantic dinner and an even more romantic evening.

Chloe Sullivan does not give up. She always gets what she wants.

Operation get-this-show-back-on-the-road has begun.

Fifteen minutes later

I press the elevator button with my elbow, balancing my box from work, the pink bag from Victoria's Secret jammed inside it, groceries precariously plopped on top, my backpack with my laptop, and the bottle of wine acting as a counterweight to all the shit I'm carrying in my arms.

The doors slowly open, then close on me. *Breathe in, breathe out.* Another elbow press on the panel, the elevator hiccups up, and I clench my jaw.

But I've hit rock bottom already this morning. I'm not getting stuck in the elevator now. The Law of Averages says so.

I get to my floor, no problem. See?

Steadying my box on my hip, I unlock our front door and enter the apartment backward, pushing the door open with my backpack, then letting it shut softly. I close my eyes.

I can do this. Being let go is not the end of the world.

For most people, Chloe, but for you? Pretty much is.

I turn the little voice off.

Reality is beginning to catch up with me, and I need to get a grip.

Eyes still closed, I focus on my breathing. On the smells.

There's a weird smell.

Something sweet. Flowery.

I open my eyes.

What.

The.

Fudge.

I kick my shoes off and set my stuff on the kitchen counter. I resist the urge to call Tucker to bitch about him lending our apartment as a fuckpad to his loser brother.

Whatever.

There's a bra on the back of the couch, a blouse on the floor, jeans on the coffee table, and the trail of shoes and underwear continues down the hallway.

To

our

Bedroom.

G-ross.

And really—*the nerve!*

I stomp down the carpeted hallway, dark except for a ray of light seeping from our half-open bedroom door. Not enough for me to see inside the room.

Plenty enough to hear.

The woman has her full volume on.

Come. On.

This is like a porno soundtrack, without the lounge music.

No music? The guy is lacking in the atmosphere department. I'll have to tell Tucker that. We'll have a good laugh.

Meanwhile, this is my place, and I need them out of here.

I'll clear my throat, knock on the door, push it open, say a few words, then retreat to the kitchen so they can leave decently—I hope. It'll be awkward but what the heck. Not *my* problem.

I'll have to wash the sheets. *That's* really annoying.

I'm getting pissed at Tucker now.

The woman picks up her moaning, and the guy grunts.

He grunts just like Tucker. Brothers, I guess.

God! I so do not want to be here right now. I train my eyes to the floor as I prepare to push the door wide open, not wanting to see anything. Still wanting to get them out of here right. Now.

But then the woman moans, "Oh, Tux... my god... Tux!"

My hand pushes the door, my eyes fly up to the bed, and the thump of my heartbeat covers the rest of their sex noises as I struggle to just stand there. To not collapse, or scream, under the humiliation.

The anger.

The shame.

I expect them to jump and grab the sheets to cover themselves and say something absurd like "It's not what you think," but they're so deep in it. And I'm so totally in the dark of the hallway, I go unnoticed.

I've lost all sense of touch, as if my skin were building a shield around me. There's a voice-over in my head making commentaries, helping me process what I'm seeing.

Tucker has his face snug between her legs. She's undulating under his mouth. They still have no clue they have an audience. At some point he lifts his face and says, "On your knees," and they end up both facing the oversized mirror on the side of the bed. I have a prime view of his narrow ass ramming into hers. Her face looks vaguely familiar, but she has one of those pretty blonde faces. Could be anyone.

Is she faking? He's not that *good.*

When I'm close to throwing up, I go back into the kitchen on wobbly knees, shove my box with my fern in the pantry, the pink lingerie bag and the brown grocery bag in the trash, and quietly leave the apartment, taking the emergency staircase down to the street, blood swooshing through my ears, my mouth dry, my eyes wet.

I walk the streets for hours, trying to quiet my heart. Trying to shut down the thoughts in my head. When did I start meaning so little to him that he could do… *that*? Why am I feeling dirty and ashamed? Like I did something wrong. Something to deserve that. God! This has to stop.

And why did I leave the apartment instead of yelling at them? I wish I'd had the guts to throw them both out. I don't like confrontation, and I always thought that made me a better person. Until now. My fingernails dig into the palms of my hands, forming pitiful little fists.

Eventually I end up at a coffee shop and wait until it's my usual time to come home. I don't have the energy for a fight. I'm too defeated.

We never have sex like that. He says he doesn't like going down, that it's gross. But he sure didn't mind going down on another woman. In our bedroom.

I guess I'm the problem.

And then there's the matter of losing my job.

My throat tight, I swallow my shame.

Eventually the sun dips over the buildings, and I walk into the apartment. Tucker is at his usual station on the couch, watching a game on TV, fully dressed, no trace of any woman. Not even a faint smell.

He looks so *normal*. Does this happen often? Like, regularly?

I sit on the armrest of the couch. His gaze cuts to me. "Hey," he greets me and looks back to the game.

I wipe my hands on my thighs. "Hey… So. I was here earlier," I say, struggling to keep my voice from trembling.

His face whitens. "*Why* were you here?"

I fight to control the quiver in my voice. "I *live* here." Again, I can't believe his nerve. Really? *Why* was I here? I stand from the armrest. "You have thirty minutes to pack your shit."

"Come on, Chloe. It's not what you think."

I knew it! I knew he'd use that stupid phrase.

"Tux? She calls you Tux. You need more details?"

He stays silent but still doesn't budge from the couch.

"Thirty minutes, Tucker. Get the hell out of here."

He doesn't bother looking at me. "It's my place, Chloe."

"What?"

"Lease is in my name."

A-hole. Crapcrapcrap. "I'll take it over," I say with way more confidence than I feel. Sure, I already pay two thirds of the rent because Tucker makes way less than I do. But paying the extra third will be a stretch, and then there's the matter of losing my job.

"No you're not. Like I said, it's my place. You can't find it in your heart to be cool about what happened, feel free to go."

"Cool about—" Is he effing nuts? I don't want to argue about the blonde in our bed. I can't believe he'd even—actually, yes, I can believe it. But I'm not leaning into the argument going that way, because I know what lies there: my responsibility. "You can't afford the place," I say instead. "Don't be a dick."

He stands and towers over me. "Gave you your chance, Chloe. You just burned it. Now *I'm* breaking up with you, and *you* got thirty minutes to get the hell outta *my* space." He plops back on the couch and adds, "Sick of your shit."

Sick of *my* shit?

What shit are we even talking about? Me working too much?

This argument hasn't even started yet, and I can see how useless it would be. There's nothing to discuss.

I cross my arms. "I'm going to need to rent a U-Haul. And I'll need time to pack. And it's already night."

He disappears into the bedroom and comes back with a duffel bag. "Move out by tomorrow night," he says before slamming the door on his way out.

My eyes well up. Three years together, the last six months not so great, but *this*? I never saw this coming. What did I miss? How can he just write me off like that? My vision blurs as I think back to the blonde. And here I was thinking he'd be proposing soon. What an *idiot*! I don't know if I'm more hurt or ashamed.

I shake myself out of my pity party and call my mom. I misjudged the situation, me, Tucker. Clearly, I missed so many things. I need to focus back on my family. Starting with Mom, who's just lost her brother.

She's shaken, and I hardly recognize her voice as she tries to quell her sobs. "I wish I'd seen him more often," she manages to say.

"They lived far away. Don't beat yourself up."

"Not that far. Anyway," she continues, forcing fake strength into her voice. "The funeral is next week. Do you think you can make it? Maybe Tucker too?" She likes Tucker, and so does Dad. He's everything they want in a son-in-law. Good family. Successful, even if he makes less than I do. It's only a matter of time for him to be fast-tracked by his father into a brilliant career.

Shame washes through me when I tell her what happened—the PG-13 version.

"Oh, honey." Is that disappointment in her tone? It can't be. She's probably sad for me or upset. "Boys will be boys. And men have needs. Are you sure he was getting what he needed at home?"

My toes curl. No, he clearly wasn't getting what he needed, or wanted. But is it entirely my fault? Really? And can't my own mother stand by my side, even if I'm to blame for Tucker straying?

Also—cheating? Is that something she would let Dad get away with?

And in our bed? Not that that matters.

God, I don't even know what to say to her.

My voice is unsteady when I ask her, "Um... do you know what day Uncle Kevin's funeral will be?" That's a safer conversation than discussing if my dreams of a blissful marriage were shattered by my callous boyfriend or by me being too self-centered.

"Next Monday. Daddy and I will be staying at the lake house. It's only an hour away from Kevin's. Why don't you go there right away, get yourself centered. Maybe see if Tucker will come to his senses and join you there. It's very romantic. I always loved it."

I didn't know Mom loved the house on Lake Champlain. It must be the recent loss of her brother that's making her sentimental. Dad and she bought the house fairly recently, and I'm not attached to it. But it'll be a perfect place to lick my wounds while I look for another job and another apartment. "Thanks, Mom." And no, I won't be asking Tucker to join me and reconsider.

"I'll text you the door code."

"Thanks."

"And talk to Tucker, honey."

"Bye, Mom."

Breathe in, breathe out.

I go to the bedroom and pack my clothes in suitcases. Then I make a mental inventory of all the things that are mine here, the things that made this apartment feel like a home—at least to me. I don't want to leave anything behind.

At least not objects.

My disillusionment can stay behind. Because really, what does it say about me that I just didn't see it coming? Didn't suspect anything was off? Dry spells happen, don't they? It shouldn't be anything else than just that—a spell.

The next day, after a few short hours of restless sleep on the couch, I buy packing supplies and rent a U-Haul, thankful my secondhand Honda Civic came with a hitch.

I'm on autopilot while I sort through three years of a life in common. The Moroccan carpet is definitely mine. The coffee table, too, and I'm not leaving it here, even if it's a nightmare to carry down the steps alone.

While I pack the rest, I try to shut down Mom's voice in my head. Try to ignore her questioning, but still it pops in my thoughts. What did I do wrong? Was working long hours to make a good living a wrong thing to do? Is being ambitious and driven wrong? Was it wrong to want it all? The career, the husband, and happiness to top it off?

It looks like it was. Because it's all gone now. Even our friends, I realize, are really all his.

Guess what, Chloe? It's time to let that go.

Driving out of the city, my nerves are raw. But it's only because of the trailer behind my car. Because thinking about Tucker as I glance in my rearview mirror before changing lanes, a sense of relief washes over me. It's over.

And what does that say about me?

On my way to the lake house, I stop by Aunt Dawn's. Her pain is fresh and raw, her house is full, and I feel awkward for only a minute. I haven't seen my aunt and uncle and my cousins since I was a teenager, and I feel guilty that these are the circumstances that bring me back to them. I used to spend time here a lot during the holidays and summer vacations. Somewhere during my teenage years, that stopped, and I'm not sure why.

I stay only long enough to hug them all, drink some apple cider, and be on my way. Aunt Dawn and my cousins Brendan, Daphne, and Phoebe are still in shock from their sudden loss. But their welcome is genuine, and I leave their home feeling their pain but also feeling the warmth of reconnecting with family.

I've missed that.

Then I'm alone at the lake house. I spend my days applying to jobs in a desperate, frantic, and therefore random manner. I spend my evenings drinking too much wine, alone.

I know, I know.

But this is temporary.

Mom and Dad and Fiona eventually get here, and the loneliness is replaced by some massive family tension.

"Did you talk to Tucker?" Mom asks for the umpteenth time as she's preparing a dip platter.

I throw my head in my hands and scratch my scalp. "What are you doing, honey?" Mom asks softly, seeing that I'm about to lose it but not seeing that it's over her reaction and not Tucker's effed-up behavior.

"Gonna catch up with Fi," I say, then go down the wooded path where Fiona disappeared.

I find her throwing stones in the lake. "Hey."

"Uncle Kevin is still dead. Shoulda stayed home, woulda saved you a load, woulda saved my nerves." She throws another pebble, watching it ricochet.

She's had the usual lecture about her looks—piercings, tattoos, and colored streaks in her hair. Nothing out of the ordinary, especially in her world. Why can't they see that? "Maybe there's a song in there," I say to try and lift her spirits.

A bitter chuckle escapes her lips. "Yeah, maybe." She turns to face me. "I'm too old for that shit, Clo. I don't think I'll ever bother coming back."

My heart constricts at her words, but I understand her, I really do. Still, I try. "They mean well."

"Mom and Dad treat you like shit, and you, of all people, should see that."

"They treat you just the same."

She turns her back to the lake to look at me. "Right, and I don't put up with it."

Right. "I just don't want the confrontation."

She closes the space between us to hug me tight. "I'm sorry that asshole hurt you. But I'm not sorry you broke up. Please tell me you're not getting back with him."

"Of course not," I reply without hesitation.

She settles her face in my neck. "Good," she mumbles on a last squeeze before letting me go and throwing stones in the water again. "How about the job hunt?"

"What about it?"

She shrugs. "How's it going?"

"Um... I been thinking."

She turns to face me, pebble in hand. Tilts her head and reads my mind. "Fuck no."

"I'm tired of working for strangers. I want to work for myself, and at this stage in my life, working for Dad is the closest I can get to that."

Fiona rolls her eyes dramatically. "UGH," she yells, her bark echoing on the hills. "*You* are your own woman. *You* don't need anyone. *You* are the kick ass person who inspires me daily."

She's right. No offense, but I am all that. So why do I hope against reason that working for my father is a good idea? "He's our dad. You don't get to choose your family."

"You won't change him, Chloe. And maybe he *will* show you more love and appreciation if you work for him. I really hope he does. But I'm not holding my breath. And, Chloe? I love you. I really do. I'm proud and fucking happy you're my sister. But my family? My family is my band. I hope you find that someday."

Something breaks inside me at her words. We exchange a long glance, defiance, and anger, and in the end love, so much love. When our eyes water, Fi turns back to throwing stones in the lake, while I go back up to the house.

"Rhonda is retiring at the end of the month," is my father's answer to my carefully worded opening about me having an interest in joining his firm.

"Rhonda is your receptionist," I answer stupidly.

"Start at the bottom, show your worth."

I take a deep breath. "I have an MBA, Dad. Maybe I can start at the bottom in an actual department? Or as Luther's assistant?" Luther is the CFO. Being his assistant would at least put me in the mix of things, get me acquainted with the business. I mean, surely Dad is thinking about a succession plan or just retirement down the road? I know there's time. I'm in no way thinking I should push him out the door. But look at Uncle Kevin. He died suddenly, and now they're scrambling to figure out who's going to run the restaurant in Emerald Creek.

Just that should give Dad pause.

"Darling, you don't know your place. If I hired you for one of them top jobs, guys would talk. Nobody cares about your fancy em-bee-ey. And, I'll have you know, a receptionist *is* important."

My toes curl in my shoes, and I can almost feel the hair raise on the back of my neck. There's no point arguing. Just like I did with Tucker, I shove the feelings away, and put a thick lid on them.

"I'm not sure that's right for me, Dad."

"Didn't think so, honey."

"What's with the U-Haul?" my cousin Brendan asks. Uncle Kevin has been laid to rest. Aunt Dawn and Mom face their grief together, both heavily medicated and slightly inebriated, which is not the best combination but the one that works right now. Brendan and I are sitting on the steps that lead to the wraparound porch of his parents' house. The reception is coming to an end, but despite the reason I'm here, I find peace. I don't want to go just yet.

Fi and I drove here in my car so we'd have some alone time before she flies back out, and so we don't have to spend another hour or so in a confined space with our parents. And yeah, I'm not dealing with unhooking and re-hooking the small trailer, so it's here with me.

"Broke up with my boyfriend."

"So you U-Haul your shit everywhere? That's kinda dramatic," Brendan says sweetly. He's always been nice in a quiet, mountain-man kind of way.

I count on my fingers. "I lost my apartment. I lost my job. I don't know where I'm going to end up. And I didn't have time to plan, what with Uncle Kevin passing."

"His timing was shit, I'll give you that," he manages to joke.

I place my hand on his forearm. "I'm really sorry about him, Brendan. I mean it. I'm sorry I didn't keep in touch more, but you guys mean a lot to me. If there's anything I can do, you know, just… I'm here." That's the kind of stupid thing I'm prone to say at a funeral. What the hell can I do now? "I can stay a few days and check in on Aunt Dawn while I'm at the lake house, you know. In case you need to go back to your cows or..." What does Brendan do again? Some real Vermonty stuff.

"Sheep," he volunteers with a smirk.

"Right. Sheep."

We fall silent for a while in the gentle glow of twilight.

"Actually, there might be something you could help with while you're here."

"Yeah? Great!"

"I don't know anything about restaurants," I say. After everyone left and Fiona got a ride to the airport, Brendan and I moved to the study, a dark paneled room with a legit desk, shelves with trophies, deep leather armchairs. Aunt Dawn is there, too, and Brendan's younger sisters Daphne and Phoebe. They see this as a business meeting.

"But you're a businesswoman, sweetheart," Aunt Dawn says. "A restaurant is just a business like any other. It's actually much simpler. Just a few employees. One location. Preparing dinner. How complicated can it get? I mean, you've managed whole departments. And your recent bump in the road is not on you."

She knows all this about me, and I haven't even stayed in touch? The warmth of her love spreads through me like sunshine. She continues her plea, but she's already won me over. How could I let her down? She needs someone to run the restaurant while they put it on the market. It needs to stay open for them to get the best price out of it. They believe that considering how well the restaurant is doing, it shouldn't take more than a few months to sell. I'll be paid a fair salary. And it'll add hands-on experience that would factor favorably on my resume. "There's a chef, right? No cooking involved on my end?"

She cackles. "Your uncle Kevin couldn't cook to save his life, bless his heart." The meds are definitely at work in the relaxed way she's dealing with all this, but she still has her wits about her. "It's just a numbers game, honey. I'm sure you'd have a lot of fun doing it while you get back on your feet."

I sometimes watch reruns of *Restaurant Disasters*. It doesn't look remotely fun. But I get what she's saying. And from what I know, the restaurant my uncle owned is a small, fine dining place with a stellar reputation. Not the stuff that draws audiences on TV.

I'll just be tucked away in the office, making sure bills are paid and remittances are posted.

"The restaurant lease comes with the cutest cottage, so you won't have to worry about finding a place to stay. It's adorable, and your uncle Kevin barely used it. It's all yours!"

I glance at Brendan, and see him nod, visibly relaxed.

"When do you want me to start?"

CHAPTER TWO

Justin

"What else d'you need, son?" my father asks, and I feel like a kid again. He interrupted the work he was doing on the fence with my younger brothers in order to select his best cheddar and ice cream himself and hand me twice the amount I need.

"That's it. I could have gotten it, Dad. You didn't need to stop workin—"

"'Course I did." He slaps me on the back, a big grin on his face. "Proud of everything you do for the community, son." He turns his side to me, looking to the pastures in the distance, the woods bordering them, the outbuildings he added over the years. "Can't say I don't miss you working on the farm. Hell, can't say I understand the appeal of owning a pub, but I'm proud of you no matter what."

I stay quiet, not knowing how to answer that. *No matter what* probably means *despite what you do*. Every time he tries to say something nice, doesn't matter how he phrases it, it always ends up stinging.

He finally breaks the charged silence. "How'd you think our boy is doing? He gonna win?"

By our boy, he means Christopher Wright, my best friend and Emerald Creek's baker. He's currently competing for *New England's Best Baker*, a TV show being shot in Boston. I drove him there a few days ago, and he sent me back for the last day of the show to get a bunch of stuff locally made in Emerald Creek. His cousin, Colton, and I split the work and are doing the rounds as fast as we can so we can get back to him this afternoon with all he needs for the last leg of the competition. Ice cream and cheddar from King Knoll's farm being two of the items he needs.

We're all proud of him and rooting for him. Dad is no exception. Emerald Creek takes care of its own. We're a small community in Northern Vermont, we attract a lot of tourists, and we need it to stay that way in order to survive and make a comfortable living in the most beautiful, secluded place on Earth.

Christopher's fame will help us do that.

"He's gonna win," I confirm, not knowing how but knowing it in my bones.

"Proud of that kid."

We're no longer kids, but in a sense, we'll always be to him. I just wish I could make Dad proud the way Chris does.

My next stop is Cassandra's store in town to pick up the garlic scapes she grows in her garden, and I asked her to bring for me. I knock on the door of her lingerie shop, feeling awkward about going in.

But she pulls me inside. "No customers yet," she says. "Wait here, I'll be right back." Before leaving the room, she turns around and adds, "Feel free to browse."

My feet stay firmly stuck to where she left me. I check out the sexy apparel displayed in frames against the exposed brick walls like works of art, and my dick approves. I chastise it back into dormancy, but fuck. Me. She has some real nice shit.

No way am I roaming through her hangers, though.

But tonight? Action. Tonight, back in Boston, I'm hitting the hotel bar and having a good time. Don't care if Colton is there, or if Christopher gets out early. I'm a proud one-night-stand guy, everyone knows that, and they better not give me shit for getting my rocks off tonight. Not after everything I'm doing for Christopher right now, including standing in a place full of frilly lingerie.

"See anything you like?" Cassandra's amused gaze meets mine. She's in her forties, attractive, single, and she has a reputation of being a little witchy. I see it now in the way she's looking at me.

"Nothing *not* to like," I answer.

"Mmm. Still no one special in your life?"

"Lots of special ladies in my life." I grin back.

"You'll eventually find out, less is more."

"I sure hope not," I say, chuckling and meaning it.

"We'll talk again when you meet the one," she replies, handing me a small cardboard box. "For now, here are your garlic scapes. More than enough, the freshest—gathered them right when you called, so two hours ago. Keep this upright, they're in a glass of water, and the whole thing is wrapped in a plastic bag."

"Thanks."

She sets her hand lightly on my forearm. "No. Thank *you*, Justin. Thank you for being such a good friend to Chris, the best."

I shuffle my feet. The hell is she getting all emotional about? "It's alright, pub is in good hands, I can—"

"No, no. You've been the best to him for years. You were exactly what he needed, and he knows it, but he doesn't know how to tell you. So this is me telling you thank you on his behalf. And on behalf of the whole community, for everything you do for us. Starting with your community dinners. They've been a game changer for a lot of people around here."

Alright now, woman's getting all mushy on me.

Gotta go.

"You're so focused on making everyone happy, you've lost sight of making yourself happy. So please, take a moment. Soon. Do something different. Look out for yourself. Do something selfish. *Please*."

Got a tall order of selfish stuff to do right about tonight, but I'm not discussing that *with her*, and *not here*.

"Yeah. I better get going."

"Justin," she orders, startling me. "You have to let the past go. You did nothing wrong. Stop punishing yourself."

Fuck. I knew it. Total witch. "I don't know what you're talking about," I lie, but her eyes hold mine longer than I care for before I finally find the strength to turn on my heels and leave, long strides taking me away from her store.

Colton is on his way back from the Henderson's farm with smoked trout, but still a ways away, so I have just enough time to swing by the pub, give my dog, Moose, a belly rub, check in with my chef, and swing into my office to sort my mail.

Giving Moose a belly rub was a good call. Always is.

Checking in with Shane, my chef, isn't the same as petting my dog, but on a different scale, it scores just about as high. Shane knows what he's doing, he's been trained to run things way more sophisticated than a pub in the middle of nowhere, and he enjoys the lack of pressure and the freedom I give him. That means he deals with whatever kitchen problems arise like the freaking adult he is, which is, believe it or not, rare enough in this industry to be noted as a bonus point.

Now, going through my mail was not a good call. My tenant's check was returned with insufficient funds. That's three times in as many months. Three months that the fine dining restaurant next door to my pub, located in the large building I own, has defaulted on their payment.

I should have broken the lease sooner. Should have found any excuse to drive this fucker out of town. People might say the bad blood between us is ancient history, but it doesn't feel that way to me.

He never should have been here in the first place.

Now I'm fucked.

He must have sent the check right before it happened. I heard he had a heart attack.

I can't decently break the lease of a new widow. Not until I know what her circumstances are, if this was her only source of income. I can't hold her responsible for the sins of her husband.

I hear Cassandra's voice in my head again, and I know being selfish is the voice of reason, but I'm at least going to give this widow a little time to get sorted before I ask for what's due to me.

This month is going to be tight. Not something I like. Another reason to look forward to tonight, before I go back to reality.

Hotel bars in big cities offer just the right amount of anonymity.

A place to hide and be a different person. A place where no one knows your name. A place where you can be totally yourself, or an entirely different person.

That's where I find the most interesting women. The most interesting experiences.

The only ones I allow myself.

Take tonight.

It's hot outside, a storm brewing, but cool inside. There's a food and beverage conference starting tomorrow at this hotel. No one knows anyone else yet.

I'm following Chris's show on my phone, but my intention is already set on the stunning woman with dark brown hair and blue eyes sitting at the end of the bar, legs crossed, her eyes fixed on her screen, earbuds in. She's chatting on her phone. She looks a little sad, closed off.

She's not looking for a hookup.

I like a challenge.

She frowns and taps her earbuds as the sound comes in and out of her phone. Purses her lips as her frustration mounts.

Man, she's sexy. She's wearing a tight skirt with a slit on the side and a sleeveless blouse. She dropped the matching jacket a while back, once she hit the midway mark on her Jack Daniels.

I can't wait for her call to be over.

I glance at Chris's live streamed show. He's doing good, but we're still far away from the ending, the judging.

It's going to be a long night. Colton is in the studio. They only allowed one guest per contestant, and I 'volunteered' to not go.

What can I do to get her to look up?

"What?" she cries into her screen, tapping her earbuds again.

"You need to get laid! Tonight!" the voice comes out of her phone, full volume.

Hallelujah.

CHAPTER THREE

Chloe

I t might be a numbers game, but I like to know the basics of the industry I'm going to be working in. So I booked myself a food conference in Boston that lasts several days and covers everything from finance to marketing to, well, food itself.

I left my U-Haul at Aunt Dawn's, drove back to Massachusetts, and now it's the night before the conference and I'm sitting at the hotel bar, on the phone with Fiona who's in her hotel room after another concert. It's already tomorrow for her, wherever she is.

We're trying to have a chat, but my earbuds keep going in and out of sync with the phone, and it's getting annoying. I should hang up, and I tell Fiona as much.

"You go, girl!" she says, then brings her face so close to her phone it looks distorted on my screen.

But I barely hear her when she adds, "You need to get laid! Tonight!" She has her screaming face on, but her voice sounds muted to me.

Oh crap. *Crapcrapcrap!*

I fumble with my phone, but it's too late. The damage is done. Everyone within a large earshot heard what Fiona thinks I should do with my night. The bartender jolts, and it's like everyone in the bar freezes to see what I'm going to say.

Including the hot-as-sin man sitting four stools down.

He's not dressed in the usual conference attire. Instead of a suit or dress pants and a blazer, he's wearing black jeans and black leather boots, and a dark cotton shirt with the sleeves rolled up to reveal muscular forearms, one of which is tattooed down to the back of his hand. Since I got here, I've been eying him—discreetly I hope—and I can't say that my mind didn't jump to him when Fiona blurted her now very public suggestion.

To my horror, his green eyes slice sideways to me, his mouth twitches, then he drops his gaze to my legs and takes a sip of his drink.

But before I can figure out what to do or say, his gaze flicks back in front of him.

He slams his glass on the counter. "Shit," he growls, jumps down from his stool and rounds the bar. I freeze as my eyes narrow on the bartender dropping a lime, holding a knife in one hand, his other hand gushing blood, the gash profound. "I'll call you back," I tell Fiona and hang up. Hot-as-sin is running the bartender's hand under water, then wrapping it in a rag that I hope is clean, then he leans through a door at the back and barks orders.

"Shouldn't we call 911?" I say when he gets back.

"Paramedics in a hotel bar isn't a good look."

The bartender nods his agreement.

A young guy comes out of the back, wearing a long white apron and a skull cap. He takes one look at the bartender's hand and winces. "Yeah, let's go."

The bartender seems to hesitate. From where I am, he's bleeding out. What is he thinking?

"I'll cover your shift, man," hot-as-sin slash awesome guy says, and it hits me.

The bartender needs his tips.

A discussion follows between the three about the floor manager being gone for the night, keys change hands, and codes are scribbled on paper napkins. Seemingly halfway satisfied, the bartender leaves with the prep cook for an urgent care place, and hot-as-sin is clipping a name tag that isn't his on the dark shirt that hugs his muscles in a way that should be illegal.

"D'you actually know what you're doing, or is bartending on a bucket list of yours?" I say in a voice that's way more assured than I'm feeling.

Fiona's comment notwithstanding, I've always been curious about guys the likes of him. The muscular guys who don't spend their days in an office. Chatting up the bartender is almost an expectation. Now's my chance to flirt with a guy like that.

His gaze drops quickly to my lips, and I wonder if he's still thinking about what Fiona said to me. He's probably judging my likelihood of going with one of the men who just walked in, all suited up.

"We're about to find out." He smirks with a chin tip to the group of men coming in.

The men order drinks I've never heard of, with modifications or specifications that sound only meant to make them look important—a twist, a dash of this, a splash of that—and he takes it all in stride.

For the next hour or two, the ambient music mixes with the rhythmic sound of ice shakers in the guy's long, muscular hands, the thud as he plops them open, the jingle of the expert pour in the iced glasses, the woosh of beer as he fills glasses.

He owns the length of the bar, here one second, there the next, pushing back his thick hair, flashing his boyish smile at patrons as he hands them their drinks, swiftly followed by their tabs. Women's eyes follow his every move. Men engage him in conversation, and he responds easily, all while serving a seemingly endless stream of people.

Finally a lull hits, and he leans toward me across the bar, his mouth twitching into a cocky smile. "How am I doing?"

I'm caught by the green in his eyes, and my core heats up. "Better than bucket list."

"Yeah?"

"Is this your day job, in real life?"

He pushes himself from the bar to run a tray of glasses through a small dishwasher. "Kind of."

I'm insanely curious about him now. "What brings you to Boston? Or are you from here?"

"I just had an inkling I'd be needed here, so I walked in."

I giggle. "So you're what—like an angel bartender?"

He cocks the most adorable slow grin. "I wouldn't say that."

"Well, you have the hair for it." And he does. Thick, dirty blond curls that frame his strong face, curl up his ears, slightly bunch at his collar.

Call for my hands to run through it.

"Shit." He chuckles and combs through his locks as if he could tame them. "Last person to call me an angel was my mom, and I didn't even like it then."

Ohmygod. Straight up adorable. There's nothing like a man who's all man and still brings up his mom without being a mama's boy.

I fiddle with my phone with unsteady fingers. Fiona's text messages echo her last words to me. "Get laid! That guy is so into you!" She had a glimpse of hot-as-sin in the background before he jumped to the other side of the bar.

And I considered it, I really did, until he chose to play savior of the day. Which I can't blame him for. Who doesn't like a guy who saves some stranger's day? But that doesn't help Fiona's mission, which was to get me laid.

And it's not like *I'm* going to proposition him. Not that there's anything wrong with a woman making the first move, but that's not what I need right now. Right now, if I'm engaging in anything with a guy, even if just for one night, he's going to have to work for it. I'm going to make sure I'm his priority.

Who am I kidding? This guy wouldn't possibly be into me. I'm wasting my time.

I pocket my phone and stifle a yawn. "I'm going to settle," I say, and watch his face fall.

He leaves his station across from me and takes purposeful steps to go dim the bar lights. "Last call!" he bellows across the bar as he gets back to standing across from me. He scans the room to see if anyone needs a last drink. Seeing no one, he scribbles something on a napkin and tucks it on the register's screen. He prints what I assume is my receipt, but then pulls cash from his pocket and stashes it in the register, which he locks before rounding the bar and ending up at my side.

"I need to settle," I say, pulling my credit card from my wallet.

"On me. As a thank you for keeping me company tonight."

My cheeks burn. "I didn't keep you company."

He takes two more steps that place him squarely in my space, and I can't say that I don't like it.

It actually feels really, really good to have all his attention. All six foot something, lean muscle, tousled hair, dancing green eyes, square jaw animated by a mischievous grin, focused solely on me.

And he says, in a soft and low rumble, "I was hoping to make small talk with you, get to know you a little, see if maybe you were on the same page with your friend as to what you should do with your night, but duty called." He extends a hand to a spot right above my shoulder and touches a strand of hair. Not tucking it behind my ear like he's trying to fix my appearance, not pulling on it like he's just an overgrown kid. No, he just touches it like it's the first time he's seen hair, and he's amazed by it. Like he can't believe his eyes and is calling his hands to the rescue. "And instead of leaving, or chatting with any of the other customers, you followed my every move with your gorgeous, deep-blue eyes, gave me a smile when I needed one, and just stayed there in my corner when I had no clue how many rules I was actually breaking for helping a guy in need and how much trouble I might get into."

I swallow with difficulty. And then I confess, "It was a real pleasure," as raw desire zings through me.

His voice is coarse as he says, "So... What are you doing with the rest of your night?" He extends a hand to me as if inviting me to dance. "And whatever it is, can I join you?"

He's pulling my leg. He has to be. "I... I was going to go to bed," I blurt out.

How did I think this could possibly mean "No thank you"?

"Perfect," he whispers, his eyes getting deliciously dark. "Let's go."

I straighten my spine. "That's... that's not what I meant," I stammer.

His face does the falling apart thing again, like it did when I asked to settle my bill, right before *he closed the whole bar to be with me.*

"How about I join you..." he starts.

My eyes bulge but my body... oh... my body is all in.

And maybe parts of my brain too.

"... in the elevator," he finishes with a smirk.

That's more like it. He *was* kidding. Or was he? But what would a guy like him possibly want with a girl like me?

The elevators are far down the hall. I'll have time for an executive session with myself on the way there. "Okay," I whisper, but stay glued to the bar stool.

"However, your friend has a point."

"Yeah?"

He takes my hand between his fingers, like he's afraid to break it, and with the pad of his thumb draws circles on my palm that send ripples of pleasure through my core, down to my toes, and back up to my scalp.

God. He has no right being that good with *just his fingers* being *just on my hands.*

"Nothing to lose," he adds.

My pride. My dignity. *A good night sleep, if he's a tool in bed.* Which I'm sure he's not, if whatever it is he's doing to my hand is anything to go by.

"I've never had complaints."

Shit. Is my face so expressive?

He chuckles, a bitter sound.

Then lets go of my hand as his face does the falling apart thing *again*.

And he walks out of the bar, long purposeful strides taking him toward the elevators, his hair like a halo, his shoulders rolling, his muscular frame filling the whole space by his mere presence.

I've never been with a man like him. Built like he works outside. Strong and confident.

This is a one-time opportunity, Chloe.

I jump down from the bar stool and run after him, my heels clack-clacking on the marble floors.

He doesn't turn around. He doesn't slow down. He just extends his hand, and I slip mine in, and he clasps it around and tugs me to him.

Panties on fire.

We stop at the bank of elevators. He doesn't hit the call button. "Look. I get it. It's not for everyone." He dips his head to look at me. "If we're going to sleep together, we're not doing this getting to know each other thing."

"No?" That's the weirdest thing.

"Nope. That's the whole point. Forget about everything you are. Everything other people think you are or think you ought to be."

That sounds *awesome*. "Okay, I'm in."

He flashes his beautiful smile at me. "Just like that? You sure?"

It's not just that he's hot as sin. There's the way he was looking at me at the bar, and the way he took charge when the bartender got hurt—and did it only to help him. And then there's the fact that when he looks at me, he doesn't just *look*. He engulfs me in his attention. And that he doesn't just *hold* my hand. He embraces my palm and fingers with reverence, in a soft and strong way that speaks of respect and desire at the same time. I tilt my head back at him. "You having second thoughts?"

He laughs. "Hell no."

His laughter is infectious, and I giggle like a teenager as he hits the call button.

"Rules," he says. "No names, no phone numbers."

What am I going to call him? "Okay," I whisper.

"And tomorrow, we're two strangers again."

Excitement courses through me, tamping down the tiny disappointment I feel. It'll really just be the one night, then. "'Kay."

The elevator dings and the doors swoosh open. Why is he doing this? My blood turns to ice as the obvious becomes clear to me. I pull my hand from his. "Wait."

He turns to me, blocking the door with his foot.

My heart hammers in my ribcage. "You're not cheating on your girlfriend, are you?"

His jaw sets, and he looks me straight in the eye. "I don't have a girlfriend. Never did, never will." The elevator doors slide back open.

"What? Why?"

He shrugs. The elevator doors bump against his foot again. He doesn't answer.

"Why not?" I try again.

"You ask as many questions as a six-year-old."

I gasp. "Are you divorced? Do you have a kid? Is that why you don't want a girlfriend?" That's it! That explains the no-girlfriend rule. Ohmygod he must make an *awesome* dad. My ovaries are in turmoil.

"Never been married, never will be, and certainly don't have a six-year-old. But my best friend does. And she's a handful. Asks almost as many questions as a certain young woman I just met."

He gives my hand a squeeze. "You're beginning to break the rules, here." *Are you in or not?*

I take a deep breath as I step in. This is good. This is going to be great.

I focus my gaze on his long, strong fingers as he bleeps his room card and hits the button for his floor.

Twenty. Holy shit. That's going to be a long ride.

But then he wraps his arm around my waist, pulls me to his side, and kisses my head. "You nervous?" he whispers.

"No."

"You're trembling."

"I hate elevators."

"You're a bundle of nerves. You sure it's the elevator?"

"Happens every time."

"Shit," he whispers. He turns me to face him and places my hand behind his neck. "Hang tight. I'm gonna change your mind about elevators."

His nape is corded and warm, his fabulous hair brushing against my knuckles as his face slowly tilts down to meet mine. Between the warmth of his body and his scent of spice and soap, I'm a melting mess. Taking hold of my free wrist in a firm grasp, he brings it up above my head, against the mirror, and growls as my breasts brush against him. He ropes his other arm around my waist to pull me tight against him, his whole, strong, warm body encapsulating me, begging me to surrender my need for control.

"You're safe with me," he says and brushes his full lips against mine, sending fire through my core. Needing more of him, and needing it now, I lift a leg and twine it behind his, and his hand on my back slides down to my ass to give me a lift. I give into my instincts and rub myself against his muscular thigh. God, it feels so good. "That's it, baby. I got you," he whisper-growls. "You can let go with me."

My tongue wets my lips, and a slow whimper forms in the back of my throat as he leans into me, his gaze narrowed on my mouth.

Nothing exists except the two of us, his desire throbbing against my belly, and our impending kiss.

Until the lights flicker and the cab hiccups and stops amidst the terrible sound of machinery going dead.

Then all I hear is faint beeping in the distance and the thump-thump-thump of my heart.

Darkness shrouds us, except for the emergency light.

He tilts his head up, giving it a few seconds. Then a few more. Then he gives me a quick squeeze to the waist and lets go of me to reach for the call button.

Everything around me starts to sway, nausea grips my stomach, and as my legs give out under me, I slump to the floor, my heart pumping to fly out of its cage. I close my eyes.

Breathe in. My mouth is like sandpaper.

Breathe out? I have no air.

I breathe in again. And again. Still no air.

Warmth spreads through my back as his voice echoes in my brain. "Hey, hey, hey. It's gonna be alright." He leans into my space, the warmth at my back registering as his hand stroking me. Two fingers gently pull my chin up. "Open your eyes. Come on. Please. We're gonna be alright. I'm here. Come on. Open your eyes. Clover..."

My eyes fly open at his use of the nickname my grandmother gave me.

His worried eyes are locked on mine. "Hey. Welcome back." His hand locks behind my nape, bringing our foreheads together. "You okay?" His voice sounds distant, unreal, but his breath on my mouth warms me.

Then he starts kneading my skull. Ohmygod. I've never felt anything like it. It's like his fingers know exactly how much pressure to add and where. The effects spread to my entire being.

It's divine.

Yes, I'm going to be okay. Just keep doing that.

After a while he moves to sit cross-legged on the floor, and I lose the connection to his hand. My breathing becomes more difficult. I lean my head against his chest, grabbing his shirt for purchase.

His voice rumbles softly under my ear. "Wow, wow, wow, come here." He lifts me and plops me on his lap, cradling me.

"I'm s—sorry," I whisper.

"Shhh." He rocks me in his arms, his warmth enveloping me, his scent of spice and soap comforting, his slow heartbeat a rhythm mine tries to emulate. He drops a kiss on my hair.

I relax, just a bit. Open my eyes and fix my gaze to the point where his shirt is open, revealing tattooed skin.

We're still in a tiny, locked space, suspended midair... oh god. *God.* I shut my eyes.

He gives my whole body a squeeze. "Hey, where'd your mind go just now."

I move my tongue in my mouth to try and get everything to work. "Here. It's right here," I croak.

"Okay then, let's talk about other things. Tell me about you."

CHAPTER FOUR

Justin

I say a thank-you prayer to a god I'm not sure I believe in. And then I hate myself for being thankful for someone's distress. But how else was I going to hold Clover totally abandoned in my arms?

I might be cocky and say that one-night stands are the best because you can be entirely yourself, I'm kidding myself. It's not true. The women are either self-conscious of their bodies, or they're trying to be who they're not, and often they're trying too hard to please me, when really all I'm after is actually a genuine connection. Something that would feel like a relationship, if I allowed myself to have one.

I never get that. We're playing roles. We obey the rules. It's fun for the hours it lasts, and then it ends, and then the game starts all over again.

Clover is different. I could tell immediately she was intrigued, attracted by the concept of not pretending to be someone we're not.

I wonder who she's pretending to be, out there? When she's not in my arms.

I feel more than see her eyes flutter open and snap my gaze back to her face. I trace the silver chain around her neck and follow it to her back until I find the clover pendant tucked under her blouse and slide it back to her front. "Can I call you Clover?"

"I thought we weren't doing the getting-to-know-each-other thing." Her voice is raspy.

"We're past that." We were past that the moment the elevator stopped.

The moment I broke my promise to keep her safe.

"I like it," she whispers. "Can we stick with it? I still want to sleep with you," she says in a begging tone that sends my dick on a murderous trail. She's all soft curves and softer skin, long legs, and full mouth. She's a wet dream come true. She runs her hand inside my shirt. "I want to see your tattoo," she says.

My voice a rasp, I answer, "Later, I promise." I'm not getting half naked in an elevator with her. Not only because of the cameras or the fact that this thing is going to spring back to life at any time. But because she deserves better than that.

"'Kay, you can call me Clover." Then she takes a deep breath. "You're the only person besides my sister who knows about my claustrophobia. And you're the first one to actually see it."

Shit. "Not even your parents?"

She shakes her head.

"Not even douchebag?"

She frowns, then chuckles as understanding hits her. "How do you know about Tucker?"

Tucker. His name is Tucker. "I thought you wanted no names."

"That's *his* name. What difference does it make to us?"

Us. The word hangs in our bubble, its weight everything I've always wanted. A connection, even if just for one night. She doesn't know it, but she's picking my heart apart already.

"I might break the nose of every Tucker I meet from here on out," I say, and she giggles again, and I smile back at her.

"So—what happened with douchebag?"

"How d'you know about him?"

"Your earbuds are shit."

A smile dances on her face. "They are." Then her eyes darken. "He cheated on me." She turns her gaze away from me and her body tenses. "I saw them. In our bed."

My jaw tightens "Fuck."

There's fire in her gaze. "Never going through that again. I'm getting your point. Although I should have seen it coming. I should have known. I should have done something earlier to fix our relationship. He fixed it for himself, I suppose. Got what he needed somewhere else."

Now I want to punch something. Someone. "Who put that shit in your brain?"

"Facts."

"Wasn't facts." She needs someone to build her back up. "I can tell you this. If you were mine, and we had hit problems, I'd take you on my lap, like how you are right now, and we'd talk it out. I'd take you on a long vacation, somewhere on the beach, somewhere sunny. Somewhere we could just be us again. I'd take you to dinner more often. Or dancing. I'd send flowers to your work. And if all that wasn't enough, I'd sign us up for couple's therapy. I'd do something, fucking *something*, to save us."

Her jaw slackens, and she arranges her body against mine, her ass flush against my raging boner.

"What if you didn't like having sex with me anymore? What if you wanted variety?"

Variety? A deep belly laugh escapes me. I have variety more than most guys, and that doesn't fill the void. My laugh strangles in my throat. "Douchebag didn't see the treasure he had in his bed, in his *life*, he can fuck a different woman every night or more, he's never gonna find what he needs." I have my reasons for not wanting a relationship, and I made peace with it. It doesn't mean I can't understand what it's about. What I'll never understand, is people who selfishly hurt others just to satisfy a basic need. It's easy enough to be forthcoming. Look at me right now. No harm.

She stays silent for a beat, and it's almost like I can see the wheels turning in her beautiful head. "You'd make a perfect boyfriend. A perfect life partner. We've already established you'd make a perfect father."

"We?" I laugh, trying to make light of what she's saying to me.

"Royal we," she answers without missing a beat. "We need to find you someone."

"Is that a royal *we* too? Or do I get a say?"

"I suppose you get a say."

"Then I say no. I'm fine just the way I am."

She tilts her head sideways. "You do look fine. Just the way you are. But do you have everything you need?"

"I have everything I need," I boop her nose, "especially right now."

Her lips purse adorably. "That's a cheap save. But I'll take it." She takes a deep breath. "I don't think I want to stay single, long term."

My chest tightens. "Would be a shame," I concede.

"But I'll choose better next time."

"Thought we'd already established that."

"Royal we?" she smiles.

"No. *Us* we." Warmth spreads through me as I capture the recognition in her features. "Tonight, it's just us. And from then on, you're staying away from assholes."

"I'll try."

Time to be arrogant. And truthful. "*We* are going to show you what a real man is like, and if you can get someone half as good, you should be all set. Royal *we.*"

She blinks several times and wraps the hand that was on her belly inside my shirt. "You already showed me what a real man is like. I know."

Something stirs deep inside me. "You haven't seen anything," I shoot back, trying to sound playful.

"Cocky."

"You have no idea."

She wiggles her ass against my dick again. "I think I do."

Then I can't resist it. I lean into her and take her mouth, bringing her up to me, and she gives me her tongue, and her whimpers, and her heavy breathing, and both her hands tied behind my neck. I explore her slowly, commit her taste to memory, breathe her in, drink her in. Enter her slowly, then harder, then nibble her lower lip as she digs her nails into my back and lifts her body to be flush against mine.

Fuck but she feels so good. So right. All this while we still have our clothes on, sitting in an elevator.

I break the kiss slowly, letting her come down gently from it, trailing kisses down her jaw, positioning her back into the nook of my elbow, one of her hands loosely around my neck, the other limp on her stomach, my other arm back under her knees.

Cradling her.

Committing to memory the feel of her body, of her entire being, nudged against me.

"Did something happen to you?" I ask to cool down the moment. And also because I desperately want to know, so I can help her better. "Were you stuck in a closed space before? An elevator?"

Her eyes latch onto mine. "Nope."

"Locked in the broom closet for being a bad girl?"

"Not literally," she answers, missing the humor in my tone.

I give her shoulder and her hip a soft squeeze that brings her tighter against me. "Tell me."

She takes a deep breath, her head rolling against my arm as she seems to look for answers somewhere on the elevator walls. Finally, she settles for a point on my shirt, and she starts worrying the button with her fingers. "Sometimes it feels like whatever I do, it's never good enough. Or worse, it's wrong. I try and try and try to please, to do the right thing, but I end up rejected anyway."

My heart clenches. "We're not talking about douchebag anymore, are we."

"No." The word barely comes out of her mouth.

My mind returns to my father's words earlier, and I measure how lucky I am to have a family who loves me unconditionally. Despite all my fuck ups. Despite how I let them down.

Despite how I don't deserve them.

How can anyone treat her the way they do? I don't get it. I feel anger and something else I can't quite identify taking ahold of me. "They don't deserve you," I say as I bend over to gently brush her lips with mine.

Chapter Five

Chloe

"They don't deserve you," he says as he leans in for the whisper of a kiss.

His words mean more to me than the fact that he's holding me in his arms, carrying me through the night, through my night. And that's already more than anyone—*anyone*—has ever done for me.

So when he says that they don't deserve me, instead of arguing like I normally would, I let it in. Hear it. Accept it for what it is—a measure of my value for this stranger, in this moment, just tonight.

The grip around my chest is no longer there. And god, I feel so good in his arms. Warm and safe and cherished.

"Are you comfortable?" I've been slouching on his legs for a while now, and he must be starting to feel stiff. "I'm feeling a little better, I could—"

His gives me a squeeze. "Stay here." His eyes are pleading. "Unless you don't want to," he adds and starts moving.

I shoot my arm up his neck. "No. I like it here."

He dips his face to mine. "I like you here too."

My mouth opens, our breaths mingle again.

He closes his eyes. Rubs our noses together.

"Your turn," I say softly against his mouth. "Why no girlfriend? Why the one-nights only?"

"I love women, don't want the heartbreak."

I try to ignore the plural, *women*, to focus on what's important to him. "What heartbreak?"

"Losing someone."

"So you had a bad breakup," I prompt him. He's not getting away with it so easily, not after what I shared with him. Not after how he talked to me about it.

"No. I caused heartbreak to my brother. He never recovered."

My heart thumps hard in my chest, and it's for him this time. How did he cause heartbreak to his brother? "Wh-what happened?"

He shakes his head. "Long story."

I look around. It's still dark, there's no voices or sound of anyone trying to fix anything yet. "We have all night."

He huffs an exhale. "I'm not sure where to start."

"Let's start with the girl. Who was she?"

He tilts his head back against the faux wood panel. "Her name was Audrey. She was very pretty, and she was very much into my brother." His voice is low and almost remote.

"Younger or older? Your brother."

"Older brother."

"How old was Audrey?"

"His age."

"So older than you."

"Right."

"How old was everyone? I need context."

He shuts his eyes and shakes his head with a chuckle. "You're worse than Skye," he says.

"Your friend's six-year-old?"

"Right."

"'Kay, back to Audrey. How old was she?"

"She was twenty-one, my brother was twenty-one, I was eighteen."

A very pretty twenty-one-year-old who was into his brother. How does hot-as-sin fit into that? "Keep going."

"We were at this party... and... I saw her crying in the corner... and I offered her a ride home." His voice breaks a little. "That's it."

That's it? "What happened?"

His gaze flutters around the elevator before settling on mine. "We got into a car accident."

Oh crap. "She didn't make it," I whisper, hoping he'll have another answer.

He shakes his head.

I want to ask him about the accident, what happened exactly, but I'm afraid of what I'll hear. Maybe he was intoxicated? Maybe he was just too inexperienced and made a fatal mistake? "And you were driving," is all I volunteer, just to make sure I got the basic facts right. The root cause of his guilt.

"Yup. Got hit. Couldn't get her out of the car soon enough. Car caught up in flames. I tried." His jaw clenches, the muscles rolling as he grinds his teeth.

I nudge my head against his chest and rock us back and forth. He leans over me to hold me tighter, and his arms crush me. His whole body is trembling, just like mine was before.

Two messed up people clinging to each other in a dark box suspended in midair.

We could be having sex right now.

I'll take this instead, any day. With him, I'll take this. This connection, this understanding. It's more than I ever had with Tucker.

It could be because we'll never see each other again.

Or it could be because of him. Of us.

I go over what he told me about the girl and the accident. He probably heard a thousand times that he wasn't to blame. But I get it. He has survivor's guilt. "Where does your brother fit into all this?"

"She was with him. I had no business driving her home."

"But you found her—"

"I had no business doing that," he bites.

Screw that. "You said you found her crying..."

"And I took advantage."

More like, *came to the rescue.* "I bet it didn't take much convincing for Audrey to get into your car."

"I was always trying to one-up him."

"So what? Seems like what any little brother would do."

"It was selfish."

"You were *eighteen*. You saw your chance to hook up with a beautiful twenty-one-year-old girl. I bet you already had game, back then."

A sad smile shadows his face. "I saw her crying at the party, my brother nowhere to be found, and I saw my chance. I offered her my shoulder to cry on. Then I danced with her. Then I took her home, hoping to get lucky."

"I don't think she was *that* into him anymore." It's obvious to me his brother had just broken up with her.

"Doesn't matter. She died, and the next day he enlisted."

My throat tightens. His loss, his misplaced guilt, all that he's bottled up. He has it way worse than I do. What could I possibly say or do right now, right here, to help him through this? "Maybe it's time to let all that go," I offer.

His soulful eyes meet mine, gutting me. "Yeah, maybe. Some-day." He shuffles his legs. "Looks like we're in this for a while. You cold?"

"No. But I should get off you." I start to wiggle, but his arms keep me right where I am.

"Not if I can help it." Lifting himself on his heels, he slides us to the corner of the elevator and arranges me so I'm stretched out on him, my back to his muscular chest, his legs stretched under mine, his arms encapsulating me, my head leaned back against his throat, his chin on top of my head. His heartbeat is slow and steady, and his voices rumbles into my own chest when he asks, "Comfortable?"

"Never been better," I whisper and close my eyes.

A flutter of lights blink on and off, waking me with a start. My eyes lock onto dark fabric, I register the inebriating smell of spice and soap, and I latch onto the arm holding me tight. I push myself up on him, and he lets me.

He blinks. "Did you get some rest?" He chases a stray hair out of my mouth and traces my cheek with his knuckles. Not '*Hey, power's back.*' Not, '*Finally!*' No. He wants to know if I got some rest.

"I did." I push myself off his chest and smooth his shirt. "You?"

His gaze roams my face, and his voice comes out raw when he says, "Best night of my life, Clover." He doesn't say it like it's a joke.

He means it.

"Me too," I whisper.

We should probably stand and get ready for the elevator to start, so I get up and hold the handrail while he stands and stretches. He puts his key card against the elevator panel, but nothing happens.

I take a shaky breath, needing to say what's on my chest before the night gets away from us. "If we don't get to sleep together. As in, you know..."

He takes my waist in his hands and brings me to him. "Still the best night of my life. By far."

"Yeah, me too." I swallow, a lump forming in my throat. "Umm... if we don't, you know.... Does your rule still stand? The no names thing. The never seeing each other again. We could be just friends?"

He turns to face me, rakes his fingers in my hair as if he's combing it, and this time he tucks it behind my ears and smooths it continuously, like a nervous tick. Like he's thinking things through. "I could never be just friends with you." With both his hands behind my nape, he brings me up to him and takes my mouth in his, a slow, soft, sad kiss. I strive to keep my eyes open, to commit him to memory. His eyelids are shut tight like someone who wants to—needs to—bottle everything up. Then he lets go of my mouth and holds me tight in his arms. "Never told anyone what I told you tonight. I want you to carry this for me. But I can't be anything more. Can you give me that?"

I hold in my tears. "Of course."

"One more thing," he adds with a smirk. "No more assholes. Promise me."

I force a chuckle. "Promise."

Seeming satisfied, he tries the key card again, and this time it bleeps.

His hand freezes on the panel. "I don't want to presume... it'd be understandable if you wanted to rest... you know. We already spent half the night together," he whispers, the tickle of his mouth against my temple sending delicious shivers down my spine. "What do you want from the other half?" He sets his chin on the top of my head. His heartbeat drums against my core.

I tilt my face up to meet his eyes, now clear green in the bright light. My mouth goes dry. "I want more. I want everything. I want all of you."

CHAPTER SIX

Chloe

His room has the same layout as mine, but flipped. It's a nondescript, middle-of-the-line chain hotel room, and it should feel sterile and temporary, but it doesn't.

Maybe it's because he's been here a few days. There's a pair of jeans on a chair, running shoes in a corner, and a travel bag shoved under the writing desk. And the shape of his head on one of the pillows. And his subtle, manly scent floating.

Or maybe it's because we have a few hours to ourselves, a few hours to be us, here. Like one lifetime encapsulated in another, in this space.

I'm tempted to push him on the topic of not seeing each other after tonight.

But he's right. I'm myself only because I won't see him again. I can let go. He's giving me this amazing gift, and I'm going to enjoy it. I kick my shoes off and put my phone on silent as he hands me a bottle of water. I take a long gulp. Then another. I was parched.

"Better?" he asks, his face gentle and caring, making my heart skip a beat.

I give him a smile and slip into the bathroom first. When I come out, he has the lights dimmed, his stray clothes stored away, the pillow fluffed, and music seeping out of somewhere.

He slips into the bathroom and comes out of it barefoot and hair half-tamed like he might have tried to run wet fingers through it.

"Where were we, earlier? Before we got all deep into our shit," he growls as he pulls me into him.

My core warms. *You had me pinned between the wall and your hard body, my wrist in your strong hand, and I had my other hand around your neck.* "You were going to change my mind about elevators."

His gaze turns molten. "Totally messed that one up," he mumbles.

Totally *did not* mess up. But before I can argue with him, he seals his mouth to mine and wraps his hands around my waist, up my back, in my hair. His tongue takes my mouth without asking, and I let him, my body pressed against him, begging for more. He finds the top button of my blouse and opens it without breaking the kiss, sliding his hand inside, letting out a low growl when his fingers find my nipple.

A moan escapes me, desire zinging down to my center. I reach between us to undo the rest of my buttons and wiggle out of my blouse, letting it plummet to the desk. He pulls away from me a bit, his eyes widening as he looks at my chest like it's the most beautiful thing ever. He's so in awe of my body it's intimidating, and I fleetingly wonder if he's so enthralled with every woman. If he's into women as a collector would be.

I open his shirt, button after button, down to his navel, and push it off his arms, letting it gently fall to the floor. I trail the designs on his skin with the tip of my fingers—leaves and tree bark and animals—and shiver as the uneven surface under the ink tells the story of the wound on his soul. The red, tortured scars of his skin, turned into a work of art.

His pain a secret hiding behind ink.

I trace the shapes covering his tormented skin with my tongue, committing them to memory. Then I press my lips to the center spot, untouched, unscarred, and naked of ink, feeling his heartbeat right under my kiss.

He gently presses my face deeper into him, and I feel his heartbeat pick up and his chest rumble when he says, "I want to make love to you, Clover."

Isn't that what we're doing?

"I'll fuck you later, but right now, I *need* to make love to you. Do you get me?"

I lift my face to his and twine my hands around his neck, then nod silently.

"Good, 'cause I'm not sure I get it myself."

He wraps my legs around his hips and sets us softly on the bed, then carefully takes off every piece of my remaining clothing, one after the other, kissing every square inch of skin he bares. My eyes are glued to his washboard abs, to the intricate tattoo that starts on his left side and covers half his torso and his left arm, all the way to his wrist.

I might just come from the sight of him, so I close my eyes.

My body hums under his kisses, my back arching into his touch, his lips, the feather licks he deposits everywhere.

At some point he got rid of his clothes, and he's down to his briefs.

And that won't do. I trail my fingers along his erect shape, stopping him from kissing my neck. His eyes lock with mine. He hisses. I snake my hand inside his briefs. More hissing. I stroke his long, wide cock and lick my lips.

He kicks off his briefs. "Fuck, Clover." He grabs a condom from somewhere and sheathes himself. Then he slips into me, slow and gentle, adjusting himself to the sound of my breathing, to the tiny signs my body gives him of how good he feels inside me. His eyes barely leave mine, only to trail sideways to my temple before kissing me there, or down to my mouth to take it in his.

I wrap my legs around his waist, tight, and pull him in. Run my hands up and down his back, my back arching into him.

He drops his head to my neck. "Clover," he breathes, and increases his rhythm inside me, deepens his possession of me. Then suddenly he slips out and slides down to bury his face between my legs, laves my center, runs circles around my clit, then sucks it gently until I wail, and he pulls up and he's inside me again. My legs are around him again, and I come again, a deep orgasm brought on by his powerful, fast strokes.

He wraps his hands around my head as he stills inside of me and growls, "Clover." Then he rolls to his back, bringing me with him so I'm nudged on his chest, knees bent, my legs encapsulating him.

His heartbeat is fast and loud, and his hands caress my back and massage my head and trail down to my butt and back up. Then he pulls a sheet over us, and everything goes dark.

I startle awake to low whimpers and a hard, shaking body.

Not mine.

A body that smells like spice and sex, and a touch of soap. One with uneven skin on half the torso.

It's still dark out. I must have just dozed off. But he's asleep, in the throes of a nightmare, his arm around me clenching, his whimpers becoming more desperate. I tilt my head to kiss his jaw and stroke his chest and say little soothing silly things like, "It's okay, it's okay," in a whisper voice. His legs jerk around until I tie them down with mine, still whispering, still kissing his jaw, wondering if I should wake him, then remembering you shouldn't wake someone having a nightmare, then thinking that might actually be for sleepwalking.

Or is it?

He grabs me tighter to him and quiets down, and I fall back asleep.

Then I again startle awake, this time to his cock beating against the inside of my thigh, and I lift myself off him. He's spread-eagle, one arm lazily holding me near, the other thrown over his head, hooded eyes trained on my face. "Hey," he whispers.

Oh god.

God.

No one has ever looked so good, and no one ever will.

I lick my lips and with one finger trace the design of his tattoo from his arm above him, down to his chest. I kiss his chest above his heart, now beating slow and hard, and lick my way down to his cock. He holds my hair in his fist so he can watch me.

I lick his tip, a pearlescent bead my reward, then take his base in one hand and stroke him slowly. He grows thicker, making me wet and needy.

I take him in my mouth, as deep as I can, licking and sucking and moaning, a horny mess so into her own power over a man like that.

A man I should never have.

A man too good to be true.

I bob my head and moan around him, and he hisses "*Clover*" like it's a curse, and then he picks me off him and jackknifes up, and my face is on the bed, my ass propped in the air, there's the sound of a condom wrapper being torn open, then his hands around my hips putting me right where he wants me, and he fucks me so hard and so good I blubber when I come.

Then he flops me around and kisses me. A deep, long kiss. A soft kiss.

It's a goodbye kiss, I know it.

Then he tucks me under his arm, and I curve my leg over his.

"Can I ask you a question?" I say.

"What do you want to know?"

"You have experience with women, right."

"What do you want to know, sweet Clover?"

I take a deep breath. Not the kind I need to take before I get in an elevator, but close. "On a scale of one to ten... where do you put me?"

His hand sifts through my hair. "I don't grade women, Clover. That's disrespectful."

I roll my eyes. He would say that. But come on. "I mean, not saying you give them grades, but... some people are better in bed than others."

"Right. What do you want to know?"

He said we should be truly ourselves tonight, and that's why we're doing the no names, no numbers things. So I put myself out there. I hope he doesn't make fun of me. "Where—where do I need to improve? Like, could you show me some tricks? Or whatever."

His arm around me tightens, and I lift my face to his.

Something dangerous passes through his gaze.

"You know, for—"

"Yeah, I think I know what you mean." He dips his head to kiss my temple and doesn't say a thing.

Then he lifts me in his arms and takes me to the bathroom. He runs a warm shower, and we both step in. He washes me and lets me lather his whole, beautiful body. He's careful not to get my hair wet because I said I don't want to deal with the whole drying part of it.

Also I could keep his smell on me a little longer, but I don't tell him that.

And then he fists my still-dry hair so he can kiss me long and hard this time, and he presses me against the tile, and he lifts one of my hands above my head, like he did in the elevator. I hike one leg around his hips, and his hand shoots out of the shower to grab a condom. Before I have time to fully revel on how prepared he is, he's pumping in and out of me. My raw insides clamor for more, my legs shake, my toes curl, my scalp tingles. As I scream and fall apart in his arms, and while he's still fucking me against the tile, I wonder how it is that each orgasm is stronger than the previous.

You'd think I'd be out of orgasms for a while.

After he comes and dries us and gets us back to bed, I say, "I get why you only do one nights. It's better and better each time. I'd end up just wanting to have sex with you all day. Wouldn't get any work done."

He chuckles and pulls me into his side and sets his alarm. The pale gray light of dawn is seeping through the curtains.

He closes his eyes and plays with my hair for a while. Then he says, "You're off the charts, Clover. Totally off the charts. I'm not saying that to make you feel good."

I kiss his cheek and settle into him and wait for his breathing to steady. Then when I'm confident he's deeply asleep, I slowly worm my way away from him so we don't have to say goodbye. Then I get dressed, and I leave him forever.

CHAPTER SEVEN

Chloe

O *ne week later*

Why didn't I push back? Beg him? Stalk him? Try to find out from the desk clerk who the man in room 2037 was? I could have done so many things.

Instead I kept my promise to him.

The days that followed our night in the elevator, I went through the conference like a zombie, my thoughts full of the feel of his strong arms around me. Of his deep green eyes, full of so much care. Of his voice carrying me through the night.

I took notes in sterile, windowless rooms, exchanged business cards, all the time peeling my eyes in hopes that he would be here too.

He wasn't, or I didn't see him.

After the conference I stayed in Boston a few more days.

I stayed at the same hotel. Lingered at the same bar. The bartender's wound was healing nicely. And the bartender had no idea who my mysterious stranger was. Or if he did, he hid it well.

He never came back.

I met with vendors and restaurant owners who were kind enough to show me how they operate, so I'm not too green when I get to Uncle Kevin's restaurant.

Now it's time to go, and as I'm driving away, I blink back the tears threatening to fall again at the thought of everything I had that one night and lost right away.

Boston fades away in my rearview mirror, and with it, any chance of seeing him again. He truly is gone from my life forever.

It's time for me to put that away and to move forward.

Like Fiona said when I called her to tell her (most of) what happened, rebounds aren't meant to last.

He was the perfect rebound from Tucker. Time to move on.

Breathe in, breathe out. I turn my mind to what awaits me in Emerald Creek.

First impressions are everything, and I don't want my uncle's staff to realize immediately that until a few days ago I'd never set foot in the kitchen of a restaurant or behind a bar. So I mentally review the vocabulary I recently learned and put myself in the shoes of a restaurant owner.

Aunt Dawn can say all she wants that it's a numbers' game; I know for a fact that every business is a people's game.

After two hours on the interstate, nondescript malls and highways and billboards disappear, giving way to rolling hills and farm stands and horses and cows grazing lazily.

I stop at Aunt Dawn's to reattach my U-Haul and get the keys to the restaurant and the cottage.

"I haven't been there in years," Aunt Dawn tells me over coffee and pie. "I hope the cottage isn't too dusty. I don't know if your Uncle Kevin paid much attention to it. It's only about an hour drive from here, so he barely used it at all. Only in case of a bad storm on a late night. He didn't want me to fuss over it."

"Don't worry about that, Aunt Dawn. I'll be fine."

"And don't let that landlord get to you, honey. He was Kevin's bane."

"How so?"

She turns her coffee cup in between her hands. "Kevin never really said. At some point the building was on the market, your father was thinking of buying it as an investment, but there was some funny business, and it was that man who got it instead. After the sale, it got so bad that Kevin was concerned he might lose the lease, but 'parently, the lawyer did a good job, and that lease wasn't easy to break. But he and Kevin never saw eye to eye. There was always something, he would never say what. But I could tell it was eating at Kevin." She stops worrying her coffee mug to put a hand on my arm. "That man all but killed my Kevin with his own two hands." Her eyes water.

"What—what do you mean?" I ask under my breath.

"Stress, honey. Uncle Kevin was under a lot of stress, I could tell. He kept saying everything was fine, but it wasn't. Now, the restaurant is doing fantastic, so what else could be eating at him? The *landlord*. That man caused trouble for years and years. It never got better. But recently, it got worse. Much worse. I bet you it had something to do with the lease renewal."

Shoot. The lease is up for renewal? What else did she forget to tell me? "Aunt Dawn, the lease is a pretty important part of the sale you're planning."

"Uh-huh," she says, nodding. "Careful with the pub owner."

I scoop the last of the pie crumbs and ask, "What pub owner?"

"The landlord! He opened the pub right next door to Uncle Kevin's restaurant."

"Wait—the landlord opened a pub right next to Uncle Kevin's restaurant?"

"He did. Caused your uncle to lose a lot of business. Used to be something or other. A garage, maybe? Or a store. I don't remember anymore."

A pub next door wouldn't necessarily harm a restaurant. If the style and the price point are different, they could actually benefit from each other's presence. But Aunt Dawn is saying it caused Uncle Kevin to lose a lot of business, and I have no reason to doubt her. I guess I'll find out once I get to Emerald Creek. "What else did Uncle Kevin say about this man?" I'm more concerned about having a landlord in my face all day.

"There was always something. The garbage wasn't disposed of right. Something about window boxes." She fidgets. "And then he stole his chef."

"He what?"

She nods. "The chef before this one went to work for the pub. Would you believe it?"

Hmm. Well that could account for actual competition. If the chef moved next door, he could have brought customers with him. "Why would he do that?"

"Why do people do the things they do, honey?" She gives me a sad smile, and then pats my forearm. "But the new chef, Samuel, is fan-tas-tic. Uncle Kevin loved him. Just *loved* him. He took care of *everything*. You'll be fine."

"I know I will," I say, reassuring her as much as myself. I have my work cut out, but it's just as well. I'm not sure just showing up to pay bills and tally up deposit slips would be enough for me. I pat her hand. "Don't worry, Aunt Dawn. I'll show him a good time if he makes trouble." I'm actually looking forward to a showdown with the man who caused so much grief to my family.

She cackles. "You do just that."

The road to Emerald Creek is a winding, narrow ribbon nestled in between trees that shade the sun in green freckles. For the most part, the road follows the river, which early in summer is still full and bubbling. A split in the road indicates Emerald Lake and Emerald Lake Resort, but I keep going. A clearing in the woods reveals a rocky beach on the river. Dogs and kids are splashing in it, while adults chat, water to their knees. A picnic table on the embankment is laden with wicker baskets and boxes.

Then the woods clear, and the landscape turns to farmland again. Cows grazing in fenced pastures, huge red barns, their mouths open to the summer air, white farmhouses with wraparound porches, chicken coops in the shade of trees.

A pullout on the side of the road beckons to a farmstand. I stop the car and stretch. No one is manning the stand, but a sign announces *'Fresh eggs, bacon and salad in the cooler'*, and prices are written in an even handwriting on a lined paper taped to a metal box. Strawberries, peaches, cherries, zucchini, and maple syrup are neatly arranged on a wobbly wooden table, protected from the sun by a couple of umbrellas. I take one of the neatly folded paper bags tucked under the table, get some salad, eggs, bacon, strawberries, and zucchini, add my total to the bills stashed in the metal box, and plop my bag in the back of my car.

Then I close my eyes and pause in the warm summer sun.

The sweet smell of flowers. Wind rustling in the trees, cooling my cheeks. A dog barking. Insects rattling, butterflies tickling my arms. Birds chirping. The river flowing in the distance.

I take a deep, cleansing breath and drive into Emerald Creek.

Why has no one ever told me about this place? I take my foot off the pedal, lower my windows, and take it all in. Houses of all styles—mostly white or pink Victorians and brick Federals—with lovingly maintained gardens and colorful window boxes line the main access road, which turns into main street, where people are strolling, holding hands, coming in and out of the ice cream shop, the general store, an antique shop.

There's not a chance in hell I'm even attempting to park here with my U-Haul, so I'll just have to come back later.

But before heading to the cottage, I drive to The Green.

I want to scout the restaurant. See what it looks like. What first impression it gives. My aunt and cousins were proud of it, and I'm looking forward to being impressed.

The Green is a small park in the center of Emerald Creek. A white steepled church stands proudly at its top. Large houses and businesses line its sides, separated from The Green by a one-way lane and large sidewalks. A live band is currently performing at its center. Children are dancing and adults are loosely circled around the low stage, and a woman's melodious voice fills the air with the sound of soft rock.

Small Town America. So utterly perfect.

I look for the restaurant but can't find it. I see the pub alright, The Lazy Salamander, occupying the left side of a brick building, its large windows lined with flowers. There's a big-ass dog sprawled on the sidewalk, and people step over it to get in. They have outdoor seating as well, a row of cafe tables with bright green-and-white umbrellas. It's cute. It's the kind of place I'd go to without a second thought. In fact, I'd go now if I didn't have my U-Haul strapped to my car. Just to check it out. See what the owner is like.

Who I'm up against.

But I digress. I'm not here to get into the neighbor's face unless I need to. I'm here to temporarily run a restaurant that should be right there but for the life of me, I can't find. Was I given the wrong info? Could it be elsewhere? Aunt Dawn said it was next door, and next door to the pub there's ... a dusty door and a row of dark windows. No sign. No outdoor seating.

The dusty door opens, and I slow down. A guy in jeans and a gray T-shirt comes out and lights a cigarette. I squint. Turns out, there *is* a sign. *'Emerald Creek Fine Dining.'*

My belly clenches. Shoot. *Not* what I expected. Does Aunt Dawn have any idea?

This is going to be a lot of work. Which in a way, is good.

Work has always been my salvation.

Or so I tell myself as I continue driving through Emerald Creek to where my GPS indicates the cottage will be.

Right after The Green, the road narrows and hugs the river, then curves away from it to leave space for a stone building built right on the water and a large, shaded parking area. A cheery hand-painted sign announces, *Easy Monday.*

Ahmayzing Juice Bar, Best Coffee in Town, Cupcakes and such, Books and More Books.

A second sign, attached below the first one, reads, *420*

With a bunch of happy flowers all around it.

My GPS takes me under a one-way, wooden covered bridge with a red roof and hanging flower baskets on each side of it, and I smile at the care the people here have for their town.

My first order of business will be to introduce myself to the other business owners, find out if there is a chamber or other organization I should join.

I find the cottage easily, up a country road just like Aunt Dawn said, a short drive from The Green. It's on a hill, with views of the lake in the distance and open fields around it. The neighbors are invisible, although I passed houses close by.

It's a small, white cape with an overgrown yard. I pull all the way up the weedy driveway, to the cobwebby porch with peeling paint. I brace myself. Aunt Dawn didn't say anything about the restaurant needing TLC, but she had reservations about the cottage. I wonder what awaits me.

The screen on the front door opens with a wail, and the front door needs a shoulder push.

The inside smells dusty, but nothing worse, and I breathe in relief. The downstairs consists of an open kitchen on the left, with a round plastic table and four chairs defining an eating area cornered by grimy windows on the side and front of the house. On the right of the front door, there's a brown-ish couch smack in the middle of an empty space.

In front of me, dividing the house, a carpeted staircase leads to two bedrooms and a bath.

One bedroom is empty, its wallpaper peeling. The other bedroom boasts a queen-size frame and mattress and received a coat of paint in the last decade. There's even a set of linens and towels in the closet.

It doesn't look like anyone has lived here in a long time. Years ago, someone had the idea to do something with it, and then they changed their mind. They brought a bed, a couch, a table and chairs, and then found better things to do. Or ran out of energy. I wonder briefly if that someone was Aunt Dawn, and then I focus on other things. Like making this space mine for now.

With what Aunt Dawn said, and Uncle Kevin passing away a couple of weeks ago, I was dreading long-forgotten, overflowing trashcans. A fridge with brown leaks where there once was food.

I was expecting mice.

There is nothing of the sort.

I prop all the windows and the front door open to create a nice airflow, bring my luggage in, then get to work.

I vacuum and mop and dust. Clean the windows. Wipe the fridge. I find a single-use packaged powder detergent that smells fantastic and run the kitchen curtains in the washer.

Then I unload my U-Haul and unroll my Moroccan carpet—that Tucker had thought was *weird*—in front of the couch. With its blue and green hues, it looks *awesome.* My off-white, distressed coffee table I set right smack in the middle of the carpet and proceed to place three candles at an angle on it. Tucker didn't like the candles. He said they got in the way of watching the game.

Well, there's no TV here. Not that I need one.

I drag one of the four kitchen chairs next to the couch as a makeshift side table and plop my tiffany lookalike lamp on it, plug it in and turn it on, for effect.

Then I proceed to carry my bookshelves inside, assemble the shelves, stack my books, arrange my knickknacks, and then plop on the couch for a beat.

It looks like home.

I thought I'd miss my apartment, with its high windows and airy views and open space. It felt like I was making a home there, and that that home was ripped away from me.

It wasn't. Home is where I decide it is.

I get my ass off the couch, set my laptop on the kitchen table, and plug it in.

I had left my fern inside Aunt Dawn's house for her to babysit, which means it had plenty of water and regular misting. It looks fantastic. I set it on a chipped plate on the floor next to the couch, for now.

I bring all my kitchen stuff and store most of it in the empty cupboards and drawers, set my red and white ceramic vase on the countertop. After I wipe down the bedroom closet, I hang and fold my clothes there. Make my bed with my own sheets. Again, a feel of home.

Then I move to the bathroom, give everything a wipe, and open the faucets. While they do their coughing and gurgling from going too long without being used, I set my toiletries on the side of the sink, under the vanity, in the medicine cabinet, and in the shower.

When the water flow is nice and even and the bathroom is steamy, I strip out of my sweaty clothes and get under the warm shower. Shampoo and conditioner have never felt so good. Shower gel so indulgent. The weariness from travelling and setting up, washes out, and I'm left with only a feeling of peace.

The sun is setting when I walk back downstairs. The place smells fresh and clean.

My new home, sparse but cozy.

A new start.

I close the windows and take one of the three remaining kitchen chairs to the porch. Finally sitting down, I plop my feet on the railing and bask in the landscape turning crimson while I snack on strawberries.

The next morning, after a restful night, I take a minute to truly enjoy the coffee from my own espresso machine. And the unbeatable taste of a scramble made with fresh farm eggs.

And I'm glad I did, because the minute I walk into the restaurant, holy crap.

It's going to take more than a good wipe.

CHAPTER EIGHT

Chloe

I don't need the key to the employee entrance Aunt Dawn gave me. That back door isn't locked, making me briefly wonder if someone might have just stepped out and will be coming back at any moment to finish what should have been done last night.

Bags of trash are piled next to the back door, waiting to be taken out, spreading their foul smell throughout the whole restaurant.

The dish pit is overflowing, dried food caked everywhere, a blatant health violation on top of being the mark of disgusting laziness.

Is no one actually in charge here? Did no one step in to fill the void? Who was here last night, smoking a cigarette on the sidewalk?

My sneakers slipping on the greasy floor, I find my way to the unlocked office.

There's a desk disappearing under wobbly piles of paper and un-opened mail and a desktop computer—the kind that's hooked up to a tower on the floor. I press the 'On,' button and while it whirs to life, I sift through the storage boxes lined on the shelves, labeled by year.

The swivel chair in front of the computer sighs when I slouch in it. Uncle Kevin's list of passwords is taped under his keyboard. People can be so painfully predictable.

It takes me less than an hour to establish that the restaurant's financial situation is worrisome, to say the least. There's a little money in the bank, but only because vendors haven't been paid and rent is three months behind.

Payroll is due.

I already know from the online reviews I finally looked up last night that quality is lacking and has been steadily declining for at least a year, if not more. I don't know if Aunt Dawn and my cousins are in denial, uninformed, or weren't entirely forthcoming with me. But I do like a challenge, and fixing up a flailing business is right up my alley. I've done it for corporations where all the numbers on the P&L had two or three more zeros than this restaurant.

I can do this.

The first order of business is to tend to the lease. Aunt Dawn cautioned me against the landlord, but what else can I do? I fire him a quick email. Who knows? We're neighbors. He might be yearning for a good relationship. He might be understanding. And he definitely has a lot to gain by letting us stay in business. After all, I only need a few months.

From: Chloe Sullivan
To: Justin King
Subject: Intro and Terms
Dear Mr. King,

I am writing to introduce myself. I am the niece of the late Kevin Murphy and have been appointed by the family to fill in for my uncle while we look for the restaurant's next owners.

I would welcome an in-person meeting at your convenience to discuss pending matters and generally establish the groundwork for a mutually beneficial collaboration.

I look forward to your response.

Chloe Sullivan

Minutes later, his answer pops up.

From: Justin King
To: Chloe Sullivan
Subject: Clarification

Ms. Sullivan,

There are no pending matters other than the late rent. This meeting doesn't even need to be an email. A wire transfer will do.

Justin King

That's not good. Let's see... I start typing.

From: Chloe Sullivan
To: Justin King
Subject: Wrong foot

Dear Justin,

I'm afraid we started off on the wrong foot. I understand you are upset about the late rent, and I just want to discuss terms of payment that would be acceptable to you without threatening our family's business.

Would you care to join me for a glass of wine so we can break the ice? And I'd love to pick your brains about having outdoor seating that would complement yours and elevate the experience for your customers as well as ours.

Chloe

From: Justin King
To: Chloe Sullivan
Subject: Rent

Ms. Sullivan,

Only my friends and family call me Justin. You are neither.

You are three months late on rent.

Because I am not a monster, I will grant your aunt thirty days to get up-to-date on her late and upcoming payments.

Sincerely,

Justin King

Wow. That went off the rails real quick.

It's time for Chloe's charm offensive. I push up from behind the desk, smooth my hair, and walk out of the restaurant.

A young blonde woman is wiping down the outdoor tables.

"Hi, I'm... uh... Kevin's... niece?" I point my thumb behind me. "The new manager for the restaurant. Just temporarily. I—I just got here."

She frowns at me.

"Kevin Murphy? The restaurant?"

She blows a lock of hair off her forehead. "Oh, yeah, yeah, yeah. Hi." She straightens and tucks her rag in her jeans buckle. "Welcome to Emerald Creek. And sorry for your loss." Her eyes dart to the door of the restaurant. "Temporarily?"

"Just helping out the family. You know. Giving them time to get their bearings. Love the setup you have here, by the way. The outdoor seating?"

She beams. "That's all Justin. He's got a sense for that."

Justin, right. "I was hoping to... I—I just need to have a quick word with Mr. King? He's in, right?"

"Mr. King?" She bites her smile. "You mean Justin. No one *ever* calls him Mr. King." A wide smile spreads across her face, and she extends her hand. "I'm his sister, by the way. Haley."

We shake hands, ice broken. "I'm just helping him out for a while. Not sure I know what I'm doing, but family's family," she adds.

I smile wide, her empathy hitting the right chord. "I totally get you. Not sure what I'm doing here either. But don't tell anyone!"

She giggles. "Pinky promise. Fake it till you make it."

Right on. "So... *Justin.* Can I pop in and... say hello?"

Her face scrunches. "Um, he's not in right now... we're not technically open. Like, we open at twelve?"

I wave like it's no big deal. "We've been exchanging emails, and I figured it'd be easier if I just popped in to introduce myself."

"Oh. He must have answered from his phone."

He's in the middle of something. That explains the curt responses. "You know what, I'll come back later. It was just a neighborly visit, no big deal."

Pink tints her cheeks. "We had no idea you were coming, or *we* would've welcomed *you.*"

I backpedal to my portion of the sidewalk, the one without cute tables and umbrellas. For now. "Is twelve a good time? One?" I really need to get the rent problem crossed off my list of things to worry about for now.

She waves me back to her. "Hold on," she says, pulling out her phone. "Let me tell him you're here. I'm sure he'll—" She puts the phone to her ear, opens the door, and ushers me in. The 'Sorry, we're closed' sign bangs against the glass pane.

"Moose, behave," she says as the dog I saw yesterday lifts his massive head my way, then gets up slowly and ambles to greet me. He's not just big. He's huge. His head is about level with my waist. "Hey, buddy." He closes his eyes while I give him a skull scratch.

"Hey, so... the lady from the restaurant is here?" Haley says into the phone, looking at me. Then she dips her face and turns around.

I take a few steps away to give her privacy. Moose nuzzles my hand, so I resume my petting while I take in the pub, Haley's conversation inaudible. Dark wood paneling, shiny brass details, comfy booths, small ambiance lamps, local photographs: everything imparts a feeling of relaxed comfort. The floors are old, waxed wood planks. Behind the long bar, bottles are neatly lined, and there's not a speck of dust on the shelves.

Haley pockets her phone and turns to me, embarrassment painting her features. I hate that I've put her in a difficult situation. She opens her mouth, but no sound comes out. Clearly, *Mr. King* doesn't want to talk to his neighbor and tenant.

Clearly, I should be gone already.

I give Moose one last scratch between the ears. "Thanks for trying," I say to Haley. "I'll come back."

I turn around and slam into a mass of muscle. "You need to leave," a familiar voice says.

CHAPTER NINE

Justin

I lean against Chris's prep table in his bakery, the cold metal digging into my hips. "What are you doing?" It's a rhetorical question. I wave my phone to indicate I'm onto him. How do I keep him from totally messing up his life after he and his girlfriend, Alex, had a falling out, when I'm having trouble keeping my own shit together? Truth is, it's been a week, a whole week of beating myself up for letting Clover go. For my stupid rule: No Name, No Number. A week of wondering.

Does she think about me?

When she falls asleep at night, do I cross her mind? Or am I already just a blip in her past?

How does our one night together compare to her nights before?

To her nights now.

Does she think about it like I do? Like this was the one and only night I felt truly alive.

It can't be, or I wouldn't have woken up to a cold bed. To a morning without someone to share my coffee with. I've played this in my head over and over. I would have brought her a cup in bed. We would have kissed and cuddled and made love, and then I would have said, or maybe she would have said, '*To hell with that stupid rule. I want to see you again.*'

And she or I would have said, '*Thank god. I was hoping you'd say that.*' And then we would have kissed again, the kiss to end all hopelessness, and...

My phone lights up with an email from my tenant.

I fire a quick reply and get back to the reason I'm here. Alex left without taking her phone, and Chris has been trying to get in touch with her via his social media. He thinks she's with her best friend, and somehow a plan formed in his mind to get through to her that way.

It's not pretty.

The guy knows nothing about social media. The little he does know, he learned from Alex who came to Emerald Creek for an apprenticeship at his bakery.

Now he's live, insulting his customer base, and he doesn't even know it.

"Dude, what are you doing?" I close my email icon, trying to get past the fact that my tenant is trying to get an extension on their rent. After what they did to me, they have some nerve.

"I'm banking on a bunch of losers to help me find Alexandra," Chris says, talking straight into the camera. That's live, too, as my phone screen attests a split second after he talks.

It's time for an intervention, so I talk him through what he's doing. Meanwhile, the email icon lights again. Another pushback from the new manager at the restaurant.

Really? The woman has no shame. I type a quick response and clear my mind by bombing Chris's video, my head over his shoulder as he talks.

Chris finally gets the idea that he's not going about it the right way, and he logs off.

"Hey, man, when are you going to reopen the bakery?" I ask him when he puts his phone away.

"Not 'til I get Alex back."

I sigh and cross my arms, feeling his pain. I'm about to try and talk some sense into him, but he says, "What's up with you? You look like shit."

"Nothin'," I lie. He sees right through it, so I offer, "The restaurant has a new manager. She's busting my balls about the rent." I'm not going to tell him I'm bent out of shape over Clover. And if this Chloe Sullivan keeps at it like that, she might become reason enough for me to be pissed all day, anyway.

"What about the rent?"

I tell him the situation in a few words, then move onto the real reason I'm here: talking my friend into reopening his bakery, into getting his life back on track, but before I can get too far, my phone rings. *Haley.* This should be quick, so I pick up. "Whassup?"

"Hey, so... the lady from the restaurant is here?"

You gotta be kidding me. "The fuck does she want?"

"Um... to talk to you?" She lowers her voice. "She's really nice, and she wants to fix up the restaurant. I think you should talk to her."

That's not going to happen. "They want to fix up the restaurant on my money so they can sell it at a premium."

"What do you mean?" she whispers.

"They're late on rent."

"Yeah! Like half the country," she hisses.

"Three months, going on four, and asking for more."

"Oh."

Yeah, *oh*. Does my sister really think I'd be an asshole for one month late? "Why did you let her in?"

"She was super nice."

More like, super pushy. "Really."

"Yeah, really," Haley insists, still whispering but in an angry way. "What do you mean about the selling stuff?" she whispers.

I can't believe they're actually hoping I'll give them another extension so they can *sell* the restaurant instead of just folding like he should have ages ago. The guy was a permanent insult to me. To this whole town. After everything he did, I couldn't believe he had the balls to stay in town, when he didn't even live here. No wonder none of the locals ever went to his place. They knew the history. No matter how good his food was—when he was able to keep a decent chef around—they weren't going to give him their business.

"What's going on, man?" Chris asks.

I cover the phone's mic. "The restaurant's new manager, Murphy's niece. She's at the pub. Pain in my ass."

He lifts his chin. "Shit never ends, does it."

"You got that right."

"Runs in the family. Nip it in the bud," Chris says just as Haley tells me, "What do you want me to tell her?"

"Tell her I got nothing to add," I tell Haley. "Tell her we're closed."

"I said that already, but now she's *inside*," she whispers, while Chris says, "Man, just tell her, her uncle was a criminal and an asshole, and there's nothing to negotiate."

"Why'd you let her in?" I snap into my phone.

I can sense Haley's frustration. "I don't know! Trying to be *nice*?"

Why would she care about being nice to that family? "Fuck," I say and hang up before I add something I'll regret, something that would hurt my sister. Did Haley already forget what Murphy did? Because I have the scars and the phantom pains that never let me forget.

"Telling you, man, just get in her face and make it clear," Chris says. "She probably doesn't know half the story, or she wouldn't have made nice with Haley."

"How'd you know she made nice with Haley?"

"Why else would she be inside the pub?"

"Maybe she's as entitled as Murphy."

The idea that anyone from that family is inside my pub is enough to enrage me. "That too." Chris is right. I need to end this before it even starts. "Be right back," I tell my friend, my long strides taking me across The Green, yet doing nothing to calm my rising anger.

So when I get to my pub, even though I'm blinded by the outside sun and can't see who's inside, I don't need to think twice about what I say to the person slamming into me.

"You need to leave."

CHAPTER TEN

Chloe

The silhouette is dark against the blinding sun outside, but for a moment I'm paralyzed.

That voice.

That smell.

I'm hallucinating. Time to get a grip.

I turn to Haley and then to King, still a dark mass against the bright outdoor. My heart bangs against my ribcage and my throat constricts. Sure, I'm disappointed that my first interaction with the locals is going so poorly. "Nice welcome committee," I mutter. "No wonder Uncle Kevin had a heart attack."

But also, I'm having an overwhelming response to this shadow of a man. Clearly, I'm not over my rebound if I'm seeing him everywhere. "I'll get out of your way now." I inch toward King, who's still blocking my exit.

"You Chloe? Sullivan's daughter?" That voice... it's uncanny. My breath catches. God, what is happening to me?

But also, how does my father factor into this non-conversation? I need to get out of here.

"You have some balls getting in my face," he adds, still blocking my exit.

"I'm trying to leave," I snap at him.

King steps aside to let me go. I look out the door, meaning to ignore him, but as I walk past him, his scent shakes me to the core, bringing me back nights ago.

"Don't come back unless you have a certified check," he snarls, his voice tingling my spine despite the bite in his words.

My knees buckle at his words, and my heart stutters. I look up at him, and my breath hitches. Now that he's stepped inside the pub, I can see his features. His dirty blond locks curling at his collar. The set of his jaw. The curve of his lips.

It's *him*.

It's him!

All of him.

My insides fire up, and my mouth gapes as my gaze trails his wide shoulders. Any strength I had leaves me at the sight of his strong arms, remembering how they held me all night. Remembering the feel of his wounds under my fingers. Of his skin against mine.

Remembering him inside me.

I fight the urge to throw myself at him.

Because the way he wanted me is etched into my memory.

And now? Now, he doesn't even look my way. His beautiful green eyes are dark and cold. I run out the door before he turns his gaze to me.

CHAPTER ELEVEN

Justin

The shock wave hits me first in the gut, then knocks the wind out of me.

I'm frozen in place once she steps out of the darkness of the pub, and I recognize her. But she's already fleeing me, her beautiful blue eyes watery, the dark brown waves of her hair flowing behind her as she runs outside, her hands clenching at her heart.

Hands that were once grasping at my shirt, at my neck.

How could this happen? Who did I piss off in the universe to always, *always* mess shit up spectacularly?

Anger balls my hands into fists and clenches my jaw.

"What is *wrong* with you?" Haley's mouth is hanging open, her hands on her hips, her head tilted just like Moose's.

Clover is already gone, storming out of the pub, head down, shoulders hunched, steps hurried.

Defeated.

My heart hammers inside my ribcage. What *is* wrong with me? "Did you hear what she said?"

"Yeah, that we weren't welcoming." She crosses her arms, daring me to question that.

"She insinuated I had something to do with her uncle's heart attack."

"You're exaggerating." She straightens her spine. "It maybe wasn't very... tactful, but... she seems like a lovely person—"

"Nice tits and ass alone don't make you lovely." The way this is going, the fact she's who she is, I might as well get her out of my system now. Because this is not happening.

Matter of fact, this was never meant to happen.

Haley crosses her arms and juts her hip out. "I wouldn't know about her tits and ass. Glad we got that straightened out. So a woman can't have nice tits and ass without being blamed for it?"

"Holy fuck, Haley, that is not—"

"That is *totally* what you said! And stop swearing! It's not good for business."

I roll my eyes. Hiring my sister for temporary help might have sounded like a good idea, but sometimes it's like having my mother in my face. I love my mother and all. But fucking Christ. Can I get a break? "You know who she is?"

She rolls her eyes. "Yessss. The new restaurant manager or... something."

My Clover.

"She seems nice and... it looks like she will fix up the dump the restaurant became."

One night.

"She'll make the whole block look nicer. That'll be good for you."

The one woman.

She throws her hands in the air. "What is *wrong* with you?"

And I shouldn't want her. "She's Murphy's niece."

She fires back, "So?"

"So!?" How can my own sister be so aloof?

Haley's face softens. "Oh." She takes two steps toward me. "Gosh, Justin, you have to let that go."

Easy for her to say. "Don't you have tables to wipe out there?"

She ignores my jab and plants herself on a barstool. "Is it a girl? Is that why you've had your panties in a tizzy since you came back from Boston?"

A girl? My panties in...? "The fuck you talking about."

"I didn't want to say anything, but I'm not the only one seeing it. Since you came back from Boston, you're... not yourself."

Not this. "I have a mortgage to pay. No rent coming in."

"Is it because Alex broke up with Chris and went back to New York?"

What is she talking about? "Business is slow."

She waves her hand around her. "Business will pick up after the Fourth. It always does."

My eyes keep going back to the door, to the window at the back where I last saw Clover. I feel a pull. And a weight on my chest. "How would you know?"

"Ohmygod, don't tell me you fell for Alex. Justin, she's... she's Chris's, if he can get his shit together. Is that why she left? Is that why Chris is so depressed? He lost the love of his life and his best friend at the same time! That's not how you treat—"

The fuck is she talking about? "It's not *Alex*!" I boom.

"Ha!" She jumps off her stool and slams her hand on the bar. "I knew it! It's a girl. I knew it!!!" She throws her head back and releases a demonic laughter. "Admit it."

"No!"

She raises a victorious eyebrow. "Colton told Grace."

"Colton?" I narrow my eyes. I might have had an argument at the reception desk, trying to extract Clover's real name, seeing as I had to drive my friends back home and therefore couldn't register for the freaking conference I assumed she was attending. And Colton might have been nearby. Who cares? Can't a man have a private life? I wait 'til I'm in fucking Boston to get laid, and my friend tells everyone in town the minute we're back? What fucking world do we live in?

"Grace extracted it from him. We've been sleuthing. It wasn't easy."

That's more like it.

"You are... ohmygosh." She breaks in a fit of giggles. "You fell for a girl! Where does she live? Come on! You can tell me. I'll help you out."

"Help me out?"

"Yeah. You need to court her. Romance her. You had a one-night stand with her, and now you want to see her again, but you don't know what to do. That's where your little sister comes in. Gimme your phone. Gimme, gimme, gimme." She wiggles her fingers toward me.

I pinch the bridge of my nose.

"Justin, seriously. Tell me. What's her name? I won't tell anyone, pinky promise." She plucks her phone from her back pocket. "Just need to find out where she lives, where she hangs out, what she likes. So we can hook you back up. Get this show on the road. Come on." She does some come-on gesture with her free hand.

Fuck me. "Where's the aspirin?"

Haley huffs and turns up her attitude dial. "I dunno. I got tables to wipe, 'member?" She whips around, then stops with her hand on the door and turns around again. "And when you're done moping over some slut, you might wanna apologize to the *perfectly nice woman next door*!"

"She's not a slut!" I snap and register my sister's victorious look.

Instead of basking in her *I-was-right* attitude, she provokes me further by adding, "Anyone who would have a one-night stand *with you* is a slut." She makes a disgusted face, totally trying to get a rise out of me. Or information.

I clench my jaw. "Haley."

"Then prove it. Tell me who she is. Bring her to Emerald Creek." Then she heads outside, and Moose worms his way through the door with her, leaving me alone in the pub.

My brain is a mess, my thoughts raging with anger.

'Bring her to Emerald Creek.' The irony.

I can't believe what just happened. I can't believe I found Clover, only to lose her again. Clover is Sullivan's daughter.

Shit.

Fuck.

The words she told me in the elevator, the ones that made me want to punch the wall, surge back in my memory. *"Sometimes it feels like whatever I do, it's never good enough. Or worse, it's wrong. I try and try and try to please, to do the right thing, but I end up rejected anyway."*

And now I've done this to her.

And why is Clover running her family's restaurant? Is that her trying to please? Fuck, she came to the pub, and Haley said she was so nice. Trying to please again. And she ended up being rejected again. How could I mess up so spectacularly?

I'm too fucking angry to stay at the pub now. I turn around to go back to Chris's. Maybe I can help him fix *his* relationship. One that took almost six months to build. He has something solid.

Not like me.

As I hit the sidewalk, I see Haley and Grace, who is Chris's cousin and also Colton's sister, knock on the door of the restaurant. Haley purses her lips at me and turns her head to Grace, who gives me the stink eye.

Of course the girls are going to meddle.

Well, hell.

Chapter Twelve

Chloe

I deadbolt the restaurant door, lean my back against it, and slide down to the floor, closing my eyes. My heart thumps loudly.

Justin. His name is Justin.

Ohmygod. What a mess.

What did he say in Boston? *'Tomorrow, we're two strangers again.'*

So we're strangers. Okay. Oh god. I just need to keep it together when I see him. It won't be hard, given what just happened.

And he also said, *'I don't have a girlfriend. Never did, never will.'*

Okay. That's good, right? I won't have to see him in town with another woman. *If it's true.* After what happened with Tucker, can I even trust him? Maybe he lied to me. But also, I need to forget about having *anything* with him now. What am I thinking? With what just happened, there's nothing to be had. He couldn't get rid of me fast enough.

What do I care anyway? He was a rebound, a one-night stand.

Right?

A big fat tear rolls down my cheek.

I wished I'd never seen him again. I could have kept fantasizing. Now even that is lost.

I wonder what would have happened if I'd broken my promise to him, that night? If I'd told him who I was? Would we have figured out our differences? Would he have given me a chance?

Breathe in. Breathe out. I can't do the what-ifs. It's too painful.

I need to forget about my night with him. Fiona was right. He was a rebound, and nothing more. I need to move on.

And I need to focus on the reason I'm here. Initially, to keep the restaurant running until a sale. And now that I know the real situation, to bring it back comfortably in the black so a sale can actually happen.

Focus on work, Chloe. That's always the answer.

A knock sounds, and the door reverberates through my body, startling me. *Shoot.* Is that him? What does he want? I scramble away from the door.

The knocks become louder. "Chloe!" It's a woman's voice. I tiptoe to the side window and peek at two women—Haley and another woman our age.

I open the door and force a smile. "Hey," I say, unable to keep the defensiveness from my voice.

"Are you alright?" Haley says, gently pushing the door wider so she can storm inside. "That was nuts! Grace, swear to god, never seen him that way. This is Grace, by the way. Chloe."

Grace has a lock of shiny black curls and soulful eyes. She immediately envelops me in a hug. "Welcome to Emerald Creek. Haley told me everything. I sent Ms. Angela home, told her I'd finish her pedicure later. I'm sure she stopped at Cassandra's on the way." She says all this like I'm supposed to know who these people are, then finally releases her hug but holds onto my shoulders. "I can't believe Justin wouldn't even want to talk to you. I'm embarrassed. Please don't judge us for how he's behaving. How can we make this right?"

"I'm telling Mom," Haley drops.

"Oh wow. You are? Oh well, then." Grace pulls a chair and plops onto it like she's exhausted. She looks around the dining room. "I've never been here. It's... not what I expected."

"Not what I expected either," I confirm, happy to change topics.

She scrunches her nose, pulls out her phone, and starts clicking on it.

"How is your chef treating you?" Grace asks.

"I haven't met him yet."

Haley crosses her arms. "To be a fly on the wall when that happens." She sits next to Grace and pushes a chair out for me. "Girl talk. So. What went down today with my brother. That's not him. You need to know that. He's a sweetheart."

Really.

"No, for real. I know where you're coming from. But that's not him. You just need to clear the air about the bad blood between him and Murphy. He'll get over it."

"Totally," Grace says.

Bad blood? Is there more than unpaid rent? Aunt Dawn did warn me against him. Seems she was spot on.

"I've never seen him this mean," Haley tells Grace.

"I've never seen him mean, period," Grace answers.

"It's a girl," they both say, still looking at each other. Then they laugh out loud. Then Haley takes my hand, because I'm not laughing at all. I'm on the verge of throwing up, of loading my U-Haul, and of telling Aunt Dawn, *'Sorry—not sorry.'* Because how am I supposed to work with him being like that and being right next to me?

"He really rattled you," Haley says.

"Yeah, those King brothers, they can be something else," Grace whispers. "But it's not like you two have history or anything."

My blood freezes.

"He's still the same?" Grace asks Haley.

Haley nods. "Since he and Colton brought Chris back from Boston. Which, you should know—my brother normally comes back very pumped up from his 'Boston trips,'" she adds with air quotes.

Grace waves her hand in front of her nose. "Eww. I don't want to know."

Heat creeps up my chest. Yeah, no wonder he was upset at seeing me. He doesn't want whatever he does in Boston to seep into his real life.

"Yeah. But this time, he *admitted* it."

My pulse quickens.

Grace's eyes widen. "He *did*?"

"I trapped him, he fell right in it. I might have pushed Colton in it too."

The two throw their heads back as they laugh uncontrollably. I'm not sure I'm following anymore.

"We're boring you with our gossip about Justin. Sorry." Haley dabs her eyes as Grace checks her phone. "He's got to be the last thing you want to hear about right now."

"It's fine," I lie. "I just should probably get ready for the staff to get here any minute now."

"Oh, honey. No. They don't work today. Only Wednesday through Saturday nights."

I try hard not to show my shock. "I'm sure someone'll be in. The employee entrance in the back was unlocked. They might be running an errand." And there's the matter of the freaking mess in the kitchen.

Surely that hasn't been in there since... Yeah, it's totally been there since Saturday night. The way everything was caked. And there were a couple of flies.

And the garbage.

"Crap."

Grace takes my hand. "You need help, honey, you let us know."

"Sure."

She squeezes my hand.

"Um...?"

"You need help."

"I do?"

"Garbage's been rotting in here for days. Floors are sticky. You need help."

"You can't help me with that."

"We know people who can."

Oh. "I was thinking of having a little come-to-Jesus talk with my staff. Don't want to be seen as doing their job. Make it a statement."

"I like that." She squeezes my hand again and smiles. "What if the health inspector comes in?"

Crap.

The front door flies open, two young guys darkening the entrance. "Holy shit, Grace! You didn't say we needed hazmat suits."

Grace lets go of my hand. "Boys. Language."

"That was Trevor. I... brought hazmat gear." Not-Trevor turns to me with two fingers to his head and a disarmingly cute smile. "Ma'am." He pulls out a box of gloves.

Upon second look, the two very young men are identical twins with very different vibes.

Trevor pulls out his phone and does a sweep of the restaurant, walking toward the kitchen.

"What are you doing? You can't post this on social," Haley says.

"Just doing a before and after for...?" He turns to me.

"Chloe. And you are...?"

"Trevor and Ryan. Grace's cousins. Currently unemployed because our half-brother, Chris, who hired us for the summer, closed down his bakery until his girlfriend comes back."

"Long story," Haley cuts in. "You don't want to know."

"Bottom line—" one of the twins start.

"We're happy to help," the other finishes.

"You're in good hands," Grace tells me as she stands. "I should get back to the spa. Got a massage client in twenty."

"I need to leave too," Haley says.

They give me side hugs and leave me with Ryan and Trevor, promising that Justin will come around.

I sure hope that *doesn't* happen, seeing as I'm *done* with him on sooo many levels, but I manage a tight-lipped smile that almost convinces them I'm beyond The Incident. Also, my head is spinning with all their instructions. *Thursday Game Night. Back of Cassandra's boutique. Bring the girls.* At least that could be fun.

The boys start by gutting the cooler and then make their way back through the kitchen. They convincingly and politely suggest I'd best be out of their way, so I retreat back to the office, make phone calls to providers, grab a menu from the hostess stand, and start brainstorming ways to spend less and make more.

That right there always brings me joy.

Trevor and Ryan are loud in a happy way—music booming, garbage cans clanking, dishes clattering. At some point we regroup in the kitchen and drink sodas. The surfaces are shiny, the floor is no longer slippery. Whatever is left in the walk-in is not past its due date.

There's hope.

After our break, they move onto the dining room, which should be a piece of cake after the kitchen situation they dealt with. I insist on doing the windows. They cave, and at five we're done.

I take cash from my wallet, which they firmly refuse to take. A semi-argument ensues in which I learn that the restaurant having been an eyesore for everyone, they're thrilled to be part in the Great Revitalization of the King Block, and that is compensation enough for them. I threaten to never hire them again if they refuse my money.

Once they accept, I further threaten to never hire them again if they keep calling it the King Block.

They give me quizzical looks, so I give them the short version of my encounter with King.

We conclude the block shall be known as The Queen Block, and we part best friends.

I haul myself to the cottage, roast some zucchini, whip up an omelet, plop my butt in the plastic chair and my feet on the porch railing, and make a list of things to get done tomorrow.

Then I go to bed early because tomorrow will be a long day.

Tomorrow's Wednesday.

CHAPTER THIRTEEN

Chloe

A loud flock of birds wakes me before the sun is up. I try to smother the outside sound with a pillow on my head, but the bitter memory of yesterday twists my stomach.

Not the unkempt restaurant.

Not the concerning financials.

Not the fact that my aunt was either clueless or not entirely forth-coming—or possibly both.

What twists my stomach is *his* voice. *'You need to leave.'* The tone he used to speak to me, as unforgiving as the crying birds outside my window.

Did he not recognize me? Did he even look at me?

God, I have to stop these thoughts.

I take a quick shower and skip my morning espresso machine rou-tine. Instead, I head out to Easy Monday.

I need my coffee, and they claim it's the best in town. I want to put that claim to the test. I also need to forget about who my neighbor is, and exploring the town and all it has to offer should help me do just that.

The wooden door is painted a bright yellow that dings when I push it open. A young woman with long flowy hair, a long print dress, and actual flowers in her hair comes from somewhere in the back and says, "How can I make your day awesome?" with the most genuine smile.

"You already did." I smile back and focus on the blackboard menu above her head.

"Cool!" She turns around and skips to the back, leaving me alone at the counter.

"Millie!" a woman with long, blue-streaked hair calls out. I hadn't seen her when I came in. The place is a hodgepodge of beanbags, shelves stacked with books, wooden tables and chairs of all sizes and heights, artwork on the stone walls, and sculptures hanging from the ceilings, some, but not all, doubling as light fixtures.

Nudged between a table with a puzzle in progress and an easel with the half-finished canvas of some goddess or mermaid whooshing out of the river, the woman is deep in a couch, a coffee in one hand, a cupcake in the other, a book balanced on her knee. She looks at me and shakes her head, a *you gotta see it to believe it* look on her face.

"Over here!" a voice singsongs in the back, and the first young woman returns. "'Sup, Cass?"

"I think your customer might want more than your sunny presence."

"Oh cool!" Millie says, a huge smile on her face, like someone ordering anything from her store is a complete surprise to her. "What can I get'cha?"

I read from the blackboard over her head. "One large Road to Heaven." As the words leave my mouth, doubt strikes me. "That's not... there's no..."

Millie tilts her head patiently, waiting for me to find my words. I'm not even sure how to ask this.

"The weed place—420—is on the other side. Different entrance. Regulation," the woman called Cass offers. "Here it's straight up coffee."

Millie frowns and smiles at the same time. "I can add a shot of CBD?"

"No, no, no, no. Straight up coffee is what I need."

She leans over the counter. "You sure? Cos I heard about Justin. And his... you know... with you?"

I open my mouth, but no sound comes out. Small towns are known for spreading news like a bushfire, but this is a whole 'nother level.

And hopefully she means yesterday's argument with Justin.

Not the rest.

She has to, right?

"I can... *not* believe he wouldn't talk to you!" she whispers. "He is *such* a nice man. *So devoted* to the community! *Always* lending a helping hand."

I almost breathe easy. She does mean our argument. "Hey, we all have our limits."

She drops the to-go cup she was about to fill. "Ohmygod, you are *So. Right.* I can... not believe *you*, of all people, would understand that. After how he treated you, I mean," she adds quickly, like she just said something extremely offending.

She gets back to preparing my coffee, mumbling, "Maybe I'll just bring him a gummy today." She hands me my coffee and says, "Let me know if you like it," looking at me like she really expects me to give her a full feedback on my cup'o joe.

What can I do? I indulge her. "Ohmygod." I'm *so* not faking this. "Millie. It's Millie, right?"

She blushes and nods.

"Are you for real?" I laugh for the first time in... a long time. "This is... heaven!"

She swipes her hand sideways. "That's what it's called."

"You're my new best friend. By the way, I'm—"

"Chloe."

We both smile, big stupid grins, warmth spreading inside me. Day two, and I've already made three friends! "I should go. Big day ahead of me." I pull out my wallet.

"On me," she says. "Welcome to Emerald Creek."

I fold a bill in the tip jar as she says, "Have an awesome day!" twists around and disappears in the back.

"Bye, Clover!" I swear the woman with blue hair says to me. I whip to look at her, but she pretends to be reading her book. I pause with my hand on the doorknob, my gaze fixed on her. She finally lifts her head and says, "Good luck today."

That was... weird.

But I'm holding the best cup of coffee in the world. I have three new friends.

Life is good after all.

The restaurant is open when I get there, a radio blaring in the brightly lit kitchen, a man chopping vegetables. He looks like he could be the man I saw standing at the door when I drove by the day I arrived in town.

"Oh. You're here," I say. Life might be good, but it's no thanks to him. As I get closer, the smell of cigarette emanating from him further confirms my suspicion.

He twirls his knife on the chopping board without really looking at it. "This is my kitchen. Why wouldn't I be here?"

Are all men assholes in this town? They should have a sign at the entrance. This is not what the Hallmark movies prepared me for.

I love Aunt Dawn, and she needs the money.

"Right, good point." I extend my hand. "I'm Chloe Sullivan, I'm here to—"

"—Yeah, Brendan said you might show up." He looks down at my extended hand, and after a beat, extends his elbow for me to shake.

Sure, why not. "So. What happened?"

He starts doing the chop-chop-chopping of vegetables. I sip my to-die-for coffee. "Say what?" he says after such a long time, I thought he was either ignoring me or didn't hear my question.

"I came in yesterday, and the place was... dirty. What happened?"

He stops chopping, knife pointed at me. "That's for you to figure out."

Um? No. His kitchen, his responsibility. "It is. You're right. That's why I'm asking you. Since you must have been here the last evening the restaurant was open. That would have been... Saturday?"

"Saturday. Saturday. Yeah. Well, if the place was dirty, you could ask Shoshana. She's front of house."

"How about the kitchen?"

"What about it?"

Anger starts coiling somewhere deep inside me, but I manage to keep it in check. "It was dirty."

He drops the knife with a loud clank on the metal surface. "Are you questioning my work?"

Well, yes. And your attitude. "Not at all. Look. I'm just asking for help here. The reputation of my uncle's restaurant rests... ninety percent on your shoulders." A little ego stroking never hurts assholes.

"I'm sure it hasn't been easy for you. For the whole team. To keep going when there was no clear direction. When you didn't know what the intentions of the owners were, if your jobs were secure—"

"Lady, I can find a job anywhere else. Tomorrow."

"Chloe."

"Huh?"

"My name. It's Chloe."

"Whatever."

"Or Ms. Sullivan. Whatever you're most comfortable with, Samuel."

"I'm most comfortable with Chef." I stifle my amusement, but he catches it.

"If you had any experience in the industry, you'd know to call me Chef."

Right. "So. Back to the kitchen. *Chef.* Who am I supposed to have a talk with?"

"You can talk to me."

At last! Ownership. I think? "Good. The kitchen was filthy. Dirty dishes. Greasy surfaces. Spoiled food in the cooler."

He looks around. "I don't know what you're talking about. Looks pretty good to me."

I see what this is. We're playing games. Maybe I should have left it the way it was, after all. "Who cleaned it?"

"Whoever was supposed to. It was done."

"No, it wasn't."

"A'right, then, I'll talk to them."

"And who's them?"

"Eric," he says, pointing his chin to a young guy who just came in. "He reports to me. You have something to tell him, you go through me."

"Great. So this is me telling you." I lower my voice so Eric doesn't overhear. "Party's over. Do your job."

His shoulders stiffen. "Anything else?"

"Yes. We need to discuss the menu."

He swiftly uses the flat of the blade to slide chopped carrots into a large metal bowl. "There's nothing to discuss. It's set for the season."

"Right. When is a good time?"

"For what?"

"For you and me to have a meeting." Something about Samuel and a knife doesn't sit well. Best have a talk when he's not working.

"Next week?"

"Why don't we make it Sunday?"

"We're closed Sunday."

"Exactly. Less distractions. Tell you what. I'll take you out. Brunch?"

"Lady, I don't brunch."

"Your loss, Samuel. Next Sunday at noon, here. We'll be discussing the menu."

What a piece of work! But I'd say I didn't do too bad. At least I didn't lose my patience, and I showed I was no fool.

I think.

On my way out of the kitchen I introduce myself to Eric, the kitchen prep guy, if our pay stubs are anything to go by. Eric is a young guy with skin problems and a clear fear of Samuel. He walked into our conversation and has kept his head down the whole time, shoulders hunched.

Then I almost literally bump into a young woman in chef garb, and that would be Corine, our sous-chef. Corine is red and out of breath. She barely glances at me and beelines for Samuel. "Fudge, Chef, I'm sorry, won't happen again. Daycare wouldn't take Theo with a fever and Mom—"

"Strike three and you're out," Samuel cuts her, jaw clenching.

"Yes, Chef."

"The boss here," he says with a smirk my way, "is pissed about last weekend. So I guess that means no more leaving early for you guys."

Eric and Corine both startle at his comment, widening their eyes at him like you would when someone is blatantly lying but you can't call them out on it.

I'm pissed and uneasy and not sure how to handle all this. I can't stand Samuel, but I need a chef. I need him to run his kitchen professionally, but I can't undermine his authority in front of the staff.

I introduce myself to Corine, we exchange a brief handshake and a small smile, and I leave it at that.

For now, I need to ride this out. Make some cash. I hope I made my point with Samuel.

I still put out a job offer for a chef on a couple of specialized websites. Then I pay some of the bills to keep the providers happy, and call Aunt Dawn to lie about what a wonderful time I'm having.

My next call is for my cousin. "I don't know how to put it other than, the restaurant is in the red. Pretty bad. Defaulting on payments."

"Shit," Brendan mutters.

"There's no reason an establishment like that can't do well in a place like Emerald Creek. There might be some tweaks needed," I add, thinking about the sad décor. "And I need to investigate our costs."

"What should I tell Mom?"

"Nothing until I know more. There's no point alarming her until I can offer solutions." For some reason I hold off on bringing up Chef Samuel's attitude. I'm still hesitating between looking for a new chef right away and figuring out what's wrong here. And there's the fact that Aunt Dawn pointed out that Uncle Kevin relied entirely on him. I can't just barge in guns blazing and fire the first person who crosses me.

Brendan grumbles something unintelligible, then says, "Makes sense."

After we hang up, there's still two hours to go before opening. I head to the cottage and take a shower and slip on my favorite little black dress. I tie my hair in a loose bun, strap on my three-inch heels and add a discreet gold bracelet and thin gold hoops to the clover pendant I always wear. Then I do my eyes a little smoky and my lips a little glossy.

I need the staff and the customers to believe the place is in good hands.

I pull into the back parking lot, close to the restaurant's employee entrance. A door to the right opens, and Moose steps out of what must be the pub's loading dock. I avoid looking that way, expecting to see Justin right behind him.

I slide out of my car, keep my head down, and hurry my steps. A warm and moist bump lifts my elbow. "Hey, buddy," I whisper.

Moose whines.

"Yeah, I know." I can't help but pause a second to plop a kiss on his muzzle and give him a behind-the-ears scratch.

Then I half-run inside and slide into the office to calm my heartbeat.

"I can't run tickets. The POS is glitching," Abby, our server, says as she passes me, carrying four plates at once. She stops for just a beat to make sure I understand what she's saying, then delivers her food to the back of the room.

Crap. The... what? Right. Point Of Sale. "Ok—what... what would you normally do?" I look around for help. Abby is already back in the kitchen. David, the bartender, is mixing two drinks at once.

Shoshana, our tall, thin, blonde and by all other accounts perfect hostess, lifts her shoulders. "Last time, we just cancelled people."

David seems to listen in, but he says nothing.

Cancel people? "Why?"

"Because... we can't track orders, and run food—"

"What's wrong with paper pads?" They had restaurants before the internet.

"—and print the tickets, and run the credit cards," Shoshana continues.

Um. Wow. "Hold on." Shit, shit, shit. "We're not canceling anyone. Office, now."

"Am I in trouble?" she whispers as she follows me, teetering on her heels as we both rush to the back.

"We're going to make manual receipts. Grab paper, scissors, pens, whatever you need. I want it pretty, and I want it neat, and more importantly, I want all the tabs to be perfectly correct, starting with our name at the top. Got a phone?" I ask on our way back to the front.

"Yes, ma'am."

"Use it to add up."

"On it. Anything else?"

"D'you know if Uncle Kevin might have kept a knuckle buster?"

"Who?"

"Mr. Murphy."

Her face falls. "Oh... right. Sorry—kept a—what?"

"The thingy for the credit cards." I make a sideways motion with my hand like I'm scraping something off the table.

Her face lights up. "Oh, yeah. Under the bar." I follow her, and we find it right under the bar register, with a neat pack of blank carbon slips.

"What's all that shit?" David asks, pointing to the paper and scissors and pens.

"It's for—"

"I get the intention. We got manual ticketing stuff down there too." He crouches and pulls a bunch of booklets with carbon copies and flops them on the bar.

I flash my smile at Shoshana. "Back in business."

"Yes, ma'am."

"Shoshana? Drop the ma'am please, you're making me feel old." She blushes. "Sorry."

With Abby reassured she'll be serving dinner all night—therefore getting her tips—and Shoshana hopefully learning a lesson on resilience, and David not a grumpy asshole—a refreshing change from the other men I've met here so far—I'm about to go sit in the office for just a second.

My feet are killing me.

I'm paying the price for wanting to look nice on my first day. Tomorrow, we're downgrading to what Aunt Dawn would call sensible shoes.

"Behind!" A flustered Abby storms past me toward the kitchen, holding a barely touched dish that I swear she just delivered to table nineteen.

I slow my pace and linger next to the kitchen door. "The fuck?" Samuel yells. "The fuck it's overdone. Tell 'em there'll be a wait."

Abby comes out of the kitchen, eyes bright and lips pursed. "I got it," I tell her. "You take five. Give me your apron."

Samuel barks at me. "You can't be in my kitchen! Not during service!"

I cross my arms, widen my stance, and look up at him. "How much?"

"Say what?"

"How much d'you pay for that kitchen?"

He looks at me like I have three heads.

"How much d'you pay for the food that was sent back?'

Now he's looking at me like he's ready to murder me.

"How much d'you pay for rent?"

I pray to god he doesn't know about the rent situation.

"That's what I thought." I get closer to him, so close I can smell his armpits and cigarette breath, so close I can feel the anger radiating, so close I could count the number of sweat beads pearling off his forehead. So close I can whisper, so this is just between him and me. "You get that salmon done right now, and you get it done so frigging perfect the guest will write us a five-star review that will erase the memory of all the shitty reviews we've gotten because of your crappy work ethic. And from now on, you're dropping the shitty attitude and you. Are. Focusing. On. Work."

His nostrils flare and his jaw clenches, and I see it coming, so I cut it short before the thought forming in his lizard brain makes it to his mouth and he does something we'll both regret. "And if you so much as think about quitting without giving me a proper two-week notice, swear to god, you will find no work in this state, no work in the northeast, no work on the East Coast, or the West Coast, or the Midwest, or the South, or Canada, or anywhere else in the frigging world because swear to god, I made a promise to my aunt and I. Always. Keep. My. Promises."

He holds my gaze in a stare-down contest.

"I'm waiting for the salmon," I say in clenched teeth.

"Salmon!" he barks, still in my face, still staring at me, but I manage not to blink.

"Salmon, coming up!" Corine answers from somewhere.

"Hands!" Samuel barks in my face.

I break into my sweetest, fakest smile. "Thank you, Chef."

I deliver the salmon cooked to perfection by Corine, comp the whole table, and we send in desserts and after-dinner drinks. Three hours later, while I'm reconciling receipts in the office and the kitchen crew is cleaning the kitchen and the front of house has the chairs on the tables and the lights on super bright so Trevor and Ryan—my newest recruits—can actually see where they're mopping, we get our five-star review.

The first in over a year.

I get to the cottage at two in the morning. Too wound up by the night, I open a bottle of Prosecco to celebrate.

There's not much else to celebrate than the review. We're more in the red tonight than ever, what with that big table entirely comped and all the extra stuff we sent them.

I can't make that a habit.

Samuel is going to have to suck it up and learn how to cook salmon properly the first time around.

CHAPTER FOURTEEN

Chloe

The rest of the week goes okay-ish. On Thursday I discover that when Samuel has arguments—he calls them meetings—with his staff, he conducts those in the cooler.

I ask Abby what's up with that, and she informs me that everywhere she's worked, chefs have held their heated conversations this way. Apparently, it's a thing.

Corine confirms.

Corine, Abby, and I run into each other at Easy Monday more than once, and that's where we've had *our* private conversations. Shoshana was there once or twice. In fact, all of Emerald Creek congregates at Millie's café throughout the day.

It turns out that by a streak of marketing genius, Easy Monday also carries used books, including a large selection of romance. The genius part of it is that the local library is heavily financed by someone who forbids 'dirty books.' Millie saw the opportunity and seized it. By creating a romance exchange, she ensures a steady flow of mostly female readers who consume her coffees and cupcakes while there. As they sample the books, they stay around in the comfy couches. They order more food and drinks as they turn the pages. This in turn has the effect of attracting the other half of the population at a higher rate than coffee alone would.

"It's kinda like Ladies Night all day long and every day," Millie informs me. "Except I'm just out books that were actually donated or bought by the pound. And instead of giving them away, I loan them out. When it's time for me to close, they leave with a book or two they have to come back to exchange or return."

Abby lifts her eyes from the title she's selected, *Your Place or Mine*, to inform me that not all men in Emerald Creek are assholes. All the women agree. Quite the opposite, they assure me.

I've just not been lucky, they say.

I would agree with that.

They further press that, actually, most men, including Justin, have high romantic potential and all sorts of bonus attributes. They seem to speak from experience. "You just caught him on a real bad day."

Moving on.

On Friday, Cass, aka Cassandra, the woman with the blue-streaked hair, joins our little circle at Easy Monday. She's some sort of business leader in Emerald Creek, being the owner of a famous lingerie shop in the back of which she hosts Game Nights. She broaches the topic of an upcoming town fair in which she strongly suggests the restaurant participate. "It would be great exposure for you."

I glance at what I consider my team. "We always told Kevin he should do it," Abby ventures. Corine nods.

I turn to Cassandra. "Done."

"Fantastic! The Events Committee will be meeting about this. You'll need to come. Details will be in Echoes."

This is when I learn that Echoes is Emerald Creek's own Social Media platform. Cassandra blushes when she realizes I haven't been invited yet. This is remedied within minutes, and I am now flooded with notifications of the latest gossip as well as important news such as, *Daisy has been sighted next to the covered bridge. Please slow down.*

I'm informed Daisy is a cow with wandering tendencies.

On Sunday, to my surprise, Chef does show up at our work meeting. I ask him for his menu costing, which he doesn't have. I ask him for his recipes, so we can start working on costing. He points to his head. "All in here."

"That needs to be written down. Standardized. I need this by Tuesday. And Wednesday we'll do some menu training. Abby and David need to be able to upsell."

He clenches his jaw, again, but he knows I'm right. There's always a lot of jaw clenching where Samuel is concerned.

Then I broach menu changes, and he pushes back. I let it go for now. Until I have the menu costing, that is.

We manage to part amicably.

I'll call it a win.

It's the middle of the day Sunday when I walk into the antique shop.

It's hours later when I walk out, squint in the dipping sun, and smile like a goof.

I found a pine chest and two night tables for the bedroom. A small farmhouse table and four adorably mismatched chairs to go around it with little flat cushions in sage green attached to them with bows. Two cozy armchairs for the living room and a boho throw for the couch. Two fat tree stumps polished to a shine that are almost free and will be perfect as side tables. A set of four plates with a hand-painted, red covered bridge and three matching mugs. Seven silver-plated spoons and five stem glasses.

With no rent to pay since it's included in the restaurant lease, and a cushy severance package, I can afford the indulgence.

Also, I deserve it.

My little cottage is going to be so cozy!

I've already returned the U-Haul, but the owner of the antique shop offers to deliver everything for free that very afternoon. "Autumn, my daughter, will help me. You go on and relax. I know exactly where you're at," he tells me just by seeing my name on the credit card. "We close at five. We'll be at your place around six."

I spend the rest of the afternoon exploring. I eat ice cream, dip my toes in the river, and promise myself to always have a bathing suit with me this summer.

I drive back home, take a shower, and wear cutoff shorts and a tank top. The antique shop owner and his daughter arrive, as promised, at six. Autumn is in her twenties, with a mass of copper curls cut to her shoulders and beautiful freckles all over her porcelain skin. She compliments me on my choices while I help them unload the truck.

"A little welcome gift for you," Autumn says, setting three wooden candle holders and three natural wax candles on the farmhouse table. She steps back to look at the space. "Amazing what a little furniture can do!"

My cottage does look more and more like a home. *My* home.

We did good work, and it's the end of the day. This calls for something. I open the fridge. "A beer?"

They exchange a glance. "We need to be somewhere," Autumn says. "Next time? We might have just the right wicker furniture set for your porch."

"Next time, for sure."

After they leave, I sit on a plastic chair on the porch, drink a beer alone, mesmerized by the view on the rolling hills set ablaze by the setting sun. Porch furniture would be nice, but this is close to perfect already. I'm having a slice of quiche from Easy Monday when Moose ambles up the driveway, to my porch, and lies with his head on his paws, tongue to the floor.

I bring him a bowl of water and pet him. He drinks and flops himself on his back for a belly rub.

I scratch and pet his tender skin.

So Justin is a dog person. On top of being an incredible, generous bartender. And a mean asshole. At least to me. I chase the thoughts away and retreat inside the house, or Moose will stay here all night.

I figure he'll walk himself back home when he gets bored of being alone.

But he doesn't, and it's getting dark. Cars might not see him. I try shooing him away, but he just smiles at me—I swear he does—his long tail wagging loudly against the porch floor.

"Go. Go see your daddy."

More smiling. More tail wagging.

"Shoo!"

At that, he rolls onto his back, a gigantic beast acting like a puppy. Shoot.

I open the passenger door of my car, he hops in, and I drive back toward the village. It's a short drive to Lazy's, but my nerves are shot. I'll just open the car door real quick, make sure he gets inside the building one way or another, and drive away.

I *do not* want to see Justin. Not now, and if can help it, not ever.

Chapter Fifteen

Justin

Knowing she's alone tonight when the whole village is invited to my community dinner is making me feel all kinds of shitty. It's one of those nights when I should feel good about myself, but I can't.

I've been doing these for as long as I've owned Lazy's. My chef, Shane, prepares a main dish. People can bring food and wine, but if they don't or can't, it's all the same.

The register stays closed. No one pays for anything. All the food goes on the bar, buffet style. People help themselves and sit where they want and catch up with friends they haven't seen in a while or make new ones. There's an anonymous donation system that goes straight to the people who really need it.

So usually, on Community Dinner nights, I feel pretty damn good about myself.

But tonight I feel shitty. There's one person no one dared to invite, because of me. The only person I really would care to see tonight.

And where is my damn dog when I need him? I peek out the back parking lot, but it's empty. I linger alone in the kitchen, nursing my shittiness, drawing on a bottle of soda.

It's one of those nights, I guess. I should get back to the pub, or I'm going to start thinking about why I feel like this.

About how I break everything I touch.

I never should have slept with Clover. From the moment I slid behind the bar in Boston and she still kept her eyes and her smile for me, I knew I should have stayed away.

She could have gone with any of the guys I made drinks for that night. It's not like they weren't giving her the right signals. But she chose to stick with me.

That made something stir inside me. I should have let her go when she called it quits and asked for her tab. But she'd already moved me. She'd already planted her sweet hooks in me. And I wasn't brave enough to fight it.

I wanted to taste that connection, for just one night.

For once in my life.

Truth be told? I think someone was looking after me, the other day in my pub, when I lashed out at her. Someone was making sure I broke our connection, forever. No going back. No daydreaming about what ifs. No trying to woo her now.

Good.

Moose's bark pulls me out of my thoughts. He *was* outside. I knew it.

I open the back door, car lights blinding me.

Squinting, I make out Moose's goofy head hanging out of Clover's car window, like he's played the best joke on me. Then my eyes slide to the driver's side. The light is bad, but I can sense more than see her closed-off face, the set line of her mouth.

I set my soda down and walk the few steps that separate me from her car, aiming for the passenger seat. How do I even begin to apologize? To explain what was going on in my fucked-up head?

"Where d'you find him?" is all I manage to say as I release my dog.

"On my porch." Her eyes barely slide to me before locking onto the emptiness in front of her. She puts the car in reverse, waiting for me to shut the door.

I hold it firmly open in my fist, my other hand against the roof of the car, my head leaning against my arm as I take her in. The outline of her profile. Her lush hair cascading down to her shoulders and her back. The seatbelt pressing between her breasts and across her hips, where my arms and my hands and my face were two weeks ago.

The bitter curve of her smile.

"Clover," I whisper.

"Don't. Don't you dare." She bats tears away furiously and releases her foot from the brake, the car backing up, taking me with it.

She hits the brake again and turns a deadly gaze to me. "Shut the door," she snaps.

No, no, I won't shut the door. She's hurting, and I did this, and I need to fix this.

"Shut. The. Door."

I slide in the passenger seat and shut the door.

She recoils against her side window, disgust, *actual disgust*, painted all over her face. Her hand creeps to the door handle, but her gaze stays locked on mine. She's giving me a chance. At least that's what I want to believe.

"I want to apologize about the other day. I didn't mean to—"

"Please leave."

"I don't want to leave, Clover. I want to make this right."

"Is this always about what *you* want? *You* only sleep with women once. *You* don't want to exchange names and numbers. *You* only want your rent. And stop calling me Clover!"

She stops there. I wait for the final blow. What will she have to say about how I told her to leave my pub? The way I spoke to her.

Nothing comes.

"So?" she prompts me, crossing her arms, one knee folded on the seat so she can face me.

"I... it was... I mean... Is this about *Boston*?" How about what happened at the pub?

"What do you mean," she hisses.

"I—I wanted to apologize for what I said to you, the other day. You know."

"Right."

"So?"

"So what," she bites.

"I'm apologizing."

She narrows her eyes on me and scoffs. "You mean, you wait until you run into me, force yourself into my car, and just say the words '*I'm apologizing*,' and expect everything to be fine? I got news for you. Forgiveness takes a little work."

"Right," I mumble. Heck if I know what kind of work she's talking about. But she's right. What was I expecting?

I step out of the car and shut her door just as light spills out the pub's back door, and Shane comes out. "There you are." His gaze turns to Clover. "Oh good! You came. Haley will be happy. I mean, everyone'll be happy, but she was just talking about you." His gaze slides to me.

Clover blinks several times, like she needs to adjust back and forth to what just happened in the car, between us, and what's going on outside, in the real world.

Music and voices and laughter seep from the open door while Shane stands there, waiting for us. "I'm going home," she says. Her hand closes on the gear while the passenger window starts rolling up. The hurt in her eyes nearly kills me. I did this to her. I excluded her from this community dinner. This is not who I am. Whatever happened between us shouldn't affect her experience here in Emerald Creek. This is the most inclusive, wholesome event, one I'm proud to have created.

She belongs here.

"Clov—Chloe. Come in."

Shane strides to us. She kills the engine as he opens her door and extends his hand. "Chloe, pleased to meet you. I'm Shane." The smile in his voice drips to his whole body.

His eyes trail down her while she gets out of the car, and I can't fucking believe it, but for a second there he sets his hand on the small of her back as he nudges her inside my pub.

The rest of the evening, I get to watch Clover fit into my universe perfectly.

All while avoiding me entirely.

Chapter Sixteen

Chloe

It's impossible to resist Shane's easy charm, so moments after saying I was going home, I step through the pub's backdoor and into its kitchen. The space is calm and orderly, all gleaming surfaces and neatly stacked plates and clean pots hanging by size. Nothing like the madhouse that the restaurant kitchen always seems to be, even when it's empty.

A heavenly aroma envelops me, and my mouth waters. The one slice of quiche I had on my porch was delicious, but it's clear it wasn't enough. At least not compared to what's cooking here.

The swing door to the dining room bounces open, the low hum of conversations suddenly spilling into the quietness. "Ohmygod, you're here!" Haley shrieks. "It's Chloe!" she tells Shane as if I'd just materialized in here on my own.

He smiles at her. "I know." He grabs a bowl, then dips a ladle in the simmering pot. "How are we doing over there?" he asks Haley as he hands me a steaming bowl of chili. I wrap my hands around it, its warmth giving me inner comfort.

"We'll need a refill soon, but we're still good. I was just wondering where you'd disappeared to." Then turning to me, she adds, "Follow me, m'kay?"

We enter by the side of the bar, which is laden with food in an assortment of dishes. "It's a potluck, but Justin always provides a main dish," Haley explains. "He can't help himself. Soft drinks are also free during Community dinners."

As we make our way through the crowded dining room, Haley stops in front of a middle-aged couple carrying their empty plates toward the bar. "Mom, Dad, this is Chloe," she says with a smile my way. "*Restaurant* Chloe," she adds, wiggling her eyebrows.

I dart my eyes around, ready for anything. They're Justin's parents too. Maybe they know about the persona non grata order. Maybe they'll tell Haley she has no business—

"Darling, we've heard so much about you already but not enough. I'm Lynn," Haley's mom says. She's tall, thin, and fit, just like her husband, and unsurprisingly, considering the looks of their children, they're both blond. "And this is my husband, Craig, and we'd love to catch up with you, but we hold farmers' hours, and it's well past our bedtime," she explains with an apologetic smile. "But you *must* come to Sunday dinner next week." Turning to Haley, Lynn strokes her daughter's cheek with her free hand. "Princess, you'll make sure she comes, right?" She smiles at her daughter like she's the most precious thing on Earth—to her, she clearly is.

"I will," Haley answers, giving each of her parents a soft peck on the cheek. Craig has stayed silent, I notice, with a dreamy smile on his face as he watches the interaction between his wife and daughter.

My heart warms at their easy happiness.

Haley guides me to a table where Grace and Autumn are seated with another woman I don't know.

Grace smiles at me. "You came!"

"Hey again!" Autumn says.

"I'm Kiara," the third woman says with a wink. She has delicate features and a pixie cut that makes her look harsher than she needs to, and makeup that's a little too heavy for my taste. But her gaze is full of good-natured mischief. "I heard you had quite the welcome committee here the other day. Glad we're past that now."

Just then, appearing out of nowhere, Shane reaches over to set cutlery and a glass of wine in front of me. He gives my shoulder a friendly squeeze and leaves before I have a chance to thank him.

"Uh, yeah," I answer Kiara, glancing toward the bar against my better judgement. Justin's unhappy glare is on me. Seriously! What's up with him?

Haley slides her own glass of wine my way. "Try this first, and tell me what you think." I take a sip from her glass. "So?" she asks expectantly.

"It's good!" I'm not a big wine connoisseur, but I know what I like and don't like. And I like this wine.

"It's blueberry wine!" Haley exclaims.

"Meaning...?"

"Not made with grapes, but with blueberries."

"That's... interesting. It tastes just like a... different wine."

"I know!" She starts telling me about her plan to create a vineyard on the farm, and her current explorations into the different forms it could take. Including a cidery. And blueberry wine. Or a straight-up blueberry farm within her parents' farm. "I'm just struggling with the concept. I don't want to exclude anything. I want to explore. But I can't call it a winery if I'm making beverages that are not from grapes. Right?" She looks around for help.

Grace widens her eyes.

Kiara says, "Just get started. Once whatever it is you're doing comes into existence, you'll find the name."

"I don't know," Haley mutters. "I feel like an all-encompassing name would help."

"How about a fermentory," I suggest. "*'The Fermentory,'*" I add with air quotes. "The King's Fermentory." Ideas start flowing. "The Princess Fermentory."

Haley looks at me with awe. "Put a pin on all that. I looove it. It'll be called The Fermentory." She makes a big sweeping gesture like she's seeing the sign already. "And we'll have vintages or reserves that will be "The King's, The Queen's, The Princess's, etc. Woohoo!"

"So when is this happening?" I ask.

Haley's shoulders sag. "Someday."

Kiara rolls her eyes. "Right now, only in her dreams," she tells me. "You're not getting any younger," she says to Haley. "Get on it, sister."

Grace has a small smile. "I can't imagine the work and the investment that must be."

"I can visualize it now. You know what that means? It will *happen*," Haley declares.

"Does that mean if I visualize the restaurant's street seating it will materialize?" I half joke.

"It might," Autumn says. "What are you seeing?"

I think about this. "I don't yet have a vision—literally—for what the place should be. I'd want something relaxed but with a chic feel. Laid back but still making people feel special. It would help if I knew the area a little better."

"Makes sense," Haley says. "I'm your guide if you want to explore."

"Careful! I'll take you up on that."

"I sure hope so."

The rest of the evening goes by real fast. People stop to say hello to the girls and welcome me to Emerald Creek. Everyone wishes me success. At some point Grace and I slide out of the booth to use the restrooms. As we're washing our hands, I notice a wooden box with a sign that reads, "Leave what you can, take what you need." Curious, I open it and see bills—some folded, some rumpled, some crisp—and loose change.

"What's up with the cash in that box?" I ask Grace.

She adds a bill to the small stash. "It's Justin's way of helping people who are too proud to ask," she says like it's no big deal.

"Wow, that's..." Thoughtful. And helpful. I settle for, "clever." I dig into my handbag and add my own contribution. "No one steals anything?" I ask as we leave.

"Why would they do that? It's neighbors helping neighbors without making them look like a charity case. Anyone who would take from those boxes without needing it would have a meeting with karma real quick." She says that like it's common sense, and god it feels good to hear. It restores my faith in humanity.

And maybe a little bit of my faith in Justin, for doing that.

"The nursery at Dewey's Hollow is having a summer sale," Haley tells me when we get back to the table. And after that, we could hit The Grange."

"What's the Grange?"

"Oh I loooove the Grange," Autumn says. "Always great finds there. Let's all go tomorrow!"

"I'll have to pass," Grace says. "Everyone's booking facials and pedicures. Getting all spruced up for summer."

"Let's meet up at The Growler when we come back," Haley says to Grace.

Our plans set for the next day, we stack our dishes and bring them back to the kitchen where Trevor and Ryan are manning the commercial dishwasher.

Then I slide out to my car, both relieved and disappointed that I've managed to avoid talking to Justin again.

The next day, Haley, Kiara, Autumn, and I pile in a pickup truck Haley borrowed from her parents' farm. Kiara feeds us scones, and I make them stop at Easy Monday on our way to buy us all a round of Road to Heaven.

The nursery is having a sale—all their annuals for a dollar each—so I splurge. Autumn helps me select them according to orientation (morning sun only), shape and color. We combine English ivy, impatiens, fuchsias, and a couple little white trailing things I promptly forget the name of. It's romantic and colorful. "It's so... chic and laid back at the same time," I comment as we load them in the truck bed next to the big bag of soil I purchased. Just looking at the flats of plants, I get a happy feeling deep in my gut.

"Grange now?" Kiara asks.

"Grange now," Haley answers.

"Last time I was there, they had these adorable metallic window boxes that would look stunning for the restaurant," Autumn says. "What do you think of metal?"

Metal would look awesome. "Oh, whatever's already there is fine, but thanks. That was a great idea." I'll put a coat of paint on the chipped wooden boxes affixed under the windows. It won't look stunning, but it will look clean. It'll blend in.

Of course, it won't stand out like metal. Won't make a statement.

But it'll cost almost zero dollars.

Five minutes after we pull into the place, I get lost in the alleys, gaping at treasure after treasure. Haley follows me, occasionally taking pictures of things for sale. The Grange only sells items salvaged from old buildings. No knickknacks or piles of refuse from estate sales. Instead, pedestal sinks, antique claw-foot tubs, children's school desks, antique lamp fixtures, antique doors, stained glass windows, mantels, and even cast-iron radiators. The occasional set of furniture from a hotel. Kiara disappeared in the upper level.

Autumn slides next to me. "You getting a vision now?"

"Totally." Just, not doable by me. But I know how I could sell the place to potential buyers. I know how the restaurant could look. "Where are those window boxes you were talking about?"

"They're gone," she says with a shrug.

"Oh. Alright." I shouldn't get so excited, so quickly. Over a concept. An idea. A vision.

I need to tamp things down. I'm only here to run the restaurant for a while. I'm not in charge of giving it the new life it deserves.

"Found an awesome mirror for my place. I loaded it in the truck," Kiara says, her forehead blackened.

"What do you think of these for the sidewalk?" Haley is pointing to a set of round metallic tables with matching folding chairs.

They would be *perfect*. They're cheap. But they're rusted. "I guess I could throw a coat of paint on them." I'm not sure how good I'd be at that. That would require sanding, I suppose? I don't have a sander. I can't buy a sander, that wouldn't be a wise expense. And what do I know about painting metal? I'd need pillows for the chairs. That's an additional cost. And the time it's going to take me? I have more pressing things to do. I'll have to settle for some standard issue restaurant furniture. "I'll think about it."

We pile back into the truck and stop at a small café alongside a brook. We order sandwiches and eat them sitting on the grass, our bare feet dipped in the cool water rushing down the hill. Then we lie on our backs, the hot summer air getting the best out of us while the hum of insects acts like a lullaby, at least for me. I close my eyes, the sound of Kiara cleaning herself in the brook the only thing occupying my thoughts. Turns out, her arms were dirty too, all from the mirror.

"How is your space coming along?" Haley asks her.

"Ugh. Slowly. It'll be awesome. Someday," her voice drifts to me.

"Are you doing a float this year?" Autumn asks her.

"It's up in the air at this point. What with Chris being closed."

A float? "A float for what?" I mumble, half asleep.

"The parade."

The parade? I lift my head and squint at Haley.

"On the Fourth? There's a parade on The Green," she informs me. "With floats, the high school band, and carriages. It's awesome! You should come and check it out. It gets crowded, but I'll talk Justin into letting you go to his rooftop, since you'll be closed anyway," Haley says.

I sit up straight. "Not anymore I'm not."

"It's a Tuesday," Kiara observes.

"I decided to open. We'll serve small bites." *No need for a chef.* "Fruit punches." *More profit.*

"Cool! When did you decide that?" Kiara asks.

"Just now." The sidewalk will be crowded.

Autumn claps her hands. "I love it!"

"Good for you! Will your staff be good with that?" Haley asks.

I'll find out soon enough. "Worst case, it'll just be me. Whatever I can do will be better than nothing." Now that I know there's a parade right in front of us, attracting maybe hundreds of people, I am not letting this opportunity pass.

"You have to get the tables and chairs. Come on. We'll help you paint them," Autumn says, getting to her feet.

I jump up. "Let's go."

Half an hour later, I'm paying for the furniture while the girls arrange everything in the flatbed.

"I'll never have those ready by the Fourth," I mumble as I hop back into the truck.

"I'll make the cushions," Autumn says. "I have leftover fabric from the resort renovations last winter. And Kiara will talk to Colton, right?"

"Sure, but why me? He's not *my* brother."

"You're the Colton whisperer," Haley says.

Kiara stays silent.

"Colton is Grace's brother," Haley explains to me, "and he's also a bit of a grump."

"He also owns a fabulous garage where they do custom works. So he'll have all the paint and buffer stuff you can dream of," Autumn adds.

"Are you sure?" I ask. That feels very imposing to me.

"Believe me, he'll be thrilled," Kiara says. "The guy lives for that kind of stuff. He'll do your tables and chairs with one hand while he redesigns the interior of a vintage convertible for his next client."

"He has those kind of clients here?"

"Canadians. Second homeowners."

"Call it third homeowners," Haley giggles, rubbing her finger and thumb together. "Money, money."

I didn't realize there was that much money in this small, sleepy town. It explains the quality and abundance of shops. It also begs the question: why isn't the restaurant doing better? The market seems to be there.

After we offload the flowers at the restaurant and the mirror and my furniture at Kiara's place, the girls drop me off at the cottage and we make plans to meet up with Grace in a couple of hours.

The Growler is an event space lost in the hills, with food, several bars, a stage, outdoor seating, and games. It's still light out when we meet up. "Let's keep this low-key for tonight," Grace says as she points to the outdoor seating area. "This place can get a little rowdy."

"You're right, sis. It's only Monday," Kiara says. "'Member when we brought Alex here for the first time?" She chuckles.

As they reminisce, my attention drifts and I take in the moment. The dipping sun creating a gold halo on the hills. The sound of music drifting from within. The crispy yet soft, hot, and tangy nachos hitting my tongue, chased by a maple margarita.

It's a perfect evening after a perfect day with girlfriends. I bask in the easy happiness, shoving down the thoughts of Justin that threaten to ruin it all.

On Tuesday, I wake up late, make a quick stop at Easy Monday, and get to the restaurant mid-morning, dashing straight from my car to my office through the back entrance.

I email David about my July 4th plan for the restaurant. Surprisingly, he replies quickly, and he agrees to work that day. He even suggests some fruit punches and specialty cocktails we could offer to up our margins.

We're on the right track.

Next, I email Samuel, feeling karma on my side, but I don't hear back from him. I call Corine and tell her my plan. "I can't make it Tuesday. Mom has plans already, and I won't be able to find a babysitter on such short notice. But if Samuel can't help out, I'll do a bunch of prep for you on Sunday and Monday. Next year, for sure, I'll make myself available!" My heart pinches at the idea that I won't be there to witness it next year. But I store the information that she and David have no problem working more.

Finally, I text Trevor and Ryan to find out if they're available to work next Tuesday. "No problem," Trevor answers, just as Ryan texts back, "We're working at the pub that day."

"Never mind! Thanks :)" I text back.

These are just minor setbacks, I decide. Not everything can go according to plan. I post on Echoes that I'm looking for extras on July 4th, but I'm not holding my breath. People either have a job lined up or fun plans.

To make myself feel better, I grab the trowel I found under the sink at the cottage and set out to fill my window boxes with all the flowers I bought yesterday. As I hit the sidewalk, I stop in my steps. The wooden flower boxes have been replaced with vintage aluminum boxes that seem to come straight out of a home decor magazine. They create a stark contrast to the building's exposed brick, giving it a retro-hip look.

It looks *awesome*.

And so nice of my friends!

I send a frenzy of excited group text messages and set out to garnish the boxes.

An hour later, I send them pictures of the finished product.

Once the tables and chairs are done, the sidewalk is going to look *fabulous*. And that will signal the restaurant's comeback.

I have a great feeling about that.

On Wednesday, *Chef* comes in and informs me that no, he won't be working on Independence Day.

Not everything can go according to plan.

On Thursday, Colton and Autumn deliver the tables and chairs, and they are more than fabulous.

They are works of art.

The metal is painted a slate gray, polished to a shine, the flat surfaces of the tables reflecting the sky and clouds. The chairs have thick cushions in a yellow and cream stripe.

Once all eight tables are on the sidewalk, with the chairs around them providing a pop of color, Autumn sets the cutest flowerpots, painted in matching stripes of yellow and cream, in the center of each table. "I was thinking herbs would look cool, with a holder for a drink menu, but I'll let you decide. Happy to brainstorm if you need!" she says, wiping her hands on her jeans.

Too stunned to talk, I lean into the impulse to hug her. Then I turn to Colton. Grace's brother is tall, dark, and sinfully handsome. He takes a step back, hands in front of him as if to say, 'I'm good.' I can't help but laugh. "Thanks so much for doing all this so quickly," I tell him. "How much do I owe you? Lemme get the checkbook in the office."

"Nah," he says. "Was nothin'."

"Oh come on, it was not nothing."

He looks at Autumn and shrugs. "I gotta go."

"Please. Let me at least pay for your time and paint."

"Paint was left over from a job and time was... nothin'." He ends this on a shrug.

Autumn gives him a friendly slap on the arm, and he slides into his truck. "He's good," she tells me.

That's super nice. But also, it's super embarrassing. How can I thank him?

The restaurant doesn't even have a gift certificate system.

We need gift certificates.

Another thing on my to-do.

Chapter Seventeen

Chloe

"My parents said you're coming. Plus, you have no excuse. Your restaurant is closed on Sundays. They're expecting you."

That was Haley, yesterday morning at Easy Monday. There was no mention of Justin, and his pub is open on Sundays.

Plus, why would they invite me if he'll be there? He's their son. They wouldn't do that to him.

Ergo, Justin won't be there.

The town is all decked out for July 4th celebrations as I drive through it—flags and banners and red-white-and-blue flower arrangements. I'm proud the restaurant will be part of the festivities. Corine and David worked extra to create small bites and fruit punches. Samuel won't work it, but he's stayed courteous through the tasting, not exactly partaking in it but not shooting it down either. Corine will come and prep on Monday. I'll make it work with just Abby and

Shoshana. It'll help our bottom line and bring the restaurant back into the community.

Why wasn't Uncle Kevin more invested in Emerald Creek? And why didn't Aunt Dawn ever go to his restaurant? Surely she would have done something about it's appearance. It's a moot point now anyway. How well did I really know them? I spent a few summers with them, but that was a long time ago. Things change. Children's perception of things are just that. Children's perceptions.

I veer under North Bridge onto a long, bucolic country road which Haley said leads straight to the farm (*'You can't miss it')*, but first winds through a spectacular landscape of lush pastures and thick woods. A sign at the bottom of a hill indicates I am entering King Knoll Farm, but with no sign of a farmhouse, I keep going. Just one soft hill after another, the rocky road dipping under the canopy of trees, then hopping over brooks that bubble down to the Emerald Creek.

The peacefulness of it all calms my nerves. My windows are rolled down, the air playing with my hair, bees zipping in and out of the car.

This will be fine. Having Sunday dinner at Justin's parents will be nothing. Correction. At *Haley's* parents. And Justin will not be there.

After one last turn, I happen upon a vast clearing, in the distance, a massive red barn built alongside the slope of the hill. Pastures delineated by white fencing. Woods framing the whole. In the forefront, a large, white farmhouse surrounded by a wraparound porch. People standing on the porch, looking in the distance or chatting or lounging in one of several porch swings. Around the house, children running after one other, chickens flying away as they approach.

In front of the house, a variety of cars parked haphazardly.

And Moose, his tongue lolling out, ambling like a goof to greet me. Shoot. Nope. I can't do that.

Luckily, no one's seen me—I don't think—so I put the car in reverse and twist my neck around to see where I'm going.

Just as I think I can make my escape unnoticed, Craig King waves at me through the rear window, a big grin on his face. I hit the brakes.

"You're fine right there, sweetheart," he says as he walks up to my open window. "No one cares about parallel parking here."

"Um... actually." My eyes dart to Moose, dreading seeing Justin come for him. "Something came up, and I have to go. I'll—I'll call Mrs. King to apologize, but it's rather urgent." I lift my foot off the brake, giving Mr. King the hint, I hope.

He backs up with me, his hand on the window.

"This about my son?" he asks.

"Um..."

"Justin. Knucklehead. This about what he said to you?"

I feel heat running up my face. "I'm sorry, Mr. King. I didn't—yes—no," I shake my head. "I really should go," I plead on a whisper.

"Craig," he corrects me. "You're gonna hurt Lynn's feelings—Mrs. King. But if that's what you want." He lets go of the window and stares at me like he's the one who's hurt right now. "My son is really an idiot. The rest of the family, we're okay. Why don't you find out for yourself? It's just us and a few close friends. I understand you're close to Haley now. She'd like to have you. Poor girl has four brothers. You can imagine."

I glance out my windshield. Haley's infectious laughter trills all the way here. Two little girls chase each other. Moose sets his head on the car's windowsill.

"Made a mean brisket," he adds sweetly.

How bad can it be? I kill the engine, grab the dish I made, and breathe in—breathe out as I follow him.

I'm barely on the front porch when Haley takes my dish and brings it inside, Mrs. King greets me with a side hug and reminds me to call her Lynn, and Cassandra ambles to me, her blueish hair flowing around her, her mysterious smile comforting me. "Every Thursday we have Game Nights in the back of my boutique. You *have* to come. It'll be so fun. We'll find someone to come and help close the restaurant so you can bring all your girls too."

My girls? Does she mean the women in my staff? "Where...?"

"Corine knows. Bring Shoshana and Abby too. Promise?"

What can I say? "Promise."

Grace walks up to me, shoves a glass of lemonade in my hand, and introduces me to Emma, a young mother who's the only CPA in town. I swap phone numbers with Emma, and she promises to come by the restaurant to sort things out during the week, when we're closed.

"Enough talk about work," Grace says. "Come, let's grab food. Sides are in the kitchen, barbecue is outside."

The farmhouse is stunning, with its wide floorboards, rehabbed fireplaces, and simple decor incorporating natural elements in an understated elegance.

We load our plates with sides in the kitchen. Grace takes a bite of the dish I brought—maple glazed veggies on a bed of herbed quinoa—and loads another side plate with just that, then we make our way outside through the back deck.

I tense as I see Justin manning the barbecue, stopping on the top step. His back is turned to us as he crouches to talk to a little girl, his muscles straining under the dark tee, the faded jeans. My heart flutters at the sight of him, then leaps when the little girl wraps her arms around his neck and gives him a kiss, then runs away.

Grace leans into me. "He makes the best barbecues," she whispers.

Justin stands and turns, and our eyes meet. His body tenses, his lips straighten, his face shuts off.

He didn't know I was coming.

And he does not want me here.

My stomach clenches, and I turn around and go back inside.

"You okay?" Haley asks. "You look like you need a real drink. Here," she says, "Bees Knees."

Fifteen minutes later, I've forgotten all about Justin. That's because the girls commandeered the front porch, and me, Haley, Grace, Emma, Cassandra, Lynn, and girls I'm just meeting now—Willow and Thalia—are sharing Bees Knees, and Autumn is telling us about her latest dating disaster.

After that, we all help ourselves to sides in the kitchen, everyone but me goes to the barbecue station, then we convene around the long trestle table set outside. I find myself between Hunter and Logan, two of Justin and Haley's brothers. They share the family's fair complexion and easy-going attitude (that is, except for Justin, as my internal jury is still out on that), and I'm beginning to warm to their presence, their easy banter, to the point where I don't *forget* Justin (how could I ever?), but I'm able to somewhat enjoy my time without wondering what to do with myself.

Until a distinct scent of spice and soap mixed with barbecue smoke fills my lungs, and a corded forearm with tattoos I'm intimately familiar with gently sets a plate of brisket in front of me. "You forgot this," Justin says softly, then disappears and doesn't come back to the table for a while.

And when he does, it's with what's left of my veggie and quinoa dish. "Anybody know who made that?" he asks. "And who wants more before I finish it?"

"Ohmygod, yes? That was the bomb," Haley says, extending her plate.

"Mom? There's only a bit left."

"You go ahead, honey."

"You sure? It's... spectacular. Have you tried it?" Justin insists, my inside warming at his words.

"No." His mother extends her plate. "Okay, just a bit, I'm really full."

"It was yummy! I finished it aaaall," a little boy declares from the kids' table.

"Anybody else?" Justin looks comically worried that there won't be any left for him, and I begin to feel heat creeping up my forehead.

"We're too full," several voices whine.

"We wouldn't want to take any food from your mouth," Hunter says. "You finish it."

"I'm offering it to you, dummy. Did you even try it?"

"Nah, I'm good. Veggies..." He makes a face.

"Don't know what you're missing." Justin slides three seats down and across from me, squeezing a stool between Haley and Cassandra. He chews slowly, eyes half-closed. "The vegetables are... they're perfectly cooked yet not soggy. I wonder..."

A la minute seasoning. Draws out the excess moisture.

"And then they're perfectly coated."

Well duh, tossed them, didn't drizzle them.

He continues, turning his forkful in front of his eyes. "And look at those colors! And the way the flavor just bursts in your mouth! It's like walking in a vegetable garden and eating right there except there's the caramelized taste..."

High-heat roasting. Best way to do it.

"Balsamic vinegar. They added balsamic to the glaze," he says.

Balances out the sweetness of the maple syrup.

"And the *coup de grâce...*"

Saffron.

"Get him his meds!" Logan jokes. "When he switches to French, he's about to have a food seizure." Laughter ripples around the table.

Justin closes his eyes, exhales through his nose. "What is it?"

Saffron!

"Turmeric," Justin drops.

Oh no! Justin.

"Turmeric. Interesting. I'll try that in my casseroles," Lynn says.

"This isn't just veggies. This is... poetry in the kitchen. This is love." His eyes slice to Lynn. "Seriously, Mom, you made this. Come on, admit it."

"I did not!" she shrieks and laughs at the same time.

"Jeez, Just'," Hunter says. "Why do you get so bent out of shape over a dish?"

"Food is love, and I need to know who made that freaking amazing dish."

I'm burning right now. I should have come out and told him right away. We wouldn't be having this conversation at all. Now, by not saying anything, it's pretty much the equivalent of lying. Thank god no one is paying me any attention.

Hunter rolls his eyes.

"How can you work on the farm and have that perception of food?" Justin asks his brother.

"He's good with fences," Craig tells Justin, and I feel Hunter tense next to me.

"Fences are important," I whisper to him, hoping to help avoid a family-wide brawl that I feel responsible for creating. I don't think he heard me, so I repeat, "No fence, no farm animals," louder this time and of course, this happens right in a sudden beat of deadly silence.

"Well said," Lynn says. "Thank you for keeping the peace among my boys. Sheesh! You should come more often."

My eyes glide involuntarily to Justin. Our gazes cross for a split second, then he clears his throat and looks away as I stay frozen, his profile doing all sorts of funny things to my insides.

"So, Chloe," Lynn adds, her tone suddenly serious. "How long will all this... take?" she asks, her fork twirling around the air like it's supposed to indicate what "*this*" is.

"Um...sorry?"

"This closing down the business." Conversations around us die down.

My head spins. What is she talking about? "Wh...?"

She leans over to make her point clearer. "Closing down Kevin's Fine Dining. What does it entail? I've been wondering why they had to send someone to do it, instead of just, you know—putting a sign on the door, emptying the fridge, turning the lights off, and leaving the keys with Justin."

Wh... what?

My gaze turns stupidly to Haley, who's looking at her mom like she's growing another head, then back to Lynn. Does she know something I should know?

Around the table, an embarrassed silence settles in. "Mom," Justin growls, his eyes closed, his fingers pinching the bridge of his nose.

Yup. There's definitely something I should know. Blood wooshes through my ears, and my vision narrows to my glass as I try and make sense of what she's saying.

Lynn is still looking at me like she asked the most innocent question. I'm sure she has, in her mind. I just wish I'd been sent the memo.

I don't want to look stupid. I don't want to create a scene. I just wish this dinner could continue the way it started.

"Oh, yeah, yes-yes-yes, of course." I nod and wipe my clean mouth. Take a drink of water. "Um," I shake my head, "There's still some loose ends and uh—" My cheeks burn. *Ohmygod. Is he breaking the lease? What will happen to Aunt Dawn?*

"The restaurant will participate in the fair," Cassandra cuts in.

"Right, and next week we'll be open on the Fourth, although it's a Tuesday and until now the restaurant's been closed on Tuesdays. Trying to make a little extra money." I feel all my eyes on me when I continue rambling. "Anybody who wants to work a couple of hours instead of having fun on a holiday, just pop into the restaurant!" I force a laugh. "But basically yeah, you know," I glance at Justin, who's studiously avoiding my gaze by scraping off the rest of my veggie glaze with his fork, sticking, it seems, individual grains of quinoa to the back of it, "we're in the ironing-out-details phase of it."

"Interesting! So how are you going about it?"

"Um... well, we—um. It's... lots of moving parts."

"But what's the target date?" Lynn turns to Justin. "Don't you need a date?"

He clenches his jaw. "Nothing's set in stone yet, Ma. We're still just talking things out. You're getting a little ahead of yourself," he adds with a bite in his tone.

"Well, I'm just asking a perfectly valid qu—"

Craig sets a hand on his wife's hand, a gesture that carries enough gentle force to make her stop talking and turn to him. "Honey," he says. "He'll figure it out. Like the kid says, you're getting ahead of yourself, and you're not helping."

"Oh okay," she says softly. "I was just asking because, you know, Justin needs... and um, I thought that's why Chloe was here, to you know, *iron things out* like she said."

My heart stammers and my throat tightens. Luckily people are politely avoiding looking at me, and the general conversation now moves on to Justin's community dinners. I take a sip of water, then another, the voices around me fading.

Is Lynn just ill-informed? Is Aunt Dawn unaware of something? Or was she aware of the agreement to close down the restaurant, and she didn't want to tell me? But then why bother? And surely I would have found something about it, some correspondence, emails, notes. *Something*.

I didn't.

Who's keeping what from me?

Just as my thoughts are taking a dark turn, I'm jostled back to the present by Craig's question, "Why don't we ask Chloe what she thinks?" and everyone falls silent as their eyes narrow in on me.

CHAPTER EIGHTEEN

Justin

She nearly chokes on her water when Dad calls her out. Jeez, can they leave her alone? Don't they see she's trying to figure out what's going on with the restaurant that she didn't know? Mom always puts her foot in her mouth—usually in a funny way—but this time she went too far. I need to put some distance between them and my business.

Clover is getting caught in that mess.

God, I'm the reason she's stammering through dinner, feeling awkward as fuck, avoiding my gaze when she thinks I might be looking at her.

I could feel her staring at my back, at the barbecue, her presence like a warming fire, an overall tingling. Then I saw her leave, and I know why she did it.

She doesn't know who I am anymore. And fuck, neither do I.

Now Dad wants her opinion on my community dinners, something my parents think I should stop doing or at least, scale back to just once a year.

Not a chance. But why are they putting Chloe on the spot for that? Are they trying to pit us against each other?

"Sorry—what—what is this about?" Clover says as she carefully sets her glass on the table.

"My son here," Dad says, pointing his fork at me, "maintains that his community dinners, where he actually *gives* out food and *closes* his establishment to paying patrons, are good for his pub. Now, you're a restaurant person, what are your thoughts?"

Her eyes lock with mine for a beat, and her breath catches. She turns her gaze back to Dad and answers, "Um... I think... I believe the restaurant business is about generosity and community building. It's hard and unforgiving and stressful. The margins are ridiculously low. You definitely don't go into that business to get rich, right? It seems to me that it shares a lot of similarities with farming? Which I know nothing about, so I could be wrong. But basically, we're all doing this to provide for the community at large, not only food, but the communion that food makes possible among humans. Bringing us together. Like we're doing right now, around this table. Without that, what do we have? Nothing." She stops and finally takes a small breath.

The room is quiet, everyone looking at her. She could be intimidated, especially after what Mom said, and given that she's contradicting my parents, but she soldiers on. "So yeah, having witnessed only one of Justin's community dinners, I would say they are in line with his mission statement. If he has one, that is. I mean being the village pub, the mission statement would have to include something about community building? No?"

Dad grunts. "Makes me see it in another perspective, I suppose." He lifts his beer to her, a toast of sorts, then slices his gaze to me, a twinkle in his eye.

"You have three months of reserves, Justin," Emma states.

It's three days after the barbecue at the farm. I'm in my office with my accountant.

A month ago, we'd decided to kill the lease and rent the restaurant out to another person.

Someone who'd know what they're doing.

That was before Chloe.

Before Clover.

The woman who gave me love and connection. Who gave herself entirely to me. Who trusted me to carry her through her night, through her fear. Through the night her life had become. In doing that, she gave me purpose. Validation.

She made me feel like a man again. Someone who could care for a woman, and that care made me better.

Made me feel alive again.

At the same time, she's the woman whose family took a life and threw money at it to make it better.

"Justin?" Emma repeats.

Was she saying something? "Yeah?"

"We can discuss the restaurant situation. She's not my client yet. This will be between you and me. I gathered from what your mom said..."

Her voice fades out again as I think back to Clover's reaction when Mom asked her her timeline for closing the restaurant. She clearly had no idea that was my plan.

Murphy should have pulled the plug earlier, because he was clearly not managing his restaurant anymore. He missed the mark of selling the business at a top price, when it was performing really well. That would have been several years ago, but he's always been stubborn and entitled.

Unable to see the tide was changing.

I've been wanting that space from the beginning, to add a different offering to the town. Something more in line with its vibe. Given our circumstances, my offers went through a realtor, but Murphy refused each one.

Then he started defaulting on his payments.

Then he died, and yeah, I thought that'd mean I'd finally have the space revert to me once the family realized their restaurant wasn't viable.

But then Chloe came in, and everything changed. Not just for me, but also for the restaurant.

Take yesterday, July 4th. Chloe saw an opportunity for exposure and quick cash, and she opened the restaurant. With no guarantee that her staff could make it. She was ready to shoulder the work all by herself.

When I saw her out there in the early morning wiping the tables outside, I asked what was going on. Ryan and Trevor said she'd asked if they were available to help, but they had to decline because I'd asked them to come in that day. I heard Corine had been looking for a babysitter.

I sent Ryan and Trevor over to help her, asked Chris and Alex if they could babysit Theo for Corine (I figured Alex could use the training and Chris was a veteran in baby stuff) and fielded Haley's devilish smile. "What?" I said. "Just being a good neighbor. Isn't that what you wanted?"

Soon enough, we were slammed to the point where we communicated with single words and only to get orders out, so Haley's attempts to tease or downright torture me were put to an end.

But I kept an eye on Chloe's portion of the sidewalk, and I can't say that I wasn't stoked to see it full, that my heartbeat didn't pick up when I saw Chloe delivering apps and cocktails, that I wasn't proud to hear people complimenting her.

And yet I can't stop wondering, how did Chloe get roped into managing the restaurant without knowing the whole history between me, Murphy, and Sullivan—her own father?

Is it even possible she doesn't know anything?

Does it matter?

"Justin?" Emma snaps me back into the present. "I'd be happy to act as an intermediary between Chloe and you, but you need to tell me what you want."

Fuck if I know.

"Do you want to try and get the back rent now? Do you want to give them a chance to make some money over foliage?" she asks, using our term for the fall season, when leaf-peepers flock to Vermont. "How quickly do you want to act? You could probably get a court order and have a new tenant in place come September."

Until Chloe rolled into town, I would have said yes to everything. The sooner the better. Now, I don't know.

I want her here.

I want her gone.

I wish I'd never met her.

I wish we'd never left that hotel room for the rest of our lives.

In the elevator, the weight of her body on mine grounded me, gave me a purpose, a reason for being. Her. She was my reason. Clover was all I needed.

Forget whose daughter she is. I'm over that.

The truth is, in the real world, I know I'll never be enough for her. I can't have someone in my life. Everything meaningful that I touch, I break. The most I can handle is my dog to care for.

Who am I kidding? He's the one taking care of me.

"Let's table that for after the fair," I tell Emma.

I can't even make a freaking business decision anymore.

That afternoon we're all gathered on The Green for a merchants' meeting called by Cassandra. The order of the day is coordinating the summer fair taking place next week. With Christopher winning the TV competition, we're expecting more visitors than we usually get, so there's a little added pressure. The good news is, he's back on his game, his girlfriend, Alex, is back, and we can put all their drama behind us.

Cassandra is standing on a bench and waves at us to get closer so she doesn't need to shout. Millie from Easy Monday is there, and Kiara in her capacity as pastry chef who works for Chris and for the resort. Christopher's half brothers, Ryan and Trevor, are standing in for him since he and Alex drove down to Maine to pick up Skye at his parents'. Ryan is ready to take notes on his phone while Trevor flirts with a recent high school graduate. The food group automatically stands together at these meetings, because some level of coordination will be required of us.

Kevin Murphy's restaurant is not represented. Did someone even think of telling Chloe? At dinner the other night, Cassandra mentioned the restaurant participating in the fair, but I felt she said that as a save. She read Chloe's confusion and my embarrassment at Mom putting her on the spot.

"For the most part, we want variety," Cassandra is saying to the shop owners, artists, and makers. "So we've assigned you booths to make the guest experience varied and interesting." She goes on and I tune out.

I glance toward the restaurant. No sign of movement. But her car was there earlier.

"Food providers, listen up!" Cassandra scans the crowd. "I don't see anyone from the restaurant," she says, looking toward Kevin's place. The door and window are shipshape clean now, with a fresh coat of paint and window boxes filled with colorful flowers and even tables and chairs.

"Last I heard, Chef had her cornered in the cooler, bitching about something or other again," Trevor says matter-of-factly. He's been working part-time for Chloe.

My blood runs cold. Chloe locked in the cooler?

"She can't stand that," I say.

"Say what?" Trevor asks.

"Closed spaces. She's gonna pass out." My eyes dart to the restaurant. Please let her come out, now.

"I'm not going in there," Trevor says. "They were going at it pretty bad. He has a way of twirling his knife... not for me, dude."

I elbow my way out of the crowd and run across The Green, nearly tear the door to the restaurant open, and jog into the kitchen.

"The fuck are you talking about?" Samuel's yelling comes out muffled.

Chloe's voice is barely audible. I can't make out what she's saying, and I don't care. I stomp through the kitchen, the sous-chef, Corine, and the prep cook ogling me like the crazy man I feel like right now.

"I will not compromise my name!"

I push the prep cook aside and rush to the cooler.

"Then do your effing job! All I'm asking is menu costing! I can't do mine if you don't do yours. I'm here to save th—"

I swing the walk-in door open, fuming. Samuel has his back to me, hiding Chloe from my sight. His chest is heaving, his knuckles white from holding onto the shelves, boxing Chloe in. Chloe stops talking, but he doesn't move when I open the door.

"Privacy!" he booms.

Chloe's sharp intake of breath is what does me in. I grab the collar of his chef shirt and drag him out. He's about my height, but thicker, heavier. He stumbles back, almost knocking me down, but turns around, enraged, his red, meaty face distorted in anger.

I get a glimpse of Clover, pale, shaking, barely holding it together, and my fist flies automatically into the pig's face, making contact with his nose in the most satisfactory crunch. Blood spurts as he buckles over.

I lean into the cooler and take Clover's hand. She follows me out, barely looking at her chef.

I drag her to the dining room. "You okay?" My hands fly to her head, treading her hair, searching for I don't know what, going down to her shoulders, her elbows, pulling her into me. Her sweet scent wafts in a wave, making me teeter.

She stiffens.

I pull away. "Sorry," I mumble. "Are you okay?"

She gives me the standard answer of an upset woman. "I'm fine."

CHAPTER NINETEEN

Chloe

I cross my arms on my chest to keep myself from jumping Justin after he's roamed his hands all over me. "I'm fine." I swallow with difficulty. Why is he here? Not complaining about him saving me from crazy Samuel, though. The guy was scary. He refused to meet in my office, so I brought the topic of menu costing to the kitchen, asking him, kindly I might add, when the eff I was going to get that breakdown?

I didn't use the eff word. Only in my mind and very quietly.

Before you know it, I was shoved inside the refrigerator, but worse than last time. He didn't waste time, started yelling in my face right away, cornering me, trying to scare me so that—what? I let him go on without doing his work?

If only I could have had more control over myself. But I got dizzy, I couldn't breathe, and he took it as a sign of weakness. A sign he won our argument. In one last-ditch effort, I yelled back at him, and that's when the door flew open, Samuel disappeared from my sight, and Justin finished him with the knockout for the records.

And then he checked me *everywhere* to make sure I wasn't hurt.

Oh god.

God!

So good I almost died.

So good I almost forget I hate him now, just like he hates me.

Luckily, I remember before I do something stupid like lace my hands behind his nape and fist his hair and rub my needy body against his muscular body and kiss him thank you.

I tell him I'm fine so he stops touching me, at the same time wishing he would see straight through my lie. Wishing he'd cradle me in his arms. Wishing he'd take care of me like he did in the elevator.

But that will never happen, and not only because he's a rude asshole who only wants his rent. No, that won't happen because he said in Boston that he doesn't want a relationship or a girlfriend. He doesn't even want the flavor of the night to know his name!

So why is he here?

"There's a meeting... on The Green," he says.

I blink outside the window. There's a group assembled around Cassandra.

"Oh, right." The events meeting for the fair. I tug at my T-shirt and run my fingers through my hair to smooth it, struggling to keep my eyes off Justin.

Breathe in, breathe out. Justin's scent hits me like a painful memory.

I straighten my shoulders and walk out without making a fool of myself.

"Chloe, you made it!" Cassandra beams. "Let me summarize things for you and Justin. This year we're shaking things up. We're teaming you up. Easy Monday will be paired with The Wright Bakery to create snackables with a Vermont flair. The King Farm will work with Kiara for an ice cream and dessert stand. And The Lazy Salamander and Kevin's Fine Dining will be working together to create a signature dish that blends comfort food and creativity." She takes a deep breath, her eyes darting between the two of us.

"Justin, can I count on Shane for that?"

"Absolutely," Justin answers, so close to me his deep voice does illegal things to my panties. *Remember: we hate him! I chastise my body.*

"Chloe, can we count on Samuel to work with Shane on this creation?"

Not over my dead body. I don't even know if I'll still have a chef tomorrow. Or tonight. "I'll work with Shane," I answer, my voice showing way more confidence than I feel.

A few faces turn my way. Cassandra is beaming. "Excellent! Duly noted." She scribbles something in a ring binder. "You and Shane will get back to me in the next few days to update me. I'll need the name of the dish, a brief description, and pricing. Feel free to create more than one dish."

"Strike that, Cass," Justin cuts.

More heads turn our way.

"I'll be working with Clov-Chloe."

Cassandra tilts her head. "How nice! I love it. Also heads up, you'll also both be assigned to a common booth at the fair. Next up, ticket sales! We need twelve volunteers..."

My ears buzz. My head is spinning. My heartbeat increases and my palms are sweaty.

Yet I'm in the middle of a park, in the heart of a small village, under a great, open sky.

I'm going to be working with Justin.

How did that happen?

"Give me your phone," Justin says.

I snap my head up. His sparkling green eyes are trained on me, his blond curls form like a halo, and I know exactly how good his mouth feels, yet my gut clenches.

"What?" I say on an exhale.

"Your phone."

Is he crazy?

"I just want to put my number in it." My throat tightens and my thighs clench. Does he not realize how inappropriately sexy his suggestion is?

I square my shoulders. "That's not necessary."

He dips his head. "Right. Do you want to set a meeting now?"

"Nope. *That* meeting can be an email. No point wasting each other's time."

He kicks the grass with the tip of his boot. "Gotcha." Then he spins around and walks to Lazy's, ass molded in his faded jeans, shoulders rolling under his white shirt, his ink showing on his tan forearm.

God. What am I going to do now?

To: Justin King
  From: Chloe Sullivan
  Subject: Dish collab

Dear Mr. King,

Following up on the request from the Chamber of Commerce, I'd like to suggest a brown butter lobster roll, served with a side of sweet potato fries with maple bacon aioli.

I look forward to reading your thoughts.

Sincerely,

Chloe Sullivan

To: Chloe Sullivan
From: Justin King
Subject: Definition

Dear Clover,

Collaboration: "the action of working with someone to produce or create something." (Oxford English Dictionary)

Yours,

Justin

To: Justin King
From: Chloe Sullivan
Subject: Rethinking this whole collab

Mr. King,

I will be informing Cassandra that I am delegating my chef to collaborate on this project with you.

Sincerely,

Chloe Sullivan

To: Chloe Sullivan
From: Justin King
Subject: Fate

Dear Clover,

The fate of poor Samuel is in your hands. His ego will not survive working with me.

Yours,

Justin

To: Justin King
From: Chloe Sullivan
Subject: Egos

Mr. King,

Your ego is on par with Samuel's, and this town could use a cleanse. I look forward to seeing both my problems obliterate each other.

Sincerely,

Chloe Sullivan

Hmm. No answer. Fantastic! I'll email Cassandra in the morning. Or the next day. I still need to tell Samuel.

Ohmygod, how am I going to tell Samuel?

Maybe I could delegate Corine instead of Samuel?

Nope. I can't do that to her.

Or could I?

I poke my head in the kitchen. Samuel might have gone to urgent care. I don't want to know. "Corine?" I ask softly, in case the bear is still there.

"Yes, m'a—Chloe?"

"Come here a sec." I close my office door behind her. She stands like a good little soldier, hands clasped behind her back, feet hip distance apart. "How would you like to work with Justin on a project?"

"Justin? As in, the owner of…?"

My thumb indicates the wall behind me that separates the restaurant from the pub. "That Justin." I explain to her what Cassandra wants. A collaboration.

"Why me?" she asks.

"I know, I know, it's a lot to ask. I didn't want to ask that of you, at first. It's... I can't have Samuel do it, obviously."

"Obviously."

"And I volunteered—to work on the dish... with Shane. But... there's been a change, and Justin stepped in, and I... I just can't."

"Oh—but that'd be great!" She beams.

No! No. It's the opposite of great. "Why don't you want to do it? It's an opportunity for you to create something."

"I don't think it's a good idea."

"You don't like him? He's mean?" I knew it. He's mean. I need to get him out of my system. A major reboot. Boston was an illusion.

Red spreads from her forehead to her chest. "Oh gosh no. Justin is... he's..." She bites her lip.

Is she crushing on him? She's totally crushing. That's good, right? "He's what?"

Corine clears her throat. "It's just that, Shane used to be our chef, and then he left to work for Justin, and so... I'm just concerned about rumors and such."

I remember Aunt Dawn saying something to that effect. "Justin poached Shane from us?"

She tilts her head and moves her mouth around, in a *'it's more complicated than that'* expression.

"Alright, whatever. I don't care what people think. You're not going to leave, are you?" I ask.

"Can I be honest?"

Shit. "Sure, of course." She's going to tell me she's leaving. I wouldn't blame her. I wouldn't want to work for effing Samuel.

"I think you should go for it," she says.

"For what?"

"The way he pulled you out of the walk-in?" She fans herself. "If I were you, I'd give anything to be working with him."

"That's—I just asked *you* to do that. As a favor for me."

"But I'm not you."

Okay, totally confused here. "Do you want to work with Justin or not on creating a dish for our town, gossip be damned?"

"No."

"Why not?"

"Because." Her face crunches like that of a stubborn child.

I rub my eyes.

"Because he cares for you, and you should give him a chance. I know he said mean things to you, really mean things, and he should pay for that, but how is he ever going to be able to make it up to you if you keep pushing him away?"

Why is my sous-chef so informed about my would-be romantic life? "Where is this all coming from? It can't be on Echoes!"

Full blush again. Her hands twist nervously in her apron now. "I really should get back. It's getting late, and I'm not sure Chef will make it back on time tonight."

"Right." The poor girl is going to take over service tonight, and I'm bothering her with my silly nonsense. "You'll do fine. I'll tell Shoshana to turn walk-ins away tonight."

She's already half gone but she turns around. "I can handle... a certain number. I know we need to reach our goals."

Thank god for Corine. "I'll check in on you throughout the evening. I want you to let me know *before* it gets too much. And Corine? Do you go to these Game Nights? I hear there's one tomorrow."

Her face lights up. "I'm always pumped up after dinner service, and Mom has Theo, so yes, I always go. I catch the end of it, and it's the most fun. The older ladies are tipsy by that time, and they always have the funniest stories. You should come!"

I beam my first big smile of the day. "I will."

CHAPTER TWENTY

Justin

I don't want to be her problem.

And fuck if I'm going to let her put me on the same footing as that shithead Samuel.

But I get it. I need to stop messing with her. She has enough on her plate right now.

When she said she was going to be working on the dish, I knew where she was coming from. It was never about Shane. No. She knows her chef is a dud, and she cares about the restaurant's reputation in this town.

She can't trust him.

But fuck. She doesn't even want to work with me. And no, I'm not talking to Haley. I don't need romantic meddling. I need sound advice.

So I walk over to Cassandra's.

It's the second time in my life I go into her store. When I was younger, we'd linger around, elbow each other, peak inside.

Cassandra owns an internationally famous lingerie shop. By international, she means people come from Canada to shop there. That's international. Even if it's just half-an-hour or so away.

My first time there was not so long ago. I stopped by to pick up garlic scapes she grows at her home.

This time, I need her help. Some sort of intervention.

I don't think I'll ever go there to shop for lingerie.

Although, looking at what's artfully displayed on the exposed walls of her boutique, framed like the art pieces they are, I picture Clover in them.

And waiting for Cassandra, I thumb through the garments that are on hangers, wondering which one I'd prefer Clover in. There's a deep red set that feels like silk. It's not an undergarment, I don't think—rather something she'd look great wearing in my apartment, strutting around. Or in her house, as long as I'm the one there to watch it.

I never thought I'd be that guy, but now I wish I were in the position to buy lingerie for her. I certainly screwed that up, big time. I adjust my jeans and scold myself as Cassandra approaches.

"Justin!" Cassandra embraces me. She's in her forties, slim and fit, with long, blue-streaked hair. How she's still single, I don't know. "That's quite the bold move, but I love it!"

What? "Hi, Cass."

She takes a step back, holds me at arm's length. "You're looking for an apology gift?"

An...? Shit.

"Oh. I misread you. Sorry."

Cassandra prides herself on being some sort of witch, and according to Haley and my mom, she is. "I'm here to discuss the dish. For the fair."

She lifts an eyebrow. "Ooooh. Not sure how I can help with that. I thought this was about Chloe."

Yeah. "She doesn't want to meet in person."

"Uh-huh? I wonder why."

I rub the space between my eyes. "Could you—could you help with that? Like, tell her she can't go back on her word or something."

"Her word?"

"She emailed you that she was going to send Samuel to work with me."

"Uh-huh."

"She did, right?"

"What's on your heart, Justin?" She gestures to a couple of light gray chairs that are way too dainty for me and perches on one.

I sit at the edge of the other, set my elbows on my knees, and let my head hang, my gaze on the wide, polished floor planks. "I messed up."

"Uh-huh."

"I just don't know if I can fix this."

Cassandra smooths her long silk dress absent-mindedly. "How bad did you mess up?"

"Real bad."

"So what Haley said was true."

I sigh. "She doesn't even know the whole story."

"Uh-huh. And you're coming to me because...?"

"The whole village won't know I'm asking for advice."

"M-hmh."

I'm waiting for her to speak here, but swear to god, she doesn't say more than the therapist Mom forced me to go to after the accident.

Finally, she breaks the silence. "Just put yourself in her shoes, and you'll be fine." Then she stands and goes to the back of her shop.

Looks like I've just been dismissed.

Back in my office, I reopen our emails. Reread them. Try to put myself in her shoes, like Cass said.

Well hell.

I've been one cocky dick. I need to fix this. Start from zero.

From: Justin King
To: Chloe Sullivan
Subject: Blank Slate

Chloe,

Rereading our emails, I realize I might have come off a bit cocky. Maybe even a lot cocky. And pushy.

I want you to know this was never my intention, and I'd do anything to start with a blank slate.

Justin

Two hours later, no answer. At least she didn't tell me to get lost. I think back to the scene at the pub. To the way I talked to her. All but threw her out.

I judged her based on who her family is. But she is *not* her family. I ball my fists, angry at myself. How could I do this to her? I know how she feels about her family. About her parents. Christ, she told me as much in the elevator. And yet I marched in on her, judging and berating her for something she never did. Doesn't matter that I didn't know who she was.

She's their victim too.

From: Justin King
To: Chloe Sullivan
Subject: Apology

Chloe,

I owe you an apology.

I want you to know I am deeply sorry for the hurt I caused you, and I'm ashamed of myself. I passed judgement based on who your family is. I, of all people, know how wrong and hurtful this must have been to you. I would do anything to take these words back if I could.

How can I ever make it right by you, Chloe?

Justin

"Just'. Bar's getting busy and I'm headed out."

Why is Haley leaving? What time is it?

"It's Thursday. Girls' Game Night. I'm late already."

"Right. Right. At Cassandra's, right?" Fuck. I hope they invited Chloe.

"Is everything okay?"

"Close the door."

She does and sits down, always game for some juicy gossip or drama.

"Hypothetically..." I start. I have to be careful, because Game Nights is gossip town on steroids. "If a man were to do a gesture to apologize..." I let her fill in the blanks.

She tilts her head at me, watching me squirm.

"What..." I continue. "What should he do."

"What did this *hypothetical* asshole do?"

Aww fuck. Can't she just help me out?

"This *is* all hypothetical, Haley."

"Well, if this hypothetical asshole hypothetically broke a teacup she really liked, he could go out of his way to find a hypothetical replacement teacup, and with the new teacup send along twelve or twenty-four very real, long-stemmed roses."

"Let's say he didn't break a teacup."

"Okay. So he rear-ended her. He could send a gift certificate to get her car detailed and twelve or twenty-four long stemmed roses."

"Let's say—"

"Just get off your ass and send her two or three dozen roses."

"I can't do that! That's a romantic gesture."

She rolls her eyes. "Women love roses, and it depends on the color of the roses, but fine. Send her an *expensive* bouquet. Don't be cheap, for chrissakes. And look up the meaning of flowers."

"The what?"

She stands and raps her fingers on my desk. "Google the language of flowers. You need to work at this."

Then she's gone, and I get behind the bar, thinking about Chloe the whole time. The evening drags on.

That night, from my apartment right above the pub, I start my internet search about the meaning of flowers.

Let me tell you, I had no idea.

It's past two in the morning when I hear voices and engines running in the back parking lot. It happens a lot with the restaurant staff. They're never loud, but in the middle of the night, you pick up on things.

I never paid attention to it when Kevin Murphy was still there. His business, not mine. Now I feel differently. And I know the restaurant's been closed for a while. At least three hours, if not more. The twins swung by after they helped close the place so the girls could go to Game Nights.

I leave the lights out, the glare from my computer screen and the reflection from the streetlamps guiding me through the open space of my apartment.

Samuel and David are hauling cases in a car. Not empty cases. The guys are straining, and the car does a little thump when they drop the cases in the trunk. It looks like bottles, but they're not empty. Not for consignment. The two guys go back inside.

Besides, I thought Samuel was out tonight. That's what Trevor said. I'm sure he did. Hospital. Made me proud, but I'm not stupid enough to brag about it. He even said Eric, the prep cook, had commented on how well dinner service had gone, considering they were down their chef for the second night in a row.

Samuel and David are coming back out, each carrying a bulky package. I can't tell what it is. Food? Linens?

They close the trunk, get in the car together, and drive away.

Maybe they're catering a dinner tomorrow? Maybe it wasn't booze, but... what? Tools?

Maybe.

Or maybe not.

I wish I could talk to Chloe about it. But the way things are between us now, she wouldn't even believe me. And I can't blame her.

CHAPTER TWENTY-ONE

Chloe

Shoshana, Corine, Abby, and I all go to Game Night. We had an okay evening for a weekday. Corine handled some walk-ins, I told Shoshana to turn the rest away without telling Corine, and dinner service went without any yelling or dishes returned or any other glitches.

We were closing the restaurant when the twins, Ryan and Trevor, showed up saying they heard we needed help with clean up since "the ladies" were going out. No questions asked, we left them with David and Eric and headed out earlier than planned.

Cassandra's lingerie boutique is like a mini art gallery dedicated to showcasing the woman's body. I've eyed it a couple of times already, but tonight we enter through the back door, which leads us to a hallway with the most extravagant she-living room on the left.

A number of women in varying states of tipsiness are sprawled on white couches, their pedicured feet propped on golden tables, twirling girly drinks in their hands, laughing and mock arguing about some version of a game of Clue.

"Yayyyy! The restaurant gang! You made it!" Haley shrieks and hurls herself at us. "Get them something to drink! Get them a foot massage by a hot guy! Get them..." She turns around and lunges to a mirrored bar in the back. With steadier hands than I would have credited her for, she starts mixing drinks for us.

I'm introduced to everyone, and minutes later we're plopped in adult versions of the bean bag, our feet are bare—but no hot guys to massage them—and the whole room stops its chatter when our hostess, Cassandra, says, "I am elated that you and Justin are going to be working together. I cannot *wait* to see what you come up with. There's nothing like the creative sparks that fly when inventive minds join forces." She turns her attention to a group of women lined up on a couch, one of them Grace. "Alex!"

A young woman with long, honey-colored hair perks up. "I know you just came back, and thank god for that, but—would you be able to film these two working on the new signature dish for the fair? A sort of *making of?*"

The woman named Alex leaves her friends to crouch next to me. "I'd love to. I've heard so much about you already. When are you and Justin working together?"

"I—I'm not sure... We might..." The room is dead silent. I glance at Cassandra, who's looking at me intently. "I might have been roped into something I'm not sure I can handle. I was fine working with Shane, but Justin, I don't know."

Cassandra smacks her lips. "I think I know where you're coming from. Justin was rude—"

"Justin?" Alex exclaims.

"Girl, you missed some action," Grace says, and Haley uh-hunhs.

"Justin was rude to you," Cassandra resumes, "but you need to keep that door just a crack open. Give him a chance."

"He hasn't really apologized."

"But he punched Samuel in the nose, and *there was blood everywhere*," Corine cuts in.

A few gasps come from the audience, from those who aren't twenty-four-seven logged into Echoes. There's no way that's not in there.

"Is he pressing charges?" someone asks.

"Nothing on the police blotter yet, and no radio chatter about that either," one of the older women says. "Looks like no one bothered calling it in," she adds, looking at Corine, who raises her hands as if to say, *I don't want anything to do with it.*

"I don't think punching someone in the nose counts as an apology, Corine," Cassandra brings the topic back to where she seems to want it.

"Wait. I'm missing pieces of the story," Alex says. "Why would this have anything to do with an apology?"

"Because," Corine swoons, "you should have *seen* him."

A lengthy account of my rescue from the walk-in cooler follows, after which Cassandra asks me, "Did he ever formally apologize for what happened at the pub?"

"Days later, he said, 'I apologize.'" A disappointed chorus answers me. "And that's only because he... we... bumped into each other."

"Yikes. I wouldn't settle for less than an extravagant bouquet of flowers," Haley says.

Grace and Shoshana and others I don't remember the name of approve loudly. Corine is beaming.

"But what happened?" Alex asks, getting frustrated.

"He's been totally out of control since he went to Boston. Before he knocked out Samuel, he yelled at Chloe."

"*Our* Justin? He's the sweetest man on earth," Alex says.

"I'm sure it's a girl. He all but admitted it to me."

Alex snaps her head to Haley. "A girl? Justin? For more than a night?"

"Ooooh. You might be onto something," one of the more mature women says.

"Grace, honey, find out from your brother if he noticed anything in Boston. Alex, ask your man if Justin let anything slip during one of their much-imbibed pity parties," Cassandra says.

"Imbibed? Justin?!" Alex's eyes are like saucers. "Oh my god, what happened to him in Boston? You're right. It's gotta be a woman."

My heartbeat drums in my ears, and my palms are sweaty. This is bad. Really bad. Could they find out it's me he slept with in Boston? And at the same time, I'm getting a hum. A nice hum all over. Is he really out of sorts because of our night together?

And what if they find out? Will they get in Justin's business even more than they are now? "What if... what if you find out and it upsets him even more?" I venture.

"I heard he got a new tat," Millie says, ignoring me.

"What?" This time it's Haley who can't believe what she's hearing. "The only tats he has are..."

"Those that cover his scars," Grace finishes.

A deadly silence follows this realization.

"Ladies, we need to sort this out. I went without bread for two weeks thanks to Ms. Alex here who thought it was cute to literally take a hike. I am not—not—going for an indefinite amount of time without a pub," Ms. Angela says.

"Hear, hear!" the whole group approves.

"Haley, try and find out what the tattoo is," Millie says.

"And where it is!" Corine shouts and holds her glass out for a refill.

"Hear, hear!"

"Did you hear about the potatoes at the Silver House?" a lady with white, curly hair says, moving the conversation away from Justin.

"It was in the police blotter!" Ms. Angela confirms. "I read Declan went in to check that everything else was okay. Lemme tell you, I had dinner there with Abigail last week—she moved in six months ago—and it's not just the potatoes," she adds firmly.

"What's the Silver House?" I ask Alex under my breath.

"The retirement home," she whispers back.

"Anyhoo," the lady with white, curly hair continues, "Declan sat with her to make sure nothing else was wrong. Turns out, that was it."

"Well, their food really *is* a crime, if you ask me," Ms. Angela sighs.

"Oh—the people at the Silver House are sweethearts. It's just the food is—"

"That was in the police blotter?" Haley asks, incredulous.

"Has to be, if someone calls the police," several older voices say.

"Man, I should have reported my brothers more often when I was a kid. Can't believe I missed out on having Declan check in on me!" she teases, oblivious to Corine shooting daggers at her.

"It would have been old man Frank, honey," Ms. Angela tells her. "Not handsome Officer Campbell at the time."

"Uh. Still worth the annoyance to my brothers. Wish I'd known you could do that."

"Chloe, dear, come here," Cassandra says once the commotion recedes, and some ladies are either being picked up or walking to their homes after we say our goodbyes.

What does she want from me?

She takes me to the boutique side of her house. "I'd like to give you a welcome gift. Something you would wear... to relax, at home, when you're in good company. If you get my drift." She winks at me.

"Um... no, I don't. I don't plan on having that type of company anytime soon. Or, like, ever."

"Ta-ta-ta-ta-ta. Nonsense. Turn around." She holds my hand and twirls me around. "Build it, and they will come. Pun intended."

"I don't want them to come!" I chuckle but still look at her stuff. It's absolutely gorgeous. There're all sorts of shapes of bras, all in beautiful fabrics—lace and silk, see-through or padded, demi-cup, full cup. Matching panties with various degrees of reveal and more elaborate contraptions that might have been worn by the women who inspired Bridgerton.

"You'll come around. Meanwhile, consider this. Wear beautiful lingerie for yourself. Every single day. You may be the only one to see it, but it will give you confidence, a sense of your worth. They say true beauty comes from within. Then wrap it up with a bow to match it."

"I like the attitude." I discreetly look at the price tags.

"There's a forty percent discount for locals," Cassandra says, then adds, lowering her voice as if there was anyone to hear us, "and I mean, us working people. Second homeowners consider themselves locals, bless their heart, but if I gave them a discount, I might as well close shop."

Smart woman. At a forty percent discount, I'm sure she still has a margin, if slim. It keeps some money coming in. "Are there a lot of second homeowners here?"

"Oh, baby. Yesss. The Boston and New York creme de la crop. How do you think I can have a shop like this here? Them and Canadians. They come here on the weekends, and they *shop* like it's their job. Which for some of them, it kind of is their occupation."

She's giving me a lot to think about for the restaurant. Data points I didn't have. Creative ideas to bring in more money. No matter what Lynn may know or think she knows, I haven't been tasked with closing the restaurant. But what she said put a fire in me, and I'm working double to make it profitable much earlier than planned.

Cassandra hands me a purple bag with *Cassandra's Lingerie* written in golden ink. "I can see the wheels turning. Here's a little welcome gift for you. Something to relax in after a hard day of work."

CHAPTER TWENTY-TWO

Justin

The next morning, I call Randy, the florist, and we have a lengthy talk about the appropriate flowers I should send to Chloe, all this, supposedly, confidential.

"I get my deliveries only once a week—Wednesdays," Randy says when we've decided what the flowers will be.

Shit. I'll have to wait another week? This isn't going to work out. I need to find another way to apologize. "I can't wait another week."

"I hear you. If you're willing to reconsider what flowers to include, I have a wedding this weekend. I can put together something to die for. But I won't have yellow roses or blue delphiniums."

Thank god. "Do people really care about the meaning of flowers?"

"Not if they were born in the last fifty years."

"Are you sure? I've been told it's important."

"If it's important to you, I can have them delivered a week from today."

Nope. "And you said you can do a bouquet to die for today?"

"She'll be talking about it 'til Christmas."

"Alright, deal."

"And what should the card say?"

Right. I'm keeping that part private. "I'll bring it to you." I run to the bookshop, pick up a cute little card with a puppy holding a 'Sorry' sign. Then I put it back down. Pick one up that says, 'Sorry' in gold cursive. Then I put it down. Grab one that has a novel written inside, a bunch of cheesy crap. I can find my own words, thank you very much. I put it back down, but I'm at a loss.

"I'd take the blank one inside with the watercolor of the covered bridge," Ms. Angela says. I hadn't seen her when I came into the bookshop. She must have been between bookshelves. She was my second-grade teacher, and now she runs a bed-and-breakfast. She's also in everyone's business, but that's okay.

A watercolor of a bridge? "I like it. Great imagery," I say. "Thank you."

"Good luck," she cackles.

Yeah, totally in everyone's business.

I get back to my office, write my apology, and seal the card. Then I bring my card to Randy, pay him, and rush back to the pub.

He was working on the bouquet and said she should have it within the hour.

I pray to god I'm doing the right thing. That it's not going to backfire on me. That I'm not coming on too strong.

My phone dings with a text message I don't recognize, with a 617 area code. It could be a food provider. Or someone looking to cater an event.

Hey, Justin, hope you're well. I need to talk to you.
Gisele

My phone dings again, a picture this time. A blonde who looks familiar.

I don't know a Gisele.

Do I?

No. I don't.

Haley barges into my office, looking flustered, so I pocket my phone. "Hey, boss, Declan wants to talk to you."

Declan is our police officer. What's going on? "Let him in."

Ten minutes later, I'm surprised. I shouldn't be. That little piece of shit Samuel pressed charges.

"The guy had a woman cornered in a locked space, and he was yelling at her. In her face. I'm asking you, Declan, what would you have done?"

"I hear you," he says, looking at his notepad, pen at the ready. "Did you have any particular reason to believe she was in danger?"

Hell yes. She's claustrophobic, and that alone is dangerous. But the guy was verbally abusing her. "He was *in her face*." She was seconds away from fainting. She could have hit her head. Just having a panic attack is terrible enough. I can't think of the consequences if I hadn't been there.

"So they were having an argument." He scratches his head. "Heard you had an argument with Ms. Sullivan as well. Hmmm."

Shit. I hate that he's making the comparison. I hate myself for what I did to her.

"Point is, people have arguments all the time," Declan continues. "Her staff was there, they didn't seem to think she was in danger. They actually said it was customary for Mr. Reynolds to have his 'private' conversations in the walk-in refrigerator."

"You find that normal?" I snap at him.

He leans back in his chair. "Help me out, Justin. The guy is pressing charges against you. If you're not telling me why you jumped him without warning and nearly broke his nose, there's nothing I can do. Who'll run the pub when you're locked up?"

Fucking locked up? Is this guy for real?

"Lemme ask you again. Was there anything to make you think Ms. Sullivan was in actual danger?"

"Yes," I reply without thinking.

"And what is that."

Fuck. "I can't tell you."

He snaps his notebook shut. "You guys are a bunch of school-boys. But I have to follow procedure."

"Sure."

"Don't wait too long to change your mind. I'd hate to see your mugshot in the paper."

Fuck. Me. My fists clench.

"You know where to find me."

Yup. South access road in the morning, Easy Monday parking lot around noon, outside the high school at three in the afternoon, around Emerald Lake Resort at five, and tucked behind a copse near The Growler after ten at night.

He tucks his notepad and pen in an inside pocket. "I never thought I'd say this, but between you and me?"

What?

"You should hit 420. You need to calm the fuck down."

Right. "Hey, Dec."

"Yup?"

"Supposing I suspected someone of stealing from someone else, how would I go about it?"

He leans his impressive stature over my seat. "Supposing you'd grow up enough to not keep secrets from law enforcement, you'd get your thumb out of your ass and get to the station with *specific, demonstrated* information, and you'd *let us take care of it.*"

"Gotcha."

CHAPTER TWENTY-THREE

Chloe

Samuel hasn't answered the text I sent him yesterday asking how he was doing, so I'm assuming he's not coming in today. This means my Easy Monday pit stop will have to wait until after I swing by the restaurant and get the day started.

"Great minds think alike," I tell Corine as a matter of greeting. She's here earlier than usual as well, chopping herbs. Eric comes in right after me. "Your usual from Easy Monday? How about you, Eric?"

Corine looks up from the marinade she's preparing, and blushes. "Um... there's someone in your office."

Why is she blushing? Could it be Justin? What would he be doing here? What am I going to do if it's him? And what if Samuel comes in? I swing the door to the office open and find a police officer occupying the whole space with his mere presence. His dark eyes pin me in place, and his stature is intimidating in a good way. The way you'd want a man of the law to be intimidating. The way, I might add, any man should be, if he's to be intimidating.

I get where Corine is coming from.

"Ms. Sullivan, I'm officer Declan Campbell." He gestures to my seat, so I sit down. Like I said, intimidating. Not going to question him.

"What can you tell me about the incident involving Samuel Reynolds and Justin King?"

Oooh, I don't like this. Don't like it at all. Specifically, I don't like the word *incident* associated with what I consider to be my restaurant, at least for now. I play stupid and frown. "What... *incident*?"

He smirks at me, tilting his head. "I thought you were smarter than that."

Ouch. Tall, dark, and handsome men in a position of authority and not wearing a wedding band should not show women they're seeing straight through their lies.

It's just plain cruel.

Luckily, I'm not interested, so I just make a mental note to not mess around with Officer Campbell and answer, "Oh, *that* incident. What about it?"

He sits comfortably back in his chair and produces a notepad and a pen. "What can you tell me about it?"

I blow raspberries. Really, what is there to tell? One asshole hit another asshole. I lift my shoulders. "Boys will be boys."

"Mmm, I see." He scratches his head. "Were you ever in any danger?"

I poke my thumb at my chest. *Me?* "Nah."

"Mr. King seems to believe that he went to rescue you from a potentially dangerous situation."

I squint. Mmm. "Did Justin say that?"

"Were you? In a potentially dangerous situation?"

Well—Samuel was in my face, but he didn't touch me. The only dangerous thing was if I were to fall because of a panic attack. "I suppose it's a matter of perception."

"Could Justin have *believed you* to be in danger?"

"Justin could have, yes," I answer carefully, noticing he switched from *Mr. King* to *Justin*. "Potentially."

"And why would Justin believe you to be in danger, and not your staff, who were right there?"

Shit. I can't tell him about Boston. About our history. That's not for me to tell. Declan Campbell might be an officer of the law, with rules around confidentiality and such, but he's bound to talk to a girlfriend, a mother, a sister. He'll put it in his report, which might be typed or printed or filed by someone other than him. Someone with looser confidentiality strings.

That stuff's going to be all over Echoes if I say anything. There's also the matter of Samuel. If I provide Justin with a valid reason for hitting him, I will lose my chef. Best if I stay out of this. "You know... Did you ask him?"

Declan's face closes down, but we're interrupted by a knock on the door. An impressive bouquet moves into the small office and is deposited on my desk. A man emerges from behind it, his eyes dart to Officer Campbell, and he quickly leaves.

Corine is closing the door, her eyes on the bouquet as wide as saucers. "There's a card," she whisper-cries.

Any flowers delivered to me would be fabulous, since that's never happened to me, but these are *truly* fabulous. I didn't think I'd ever be that woman, but the pink peonies, the blue delphiniums, the white lilies, all tied together exquisitely with airy little white thingies, spectacular greens twirling around, and a myriad of other flowers I don't know the names of, make me blush and ooooh and aaaaah.

Officer Campbell clears his throat, but I *have* to know.

Who sent these to me? Aunt Dawn as a thank you for running the restaurant (she has no idea what I'm going through)? Mom as a sorry for being a bitch (a daughter can hope)? Hopefully not Fiona as a thank you for the plane tickets, because I'll ream into her if that's where she spends her/my money.

I pluck the card off and tear it open.

As I'm reading, I feel the heat creeping from my center to my torso, my legs, my head.

I quickly slide the note back in the envelope and the envelope into my handbag and try to steady my breathing as I blink my eyes back to Officer Campbell.

He shuts his notepad and stands. "Mr. Samuel Reynolds pressed charges against Mr. Justin King. I'll just let Mr. King and his lawyer decide how many billable hours they want to expend on this."

I hesitate. Should I tell him that Justin is the only one who knows about my claustrophobia?

But Officer Campbell is already out the door, and I'm left alone with the spectacular bouquet.

I shut the door, pull the note back out, and read it over.

Chloe,

I am truly, profoundly sorry to have hurt you and ashamed of how I talked to you. Please know that these words were merely a reflection of my dark soul.

I understand that nothing I do can ever erase how poorly your first day in Emerald Creek went, but I hope these flowers bring you joy today.

Justin

I lick my lips and smell the flowers. I read the note again before sliding it back into my handbag.

Then I think back to what Officer Campbell said. That Justin believed me to be in danger, and I have to suppress images of him cradling me in an elevator.

I need to clear my head with work and coffee, so I call Corine into my office.

While she wraps up in the kitchen, I decide to send Justin a quick thank-you email. Email is safe. You'd have to put some effort into showing emotions over email, and I'll put effort on being businesslike. I can't have him thinking I'm seeing anything else in this gesture. Surely for him it was a formality, a way to get us back to normal, and I'm grateful for that. But it's nothing more, and I don't want to make it awkward for him. He doesn't want more. Never did, never will.

I open the email icon and see I already have two messages from Justin. My pulse quickens.

They're dated yesterday. *I should add my work emails to my phone,* I think as I click it open.

Chloe

Rereading our emails, I realize I might have come off a bit cocky. Maybe even a lot cocky. And pushy.

I want you to know this was never my intention, and I'd do anything to start with a blank slate.

Justin

A blank slate.

Last night, Justin wanted to start with a blank slate.

This morning, he sent me gorgeous flowers and the most touching note—though I'm not sure what he meant with his dark soul comment. Why did he send flowers? Did he think I was ignoring him after his emails? Is that why he escalated the apology?

Or did someone from Game Night give him an earful?

Did Haley say something to him?

That has to be it. Maybe she even wrote the note! Who knows? Why else would he talk about his dark soul?

I'm so confused.

When I click on the icon for his other email, I'm even more confused:

Chloe

I owe you an apology.

I want you to know I am deeply sorry for the hurt I caused you, and I'm ashamed of myself. I passed judgment based on who your family is. I of all people know how wrong and hurtful this must have been to you. I would do anything to take these words back if I could.

How can I ever make it right by you, Chloe?

Justin

My family? What's wrong with my family?

Well, lots of things, but as far as Justin is concerned...?

It can't be about his friggin' rent again, can it?

So confusing...

Also, so much for email not carrying any emotion.

Is it just me, or are his emails highly emotional?

Or am *I* highly emotional just because it's Justin?

The one thing I'm not confused about, is that I need to protect my heart. No jumping to conclusions. I'm the only one who made a whole thing out of Boston. He didn't. When I brought Moose back to him the other night and he was having his Community Dinner—to which he did not invite me—he was all like, '*Is this about Boston?*' like what happened between us was the most trivial thing.

God, I was so embarrassed.

Moving on.

I'll shoot him a thank you email so I can cross that off my to-do list. I need to keep on keeping on with my life.

It takes me the longest time to figure out what to write, though. As much as I should not care and just get it over with, I can't bring myself to hit *Send*, knowing Justin will be reading my words.

I may not matter to him, but what he thinks of me matters to me. Go figure.

When Corine comes in, I hit *Send* on the email ("Thank you for the gorgeous flowers. Definitely brought me joy today." I know—how original) and gesture for her to sit down at my desk, moving the bouquet aside so she has space. "I don't know when Chef will be back, so I'd like you to work on menu costing, please. It's one of the first things I need in order to get the restaurant on the right track."

She dips her nose in the flowers before sitting down. "Of course."

"Do you have everything you need to do that?"

"Yep."

"It's going to take some time, but if you could get started now, that'd still be progress. Use my computer. I'm going to run to Easy Monday. It's about time I get you and Eric your coffees," I say, smiling. "You're in charge while I'm gone!"

She looks a little panicked.

"I'll be gone thirty minutes, tops. Just do whatever I'd do. You got this."

Coffee and work. This is what I need to keep it together.

I return an hour later. It's a gorgeous morning, Millie was in an even better mood than usual. She introduced me to the owner of the general store, and we started talking about ways to promote the restaurant to locals during the week.

Yes. The restaurant will be open seven days. The staff just doesn't know it yet.

Oopsie.

To be fair, we'll be hiring more people. The goal is to make a profit, which means a raise for all of them. Win win.

Then I bumped into Craig on the way out. We said a quick hello, but I didn't get to chat with him seeing as he was on his phone.

It's best he doesn't know yet about my plans for the restaurant.

I bring Eric his iced latte with a double shot of espresso, get to my office, and plop in the chair where officer Campbell was earlier. Corine is squinting over the computer screen. "Here's your iced chai, dirty. How's it going?" I don't expect her to be done. Just to have started.

She keeps her gaze on the computer and takes a long pull on her paper straw. "Um... I might have gotten sidetracked."

"Sure. What's up? Anything I can help with?"

Slurp. "Remember when you said I should do whatever you would do?"

Hmmm. "Un-hunh."

"Well, I might have answered a message for you."

Umm. What?! "That's... fine. What was it?"

"And then I might have entered a chat..."

"M'kay..."

"And... Okay." She makes buggy eyes at me. "Hear me out. It's gonna be *fine*."

"Sure."

"I promise."

"I trust you." What else am I going to say? I like her, I need her, and I gave her unclear instructions.

She slurps her drink, toying with a little green thingy that springs out of the bouquet, looking all dreamy and stuff.

"I was creating all the columns in Excel, and that went well. And then I started on the rows, and that's taking me a whole lotta time, 'cause there's stuff on the menu that we don't ever sell, but it's there, so I have to price it, right?"

Oh. We'll get to that later. "Un-hunh."

"And your email thingy popped up."

"Right."

"And it was right in my face, so I read it."

How bad can it be? A delivery pushed back? A provider cutting us off? Samuel resigning? She'll find out anyway. "Okay."

"Actually it was a chat, and you said I was in charge and to do whatever you would do."

Right. But really?

Moving on.

"Right?" she insists.

"Sure." Note to self: Corine takes things literally—act accordingly.

"And so I thought you'd want to answer right away... since it was a chat." She dips over her chai so she doesn't have to meet my glare. "And so I did."

"Sure!" I chirp. "Wanna fill me in? What was it about?" I should have ordered a green tea with an extra shot of CBD.

"Maybe... maybe you should just read it yourself?" She grabs her drink and stands.

"Corine, its fine, I swear. Stay here and use the computer for your spreadsheet. Just tell me what's up."

"You're meeting with Justin tomorrow."

Whaaaat? I choke on the Road to Heaven, and she takes that for my answer. Rightfully.

"At your house. Nine in the morning."

My ears are ringing with the sudden upsurge of blood. That's... that's just not possible. Not gonna happen. I take a deep breath to keep my voice steady and *kind. Kiiiind.* "Lemme—lemme take a peak at the chat."

She scurries up so I can see the screen. "Technically, I signed C, so you *could* say it was me. If you wanted to... you know... get out of it." She slurps again. "I wouldn't, if I were you. But I'm..."

I must be giving angry vibes now, because she doesn't finish her sentence. *I am so stopping at 420 today.*

Justin

> I'm glad you liked the flowers.

Chloe

They are gorgeous. And they smell so good.

C

Justin

> Now that we've cleared the air, can we revisit working together on the dish for the fair? Cassandra has been busting my balls about it, and Alex (Have you met Alex yet?) wants to take photos and videos of us making it together.

J

Chloe

Of course! I'd love to.

> **Your place or mine?**
>
> C

Seriously, Corine? *Your place or mine?* God, I'm pretty sure that's the title of one the romances they were talking about at Easy Monday the other day.

Justin

> **I'll be at the cottage tomorrow morning. Nine okay?**

Chloe

> Perfect! <Happy emoji>
>
> C

And the happy emoji? I don't know if I'm more embarrassed by the content of the messages or by the fact that "I" have so easily accepted to meet with Justin.

You know what? It doesn't matter. It doesn't matter that my heartbeat picks up when I look at the flowers he sent. It doesn't matter that my palms are sweaty when I think about him coming to my place tomorrow. It doesn't matter that I'm already thinking about what I should be wearing for our meeting.

I doesn't matter because that's not what he's after.

And so I can just relax and focus on work.

We're just two business owners doing the right thing for our small town.

I should focus on the dishes I want to propose. I should start a shopping list and actually go shopping so I can show him that I can hold my ground when it comes to food. Even though I'm a numbers person, I know a thing or two about food and I intend to show him.

I'm so wound up by the end of the day, I definitely stop by 420 for gummies, or else I won't sleep. And this girl needs her beauty sleep.

CHAPTER TWENTY-FOUR

Justin

I know she's an early riser, and she slipped away from me once before, so I'm not making the same mistake twice.

I show up at the cottage at eight. Moose scratches the door while I knock. After a couple of minutes, the door opens, and I almost drop her Road to Heaven, my double espresso, and the bag of croissants I brought.

She's mussed up from her night, dark hair a sexy mess, blue eyes puffy from sleep, pink lips a little swollen. She's wearing... holy shit she's wearing that little nothing I saw at Cassandra's shop, and I was *right*. That thing looks like it was made for her. Shoulders bare except for two thin straps, legs naked up to where it's indecent, the red thing clinging to her tanned skin, taunting me.

She looks at me with a gasp, and I don't know if it's me or the cool morning air, but her nipples pebble.

I shoot my gaze right back up. "Morning!" I smile, trying to sound casual.

She blinks and frowns, and her mouth does those little waking up sounds. Sounds she never got to give me in Boston. Sounds I always thought as a little gross coming from others. Don't ask me, but coming from her, those sounds shoot straight to my dick.

Her gaze drops to Moose. "What are you doing here?" Awww, man. That just-awake, raspy voice.

"Coffee!" is all I can say.

"What time is it?" She blinks at the bright sky behind me. Then, narrowing down on the cups asks, "Is that a Road to Heaven?"

She moves from the door to let me and my dog inside and snaps her mug from the tray. Moose goes straight to the oversize bowl of water on the floor next to the refrigerator. "I see you have a regular visitor."

She gives Moose a scratch between the ears.

Damn it's hard to keep my eyes on her face and not let them drift to the rest of her, so I just turn away from her to look around her place. She's slowly making it into a home, and I see a side of her I didn't know.

Of course I didn't.

The cottage is still a little bare, there isn't any of the shit that people accumulate over time, but it's comfortable and welcoming. She has a little dining set, some decoration stuff. A thick area rug with some unusual motif. Nothing pretentious. I would have taken her for a more sophisticated type. I like this side of her.

"I had a gummy... or two last night. Best sleep ever," she confesses.

As I look at her, my gaze drops to her endless legs. My breath catches. and it becomes hard to breathe and hot in here. My eyes lock on hers. She crosses her arms for a beat and then points her thumb to the staircase. "I'm gonna take a shower. I'll be real quick." She grabs her to-go cup and stops on the bottom step. "We did say nine, right?"

"Yeah. Your assistant." I know it wasn't her answering her chat, because I was on the phone with Dad while I was on the chat, and he mentioned holding the door for Chloe who was walking out from Easy Monday with a tray of drinks.

Her eyes flash between annoyance and amusement. She purses her lips. "My sous. Corine. I don't have an assistant."

That's what I thought. She wouldn't have agreed to a meeting like that. I'll have to thank Corine, some day.

But also, she didn't cancel. That has to mean something, right?

The shower goes on and I can't help but fill in the visual, so I take Moose to the porch before I completely lose it.

What am I even doing here? What am I hoping? I don't want a relationship. I don't want a girlfriend. I'm not going to sleep with her.

I just want to be with her.

She comes back in a baggy gray track suit, her wet hair braided tightly on her back, leaving a dark straight mark between her shoulder blades. No makeup, of course, and no jewelry, except her clover pendant. She's trying hard not to look sexy. *E* for Effort.

No trace of the floral scent she wears, but the coconut note is stronger. I'm guessing it's her shampoo for sure and maybe also her shower gel. I don't know about that.

I'd have to taste her.

She sets a thick notebook on the table. "More coffee?" She's already at her espresso machine, so I just nod. "I need to find out what's in that Road to Heaven," she mumbles. She grabs a pen from a kitchen drawer, sets it on her notebook, and returns to making coffee, all without ever making eye contact. "So I was thinking," she says loud enough to cover the hissing and grinding of the espresso machine, "we should try and produce something that's halfway between comfort food and sophistication." She plops our cups on the table and brings a cute little pottery bowl for the sugar and a matching pitcher for cream. "Yeah?"

She sits at an angle from me, our knees not quite touching yet, but they could. She did it so I could follow on her notebook, which she opens. Or maybe it's so we're not facing each other, and she can keep looking out the window, which is a much more interesting view than me.

I'm interested in her, so that's where I'm looking. Right at her profile. She pours sugar and cream, takes a spoon in her dainty hand, stirs, licks the spoon, sets it down, brings the cup to her lips, blows on the hot coffee, then takes a careful sip. Her eyebrow raises. "What do you think?"

What was she saying? '... *between comfort food and sophistication*' "Absolutely. Something that expresses the identities of both our places." I take a sip of my black coffee, the bitter taste hitting my tastebuds in a satisfying manner. "We should incorporate clovers."

Her cup hits the table loudly, a few drops of coffee jumping out.

"Don't, seriously," she pleads, giving me a glimpse of something unexpected. Something that pierces through me, making me believe for a fleeting instant that given the choice, that morning, she wouldn't have... *I need to stop.*

"Sorry. I mean—your uncle's restaurant. The sign has a clover, right?"

She's back to looking out the window. "A shamrock. We can incorporate a shamrock."

"I dunno. The word shamrock doesn't really—it doesn't sound great in a dish, you know? *Sham* and *rock*. Could we...? Clover is such a better word." I wanna add that it has the word lover in it, but I don't want to push my luck.

"Sure! Clover. Why not?"

Well that was easy. I'm almost disappointed.

"As long as we incorporate salamanders in that dish."

"Salamanders? No one eats salamanders."

"Why not? A bunch of people across the globe eat insects. The French eat frogs. Why wouldn't we create a dish with little salamanders?" Even when she says something so disgusting, she manages to make cute little gestures and faces, like that chick on the Schitt's Creek series that Haley used to be so hooked on.

"How would we prepare salamanders?" I wonder how far she's going to take this.

"We could try roasting them. Little baby salamanders roasted like marshmallows, on a toothpick for apps. With a clover leaf at the base. We could boil mommy salamanders and roll them in sushi rice and wrap them in clover leaves. Take big daddy salamanders and chop their heads off, filet them and eat them raw with just a little lemon and freshly chopped clovers."

"Like an oyster," I play along.

"Yes! So. It's set?" She dips her head to her notepad and starts writing.

"What are you doing?"

"Starting on our recipe."

"Chloe."

"Mmm?"

"Salamanders are a protected species."

"They are? Why?!"

"Because..." Hell if I know. I go for the obvious. "They're going extinct."

"Well, that's because they're lazy. Humans are never going extinct because we're always working-working-working. Salamanders should get a hint."

My mouth twitches, but I want to keep this going. Chloe on a black humor streak? Priceless. "Salamanders aren't lazy. They're... animals. They just *are*."

She narrows her eyes at me. "Your *sign* says they're lazy."

I give up, bend my head, and pinch the bridge of my nose, the low chuckle inside me building up to full-blown laughter. My whole body shakes, and my eyes tear up.

"It's not funny!" She mock-slaps my shoulder, and I throw my head back and laugh out loud. It's not *that* funny. I just need the release.

My laughter shows no sign of receding, and she turns to me, her knee pressing against my thigh, and she mock-slaps me again. This time I'm prepared, and I grab her hand. My laughter dies down instantly, and I twine her fingers in mine.

Our eyes lock while my mouth dips to her hand and my knee nudges between her legs.

"You're right, it's not." I run my lips on her knuckles.

Give it a little tongue.

She *lets* me, her knees squeezing mine for a beat.

I continue. "I bet you salamanders are bony. No flesh. Just as gross as licking your fingers." And I let her go, but not before I see the heat of lust in her eyes before they turn murderous on me.

She whips her face from me to hide her emotion and stands. Good, because I'm getting a hard-on, and I need to hide that from her.

If she's into me, she's going to have to show me.

"Fine. No salamanders."

Fuck. "What happened to me telling you your fingers are gross?" I stand and grab both our cups.

She moves to the refrigerator. "What about that?"

"Aren't you upset?"

She's rummaging in the fridge, her back to me. "No. My fingers aren't gross. I know it. *You* know it." She pauses to let that last bit sink. "You're just being an asshole."

"Good," I say, running our cups under water.

"Why?" she asks, this time clearly annoyed.

"Just got another reason to send you flowers."

She startles and keeps her head in the fridge. "We should really get to work. Here's what I'm thinking. We start with the comfort foods, and we elevate them." She takes out a long, covered dish, square containers, a block of cheese, and goes back to the fridge.

"Chloe, there's something I need to tell you."

CHAPTER TWENTY-FIVE

Chloe

While I'm trying to literally cool off by popping my head in the fridge, Justin steps next to me. "Chloe, there's something I need to tell you."

"M-hm?" I pop my head out of the fridge but hold onto the door to steady myself. His gaze is boring into me with more force than I can handle.

"I really *am* sorry, more than you can imagine. I wanted to tell you in person. I'm glad you liked the flowers, but I don't think that's nearly enough. I'm ashamed. I'm sorry. I want to make this right." He stops and just looks at me, waiting for me to say something.

My breath comes out shaky. "Water under the bridge, Justin. Apology accepted."

"Bullshit," he whispers. "You're still on the fence."

I lower my eyes. He's right, I'm not sure about him. But not in the way he thinks. It's going to be hard for me to be just business acquaintances. I'm going to have to reframe how I feel about him, and I'm not sure I can do that easily.

His voice comes out raw when he continues. "There's no excuse, only an explanation. I hadn't been myself since Boston. I was angry at myself. I took it out on others. Like I said, it's no excuse. I need you to know, this isn't who I am. That's all I have to say."

I want to ask him what he means exactly, that he's been 'angry' since Boston. I want to know everything he feels about Boston, but he's not volunteering that. What he did volunteer in Boston, was that he didn't want a relationship. Ever. So I'm definitely confused over what he's talking about. "Apology accepted. Truly." I lift my eyes to him and meet his, appeased.

"Thank you. From the bottom of my heart."

My heart bottoms out. Why isn't he saying more? Why does this seem to be so important to him?

He turns on his heel and steps outside. The door of his truck slams, then he comes back with a bag of food. "Christopher's breads, herbs from Cassandra's garden, and my sauces," he says with his half-grin that shoots straight to my panties as he plucks Mason jars from the bottom of the bag.

My mind and my heart battle over what to do.

Focus, Chloe.

Work is the answer. And the good news is, cooking has never been work for me. It's always been a hobby, a relaxation, so now that it's work as well? Double win.

It should help me focus on something other than my attraction for Justin. I mean, you would think.

Except, of course, he's here, in my space, close—too close—his scent all around me, leaning over me to help assemble mini BLTs and short rib sliders, teasing me endlessly over the way I beat the mayonnaise ("*like a miniature boxer hitting the punch ball*") or the way I pull apart the meat off the marinated short ribs ("*like you're ripping off a Band-Aid. Scrap that. Like you're plucking out your worst enemies' eyes.*").

"So you're saying, I'm aggressive when I cook."

"More like, you're letting off steam."

He's so right, though. I stay silent.

"My friend Chris—"

"The baker?"

"Yeah. He has this thing about the dough sensing the mood the baker is in, and how it impacts the result. He says the dough is alive."

"Lemme tell you, nothing I'm touching here is alive, m'kay? We can all take a deep breath."

He chuckles, a deep rumble that resonates deep inside me. My toes curl like they're on autopilot and we're in for a good orgasm. Darn it.

He leans over to grab one of his homemade sauces, his forearm brushing against mine, his front so close to my side we're almost touching. "How about the Mamamia sauce for the pork belly sliders?"

"What's the Mamamia again?"

"Maple Mango Madness."

"What's the Madness part?"

He shrugs. "I dunno. It's just a name. Haley was going through her Abba phase at the time."

"That doesn't answer the Madness question."

He chuckles. "Shit, Chloe, you never let go, do you? I made it in March. There. Happy?"

"Yes, happy." I take my mac'n cheese out of the oven and set it to the side to cool. When I turn around, he's scooping his Mamamia sauce onto an open-faced pork belly slider. My pork belly, marinated, his friend Christopher's brioche bread, and coriander from Cassandra's vegetable garden. He hands the bite-size slider to me, one hand under it so the sauce doesn't drip on the floor. I meet him halfway, my gaze hesitating between his green eyes and the food he's finger-feeding me. He could have set it on a plate. On a napkin. He could have let me take it myself.

He probably should have.

Because now, my mouth is closing down, his fingers are caught in, and his gaze is searing into me. What is he *doing*?

He wipes his fingers on a dishtowel and turns his back to me to fix himself the same bite. "So? What do you say? Good?" His voice is detached. This must have been nothing to him. I need to cool down.

I swallow and take a long drink of water. "It's heavenly." The pork belly is a perfect balance of crispy and soft, the coriander adds depth, and his sauce is equal parts sweet and spicy, in tune with the dish, enhancing it without overpowering it. The brioche bun provides a sweet, soaking vessel.

"Umm, good," he agrees. "Yup. That's up there. Lemme write it down." He grabs my notebook and the pen.

My fingers tingle as his decisive handwriting fills my notebook with the recipe we just created. I can't help but recognize it—so he did write the apology note himself.

This is ridiculous. I'm like a schoolgirl watching her crush fill her yearbook. Next thing you know, I'll be carving our initials on a tree. *Rolls eyes inwardly.* I grab our glasses and refill them with water, then set his next to him.

"Thanks," he says.

The countertops are full. We're not in a professional kitchen, so we have to make do with the space we have, which isn't much. It's cramped and messy but it's fun. And Moose can be with us. I throw him a lean piece of meat, which he swallows in a fraction of a second.

My phone dings with a text message from Corine. *Sam is here.* Hm. She doesn't call him Chef.

Me: Okay. All good?

Corine: Yes. Just wanted to let u know.

Me: thx

I'm not looking forward to going to the restaurant today. Samuel hasn't answered my messages checking in on him, and I'm not sure how to navigate that situation with him. He did lock me up to yell at me, after all. I don't want to blow it out of proportion, but I can't accept that. On the other hand, he was beaten up pretty badly by Justin for doing just that, so it's not like I feel super comfortable addressing that again.

What bothers me most is what Corine said about menu items we never sell. And I know we order a lot and should never be short. I'm going to need to look into that.

"Almost done with the pork sliders," Justin says, cutting into my thoughts. "What next?"

Me: Might be running late today

I put my phone down, stress from the day ahead lodging right between my shoulder blades. The restaurant can wait, for now.

The mac 'n cheese has cooled, so I grab a fork and dip in. "Holy crap. It's the best I've ever made."

"Is that your specialty dish?" he asks.

"Nope. My specialty dish is a lobster risotto."

He stops with his pen midair. "Why didn't you make that today?"

Last time I was going to make it was for Tucker. "It brings back bad memories."

"Lemme guess. Douchebag?"

I nod.

He shakes his head, writes more stuff in the notebook, then puts the cap back on the pen and comes to stand next to me. "Don't tell me you're going to let some asshole dictate what makes you happy."

"Makes me happy?"

"Cooking."

Hmm. He noticed. "I thought you said it made me angry."

He hands me my glass of water, and our fingers touch briefly. He keeps his hold on the glass and answers, "I said you were letting steam out. That was phase one. Now we're onto phase two. Happy Chloe." His voices dips a little, and so does his gaze, down to my lips. "Now drink some water."

And I do, and you'd think the cold would douse everything he does to me.

Nope.

He picks up a fork and digs into the mac'n cheese. I eye him sideways to test his reaction. "Holy fuck," he mumbles, then looks at me. "Clover—" he starts.

I can't. I can't take it. I can't have him call me Clover. "Please, don't," I plead. I feel my eyes betraying my feelings, and I hate myself for that. I'm going to pay later, I know it. But I need him to stop reminding me of everything he gave me that night.

Everything I'll never have again.

His gaze latches onto mine. "Sorry, I slipped." His gaze drops down to my mouth, and I turn around to break the connection. To breathe. Does he want this? Do *I* want this?

His phone buzzes on the counter with an incoming call, and he shoots his hand over to silence it. Then it dings repeatedly with a slew of messages, and I can't help but look when he grabs it, swipes the messages open and closed, but not quickly enough that I can't see the picture of a blonde in a suggestive selfie pose.

"Seriously?" he mumbles and starts doing stuff in his phone. "This phishing shit is getting out of control," he says, and I breathe better. Why am I feeling possessive of him?

"Where were we? Right. Your mac'n cheese." He takes another forkful and closes his eyes, giving my eyes freedom to roam his chiseled jaw, the gold stubble that grated my thighs not so long ago, his Adam's apple bobbing when he swallows. "That's the shit. We're keeping that."

"I dunno. It's not easy to eat at a fair. People would have to sit down. Use forks and stuff."

"Then why'd you make it?"

"As a starting point."

He snaps his fingers. "Let's make breadcrumb-coated balls of your mac'n cheese. Deep fried. Bam."

I dip my fork in the dish and take a bite. "I like the idea." What could we serve this with? "With tomato soup?" That's a little basic. I can do better. I load my fork with a heaping serving. The shit *is* good, and it's getting to midday.

"Gazpacho," he says, his eyes shiny.

"Ohmygod—yes! That's genius," I spurt with my mouth full. "Little shots of gazpacho!"

He takes a mock bow, his messy blond hair falling all over, and when he straightens, somehow he's gotten closer to me. Very close. So close it's hard to swallow.

He flings his finger to the corner of my mouth, wiping it. I stop breathing, my body humming with desire for him. For his touch, his gaze.

His friendship.

All of him.

I know he doesn't want a relationship. A girlfriend. A date. I could want all of that, with him. But right now, I want his finger back on my mouth. I want it *in* my mouth.

Is my lust for him going to ruin our new friendship?

He licks the finger that was on my mouth, taking his time, his gaze caressing me, making me miss a heartbeat or two.

"Are you eating food that came from my mouth?" I blurt on a whisper.

He removes his finger from his mouth with a pop and places his hand against the counter, right by my side, his forearm brushing against my waist. "I wish." His eyes drop to my mouth as he inches closer.

Oh.

My.

God.

My tongue wets my lips.

"Yoo-hooo! Anybody home?" We both jump apart as the front door slams shut. "I saw the two cars, and no one was answering the door. I wondered if you'd killed each other alr—" Alex stops in her tracks, a knowing smile spreading slowly on her face. "You're alive! The two of you!" She sets a tripod on the floor and fusses with Moose while I get myself together.

"Nice braid," I say. "Coffee? Water?"

"Hungry yet?" Justin asks.

"Starving. Chris has been up since three."

"Bet you were with him," Justin says as he hands her a pork slider. "I'm surprised you made it out of the house at all."

She blushes. From what I heard, she and Christopher are finally together after a love story that was so hot it made the news. "I was—ohmygod these are the bomb," she says with her mouth still full.

Her eyes dart between the two of us. "Who made these?" She takes her phone out and starts filming us.

"Team creation," Justin answers her as I say, "I'm not—I'm not camera ready."

Justin trails his gaze over my track suit, lust in his eyes, and Alex giggles. "You so are. Totally authentic, you two. Love it. Just ignore me and keep doing what you were doing before I came in." She lifts her gaze from the phone to set it on us. "Just keep it PG and throw in some cooking, ya know?"

CHAPTER TWENTY-SIX

Chloe

We end up making the mac'n cheese balls and the gazpacho while Alex films us and takes close-up photos of the foods, standing on a chair so she can have a perfect looking-down angle. We drink more coffee, make more food, and finally end up having a late lunch on the porch. At some point Justin carries our plates inside, and Alex and I get lost in our chatting. Then Justin comes back out with glasses of water for the two of us and says, "This was fun."

Then he hops in his truck with Moose on the passenger seat.

And then he's gone, and I feel a little lost. He didn't even look directly at me before leaving.

The dust isn't yet settled on my dirt driveway when Alex says, "You guys worked out okay, after all."

Us guys? Justin is going to hate that. "Oh—you got the wrong impression. I could tell you thought something was going on when you came in, but—there wasn't."

She looks out to where the truck disappeared, mischief in her gaze. "Does Justin know that?"

"Justin doesn't want anything," I say and immediately regret it. I've exposed myself. Oh well.

She stands and stretches. "Yeah, we'll see about that." My heart does a little skip at her words. She has a glow about her that's a testimony to how happy she is in her love life, and while I'm envious of her in a good way, I'm also aware that she's bound to look at everything with rose-tinted glasses.

We both go inside with our empty glasses.

The kitchen is shipshape clean, the leftovers boxed and labeled in the fridge, my notebook closed with the pen on top of it the only trace of what happened here.

"Holy crap!" Alex lets out a cascading laughter. "He's definitely a keeper," she adds as she bags her tripod.

"Alex," I say as I walk her to the door. "I'm—I'm serious. About earlier. Nothing happened between Justin and me." I can see where Justin is coming from. Small towns have a way to obliterate your privacy in a way that can seem stifling, and maybe that's one reason why he's so careful about not having any crossover with whatever he does when he's not in Emerald Creek. I don't take Alex for a gossip, but I'm feeling oddly protective of Justin. "Nothing happened today," I hammer. At least that's the truth.

Her gaze, playful earlier, gets deeper as she pauses on the threshold and turns to me. "Okay," she says softly. "But I hope something does. Fast."

I let out a deep sigh once she's gone.

Justin nearly kissed me, and I wanted him to.

So much.

Was it just the heat of the moment?

Will we have this again?

Will he create the opportunity again? Should I tell him something?

And why is he flirting with me? He knows who I am. He has to know I want him, right? There can't be a doubt in his mind. I'm like a blushing teenager around him. He has to see that.

I wipe my hands on my thighs as I stand right where we were when he licked his finger, set his arm against the counter and against my waist, drilled his gaze into my eyes and all but told me he wished he was eating food out of my mouth.

My inner parts beat painfully at the memory.

My horniness is embarrassing.

The truth of the matter is, I had fun today. For the first time in a long time. I had fun doing a simple thing I don't get to do enough: cooking. And it was effortless with Justin. We fell into it like two old friends. We shared the same codes, laughed together.

It felt so good. So easy. So natural with him.

I wrap my arms around my middle, suddenly feeling lonely without him. I shake myself together, go upstairs, and take another quick shower. I swap the bulky track suit for capris and a T-shirt and head to the restaurant. I'm confused and hopeful about how my relationship with Justin has taken a turn for the better. I take my time driving to the village, windows rolled down, air in my hair, noticing the lush pastures, two horses galloping playfully, the lake glistening in the distance.

Life is beautiful.

Rosy glasses, Chloe.

Samuel is there alright, two black eyes and a big-ass cast on his nose. I almost feel sorry for him—that's how bad he looks. "Chef, you look like... like you should stay home. For a couple more days at least."

He slices his gaze at me. "Got a job to do." He hands me a wad of papers. "Here you go." It's the menu costing.

"Are you cleared to work?"

"You don't want me here?"

"Of course I do. I just want to make sure..." This guy's ego is so oversized, I'm not sure how to handle it. "You know what, never mind. Thanks for being here. Let me know if I can do anything."

I retreat to the office and open his menu costing. Then I open the file Corine created on my computer and compare the two.

And they're very different.

Samuel's recipes include a lot more of the expensive ingredients, like saffron. His foie gras appetizer calls for one-hundred and twenty grams of the duck delicacy, when Corine's inputs it at forty grams.

I go back into the kitchen.

"Guys, we need a recipe book. With weights and all that shit." I make it sound like I don't know what I'm talking about. Then just to show solidarity, I add, "Owners request it." I do know a little more than what I'm letting on, and Brendan and Aunt Dawn gave me free rein, but keeping Samuel in the dark about where my mind is, is key. "Chef, I think Corine could use the overtime hours, if you want to delegate that to her."

"Nah. I'll do it."

"Great. You and I need to meet about the fair. When you have a minute."

He drops his knife and turns toward me, leaning his hip against the prep counter. "I'm running a fine dining kitchen. You want to have fun, go for it. But don't think one second I'll have my name mixed into that."

I let his snarky remark about me having fun slide. Actually, I do plan on having fun. And I'll also work my ass off, but that's beside the point.

I pretend to look relieved, and maybe I am. "Glad you said that. I'll take over the fair. We're expecting an influx of visitors in town as well as on the grounds. So be ready for a larger than usual crowd. Can you handle being open all day that Saturday? We need to start bringing in more revenue."

The *'Can you handle'* provokes him in a good way, just like I anticipated. "Whatever you need, boss."

"Thanks."

"Anything else?"

"Nope! Just the recipe book. My uncle's family is expecting my report by early next week," I lie. "And that analysis needs to be part of it."

He nods. "Talk to you for a second?" he asks, his chin pointing to the walk-in cooler.

"I'll be in my office."

Surprisingly, he follows me. I flop into my chair. "Take a seat," I say. "What's up?"

He leans his imposing stature against the door, towering over me instead of sitting at my level and effectively preventing anyone from coming in. I don't know if that's a strategy or second nature. I'm thinking the latter. "You're getting awful cozy with Justin King."

Um... define cozy? "What do you mean?" I cross my legs but catch myself before I cross my arms. I need him to feel like he can talk to me.

"The whole fair thing, that's not something Kevin would have done. Ever. And it's not because I don't like it. I mean obviously, it's not the right place to be for an establishment of our caliber. But besides that, Kevin would never have cozied up to King."

"I'm confused," I admit.

He narrows his eyes on me. "King has been trying to get the restaurant closed for a long time. Started before my time. Kevin told me about it. When King bought the building, Kevin already had the lease, and King tried to get out of it, but it was locked down. I'm not sure how, I don't know the specifics, and it's none of my business. But I know what Kevin told me, and I'm thinking he might not have told his widow, so maybe you don't know either."

"Go on," I say, leaning back in my chair.

"For starters, you need to know King wants this space. To expand his pub, or for a wine bar for his sister. And he's stopped at nothing to try get it. He's sent us the health inspector under bullshit reasons. Took ages to repair a pipe leak that caused damage to our kitchen equipment. Had his friends post one-star reviews. Lets his dog shit on our portion of the sidewalk. You name it."

"Okay," I say, not sure what he wants me to do with this information.

"It may not seem like much, but I'm sure there was a lot more going on. That man," he says, pointing to the wall separating us from the pub, "was constantly harassing him for no reason and didn't act like a decent landlord. He stops at nothing to get what he wants." His jaw twitches with anger. His nose and black eyes are testimony to Justin's determination. Suddenly I'm back in the pub, Justin yelling at me when all he knew about me is that I was the new manager for the restaurant.

"I mean, there's a reason why Kevin had a heart attack," Samuel finishes, pushing himself from the door. "Days before it happened, King told Kevin it was only a matter of a few weeks for him to be shut down. Honestly, after Kevin passed, we were getting ready to close when you strutted in here with all your fancy ideas."

Fancy ideas? As in, a menu costing? Cleaning the kitchen? I hide the sarcastic thoughts overwhelming me. The more I know Justin, the harder it is for me to believe what Samuel and Aunt Dawn are saying. Forget my attraction to the guy. He's an all-around good person, and I'm not the only one to see it. "Thanks, Chef, appreciate the input."

"Anytime," he says, pushing himself from the door to leave.

"And, Chef? We'll soon be opening seven days a week. I'm hiring all positions. You won't have to work more days, unless you want to."

He says nothing for a beat, then, "I'll let you know."

"Sure. Take your time."

He nods and leaves, his slow, loud footsteps sounding through to the kitchen like he's trying to mark his territory.

He didn't express interest in the new hires. Didn't ask to interview them.

Which can only mean he has no interest in the restaurant.

But Samuel's admission that they were getting ready to close the restaurant nags at me. It fits with what Lynn said at the farm, but not with what Aunt Dawn and Brendan imparted to me. At all.

Then again, they knew nothing about how bad the restaurant's situation was. They knew nothing, or didn't tell me anything, about Uncle Kevin considering shutting down the restaurant. Or being forced into it.

Justin wants the space back. Could he have pushed Uncle Kevin too hard? Caused his heart attack, like Aunt Dawn and Samuel suggested?

Like I said to Justin my first day here, without really believing it myself.

But what if it was true?

Should I feel guilty for being attracted to Justin?

Chapter Twenty-Seven

Justin

From: Chloe

To: Justin

Subject: Follow up

Hey

Today was fun!

Cassandra was asking for names of the dish(es)... What do you think?

Anything else you need from me? Do we need another prep session?

Let me know...

PS My cell number is in my signature line.

Chloe

I enter her number in my phone, then hover my finger over it, wanting to call her. To hear her voice. To know how she's doing.

No, we don't need more prep. I took pictures of our notes in her notebook, I'll place orders with my vendors on Monday.

We're all set. Nothing more needed.

I do want to answer her, though. Engage her. Continue the conversation.

Maybe I should just stick to email for now.

"Two Heady Toppers and a Sip of Sunshine," Haley announces. She wipes her forehead and assesses the crowd outside. "What'd I tell you? After the Fourth, it always picks up."

I look out to the sidewalk where our tables are full. Inside is getting packed as well.

"How's the restaurant doing?" I ask like I don't care, while I pour her first two beers.

"They're slammed too. Those cute little tables are working. Even Chloe is on the floor."

And yet she finds time to email me... Something funny moves in my stomach.

"Being open on the Fourth was a good call," I say like I don't really care, when I'm bursting with pride at Chloe's resourcefulness. A lot of locals attend the parade, and they got to see another side of the restaurant—an approachable side.

"Where were you earlier? It got a bit crazy here for a minute," Haley asks.

"I had shit to do. For the fair." I set the two beers on her tray and start on the third.

"Oh right. Why'd you have to do this on a Saturday?"

I shrug like I have no idea. Like this was never in my control. "Cass said so."

"Cass?" Haley frowns, seeing straight through my bullshit. Cassandra is the opposite of a micromanager. She's actually great at suggesting to people what the end result should be and nudging them to figure it out on their own.

I set her Heady Topper on her tray and grab a rag. "Beers are getting warm," I growl at my sister.

She rolls her eyes, balances her tray, and leaves.

'Even Chloe is on the floor.'

I want Chloe to be successful. Not so she can pay the rent.

For her.

I've seen what she's capable of in a kitchen, and sure, that doesn't make her a chef, but that makes her a restaurateur. Someone who understands how the end result should be. Someone who would be fantastic at gently guiding a young chef, or, why not, a team of cooks with manageable egos into producing quality food without any fuss or drama.

Damn, her food was good. Great.

And her mouth. Fuck! *Her mouth.* My finger on her plump lips, her hitched breath... I'm getting a hard-on again.

If Alex hadn't come in, who knows what would have happened.

I need to get that shit under control. I can't go there with her.

Or with anyone.

"Hey, man."

"Uncle Justin!"

I jump at the familiar voices.

"Are we interrupting some daydreaming?" a third, teasing voice adds.

Chris and Alex are standing on the other side of the bar, watching me with amusement, while Chris's daughter, Skye, darts to the hallway leading to my office, where she knows she'll find Moose. When we're full of tourists, he knows to retreat to the back, where his presence is not a health code violation. When it's slower and mostly locals are around, my dog plops himself next to the door so people can get their daily dose of canine loving.

"Heard you had a productive morning," Chris says as he pulls a stool out for Alex.

"I guess."

"Oh yeah," Alex says as she pulls out her phone.

Chris is standing next to her, boxing her with his arms on either side, his chin on the top of her head. He can't get enough of her since they're back together, and I get it. I totally get it.

I know the feeling.

"Holy shit," Chris says. "That the new girl?" He cocks an eyebrow at me.

A slow grin spreads on Alex's face.

I set my hands flat on the bar. "What can I get you guys?"

"W-w-wait," Chris says. "You never said anything."

"About what?" I look at Alex, mildly alarmed. Is Chris about to say something sexual and highly inappropriate about Chloe in front Alex? What is he thinking?

"About how you can't keep your hands off her?"

I huff. The hell is he talking about?

"Or she's checking you out every chance she gets?" He points at Alex's phone.

Shit. Really? "Knock it off." Pretending like he's just pulling my leg, I go to the other side of the bar to fill an order for a couple who's just arrived. But seriously? Now I can't wait to see the video.

"Don't worry, I'm editing those parts out," Alex says when I return, her fingers flying on her phone. "There. All gone."

My stomach bottoms out. What did she just do?

"Babe," Chris growls, stifling laughter. "That was just plain cruel."

Wait. Did she actually delete those parts or is she pretending she did only to test me?

"Two Arnold Palmers, a Bees Knees, and a Thyme Will Tell," Haley calls out. "Hey, guys! What's up?"

Alex's answer is to show her the phone.

While I mix her drinks, I brace for the worst.

"Uncle Justin," Skye's little voice pipes in, "may I please have a grilled cheese sandwich and—"

"And French fries. Already placed the order with Shane, sweetheart."

She hoists herself on a barstool, a big grin on her face.

I finish up Haley's drinks, then set a Shirley Temple for Skye on the bar. Haley hands the phone back to Alex and takes her tray without a word. I risk glancing at her. I was expecting a lot of ribbing. All I get is tight lips, rosy cheeks, and laughing eyes.

But she says *nothing* to me, and that tells me I should be concerned. I'm just not sure about what.

"When are we tasting all that stuff?" Chris asks.

"What stuff?"

"Your food for the fair. You're not gonna go blind, are you? Let's do a tasting."

I rub the back of my neck like that's a complication I could do without, when since I've read Chloe's email it's all I've been wanting to do.

A repeat session with Chloe.

But with people around. No wandering hands. Or thoughts. "I guess that's an idea," I finally drop. Inside, I'm like a kid in a candy store. We'll do this here, in my pub. It'll be just Chloe and me in the kitchen. In *my* kitchen. "Sure," I add with a shrug.

The following Tuesday, Chloe is in my pub, in my kitchen, in fucking shorts and a tight tee on account of the heat in and out of the kitchen. "Did you see the videos Alex made of us? They're so cute!"

I did see the videos—the unedited ones. Alex sent them to me right after leaving the pub, the other day. There's over an hour of footage, maybe two—and I watched it all. And might have zoomed in. And might have sought and found release. More than once. "I haven't really paid attention." I hand her a chef's apron, but it does nothing to make her less attractive.

"Right, course," she says, seeming disappointed. "What are we working on today? Why did you need my crew to come in later?"

I get to the walk-in cooler and hand her containers. "A practice run. I had the kitchen here make those preps following our recipes. That's how we'll do it for the fair. Most of the stuff will be made in advance here at the pub, by Shane and his team. We'll shlep everything down to the fairgrounds the day of. We'll just heat up, fry a couple things, assemble. Basic stuff. You and I'll do that today to get our sea legs, and then we'll have a bunch of people taste and give us their opinion."

"Oh." Her shoulders tighten and her face closes up.

"It's gonna be fine." I hand her the meat container. "We'll reheat that and keep it in a chafer today. I'll be borrowing food warmers for the fair. It'll be similar. The main thing is the *mise en place*. It means setting out every ingredient in advance and logically on your workspace so you're not scrambling when an order comes in."

"I—I've never done this before. I'm not—I'm not—"

What is she talking about?

She lifts panicked eyes to me.

"The hell is going on?" I say softly. Hell, I do want to take her in my arms, and we're just getting started.

"I'm not qualified!" she blurts. "These are... professionals," she adds with a sweeping motion of her hand.

I pour the meat in a large pot, cover it, and set it on the range at low temp, then get a chafer ready and turn the deep frier on. "Right. And neither am I. I learned by watching, and that's what you're doing too. We're both restaurant owners lending a hand so we can run our businesses in two places at the same time. See, I love Cass and all, I really do, but the thing she doesn't realize with the fair, is that we all need to split ourselves in two. It's not like we're going to close our restaurants while the fair is going on.

"But you know who knows that? Our staff. And they appreciate that we're stepping in, taking on something that's not glamorous so they can continue to do their jobs and the town can have even more visitors. So believe me when I tell you, there will be no judgement on their part. Only encouragement. And let me just finish by saying, there's nothing kitchen staff appreciates more than to put their feet under the table and enjoy a meal they had no part in preparing. Especially if their boss is doing the cooking."

Color tints her cheeks. "Okay. I guess."

"Besides, you're an awesome cook." I set up the herbs and chopped veggies and brioche buns on a prep table.

She doesn't protest. At least there's that. Then after a long silence where she seems lost in contemplation, she whispers, "Thanks." Then she whips around and blurts the weirdest thing. "Saffron."

"Huh?"

Her eyes are like saucers, like she's confessing to some crime. "The maple glazed veggies on herbed quinoa. It was saffron. Not turmeric."

Of course it was her. Warmth spreads through me. "Why didn't you say anything?"

Her throat bobs. "I was embarrassed."

Embarrassed? What the fuck?

"You were going on and on about how good that dish was, and only after that did you ask who made it and at that point I was just overwhelmed," she blabbers.

"You're not good with compliments," I say, stating the obvious.

"You said other embarrassing things."

I did? "What'd I say?"

She waves my question away. "It was in the heat of the moment. It doesn't matter anymore."

"It matters to me."

"Oh. You said something about how the person who made it... I don't remember your exact words, but it was something about love, and well, it got a little embarrassing. For me. You know, if I'd said something at that point."

I set the chilled gazpacho on a prep table with the small shot-like containers next to it. "Grab that ladle there and set it over there?" Once she does, I ask her, "Why was it embarrassing to you? It was a compliment."

She shakes her head. "It's silly... I just... just took your compliment to heart, and I figured everyone would see right through me if I said anything. You know, like, they would *see* that we shared... a *moment* in Boston, and I know that was totally me extrapolating, but that was how I felt, and I couldn't help but be panicked at the idea. I didn't want to upset you any more than you already were."

"Upset me?" She's making no sense at all.

"You were super upset at me for showing up at your pub, and I know the whole rent mess wasn't helping my case, but well, when I saw you, I figured it out."

"Figured what out?"

"Why you were so angry at me. It wasn't just the rent. It was mainly because you thought I wasn't holding my end of the promise we made in Boston. So I just wanted to clarify, your secret is safe with me."

"My secret?" I can't believe what she's saying right now. The reason for my No Name, No Number rule was that I didn't want any complications. No expectation of any sort of follow-up ever happening. And certainly no assumption of any commitment of any sort. Not because I was hiding something from the gossips here.

"Well, you know, Bost—"

"It's not a secret what I do on my trips," I say, and immediately regret it when I see the hurt shadowing her face, quickly replaced by a brave yet tight little smile.

"Oh, good," she squeaks, then clasps her hands and says, "Should I check if anyone's there? It's noon already."

Thirty minutes later she's laughing out loud as she's retelling the story of how she pretended to want us to serve salamanders.

"He thought I was serious!" she hiccups, her gaze briefly crossing mine before settling on Alex, who's finger-feeding Chris. Those two can't keep their hands off each other now that they're back together and there's no reason for them to hide their relationship.

"I would've believed you," her server Abby says. "You're capable of anything," she adds with admiration.

"Remember when our POS stopped working?" Shoshana asks around. Chloe's front of house staff starts telling a story that happened when she was just starting out, while Chloe shrugs it off, laughing a bit.

She's back from the freak-out moment she had in the kitchen, and I can't say that it doesn't mean something to me that she shows her vulnerability to me. I'm fucking proud that her staff thinks she's this badass boss who isn't afraid of anything, and I know deep down she is that.

But it rocks my world that she shows me another side of her. She showed her true self to me in the elevator, and she never put up that wall again. Not with me. And what am I supposed to do with that?

CHAPTER TWENTY-EIGHT

Justin

A week later, I'm at Clark's Meadow, wiping the sweat trickling down my forehead as I hammer the last stake into the ground. It's my least favorite part of the summer fair. We can't afford to hire people to set up the equipment, so we do it ourselves. And the food tent is the largest one, bulky and heavy. We start with that one, so the rest seem easy in comparison.

I stand and look at it. Mission accomplished. I step in the shade and reach for my bottle of water. Chloe is helping carry the trestles inside, and I do a double take at the way her T-shirt clings to her breasts and lifts, showing her narrow waist.

It's been ten days since our first cooking session at the cottage. Ten days since I almost kissed her. And thank fuck I was interrupted. Since then, I've been managing. Being close to her is part torture, part dream. I want more with her, but I can't have that.

I know it sounds weird, but I can't get past the fact that it'd be wrong. And not because she's Murphy's niece. Or Sullivan's daughter.

Fuck these people. No, the real reason is all about me.

A powerful backslap interrupts my daydreaming. "Stop gawking!" I jump in disbelief at the familiar voice, dread and happiness fighting for control over my feelings.

Before I can decide which it will be, I'm taken in a bear hug.

One I reciprocate, not believing it's finally happening.

My older brother, Ethan, is back.

I never thought I'd see the day.

He left ten years ago without saying goodbye to me.

After what I did, I can't blame him.

He releases his grip on me and holds me at arm's length. "You look good, brother. Damn good." He fist-bumps my pecs, and it's just like old days. I don't know if he's serious or teasing or making fun of me.

Because I may look good, but Ethan is a hunk. He's chiseled. He's beefed up. He's taller than me. He's always been, but he seems taller than last time I saw him, if that's possible. He's scary.

And I'm his little brother again, and I'm not sure how I feel about that.

"Tell me what to do," he says, squinting in the sunshine. "We'll catch up later."

He's been in the military for the last ten years. Surely there's other things he'd rather do now than set up tents?

"Seen Mom and Dad yet?"

"Course! Mom started cooking. Dad said you guys would all be here." He grips my shoulder like he wants me to relax, and maybe I should. "You look great, man," he says again. "Fuck, I missed you."

My gaze wanders to Chloe. She's laughing heartily with Autumn. They've already decorated the tent with a bunch of wicker baskets and garlands of flowers. Chloe is describing something to Autumn, using her hands a whole lot and making faces. "Missed you too, man." Guilt creeps through me at the thought of why he left, and I look away from Chloe, to the shrieks coming closer and closer.

Hunter, Logan, and Haley come running, and for a hot minute it's a jumble of King family hugs. Haley wipes a tear away and stays tucked under Ethan's arm. "Alright guys, tell me what to do," he says again.

"Jeez, they really brainwashed you! All you do is take orders?" Hunter jokes.

"Yeah, you little fuck." Ethan laughs. "By the way, Dad said to ride your ass for the piss-poor job you did cleaning the stables. Wanna give me a hundred push-ups?"

We all laugh and move to set up the next tent. I'll return to the food tent later to finish hooking up the generator I borrowed and all the portable kitchen equipment.

I glance toward Chloe, who's now helping Autumn write shit on blackboards. She lifts her head toward me, and our gazes lock for a brief moment before I'm pulled into setting up the next tent.

And now I feel guilty about her too.

When will this ever stop?

That evening the whole King family is having dinner together at the farm. Mom made a pot roast, and Dad is liberally serving wine and beer. It's only us for once, and it's all of us. Their monthly Sunday dinners, pretty much half the town has an open invitation, so we do get together a lot. But just Mom and Dad and us 'kids,' it doesn't happen often. And I can't remember the last time Ethan was here. It seems he came once during all the time he was enlisted, but we were tied up with some function or another, and I can't remember being seated like this, around the family table, since... since *before*.

I don't know when it will ever happen again.

Ethan is quiet about the stuff he does while he's away. He just says he's glad to be back and that it was time.

"So how long you staying this time?" I finally ask. I'm the last person who should fault him for enlisting, but I know Mom—and also Dad, although he doesn't show it—miss him a lot. It has to be bittersweet for them to see him, only to have him leave again, not knowing if this might be his last time with us.

He shrugs and looks at Mom and Dad. "It's kinda open right now. Don't have a timeline yet."

"You can stay here as long as you like," Dad says. "I'll keep you busy." He's always wanted all of his children working on the farm. I know he doesn't understand my commitment to the pub, but at least I stayed in town.

Mom shrieks, drops her fork, and clasps her hands to her heart. "Ohmygod, my baby is staying!" she says, and we all laugh. Ethan looks nothing like a baby, at least not to us. I don't even know how Mom can still see him that way.

"Mom, I just said I didn't know how long I was staying," Ethan says with a sad smile for Mom.

She waves his argument away. "That's a good start, honey. A very good start."

After dinner, Logan says, "Let's go to The Growler."

"How about Lazy's?" Ethan asks. "I wanna check it out."

Something warms in my core. Something that feels like pride and... affection?

Haley doesn't want to come with us, and I can't blame her. It's where she works most of the time, these days. Mom and Dad pretend to be tired, but I think they want to give their sons some time together. So it's just us guys.

Once at the pub, I manage to not get roped into the operation, to just sit back and relax in my own place, to watch my brothers have a good time in my pub. Girls take notice of the four King brothers hanging out together, but we're too into ourselves for anything to get any further.

And thank god for that.

It's late at night when we get home. Mom, Dad, and Haley have already gone to bed. Hunter and Logan stumble drunkenly up the stairs.

I'm on a different schedule, what with the pub opening at noon and staying open late into the night. I'm not tired yet.

"A beer?" Ethan asks.

"Sure."

We sit on the porch, Moose at our feet, and pop our beers open, looking out into the dark fields, the shape of the barn against the moonlit sky. "So fucking proud of ya," he says after a while.

"Proud of *what*?" I ask, almost offended. I run a pub in the middle of nowhere while Ethan is risking his life on the daily to keep us all safe.

He turns his face to me. "The way you rebuilt your life. The way you created something for this whole town."

His compliment sits uneasily with me. I know he doesn't mean it sarcastically, but I'm the reason he left the family and Emerald Creek.

He was the firstborn son. He went to UVM on a full athletic scholarship. I thought he was going to take over from Dad when the time came, and in between, they were going to work together on expanding King Knoll Farm.

Then I fucked up, and Ethan left.

"Anybody did something good with his life, it's you, man. I just sell beer."

His grunt tells me he doesn't agree but won't debate me on that. Not right now. "You ever think of settling down?"

I've lived in Emerald Creek my whole life. How more settled down does he want me to be? "I don't follow."

"Settling down. Having what Mom and Dad have. A family. That sounds pretty awesome to me. You?"

I don't know how to answer his question. Until the accident, I didn't project myself into what my adult life would look like. After the accident, I worked on fixing things. Making life better for others.

I knew I messed up Ethan's life. His love life, and his whole, entire fucking life. He needs to know that I know that. That the way I'm living my life, is my apology to him. Because if he doesn't know that, how can he move on?

"I—I can't do that. Not after what happened. Not after what I did to you. It's just not gonna happen." I'm happy, so fucking happy he's here, alive, and healthy, and I hope he gets the life he wants. The life he was meant to have. But until that happens, I'm not thinking about building something for myself.

He pinches the bridge of his nose between his fingers, looking just like Dad when we used to mess up. It tugs at my heart how alike they are. I used to be jealous of it. Hell, a part of me will probably always be jealous. "Fuck, man. What are you talking about?"

He turns to me like someone who knows exactly what I'm talking about. "I ran away like a fucking coward when you were in the hospital. I didn't even know if you were gonna make it. I can't believe you never said anything about that. *I* failed *you*." He pets Moose, his gaze turning to the night. "But you know what? I forgave myself. I was just a kid. Scared. I messed up. People mess up, bro. The only thing to do is pick up the pieces and keep going."

"Yeah, except not everyone got to do that," I croak. I don't remember her face. I only remember the stench of burning flesh. Hers. Mine. It stuck to me for a long time.

"It wasn't your fault," Ethan says. "You almost died trying to save her. You did everything you could and more."

"It doesn't matter. I shouldn't have... driven her home."

Ethan exhales loudly. "We were kids, Justin. You were a baby. But if you want to go down that road, then—you... you did right by her. I didn't. She came to the party to find me. I should have been looking out for her."

"What do you mean? She was your girlfriend. I hit on your girlfriend. I took her home to get lucky and—"

"She wasn't my girlfriend. I didn't even know where she lived! We'd hooked up once before and I'd called it off. Then she came onto me a little strong at the party, and I told her off a little strong too. There was nothing between us."

My heart skips a beat, and my blood runs cold. "I thought... I thought... I thought that's why you left."

"Yeah, I heard that before. But naah. She wasn't the one." He hands me another beer, and I take it without thinking, downing it in one long gulp. He continues. "Did you know... shit, I can't even remember her last name right now, isn't it weird? Oh yeah... Ward. Audrey Ward. Did you know the Wards met with Murphy? Couple years ago, that is."

"Couple years ago?" I knew about formal meetings in the weeks following the accident. Mom and Dad represented me, as I was in the hospital. Our lawyer negotiated the settlement payment with Murphy's lawyers, and as it was, Sullivan's since he was the one with the deep pockets.

Wish I'd known then that once I got out of the hospital, I'd set my eyes on the old forge for a new pub in town. I'd have negotiated kicking Murphy out as part of the deal.

"What about?" I ask him.

"Wanted to let him know they forgave him."

Well fuck me. They forgave the asshole who drove too fast on a winding country road at night during a storm, leading him to skid right into my car and kill their daughter?

"Made me think. 'Bout forgiving myself, you know. You might wanna think about it. Maybe you should talk with them."

The second beer is hitting me strong. "Who?"

"The Wards. You should give them a call. Have lunch or something. Who knows? Might help you."

"I don't need help. And if I did, they'd be the last people I'd turn to." Is he out of his mind?

He stands abruptly. "A'right. I'm gonna hit the sack," he says. "You okay to drive?"

No, I'm not. I had two beers back-to-back after drinks at the pub, and visions of a burning woman next to the wreck of my car more vivid than they've been in years. "I'll crash on the couch."

He stretches his impressive body, his fingers touching the porch ceiling. "That new girl..."

New girl? "Yeah?"

"You're doing something about her, right. The one at the fairgrounds. You know who I mean. New girl," he repeats.

Chloe. Bringing her up after we talk about the accident is like a literal balm on my gaping wound. But I'm not talking about her with Ethan. What are we, middle-school girls? "'Night, bro."

"'Night, asshole."

I settle on the couch, Moose at my feet. It's good to have Ethan back. But what he just said, the whole forgiveness from the Wards? I had no idea.

They reached out to Murphy, but not to me. Do they still hate me for what I did?

CHAPTER TWENTY-NINE

Chloe

I haven't seen Justin since we set up the tents. He said he'd take care of the equipment with the guys later, and now it's the night before the fair. At the thought of working next to him all day, I can't sleep. Did I dream our almost kiss at the cottage? Did I imagine the gentle way he talked me off the ledge, when I freaked out in the pub kitchen? Did I make up the way he looked at me when we set up the other day? Yet he hasn't reached out for more time together.

I toss and turn all night, and when dawn breaks through my blinds a little after four, I give up.

I'm too ramped up to sleep.

When Justin and I assembled poles and hauled tarps and set up tables, it was hot and messy and fun.

But mostly, it was hot. And yeah, the temperature was hot, but also Justin. The only time I'd seen him break a sweat like that was in our hotel room. Not that I need the visual reminder to think back to those moments, but fresh memories assailed me. His locks of hair matted around his face. His heavy breathing.

His smell.

I clasp my thighs together under the sheets, but that doesn't help, so I snake a hand down and take care of my needs. If not me, who? Justin hasn't made a move. It's like he's avoiding me.

And I get it. His brother Ethan came back, the one he told me about in Boston. I saw it happen. I saw the look on Justin when that hunk of man slapped his back. Justin was shocked, and elated, and in pain. His carefully constructed universe flying open, and he didn't know where he fit in it. My heart clenches. If he'd let me in, I could help him. I want to.

He's the best I've ever known.

And damn, the look in his eyes when we were alone in the cottage. His breath on my face—I could almost taste him. I *wanted* to taste him. And he said as much.

I come with his name on my lips, the tremors a temporary relief.

After a quick shower, I take time blow-drying my hair so it looks real good, and put some effort in my makeup. Then I snatch the summer dress Fiona made me buy last year that I haven't worn yet.

Fiona said it was sexy as hell and I should buy it.

Which, in the out-of-body experience that shopping with Fiona can be, is why I bought it.

Which is also why I never wore it.

Until today.

"How can I make your day aw—*Holy smokes*!" Millie exclaims when I walk into Easy Monday minutes later.

"You're open! Thank god," I answer, ignoring her comment. I guess I do look hot. Good.

Her mouth gapes. "You look fantastic!"

It's just us in the shop, so I do a little twirl, the skirt of the dress flying up and around my thighs.

The dress is a cream color with tiny flowers all over. The color looks great with my dark hair and summer tan. But what really looks awesome, and the reason I haven't had the guts to wear it yet, is the way it cinches my waist and pushes my boobs up.

And then it has those little lacy things at the cleavage that make it look innocent and all. The same lace ribbons are repeated on the shoulder straps, and again at the hem.

Said hem is mid-thigh, and the dress closes with a series of buttons all the way down. "Thank you! I thought I should put in a little effort for the fair."

"Un-hunh, for the country fair with an ox pulling demo and an ax throwing contest and pigs rolling in mud."

Right. "I'll be serving food." I smile.

She fans herself and rolls her eyes. "Road to Heaven, iced?" She turns around before I answer and busies herself at the coffee machine.

"Please. And..." Should I bring something for Justin?

She smiles over her shoulder. "Double iced espresso? Haven't seen him this morning."

My stomach flutters at her question. "Y-yes. Please."

She sets the two containers on the counter. "He deserves to be happy, after everything that happened to him. You take good care of him, yeah?" There's something in her eyes that makes me stop, and I want to ask her more.

Suddenly I'm back in the hotel room with him telling me about his accident. I'm back at the pub, with him yelling at me. With Haley more concerned than angry at him.

But I won't ask Millie, as sweet as she is. And as I drive to Clark's Meadow, the field where the fair is set up, I decide I'll do everything I can to get through to him.

Even if all I have is a cup of coffee as an offering.

I park my Honda on the expanse of grass marked 'Parking' and grab my jean jacket from the backseat. It's still early enough for the air to be chilly. As I step out and the dewy grass soaks my toes, I catch a glimpse of Justin at the food tent, then he disappears behind it.

I take quick steps to our stand and find him connecting the generator to the fridges and a deep fryer. He's wearing faded jeans and a tight T-shirt with his restaurant's logo on it. He smiles at me, a big, spontaneous smile I didn't see coming.

"Perfect timing," he says, his gaze doing a double take the length of my body, his hand shooting out to grab his iced espresso. "Thank you." He gestures to a wooden bench just outside the tent.

I sit first, my dress inching up, and register him clearing his throat. Oh well.

Taking a deep breath, I let the early morning sounds take over any conversation, for now. Distant voices calling to each other. A hammer clanking against metal. A dog barking. Generators springing to life.

I point my mug to a low corral being set up by a few guys. "Is that your brother, over there?"

"Ethan." He takes a sip of his coffee. "I—sorry, I should have introduced you the other day."

"Oh, no! No, no, no. That's..." *That's not why I'm bringing him up.* "You guys looked so happy. All of you." They looked like a pack of oversized puppies, running around and ribbing each other. But Justin had this air about him. He seemed worried. Tormented. Like he wasn't sure what was coming next. I think back to Millie's comment. *'He deserves to be happy, after everything that happened'.*

"He seems happy to be here," I insist, thinking that might start him opening up.

"Yeah," he says in a low growl.

"You know, what you told me in Boston—"

"Shoulda stayed in Boston," he snaps.

His anger catches me off guard but doesn't surprise me. "To be fair, it was meant to stay between us," I say softly. "If you remember correctly—"

He shuts his eyes. "I remember everything from that night, Clover."

He remembers everything. I whisper, "You said you wanted me to carry this for you."

"I did."

"That's the opposite of leaving it behind. Leaving it in Boston."

"So?"

"I'm carrying it for you. You're not alone in this."

After a long silence, Justin glances at his army green watch and stands. "We should get started."

I stand to face him and set my hand on his forearm. Then I let my finger run up the intricate tattoo designs that cover his scars. He shivers but doesn't move away from me.

He tilts his head down to me, his gaze drops to my lips, then peels itself from me to look over my shoulder into nothingness. The tents across the field. The vans bringing in chickens and pigs and horses. The trees in the distance.

Or maybe his brother.

"What happened in Boston stays with us," I say. "Forever. No matter what may happen between us."

His throat bobs.

"But you kept something from me, didn't you?"

His voice is raspy, like he's on the brink of tears when he answers, his gaze slicing to me. "That night meant the world to me. Don't take it away now."

"I'm bringing it back," I whisper. "Talk to me." My head is tilted to his face, my shallow breath taking in his scent.

He places his hand on my hip and pulls me close to him. My traitorous body almost gives in. I almost mold myself to him.

I almost ruin it.

But I need something more important from him. So I twine my fingers in his wandering hand and bring it up to his heart. "What aren't you telling me?" I ask. His heart beats hard against the back of my hand. "We were supposed to be our true selves that night. But you left something out, didn't you? You owe me."

"Nothing is ever just what it seems." His fingers clench around mine. "I messed up." He lifts his gaze to meet mine. His brows are furrowed, and there's pain, so much pain that tears spring into my own eyes. "And as hard as I try, I can't fix it."

My mouth is dry, and the words are hard to come. "Then if you can't fix it, you keep going. You have no choice." When he doesn't answer, I take a gamble. "Or else you die, too, in a way," I say as softly as I can.

He takes a deep breath and straightens himself. His eyes are bright. He looks around the vast field that's being turned into a fairground as more and more people arrive and finish setting up their stands. His lips curl up and his hand lets go of mine. He takes a step away from me, but his gaze caresses me top to bottom.

"What the fuck is that dress, Sullivan." Totally changing the subject. Totally throwing me off.

It works. "I... I wanted to look cute for the fair. I don't have branded T-shirts," I offer as an excuse.

"Cute for the fair," he repeats, his body shaking with laughter. "Come on, let's get this show on the road."

"We're not done talking."

"For now, we are, yeah." He gives me a playful grin. "Let's set up."

We go over the process, set up our stations, and I'm more relaxed than I was at the pub. I think it has to do with the setting. There's something so down-to-earth about making food in a field. How can you mess it up?

"Containers for the fries, wrappers for the sandwiches. And gloves. Always wear gloves, change them often. Not much running water here."

A part of my brain registers what he's saying, while another part is somewhere else.

He takes a break, fists on his hips. "I think we're in good shape," he says.

Four hours later, the line snakes all the way to the next stand. My feet are pulp. My dress clings to me from sweat. At some point I twirled my hair on top of my head and secured it with toothpicks.

"A Vermonter, a Crispy Creek, and two Flatlanders," Justin calls out.

My fingers fly on the register. "Seventeen." I grab two flavored still waters from the cooler behind me, add them to the bag, and raise my head to smile at the couple in front of me. "Here you go." I hand them their change, and the guy plops it right back in the to-go mug marked Local Food Bank. "Thanks!"

A group of teenagers huddles to where Justin is. "Um... Three Salamanders. And four Clovers. No. Hold on. Four Salamanders. And four Clovers." Justin glances at me, and I move from the register to the prep station, slide on a pair of gloves, and start on the Salamanders as they continue with a drink order.

No actual Salamanders are involved. Lol. Cassandra asked that we actually come up with several dishes, and names for all, and Alex advised us to make them catchy for social.

There *are* clovers involved in the Clover however—our vegan wrap.

"Chloe, you with me?" Justin is sliding the Clovers my way.

I jump. "Yep! Got it." I finish scooping the pulled pork on the second brioche bun, and wrap it carefully, then move onto the third.

Justin slides behind me to grab the drinks for the group, his hand on my hip lightly moving me to the side as he does, his touch setting me on fire.

He bags the drinks as I wrap the third sandwich, then moves to the register.

I hurry through the last bun but still want it extra yummy with his sauce and the herbs that go on it. "I got it."

"I know," he says softly. "Take your time."

My throat catches at his gentleness. He rings up the big party as I put the last sandwich in their bag.

Then he moves me back in front of the register, his hand falling naturally at my hip again, lingering there for a beat more than is necessary. He keeps me in front of him as he says, "Have a nice day," to the group, his voice gliding from my ear to my neck and all the way down my spine.

Then I process their credit card, my hip both burning and feeling cold from his sudden move away from me.

The whole time, it's a steady trickle of people, sometimes a longer line. Toward the end of the morning, Haley and Ethan come by and order an early lunch. They both look between Justin and me with clear interest and amusement, but neither says anything. Cassandra, Kiara, and more people I know, and a lot more I don't know, keep us busy nonstop.

We go on like that for a while, until there's a sudden lull. "Where's everybody?" I ask.

Justin grabs a water from the cooler. "The ox pull. That's an all-time favorite. You should go and check it out. I'll hold down the fort here."

I look around. Our corner of the fair is deserted. We have time to talk some more. I take careful steps toward him, grab a water, start sitting down on the cooler.

"Chloe."

"I'd rather stay here."

"Cool, then I'll go to the ox pull," he says but doesn't move. His gaze on me is both annoyed and defiant.

"Fine," I huff and reluctantly walk away.

"Come back before the end of the pulling contest. We'll have a crowd then," he calls after me.

Okay so, he doesn't want to talk now.

It's fine.

I'll get through to him.

I elbow my way to the stands and watch as two oxen, harnessed together, are pulling a contraption that has a bunch of huge rectangular stones on it. Three guys surround them, seeming to coo, or maybe yell, at them. It's hard to tell with the crowd's cheers and whistles, and the commentator's voice coming out of the subpar loudspeakers. I can hardly make out what he's saying.

What I can make out, is my mother's voice. Straining my vision, I look around, but the only thing that catches my eye is movement in the back of Grace's massage tent. It looks like she's taking five, but not in a good way. Before I can worry about what's wrong with her, my mother's voice sounds louder.

"Why there she is!" I jump and look behind the bleachers. Mom, Aunt Dawn, and Brendan are standing there, all looking at me. Mom has one eyebrow disapprovingly twitched up. No surprise there. Aunt Dawn looks downright worried, and Brendan's fists are shoved down his pockets.

I square my shoulders, ready for the family firing squad, and elbow my way down to them.

Aunt Dawn's eyes are batting like mad. "I couldn't believe it when Chef Samuel said you were here."

I let that slide for now. "Why has no one called me?" I look for my phone in my back pocket, but I'm wearing a dress with no pockets, and it hits me that I've left my phone in my car. *Shoot.*

Mom's lips are pinched disapprovingly. Why does my gaze even glide to her? Of course she disapproves.

"It's good to see you!" I say and give them each a peck on the cheek, getting only a lukewarm greeting at best.

"I wanted to show the restaurant to your Mom, and Brendan needed to meet some people here, so we decided on a whim to make an outing of it... We'll let you to it," Aunt Dawn says, taking Mom's arm under hers and stepping away.

"We'll be right back!" Mom says over her shoulder. "Just want to check out this custom jeweler."

Brendan shuffles his feet.

A little advance notice would have been nice. I'm not sure how much I believe this visit was unplanned. "The reason I'm at the fair—"

"Chloe, you don't need to explain yourself. I trust you."

"Really? Because," and I try to keep my voice in control. Kind and gentle and understanding, "because it doesn't look like it."

"I know. Mom... Mom wanted to show her sister-in-law the place. And I guess Aunt Pamela seemed excited to see where you worked, and I wanted to come to the fair anyway to meet with some folks I don't get to see that often, so it just happened. They tried to call you all morning to tell you we were on our way, but you weren't picking up. And while we were here, Samuel—Chef," he corrects himself, "kinda..."

"Yeah?"

Brendan crosses his arms. "He kinda let it slip that in his opinion the restaurant shouldn't be represented at the fair."

Samuel's opinion is worth shit, but it's my fault for not sharing my suspicions with Aunt Dawn earlier. I should have spoken up right off the bat, hired a new chef. But would she have agreed to it? It's almost like she was brainwashed.

Brendan continues, "And then something caught fire in the kitchen—"

"What caught fire?"

"I wasn't there. Someone in there took care of it. Clearly. And then Chef said if you weren't there when there was a kitchen fire..." He lets the sentence hang, his hands parting.

"He said that, huh?" Samuel totally hyped up the whole thing.

"I'm sorry, Chloe."

This is beginning to sound like a letting go meeting, and I know it isn't. But it could be. "Look, Brendan. I'm not Uncle Kevin. I'm bound to do things differently. And I've never owned a restaurant. I was clear about that, going in. The reason I accepted, is that I know how business works. I can read a P&L Statement."

"That's not why we needed you, Chl—"

"But you see, Brendan. That *is* why you need me. I walked in here thinking I would just tick boxes on a daily to-do list. And it took me only two hours—two hours—to find out that you guys are deep in the red. *You* know that. So I'm looking into why that is. And I don't have all the answers yet. But I will."

"Appreciate it," Brendan says.

"Your dad was having a lot of problems." I'm not sure how much he knows. At some point I'll have to share everything with him, but I'd like to have some answers first. Solid solutions. And I'm getting more than annoyed at Samuel for not giving me the financials I need from him—mainly, a reliable costing. So the fact that he threw me under the bus with my family is not helping his case.

Brendan narrows his eyes on me. "He mentioned the owner of the pub, a coupla times. His landlord. That the fellow you're at the fair with?"

I nod. "The town asked that we put something together. I didn't think it'd be a good idea to say no. I'm getting a vibe of some kind of... rift between the restaurant and the town. Any idea where that came from?"

He shakes his head. "Never heard anything of the sort. The only problem Dad ever had was with his landlord, from what I know."

"We need to think more local," I say, jumping topics. Something's been bothering me, and I have to ask. "Why... why didn't Uncle Kevin get some meat from you?"

He shrugs. "He always let his chef do the ordering."

Uh-huh. "Does Samuel know what you do?"

"Oh yeah, yeah. I think he likes to always go through the same wholesaler. Can't blame him. It's simpler."

"Uh-huh." I look at the food tent and decide against walking back there with Brendan. He doesn't like Justin. There's no point making waves now.

Aunt Dawn and Mom return.

"Dad trusts—trusted him," Brendan adds.

"Samuel? What a darling," Aunt Dawn says, like she knows exactly what we've been talking about. "I don't know what we'd do without him. Did you know he offered to manage the restaurant for us?"

He *what*? This isn't a standing-up conversation. And I really need to get back to Justin. "Are you guys staying the night? Can we continue this conversation later?"

"We actually need to leave," Aunt Dawn says.

"Chloe!" Mom gasps, ignoring my question. "Why you could go back to the City!"

My jaw drops open. Yes, I could. But Aunt Dawn can kiss her restaurant goodbye. "I—I don't think running the restaurant without a manager is a good idea. Unless..."

"Unless?" Aunt Dawn and Brendan ask at the same time.

I lower my voice. "Unless Samuel is offering to buy into the restaurant."

Aunt Dawn raises an eyebrow. "No. He's... he's not ready to do that."

"He's mentioned he might be considering... leaving," Brendan says under his breath.

"Brendan!" Aunt Dawn chastises him.

"We didn't tell you anything. This stays between us," Brendan adds.

"Did he say why?" People start coming out of the ox pull, which means Justin is going to need my help, but I need to know.

Aunt Dawn clears her throat. "Your name came up."

Of course.

Mom gasps. "I can't believe this man is-is-is questioning Chloe's abilities. It's preposterous! No offense, but Chloe is doing you a favor. She's overqualified here." Wow, Mom is defending me? I wonder why she can't do that in front of Dad.

"Mom, it's okay. I'm fine helping out family." I give Brendan and Aunt Dawn a sweet, genuine smile. "And I'll be sure to be more mindful of *Chef* Samuel. I'll leave my corporate habits at the door."

"That'd be lovely, honey," Aunt Dawn says, clearly unphased by her sister-in-law's haughtiness.

"Dad always said the restaurant would be nothing without him," Brendan says. "He nearly lost it when the other guy left to go work next door."

Aunt Dawn wraps me in a goodbye hug. "That King man hurt your uncle a lot, Chloe. I warned you about him. Be careful."

Brendan gives me a quick hug. "We should head back."

Mom lets Aunt Dawn and Brendan leave before giving me her air kisses. "It breaks my heart to see you here, honey. This is not your place," she murmurs.

"I like it here, Mom. It's not that bad."

"Oh, stop it!" She laughs her airy laughter like I've cracked the funniest joke ever, then her laughter dies, and she says, "Daddy was *very* upset to hear you were going to work here. We even got into a *fight* about it, if you can imagine. Both agreeing, actually. Daddy... your father always had something against Kevin, never understood it, but anyhoo." She takes a deep breath and looks at me straight in the eye, no BS. "He's agreeing to take you on at the office, if that means you won't be working in this village."

"I really have to get back to the tent, Mom, but... is this why you came? To tell me that?"

She does a little tip of the hip, a dip in her knees, that's meant to look cute but is just annoying. "I told Daddy I'd talk to you. He hates knowing you're here even more than me."

Seriously. What is wrong with them? "Tell Dad it's a temporary job. Just a few weeks, couple months tops. He has nothing to worry about." This is not a lie.

Her features relax. "Okay, dahling, I have to run. Your aunt Dawn and her *shepherd* son are waiting," she says, thinking she's amusing. "Ladi-da!"

I walk quickly back to the tent.

"Sorry," I mutter as I take my place behind the register, smiling at strangers while trying to read Justin.

We fall back into our teamwork, saying nothing, occupied with the constant orders.

"Cooler's almost empty," I inform Justin at some point.

"We'll be sold out of food soon," he answers.

"Oh."

He shrugs. "Getting late anyway." Then, with a wink, he adds, "We'll just send them to town."

We close the tent fifteen minutes later.

"Sorry I dropped the ball on you," I say when we're alone.

"Figured something happened, and then Alex said she saw you talking to a guy?" he tells me as we're cleaning the space. Not exactly angry but not exactly happy either.

"My cousin."

His features relax. "Everything all right?"

"Yes. No." Someone's playing me. My family? My chef? A little bit of both.

The knot I feel in my gut feels oddly familiar.

He smirks. "Yes or no? What was the problem?" His gaze on me is like a light blanket, shielding me from the world out there. He stops what he's doing, waiting for an answer.

"Um." I blink several times. What was the problem again? "Nothing. Just a misunderstanding."

"Great," he says, his warm gaze all over me. "We'll break this down tomorrow," he continues, gesturing at the tent and all its contents.

"But I need to bring the generator and a couple things back to the dude who lent them to me."

"Now?"

"Yeah. He needs it for tomorrow."

"How far is it?

"Couple hours away, over the mountain. Couple hours to get back."

"I'll come with you." Fours hours on the road. Lots of talking time. Lots of being together.

He blinks at me, and I brace for his pushback.

It doesn't come. He just shrugs and mumbles. I take it as a yes.

This time I pluck my phone out of my handbag and text the group chat I have with the restaurant.

Me: Something came up. See you tomorrow.

Samuel: We got you.

His answer sits uncomfortably with me, and I decide to forget the restaurant for tonight.

I don't feel supported. I thought I was leaving that life behind, the double standards, the betrayals.

But no.

The only place I feel safe right now is with Justin.

CHAPTER THIRTY

Justin

I don't care that my truck makes a funny noise or that Moose is drooling over my shoulder.

Chloe is sitting right next to me, and nothing could be more perfect. I peel my eyes off her pretty little dress creeping up her tanned thighs and adjust my jeans, then downshift as we approach Dewey's Hollow.

A shadow catches my peripheral vision in the quickly darkening landscape, and I hit the brakes, my arm coming across to hold Chloe and Moose. "What's wrong?" Chloe asks in near panic. Her question is answered when a black cow jumps onto the road. "What's that?" is her next question.

I curse under my breath. "That's Daisy."

"Ohmygod, I heard of her. She's *real*? I thought it was some kind of urban legend. Rural legend."

I chuckle, relieved that I didn't hit Daisy. How that has never happened to her yet, I don't know. "Oh she's real, and she's a real pain in the neck." As if to prove my point, Daisy ambles in front of us, then kicks her hind legs in mock provocation before jumping over the ditch and running across the field toward the Chandlers' farm.

"My parents got her a couple of years ago, and they can't seem to keep her at the farm. She always finds a way to escape, and then either someone ropes her back in or she just shows up when it's raining too hard or the cold is too much for her."

"That's too funny," Chloe says, her gaze following Daisy up a hill.

"Not for my parents it's not. And not for Declan. He gets all the complaints. It turns out, Daisy loves to snack on flowers."

"Oh dear." Chloe laughs.

"Yup." With Daisy out of the way, I pick up speed. "Matter of fact, I think that's how she got her name."

"That's too funny," Chloe says again, then starts playing with the radio stations until she stops on country rock. "This okay?" she asks.

"Sure." I like that she asks me. I also like that she's not a music snob. People who are partial to this or that type of music get on my nerves. Music is music. A good rhythm, a melody you can hum to yourself, lyrics you can relate to. That's all I ask for. Making my point, Chloe hums softly along with the chorus, then she rolls her window down and her soft hum turns into more of a full-on bellow.

Totally off key. Totally adorable. I can't help the smile spreading across my face.

Somehow she catches me. "What?" she snaps.

"Nothing," I say. "It was a good day." I glance at her.

"Hard not to have a good day in Emerald Creek," she answers, filling my heart with pride and warmth.

"You're right about that."

She turns her head to the window, butchering the music in the most endearing way. I wish the song would never end.

But it does, and then she lowers the volume and asks, "What was it like, growing up here?"

"It was..." Where do I even start? "We spent most of our time outdoors, helping on the farm or building tree houses or swimming in the river or the lake."

"Wow. I can't imagine. What about winters?"

"Sugaring."

"What's that?"

"Making maple syrup. That only lasts a few weeks. And we'd take care of the animals—mainly cleaning stables. We didn't have many when I was a kid. A couple dozen cows, chickens, a couple of horses. When those chores were done, we'd go sledding. Snowshoeing. Late fall and winter, hunting."

"Did you go skiing?"

"Not so much." More like, not at all. "It gets expensive, with five kids. Although, the school started a program when I was ten or twelve. Mostly, we'd skate on the lake."

"You—what?"

"Lake gets frozen solid in the winter. We'd clear the snow and skate." It was the best. Mom would freak out that we would go too early, before it was solid enough, or too late, when it'd started thawing, but we were smart. We'd heard the horror stories. That's how Ethan got picked up for hockey, actually. A rich tourist was staying at the resort, and he saw him skate. At the same time, the town got some trickle of federal money, and with it, they built the arena. They put together a team, and Ethan became the golden boy. Emerald Creek won game after game. We won the national championship. *Ethan* won the national championship.

"Hey, where'd your mind go?" Chloe interrupts my thoughts.

"Skating," I semi-lie.

"That good, huh?"

"Most of the time, yeah." The times Ethan wasn't there to cast his shadow over me. I shake the feeling away, guilty about it. *I'm always guilty when it comes to Ethan.*

"I haven't gone skating in I don't know how long." I catch her pensive gaze on me from the corner of my eye. "Never on a frozen lake," she adds.

Man, I'd love to take her skating. "Something to look forward to," I venture. What am I doing? I need to stop thinking about her that way. I will *not* take her skating. Skating with a girl is a... it's a first date thing. And then it's a repeat date, or maybe a nice proposal idea. Shit. *She's a friend, Justin, think about her as a friend.*

She gives me a big smile and it's hard to get my focus back on the road entirely, so I slow down a little. "How's it going at the restaurant?" I say to bring the conversation back on safe territory.

She shakes her head. "I don't even know where to start."

"About what my mom said the other day..." Fuck, where do *I* even start?

"It's okay," she interrupts me softly. "Parents don't always know what they're talking about." She tucks her hands between her knees.

The thing is, although Mom shouldn't have said anything—but being Mom, how could she not?—she was right. My plan is—was—to take over the space.

"I don't get it... Why did they bring you in?"

"Who? My aunt and cousin?"

"Yeah. As a restaurant manager."

She pulls her hands from between her knees and crosses her arms. Squints through the window. Licks her lips. "The day... the day I found Tucker..."

The day she found her ex cheating. "Yeah?" I prompt her gently.

"I was coming home early because I'd been let go." *Fuck. What a shit day.* She blinks and her eyelashes flutter. "Then it was the funeral, and uh... I guess my cousin found out everything that had gone down with me, and he asked for my help. He wanted to help me get out of my funk too. First I didn't want to do it. I was already job hunting. But then I figured, you know what? They're family, they need my help, and I could use a change. I should do this."

"So they hired you—what? Full time?" What I really want to know is, if she's staying here for good.

"Yeah, you could say that. The plan initially was for me to run the restaurant as they looked for a buyer. But then I convinced them to give me time to bring the restaurant in the black before putting it up for sale."

So she'll be leaving at some point? I want to punch something.

She continues, "I went to that conference in Boston to get some basic food industry knowledge and contacts."

"What did you used to do?"

"Business development for a beverage company."

"That's not too far out," I point out, my mind turning the phrase she said before, *as they looked for a buyer.* "Seems like you have exactly the skillset for the restaurant."

"Yeah, I dunno." She plays with the last button on her dress, distracting me from the conversation. "I'm used to corporate environments. This kitchen power play... too much bullshit for me."

My knuckles tighten on the wheel. "Samuel giving you a hard time?"

She chuckles, but it's a sad little sound that I hate for her. "Not that kind. He's moved to mind games now."

I hate that guy. I need to nail him stealing from her, get her rid of that asshole. "Fuck," I growl. "How 'bout the rest of the crew? Those who came to the tasting seemed cool."

"They're great. I mean, they all have their quirks, right—we all have—but we're a good team. I think they trust me, and I trust them. Abby and Shoshana kill it in the dining room. Corine and Eric do a great job in the kitchen. I mean, the nights that Samuel was out because of you-know-what," she adds with another chuckle, a happy one this time, "they did fantastic. I'm actually thinking of promoting Corine to Chef de Cuisine."

"You wanna get rid of Samuel?"

"Just thinking ahead. Anyway, my aunt wouldn't back me if I decided to let Samuel go. But I opened up the conversation with Corine about it, and she freaked out. I just wanted her to have a nicer title when Samuel isn't working, and I want her to build up her confidence. She'll get there. I just want her to start thinking about it. Projecting herself."

I love how she appreciates her staff. I used to think they were a lazy bunch, but all they needed was a better leader. Is it weird that I feel proud of Chloe for how she's turned them around? I glance at her, the way she talks about the business and the people, the care she shows.

Shit. It's making me hard. Not her naked legs and bare arms, not the cleavage she's showing, not her dark hair and the memory of how it looked wrapped around my cock. What's making my cock hard and my heart soft is the care and passion she's putting into what she's doing, although I know it's not what she would choose to do if she could. She did it out of a sense of duty to her family.

She's the kind of person who goes all in. Gives herself entirely.

Gives herself entirely.

I'm having trouble swallowing.

She's still talking. "David keeps to himself, and I have to say, that's kind of a relief. No drama. No questions. Last one out every evening. Does everything he's asked to do."

I bet he is. He's smarter than Samuel. He knows better than to antagonize the boss when he's stealing from her. I keep my thoughts to myself. Like Declan said, I need something specific, and proof.

CHAPTER THIRTY-ONE

Chloe

Justin doesn't comment on my somewhat lengthy description of the restaurant staff, and I think I know what he's thinking.

That I owe him three months' worth of rent.

I still wonder why Lynn said what she said to me at dinner the other night. All those questions about closing down. There's no smoke without a fire. And her questions were super specific. These types of questions don't pop up without something to fuel them.

"About the rent..." I start. We need to have this conversation. "We really need to talk about it."

He flips his blinker and pulls into a parking lot next to a warehouse. Ignores my question, opens his door, opens Moose's door. A guy comes out of nowhere, they do the backslapping thing and move to the bed of his truck.

Oh well. I slide out of my seat and stretch my legs. It's getting very dark now, not quite night yet. The sky is a deep blue, the new moon a slim sliver casting no light. Its delicate shape reminds me of a print in my childhood bedroom, of a girl sitting on the moon, the stars all around her. I wonder what became of that print, and stupidly my heart clenches. What became of all the dreams I had, growing up?

Time to be adulting, Chloe. Life is tough, and then you die. Deal with it.

"Ready?" Justin asks after he's dealt with the guy and the equipment, and I've had my little dreaming awake session. "Let's have a burger before we head back. I know the best place in the state."

"Best burgers in the state? Coming from you, must mean something."

We drive down a small road and park next to a red barn-like building. The Mighty Burger—that's the name of the place—delivers on all fronts. Rustic, mismatched tables and chairs, menus in neat handwriting on massive blackboards above the ordering station, a huge selection of draft beers—mostly local—and merchandise. And the burgers! My god the burgers. Now *that's* a brand. "Wish I could do something like that with the restaurant," I mumble between two bites, really talking to myself.

"You want to turn Kevin's Fine Dining into a burger joint?" Justin teases.

"Branding. Everything here is on point." I take another bite and wipe the sauce dripping down my chin. "Need to entirely rethink the restaurant placement in the market." Justin is not saying anything. He's glancing at me like he's waiting for me to say more. Almost like he's afraid of what he's going to hear.

I really do need to get to the bottom of what his mom said. I interrupted him earlier, when he brought up what Lynn asked me, because I was afraid of what he was going to say. Afraid to hear something I wasn't ready to hear.

I'd been let go almost two months ago. And yeah, I took this job to help my family but not without the understanding that success here would help my resume.

Then the chef gave me a tough time from the beginning.

And now I have to convince my own family to trust me.

Last thing I need is the landlord telling me he's pulling the plug.

But if that's what he's going to do, then I do need to know.

The sooner the better.

"About the late rent. And what your mom said. We need to talk."

He plops a French fry in his mouth and says, "Why?"

Um. *Why?* "I need to know what... your intentions are. If you're willing to work with us. And if you would—"

"Us?"

"Yeah. The restaurant."

He wipes his hands on a paper napkin, tosses it in his empty French fries container, moves the container to the side. "Us." His gaze bores into mine, then drips down to my lips. *Us.* We'd played with that word, with that idea, during our time away from time. He remembers. He knows I'm thinking about that too. *Yeah, we should talk about that too.*

"I'm willing to work with *you*, Chloe."

"Okay, yeah. Um." What's the difference, at the end of the day?

"I don't trust Samuel. I certainly didn't trust Murphy. And I do not trust his widow or his family. Only person I trust is you."

"Why?"

His only answer is a frown.

"Why do you trust me? I've never run a restaurant before," I insist.

"You understand business concepts. You understand food. You have great taste. You're smart. You have motivation. And most of all," he pauses, his gaze trailing down to my mouth, then up to my eyes, making me feel all sorts of mushy and warm and forgetting the conversation to focus on what might come next (his hand tucking a wild hair behind my ear? His fingers lacing with mine? His head leaning over the table to take my mouth?), "most of all, we're friends."

Friends?

Friends?!

Is that supposed to be a good thing? He says it like it is, handsome smile and all. Then why is my belly clenching, threatening to send back my burger? I don't want to be just friends with awesome, sexy, kind Justin. Justin who's hiding more than burn marks under his tattoos. Justin who does so much for his community and so little for himself.

Justin who told me himself, ages ago, in an elevator, that he could never be just friends with me.

What happened?

He's a rebound, sister.

I know, I know. But I also know how his hands feel on me, how his mouth feels on me, how awesome his kisses are and the way he grumbles against my skin and how it sends shivers down my spine and all the way to my core. I know the effect his mere scent has on me, and I've been basking in it for hours now.

Can I get more?

Just a little more.

Just another round of rebound.

That has to be a thing, right? My core feels heated and bothered at that thought.

Time to regroup and reframe. "Um, okay so, when can we talk about the rent?" Okay. Better. Breathing back in control. Topic back on work. Friends. Gotcha. "Just you and me." I wave my hand between us. "*That* us."

He winces. Ouch. That's not a friend thing to say. That was a Boston thing.

Yeah, well, Boston happened to me, too, and if he doesn't like it, I do. In case he didn't notice, I'm not letting him forget that.

Besides, he's probably going to make sure I am out of a job pronto, so who cares.

He unfolds his long, strong, fantastic body, standing and towering over me. Grabs our dirty dishes. Sorts trash from recycling and tosses them in the recycling and trash thingies they have next to the door as I follow him. Then he goes out to the truck and to the passenger door and opens it for me. "Moose, out," he says as he holds the door and helps me up with a hand lightly on my elbow.

Yum.

Once I'm seated and our eyes are level, he pulls the seatbelt out and hands it to me. "I said I trusted you, Chloe. You'll figure it out. We don't need to talk about the rent."

His eyes drop to the slit of my dress mid-thigh as I pull the seatbelt across me, then zip back up to meet mine. "Oh, okay," I breathe. "Thank you." I guess?

He pours water from his bottle into a metal container for Moose, then shuts my door while Moose runs around to get back in from Justin's side. Then he gets in his seat and starts the engine.

And I start cranking numbers and timelines in my head. I don't know what his expectations are. I just know I need to beat them.

We're back on the road we took on the way down, but now it's pitch dark. My thoughts are reeling with what he said, with everything it means. For the business. For me.

It's a lot to think about. I had a beer, Justin did not. It's been a long day, and without the entertainment of the beautiful landscape since it's now pitch dark, my eyelids are heavy.

Justin took a shortcut, same as on the way down. It's a small country road, and sometimes instead of following the curve of it, he just keeps going straight on a dirt road that goes up and down hills and eventually rejoins the larger, hard-packed road we were on. It lolls right and left, up and down. It's perfect.

At some point we lose decent radio signal, and it's crackling so much, I turn it off. Out of habit, I check my phone—zero bars. Not that I could use my playlists by connecting to Justin's truck anyway. It might be in excellent repair, but it's from a previous generation. Moose is dead to the world, his huge body filling the back seat.

The purr of the engine is our only soundtrack.

Justin's scent envelops me, and I take a deep breath.

"You okay?" he says, glancing at me.

"I'm great," I answer sleepily as I close my eyes and tuck myself deeper in the seat. I feel his gaze lingering on me, my skin reacting with tiny pleasure goosebumps until I drift off to sleep.

And then a loud grind fills the air. I peel my eyes open. We're climbing a hill, and the noise becomes louder. "Everything all right?" I ask the universally stupid question when you know something's wrong—you just don't know what.

Justin frowns and cusses as the truck slows, seeming to struggle getting up the hill. He pulls to the side, on an open and somewhat flat field, just as the truck stops.

He turns the key in the ignition. The engine cranks, and I hear the sound of something spinning. But nothing else happens. "Fuck." He pops the hood open, reaches over for a flashlight in the glove compartment, and slides out of the truck.

I come out and hold the flashlight for him and watch him check levels and wiggle wires. Then he goes to the back of his truck and pulls out things and changes things and wiggles things. Asks me to get behind the wheel and start the engine. Wheeze, nothing.

He does more mysterious things.

I turn the key again.

Wheeze, nothing.

After maybe half an hour of this, he wipes his hands on his jeans and says, "Ever slept under the stars?"

I do a little happy jump that he doesn't see while he closes the hood.

Minutes later we're on our backs in the truck bed, Moose at our feet, some moving blankets spread under us, an old jacket of Justin's spread over us. Justin took care of setting up the truck's flatbed while I did my business in the field, and that's where we're spending the night. We both have our hands under our heads for support, looking at the stars.

"Best night of my life," I whisper. The flatbed is hard and cold, but there's nowhere else I'd rather be.

Justin grunts and I laugh softly. He doesn't bring Boston up, though.

"Best night of my *real* life," I whisper again, and I feel him shift next to me, his side against my side, warming me. I want him to reach his arm around my shoulders, but he doesn't, and I don't dare move.

Friends. Get that in your head, Chloe.

But I tilt my head when I say, "Night," and catch him looking down at me.

"Night," he says back, and we roll our heads back to face the stars but neither of us close our eyes.

It's too beautiful. A myriad of constellations, the thin moon in a corner, the deep dark sky behind it like the velvet pillow to so many diamonds. The air is cool and fragrant, animals ruffling and owls tooting and Everything. Is. So. Perfect.

I drift asleep knowing I had that in my life, and it's more than most people can say.

I startle awake to the sound of Moose growling. My back is cool, but my front is warm, my cheek against something soft and that smells *awesome*. I blink my eyes open just as my arm is being lifted slowly, softly. "Baby," Justin's low voice rumbles inside me.

Oh good. I'm dreaming. Yummy dream. I shut my eyes tightly. Where was I? Justin calling me baby. Mmm. My thigh over his hard, warm body. My head over his—

"Clover, baby, gotta move you. Don't be scared, alright?"

Moose growls louder.

I push up and realize I'm tangled over Justin and it was So. Good. "Oh, sorry, sorry," I say and retreat.

"Clo, listen to me. Don't freak out. I'm gonna grab the rifle behind our heads, okay."

I sit up. "Whaaaat?" I shriek, immediately clasping my hand on my mouth. "Why?" I say, the word muffled behind my hand.

He grabs from the long box behind our heads that I thought held only his tools but turns out, it also holds a big-ass rifle that gleams eerily in the night. "There's a bear, sweetie. Don't freak out."

My hands clench in fists, my body tightens, and the most feral, primal, loud scream escapes me. "Aaaaahh!" It comes from way inside, from somewhere I didn't know existed. It goes on and on until I'm out of breath, and then it stops, and my eyes bug out of their sockets. My whole body is so tight, it shakes, ready to snap.

The forest goes silent. No more owls. Nothing but a scuttle fast disappearing, far, very far.

"Fuck was that, Chloe?"

No more "*baby or sweetie,*" I guess. Oh well, that had to happen.

"Is it gone?" I ask, my voice coarse.

Justin scoots away from me, kneels, and arms his rifle. "Looks like it. But just to be sure," he adds and shoots up in the air.

"Ouch! That was loud!" I plop my hands on my ears. Moose whines and tucks his head between his paws.

"*That* was loud? Babe, did you hear yourself?"

Babe? Hmmm.

"You were going to kill a bear. I had to do something."

He opens his rifle and removes the casing. "I wasn't going to kill it. Just scare it away."

"Scare it how?"

He chuckles. "With the sound of the gunshot. You beat me to it."

Oh. "Are we safe?" I bring my knees to my chest and wrap my arms around them.

"Oh yeah. That bear's not coming back. Plus, they're harmless." He stashes his rifle back into the box and snatches it shut.

They're harmless? "Um... are you *sure*? It's a *bear*."

"Yeah, little black bear." He pats the space next to him.

"Still. A bear!"

"Bears around here don't attack humans. Not unless it's a mama bear and you're messing with her cubs."

"So why did it come here?"

He considers me for a beat. "Probably looking for food."

"But we don't have food! Ergo, we *are* the food."

"You might have a point there," he says playfully.

Playfully! "Are you serious?" My eyes dart all around us, as if a bear was waiting to lunge at us.

"They have a strong sense of smell."

"And? We don't *have* food."

"And... you're a messy eater."

"What?" I say on an exhale, remembering how juicy the burger was and how I licked my fingers and washed my hands *before* but not after dinner.

"Probably smelled that burger on you," he continues.

What?

He chuckles. Again.

I speak between clenched teeth. "Just what I said. We are the food."

"Not what you said." And in the night, I can make out his smile, the white of his teeth.

"I said, *We are the food*."

"You said, '*Ergo, we are the food*'."

"So? It means—"

He links his hands behind his nape. "I know what it means, I just think it's cute how you use it when you're riled up."

I huff and slide to Moose, giving him a pet on the head. He exhales loudly and stretches out on his side, ready to resume his night.

"We can sleep inside the cab, if you're scared," Justin says. He's sitting upright on the blanket, his legs outstretched in front of him.

"Should we?"

His voice dips down. "Only if it makes you feel safer."

My insides melt at his concerned tone, my temporary annoyance gone. I'm not going to deny the fact that everything now brings me back to Boston. The fact that we're stranded in the night. The fact that he's taking care of me.

Taking care of my fears.

My gaze darts between the cab and the flatbed. "I like it better here."

He moves so he's lying on his back. "Come on," he says, patting that space right next to him. "I wanna get a little sleep." His voice is gravelly and soft at the same time. He smooths the blanket out for me and leaves his arm extended.

Not wanting to make assumptions, I lie on my back, farther down, my head on my folded arms and not where it wants to be—on his arm. "You didn't get any sleep?" I ask, my eyes safely fixed on the stars.

I feel his body turn toward me. "Nope."

"Because of the bears?"

"Nope."

"Then why?"

His voice dips. "Because of you." His arm nudges closer to the top of my head, his bent elbow nesting me to him.

My heartbeat is at its max. Surely he can hear it. I continue to resist looking at him, again not wanting to make assumptions. "Do I snore?" I snap.

His soft chuckle is the only response.

"Ohmygod, I snore." *Why didn't anyone ever tell me?*

"You don't snore."

Good. Then back to his answer—*'because of you.'*

"I was looking at you sleep. You never gave me your peaceful sleep, so I took it."

My head whips to him, my breathing labors, and my throat clenches. "I never... what?" I wet my lips.

"I held you while you slept in the elevator. You were tense." He trails the space between my eyebrows. For a moment, I feel like he might bring his finger to my lips, but he retreats and adds, "Then after we made love in the bedroom, I fell asleep and woke up to a cold and empty bed. Never got to see you sleep peacefully."

Is he seriously bringing up making love? Not *having sex*, not *fucking*, not *doing it*. No, he says *'making love'* and he says it *with reverence*, after he told me we're *just friends*. How am I supposed to deal with this?

Going with attack as the best defense, I answer, "Is this some kind of fetish? Like, do you have a list of things you need to check off during your one-night stands?"

In the softening glow of predawn, his eyes register hurt, and his head jerks back a bit. Then he softens and says, "You're beautiful when you sleep, Clover. I knew you would be. But then I saw it last night, and I couldn't get enough of it." His eyes roam my face, pausing on my lips. His arm that was behind my head closes in on me, trailing down my side, his fingers playing against my ribs. "And just so you know, you weren't one of my one-night stands."

Now it's my head that jerks back, caught immediately in the nook of his warm, hard arm as he clenches around me, bringing me closer to him. "You were *not*." He dips his head closer to mine, our foreheads almost touching, and his voice lowers to a murmur. "You were so much more than that. That's why I was so pissed when I found you'd left without saying goodbye. And why I was still pissed a week later, when you came into my pub to bust my balls about the..." his lips get close to mine, "fucking..." his tongue darts out, "rent." He's moved his body over mine, not touching but almost, one arm cushioning my head, the other holding himself slightly up so he's not crushing me. The stars behind him pale, dawn peeking to our right, his intoxicating scent mellowing me to the core. All I see is his face over mine, the sky, and the stars behind him, and I want this moment to last forever.

Then my hand shoots to his nape, and he dips down and takes my mouth in his, and I want *this* moment to last forever. His eyes shut, and his forehead creases, and his mouth explores mine, a slow, lush, erotic melding of tongues swirling and lips and teeth nibbling. He angles his head the other side, his kiss deepens, and I meet him stroke for stroke as his body brushes against mine. Leaving my mouth, he trails down to my neck, kissing and licking the soft skin from my ear down to my shoulder, then back up, his hands, all the while, behind my head holding me up to him. "Fuck, Clover, I missed you, baby," he growls in my neck. "Missed you so much it drove me crazy."

I hook a leg behind him, pulling him closer. "Justin..."

He lifts his head to meet my gaze, and again I see hope and pain and desperation.

"I'm right here, honey. Right here with you."

He doesn't say anything, just kisses my forehead, his lips there for a beat, his breathing deep while I rake my hands on his back, the feel of his muscles enough to make me shiver.

Then he takes my mouth again, his kiss so hot I whimper and press myself deeper against him.

He runs his hand against my naked thigh, his erection presses against my belly, then he trails under my dress up to my panties, up to my bra. Breaking the kiss, he lifts himself off me just enough to look at my body with hooded eyes. Then he brings the hem of my dress up my thighs until it bunches around my hips and runs a finger under my red lace panties. "You been wearing these since yesterday?" he growls.

"Y-yes."

"Fucking hell, Clover. When were you going to tell me?"

"W-what?"

"You had to know that dress drove me crazy, but, baby, if I'd known about this..." He pushes the panties aside so he can plunge a finger inside me. "Shit, you're so wet. So fucking wet for me. I wanna see you come."

I could come just from the sound of his voice, from his scent, from the way he looks at me, like I'm so precious he can't believe it, like I'm the sexiest woman he's ever seen. "Come for me, baby, show me again how beautiful you are when you come on my fingers."

A low wail emanates from me, and I clench my lips.

"Let it out, baby, it's just you and me. Show me how loud you are for me."

My body trembles, my orgasm shaking me, and I let it out, a long cry that swells and heaves out of my control, like I'm possessed. I've been so close for so long, being with him all this time, my release is both a relief and a disappointment. I want more. As I come down from it, I look at the beautiful man looking at me, and I wonder how it is that I'm so lucky. Then I wonder how I can protect my heart so it doesn't shatter into pieces.

"Where'd your mind go?" Justin says, peppering kisses on my cheekbones, my temple, my head, my eyes.

One-night stand rebound was safe. Pining for Justin who I thought kinda sorta hated me for a minute (maybe not that much) was safe. This is anything but safe. "I'm scared," I admit in a whisper.

He blinks several times. "Then we can be scared together," he growls and takes my mouth in his, puts his hands all over me, lifts me and sets me against him, laying me face down against his hard chest. His strong arms close around me, his warm hands roaming up and down my frame until one settles under my butt and the other across my shoulder blades. I close my eyes to the sound of his heartbeat and the forest waking up.

Then Moose lets out a deep sigh, and we both laugh.

CHAPTER THIRTY-TWO

Justin

"Wear that dress and underwear tonight." It's midday, we're hot, we're thirsty, but that's all that's on my mind right now. Her dress, her underwear, and everything Chloe. Everything I've wanted, within reach, right there, too stupid to take it. It's here, it's mine, and I want it.

Except I'm gonna have to wait. We've been squeezed in Colton's tow truck for the past hour, my truck on his flat bed. Colton bitched about me taking back roads, but overall, I think he had fun maneuvering the dips and curves and scaring tourists away. I mean the guy fixes cars for a living and does stock car races for fun, so I think he's having a little of both right now and no grounds to complain.

Now we're dropping Chloe off at the cottage. I go to the kitchen with her so Moose can get a drink. Colton's truck is idling on the road. I grab Chloe by the hips and pin her right where she was when we were tasting foods and I almost, almost kissed her.

Why didn't I?

I wasted two more weeks.

I was scared, and scared is no way to live your life.

So now I go for it and kiss her long and sweet. She twines her arms behind my neck and pulls me closer to her and fuuuuck. That right there is what scares me. How she wants me, how she almost seems to *need* me.

Am I man enough for that? For her?

She makes a little noise in the back of her throat, her leg creeping up mine, her foot hitting the back of my thigh. Pulling me closer into her. God I want her right now. Right here.

Six weeks since I had her.

No one since her.

Not that I wanted anyone else.

"Wear that dress and underwear tonight." She said something about taking a shower, and hell if I'm gonna miss out on peeling those clothes off her later today. "Gonna fuck you in that little dress," I say, and she does a whole body clench around me that just nearly undoes me. "Been teasing me thirty hours, babe." I run my thumb across her nipple, and she arches into me, throwing her head back.

Colton honks his horn, and I peel myself off her.

"Not kidding, Clo. I want you in that little dress tonight. At my place. You know how to get there, right? Staircase at the back of the pub. Gonna cook you dinner." I give her lips a quick kiss, whistle softly for Moose to follow me, and get back in the truck.

Colton says nothing, but his eyes are dancing, and his mouth is twitching.

"Broken timing belt," Colton says as he wipes his hands in a rag. We're in his garage, I'm sipping a soda while he's under the hood of my truck. "I'll keep her a coupla days tops. You can use the Chevy." He grabs the moving blankets from the bed of my truck and hands them to me. "For Moose," he says.

I glance at the vintage car he's been lovingly fixing up for years. It's proudly displayed on the patch of grass at the entrance of his shop, gleaming under the sun. "*That* Chevy?"

"Yeah."

"You sure?"

"You're gonna need something to impress your girl when you take her out." He slides back under my truck.

I roll my eyes. "Seriously, dude. I can borrow something from the farm. I'll just call one of my brothers to give me a ride." I'm dying to drive the Chevy, but from his joke, I don't know if he's serious or not.

"Keys are behind the door. Have fun with it. Just go easy on her. And keep Moose on the blankets."

I guess he's serious. "Geez, thanks, man."

"Treat her right."

The pub is busy when I get there late morning. I barely have time to update Shane and Haley on my truck issues.

"So you spent the night out in your truck?" Haley asks. "How d'you get Colton to pick you up?"

"I flagged down the first person I saw, a dirt bike. He called Colton when he got service."

"Huh. That's funny. Colton must have been busy this morning." She wipes a perfectly clean spot on the bar, ignoring the dirties piling up on empty tables.

"Yeah?" I log into our POS and check last nights' numbers.

"Yeah," she trails. "Same thing happened to Chloe last night. I was trying to reach her, and this morning she finally answered, and she said she was stranded overnight and that Colton had just dropped her off."

"Uh-huh."

She plants herself next to me, hands on her hips. "Tinman," she says, using my childhood nickname.

"What."

"Spill."

I clench my jaw but at the same time I feel happy. I'm trying to keep everything in but it's hard. I feel like a bottle of beer ready to explode from being shaken too much.

Haley shrieks and throws her arms around me, squeezing me and doing a jumping-up-and-down dance.

"What's going on here?" Shane asks, poking his head from the kitchen.

Haley lets go of me. "Nothing!" she singsongs and finally gets started on clearing tables.

I head to my office and give Declan a call. It's time I get off my ass. "What's the law about surveillance cameras?" I ask him.

"No such law in Vermont."

Huh. "So I can put cameras anywhere?"

"As long as you don't break privacy laws, yes."

"What's'at mean?"

"Surveillance cameras are legal as long as they don't capture anyone else's private area. Like your neighbor's garden or inside their house.

Just don't put cameras anywhere there's an expectation of privacy. Like bathrooms."

"Gotcha."

He stays silent for a beat, and when I don't add anything, he asks, "Does this have anything to do with what you asked me the other day?"

"Maybe." Totally.

"Don't do anything stupid, Justin."

"I'm just getting my thumb out of my ass, like you said I should."

"What happened to letting us take care of it?"

"That's actually the part about getting you specific and demonstrated evidence. Or clues, whatever. You'll be in the loop, no worries. Expect a call late at night one of these days."

"Can't wait," he grumbles and hangs up.

I spend the next hour ordering cameras online, next day delivery.

Then I head to Clark's Meadow to help take down the tents. A bunch of guys are already hard at work, and within a few hours we're done.

Late afternoon, I'm pouring beers when Haley walks behind the bar. "I'm going to let you guys handle this tonight," I tell her.

A slow smile spreads across her face. "Nice. Where're you taking her?"

"I'll be upstairs. Need some rest."

She swats my bicep. "Take her out somewhere nice! In Colton's car."

"I'm going to be at my apartment, which is right upstairs. I need some rest."

"I'm sure you do," she whispers.

"If you guys need anything, you call me right away."

"We won't need anything. It's Sunday. It'll be slow. Go have fun."

I'm about to tell her I'm not going to have fun, but that'd be a lie.

"Haley! I'm serious. You guys need anything, you call me." I know they can handle dinner service without me, but I wasn't here last night. I won't be here tonight either. I feel a little guilty about it.

"Hope you take her somewhere nice," she calls out teasingly as she walks out to the sidewalk.

I don't tell her I'm cooking for Chloe. I don't tell her I want to see Chloe in my space, in my bed, in my shower, on my kitchen counter. I want to make her mine in any way possible, and that means bringing her to my place.

I never wanted to date anyone. I never wanted to hook up with anyone in town.

But everything changed with Chloe. I want her in my world. I want her to *be* my world.

And that, I'll say it again, is scary as fuck.

The table is set, the main dish is keeping warm in the oven, apps and dessert are ready, and the salad just needs to be tossed, when a soft knock on the door sounds right at seven.

Chloe is standing there, looking shy. Pink tints her cheeks, and her smile is uncertain. Her eyelashes bat and she says a tentative, "Hey."

I feel the same.

It was one thing to fool around at her place and in the truck.

But we both know why she's here. We both know what this means. This isn't a second one-night stand. This isn't giving in to impulse.

This is us wanting to explore what we could be.

I might have talked dirty to her at her place today—telling her I wanted to fuck her in that dress—tonight means so much more to me.

"Hey," I say, holding the door open for her.

She's wearing the dress, but it looks like she pressed it or something, because it certainly doesn't look like she wore it the day before at the fair and last night in my truck. She smells like flowers, like maybe she's wearing a spritz of perfume. Her hair flows on her shoulders, and there's light makeup on her eyes. She doesn't need it, but I like that she did it.

She looks around my apartment, her smile deepening. Then she drops her handbag on the couch, kicks her shoes off, and turns to me. And I've never felt so good in my life.

CHAPTER THIRTY-THREE

Chloe

Justin shuts the door quietly behind me and wraps me in his arms, a slow, tender, deep embrace. He kisses my neck, and my center fires up, then he hoists me on his hips, our foreheads touching. I fist his hair, bringing his lips to mine, darting my tongue out. He kisses me back, a soft and slow kiss as he walks us into his apartment. Then he twirls me around and drops me on a countertop and leaves me slightly dizzy, a stupid happy smile on my wet lips.

"Mojito?" he asks.

"Yeah," I answer, craning my neck to follow his awesome body as he moves to make us drinks. He's wearing washed-out jeans, a short-sleeved button-down that's a very light shade of gray, has tiny stripes, molds to his muscles, and shows a good portion of his tats. He's barefoot and I think to myself, *He has great feet.*

I have a little internal smile at my weird-ish observation, then I turn around to take in my surroundings.

Where Justin lives.

His apartment is right above the pub. We're in a large open space with the kitchen area in one corner and sliding doors that open to a deck built on the pub's roof. There's no furniture outside, not even a single chair. Just railing all around it. Justin clearly doesn't use the outdoor space.

I move my attention to the inside. The walls are exposed brick, the ceilings high with dark beams. The floor is wide wooden planks showing all kinds of wear and tear but sanded down and polished. A leather couch faces a huge flat-screen TV mounted over a fireplace, with a battered, dark coffee table in front of it. To the side, next to the row of windows facing The Green and between shelves filled with books, there's a wood and metal dining table set for two.

My heart does a little thump as I take in the flowers in a small Mason jar, the tea light candles flickering, the napkins carefully folded over the plates.

Then I move my attention to the black-and-white pictures on the wall.

I hop down from the countertop and walk to the photographs.

The sound of a shaker fills the room, followed by drinks being poured, then Justin's steps and his warmth next to me as I catch my breath.

The first photograph shows an old building, floor to ceiling openings, about two stories high, with men in leather aprons posing with their tools. The sign above their heads reads, *Sal's Forge.*

The second photograph is the same building probably decades later. Some of the openings on the left side have been walled from the ground up, maybe to create large bay windows. It's hard to tell because it's boarded. A partial story has been added to the building, also on the left side.

The right side, about one third of the whole building, looks like it's been rehabbed into a store, or maybe a restaurant, with its own entrance and windows and awnings.

The third photograph is clearer, and that's the one that guts me.

It's a more recent photo. Black and white. Not by artistic choice, I don't think. The framing could have been better. Not a professional photographer. It's more like it was printed in black and white by choice. Maybe to match the others.

The photograph shows the same building. The boards are gone and replaced with windows. There're flower boxes now but with the picture being in black and white that's kind of lost. The main entrance for the bulk of the building on the left side is now a wood and glass door with wrought iron details I'm familiar with. There's a brand-new sign, *The Lazy Salamander.*

A group of people are assembled under the sign, ready for a ribbon-cutting ceremony. I recognize Chris, and Lynn and Craig, and Grace and Haley, Logan and Hunter, and Colton.

What breaks my heart is in the center. Justin, holding giant scissors, smiling tentatively at the camera. He's nothing like the man I know now. He looks frail and almost stooped. A shadow of himself. Like he's struggling to stand, struggling to hold the scissors, struggling and failing to really smile. But it's him alright. Those locks framing his face, wilder than now. That piercing gaze, with that sadness that usually only comes in hints, captured entirely on paper.

I can't take my eyes off the picture, even when he hands me my drink. "You okay?" he says.

I peel my eyes off the wall and look at him now, grinning, full of life, full of joy. What am I missing? How do I ask him?

He clinks his glass to mine. "Cheers." We take a sip, his eyes boring into mine, mine into his, with a lot of questions. "You look good in my place," he says, a glimmer of mischief in his eye.

"Your place is great." I turn away from the photo wall, try to make small talk. "Very manly." I smile. "Like a giant man cave."

"At least you didn't say it looks like a bachelor pad."

The word makes me shiver. Does he bring a lot of girls here? I didn't think he did, but what do I know?

He claims my waist in his free hand and brings me to him. "Hey, where'd your mind go, Clover."

I need to grow up and get rid of my insecurities. Of course he's had girls here. I mean, look at this place. Look at this *man*.

"Cave is the word," he says softly. "I never have anyone here. No friends. No family. Mom came here a couple of times when I moved in, but not anymore, thank god. Been a while since I've needed help."

I turn a questioning gaze at him.

He points to the photos with his drink. "When I opened the pub, I was still in rehab. Still had motion issues. She was worried for me."

My gaze stops on his forearm, where the intricate tattoo designs artfully cover his scars. "You never really told me how bad your accident was." I instinctively mold my body closer to his, but he shrugs, and his hold around my waist loosens. "I don't like to talk about it."

Yeah, I kind of got that. "Then why the photos?"

"I don't want to forget it either."

Here we are. "So you'd rather keep it to yourself?"

His lips tighten in a forced smile. "I have some appetizers. Don't like to drink on an empty stomach." He lets go of me, goes to the fridge, pulls out a board, and sets it on the coffee table.

"So this place was a forge?" I ask once we're seated on the couch, me at an angle, my bare feet on his lap. I pretend to forget he didn't answer my question. I'll get back to it.

He finger-feeds me a piece of prosciutto and nods. "Sal's forge. When renovations were almost done and it was time to find a name for the pub, I played with incorporating his name. At the time I used to sit in the back a lot, get some sun, and there was this salamander that kept showing up that I thought was super friendly and weirdly slow. I thought The Lazy Salamander was a cool name for a pub."

Right. So, after our cooking session, I did some research. Turns out, for the most part, salamanders are not a protected species, but, also for the most part, they're poisonous to eat.

Also turns out, they have a strong symbolic meaning.

Not saying there wasn't a friendly salamander keeping him company on his breaks. That could happen. But come on. I drain my mojito and play with the ice cubes, twirling them in the glass, wondering what will get him to open up to me. "Isn't it cool the salamander also symbolizes rebirth and... the ability to survive fire?" I narrow my eyes on him.

"Very cool," he says, unfazed.

"So, why lazy?"

"Even cooler," he answers without missing a beat, his killer smile again freezing me in place while he goes for a slow kiss.

My center is mush and my throat tight. How can I get upset at him after he kisses me *like that*? Wanting to know more about him, wanting to someday know everything about him, for now I go to a safe topic. "You did a lot of renovations?"

He sets his empty glass on the floor and starts rubbing the soles of my feet. "Place was a dump. After the forge closed down, some dude bought the building with the idea of converting it, not sure to what.

He added this apartment, then ran out of money. The whole King block and another property he had, the cottage you're living in, were foreclosed on just at the right time for me."

"The right time?"

His lips tighten again, but he answers this time. "After the accident, I got some money." He looks bitter about it. "There's things money can't buy. But then there's things money can actually get you."

On instinct, I go for the safe question. "What made you want a pub?"

He doesn't answer right away, instead he pulls me closer and starts trailing his hands up and down my legs, caressing my calves, my knees, stopping shy of the inside of my thighs. Then finally he says, "I wanted to stay in town, but I didn't want to work on the farm." His gaze wanders away from me, and my heart clenches as I listen to him trying to tone down what had to be the most difficult time in his life. "I didn't think I could pull my weight, at least in the beginning, and I wanted my own thing. I was working on getting better, getting back to a hundred percent. I knew I wouldn't get there if I lived at home. I didn't want my parents or anyone pitying me."

There are so many things I want to know about him, but I get that he's just opening up about this. Some things take a while to come out. Sometimes they never do. Sometimes the people around you need to understand the words you're not saying. "Were you in a lot of pain?"

His eyes swing back to me. "Mostly, yeah," he says casually. "I needed to do my own thing," he continues, "and I wanted to do it in this town. I got some money, saw this block in foreclosure, bought it, saw the town needed a pub, took a loan to make it a pub. The other space was already a restaurant, so I didn't touch it." I scoot closer to him, wanting to hold him, but he moves my feet to the floor, stands up, and mutters, "I wasn't the running away type."

Then he pulls me to my feet, and I land against the length of him. "Hungry?" he whispers, his hands at my back pressing me deep against him, his mouth dipping to my ear.

I tie my hands behind his nape. "Not for food yet."

"Not for food?" His eyes are dancing, his smile is deep. He's past the sadness, or maybe he's learned to live with it and can chase it away whenever it shows up. He gives my lower back another pull, rubbing his erection against me. "You're driving me crazy."

"Then do something about it."

He growls and lifts me, one hand behind my butt so I'm straddling him. In a few long steps, we're in his bedroom. The shades are drawn, the bed is a king and it takes the whole space.

He sets me down on the bed. "Don't move," he says as he yanks his shirt off, then shucks his jeans and underwear, never breaking eye contact with me.

He's so intense, his gaze so hungry, that despite feeling a pull to look at him getting undressed for me, to look at his magnificent body I've reimagined so many times since Boston, my eyes stay locked to his. Then he drops his gaze to my body, and I squirm under his scrutiny. My center pulsates, and I reach for the hem of my dress.

"Keep it on," he says as he lowers himself to the bed, trails his hands up my thighs, reaches my panties, and pulls them off. He growls as he watches them dangle off his fingers for a beat, then drops them and turns his attention back to my center. He nudges his face between my thighs, growling against me, then lets his tongue take over, swirling around my clit, driving me crazy.

"Justin, please," I beg. His hands take a firm grasp of my waist, giving me a tug, then he growls and finally, finally hits my spot. I start moaning, my release building fast, and he pulls away.

"Not without me, babe," he says as he grabs a condom.

I look at his magnificent body, so strong and full of life and ready to fill me, and all sorts of dirty thoughts run through my mind. "Hurry, baby," I say just as my eyes narrow on a spot right where his heart is that last time had no ink but now has a...

Clover.

My heart ba-booms, and my center clenches but not in a sexual way.

In a primal, existential, scary way.

I grab his neck and pull him to me. "What is that?"

"Babe, what?"

"On your chest."

His face softens, his lips dipping to mine.

Is he trying to avoid answering my question? "What is that new tattoo?"

"Clover..."

Why did he act that way with me when he had me tattooed on his heart?

"Tell me."

He doesn't tell me anything. His eyes go somewhere sad and deep again. He grabs me behind the knees and folds my legs up, bucks his hips and enters me hard, then lets go of my legs to cup my head. He leans his forehead against mine as I wrap my limbs around his body, pulling him against me, never letting him go. He's relentless in his pounding.

"Tell me," I beg, the words getting lost in my moans, my body betraying me.

He undoes the top buttons of my dress, slides a hand under my bra, flicks the pad of his thumb over my nipple and just growls, "Clover," and I come undone under him, my orgasm still rippling through me when he comes inside me in long, hard jerks.

I pull his body to cover mine entirely, but he props himself on one elbow as he catches his breath, his locks of hair caressing my face, his exhales like feather kisses down my neck.

"Tell me," I say.

"You're angry."

No. I'm freaked out. Okay, maybe a little angry too. "Yes."

"Why?"

Why? First he didn't want to take my name or number, then he yelled at me, then ignored me, then said we were friends, and for a large part of that time he had *my name tattooed on his heart*?

"Clover, you're scaring me. Talk to me."

I take a deep breath. "No, *you* talk to me. I wanna know everything. From the top."

He rolls away from me and settles on his back, trying to pull me against his side.

My body hardens.

"From the top?" He sounds freaked out and reaches for me again.

"We got all night."

He pinches the top of his nose. "Can we cuddle? I miss your cuddling."

"No cuddling with liars." I'm not as angry as I sound, but I do need to make a point.

He lifts himself halfway. "Liar? What did I lie about? I didn't know I was supposed to disclose a new tattoo."

It's not just any new tattoo. I sit up and tuck the dress between my legs. "You lied about your feelings, Justin. You made me miserable because of that. You made *yourself* miserable."

He drops a hand on my knee and caresses it gently. "I'm sorry," he says in a low whisper, so genuine I almost crumble and climb him and cuddle against him.

"Kay," I say. "Now we're gonna talk."

"Kay," he says, repeating my word. "But can we talk over dinner? I'm starving. It's either cuddle or eat. You won't cuddle, I need to eat."

I almost melt at his confession, but he doesn't give me enough time to change my mind and nudge myself against him like I want to.

He ducks into the bathroom and leaves me feeling silly. He returns moments later. "It's all yours," he says and goes into the kitchen. I slide off the bed, clean up in his very manly, very dark, very stark yet quite awesome bathroom—mostly black tile and chrome.

I find him in the kitchen tossing a salad while something that smells awesome is in the oven.

"Can I do anything?" I'm annoyed at myself for the way I talked to him. Did I push him too fast, too far?

Did I push him away?

"You can come here." His gravelly voice shoots straight to my lady parts. I make my way to him, relishing the look he gives me. He pulls me into him, one hand behind my back, the other playing with my hair. His gaze jumps from my lips to my temple to the top of my head. "I like you here, Clover. I like you in my arms, I like you in my place. I think I'm gonna like you in my life."

My chest ba-booms again. "Justin," I whisper, tilting my head back, angling it just so when he lowers his mouth to mine.

He gives me another of his full, deep, soulful kisses, then pulls back just enough to say, "I made a mistake in Boston. I told you, I was angry at myself. The one way I'm used to dealing with my wounds, is to cover them up in ink."

My knees buckle at his confession. "Oh, Justin…"

He takes my mouth again, gives me another long, deep, awesome kiss. "But I should know. Even the deepest wounds eventually heal. Sometimes in surprising ways," he adds, booping me.

We're feasting on marinated grilled chicken and herbed new potatoes when he says, "After the accident, I had to have some skin grafts. After that, physical therapy. My PT became my best friend, so to speak. He's an older dude, was in the military, then after his discharge, went back to school. He was exactly who I needed. Tough. Knew what I was going through. Knew what I could handle. Knew how to bring me back. All the way. Once I was completely healed, I just kept on going with training and shit."

I can't help but roam my eyes over his body. The training *and shit* definitely worked.

"Like what you see?" he asks, his foot under the table grazing my calf.

Heat creeps from my center to my chest. I don't know why I feel like I've been caught with my hand in the cookie jar. A smile is the only answer I can give him.

"You're so darn cute when you check me out, Chloe." He's full-on grinning now.

I want to know more about what he went through. "How about pain?"

"What about it?"

"How did you deal with it?"

"As soon as I was out of the hospital, I tried to stay away from meds as much as I could. Did mental shit like meditation. CBD. Tried weed but didn't like what it did to me. I wanted to feel fully in control. Having the pub gave me a purpose. Something to think about, worry about, that wasn't me or my body."

"It must have been hard."

"I came out alive. I was the lucky one."

Right. I almost forgot. How does he feel about that? Did he go to therapy? Does he still need help coping? There's so much I want to know. "Do you often talk about the accident?"

He looks at me like he's stunned. "No. Not going to. Thought I told you already."

Oh. I clear my throat, stand up slowly and round the table, set my hand on his shoulder and push back a little. "I think it's cuddle time," I say, pushing harder so he'll give me space to sit on his lap.

He doesn't budge. "I don't want your pity, Chloe." His eyes are softer, but still, I can tell, he's guarded.

"I don't pity you, Justin." I wiggle myself between the table and him and straddle him, running my fingers through his hair. "I just want to give you some love. That okay?" I add, bringing my forehead to his, my hair creating a curtain around us.

His hands come to my hips, up my butt cheeks, and he gives me a squeeze. "Yeah, Clover." He kisses me softly, barely any tongue, then nests my head on his neck.

We stay there for a moment, quiet, eyes closed, until he carries me to his room again and makes sweet love to me.

This time, I examine his tattoos carefully, an intricate web of leaves and tree barks covering the uneven surface of his skin. There's even a small salamander on his shoulder, and I give it a soft kiss before trailing down his chest and ending on the clover, which blends seamlessly with the leaves and flowers covering his ribs.

Then he brings us fresh berries and homemade ice cream in his bed, and after that, we fall asleep. When I wake up early in the morning, the bed is empty but not for long.

Justin brings me coffee and a warm croissant from Christopher's bakery right across the green.

"You sure you have to go?" Justin says when I get up and start looking for my underwear.

"I can't be wearing the same dress three days in a row. People'll start talking."

"They're already talking."

"Right. But not about my poor hygiene. Not yet." I snap my panties and tug them on.

He laughs softly.

I find my bra under his bed. "Does it bother you that people are talking about us?"

"Why would it bother me?" He stands and walks with me to the main room.

You used to have one-night stands outside of town? Rumor is you never wanted to date anyone here? I stuff my bra in my handbag and slip my sandals on.

He wraps an arm around my waist and pulls me to him. "I don't care what people say. And anyway, people are probably just saying the truth for once. That I'm a lucky bastard." Then he kisses me long and soft and lets me go.

I hesitate at the door, burning to ask, *Do you want to come to my place tonight?* But we've already spent two nights together. I don't want to seem needy. I don't want to *be* needy.

"You ever been in a 1956 Chevy Bel Air convertible?"

That would be a no, but I'm not sure why he's asking, so I safely settle for "Um…"

"I'll pick you up in two hours. Taking you to the lake."

CHAPTER THIRTY-FOUR

Chloe

"In two hours?" It's morning, and he wants to go to a lake already? I wasn't at the restaurant yesterday because of the fair. I need to show my face today, or my staff is going to—

"I'll bring you back by three. You'll be there before the action starts. Plenty of time to do your office work *and* do admin work *and* help your staff." He grins and slaps me playfully on the butt. "Now go get ready and pack a bathing suit."

He arrives at the cottage an hour and a half later, and the Chevy does not disappoint. For a moment, I'm blinded, my eyes dancing between Justin in a tight tee and shorts, aviator sunglasses pushed over his head, and the car fit for a movie star, stretching forever, blue and off-white with some fantastic stripes and shining chrome. Moose is on the back seat, the car's leather duly protected from the dog's paws by several layers of moving blankets tucked neatly so as not to move.

"I did run this by Colton, by the way. He said it was okay to bring Moose in the car." Justin takes my straw tote bag and holds the door open for me.

"He must really like you," I say.

"I think he likes Moose better." He shuts the car door softly after I'm in, leans in and kisses me. "And he thinks my truck isn't good enough for you." He rubs our noses together and dashes to his side, then roars the car to life.

"That's because he doesn't know how creative we can get in your truck." I lean into him to drop a kiss on his jaw, then stay snuggled against him. "Though there's something to be said about that bench seat. Definitely holds more makeout power than the truck."

A big grin on his face, he sets his hand on my bare thigh and leaves it there, moving it only to change gears, as we cruise away from the cottage, through Emerald Creek, and toward the lake.

"Canoe or paddleboard?" Justin asks. We're at 'The Beach,' an area tucked way up north on Emerald lake, where the shallow waters are what gave the lake its name and there's actual sand.

Tucked at the edge of the woods that border this corner of paradise is a shack that rents paddleboards, canoes, and kayaks. A hut on the side serves ice cream and sodas. A couple of picnic tables complete the picture.

Everything else is pristine nature.

"Paddleboard, so we can keep an eye on Moose," I say. "I don't think I can go too far on a paddleboard."

"Ever been on one of those?" Justin says, fists on his hips.

"Never."

"Me neither." He grins. "Hey, Mindy! How's it going?" he asks the teenager coming out of the shack.

"Hey, Tinman! You guys doing SUP today?" she asks, referring to Stand Up Paddle. "Fuuuun!" she adds in an upbeat tone as she hands us each a life jacket. "All about balance." She grabs a board under each arm and dashes to the water. "Grab the paddles!" she says over her shoulder.

"The energy of that kid! She makes me feel old," I chuckle.

"Tell me about it."

We follow her to knee-deep water. "Start by kneeling on the board. Place your knees on the deck, shoulder-distance apart, near the center of the board." My first try, I slip back into the water. Second, I make it. Justin is already crouching on his board, trying to stand up.

Splash!

"You wanna paddle on your knees first," Mindy says while Justin shakes the water off his body and hoists himself back up, water sloshing upward, his muscles now glistening in the sun.

My knees soften. He's too distracting.

I manage to turn the board so I can't see him anymore. I have no interest in getting wetter than I need to, and I don't mean the sexy kind.

Should have thought about that before choosing SUP.

What can I say? Seeing Justin just makes me lose my focus.

Ten minutes later, Mindy's laughing so hard it's embarrassing. For both of us. We can't stand on the freaking things. We just keep falling off. Moose barks. "Knees wider!" she repeats for the umpteenth time. "Hip distance apart. Closer to the center. There! Now. Lift yourself..." I do as she says—I think. But then I take a look at Justin, who's in the same crouchy position as me, and I laugh again.

And fall off again.

"Come on, you guys, you're paying by the hour!" Mindy says, laughing.

Shit. She's right. I need to get my head straight.

"Are we done yet?" Justin's almost upright. "This was supposed to be fun."

"That's it, Chloe! Now, hold the paddle with both hands, shoulder-width apart. Now insert the blade into the water near the board's nose and pull toward the tail."

Splash! That was Justin.

Bark! And that was Moose.

"Now alternate sides, Chloe. Justin, you might wanna look at your girlfriend. She's got it."

"She's on her knees."

"Yeah, that's how you start!"

"But it's called Stand Up Paddle," Justin replies. The surging water cascade sounds again, then "Fuck!"

Splash.

"Now, Chloe, place your paddle horizontally across the board in front of you. Bring the right foot where your knee was. There you go. Now the left. Now slowly stand up, keeping a slight bend in your knees, and look straight ahead."

That's the trick. "I got it! I got it! I got it!" The board feels steady under my feet, and I'm upright.

"How'd you do it?" Justin shouts.

His voice makes me weak in the knees. "I stopped looking at you!"

He laughs heartily, and I need to crouch again to keep my balance. Trying to ignore his sexy laugh rippling on the water, I straighten myself and paddle away.

"Moose!" Mindy and Justin both call out. "Moose! Come here!"

Suddenly my board rocks for no apparent reason.

"Moose! No!"

And then I'm under water.

"Well that was fun." We're lying on our backs on oversized beach towels, drying off. Justin pulled out a picnic basket, and he's hand-feeding me cherry tomatoes. Moose is twenty feet from us, in the shade of the trees, looking at us in case we should decide to do something dangerous again—like stand on a flat piece of wood and drift away—and his immediate intervention is again required. You never know what crazy stuff your humans are going to come up with, and you have to be there to save them. Being a dog is exhausting. Not one moment of peace and quiet.

"You hungry for more?"

I squint at Justin, his head like a golden halo against the blinding sun. "Like what?" My center heats up, and my thighs automatically rub against each other.

He leans in and whispers, "Like real food, you dirty girl. This is a public beach."

"Oh." I pretend to pout. "Sure, what you got?"

He unwraps ciabatta bread sandwiches with mozzarella, tomatoes, basil, and bacon. We share an egg salad, taking alternate bites from the same fork.

"My god, Justin, best meal in a long time. I can't believe you made all this in the time it took me to take a shower this morning."

"What can I say? You inspire me." He drops one of his feather kisses on my forehead, then puts the food wrappers away. "Full disclosure, the sandwiches were made by Chris. Special order. He hand delivered them."

"Isn't the bakery closed on Mondays?" I ask as he settles on his side, facing me.

He squints. "Not for you it's not. Chris owes me big time for closing down when Alex left, and he knows it. Put all of us here in a bind. Now it's payback time." His laughing eyes drill into mine. "Don't worry, he's fine."

"I barely know him, but Alex is great. She moved up from New York, right?"

"Yeah... You want a cremee?" he adds suddenly.

"A what?"

"A cremee." He jumps to his feet. "Course you do. Be right back." He jogs to the shack, Moose right after him. I lay on my back, watching the small cotton-like clouds slowly drift against the azure sky, Justin's voice drifting to me in waves.

He settles back next to me, handing me an ice cream.

"Oh! What flavor is that? And thank you."

"Babe. We're in Vermont. There's no question what the flavor of a cremee should be."

Ohmygod. This is heaven. So soft and, well, creamy, and sweetened with pure maple syrup.

"Can't believe you have never had one of these."

"Me neither," I say, licking the ice cream melting down the cone.

Justin's gaze heats as it narrows on my tongue. He takes a deep breath and shifts on his towel. "How are things at the restaurant?"

Brought back to reality, I take a deep breath.

"I mean in general, Clover. This is not a loaded question. I'm not asking about the rent or anything. I don't have an ulterior motive. This is me wanting to know everything about you. How your days are going. What you worry about. What keeps you up at night. Now that we're... together, I want to be there for you. For everything."

Warmth spreads through me. *'Now that we're together.'*

I blink a few times at him. I need to pinch myself. So this is what's it like to have a significant other? Someone who cares about what you do when you're not with them.

"Well, let's see. The restaurant needs a re-brand. A clear position in the market. A new menu. A redesigned visual identity, starting with décor. It also needs a new chef." I take a big bite out of my ice cream, which is in danger of melting onto my thighs.

Justin takes clean, wide, effective licks. He's almost half done with his ice cream—*cremee*. "Samuel being a dick?"

"Nope, no. Not in the way you may think." I tell him about my issues getting a menu costing that holds water. Samuel's refusal to discuss changes to the menu. And his refusal to put the recipes in writing. "I think he's being dishonest about the quantities that actually go on the plates, versus what he claims we're serving. But I can't pinpoint why he would do that and how that affects our bottom line. Because at the end of the day, if we charge the same price but put less product on the plate, we should be making more money, right?"

"Do you guys do any catering?" Justin asks.

Where is he going with that? "No...?"

He clenches his jaw, like that makes him angry.

"Should we offer catering?" I don't even know how we would manage that.

"You have a lot of waste?"

"What's a lot? Plates usually come back fairly empty." Unless the salmon is overdone, but that's another story.

"Do you see your kitchen staff throwing away food gone bad from the fridges."

"I haven't noticed. We're bleeding money, and I can't put my finger on it. We spend more than we sell. Yet it seems we're always out of some items. We can't sell some dishes because there's always something missing. Like, one week we can't sell the tajine because we're out of the lamb, and then the following week we can't sell it because we're out of cumin or saffron or more likely, both."

"Why do they run out of stuff? Did you ask?"

"Did you see who I'm dealing with? I just need to do inventory myself, and I'll take note of expiration dates." Maybe that's the issue. "We just need to run specials when the stuff gets close to expiring," I mumble, "although that's not—"

Justin cups my jaw. "I know you're not going to believe me, because of how I fucking hate Samuel, but... he's stealing from you. I'm convinced of it, and you need to believe me, so we can catch him."

What?! "How do you know?"

"There's some weird shit going on at night."

"Ohmygod, you're right. The first day I got here, I drove on The Green, and I saw him smoking a cigarette outside. It was a Sunday! We're closed on Sundays! And when I went there the next day, the place was disgusting. D'you think he uses the kitchen for himself—like to run a catering side gig?"

"It's possible. But there's worse. There's always noise after hours coming from the restaurant, and I didn't used to pay attention to it. But the other night, after I pulled you out of the walk in? I couldn't sleep, and I heard noise again, and this time I checked it out. Samuel and David were loading heavy stuff in the trunk of a car. D'you have another explanation?"

My blood runs cold. *They're stealing? And in those quantities?* It's hard to believe, even with the way Samuel's been acting. Although...

"I thought they might be doing a catering gig, and frankly, I didn't think you'd believe me if I told you my suspicions at the time." Suddenly his expression turns angry, and he punches the sand. "Fuck! I knew it. I should have done something that night."

I'm sitting upright now, legs crossed. "You had no way to know."

"I bet you if you ask him next time, he'll tell you the lamb went bad and he had to throw it. Those spices go in another dish?"

"They don't. That's why it doesn't make sense." That and the fact that he insists on featuring dishes from another continent when we should be all about local, but whatever.

"It does. I bet Murphy never checked inventory."

"My aunt said Uncle Kevin relied entirely on Samuel. I'll do inventory myself, early tomorrow morning. I'll take note of expiry dates. This way I'll know if he's lying next time he says we're out of fresh meats or produce. Do you think they run a side gig? Catering?" That would explain why Samuel doesn't want to work extra days.

"I don't know. Margins are slim in catering, and he's kinda lazy for that. Who do you use for your provisions, meats and produce?"

What difference does it make? "Some large national company." I tell him the name. "He doesn't want to go local. Says it's too much hassle, too many providers."

Justin's jaw is tight. "He's buddies with his rep. I bet you he sells the stuff back for cash to his rep, the rep sells it cash at a discount to another place with low standards."

I can't believe this.

Actually, I can.

"I'll get on it tomorrow morning." I'll have to go in super early to make sure I have enough time. I'll take pictures of expiration dates to confront him when the time comes.

"Maybe you don't need to."

What does he mean? "Of course I do! I need to figure this out!"

He takes my hand in his. "I'm installing cameras on the parking lot."

He *what*?

"I ran it by Declan," he continues. "Says it's cool. I just needed to confirm a couple of things with you first. And you just did. Once I'm done all we'll need is to sit back and wait for them to do their next run."

I'm speechless. In a good way. My lady parts do a little happy dance.

"Babe." He strokes the inside of my wrist. "I wasn't going to sit there and do nothing."

My center clenches. Sure, there's his fingers stroking my soft skin, and his bare abs showing above his swimsuit, and his boyish grin just for me, and his sparkling eyes caressing me somewhere deep.

But there's more.

He's looking out for me.

I get on my knees and kiss him softly. "Thank you."

He picks me up and sets me on his lap, and we look at the lake in silence for a moment. "How do your parents feel about what you're doing here?"

I shrug. "Does it matter?"

He strokes my arm. "I guess not." Then, after a beat, "Ready to go?"

I shake my head and laugh. "No!" But still stand up, stretch, and shake the sand off my towel.

Justin whistles softly for Moose. "Did they come and visit you here yet?"

"Who? My parents? Mom came the day of the fair, with my aunt and Brendan—my cousin."

"Not your dad?"

"He's too busy for that kind of stuff. Plus, he didn't like Uncle Kevin, and I think he's sort of pissed that I'm working at the restaurant."

Justin stops what he's doing. "He didn't like Murphy?"

"Called him a loser all the time."

He seems genuinely puzzled. "Wasn't he your mom's brother?"

I plop my sunglasses on and grab my sandals in one hand, my tote bag in the other. "Yup. Welcome to the family!"

"I—I don't understand," he mumbles.

"Trust me, don't try."

CHAPTER THIRTY-FIVE

Justin

"How's that?" Two days later, I'm holding the tiny camera inside the hollow of a tree in the parking lot. From that angle, we're catching the restaurant back door and the parking lot.

"Great," Chloe says, focusing on the image on my phone. "Can't believe how clear the image is."

"Can you see the license plate?" Chloe parked where I saw Samuel's car that night. Close to the door. The back facing the camera. Perfect.

"Super clear," she confirms. "Will it work at night?"

"It does. Plus, lights come on when there's movement. That'll help." I drill a small hole in the inside of the tree trunk and attach the camera. "Let's just hope squirrels don't shit on it."

"Oh man."

"Just kidding. They won't." They might, though, but this is the best hiding spot I found for the camera, so I'm going to chance it.

Right as we're wrapping up, Chris rounds the parking lot, surprising us both. "I thought I saw lights at your place. What you guys doing outside so early?"

"Nothing," Chloe answers quickly. "Just hanging."

Chris's eyes dart from her to me, and he lifts a paper bag. "Perfect timing. I brought croissants."

I wipe my hands on my jeans. "Where's Alex?"

"She's on a Zoom call with Europe."

I tilt my chin to my apartment. "Coffee?"

He eyes Chloe. "Oh wow. A legit invitation? Sure. Don't mean to interrupt... whatever it is you're doing."

I wrap my arm around Clover. "Come here." Nibbling her ear as we climb the outside stairs leading to my apartment, I whisper, "it's alright." We'd decided not to tell anyone—and I mean no one—about our suspicions and the fact we're installing a camera to catch Samuel in the act. We don't want to compromise an easy solution to Chloe's problems just because someone let something slip, however innocently.

"How d'you like your coffee?" Chloe asks Chris, and god—*god*—I fucking love that she's so comfortable with my best friend, but even more, I love that she acts like this is her place.

I want it to be hers.

Ours.

Any other time, I would have pulled Chris into my pub. Not upstairs to my apartment. Upstairs feels like home, now that Chloe is here.

A quick smile runs over Chris as he answers, "Black. Thanks."

Chloe starts the espresso machine and takes the croissants Chris is handing her.

"Samuel is stealing from Chloe. I'm going to nail him," I inform Chris.

Chloe freezes, the bag of croissants hovering over the plate she just pulled out of the cupboard.

"It's okay, babe. He won't say a thing."

She blinks a couple of times and gets us cups. "We should sit on the rooftop. It's gorgeous out there. Why don't you guys bring some chairs out while I get us coffee."

The rooftop is really just that. A flat roof. You can stand on it. Because of that, the previous owner installed sliding doors to access it straight from the apartment and a kickass wrought-iron banister all around it.

I never did anything with it.

Chris winks at me. "Happy for you, man," he says while we bring chairs outside and Chloe is still fussing over the espresso machine.

I don't answer.

He chuckles.

"What?"

"Nothin'. Fun to see you get a little whipped up."

"I'm not..." Yeah maybe I am. And fuck it—I like it.

"Don't ruin it with some stupid shit like I did."

"What'd you mean?"

"Don't make assumptions. Talk to her. Women need to talk shit out."

I raise my eyebrows, uncertain what he means.

"Verbalize."

Still unclear. I think I'm doing a pretty good job at expressing what I want with Chloe. Right?

"Look at the view from here." Chloe exclaims once she joins us, pointing to the mist over the lake, the mountains a dreamy gray in the back, the rising sun tinting the air pink. She lets out a big sigh. "We should make something of this outdoor space."

And fuck. The way she says it nearly undoes me. It makes me feel weak and strong at the same time.

Chris downs his espresso. "I'd take that silence as a yes," he tells Chloe.

She giggles softly, eyes me, and takes a bite of her croissant. Then she moans.

I shift in my seat.

Shit.

Chris's shoulders shake with silent laughter. "Alex is probably done with her call," he says as a goodbye.

After he lets himself out, I pull Chloe on my lap, inhaling her sweet scent. "There's a bunch of outdoor furniture stored somewhere at the farm. Why don't you take a look next time and take what you like for here?"

"Wh-why? It was just something I said. Didn't mean anything."

My hand goes up her thigh. "Would mean a lot to me."

She's quick to put her cup on the floor and turns to straddle me, her eyes searching mine, an unspoken question between us.

"I'd like you to." I want her to put her mark on my space, just like I inked a clover above my heart. I want her all around me.

Her soft mouth closes on mine, her tongue taking possession of what's hers.

Picking her up with ease, I carry her to the bedroom.

She's wiping herself down after our shower, when her phone rings. She wraps herself in a towel and grabs it from the kitchen counter. "Hi, Aunt Dawn."

I duck into the bedroom to get dressed. When I come back out, she's worrying her bottom lip. "Sure, I'll ask around. I can do that. Bye."

She looks defeated.

"What's going on?"

"My aunt is in a hurry to sell. She says it's been over a month, which it has, and she's contacted some brokers. I tried to tell her that we'd be in a better position with a healthier P&L, but... anyway, long story short, she's asking if I could get some estimates for a rehab of the place."

"She wants to put money in the place before selling? That makes no sense."

Chloe shakes her head. "She saw the place during the fair, and like everyone else, she's not impressed. She's got it in her head that if we have an estimate for renovations, with sexy renderings, it might entice a buyer. Give them a better sense of what's feasible. And I've told her the lease is up for renewal... but it's like she doesn't get it. There's nothing to sell, really. Not yet at least."

I close the space between us and wrap my arms around her middle. "She should trust you to bring it back in the black. I'm sorry she's—"

"She doesn't understand how it works. It doesn't really matter in the end. It's an awesome location, there's no reason for it not to succeed. I'll just do what she asks. And at some point I'll talk to the landlord about a new lease, I guess," she adds with a smile. "But that's not in my hands, and if she doesn't understand that, then so be it."

I kiss the tip of her nose. "I think he'd be open to that discussion." The question on the tip of my tongue is, *And then what?* Will Chloe leave Emerald Creek? Go back to a corporate job?

I can't even think about that. "For an estimate on renovations, you could ask Thalia and Lucas. I heard they're in between projects at the resort." Thalia and Lucas are newcomers in town, and they run an architectural design and construction company.

"That's a great idea. I'll ask Autumn to put us in touch." As she moves to the bedroom to get dressed, she mumbles, "I really wanted to be the one to make that restaurant *awesome*."

And that kills me more than not knowing where she'll be next. I hate for her to not be recognized for her work.

Later that day, once Chloe is at the restaurant and I'm at the bar, I catch Haley during a quiet time. "You still thinking about the brewery?" "Brewery?"

"Or winery. Was it a winery? I thought you wanted to brew blueberries."

"Oh. You've been paying attention."

"Sorry, I've had other things on my mind."

"Oh yeah. I know. What do you want to know about The Fermentory?"

"Fermentory? That's what you're calling it?" It's a pretty cool name, but I'm not going to tell her that. "Are you sure about that?"

She puts a fist on her hip. "That other thing you have on your mind?"

What is she talking about now?

"That was *her* idea," Haley says. "And it's an *awesome* idea."

I pretend like I don't understand.

"Ha. Now he shuts up. What about The Fermentory?" Haley asks.

I was going to tell her that it was right up Chloe's alley. That she used to work in developing breweries. That maybe Haley wanted to partner with her.

Anything to keep her here. But that might be a little too transparent. And it looks like Chloe and her might already be talking about it, if Chloe suggested a name.

Why didn't she tell me?

"Nothin'."

Chapter Thirty-Six

Chloe

"I don't know about this guy," Fiona mumbles. Her eyes dart right and left on the screen like she's looking for inspiration or support from her rocker posse. "He was supposed to be a rebound, and now you're practically living together."

She's right about one thing, wrong about the other.

I never wanted Justin to be just a rebound.

But as far as living together goes, since I slept over at his apartment two weeks ago, we've been spending nights together.

All the nights.

All night long.

His place, my place. Last week he stuffed a pair of jeans, T-shirts, and underwear in one of my drawers. I bought him a toothbrush and at that, he said, "Yours worked just fine."

"Oh."

"Babe, my mouth's been in your pussy and my tongue licked your butthole. That what you're worried about?"

I giggled and that was that. I use his toothbrush at his place, he uses mine at the cottage. However, I now have a double of everything else, lotion, makeup, hairbrush, and some clothes at his place.

Also, we both got tested, and we ditched the condoms.

So much better.

So much more sex that can happen on a whim. In the car, in the shower, in his office.

I sigh. "I just... I just feel so good with him. It feels right."

"I dunno. The guy's clearly afraid of commitment."

I shouldn't have told her I was his first real relationship. "So?"

"So you need someone who places you above everyone else, who's not going to bail when things aren't so rosy anymore. You need someone who worships the ground you walk on."

I roll my eyes, something she sees since we're on video.

She sighs heavily. "Look, I don't want to tell you what to do."

That's my cue to brace myself for her telling me what to do. Out of sisterly love, of course.

"But I'm not feeling this guy. Something's off."

"Um—you haven't *met* him."

"He's closed off. Cagey."

So he has stuff he's working on. Okay. But he's loving and tender, and he can't be next to me without holding me, touching me, kissing me, even in public. Especially in public. He's constantly praising the changes I'm making at the restaurant. He's helping me catch Samuel in the act of stealing so I can move forward. He once mentioned taking me on a trip to Montreal once the season is over. That means he's making plans. '*I think I'm gonna like you in my life.*' That's not someone closed off.

"He's taking me to his parents' as his girlfriend tonight," I counter. So far I've been at the Kings' once, but more as the new person in town slash Haley's new friend. Never as Justin's girlfriend.

Fiona lifts her eyebrows. "A'right, girl," and a slow smile spreads across her face. "I get full credit."

"Full credit for what?"

"You guys."

I laugh. She thinks I ended up sleeping with Justin in Boston because of what she told me on the phone that night. "You and faulty earbuds," I say.

"Mmm. Nope. I planted the seed and watched it grow."

She might be right about that. "Why does it always have to be about you?"

"You know I'm right."

"You are *so* wrong. But I'll concede, if that gets you off my back."

She chuckles. "How's the restaurant going?"

"Good. Aunt Dawn is getting ready to put it up for sale. We have new staff being trained. We're open seven days now—"

"Wow, I thought your chef was some asshole diva. How'd he take that?"

"Weirdly, better than I expected. I upped his days, he takes only two days off, relies on the sous on Mondays and Tuesdays, but he sometimes still comes around to check things out. The two sous chefs are doing awesome, and I think that sort of tickled his pride." I don't tell her that the only reason he's doing that is that he's stealing from me. We'll catch him any day now, and I can share the news with Fiona (and Aunt Dawn and Brendan) once it's done. Or else I'll never hear the end of it.

"Good. You want to keep him on his toes."

I've been monitoring inventory, and saffron has been disappearing although we haven't served the lamb tajine in over two weeks, and that entree is the only one using saffron. I'm sure there's other inconsistencies, and if we had the proper software, it'd be easy to track, but at this point good old sleuthing and deducing is all I need.

Samuel is stealing, I just need to catch him. I could just let him go, but I need closure. I want to catch him in the act, to shut his mouth and also show Aunt Dawn and Brendan what a piece of shit he is. That it wasn't Justin's fault Uncle Kevin had a heart attack. That the restaurant's problems can all be traced back to Samuel. And with Justin's help, that part is going to be a piece of cake.

And if I'm totally honest, I'm still hurting that Aunt Dawn and Brendan put his word before mine. Even if on a certain level, I understand that they were misled, I want Samuel to pay for turning my family against me. Firing him won't be enough.

But I'm not telling my sister that. She'd freak out. "Yup," I simply say. There's so much more I want to share with her, like the new midweek menu and a local's pass I'm working on, but I can tell from her fidgeting that she has to hang up.

I also finally have a meeting with my new CPA, and she just walked in. It's been a month since I contacted her, but she's been booked solid since. I feel special that she's squeezing me in.

"Emma," I call from my office door and meet her in the dining room. "Gotta run, Fi. Talk later."

Emma gives me a quick smile and throws her long, straight blond hair behind her shoulder.

"Let's meet in the office."

While we exchange pleasantries, David brings us new mocktails he's added to the bar list at my request. It's too early for food, but he knows to bring tapas for us should we go beyond two hours. I've been told

Emma works with pretty much all the businesses in town, and I want to impress her.

She seems guarded, and I can't blame her. She has to know we're behind on rent, since she does the books for Justin.

"You might want to pull the plug sooner than later," she informs me right at the start of the meeting. I sent her our financials via email, and this is to be our onboarding meeting. What is she talking about, pulling the plug? "You're bleeding money. Your creditors have to be unhappy. Once Samuel leaves, you'll be left with nothing but debt."

I let her comment about Samuel slide. I don't even ask her where she heard that—it's irrelevant.

Screw that. Because the truth is, all this place needs is new blood. A fresh menu, tuned in to local production. A different attitude.

And I have a plan for all that to happen. I just needed someone like her to bounce the financials off. Confirm or adjust my projections. Brainstorm.

She sifts through a printout of our P&L. "The owners still aren't in a position to put in more money?"

So she doesn't know about the plan to sell. Interesting. "No, but I—"

"Look. Can I be honest with you?"

"Please."

She shifts on her seat. "I'm not comfortable taking you on as a client."

What?! "Why?" I'm trying to fix what's broken. I *need* her.

"How do I say this. This is a small town. Your... the restaurant's situation is affecting some of my clients significantly."

Yes, like Justin. 'I trust you, Chloe.' "I hear you. That's one of the reasons I need you."

She leaves my financial statements on my desk and sets her briefcase on her lap. "Uhhh... the thing is, I don't think you can even afford me at this juncture. I wouldn't advise you to add to your expenses."

"But I'm working on that. We're revamping the menu, we're open all week—"

"Adding to your staffing costs," she interrupts.

Well, that's an oversimplification. With the added staff comes added revenue from being open seven days. But I can tell she's not here to discuss things. And, yup, she stands and extends her hand. "Keep using whoever Kevin Murphy had, and don't delay making the tough decisions. That's my advice."

I want Emma on my team. She knows everyone in town and in the county. She's a hard-as-nails woman, raises her daughter on her own, built her business on her own. This is the type of person I want to build a working relationship with. And not to mention, I've run into her more than once, at Game Nights, Justin's pub, or The Growler. I also want to be friends with her. Her opinion of me means something. "What would it take for you to change your mind?" I say as I shake her hand.

She gives me a tight-lipped smile. "A miracle."

I walk her out. "By when?"

She turns around, the sun shining on her golden hair. "Sorry?"

"By when do you need a miracle?"

Her smile dips. "Yesterday."

"Gotcha." Once she's gone, I close the door and lean on it for a brief moment, ideas coming to life.

Then I start working on a miracle.

Step One is a post in Echoes. It's cute, it's to the point, salesy but not too much. I hit Splash. Whoever built this app went heavy on the water references. Splash means everyone on Emerald Creek's social media gets a notification.

Step Two is in my hands, neat little flyers I've been working on, tweaking, revising, now printed and ready to be distributed.

Step Three involves Alex and a crazy, last-ditch, throw-every-thing-at-it effort.

I text her, get her overenthusiastic response followed by a *'be right there,'* and while I wait for her, I text Justin that something came up and I won't be able to make it to dinner at his parents' tonight. He's out of town today, checking out a venue he'll be catering, and that means we won't see each other until tomorrow morning. He'll be disappointed, maybe upset.

I'll miss him for sure.

But this needed to happen yesterday. And I'm the one doing it.

Tonight.

Alone.

CHAPTER THIRTY-SEVEN

Justin

I don't see Chloe's text until I stop for gas on my way back from the place where I'll be catering. Sometimes I get in my head, I space out, focus on the task at hand, and just forget to check in.

That's the scary part of being in a relationship. You need to be there for people.

Can I do that for her?

And then I read her text over, and wonder—can *she* do that for me? Be that for me?

I'm bummed that she won't be with me tonight, but I'm not in a rush to bring her to the farm as my girlfriend. Certainly not in a rush to be ribbed by my brothers about it.

But I'm *pissed* at her text message. *Sorry, can't make it tonight.* That's it? No explanation?

What's going on?

Am I going too fast? Do I want something she doesn't?

Is it the meeting-the-parents thing that's freaking her out?

Since it's just me tonight, I head straight to the farm without stopping in town.

Mom's day lilies are in full bloom. I remember when we planted those together, years and years ago. Only flower name I know are those, and for a reason. Dad dug up the border, Mom had gotten the plants from Ms. Angela who was dividing them, and we all got to plant our portion of the driveway, along a string pulled straight. I realized many years later that this was the first time we were planting something just because it was going to be beautiful, not because it would yield anything that we could sell or barter.

It meant a lot to her and Dad, and their pride rubbed off on us. We were all happy, though we didn't quite know why. We just were. I know now, it was because they felt they were doing well enough money-wise that they could raise five kids, on a farm, and spend time and energy on planting flowers just because they were beautiful.

Why they had five kids, I don't know. Dad once said, "Couldn't keep my hands off her," and we all covered our ears and yelled at them to stop talking.

But now I get it. I totally get it.

So despite Chloe bailing on me, despite the fact I'm going to spend twenty-four hours without her and that seems like a fucking long time, I'm in a great mood when I pull up to the farm behind a familiar jeep.

"Hey, Ems," I say as Emma climbs into her car. She does everyone's books in Emerald Creek, so it's no surprise to see her here too. I'm glad I talked Chloe into hiring her.

She gives me a small wave and drives away.

I find Mom and Dad at the dining room table, a bunch of papers spread in front of them.

They looked surprised to see me and exchange a glance. I go to the fridge and grab a soda. "We're on for dinner, right?"

"Yeah... yeah-yeah-yeah. We weren't expecting you this early, is all. Is your friend joining us later?" Mom asks, seeming tense.

"Chloe apologizes, but she can't make it." I sit at the end of the table. Mom looks briefly relieved. That's weird, she loves to have company.

Dad looks worried.

"What's up?" I ask.

Dad clears his throat. "Son, d'you have any timeframe on the restaurant situation?"

The restaurant situation is *my* situation. My parents insisted on lending me part of what I needed to start the pub because interest rates at the time were high, and they wanted to help. At the beginning, they checked in on me to make sure that everything was going well, but they quickly found I knew what I was doing, and I was doing great. "What's this about?"

"Well, we're worried—"

"Is this coming from Emma?" Emma knows the rent is late. But she wouldn't mention that, would she?

Mom looks guilty. "Don't jump to conclusions."

Fucking Emma. "I can't believe you guys. After the shit she pulled with Chris and Alex?" Just a few months ago, Emma tried to orchestrate a breakup between the two using confidential business information, and that did not go well. For anyone, including Emma.

We've since sorted it out, and it's water under the bridge, because that's what you do in a small town. You can't hold grudges because you don't know who you might need. But it doesn't mean we forget. "Chloe is working hard on bringing the restaurant to where it needs to be. And I know she'll be successful."

"But, honey, I thought you were going to take the space back from Kevin Murphy."

Why is Mom in my business? Where is this coming from? "And now he's dead, and Chloe has a different plan."

Mom sighs. Dad grunts.

"What is this about? You've always trusted me with how I run my business." After the accident, I received enough money for a hefty down payment on what's now known as King's Block in town. The old forge had been closed awhile, the current owner started doing something with it that went nowhere. He had part of it leased to the restaurant, didn't know what to do with the rest.

I did. I bought the whole block. The town needed a pub at its heart, and I was going to give them that. I wanted to get rid of the restaurant, because of who was running it, but folks convinced me to try and let that shit go. Be the bigger person. They said it was enough I'd become Murphy's landlord. He was probably going to leave anyway.

He didn't.

Mom and Dad insisted on helping me financially. I tried to protest but quickly understood it was their way of helping me cope with the aftermath of the accident, since they couldn't do anything about my injuries.

Who was I to deny them that?

At the beginning, they asked to be kept in the loop of how business was going, but they quickly took a step back, then stopped entirely asking questions.

Their financial assistance helped me scale up operations faster than planned. So much so that after a year and a half of operating the pub, I started investing the payments I would have normally made had I borrowed from a regular lender into an interest-earning account for the day my parents would need it. I even told Dad I could pay them back, and he almost took offense but promised to let me know if they ever needed it.

"Chloe knows what she's doing, and Emerald Creek doesn't need a larger pub. It needs more diversified restaurant options."

Mom sighs again. "We're just concerned that you're listening to your heart, maybe too much."

I clench my jaw. "Yeah, Mom, I'm listening to my heart. Darn right I am. And my heart tells me here's a woman who took a job beneath her because her family needed her. Here's a woman who rolled into Emerald Creek and was friends with half the town in less than a week. Here's a woman who's actually able to deal with a fucker like Samuel and not lose her cool and not lose her customers." I pause, my eyes narrowed on Mom, daring her to say anything about my use of curse words. "Here's a woman who gets us, gets the town, gets her staff, gets her customers, cooks like an angel... so yeah, Mom. I'm listening to my heart."

I stand and push my chair and turn my back to them then whip around and point my finger at her. "'Cause that's how you raised us." I cross my arms on my chest and brace for the response.

Mom tears up.

Shit. I went too hard on her. Why did I have to raise my voice? That's *not* how she raised us.

She walks to me and a weird smile spreads across her face, her eyes totally water, her chin wobbles, and she wraps her arms around my chest. I hug her back, open my mouth to apologize, but she says, "My baby's in love." And tilts her head back and adds, "I haven't been so happy in years."

I take a deep breath and hug her tight.

Dad clears his throat. "Well, I'm glad that's sorted out, but it was never about the restaurant."

Mom taps me on the back and takes her seat back next to her husband, wiping under her eyes.

Dad continues, "We—there's a project we'd like to work on... and, well, we were wondering what your time frame for refunding the investment we made might be."

Oh man. That's just like them to try and figure out if they can actually ask for what was always theirs. Always putting their children before themselves. "I can refund you this month," I say.

Mom's head shoots back in surprise, and Dad has a slow grin that says he's proud of me.

And I'm proud that this moment has come. At the time, I'd accepted their help only under the promise that should they need the cash for anything, they should ask me first. Not take out a loan.

They're keeping their promise.

And I'm excited for them that they're making plans. The day they stop making plans is the day they start getting old, and I don't want to think about that day.

The truth is, their loan had become an emotional burden for me, a crutch I no longer need. If anything, it was a reminder of the worst time in my life, and I don't need that anymore.

I'm ready to move on.

After dinner, Dad walks me to the truck. "Just look after yourself, son. And if she's the one, tell her she can't skip on dinner with her family."

"Right," I answer softly, feeling both warm and fucking scared again.

He stops in his steps before we reach the truck. "How'd you feel about seeing Sullivan again? And Murphy's widow?"

"Why would I ever see them?"

Dad shakes his head. "Never seen you with a girl, son. Now you're bringing her to your Mom. Or you will. You're gonna have to deal with her family."

Shit. I hadn't thought of that.

"It'll go fine. You don't need to love'em. Don't even need to like'em. But they're her folks. You might wanna have a little talk with yourself about how you're gonna deal with that when it happens. Make sure the one gets hurt isn't Chloe." He squeezes my shoulder gently. "Helps to prepare."

"Thanks, Dad. You're right." As always. As I give him a quick hug, my left side clenches, phantom pains shooting up like a memory.

"Funny how life goes, son," Dad mumbles as we part.

It's still light when I get home. I stare at the screen of my phone, the last message from Chloe sitting there like a wound. *Sorry, can't make it tonight.*

I mean, what the actual fuck kind of message is that.

We need to talk, I answer back.

My phone rings right away. *Chloe calling.* I clench my teeth and pick up.

"Hey," she says.

"Everything all right?" I ask her.

"Yeah. I uh... I had to work later than planned."

"Someone sick?"

"No um... admin stuff."

Admin stuff? That's why she bailed out on dinner at my parents? That's why she's not in my bed after close to two weeks of sleeping together? She's gonna have to give me more than that. "Yeah?" I bite.

"Yeah," she breathes. "Um... Emma's not gonna work out, and I already fired the other guys, so I'm catching up on bookkeeping and stuff."

"Emma's not working out?" That's new to me.

"Yeah, we had a um... productive meeting, and turns out, she's not a good fit for now. So uh... I can do the bookkeeping, and then I'll just hire one of the usual suspects for reporting and stuff. It's for the best."

Bullshit. I can sense the tension in her voice. Something else is up. Is she getting ready to close down the restaurant? Does she feel she can't tell me, because of the back rent that's owed? I hate that this is between us. "My dad wasn't happy about you not showing up," I say with what I hope is a lighter tone.

"Ohmygod. I'll... I'll... should I send flowers?"

What the fuck? "No, Clo, I was kidding. I mean, yeah, we missed you. But my parents don't care. I mean they care," I fumble, "but if you can't make it, you can't make it. They understand."

"Right. Good. I guess I should invite them over then, some time?"

Oh. That's new. My parents don't get invited that often. They do the inviting, and they've for sure never been formally invited to one of their son's girlfriends. I don't know how I feel about being the one to experiment with that.

"Yeah, you don't have to."

"Right," she answers softly.

Shit. Did I hurt her feelings? "Want me to come over?"

"No," she answers quickly. "I'm pulling an all-nighter."

That's not good. Not good at all. A restaurant manager shouldn't spend the night doing bookkeeping.

Something's up.

CHAPTER THIRTY-EIGHT

Chloe

My alarm blasts at ten in the morning.

It's too early.

Way too early.

At seven I plopped onto my bed. I'd stuffed only part of the mailboxes, seeing as dawn started shortly after four, but I'd been strategic about it. Some areas are more affluent than others. Even in the countryside, you can tell. Even if you can't see the house. A mailbox can sometimes tell a whole story. Not every house is the target clientele for the restaurant.

After my mailbox run, I tried to do some bookkeeping from four to seven. Then at seven I nosedived on my laptop and got the hint. Time for bed.

The thinking was, three hours of sleep is two full cycles. And that should be enough. It being seven in the morning, I should be good to go at ten.

The thinking was wrong.

I drag myself into the shower, brush my teeth, and go downstairs wrapped in a towel to get the espresso machine going. I go back upstairs to get dressed, down the espresso on my way out, get in my car, get to Easy Monday.

"How can I make your day awes—oopsie! What happened to you?" Millie rounds her eyes at me and comes from behind the counter to examine me closely.

A couple of ladies lift their heads from their books.

"Work or party?" Millie asks, zooming in on my eyes. "You're not high, for sure."

"Um..."

"Heard you missed dinner at the King's last night," one of the ladies says.

"Heard she was driving around town breaking into people's mailboxes," the other one whisper shouts.

"That right?" her friend shoots back, not whispering at all.

"Oh yeah. Frannie saw her as she was chasing a bear out the resort's dumpster, and Shannon on her way back from the hospital, and then Angela—you know Angela can't sleep and she goes on her walks—and Declan didn't deny it when he came here this mornin'."

"Oooh," Millie says super low so the ladies can't hear, "see we got ourselves a little criminal. Welcome to the dark side, sistah!" She goes back behind her counter. "I'm making you a Back From Hell this morning. You're gonna need it. And brownies to go with that. And the usual for your staff?"

The usual for my staff is beginning to cost a fortune, but they're worth it. "Sure." She's already working the levers of her coffee machines.

"People are loving the pass, Chloe," Millie says. "I'm out of brochures already."

"How's that possible? I left at least fifty last night."

"What I said. They love it."

Wow. "I'll get you more." I take a sip of the concoction she made for me and feel my eyes opening to their full extent.

"You do that. Great idea, by the way. I'm gonna do the same for Easy Monday. Call it the Easy Way."

"That's brilliant. And Mils?"

"Yeah?" she sets out a tray of to-go cups with the staff's names neatly written on them.

I take another sip of my coffee, feeling excitement course through my veins at my new idea. "You ever thought of having reusable cups? You sell your customers the cups branded to your store, with their names on it? They get a free day-old muffin every time they use it?"

"She sells'em day olds a dollar," one of the ladies in the back chimes in. "And they're goooood."

Oh. "Whatever. You'll figure it out," I say with a wave.

"We'll see you tomorrow," one of the two ladies says to me as I get to the door.

Oh? "Tomorrow?"

"At the restaurant. See you tomorrow."

I have no idea what she's talking about. Are they coming in for an interview? Shoshana mentioned potentially needing back up hostesses. For dinner? I guess I'll find out. "Oh—of course, yes."

Millie waves goodbye at me and the two ladies dig back into their books.

"I don't know what's happening," Shoshana tells me the minute I walk in. "Our voice mail is flooded. I've been calling people back since I came in. We're booked solid this week."

What?! I set the tray of drinks down and look over her shoulder to our POS. "Something going on in town?" Shoshana asks.

"Give me a sec."

I feel a cold rush, then a heat wave. Did we do it? Are people loving the Local's Pass *that much*? That can't be. It's only been a few hours since I dropped the fliers at the stores and in the mailboxes, and announced it on Echoes.

I rush to the office and close my door. Open my computer and flip one of the brochures in my hand, marveling at how the understated, classy design advertising a super reasonable prix fixe menu on weekdays and a discount on weekends for pass holders might have just saved the restaurant.

I access our payment system and let out a happy cry, clapping to myself. A big fat number is sitting there. I stare at it for a second, then hit a few keystrokes to take care of the most pressing debt we have.

A huge weight off my back, I go to Shoshana's station, holding a brochure. "The Local's Pass. I wasn't sure it would work, that's why I didn't tell you guys about it. People pay up front for a number of prix fixe dinners. That gets them a discount. There's several tiers. The more they pay upfront, the steeper the discount."

Shoshana looks at the tier levels. "People have that kind of money around here?"

"The first tier barely covers a dinner for two," I point out. "As for the higher tiers? I was wondering about that too, and we have our answers."

"So... is this just for locals?"

That's the catch. It's called a Local's Pass, but anyone can buy it. And I *may* have played on the affluent second homeowners' desire to feel like locals with the name of the pass. But there's a part that I hope will tilt the balance in favor of real locals. "There's a steeper discount on weekdays, when it's only us locals in town."

"That's really cool." Shoshana smiles.

"Thanks. I'm so glad a lot of people seem to think that way too!"

"I should get back to all these voice mails," she says.

I walk back to my office, reaching for my phone to tell Justin.

And as I hear the phone ringing, it hits me.

He was the first I wanted to tell.

That evening, we celebrate at The Growler. Justin says we both need a break from our businesses, we should dance and party, and it'd be good, anyway, for people to see me, talk to me, spread the word even more.

He booked us a table at their steakhouse, a more intimate restaurant located on the third level, where tables are comfortably set apart. White linens, candles, and flowers make the setting special, while the music seeping from the lower level still promises a good party later on.

Justin pulls my chair out for me and softly kisses my hair before sitting across from me. While we place our orders—juicy steaks for both of us—the maître d' brings two champagne flutes. "From the gentleman at three o'clock," he tells Justin.

Justin whips his head around, and a big smile spreads on his face as he recognizes a man across the room sitting with three other people. He lifts his glass, a question in his eye. The man nods toward me. Justin tilts his head, furrows his brow.

The man slides out of his chair and comes over to us. "Congratulations, Ms. Sullivan, very impressive," he says. "I'm Scott Johnson."

I turn my gaze to Justin.

"Scott is CEO of a community bank in the Northeast Kingdom," Justin explains.

"Oh—NekNest?" That's where the restaurant banks. "Yes, of course. Good evening. And thank you?"

"Like I said, I'm very impressed," Johnson says to me. "I'd like to meet with you as soon as possible. I'll email you." He turns to Justin, then back to me. "Enjoy your dinner."

"Wow," I say when he's gone.

"To great beginnings!" Justin lifts his glass to me. "But—need to set something straight." He pauses, and we both take a sip.

"Hmm?" The bubbles hit my palate.

"Got all your bookkeeping done?"

"Um... that would be a *no*. But getting there."

He sets his glass down and shifts in his chair. "I get why you kept this from me, Clo. You're too proud for your own good. But now, it's you and me together. No more secrets. No more going behind my back to fight your own battles." He twines our fingers together, his gaze somber. "I mean it."

"Kay," I say softly.

"Promise me."

My heart ba-booms as he looks deeply into my eyes, squeezes my hand. "I promise."

"You and me together, Clover."

Oh god. This man. How did I go through life without him?

After dinner, we go down to the room with a live band and sway to the music. Justin nuzzles my neck. "I missed you last night," he says.

"Missed you too, baby. I still have a lot to do," I warn him. Starting with bookkeeping.

"You're not doing any work tonight."

I smile coyly at him. "That right?"

He sets his hand on my ass, pulling me to his erection. "That feel right to you?"

I giggle, looking around us self-consciously.

"What?" He licks my earlobe. "You got a problem with how hard you're making me?" He trails his tongue down my neck, making me laugh softly. I bend in his arms and press myself against him even more. "I see you don't," he growls, moving his tongue across my jawline, nibbling at my lower lip.

"Love the pass!" someone near us cries in my ear. "Got one for me and my girlfriend, and one for my parents." Should I know who they are? I beam at them, feeling so good about myself. People know me! "Catch you later, Justin!"

Or rather, they know who Justin's girlfriend is. And that's quite alright by me. I give him a huge grin. I'm so happy my cheeks hurt.

The beats of the music engulf us, and I let Justin take the lead. Turns out, he's an awesome dancer. "How come this is the first time we've danced together?" I ask as he pulls me back into him after twirling me around his finger. He steps away from me, our fingers connected tightly, and brings me into an underarm turn, then alternates twists and turns until my head spins, and he brings me back into his chest. "Because we're trying to take some things slow," he says, laughing.

That's the only thing we take slow. Moose is at Justin's, so that's where we're headed after The Growler. We're barely past the door before we claw at each other's clothes. All that dancing was enough foreplay for me. A whole evening of rubbing against each other, holding each other, necking. Justin's hungry gaze on me almost makes me come.

There were a lot of women eying him, and I can't blame them. But Justin's gaze was only for me. A couple of women talked to him when he went to the bar to get us after-dinner drinks, and he barely responded. I wasn't jealous or worried. But damn it's good to feel secure in a relationship. I never felt that way with Tucker. Now I know why. I just didn't know how you were supposed to feel when your partner is reliable.

We're on his bed, naked, a trail of clothes in the living space, Justin's face between my legs, his amazing tongue doing a slow pass. I feel my clit pulse. "Babe, please, just take me." He lifts himself and turns me over, and I find myself with my head pressed into the bed, my arms outstretched, my ass in the air, and Justin entering me. "Fuck, you're so wet for me." He gives me a slow inside stroke. "Ah fuck, Clover, you have no idea how good you feel."

He feels awesome, his dick stretching my inside, rubbing my spot, his hands at my waist pulling me to him. I'm close to coming. "Harder," I wail.

He pounds me one, two, three, times, and I come undone, shaking under him as he grunts and stills. I feel him pulsate inside me, his hands clenching at my waist. Claiming me.

Then he plops onto his back and pulls me to his side and we catch our breaths.

Exhausted by my previous night with almost no sleep, the excitement of today, tonight's partying followed by awesome sex, I try to resist the weight of my eyelids but can't. I fall asleep against him, listening to his heartbeat.

Then I wake up to his cock pulsing against my thigh as he says, "Babe, there's something I need to tell you." His hand is playing with my hair, and it's the most delicious feeling. I'm not sure I want to break this moment. I keep my eyes closed and snuggle deeper into him. "Clover, we need to talk."

My body stiffens, preparing for the worst.

His other hand touches my bare arm, and his voice is low and gravelly when he says, "Clover... I'm in love with you."

I whip up on his chest and catch his searching gaze on me. Cupping his face in my hands, I bring my lips to his and kiss him, our tongues doing their slow, familiar dance. Then he releases my mouth, wraps his arms hard around me, and flips us so I'm under him. He takes me slow and gentle, our gazes never leaving each other. "I love you too, Justin. So much."

He continues his slow movement in and out of me. "Never thought I'd ever fall in love," he says into my neck. Then he lifts his head to look me in the eye. "Except after Boston. You're the only one for me. Was just waiting for you to come into my life."

I tear up at his admission. "Oh, honey," I whisper in his ear, and then he increases his thrusts, and we come together, our orgasms feeding off each other.

I fall asleep twirling line circles on the clover tattoo over his heart.

Then I'm dead to the world until loud bangs street-side wake me up to an empty bed.

The shower is going, so Justin can't hear. Everybody knows Lazy's doesn't open until twelve. And everybody knows if you need to get to Justin, you come through the back.

Ergo, this must be a new delivery person. I throw on my tiny pajama shorts and spaghetti strap cami, run my fingers through my hair, and rush downstairs. "I got it!" I yell for Justin, in case he heard and is scrambling to come downstairs.

I crack the door open, thinking I'm going to tell them to go around the building.

A very pretty, leggy blonde is standing at the door. Her long hair falls in straight curtains around her face. She's all cheekbones and pouty lips and eyes that totally rock the thick eyeliner and fake lashes they're sporting, even at this early hour in the day. She has the kind of physique that makes me instantly wonder why god is so unfair.

"I'm here for Justin," she says as my eyes fall on her very round belly.

CHAPTER THIRTY-NINE

Chloe

"Justin?" I repeat stupidly.

She shows most of her tan, round shoulders under the thin straps of her summer dress. She's thin and fit enough that her clavicles do that little dip, but none of her other bones show, except, as I've already noticed, for her fantastic cheekbones. Her arms are toned and tanned, a bunch of silver bracelets on both her wrists make pretty little noises that I always associate with beautiful women.

"Hello? Are you gonna let me in?" she says.

Everything in her is leggy and long and toned. Just her belly is super round, and just at the front. It pokes out beautifully, if a bit aggressively, and I take note that she shows none of the other signs of her state. Her skin in flawless, her calves and ankles thin, her boobs generous but not spilling out of her dress. Yes, god is unfair.

"And you are?"

She eyes me, top to bottom, clearly not impressed. "I'm Gisele. His baby mama."

The words hit me like an ice bath. "S-sorry, come again?"

She chuckles, a deep, bitter sound. "You're funny. I had all the coming I could get a few months ago. Now I need to talk to the daddy." She pushes by me and strolls into the pub.

My hands shake as I try to lock the door, and no air seems to fill my lungs.

She turns around several times in the empty pub, taking in, I suppose, the chairs on the tables, the lights turned off. "You guys closed?" she says, her back to me.

The entire room is spinning, while an unforgiving vise tightens around my skull. She's having Justin's child? That's what she's saying, right?

My mouth feels like sandpaper, my knees like jelly. "Um. Why don't you sit down." I turn over a chair from the closest table, then the other ones so she's not sitting staring at chair legs. "Can I get you a glass of water? Juice?"

"Water's good. Juice is full of sugar."

Good. Movement. Something to do. Need to get Justin.

I get behind the bar and come back with her water, trying to steady my hands. "Was Justin expecting you?"

Another bitter chuckle. "No, honey, *I'm* expecting *his* child, and he's been ghosting me."

I clear my throat nervously. "I mean, he didn't know you were coming today, did he?"

"You gonna be funny like that all day?"

"W-what?"

"Just get him, will ya? Please? He needs to face his responsibilities."

I fight closing my eyes. Taking a moment to myself. "Sure, sure. I'll go tell him you're here," I say, pointing to the ceiling. "Gisele, right?"

"Right."

"I'm Chloe." She doesn't say anything, so I extend my hand. "Pleased to meet you."

She looks at my extended hand like she's unfamiliar with the custom, and finally gives me a limp shake, saying "Uh, honey. No. You're not pleased to meet me. You're *pissed*."

Well, she got that right, but really?

"I'm not—" I start lying.

Her eyes soften. "He cheat on you a lot?"

My heart bangs hard in my ribcage. "What—what are you talking about?"

She points at her belly, then says, "How long you been together?"

I blink and start stupidly counting in my head. Then I stop. I'm not doing this. I'm not stooping this low. We haven't been together long, Justin slept with her before me, and shit happens. I'll be the bigger person. "Not that long," I say.

"He'll cheat. My bet is, he already did. More'n once. Men like him who need different pussy every week, they never get stuck on one woman. Never."

I swallow, not knowing what to say, just trying to process.

"You work here?" she asks.

I stupidly point to the side wall. "I run the restaurant next door." Words fall out of my mouth without my brain having a say, it seems.

She nods. "That's how come you're in his bed. 'Stead of some random hookup place." She leans back in her chair and extends her legs. "Never told *me* he had a woman at home." She huffs. "*Men*."

"I don't think..." I start, feeling the need to defend Justin.

"Honey, don't beat yourself up. Us women need to stick together, yeah?"

"Stick together about what?" Justin's voice comes from the back. In a few long strides he's by my side, wet, messy hair, faded jeans, pulling his tight T-shirt over his pecs. He curls his arm around my waist and pulls me to him, drops a feather kiss on my temple. "Everything all right, Clo?" He hasn't looked at the blonde yet.

Correction.

He hasn't looked at the *mother of his child* yet. I tense under his touch although I don't want to. Everything is about to change between us.

Everything already has.

Gisele stands. "Hey," she purrs, a hand on his forearm, the one that's not roped around me.

Justin frowns. Then his eyebrows shoot apart. "Jezebel? What are you doing here? How'd you find me?" His fingers dig into my waist, pulling me closer to him.

"It's Gisele," she answers with pursed lips. "And if you'd answer your phone, I wouldn't have to interrupt..." Her hand waves between the two of us. "...whatever's going on here."

He snatches me even tighter to him, and I crane my neck back to take in his face as recognition hits him first, then as his eyes travel down to her belly. "What do you want?"

"Introduce you to your baby."

I feel nauseated, my hold on him faltering as I see his gaze on her. He's absorbed in the observation of Gisele, of her belly. He's in shock, but there's something more that I can't put my finger on. Something that scares me more than I can handle.

I need to go.

"Yeah, it's yours. You can touch it." Gisele moves closer to him, one hand on her belly, the other extended to take his.

He recoils and steps back. "How'd you know it's mine?"

She exhales softly, something pretty and sweet going through her eyes. Something just for Justin. "I'd been months with no man before you." She giggles. "I mean, you remember. You even asked me how I was so... you know. In the bedroom."

He says nothing. Doesn't deny it.

She slides a glance my way. "You said you'd never had anyone like me."

My heart pangs, my hands dampen.

He still doesn't deny it.

"We had a great time, didn't we," she adds.

Still nothing from Justin.

My vision is blurring. "I'm gonna let you talk this out."

Justin pulls me tighter against him. "Nothin' to talk about without you."

"I have that meeting with Scott. I should go get ready."

"That right?" Justin asks.

Not really. I woke up to an email that said he'd be in the office all day, to just swing by whenever. "He emailed me last night," I whisper. "I saw it just now."

He does the thing where his mouth finds my head and kisses it softly. His heart is beating hard against my side.

"Where're you staying?" he asks Gisele.

She blinks. "Um. I just got here."

"So?" His tone is icy.

"So what," she snaps back.

He takes a deep breath. "Here's how it's gonna go. We have shit to do," his arm around me signifying he's talking about me and him. "You go check yourself into a motel or B and B or wherever the hell you want. We'll talk later."

"I don't need to check myself into no fancy place. All's I need is my kid to have a father who cares."

I feel Justin wince. "*If* I'm the father, I'll care."

"Oh, *you're* the father. No doubt about that," she says, looking him straight in the eye.

My head spins harder. I'm in dire need of a shower. Coffee. Something to clear my head. And normalcy. "So, can we just talk now? Get everything settled," she adds.

"Noon. Come through the backdoor." Justin lets go of me to go unlock the front door for Gisele.

She narrows his eyes on his back, and sadness clouds her gaze briefly before determination settles back in.

She click-clacks her way out.

Justin shuts the door on her, closes the space between us, and takes me in his arms. "I'm sorry."

"'Bout what? It's not your fault."

He grunts.

"Not really," I insist. "Stuff happens."

He clenches his arms tighter around me. "I need to get a paternity test, stat. I'm not talking 'bout anything else 'til that's settled." He rocks me gently, then grunts before peeling himself off me. "Fuck. What am I going to do? This is so unfair to you."

"Honey, we'll figure it out," I say with way more certainty than I feel. "This isn't about me." Or my feelings. It's about Justin. About helping him navigate these first few days, then the next few weeks. Get things sorted out by the time the baby is born.

After that... oh god, but what *am I* going to do? *You're going to be strong, Chloe.*

"You should go," he says, tilting my fake inner peace off balance. Sensing my confusion, he narrows his gaze on me. "To see Scott."

I'm jolted back to what I said earlier. "Oh. Yeah. It's okay, he... he said to swing by today. Anytime. I can go later. When you meet with her."

He lifts my chin so he can look me straight in my eyes. "I just got some fucked up news. I need you. Please?" He does look a little lost.

"Baby. Of course."

"I'll need you with me, Clover." Desperation and uncertainty seep through his strangled words.

"Baby." I run a hand on his cheek. "It's gonna be okay, I promise."

He takes a deep breath. "I don't know about that."

"You just need time to get used to the idea." And I do too. Truthfully, I don't know if I have it in me to get used to the idea. But I'm not going to tell him *that*.

"I can't be a father, Clo."

"Why not?"

"I'll mess up."

"All parents mess up."

"What if I hurt it clipping its nails?"

I hold my chuckle. "It's not a puppy, Justin. Clipping nails will be the least of your worries."

That wasn't the right thing to say. He looks panicked. "The *least*?"

"Raising a child… it's about talking. Setting an example. Giving life tips. You'll be great at that."

He pinches the bridge of his nose. "Life tips? *Me*?"

The idea of Justin raising another woman's child brings bile to my mouth. *I can't be that person.* "You want to drive with me to see Johnson?" The bank headquarters are about a half hour away. That would give us alone time to talk things through.

He blinks, his features set. "Nah. I'm gonna do a little thinkin'."

We go back up to his apartment, and I slip into the shower, needing time to myself. I turn the water temperature to nearly scalding but still I shake inside, and the flowery shampoo doesn't do its normal job of making me feel awesome and gorgeous and ready to take on the day.

I am not ready for this day or for the days ahead of me.

Sure, Justin and I haven't been dating for a long time, so it's not like we're a couple or anything. But we had a good thing going.

We loved each other.

What is going to happen to us now?

And as I dry off, water keeps falling from my eyes.

Once I'm dressed and my emotions are in check, I find Justin leaning against the rooftop railing, looking at The Green, or maybe farther out, to the distant hills. I wrap my arms around him, my front to his back. "I'm leaving."

"I want my kids to grow up here. She's not taking him anywhere."

I give him a squeeze and pull myself together to be the voice of reason he needs right now. "Then maybe you should calm down and be nice to her this afternoon. Also, maybe your first child will be a girl."

"I hope not."

What?! What's gotten into him? "Why not?"

He turns to face me and takes my face in his hands. "I want my daughters to look like you, Clover." He lowers his lips to mine and kisses me, hard and desperate, his hands roaming up and down my back, leaving no space between our melded bodies.

My knees are weak from his words. What is he saying? We haven't talked about the future yet, about what we want.

Maybe this conversation just started. Or maybe it never will happen, now that—"I should go," I breathe.

He gently runs the pads of his thumbs over my eyes, and from the look of him, I can tell he knows I've been crying. "I'm sorry, Clo. Really sorry."

"It'll be okay."

He pulls me into him again, his heart beating so hard it bangs through my own body.

"I'm sorry," he says again as he releases me, holding my hands as I back away from him. "Good luck with Johnson. Whatever he offers you, ask for double."

Big fat raindrops hit my windshield the minute I leave Emerald Creek, and the limited visibility forces me to slow down. Corded ropes of water hit my car when I pass a truck on the highway. The parallels to my present situation don't escape me, and my vision blurs as I indulge in a little self-pity. Just like this beautiful summer is marred by a brutal and unannounced storm, my new relationship with Justin is taking a turn I can't control.

I never saw it coming.

Am I strong enough to be the person Justin needs by his side? Can I watch him raise another woman's child? Co-parent with her?

Do I have what it takes?

I'm already jealous of her.

Visions of Tucker with the blonde blend with my overactive imagination—Justin with Gisele. Me standing on the sidelines.

Maybe I should just step aside. Fade away. Exit Justin's life.

Our relationship is just starting, right? It's not like we've built anything together yet. It would hurt, of course it would, but long term, I wouldn't have to witness, every single day, the happiness someone else's child brings him.

That makes me a bad person, I know it does.

But I've been through the pain of seeing someone I thought I was building a life with, turn to another woman. Mom thought I should be understanding. She said that people are weak, but I didn't have the strength to forgive that.

I simply could not.

I don't share.

I know it's not the same situation. But whichever way I try to look at it, I can't help but draw parallels.

Sure, I want what's best for Justin.

It doesn't mean it's good for me. Or that I should build my life around that.

I'm no hero.

I stay in the bank parking lot for a minute and gather myself. As always, focusing on work will be the answer. The CEO of the local community bank asked to see me after my resounding success with the Local's Pass. A success he must have seen the monetary result of, or he wouldn't have asked me to come in. It's time for me to reap those rewards.

I'm not wondering what he's going to offer me. I know what it is. A line of credit or something like that.

And it's bittersweet that this is happening now that the restaurant is up for sale, but that's to my credit. And I'm proud of it. I want this meeting, even if nothing tangible ends up coming from it because of its timing.

I take a deep cleansing breath, feeling better about myself.

"We'll finance the purchase of the restaurant," Scott tells me. We're sitting in his office, on the top floor of a three-story building facing the mountains. There's a serenity emanating from this place. The photos on the walls are of ribbon cuttings of local businesses. Jovial faces of hard-working people, not smug smiles of the powerful. They're mixed in with children's drawings.

No trophies. No power wall.

His smile is genuine, his hands are massive. These are the hands of generations of laborers.

"That's... that's fantastic news. I'll let the owners know right away. My aunt will be thrilled. She's antsy to sell, to tell you the truth. That'll help tremendously in finding a buyer. Thank you so—"

"We're financing the sale *to you*."

"Wh-what?" Adrenaline course through my veins.

"We'll need a business plan, just to keep our lending department happy—our *t*'s crossed and our *i*'s dotted. We've already done our due diligence on you, Ms. Sullivan, and well, while your accomplishments in the corporate world are impressive and guarantees in and of themselves, we're actually more eager to see what you have to offer in the Northeast Kingdom and surrounding counties. We need more young people like you. Entrepreneurial. With a vision. A true work ethic. A sense of community."

They want me to buy the restaurant? "I don't know what to say."

"There are a couple of conditions."

Ok, here we go. "Of course." It can't hurt to hear him out.

"We feel that it's urgent that the restaurant is renovated, at least cosmetically, before foliage starts. There's an opportunity to capitalize on the excitement of the Local's Pass and new ownership, but this needs to happen fast."

"I don't think my aunt will be amenable to spending—"

"Here's the structure we're thinking about. Your aunt and you sign a preliminary sales agreement now, with the condition that you obtain financing. With this agreement in hand, we can move forward with your commercial loan, and you'll have the authority to begin renovations. We'll immediately approve a renovation loan, since we believe this will be essential to your success."

"Wow, that's... you really thought of everything, haven't you?"

"It's what we do." He smiles and stands up. "Coffee?" he asks as he opens the door.

"Y-yeah, sure. Thank you."

Ohmygod. They are financing *me* to buy the restaurant? Shit. I can't believe it. It's so much more than I expected.

Okay, Chloe. Think.

Whatever he offers you, ask for double.

"So! What do you say?" Scott asks me as he sets down a tray laden with coffee, sugar, creamer, and two cups. It doesn't escape me that he didn't ask someone to fetch it for him. Part of it was maybe him giving me time to think things through, but most of it was him just being a down-to-earth guy.

"I think I'd love to do business with you."

Over the next hour, we hash out the big lines of their support. We talk pricing for the restaurant, look at recent comps, address interest rates, possible costs of renovations and upgrades.

And then I ask for a super generous line of credit.

He raises an eyebrow. *Did I go too far?*

"I like your negotiating skills, Chloe," he says with a smile. "Send us the Preliminary Agreement, your business plan, and let's get this deal done."

On my way back, I call Justin to tell him the news, then Brendan, and finally Aunt Dawn.

She seems surprised at first, then happy, then concerned. "I hope your mother won't hate me more than she does now."

I hadn't thought about that, and I couldn't care less what Mom and Dad think. "Don't worry about Mom. Besides, it's my life, Aunt Dawn."

"You're right, honey."

After I hang up, I call Justin back to ask him to put me in touch with a lawyer to draft the Preliminary Agreement.

Then I call Thalia and Lucas to ask them for an estimate on renovations.

And only then do I feel hopeful. I haven't thought of Gisele in the past couple of hours. Life is never perfect. Maybe I can do this after all. I just need to focus on work.

That always builds me back up.

"Fuck, babe, I'm so proud of you." Justin lifts me and swings me around in his pub—I went there straight from my appointment with Scott Johnson. "You're going to be so fucking successful. I can't wait. We should celebrate tonight."

I try not to laugh, but his kisses down my neck make it impossible. "We already celebrated yesterday, and tonight we're full. I *really* need to be at the restaurant. It's our first night hosting Local Pass holders." I brace for a rebuttal. If there's anything I've learned from my Dad and from Tucker, it's that professional success doesn't make a woman attractive or desirable.

He nuzzles me. "We'll celebrate, don't you worry. I have some very specific things I want to try on you. Was keeping them for a special occasion."

Okay, so maybe I got that wrong.

Still, Gisele's words echo from that part in my brain where I keep the stuff that hurts. *You said you'd never had anyone like me.* And then it superimposes again with the image of the blonde with Tucker.

Forget how I feel about Justin's impending fatherhood. Am *I* enough for him?

CHAPTER FORTY

Justin

S he stays quiet. I kiss her where I know she can't resist, where her neck meets her shoulder, then trail to her nape, all the while roaming my hands up and down her body.

I want her so bad. I can never get enough of her.

"What did you do this morning?" she asks me, killing my mood.

"I went to see my parents."

"How'd that go?"

"Went alright."

I wanted to break the news to Mom and Dad as soon as possible. Didn't want the gossip mill to beat me to it. Shit happens in a small town, you tell your folks as soon as you can, or someone else'll tell them for you and you won't control that information. First impressions are crucial.

"I got some bad news and some good news," was my opening. The good news was that they were going to be grandparents. The bad news, Chloe wasn't the mom. Gisele was. They didn't know Gisele, obviously, so I gave them a summary.

Dad cleared his throat. "You sure…"

I read his question. Am I sure I'm the father? "Nope. No, Dad. Not sure at all."

"Right."

Mom twisted her hands. It killed me to see her pain. She'd been worried about what she calls 'my ways,' and suddenly the weight of those were hitting me now.

"You're doing a paternity test, right? There are noninvasive ones now," Mom said on an exhale. "They take blood samples and test DNA or something. Doesn't impact the fetus at all. My cousin Jessa's son did that. You know Brian?" She doesn't wait for an answer. "When is she due?"

Hell if I know. "I'll find out."

The front door opened on a bang and Hunter barked, "Mom! You hear 'bout Justin?"

Like I said. Small town.

"Been tryin' to call'im. My friend says—"

"He's right here, honey," Mom cut him off. Ever the diplomat, trying to avoid arguments.

He skidded to a halt as he hit the kitchen. "Shit man, is it true?"

I didn't need to answer.

"Fuck," he added as he fell onto a chair, Mom not correcting his language—such was the situation—"did everything you could not to get attached and you're screwed anyway."

"Why don't you tell us how you feel?" I snarled.

"Boys. A child is a blessing. Wait 'til you hold that little bundle of joy," she said, looking at Dad.

Dad reached for Mom's hand. "She's right."

Mom turned to me. "How is Chloe holding up?"

Hunter shoved his head in his hands, and just realizing the extent of the situation, let out a slow, "fuuuck."

"You know her, Mom. She's great."

"I know she is. Doesn't mean she wants in. It's a lot to take in, and it's just the beginning."

"She's my rock."

"Dude," Hunter whispered.

"If the test confirms... you know... you'll need to bring Gisele here," Mom said. "She needs to feel she's part of the family."

Part of the family? "Maybe later."

"For the baby," she explained. "Just always have Chloe with you, obviously."

Hunter's eyes widened. "Ooooh."

"Just not right now, okay? Give it a little time." I was pushing back, but I knew she was right.

Dad growled.

"It'll be fine," I said. "We're adults. We'll do what we need to do for the baby."

"That's my boy," Mom said.

⁂

Chloe winces. "Your mom's right, you know," she says anyway, like I don't see how hurt she is. "You need to go easy on Gisele, starting now. What if you're really the father but you've been so difficult, she changes her mind and disappears? What if she bails out today and you never know if you were the father or not?"

That's too much for me to consider right now. One thing after the other. "I looked up paternity tests after that," I counter.

"Kay," she whispers. "And?"

"Found a place in Burlington where they do the prenatal testing from a blood sample. No risk to the fetus. Takes a week to process. Made an appointment for tomorrow. That's all I'm talking about with Jezebel today." I get it. Maybe I'm in denial. But something was off with that woman today. If she refuses the paternity test, then I'll have my answer. "I don't want to talk about anything else until I know without a doubt I'm the father."

"Can I say something?"

I pull Clover away from me just enough to look her in the eyes. "Always." She's my rock, and she needs to know that.

"Don't antagonize *Gisele*. What if you're such a dick to her she runs away, and you never see her or your child again?"

This again. "I'll find her."

"What if she moves across the country and raises your child to hate you?"

Shit. She could do that, couldn't she? "Yeah... I guess."

"Just humor her for a few days. Be decent. Show her you'd be a good co-parent. We don't know what she's after. Maybe it's money. Maybe it's the support of a family to raise her child. Maybe she just wants her child to have a father. Is that a crime?"

"*My* child."

"Right. You get what I'm saying?"

I'm beginning to.

We meet with Gisele in my office. I don't need to actively feed the gossip mill by a public meeting at the pub. I keep Chloe next to me, our hands intertwined. I don't want there to be a fucking doubt in anyone's mind, and especially in Gisele's, that if this kid is mine, it will have a stepmom from the beginning.

Also, Clover's presence keeps me in check.

She keeps me together.

Gisele agrees immediately to the test tomorrow, and I have to say, that's depressing to me.

It means there's no doubt in her mind I'm the father.

Fuck.

"We'll have time to talk in the car," Gisele says when I stand to show her the meeting's over.

And I feel, down to my bones, Chloe going still and cold.

Fuckfuckfuck.

After Gisele is gone, Chloe pecks my cheek. "Thalia and Lucas will be at the restaurant any minute, and then I'm meeting with Kiara about our dessert menu," she says. "I'll see you—"

"I'm coming with you."

CHAPTER FORTY-ONE

Chloe

I know what he's doing, and it's not that I don't like it. I do. But if he thinks I need reassurance, doesn't that mean there's something to reassure me about?

Am I overthinking this?

I'm totally overthinking this.

I focus back on the meeting.

"Understated chic, with natural elements pulled in," Autumn is saying while Lucas jots down measurements and Thalia examines details, takes photos, and writes notes.

I chime in, "Our target market is people coming in for a special occasion—an anniversary, a first date, a proposal—"

Thalia points to a table. "Lucas did an almost proposal to me right here."

"An almost proposal?" Autumn asks.

"Long story," Thalia says, looking lovingly at Lucas. "Anyway, I can't tell you how happy I am to be working on this project. It's perfect timing for us. We're in between projects at the resort with a lot of time on our hands." She climbs on a stepladder Lucas brought with them. "You know, ever since we had dinner here months ago, I've been thinking how gorgeous this place could be with maybe very little work." She pushes a ceiling tile in and gets on her toes to take a peek, her head disappearing in the ceiling. "Honey," she says excitedly to Lucas, her voice muffled. "Come here. I knew it."

"This looks good," I say to Autumn.

"These two are on fire. I can't wait to see what they come up with."

Thalia gets off the stepladder and starts drawing. Lucas climbs up, peeks over the ceiling, then sits next to her and starts adding numbers on his phone.

I call Millie to order some Chills, Easy Monday's version of a Frappuccino. "Dazzle us," I say when she asks what we want. "There's a bunch of us. Autumn, Lucas, and Thalia are here, Alex is coming any minute, which means Grace will probably pop in, and then of course there's my team." Somehow Haley also made it to the restaurant. "Just throw in a couple more, will ya?"

A half-hour later, Millie delivers the drinks herself, Alex enters bearing quiches made by her baker boyfriend, and as I suspected, Grace follows in her footsteps.

Thalia is scraping the wall paint with her fingernail, and tapping the floor with her foot, taking pictures and more measurements.

"How soon can you start?" Scott approved the financing for the dining room renovation this morning. Compared to the price of the restaurant, it's not a big expense, and he had authority to do that. I want to get on it asap.

Thalia glances at Lucas. "We could start demo tomorrow..."

Excitement courses through my veins at the idea of getting started so soon. "Tomorrow we have a private event I'd hate to cancel. They booked a while ago. And Saturday, we already have a lot of reservations."

Thalia thumbs through her phone. "Monday?"

"Monday is great. How long do you think it'll be until we can reopen?" I glance at Shoshana, who's already behind her station, no doubt going through our upcoming reservations.

"If we work around the clock, we should be able to complete the project by the end of the week." She glances at Justin with a smile. "Provided your immediate neighbors don't mind the noise going until late at night. Honestly, the place doesn't need the structural changes that tend to lead to surprises and delays. We're looking at creating a wow factor. Demo will be done by midday Monday—I'll order a dumpster right away. Believe it or not, that's often the hardest thing to line up around here," she grumbles. "We could use the extra day to get things organized." Then she holds up her sketchbook, her eyes darting between Autumn and me. "What do you think?"

I leave the warmth of Justin's arm around my waist to pull up a chair next to Thalia. Her drawings show exquisite natural elements—tree bark, birch branches, antlers—mixed with subtle copper accents and plaid details. The walls are natural stone, with barn wood incorporated.

"I know where to get those," Autumn says, pointing at some elements on the sketch pad.

"It's just a direction for now," Thalia says. "But what do you think?"

"I love it. I just want to make sure it's not too stuffy."

"It won't be. It'll be more on the dreamy side," Autumn says. "We could add fairy lights to the birch."

"I can have a team of painters and tilers lined up for next week, no problem," Lucas confirms. "I'm gonna head out and make some calls" he adds, grabbing a Chill. "Thanks for the drink!" he tells me while he leans over to give Thalia a kiss.

"Of course! Thank *you* for coming by so quickly."

Justin kisses my temple tenderly. "Same, babe. Gotta run. You okay?"

"Course. Go!"

He lingers. "Your place is going to look awesome," he whispers in my ear. "*You* look awesome." He squeezes my waist. "I love you."

Our eyes meet. "Love you too," I whisper back.

I catch Haley looking at us dreamily, and focus my attention on Alex, who's taking photos of Thalia's sketches. "Just for a making of," she mumbles.

"I have everything I need," Thalia says after a few more minutes, pocketing her sketch pad. "I'll be in touch with an estimate tonight or first thing tomorrow. And more defined sketches."

Once she's gone, Alex turns to me. "Ohmygod, that's going to look *fab*!"

I hope fab is in my budget. I'm about to catch up with Thalia, make sure she doesn't get too carried away, when Gisele struts into the dining room, conversations instantly dying at her arrival.

I bet she gets that a lot.

I step next to her. "Everyone, this is Gisele. Gisele is—"

"Justin's baby mama," she interrupts me.

I register the shock on my friends' faces. I take a beat, then pick back up. "Right. Gisele, this is Justin's sister Haley," I say, pointing to a tight-lipped, narrowed-eyed Haley; "Grace," with her mouth agape; "Alex," her eyes to Gisele's belly; "Kiara," her eyes narrowed on me; "Shoshana, Abby, and Corine," all three wide-eyed at me. "And finally, this is Millie, who makes the best coffee in town." Millie is squinting, her gaze darting between the two of us.

You could hear a pin drop.

"It's cool, guys," I say as I motion with my hands for them to get unfrozen and say some welcome words to Gisele.

They all wave, there are a few, "Welcome to Emerald Creek," then Grace stands to let Gisele sit down.

Gisele stays put. "Um, I was just looking for Justin," she says to no one in particular.

"He's—he's not here. Did you try the pub?"

She rolls her eyes and finally looks at me. "Um. Yeah?"

"Kay, well did you try calling him?"

She huffs. "This is useless," she says and leaves.

I pull my phone out.

Me

Gisele is looking for you

Justin

What does she want

I don't know.

Why doesn't she call me

You ask her.

Oh shit

What

I think I blocked her. <Laughing emoji>

> This isn't funny. She's the mother of your child.

> You're telling me

> Love you

> Love you more

"What was that?" Haley asks.

I pocket my phone. "Sorry, didn't have time to warn you. She got here this morning."

"But what was *that*," Haley repeats.

I look to where Gisele walked out. "I don't know what to tell you, sweetheart. It's—what you see is what you get. She claims she's having Justin's baby, Justin isn't saying it's not possible, so they're doing a paternity test, and in the meantime, we're going with the assumption it's his just so that we don't burn bridges. And we're all going to work like mature adults to give this child a fantastic life surrounded by loving, mature adults."

"Wow," Grace says. "You seem really cool with all that."

Not cool. Not cool at all. But I don't have a choice. "Justin is going to need me. I can't let him down now. I hope you guys see that. We need to make Gisele feel welcome here, so they can co-parent in the best way possible for their child."

There are some muffled *wows*, a *man,* and one *respect.*

Haley mutters, "I don't buy it. He's not the father. She's not his style."

Kiara turns to her. "Honey, did you look at her? She's *everybody's* style. Guy like Justin who didn't want to commit, he still had needs. We all know he just got them taken care of out of town, and he was out of town *a lot*. She's all tits and ass and legs and her hair is fabulous. I know you're his sister, but even you must know the guy is sex on wheels. Of course they did it." Then she turns to me. "No offense, boss girl."

I feel like I'm dying inside. "None taken."

To further soften her blow, she explains, "Sex is only sex. Makes babies. Doesn't make a man happy more'n few minutes. You make Justin deeply happy. You're at another level. He's in love with you, boss girl."

"I know," I whisper back. Still, it's hard.

"You got nothing to worry about."

"I know," I whisper again.

"He's *yours*."

"I know."

"Now, can we talk about the dessert menu?"

"Yes," I whisper even softer. "Thank you."

"Good." She shows me pictures with descriptions and pricing while I nod absentmindedly, replaying in my head what just happened. Am I going to be able to follow through on what I said? Can I even be the mature adult I'm talking about? It might be partially a *Fake it 'til you make it* situation.

"Each delivery, I'll bring extra for your servers so they know what they're selling," Kiara says.

I nod. *Okay, Chloe, back in the game.* "Appreciate that."

"Make sure they *sell*."

"Yup, none of that *ready for the bill?* business." I've already trained my staff to upsell, and as if on cue, Abby comes up to us, plops her fist on her hip with an attitude directed at Kiara, and says, "For dessert, we have our three-tiered chocolate cake, which is *to die* for (rolls eyes), comes with a side of homemade whipped cream. Or a traditional apple pie with apples from the Chandler's orchard, a flaky crust, touch of cinnamon, served a la mode with ice cream made at King's Farm with milk from their Jersey cows. Our pastry chef also made her pear and ginger souffle served lukewarm with a cardamom custard cream. You will *not believe* your taste buds if you order this one. She's won an award in France with that souffle. So what will it be? My favorite is the chocolate cake, but I'm always partial to chocolate. Yesterday we almost had a riot when we ran out of the pie. I can also ask the kitchen to do a sampling plate for you, if you *think* you're full, but honestly, I know you're going to want to go for more. So, what will it be?" she finishes by mimicking taking out her waiter's pad.

I laugh and clap at Abby's spiel. "You go, girl, that's the spirit. Don't give them an option not to have dessert."

"Holy cow, Abby! I didn't know I'd won an award," Kiara says, visibly pleased as well.

Abby flips her hair. "That was just filler text, obviously. I'll need a full prompt."

"Will do." Kiara says. "We'll go over those when we do the tastings each week."

Later that day, showered and dressed for evening service, I take a look at our guest list for the evening. "Lynn and Craig are coming?" I ask Shoshana.

She nods. "They're pass holders."

I missed that. Too much has happened, with Gisele, the meeting at the bank this morning which got the ball rolling on the renos—not to mention Samuel giving me weird vibes—I haven't taken a moment to go over the list and know who in the community has been my primary supporters. "Thanks for pointing that out," I tell Shoshana. "Table eleven, good call too. Great. Thank you. Their drinks will be on the house."

"Of course," Shoshana says, making a note on their reservation.

"They're coming late, second service. Good." That means I'll be less rushed. I'll have time to chat and apologize for missing dinner at their home the other night.

Lynn is the opposite of Mom. She hugs the staff (she knows them, of course) and makes everyone feel comfortable. She's smiling and laughing at Craig's jokes and clearly having an awesome time overall, her good vibes radiating through the entire restaurant.

Lynn and Craig are also obviously very-well respected in the community. People stop to say hello and talk with them. Their presence, I understand immediately, is a stamp of approval for the restaurant, and that is going to be another huge help in our midweek traffic.

Alex came in, took pictures of the dishes, of some patrons who waved at her, and tag notifications are starting to flow on my phone. I'll respond later. Lynn and Craig are wrapping up their dinner. I want to go and thank them properly.

"This was lovely, darlin'," Craig tells me, and it hits me how his use of the moniker is entirely genuine, the opposite of when Mom calls me *dahling*. "Gave me a reason to take my wife out. Can't pass on an excuse to save money *and* make Lynn happy. Double win." He smiles at me and taps my forearm. "Well done, Chloe. Very proud of our son's girlfriend. He did good."

He winks at me and stands. "Ladies, if you'll excuse me, I'm going to go have a nightcap at my son's establishment." He leans toward me and stage whispers, "I hear he got himself into a *situation* and needs emotional support. That boy always had to do and have more'n the others."

Lynn rolls her eyes at her husband's last remark and taps the place left vacant in front of her. "Sit for a moment?" The dining room is empty, save for the two ladies who were at Easy Monday the other morning. We chatted briefly earlier, and it warmed my heart at how happy they were to be here. They're sitting at the opposite side of the dining room, out of earshot.

"Ah," I sigh. "It's good to be off my feet. How was dinner?" I lean in and add, "Honestly."

"It was perfect, honey. Honestly." She gives me a warm smile, but her gaze seems to be evaluating me.

"Thank you," I say, returning her smile. "You're not staying to give me feedback about the food, are you?" Shoshana brings me a glass of water and I thank her.

"No," Lynn says once she's gone. "I'm here about... what's happening with Justin and..."

"Gisele."

"Right. Gisele." She sighs. "How are you holding up? Honestly."

"Honestly? I don't know. It's so new, I feel I still need to process it. I... I freaked out at the beginning. But I..." I look at her tentatively, "I love Justin. I'm *in love* with him, and I want to be here for him all the way." Her face softens at my confession. "In any way I can. I don't know what that's going to look like, but I'm guessing, new parents figure stuff out as it happens. I mean, man plans and god laughs, right? I'm thinking, stepparents should just figure it out as it happens too."

I take a sip of water. "But I'm happy to take advice." I give her a small smile. Do I even know how she feels about me? Are they traditional, and do they think Justin should marry Gisele? Ohmygod, is that why they came, to talk me into doing the right thing and retreating into the shadows? And what will I do if that's what they think is right for Justin?

"I feel exactly the way you do. I want to meet this... Gisele myself before I pass judgment, but let me tell you, Haley gave a full-blown account of her this evening right as we were getting ready to come, and she is. *Not. A. Fan.*" Lynn raises her eyebrows, tilts her chin, and takes a sip of wine. "Now of course, you're as good as a King to us. You're Justin's girlfriend, and you need to know—this means the world to us." She reaches for my hand. "You're like a second daughter for me, Chloe, and I want to get to know you as well as I know my own if I'm going to love you as my own, which I already do. So first order of business is, we schedule time alone, just you and me, and Haley sometimes, to do stuff together. Second order of business is, if anything is wrong and you need to talk to someone, a shoulder to cry on, you come to Mom," she says, pointing her finger at her chest.

My eyes well up. *Mom?*

She continues. "Things you need to know about Justin. He's loyal to a fault. Competitive like you wouldn't believe it. And he has more willpower than anyone I know."

"I've seen all this in one form or another."

"I know you have. That's why you love him." She pauses, looking for her words. "The thing you need to understand, these qualities are also his flaws. What put him in the impossible situations he finds himself in."

She takes another break, her mind going somewhere dark. "The accident changed the course of his life entirely. But it didn't break him. It made him a better version of him. He used to be so competitive with Ethan, and he never stood a chance. Ethan was a natural at sports, and three years older than him. Didn't matter. Justin always wanted to be better than him. Jump from a higher rock in the river. Pitch faster. Run faster. I watched him fail miserably for eighteen years. And then after the accident, Ethan was gone, and I watched Justin compete against himself and become...what he is now. And I'm so proud of him."

The last clients are gone, and Shoshana is folding napkins at her station, too far to hear us.

"I asked Justin to bring Gisele to the farm once the paternity test clears," Lynn says. My heart clenches. This is what my life is going to be now. "I wanted you to know that, and I also wanted to tell you, sweetheart, when that happens, I want you there too. When Justin is ready for us to meet her, you should be by his side. You are Justin's love. No one else."

My eyes well up, and I'm the one reaching for her hand now. "Thank you," I whisper.

"This is going to be hard. I need you to be strong for our son. Can you be that?"

"Of course," I assure her, praying I'll eventually become that person Justin needs.

"And always remember, you're feeling blue, you're feeling like it's too much, you need someone to talk to, you come to me."

That night, I call Justin on my way out. "I'm going to be working on my business plan tonight," I tell him. "I don't want to delay sending it, and I just don't know when I'll have time during the day. D'you want to sleep over at the cottage or...?" I have most of my notes at the cottage, and I prefer working from my laptop than on Uncle Kevin's antiquated computer.

Justin's silence on the phone, however short it is, eats at me. "I—I'm leaving early for Burlington tomorrow. Maybe it's best I stay here. If you're going to be pulling another all-nighter?"

Part of me feels like I'm falling inside. "I'm sorry, baby. I have to."

His response comes immediately this time. "I know. Don't be sorry. I'm proud of you. We'll get through this. Together."

"Kay." I hang up before my voice betrays me and he knows I'm holding back tears.

I spend the night working on the business plan and send it in the morning. Then I catch some sleep right around the time when I suppose Justin is hitting the road with Gisele.

It hurts, and I know my insecurities are to blame.

I also know it's just the beginning.

CHAPTER FORTY-TWO

Justin

"I'm gonna need some baby stuff," the grating voice blurts.

I don't remember her voice being *that* unpleasant. I wasn't paying attention to her voice, I suppose. I must have had other parts of her anatomy in mind. I wish I'd never lain eyes on her. Too late for that now.

I wasn't careful. I made a mistake. Now I need to fix it.

At least this is a mistake I can do something about. No one is dying.

This woman needs me.

I'll be there for her, all the way. No matter how I feel about her.

Because the truth is, I feel almost grateful that this is a mistake I can actually do something about.

I can prove I'm worthy.

"Jusssstin!" Nails on a chalkboard.

"Yeah, I heard ya. And I told ya, we'll go when we go see the shrink. Same strip mall."

We're driving back from the testing center in Burlington. She slept all the way down—thank god for that—but now she's fully awake.

"I just wished you'd stop saying shrink. It's a *therapist*. Don't be crass. I don't want our kid having bad manners."

I sort of thought, and probably this was wishful thinking, that she'd bail out on the paternity testing at the last moment. But she didn't. Not at all. She's pretty sure of herself.

I guess she knows.

And this means I need to get used to the idea of her being in my life for... a while. This must be god's punishment.

The child? I can't even imagine what that's going to be like. After we get the paternity test result, it'll be time for me to have a beer with Christopher. He had to raise Skye all on his own from the beginning. He'll know what I need to do.

Gisele started wanting to lay the groundwork for our co-parenting right when we left Burlington. Maybe it was because Chloe's wasn't here, and she feels more in control. Maybe it's just because she had me captive for an hour. Anyway, we're quickly realizing we don't agree on anything, and we'll need a third party to play referee. Enter the idea of a family therapist—the only thing we agree upon.

I do learn that Gisele's been kicked out from her parents' basement apartment—which she rented from them—for being pregnant. Apparently they're religious, and she didn't get the memo. Which means her bravado about not needing a place to stay was just that—bravado. According to her, Ms. Angela gave her a good deal on a bedroom at the bed-and-breakfast, so that's taken care of. She doesn't have a car, her job was next to her parents' home, which means she lost her job. But with the leaf-peeping season starting, she should be able to find work.

I hope.

"Is she looking for daycare around here?" Chloe asks me as we're having a beer on her porch before dinner. "I hear it's hard to find a spot."

I pull my phone out. "Texting mom to see if she has an idea."

Chloe settles next to me on the porch swing, her lithe, subtle body molding perfectly against mine. I lift her so she's sitting on me. We leave the lights out so the mosquitos don't get to us and so Chloe can watch the stars and the moon. Since we spent the night in my truck, she's all about that.

"I just wanna talk about something else," I say in her hair. My hand takes on a life of its own and trails under her dress, up her naked thighs. "How'd it go yesterday and today?"

"Your parents had dinner at the restaurant last night," she says with a huge smile. "They're so sweet."

It warms me that she fits so well with my folks already, but it doesn't surprise me. She's mine and they know it. They love her like one of ours, and rightfully so. My dick gets hard at the idea of spending my life with her, something I'd never thought was ever in the cards for me. Ethan coming back and the two of us talking things out put some things back in place, and the rest will sort itself out over time.

I mean, look who's sitting in my lap. Sullivan's own daughter, and I wouldn't have it any other way.

That's because she's not Sullivan's daughter to me.

She's my Clover.

"How did the meeting for the renovations go?" I ask her, breathing her hair.

"Mmm..." she purrs, "it's gonna look awesome. Alex is planning a ribbon-cutting already. We'll have press and stuff."

"Really?" That's amazing.

"It's gonna bring us a lot more business. We start demo on Monday."

"That soon?"

"Un-huh. They wanted tomorrow, but we have a private event I didn't want to cancel, plus a number of reservations Saturday. So, Monday."

I breathe in her hair. "You have a private event tomorrow?" Tomorrow I'm closed, like every year on the same date. My staff already knows. Hell, the whole town knows we're closed that day.

But suddenly I don't know what to do with myself.

Correction.

I don't feel like wallowing anymore.

"Can I take you out? Or will they need you at the restaurant?"

She trails her tongue along my neck, making my hips buck. "Mm, they can manage. Samuel will be working."

I jolt. "I wonder if—"

She nibbles my ear. "Yup. We should make sure we come back early enough."

Adrenaline courses through me. I'm taking my girl out on what used to be the hardest day of the year for me, and we might finally have an opening to catch that fucker Samuel. Because why else would Samuel agree to work on a day he's off, other than to have an excuse for staying behind after close? "Okay then. It's a date, tomorrow, on the early side."

"Dinner's ready," she purrs in my ear then stands. "I made my lobster risotto."

That sounds delicious, but then again... "Fuck. I dunno, Clo." I set my beer on the floor and pull her back on my lap, facing me this time so she straddles me, her cleavage right below my chin. "I just wanna eat your pussy."

She grinds against me. "Oh, I see," she says with a shy smile, her cheeks getting rosy. Fuck but I like the way she's coy about it.

"You little minx. I know you're having dirty thoughts right now."

She gapes and shakes her head, but a small laugh escapes her.

"Show me those tits," I order her.

Biting her lip, she unbuttons her dress down to the waist and runs her hands on top of her bra.

"That new?" I growl. The bra is light pink, sheer, revealing, and barely containing her puckered nipples. I go to unhook it at her back, but she reaches for her cleavage and unclasps it there, her breasts spilling out, offered. "Fuck, Chloe, I like this one," I say and take one nipple into my mouth, pulling on it.

She moans softly, grinds against me, runs her fingers on my scalp, keeping my mouth right where she wants it. I run a finger between us, and yeah. "You're soaked for me, aren't you?"

She grinds again.

"Aren't you?"

"I dunno," she mumbles. "I dunthingso." And then she grinds harder.

I growl and take her other nipple in my mouth.

She lowers her head to my ear, as if she's concerned someone might hear us, and she whispers. "Canyou chegagain... if I'm wet?"

I'd think it's funny and cute if I wasn't so wound up tonight. So needing to fuck her. So needing my own release. I unzip my jeans and jerk my hips up to free my cock, and register her gasp. "Yeah, babe, you're soaked. Now take your man."

She lets out a series of pants as she takes my throbbing cock in her. "That's my girl," I growl in her ear and at that, she comes. I watch the beauty of her features abandoned for me, her whole body shaking, her wet cunt spasming around me, sucking me in, sucking me dry as I empty myself in her. I give her soft hips a couple more pulls to impale her entirely on me and finish while she wraps her arms around me, and my face falls between her breasts.

"Fucking hell, best place on Earth," I grunt as I dive again between Clover's thighs and circle her clit. It's after dinner, we're in her bed, and I can't get enough of her. Her sex juices are the best nightcap I could dream of, her whimpers a total turn on. I'm hard on her sound, her smell, her taste, her feel.

"Babe," she says, and that's all I need. I slide up her magnificent body and lodge my cock where it belongs. She wraps her legs around my waist and sucks me in, body and soul, and we both find our release, sweat and grunts and tangled limbs.

Once I'm on my back and she's tucked against my chest and our breaths are slowing, I ask, "What was that all about?"

"What?" she asks with her sleepy voice.

"The new bra, the lobster risotto."

She lifts her head. "You don't like the new bra?"

I fist her hair and nudge her back on my chest. "I love the new bra."

She stays silent.

"Clover, you didn't answer."

"You liked it," she whispers, and it nearly kills me.

"Of course I liked it, and your lobster risotto could be on the menu at Per Se, but my question is, why?"

"I knew you'd like it," she whispers, and I feel her smile against my heart, my skin tingling where her lips move.

I flip us so she's lying on her back and I'm above her. "I love you, Chloe."

"I love you too," she says in a small voice.

"To me, that means you're everything to me. You and only you. You get me?"

She nods.

"So that shit about going shopping and cooking for hours when you've had the most difficult days of your life, most of it because of me, it stops now. You take care of you. Yeah?"

She makes a little pouty mouth.

She went all out tonight because she knows I'm having a shit time and she wants to make my life better. And god I love her for that. Part of me wouldn't want it any other way. But the better part of me knows she's in as much shit as I am, if not more. And I want her to take care of herself too.

"I'll take care of us," she corrects me, her tone solemn, accepting no argument.

God I love this woman. She has no idea.

CHAPTER FORTY-THREE

Chloe

I sound way more confident than I feel, telling Justin I'll take care of us. But what else can I do, in this moment? I can't possibly tell him how I feel.

Scared.

Threatened.

Like this could be the end of us.

Justin never wanted a relationship.

Now he's going to have a child.

Gisele will be in his life, forever.

As she should.

But can *I* do this? Really? And feel complete? At peace?

And how about Justin? He said he loves me, and I know it to be true. But things between us progressed quickly. It doesn't mean it's what he *wanted*. It just... happened.

The man never wanted this type of commitment.

And now, with Gisele, and a baby on the way? Is this going to be too much for him?

Gisele and the baby, he has no choice.

But *me*?

I close my eyes to hide my emotions from him and wrap my legs around his hips, my arms around his shoulders, pulling him to me.

Leaving no space between us.

His weight feels good on me, and I start dozing off.

Then both our phones chime with a sound I hear during the day, when it doesn't matter.

But it's night.

It could be what we've been waiting for.

It could also be lovers looking for a quiet place.

Justin lifts himself off me, barely enough to grab his phone.

It could also be a bear.

He jolts. "Fuck! It's them." He hops off me. I grab my phone and look at the grainy image while I slip on my clothes. The light from the restaurant's back door spills onto the parking lot, lighting a car with the trunk wide open.

I jump into my underwear, slip on my jeans and flip flops, and pull a sweatshirt over my head as we both tumble out of the house and into Justin's truck.

Checking my phone, my blood runs cold. Two men are loading the trunk of a car, the light from the restaurant's back door leaving no doubt about what's going on.

"Ohmygod, Justin, you were right." I don't care to see who it is or what they're carrying. No one is supposed to be loading stuff from my restaurant into their car.

We need to catch them in the act.

"Dec," Justin barks into his phone as he peels out of the driveway. "We're on. Got them on camera. We're headed there now."

"Wait for me," Declan snaps back, his voice audible even to me.

"Won't wait forever, Dec," Justin says, hangs up, and drops his phone on my lap.

As we approach the back street leading to the parking lot, Justin switches the truck lights completely off and slows. Then he pulls to the side and kills the engine. "Wait in the truck. If you see car lights coming down the street and Declan still hasn't gotten here, you block the street with the truck and get the hell out so they don't find you. I'm gonna go." He slices out of the car.

I hand him his phone. "Don't do anything stupid."

He closes the car door softly, and my heartbeat picks up as I watch him storm away, shoulders hunched, fists balled up, his silhouette clearly visible in the full moon.

Samuel is an asshole. And David is a wild card. What will they do if—when—Justin confronts them? God, what is Declan *doing*? How far was he anyway? I strain to listen but hear nothing but the summer trill of millions of insects in the night.

The wait seems interminable. Should I go? But then I won't be able to block their exit if they leave before Declan gets there. And if I move the truck in the middle of the street, Declan won't be able to make it to the parking lot.

God! I want to call Justin, but I can't. What if he's hiding in the bushes, collecting evidence, and his phone rings?

Ohmygod, his phone is not on silent. Oh please, please, please don't let anyone call him now.

This wait is killing me. How long has it been? My phone chimes, signaling movement again. Ohmygod, the men are coming out, carrying heavy-ass boxes. They're hunched over. And... is that Justin? What is he *doing*? He's walking to them, hands on his hips.

Oh no, no, no. *Don't!* I slide behind the wheel, deciding I'm going to pull up there in the truck. I'll improvise once I get there.

I gun it, turning the high beams on.

And finally, finally! Red and blue lights materialize in my rearview mirror. I speed up and pull to the side as I get to the parking lot just in time to see Justin stumble back and charge.

Declan sounds his siren, then jumps out of the car. Another cruiser pulls up, and the three silhouettes in the parking lot freeze. Clearly recognizable, David and Samuel are blinking, blinded, and surprised.

Justin wipes under his nose. "You wanna rewind this action and come in a little later, Dec, gimme a chance to punch this asshole in self-defense?"

"Step back, King," Declan orders, obviously not in the mood for Justin's snarkiness.

"He *did* hit me."

"Payback, asshole" Samuel snarls.

"Payback for what, you fucking moron? You're stealing merchandise, you—"

"Enough!" Declan yells. "Everyone on your knees, hands behind your head."

Justin shakes his head, takes several steps back from Samuel, and complies. David follows suit. When Samuel doesn't, Declan pulls his gun.

Shit!

"Come on, man, how much you wanna add to your situation?" Declan asks. "Do the right thing for once. On your knees."

Samuel drops to the ground.

The rest of the night goes by in a blur. Samuel and David are booked. Justin's upper lip is split, dried blood caking on it, but he won't let medics look at him.

Declan takes our statements. Photos are taken of the contents of the trunk, and I'm asked to identify them. I'll need to corroborate with invoices, but it's clear what was going on.

I'm relieved we caught them. Shocked and deeply disappointed by David, but relieved.

Justin winces as I clean his lip with a saline solution. "You okay, Clover?"

"Can't say I was thrilled to see you charge up to them, but yeah." I dab the cut with disinfecting cream.

He laces his arms around my waist. "You look pretty shaken."

"Yeah, I wonder why. Oh wait! I just saw my boyfriend get stirred like a martini no one ordered."

His lip looks painful as it splits into his killer smile. "Boyfriend?"

Ouch. "Or... whatever."

He traces my face with the pad of his thumb. "You're more than my girlfriend, Clover."

My eyes water while my center clenches. "Oh." What do I say to that? "I just saw my *person* get hurt," I correct.

His shoulders shake as he laughs softly. "No, but really, Clo, how're you feeling?"

"Relieved. And yes, shocked. And disgusted that Samuel, who Uncle Kevin and Aunt Dawn trusted, could do that, and same for David. Although David? Did not see that coming."

"You said relieved?"

"Yeah. Mystery solved. I can move on now, hire new people. Although—shit!"

"What?"

"I have that event tomorrow. They were both going to work it. I'll see if Ryan and Trevor can help out. But," I kiss the side of his mouth, "I won't be able to go out with you." I feel sad. It seemed to mean a lot to him, to take me out. "Rain check?"

"Course. Even better. I'll come bartend for you."

"Really?" That's awesome. "But—isn't it weird if the pub's owner is working next door?"

"What's weird about that?"

"Won't your staff be... I don't know..."

He runs his hands under my sweatshirt. "Don't worry 'bout my staff. I'll be there for you."

"Thank you," I breathe as he continues his exploration of my body, making swift work of the sweatshirt, and going straight for the front clasp of my new bra.

The next day flies by, and it's a good thing.

It helps me forget about Gisele. About the fact that in a few days, there will be no hoping things turn out differently. The test results will come back, and if Gisele's attitude is anything to go by, there will be no more denying that Justin will become a father soon, with new responsibilities, a new focus, a different life.

And as the months go by, will there still be a place for me in his life?

So, yes, I welcome the craziness for now.

In the morning, we go to the station to wrap up statements, charges, and other fun stuff. Midday, I stop by the restaurant to update my staff on the night's events and help them prep for the evening.

They're shocked when I tell them Samuel and David were caught stealing, but mostly they stay quiet. "Justin will come bartend for us tonight," I say.

"Oh right, he's closed tonight," Corine says.

Justin's closed? I didn't know the pub ever closed. And on a Friday?

Maybe it's a thing. Staff appreciation day or something. I'll have to ask him.

"Do we know what the occasion is for our group here tonight?" I ask Shoshana a few moments later, referring to the reservation that was made a while back at the restaurant, possibly even before I started.

"I believe it's a memorial."

"Oh, okay. I didn't see any special requests for flowers or anything.'

"Nope. They said they love the restaurant the way it is. They don't want anything special, just the menu that was agreed upon."

I check in with Corine in the kitchen. "Are you okay in there?"

She lifts her head from a sheet of paper she and Eric were examining. "All good!" her smile is genuine, and her relaxed features give me pause.

After Samuel and David were arrested, I called her before going to the station, to fill her in on the night's events. I wanted to give her the information first, and more details on Samuel's scheme.

I also offered her Samuel's job. I was expecting needing to convince her, but she accepted immediately and with enthusiasm.

And now that she's in charge, the atmosphere is much more relaxed, despite the obvious shock we're all in.

Justin gets behind the bar at five and sets himself up. I'm in and out of the dining room, and I have to say, I like him there. In what will soon be my restaurant. It also brings back great memories.

When no one is in the dining room, I sashay to the bar, hike on a barstool, and make my voice sultry. "Hey there, bartender, watcha doin' with the rest of your night?"

He chuckles at my exaggerated act, but lust still fills his gaze. "I'm getting in bed with a hot woman, lady." He pulls out a chopping board and preps his garnishes.

"Easy cutting those limes, cowboy. I've heard some pretty gruesome stories," I continue in my husky voice. Although we're being silly, bringing up the memory of our first night together fills me with desire.

I hope tonight's event doesn't last too long.

At five thirty, the hosts of the private dinner, Mr. and Mrs. Ward, arrive early, as planned, to be there and welcome their guests.

And Justin's composure behind the bar falls. He pales and freezes, as if he's seeing a ghost.

Then Mrs. Ward says, "Justin! Justin King! Oh, honey, look who's here." And she rounds the bar to hug Justin, her husband following with a small smile.

Justin's arms hang by his side as his panicked gaze is lost somewhere far. Then he awkwardly brings his hands to Mrs. Ward's back.

What the…?

Chapter Forty-Four

Justin

I find myself being hugged by the woman who must hate me the most.

Audrey's mother.

What is she doing here? And more importantly, why is she hugging me? She should be trying to pull my eyes out.

What was her name?

Anita. Anita and Clyde Ward, Audrey's parents. Whom I met only once, in a lawyer's conference room, where they and I received compensation for the accident.

They deserved it. Hell, there's nothing that could ever compensate for their loss.

Me? I was a fraud. I didn't deserve anything, other than their contempt, or hatred, or whatever horrible feelings they were in their right to nurture about me.

We didn't talk that day, and that was fine by me. I was in a dazed state, weak and probably medicated, so I could get through the motions. There were moments when I just had to take meds.

Like the day I was facing the parents of the girl I'd offered to drive home.

And the man who ran us over.

And I was getting money for this mess. Money that everyone had advised I was entitled to.

I felt dirty that day, and for all the following days. And to this day.

I also remember, distinctly, that Kevin Murphy looked relieved. *Relieved!*

And his brother-in-law, Sullivan, who had deep pockets, was paying on his behalf, and letting it be known? He looked annoyed. Like he couldn't be bothered.

I hated those two instantly.

"Finally, we get to see you and hold you and say thank you," Mrs. Ward says as she releases me, takes a step back, and sizes me up, top to bottom, her hands on my forearms. "What a fine man you've become." She says it with admiration. No animosity. Not even sadness. "Doesn't he look good?" she asks her husband.

Clyde takes my hand and shakes it for several long seconds. "So glad to see you're doing good, son. Sorry we didn't reach out sooner." His eyes are wet with emotion, but not the sad kind.

They're happy. They're genuinely moved and happy to see me.

Do they have me confused with someone else?

I shuffle from one foot to the other. I need to fix this misunderstanding, and it might turn out ugly. Chloe might lose her bartender for tonight. Shit. I should've known the private event had to do with the ten-year anniversary. But then again, I'd never thought they'd have it here, at Murphy's restaurant, of all places. "You—you know who I am?"

Anita Ward's lower lip trembles slightly. "We never thanked you properly."

What is she talking about? "Sorry?"

She turns to her husband. "Honey. We sat with Kevin, talked it out, gave him our forgiveness. I cannot believe we never spoke with Justin, when he's been in our prayers every. Single. Day."

Clyde nods at his wife and grunts what seems like his agreement.

What *the hell* is she talking about? Okay, so they forgave Kevin. Good for him. And I get that, coming from them. I suppose.

But what do they have to thank *me* for?

"I don't follow, Mrs. Ward."

"Anita," she corrects me. And then sets her hand on my forearm, looks deep in my eyes, and delivers the most bizarre statement. "You accompanied our Audrey on her path. We can never thank you enough for that."

I glance at Mr. Ward.

"Audrey didn't die alone," he says in a muted voice, a voice that still carries his pain when he says the words. But his eyes? His eyes convey relief, and peacefulness, and thankfulness. "You were there with her, you were wounded so she wouldn't die alone in... horrific circumstances. She had another human being with her. A young man who cared for her." His eyes are wet, but his mouth spreads in a genuine, if small, smile. "We're eternally grateful to you for that. You're a true hero to our family."

I reel back at their words.

Anita's hand clenches around my arm. "You cared for her in her last moments."

"Your wounds are our relief," Clyde adds, his explanation adding to my confusion.

"If it weren't for you, our Audrey would have passed alone and scared. Because of you, she didn't. She had a human connection to the end," Anita continues.

My throat tightens. I don't deserve this. I don't deserve their compassion, much less their thankfulness.

This is nuts.

"You don't understand," Clyde says. "In our darkest moments, thinking over and over that we'd lost her and how, knowing you were with her, you did everything you could, and she knew it, she knew she had someone next to her who cared enough to put his life on the line for her, that was consolation enough. Her life was short, but she was loved and cared for, to the very end." His eyes are shiny as he turns to his wife. "You were right, honey, he didn't know. I'm glad we told him."

Anita gives him a small smile and turns to me. "You're a selfless young man, a true knight in shining armor. And you almost lost your own life being that. Now be sure to look after yourself too. Don't let regrets and what-ifs get in the way of living your best life."

I shuffle my feet again, not sure how to answer that.

"We're embarrassing him, honey," Clyde declares.

Any other time, I'd be embarrassed. Now, I'm too stunned for that.

Audrey's parents are thankful. To me.

We're interrupted by the arrival of the first couple, but I stay stunned in place while the Wards welcome their guests.

Chloe slides next to me. "You okay?" she whispers.

My voice stays stuck in my throat.

"You need a moment? Wanna use my office?"

I need to snap out of it. "I'm good."

The focus back on being just the bartender for the night, until Mr. Ward stands for a moving speech about his daughter, Audrey. What's beautiful about it is the way they seem to have transcended the loss of their daughter into living life to its fullest.

At some point, he mentions me by name and points to me, and I have no other choice than to listen to him actually call me a hero again. People clap. It's embarrassing.

But it's beginning to sink in.

Live life to the fullest, be thankful for what you have, embrace the opportunities, go after what you want.

And I'm thankful for what I have.

And I know I want more, and I'm going to go after it.

I look at Chloe.

And fuck me if that isn't the moment the Sullivans walk into the restaurant.

CHAPTER FORTY-FIVE

Chloe

"Chloe?" Shoshana says quietly behind me.

"Huh?" I turn around and focus my eyes on her. "What's up?"

"Um... your-your parents are here?"

"My what? Who?" I look beyond her to the couple awkwardly standing near the entrance. Their eyes are darting between me and Justin, but weirdly it's not on me they end up focusing their attention.

"Mom! Dad! What—Hello!" I manage to smile and peck Mom's cheek, then side hug Dad.

Mom blinks and settles her gaze on me, seeming to shake some thoughts away. "Dawn told me, honey, and I said to Daddy, Honey, we *have* to go get Chloe. She cannot stay one more minute in *such* a dangerous place."

I haven't told my parents about buying the restaurant yet. I was going to keep that for later. Once it was, literally, a done deal. Less headache. I get that they're not happy. But a *dangerous* place? "What are you talking about?"

Dad clears his throat. "Your mother heard about the unsavory incident with your chef."

"Oh! Oh—that. Geez, guys, is that why you came?" It's so sweet it's not even annoying. "As you can see, I'm fine, and the good news is, the bad guys are behind bars and the mystery of why the restaurant was losing money is solved. And that is mainly thanks to Justin." I gesture to him standing behind the bar, looking utterly confused, his jaw setting when his gaze meets our group. "Justin! Come meet my parents." I beam proudly at him.

He walks straight up to me, laces his arm around my waist, lays a long, wet one on my mouth, then leaves me in an erotic daze *in front of my parents* and says, "Alan Sullivan, pleased to see you again. Miz Sullivan."

They know each other?

Dad says nothing. He looks... shrunk. Chastised. Defeated. He finally breaks the silence. "Pleasure's mine." He doesn't seem pleased. Not pissed either. Just utterly annoyed. Like he'd rather be a thousand miles away from here. "You seem well," he adds.

I mean, what is going on?

Justin tugs me so close to him he turns my front to his side. My cheek is nearly squished and my mouth feels funny.

I press my free hand against his chest to right myself. "Um... do you know each other?" It's obvious they do.

Justin's arm clenches around me. Dad does his thing where he juts his chin out and stretches his lips to the sides. Then he plunges his fists into his pockets, rocks on the balls of his feet, and avoids looking at me at all costs.

First time I saw it was when I asked about Santa Claus. He just couldn't deliver bad news to his little girl.

Now, not so cute.

Mom ventures, "We've um... we've met. Right, Alan?"

"Dad?"

Dad does his bullshit pose again.

"Justin?" I ask. "What's going on?"

Justin looks on the verge of saying unpleasant things. A lot of things. He moves his chin to the couple who are holding their private dinner here. "A reunion of sorts?"

"No. We-we were here to see Chloe..." Mom's eyes are full of tears, and her bottom lip trembles. "Such lovely people."

"That's enough," I hiss, my gaze darting between the three of them. "Justin!" He's the only one I can count on to tell me the truth.

He gives me a small shake of the head. "Not my story to tell."

Dad rubs his forehead with the back of his thumb. "Uh." He smacks his lips. "Son, mind giving me a minute with my daughter?"

Justin tenses, and not lightly. It's a full-on body reaction. At what, I'm not sure. Being called son? Being told to step away?

"It's okay, Dad," I gently nudge. "I don't keep secrets from him." I tuck my body closer into Justin. "We... we're really serious. Whatever's going on, I'll share with him anyway."

Dad chuckles. Does the back of the thumb rub again.

Mom bats her eyelashes at me. "Dahling, not tonight."

Dad looks at me. "Tonight's actually a good night. Let's go for a walk. You and I need to talk."

I glance at my staff serving dinner. "I—can this wait 'til tomorrow? How long are you in town for?"

"It's a'right, Clover. We got you covered here." Justin kisses my forehead tenderly and then turns to Dad as he lets go of me. "You handle her carefully, now."

My eyes bug out, and I lose my breath. I turn to Dad—expecting some kind of cataclysmic incident—but then Dad answers, "Count on me."

And what was that?

The conversation with Dad is one-sided and lasts more than a minute. And when it's done, my world is shattered and put back together. It looks different. Worse in some ways. Maybe better in others.

At any rate, a lot of things make sense now.

Justin hands me a beer and sits next to me on the steps off my deck, Moose at our feet. "You good?"

It's night. We just got to the cottage. The evening ended on the early side. Mom and Dad left shortly after my long talk with Dad. The Wards' memorial dinner wrapped up early. "I'm good."

"Been quite a day for you." He reaches for my free hand and links our fingers together.

"Why didn't you tell me?" I whisper, tears rushing to my eyes.

"It wasn't my story to tell," he says, repeating his earlier statement.

It was, but I get him.

Ten years ago, Dad was in Emerald Creek with Uncle Kevin for the closing on the purchase of the restaurant and the signing of a new lease on the space. They drove back at night. It was dark and visibility was low because there was a storm, but they were excited, they were in a hurry to get home, Uncle Kevin eager to celebrate. Dad was having a good day with his brother-in-law, which is not something to gloss over, since I've never heard Dad say anything good about his wife's brother. But it was one of those days where Uncle Kevin seemed to be getting his shit together, and that made Mom happy.

Dad sharing that surprised me, as it was the first I'd heard that Uncle Kevin didn't have his shit together, for pretty much all his life.

Lots of things are starting to make sense now.

Back to that night, Uncle Kevin was driving in the pouring rain, too fast, too careless, not paying attention, not having his eye on the road, not realizing the road was slippery. He didn't see an upcoming curve, and got to the curve too fast, overcompensating, hitting a car stopped at the intersection.

Hitting it full force, sending it barreling and tumbling.

It was an old car, unequipped with airbags or all those fancy systems that prevent cars from catching fire.

It caught fire.

Uncle Kevin and Dad were in a newer car. They had all the bells and whistles. Still, it took them minutes, long minutes to emerge, dizzy and confused.

They called nine-one-one.

They stumbled to the other car, maybe a hundred feet away, such was the force of the impact, hastening their steps to bring assistance, then holding back when the car caught fire, not believing their eyes when they saw one silhouette pull another one out of the inferno. Then moving again because although they'd caused the accident, they weren't monsters.

They weren't heroes either.

They couldn't bring themselves to brave the flames. It was just too damn hot. How could someone even breathe? Their eyes hurt from the smoke, their skin felt brittle, and they weren't even that close.

And so they watched, helpless.

They weren't heroes.

"We weren't criminals either," Dad said to me. "No one could establish that Kevin was driving too fast. He claimed that the kids' car had inched onto the main road, beyond the stop sign. It wasn't clear cut at all. But I was there, and I knew he'd lost control of the car. Your mom was so happy her brother finally had something he was serious about, and now everything was up in the air again. I mean, he could have faced prison. It would have killed her. And it wouldn't have brought the girl back. And so I offered them a deal." He stayed quiet for a while and added, "We met with the authorities here, and it seemed it was the best course of action. For everyone. Doesn't mean I liked it. Just means it was the best."

And so, on behalf of his brother-in-law, Dad made compensation to the Wards for the loss of their daughter Audrey and to Justin for his injuries.

"It... um... it explains a lot," I whisper to Justin. "It must have been hard for you... having him right next to you all these years." And then me, waltzing in to take over for Uncle Kevin.

He takes a long pull on his beer and exhales loudly. Doesn't say anything.

"I... uh... I don't know what to say. I guess you never uh... never talked it through with Kevin, right... and I guess uh..."

"What did he tell you? Sullivan."

"Dad? He told me about the accident, and that he offered to pay... you know, to give a monetary compensation on behalf of Kevin. To, you know..." *Make it go away.* "Make it go away," I add in a whisper.

"You ashamed?" he asks me.

"Ashamed?" *Of what?* "My dad wasn't a hero. I can't say that it doesn't hurt, that I didn't wish he'd have told Uncle Kevin to slow down, or that he'd had the guts to help you pull Audrey out and maybe do something heroic like CPR or whatever, but he is who he is," I finish, almost inaudibly.

What was left of daddy's little girl just died, I guess.

"But um... he loved his wife, and his love language," I add with a sad huff, "is money. I'm not surprised he'd throw money at a problem. I mean, I'd be surprised if he *hadn't*. That wouldn't be him. Or if it was him, if he had the means to make a problem go away by throwing money at it and he didn't, then that would be a negative trait, as far as he's concerned. He did the right thing by his standards."

"How d'you feel about that?" His question comes immediately.

I look at Justin's profile against the dark night. His strong jaw, cut cheekbones. His angry gaze. "I feel immensely lucky that I have you in my life. Despite his flaws, I love my father. But I do not envy my mother. And I would not want to share my life with a man like him. That's how I feel."

I expect this to get me a kiss, or at least a stroke on my back, a half hug. "I felt like a cheat," he says instead.

Like a cheat?

He stands, goes to the kitchen, returns with two fresh beers, one for me, one for him. He sits down and starts talking. "When I came out of the hospital, I was weak and angry and mostly felt out of control of my whole life. One moment I was this asshole stealing his brother's girlfriend, planning on losing his virginity to an experienced girl. The next I was a thief. Maybe even a murderer. A cheat."

I set my hand on his forearm, but it falls off when he lifts his beer to take a long slug. I tug my hand between my thighs, set my bare feet on Moose, and take comfort in the dog's soft grunt.

"And when I'm out of the hospital, I'm shoved into a room with my parents and a bunch of adults who tell me I have to sign here and here and here and everything will be okay. Audrey's parents were there, and they were signing. The two guys who I'm told were in the other car were there and they were signing. My dad said we were grateful. Fucking *grateful*." He plays with his beer between two fingers, his head hanging low, watching the bottle dangle. "I made money from someone's death. Real money. Too much money for an eighteen-year-old. And certainly too much money for someone who survived. She wouldn't have died if it hadn't been for me."

I don't know what to say to that, so I stay quiet.

"I still resent my parents for that. If I had to do it all over again, I'd never take a single cent from Sullivan. His money soiled me."

My stomach clenches. "You turned the money into something good. Something for the community. It did some good. It didn't bring Audrey back, but nothing could do that."

"Heard that a million times, Chloe. You wanted to know why I called the pub the Lazy Salamander? You have your answer."

"The Wards," I venture awkwardly. "What did they—what did you talk about?"

"The usual shit. Forgiveness and stuff." He takes a deep breath. "I—I didn't mean it that way. It wasn't shit. At all. I mean these people—these people are saints if you ask me. It's just that..." His words die in the night, but his pain is there, looking for a way out. "It was a lot, seeing them today. Hearing them say the things they said to me." He squints, holding tears inside. "I was looking at them, later during dinner. And listening to them. And what they said to me, they're right, you know. I need to do that too. Live my life. Snap out of it and truly live. Stop being fucking scared." He takes my hand again. "You give me that. The power to move forward. The courage to live my life." Our gazes meet. Is he thinking about his unborn child, and how I've been by his side through the curveball life threw at him? And

I'm proud I was able to do that, to be that person for him. To convince him he could do it. That he was more than capable.

That he'd be a great dad.

But I don't know how long *I* can sustain this.

My chest constricts, as if a giant vise is clamping around my heart. How do I *really* feel about Justin having another woman in his life, a woman he made a baby with? About him having this woman *in his life*, in a way, and forever.

And I hate, hate, hate myself and my stupid insecurities for that.

Why can't I be stronger?

My eyes well up just as Justin stands. I inhale slowly. I don't have the strength to open up to him about my darkness.

Justin doesn't notice my distress. He gives Moose a soft whistle, taking him to the wooded area surrounding the cottage to do his business.

I bring our empty beer bottles inside and do my bathroom routine. As I slide between the bedsheets, the domestic sounds of Justin locking the door, turning the lights off, then coming up the stairs, fill me with a comfort tinted with a shade of uncertainty.

Life can never be that simple.

He lays heavily on the bed, turns to wrap me in his arms, then falls immediately asleep. No nightmares. Not even a whimper.

I can't sleep. I want to toss and turn, but he has me tugged into him, and I don't want to wake him.

And amid all the thoughts that twirl in my mind, keeping me awake and more and more restless, my anxiety settles on one sentence.

'His money soiled me.'

Does he see Sullivan's daughter when he sees me?

CHAPTER FORTY-SIX

Chloe

The rest of the weekend, the restaurant is packed. Between the Locals' Pass and the news of Samuel and David's arrest, we're the center of attention in Emerald Creek.

Luckily, this town takes care of its own, and the way they show support, is to line up at the door and wait for a table.

Corine insists that we take in all walk-ins.

"We don't need to do this," I tell her.

"Boss, we *do* need to do this. For them, for you, and for us. Everyone's coming together. Let it happen."

And I get it. We can't turn away people who came to show support. The staff wants their tips. And they know the restaurant needs the extra money to tide us over while we're closed, even if it's only for a week.

I promised them PTOs. This is their way to thank me.

Saturday night I go to bed at two and get up at seven. Corine convinced me to offer brunch on Sunday.

And it's brilliant. With the church right up the street, we start to fill up at eleven with walk-ins, and then we're nonstop into the evening.

But all through these days, in the back of my mind, is the nagging feeling that something's going to turn ugly. That, as hard as I try, I'll lose what I want so much.

There's too much stacked against me.

Saturday night we sleep at Justin's.

Sunday, we stay at the cottage. "This way, you can sleep in tomorrow," Justin says.

Tomorrow's demo day at the restaurant. I'm definitely not needed. It's actually best if I stay out of Thalia's and Lucas's hair.

With no work to immediately tend to tomorrow, my thoughts start twirling again in my mind. Staring at the ceiling while Justin sleeps heavily next to me, I try to make sense of these thoughts. I try to analyze what's rational and what's fear-based. Who am I really to Justin? Who will I be in one year, in five years?

Can I be who he needs?

Can he be who I need?

And I fail at finding answers.

Anguish settles in the pit of my stomach. I know it's my insecurities, and they have nothing to do with Justin, and everything to do with me.

Tomorrow, in the light of day, I'll see everything differently.

I know one thing. I can trust Justin.

And that's all I really need. I spoon against him and let his warmth finally lull me to a restless sleep.

His kiss on my bare shoulder is what wakes me up from my short and agitated night. I turn slowly, the cobwebs of my insecurities pinning me to the night. Forcing myself to open my eyes, I say his name softly, hoping for an embrace, the feeling of his arms around me, the reassurance that he's real.

But all I get is the front door shutting, then his truck roaring as he peels from my driveway.

I blink. Light is pouring into the bedroom. I overslept. Pushing myself up on one elbow, I'm jolted awake by the time on my phone and a cup of coffee on my nightstand.

And I know what I was doing. I know why I was giving into my staff's insistence that we take more work.

I was trying to chase away the sense of doom. But now there's nothing else for me to focus on.

I still need to stop these thoughts.

I take a sip of coffee. Coffee at home without Justin is just plain sad. And I don't need sad right now. Feeling slightly guilty, I pour the coffee he made me down the drain. I go to the bathroom, pull on a light summer dress, my sandals, and decide to walk to Easy Monday, using the cut through the woods that continues alongside the river.

I plug my earphones in and call Fiona. I wish I could video with her, to show her the beautiful countryside, and maybe make her think over not ever wanting to come back here. But there's not enough network coverage, so we have to stick to audio.

I need to update her on the fact that I'm buying the restaurant, but more importantly, on the new family developments. Only she can fully understand me about this, and boy do I need to offload on someone right now.

"How do you feel about it?" she asks when I'm done giving her the bare facts.

I take a deep breath, focusing my gaze on the meadow on the other side of the woods, buzzing with insects. "How is it that the people I love most can just lie to me? I mean, I can maybe get that Mom and

Dad never shared that story before, but knowing I was taking over Uncle Kevin's restaurant? Knowing I was going to be right next to Justin? You'd think they'd give me a heads up. What's up with that?" Anger mixes with disappointment.

"You feel taken for granted," Fiona says.

"What do you mean?"

"Whatever happens, people think you'll be cool about it. That you'll accept it."

Yeah, that sounds about right. "That stinks. Why are they like that?"

"Because you let them?"

"I don't let them!"

"Clo, when was the last time you called them out on their shit?" She stays silent for a beat, then, "Lemme guess, last night, you just sat there, listened, nodded, and said—what? What did you tell Dad?"

What did I tell him? Nothing that I can remember. "I—what was I supposed to say?!" She's getting on my nerves because she is so *right*. I *am* taken for granted, and it's all my fault.

"It's alright, Clo, it's who you are. You have to understand that about yourself. You're a good person, and people are going to take advantage."

"But—but these are people I love! People who are closest to me." Tucker's astonished reaction when I confronted him about cheating crosses my mind, and then stays there. He, too, took me for granted. He thought I should be cool about it. Cool about it!

Am I really bringing this upon myself?

"You'll be okay, sis. The good ones always win in the end," Fiona says as a matter of goodbye. "But it doesn't hurt to fight the bad people, once in a while."

Fighting the bad people? I don't know about that.

Besides, there are no bad people in my life.

I hang up, confused and slightly disappointed from my call with Fiona. I don't feel better. If anything, I feel worse.

Easy Monday has outdoor seating next to the river, and after I pick up my obligatory Road to Heaven from Millie at the counter ("You look like you need a Back From Hell, but you're the boss", she said), I sit at a table hidden behind a large hydrangea in full bloom. Stretching my legs in front of me, taking a deep breath, I force myself to be in the moment. Nothing else exists other than the sunrays warming my skin, the river flowing peacefully below me, the hum of the bees feasting on the light pink, oversize flowers right behind me.

This moment is perfect.

"I've talked him into going to Lamaze with me." The grating voice shrills through the morning, zinging through my system like an electric shock.

Gisele. Gisele is sitting within earshot, talking to someone on the phone, oblivious to my presence right behind the hedge of flowers.

Lamaze? That's prenatal exercises, right? Isn't that for couples to attend together? Is she talking about Justin? Is he going to hold her, accompany her breathing exercises?

Does that mean he's preparing to be in the delivery room with her?

That would make sense, right?

Does that mean he'll whisper sweet little nothings to her when the time comes to deliver the baby? Hold her hand?

Oh god, god!

Of course he will. He's that kind of person.

"We're working on becoming a family," Gisele says and my heart stutters, my body goes cold. "We're going to couple's therapy... He's changed, since I'm back in his life, and... our child has matured him. I know he'll be a *wonderful* father. Very present."

My heart hammers in my rib cage, my breathing constricts, and the table looks like it's twirling below me. I lower my head between my knees, trying to get some air in, trying to shut off the outside world.

Couples' therapy?

Justin did mention going to see a therapist. I didn't ask questions. Maybe I should have. Maybe I'm not seeing what's right in front of me.

What else does a perfect dad do? My mind goes down a deadly path, filling with images that torture me. Justin sleeping on a cot in Gisele's apartment so he can help with night feedings.

I mean, why not? She doesn't have the support of her own family. So, who else? Justin won't let her deal with this alone. He's not that kind of person.

And who will change the baby after the feeding?

Oh god. I can just see it. Her breastfeeding, him plucking the child from her carmine nipples as she lulls back to sleep, changing the baby so she can get some rest.

Her arousal at the sight of Justin's bare chest, all muscles and tats, taking care of their child. What woman wouldn't want him?

His gaze trailing on her offered breasts. What man could be insensitive to that?

One thing will lead to another...

I mean, *of course*. What was I thinking?

We were supposed to be a one-night stand anyway. Life threw us back together, and okay, we have great chemistry, but between me and the mother of his child? I don't stand a chance. The man used to have a different woman in his bed every... what? Week? Day? Who knows?

If he's going to commit to someone, it'll be the mother of his child, not little old me.

I don't want to fight.

It's just not who I am.

I don't want to be the nagging girlfriend. So what if he goes to Lamaze and couples'—*couples!!*—therapy. Isn't that his right?

I've been so *stupid*.

Again.

Tears blurring my vision, I leave my coffee on the table and run back home, not caring who sees me or what state I'm in. I didn't think my legs could carry me, but somehow I find myself at the cottage, clearheaded enough to shoot a quick email to Aunt Dawn and Scott Johnson about "something coming up" and the close on the restaurant needing to be "rescheduled."

No date, nothing.

I need to clear my head before making more decisions. Before I box myself into a situation I won't be able to get out of.

I shut my phone off, get in the car, and drive aimlessly the rest of the day, thinking.

CHAPTER FORTY-SEVEN

Justin

I'm in my office, crossing off my to-do list, when Cassandra comes in uninvited and sits in front of me. *Schedule next community dinner. Check.*

"So, how does it feel, being in Chloe's shoes these days?" she asks.

"What now?" *Place job announcements for extras during foliage. Check.*

"I hear the Wards and you had a conversation last night? And Chloe's parents were there too?"

I sit back in my chair, twirling my pen, wondering where she's going with all her questioning.

"And I was at Easy Monday this morning." She scrutinizes my face. "No? Nothing?"

"You lost me there, Cass," I admit.

"Where's Chloe?"

My blood pressure pumps up. "Why?"

"You don't know where she is?"

"She had a tough night Friday. Like you said—her parents, the Wards. Lots of things came out in the open. Weekend was crazy busy at the restaurant. She's sleeping it out."

"Not anymore she's not."

"What's going on?"

"You know who I saw at Easy Monday? Chloe."

I shrug. "It's her favorite hangout. Can you please get to the point? I'm pretty—"

"*And* Gisele."

This doesn't sound good, though I'm not sure how or why. Chloe has been nothing but over the top gracious to Gisele, whether I'm there to witness it or not. "Okay." I throw my pen on the desk and steeple my fingers.

"Gisele was on the phone, or maybe pretending to be. Outside by the river. Right on the other side of the bush where Chloe was sitting. Going on and on about what a wonderful father you're going to be."

Shit.

"Explaining how you're going to couples' therapy—"

What the fuck? "I'm not—"

"Explaining how you're working on becoming a *real* family. How you're going to Lamaze classes together..."

A *real family*? La—what? What the hell is that?

"What the fuck, Cass?"

"Is any of that true, Justin? I'm not judging. It's your right to want to build a life with the mother of your child, instead of with the woman who truly loves you."

I push my chair back and roar, "What the hell?"

"So it's not true. Thank god. Sit."

I'm not sitting. "What happened?" I pull out my phone and call Chloe, but it goes straight to voice mail.

Cassandra continues. "Gisele seems to have a warped relationship with the truth. Her problem, but you are going to have to fix things with Chloe. She was hurt, Justin, deeply hurt. Chloe... she's not like Gisele. She's honest and good to the core. She welcomed Gisele and tried to include her in the community immediately. And surely she did it for you, but she did it, and she was genuine about it. She's not going to understand the depths of manipulation a woman like Gisele might go to." She looks pensively away. "Gisele probably knew Chloe was there and could hear her. She's trying to get rid of her. Did you do a paternity test?"

I'm pacing in my office, texting Chloe frantically, without being specific, just *'Where are you'* and shit like that.

I just need my phone to light up with her name.

"You need to calm down, Justin."

"You just told me the love of my life was smashed to pieces." I throw the phone on my desk.

I think about calling Gisele to confront her.

Then I think better of it.

"Focus on how to build her back up when she comes to you, Justin."

Jesus Christ. Is it that bad? Yes, of course it is. *My Clover.* "Tell me again what Gisele said." And as Cassandra does, I feel in my bones the level of betrayal Clover must have felt. The immeasurable hurt. My whole body is thrumming with a desire for vengeance.

"Think real hard, Justin. Your focus isn't Gisele, it's Chloe."

She's right. Clover's the only one who means anything to me.

The only one who means *everything* to me.

"How bad do you want her?"

A hollow sensation deepens where my Clover tattoo is etched on my skin. Where my heart beats, now frantically. The void is dizzying.

"I need her, Cass. She's truly my other half. I'm nothing without her." My eyes sting.

Cassandra stands, her dreamy smile plays on her face, the one she has when she's up to something, but fuck if anyone knows what it is. "Then make it happen."

I stare at her as she leaves the room. "Make *what* happen?" I say to her back.

She looks over her shoulder at me. "You'll figure it out."

Make *what* the fuck happen. Tell her it's not true?

She knows that. There's no way. Why would she think I'd do all that shit with Gisele and not tell her?

She was tired is all.

After the weekend she had, no wonder.

Shit.

Now it hits me.

Friday night she found out her father pretty much lied to her for a big chunk of her life. Even when she came to work here in Emerald Creek, he didn't find it necessary to be open about what had happened in the past.

Her own parents didn't bother to tell her the whole truth.

Part of her world came crumbling around her. She felt betrayed. She *was* betrayed. She'd been betrayed once before, by her asshole boyfriend.

Now her parents.

And then she hears that bullshit from Gisele.

Fuck.

She must be torn to pieces.

I know what I want with Chloe. I want everything. I wasn't joking when I said I wanted my daughters to look like her.

I want boys too.

With her.

The white picket fence if that's her preference. Or a place in a city if that makes her happier. Hell, I'd learn how to sail a boat around the world for her if that was her jam.

She'll make those decisions when the time comes.

Right now, I need to act fast.

Because when she comes to me—and she will—she needs to see I'm not messing around.

She needs to see, without a doubt, that her and me, we're forever.

I pick up my phone and call my brother Ethan.

"I have a better idea," he says when I tell him my plan. "Lemme talk to Lucas. See you up there in thirty minutes, an hour tops."

Next, I get in my truck and call my parents. Then Autumn.

I spend the rest of the day working like crazy, hurting my back, nicking my finger, sunburning my neck, but with the help of what feels like the whole town, I get it done.

Then I get back to the apartment, take a shower, and wait for Chloe to reach out to me.

And she does.

Chloe:

We need to talk.

CHAPTER FORTY-EIGHT

Chloe

I let myself into Justin's apartment and give Moose a quick scratch between the ears. He looks at me sadly and plops down with a grunt, reading my mood.

The sliding door to the rooftop is open, music from The Green seeping through. I step out.

Justin turns around, his hair bathed in a halo of light, his tan deeper, it seems, his face stern, and worried.

My eyes sting.

It's an unbearable hurt, this needing to leave, through no fault of his own, the beautiful man who now stands in front of me.

It's all because of me—me and my demons.

I can't share him. I can't live in the uncertainty of his feelings, even if he does seem genuine to me. For now.

I fear I'll never know the truth. Recent events have shown I'm not a good judge of character.

I *need* to do this, for my own good.

We don't say anything. We just look at each other for too long moments, as if we're both afraid of what must come now.

He doesn't try to kiss me. He looks at me with concern and care. Then he takes my hand.

He's going to break up with me.

I know it.

It's what needs to happen.

It doesn't make the pain any less, but it comforts me.

This is what we need to do. Two mature adults, doing what's right.

God it hurts. Why does doing the right thing need to hurt so much?

Justin guides me to the railing overlooking The Green, leans on it, his arm loosely around my back, just so I'll stay here and listen to him, it seems.

"This used to be my favorite spot. My favorite time of day," he says in a deep, gravelly voice. The sun has dipped, bathing Emerald Creek in a glow of peace and quiet. "The witching hour. Me standing here, looking down at The Green, at my friends, my community. My world."

The light is truly magical tonight. There's a live band playing covers. The townspeople, many of them my friends as well, are sitting on blankets or swaying to the music, clapping and singing along.

I'll miss them too.

"But my world is different now. It's bigger and wider."

My heart dips. Although I know what he's going to say—a child on the way, a family to build—although I've talked myself into being reasonable, I'm barely able to stand on my legs while my world falls apart.

"I want to show you how different it is," he adds.

Oh no. *God, can this please end now?* "I don't think—I can't. Please." I steady myself on the railing, bracing myself to walk out of his life.

He takes my hand again. "Clover. Come with me." And the way he says it, the way he says Clover, I would follow him anywhere, let him do anything to me, go through hell and back.

And that scares the shit out of me. That I could have a love this strong that just a few words from him and all my resolve goes up in smoke, consumed by the crazy love I've had for him since our first kiss in an elevator.

Moose following us, Justin takes me to his truck, drives us out of Emerald Creek through North Bridge, over hill after hill bathed in deep golden hues. We pass the turn for his parents' farm, continue through meadows, over brooks, past old barns still standing. At the bottom of a hill, a wooden sign indicates 'The Queen's Knoll', and Justin says, "We're here," but he keeps driving steeply up the hill, on a narrowing dirt road meandering under a canopy of trees, darkness slowly shrouding us.

The dirt path ends, and we stop at the edge of the woods. We've been climbing so much, my ears pop. Justin shuts the engine off and steps out of the truck. He quickly rounds it to open my door and lifts me off the seat as if I weighed nothing. My hands find their natural place on his shoulders, and our eyes lock as he twirls me and sets me on the soft grass, the sweet smell of summer soothing me like a slow poison.

God I'm going to miss him.

His throat bobs as he takes my hand and walks me to the very top of the hill. Moose suddenly takes off to follow some animal trail.

"Justin, what—"

"I showed you my world the way it used to be. The way I used to love it." His hand is firmly clasped around mine, his energy soft yet resolute as he pulls me up on the last of the dirt path. "But things change. People change."

My heart bleeds for him too. He doesn't deserve this.

We reach the top of the hill, our silence filled by the trills and hoots and chirps and buzzing of a million insects and small animals. The woods are far behind us now, the sunlit sky blazing crimson, the earth beneath it golden. In front of us, a vast open field spreads out, with views as far as the eye can see—faraway mountains in shades of grays and blues, the silver sky shining its pure openness over us.

As I take this beauty all in, Justin shifts behind me and sets his hands on my shoulders. "This is my queen's knoll."

I saw the sign at the bottom. It said The Queen's Knoll. I'm still confused as to why we're here. "It's beautiful. So peaceful."

He nudges me ahead with a soft press of his hands. Within the high grasses and wild flowers, a path leads to lights softly flickering in the distance. In the quickly setting sun, they shine brighter and brighter as we approach, defining the shape of a house floating way above the ground. I stop in my tracks. "What—?"

"I want to give you the world, Clover. My world. A better, bigger, wider, world. One where you are at the center. One where you never feel constricted. One where you always come first."

What is he saying? My hand shoots up to his, grasping his fingers.

We're standing at the bottom of the house in the meadows. It's not a house. It's the dream of a house.

Thick tree trunks make up an elevated platform. Birch trees loosely design the frame of the house—walls, door, a steepled roof. Ethereal fabric hangs from the branches, forming dreamy walls.

A staircase made of thick logs leads to a doorway framed in garlands of flowers and greens.

Justin takes my hand again and leads me up. As we reach the top, he lifts me, cradles me in his arms, and carries me through the threshold, his hand resting on my bare thigh.

"What are you doing?" I breathe.

"I'm showing my wife her new world. Or—an idea of it."

His *wife?*

"Justin—"

"I know what you've been through, and I know where you're coming from. I know the lies you heard today and the hurt you've felt. And I'm sorry about that. I wish you'd have come to me, but I understand why you didn't." He dips his lips to brush my forehead. "Promise me to *always* come to me now, when you're in pain, or in doubt."

"Justin, what—"

He turns me in his arms so he's holding me upright against and above him, his head tilted back to meet my gaze. "Clover, will you take me as your husband?"

My heart stutters.

"—to worship and protect you—"

Tears fill my eyes.

"—love you and care for you?"

My hands lock behind his nape as my lips open to him.

"Clover, will you take me as the father of your children?" he whispers against my mouth. "I beg you, sweet Clover. Don't leave me. I'm so, so sorry I didn't see how you were being hurt, and I swear, I have no excuse, but I'll make it right by you. You're my queen, and I'll let it be known. No one'll ever mess with you again."

"Justin—"

"As for marrying you, darling Chloe? I knew the night in the elevator that you were the one for me. No one else will do, no one else can fill my heart, nourish my soul, give my life meaning. I'm a shadow of myself without you. And I'm arrogant enough to believe that I'm not such a bad match for you either. If you'll have me."

I blink several times. Where is my resolve? In his arms, in this place, with these words, of course I want to say yes.

"There has never been anyone else, and there'll never be anyone else. And you know it. Follow my lead and don't let your fears steal your life from you. I beg you, Chloe. I will devote my life to proving to you I'm right about that."

I dip my mouth to his, our tongues softly mingling.

He nibbles my lower lip. "Is that a yes?"

I take a shaky breath and whisper, "Yes". My throat is tight, my eyes burn, and my heart is about to explode.

He wraps my legs around his waist and kisses me deeply. "How do you like our new digs, my queen?" he asks when we come up for air.

"Our new digs?"

"Look around you. What do you see?"

I stay in the beauty of his eyes for a little longer, then glance around, returning to the irises in which I want to get lost. "I see open fields and faraway mountains and nothing around for miles and miles."

"How does it make you feel?"

"Free," I answer without thinking.

"That's my wife. That's my Clover. I want you to feel free." He twirls me around once more and sets me on the platform. "This piece of land is ours if you want it. Over there," he points, "is Canada. Over to this side, is Lake Champlain and beyond that, New York. And this peak is Mount Mansfield, the highest in Vermont."

I look around, astonished.

"Way over there, on a clear day, from the window of our master suite upstairs, you'll see Mount Washington–the highest in the Northeast. You deserve nothing less than the top of the world. Let me give it to you."

I let my tears fall freely. I'm not hiding anything anymore.

I almost lost the love of my life because I hid my insecurities, my needs.

Not anymore.

I'm in Boston mode, no bullshit, nothing hidden, and at least with Justin, I'm staying myself for the rest of my life.

So I give him my tears, and my desperation, and my needs, molding my body to his.

He groans. "Stay right here." He jumps off the platform, disappears under it, and pulls an inflated mattress up, then a picnic basket. He climbs back up the log stairs, sets me on my back on the mattress. A shooting star falls through the deepening sky.

"Make a wish," I whisper.

He lays on top of me, lifting himself just enough on his elbows. "Got all my wishes." His hands frame my face, his thumbs rubbing alongside my jaw, his eyes deep in mine. "But I know I come with baggage. An unborn child that's not yours. The child's mother... well, we know who she is. Hopefully she won't be repeating that shit, once I have a talk with her, but I can't guarantee it. What I can promise you, is that you are the center of my universe. Always have, always will be. What I can hope, is that you'll help me raise that child, and we'll give it brothers and sisters soon. But that's up to you... So... is it still yes?" he asks me after a long while of me just gazing into the green of his eyes.

"Y-yes what?" A shooting star traces to his side, then another. Perfect.

The green in his eyes deepens, and his voice comes out raw. "Will you marry me, Clover?"

My heart ba-booms. Do I want to spend the rest of my life with this perfect man? Be cherished by him? Loved by him and love him in return? His limbs tighten around my body, thighs encapsulating my legs, arms cradling me into him, cock digging into my belly.

Another shooting star above us.

Perfection.

His breath tickles the top of my hair, his salty scent turns me to mush. I moan and press my hips harder against him.

He growls. "Babe."

"Mmm?"

"Need a clear answer."

An answer? Oh, right. '*Will you marry me, Clover.*' "God yes."

He takes my mouth in his, wraps one hand on my breast. I keep my eyes open just to see his eyelids hood, then close entirely, the abandon in his features so moving I nearly cry. How could I ever doubt him? From the first time he laid eyes on me, I've always been the only one for him.

We make quick work of our clothes. Justin runs a finger through my center and mutters, "Fuck, you're already wet for me."

"Just take me," I whimper. "Please." I grab him, and his hot and pulsing cock in my hand almost sends me over the edge. He's ready to explode, all for me. Only for me. I let go of him, wrap my legs around his hips, and pull him inside me.

"I'm not gonna last long," he grunts. "Fuck, Chloe, you feel so good."

He dips his mouth to my nipple, and I cry out my release, shaking deliciously under him, not knowing if the shooting stars are in my head or over him.

Then he pumps in and out of me, harder, faster, until he stills and reaches his orgasm with a grunt, and I get to witness the beauty of him coming undone for me, once again.

We fall asleep under the stars, Moose standing guard, and in the morning, we open the picnic basket. Crispy baguette, butter from the farm, a mild cheddar, and apples.

And hard cider.

Life is perfect.

"I should have brought a thermos of coffee. I didn't think we'd sleep here."

"No? Then why the mattress?"

"The mattress was for making love, or fucking, or however else this was going to turn out. I didn't think we'd spend the whole night."

I roll onto my belly. "Are you kidding? This is the most beautiful spot on earth. I'm never leaving."

He chuckles and reaches to caress my cheek. "I heard you postponed the closing on the restaurant."

I blush slightly. "Oh, right. I—I need to... I'll reconfirm."

"Do you still want to buy the restaurant? You know you don't have to."

He knows me so well. "I do, of course I do," I sigh.

"But?"

"I don't know... if it's enough? I feel I've done everything I needed, or close. They don't really need me to do well. With Corine at the helm, it's smooth sailing. Anyone could do my job."

"Then move onto your next adventure. Hire a manager, keep an eye on the restaurant, but move onto something that excites you." He pulls me in for a deep kiss.

"God, I love you so much. I want to stay here my whole life too. Can this day just never end?" I grab the pocketknife we used to cut the cheese, scoot over to one of the birch logs, and start carving our initials.

Justin kneels next to me and watches me, nuzzling my neck. "Have you thought of anything else you'd like to do?"

"Haley told me about her fermentory. I'd love to help her get it off the ground. It's more up my alley than the restaurant business."

"You would be successful in anything you set your mind to. She'll be thrilled to partner with you."

"Tell me about this land," I say.

"Mom and Dad are giving it to us to build our house on. Away enough from the farm so they won't be in our business, close enough that our kids can run to their grandparents for pie and to help with farm work.

"We can start building when you want. My personal taste? Barn style, four bed, three baths, three car garage with a guest apartment above it, but ultimately, I'll be happiest if you build whatever you want. I spoke with Lucas. He gave me numbers I like, and I think you'll like too. When you're ready, Thalia will design, and Autumn will help you decorate.

"I know Haley is already working with them on designs for the fermentory that would be a couple miles away from our site—if you want this site—which is close enough that you can ride your ATV or horse or snowmobile or fatbike or whatever you'll want to ride to go to work. I'm making Shane partner. He'll move into the apartment as soon as our house is ready.

"For the wedding, all up to you babe, but as far as I'm concerned, the sooner the better, and just so you know, there's no waiting period in Vermont, so we can get married tomorrow if you like. Again, up to you. I know there are a lot of fancy wedding venues, and maybe your folks will want something upscale, but no way, and I mean no way, are they paying for anything—I don't care that you're their first daughter getting married—so if you want a fancy wedding venue then maybe we'll hold back on the guest apartment or the third bathroom or both. Depends on how fancy you want it."

I drop the pocketknife, my eyes glued to the carved initials, CS heart JK.

"Too soon?" he asks.

Turning around slowly to face him, I take his face between my hands, and straddle him. "How long have you been planning this?" My eyes search his, uncomprehending. How did I not see this? How was I ready to say goodbye to him?

"Too much?" he answers. His hands land on my hips and trail up to my back. "It'll be whatever you want, Clover, just a few ideas I been playin' with."

I lower my mouth to his as his hand makes its way under my dress.

"You're not saying anything, Clover. Give me somethin'."

I wrap my arms tightly around his neck and say, peppering kisses all over him, "Wedding on our land. Three weeks from now. Foliage will be perfect, give us time to plan. Everything else, what you said."

CHAPTER FORTY-NINE

Justin

Sunshine's hoofs sound on the dirt road, and Moose lets out a happy yap.

I let go of Chloe and turn to see Dad in the distance, slowly making his way to us, the image of contentment.

"I think I'll commute by horse," Chloe whispers next to me.

I tug her against my side, kiss her temple, then we both stand and straighten our clothes before Dad is close enough to fully measure how fun last night was. I straighten the mattress and let it slide down the opposite side of the platform.

"Thought it was time for coffee!" Dad hollers from afar.

We wave back to him, and he pushes Sunshine to a trot. As he gets closer, all I can see is the wide smile on his face.

He dismounts, ties Sunshine to the platform, and pulls various paper bags from his saddle bag. "Are you going to invite me in?" he jokes.

Chloe giggles.

"I take it she said yes?" Dad asks me as he climbs the makeshift stairs.

"She did." The solemnity of the moment hits me, and tears fill my eyes.

"Welcome to the family, darling," Dad says, hugging Chloe. "Brought you breakfast. Fresh croissants from Christopher, a Road to Hell or whatever Millie calls'em, and a couple apple cider donuts."

We sit cross-legged on the platform.

"Oh wow, you shouldn't have gone to such trouble," Chloe says, taking her Road to Heaven with anticipation. "Ohmygod, you got us Millie's thermoses, and she *marked* them for us?" she shrieks. The thermoses have our names in Millie's handwriting, in her signature purple color.

"That's right, I shouldn't. And I didn't. This all came to me."

"What do you mean, Dad," I say as I grab the double espresso with my name on it, remove the lid, and dunk the croissant in the steaming hot liquid. I close my eyes to enjoy this pure perfection.

"Word got around. Cassandra did some work. All's well that ends well. Everyone came to the farm to get the scoop and see how you were doing. Bearing gifts."

Chloe narrows her eyes on Dad, as puzzled as I am.

"You're gonna have to be more specific," I say.

He chews his croissant slowly, washes it down with a loud gurgle of coffee, and sets his eyes on me. "Cassandra talked to Gisele. Gisele admitted you weren't the father. She left town."

The news hits me like a freight train. This I was not expecting. Is it even true?

Chloe meets my gaze, and she seems alarmed.

"Paternity test will confirm it, but Cassandra didn't seem to think there was any funny business this time."

"But—why?" Chloe asks.

Dad shrugs. "Not the sharpest tool in the shed in some aspects, surely has a twisted relationship with the truth, but also, trying to do what's best for her kid." He takes another bite of croissant, and adds, "She told Cassandra she wanted the best for her baby, and you'd be the best father from... you know... her *pool of applicants*," he ends on a chuckle.

"Oh my god," Chloe mutters. "I feel bad for her baby."

"Nah, she's resourceful. She'll figure it out," Dad says.

I blink several times, trying to get accustomed to having this weight lifted off me. "Not your problem, baby," I say, leaning into Chloe, not believing the goodness that I'm going to be sharing my life with. "Do you believe her?" I ask Dad, pointing at Chloe.

"She's the best of the best, son. Has to be, to deal with you," he adds, his eyes dancing with laughter.

Chloe laughs and I can't help but join in. Being ribbed by my father and my future wife together?

The best.

That evening, we're back at the cottage. And after I make us maple mint cocktails that are brutally deceptive in this heat. After Chloe doesn't clue in to the deception part and asks for more.

After we dine on barbecued chicken thighs that I've been marinating for two days in beer and apple cider vinegar. After we taste a new sauce I've been working on and she gives me her approval by insisting it would taste better coming straight out of her mouth, which I try and agree.

After we dig into a tub of ice cream from the farm, and Chloe decides the only way to prevent brain freeze is for her to eat her ice cream out of my mouth, which she does, straddling me and sloppily dropping ice cream on her cleavage and demanding I lick it clean.

After I oblige.

After all that, I lift her in my arms and take her to the field where I parked my truck.

"What are you doing?" She giggles, slightly tipsy.

"I put a mattress in my truck bed."

"Why?"

"Setting you on a mattress in my truck."

"Why?"

"So you're nice and comfortable."

Another fit of giggles as I set her on her feet while I bring the tailgate down. "But why?"

"So I can make love to you in my truck. That alright?"

Her gaze goes dark. "Oooo... come here. I want your *cock* inside me," she says, making the word ring. Then she slides to the ground, her fingers fumbling with my zipper.

Mmm. Tipsy Chloe has a filthy mouth. Nice to know. I lift her easily, climb inside the truck and set us on the mattress. "Now who's a dirty little girl."

She pulls her T-shirt above her head, her wild hair cascading around her face, her mouth open, and her heavy eyes falling on my lips. She frees her breasts—the little minx has another front clasp bra—and presses them between her hands. Then she lands on me, alcohol getting the better of her unsteady balance. "Fuck me, Justin. Fuck me like you mean it."

"I always mean it," I growl, making quick work of her shorts and my jeans.

"Show me those tats."

I pull my shirt off, and she goes for the Clover tattoo, licking it. "I'm tattooed on your heart," she slurs.

"Babe, you okay?"

"Just fuck me."

So I set her on her back on the mattress so she can see the stars. There's a blanket folded on the side for later. We're both stark naked. I've been waiting for this for a long time. The weather had to be perfect, warm night and clear skies. The moon had to be close to full—I want to see her.

Tonight is perfect. "I love you," I say and kiss her long and sweet and deep while her hips sway under mine. Her legs latch around my waist, pulling me to her.

Tipsy Chloe isn't into foreplay. Now, granted, this whole evening was foreplay.

My dick is at her wet entrance, teasing her. "Tell me how you want it."

As she opens her sweet mouth to answer, I focus entirely on her, on what she wants, on what she needs.

And I feel great doing only that.

I'm done with guilt.

I'm just looking at a lifetime of making her happy. Since our first night together, I've known she was the one for me. I just had to let go of the load of crap I'd saddled myself with and give in to the promise of us.

One week later

I'm so proud of her. My Clover. She's standing at the entrance of the restaurant, holding the oversized pair of scissors, lent by the Chamber of Commerce, on the green ribbon closing the entrance, flashing her smile to the press assembled by Alexandra and making sure they all get a perfect shot of her looking at them as she cuts the ribbon.

When she does, and the ribbon falls under the applause of the small crowd, I pull on the string to reveal the new name to the restaurant:

Clover's Nook

Unable to contain my excitement any further, I grab her by the waist and kiss her in front of everyone.

Fuck it feels good.

"Get a room!" my younger brothers holler.

"Finally!" Ethan bellows over them.

"Come here," Clover says, grabbing my hand and pulling me inside. Seeming to remember we have an audience, she turns around and announces, "Please come in and admire the fantastic work of Thalia and Lucas!" just as waiters I've never seen start passing champagne flutes.

"Who are these people?" I whisper into her ear.

"I hired extras for the event. I want my staff to have fun here tonight!" She pulls me toward the office, then turns around and points at the ceiling. "Look."

Thalia and Lucas exposed the original brick of the walls, and to make it cozier, they attached birch branches to the ceiling. Our initials are carved on one of the branches. "So I can see it coming out of the office." Chloe smiles. "Isn't it cool? I might want to work here for the rest of my life just to see that every night."

I curl her inside my arms. "You'll see a lot more of me, my sweet darling, but if working here every day is what brings you joy, then so be it."

Her cheeks turn pink. "You sent those flowers, didn't you?" she asks, her gaze drifting to the bar, where a massive bouquet of blush roses takes up... a lot of space.

Randy did good. "Why do you have to ask? Do you have a secret admirer?"

"There was no note." She pretends to pout. Adorable.

I nibble her bottom lip. "Oh, I see what it is. My Clover wants written declarations."

"Always," she whispers in my ear. "Flowers die, but your words don't."

Duly noted. From now on, Clover will be getting a love note every week, wherever she is.

"Chloe!" Ethan takes Chloe in a warm bear hug as we walk back to the crowd. "Congratulations—and welcome to the family."

Chloe blushes slightly as she stays under Ethan's friendly arm. She turns her head up at him. "I hear congratulations are in order for you too?" She gives him a huge smile. "Or is it too early?"

Congratulations about what?

"Not too early. Actually, I wanted to book a table here. To... celebrate. When can you fit us?"

She pulls her phone out and starts typing in it. "For you, anytime. Tomorrow?"

"What are you celebrating?" I ask my brother.

He glances toward the door and smiles at one of our friends joining our group. "Our engagement."

My jaw literally drops open. "Your what?"

"You heard me."

"You got engaged? When?"

"Last night." As Chloe steps away from him, he opens his arms and pulls our friend in.

"Wait—what—how did this happen? When?"

"Been ten years in the making, dude. You just had your head way too much up your ass to notice."

"You got that right," Haley says, worming herself between the new couple. "When's the wedding?"

"Ours is first," I grunt, pulling Chloe tight against me.

And for some reason, everyone laughs.

Sneaky Ethan! While his brother was fighting his demons to find his happily ever after, the oldest of the King brothers reconnected with his soul mate.

Read all about his "short" visit to his hometown in Return To You (scan below). Flip to the next page here for the opening chapter.

Not ready to say goodbye to Chloe and Justin yet? As a thank your for signing up to Bella's newsletter, click here for an extra chapter, type www.bellarivers.com/bonus-scene-tpoy, or scan this QR code:

Keep reading for the opening chapter of Return To You.

Return To You

CHAPTER ONE

"Ethan? Holy fuck, man!" The voice jolts me, and I nearly spill gas on the bike's tank. It was bound to happen. I just didn't think I'd be recognized as soon as I rolled into Emerald Creek.

I'm technically not even there yet. I stopped for gas on the side of the road when the village was in sight. I need a minute to gather myself.

I hang the dispenser back and turn to face whoever it is calling my name. Long, assured steps. A big smile on someone's face that used to sport a frown.

"Colton, man." I extend my hand, but he grabs me in a bear hug and slaps my back.

"Fuck! It's been what? Five, six years?"

"Ten."

He pauses, starts to say something, then stops.

I *was* here, five, six years ago. Not gonna forget that. I just spent the short time drunk so it would go by faster.

But now is different.

I'm different.

"What brings you back?" He glances at my bike. "Visiting your old digs?"

"It's Ma's birthday."

"Oh nice. I didn't know. When is it?"

"Sunday."

"I didn't know," he repeats himself. "Ten years, wow."

"I see 'em now and then," I say, feeling the need to justify myself. To explain that I'm not a complete piece of shit who walked out on his family and never saw them again.

"Yeah-yeah-yeah. Craig—uh, your dad—he likes to brag. 'Bout where they went to visit you." He lets out a short, kind laugh. "What was it...uh... Greece. Turkey. Germany?"

Yup, ten years in the Air Force, you get to see some pretty awesome places. Some not so great, too, or less exotic.

I see my siblings, too, but less often. I always find myself on a mission on Christmas and Thanksgiving, and I never complain about it. I've been known to volunteer a lot.

But I need to put an end to that.

The reasons I ran away? They're making less and less sense to me now, and that's why I'm able to come back.

I blamed myself for the accident that badly injured my brother and took his passenger's life. I wasn't driving, I wasn't at the scene, but at the time I thought, for sure, if I'd done something different that night, said something different, it wouldn't have happened.

Now that I've seen combat and operations, I can tell you: shit goes wrong all the time, and there's fuck nothing you can do about it, even with the best planning, even when you anticipate all that shit. There's more shit coming at you. And there's nothing else you can do than do your best.

So, running scared from a little town in Vermont because you think you messed up? Not worth it. We only have one life to live.

Hey, even the girl who broke my heart is gone. Married, lives in Texas. There's no chance I'll run into her. Hell, running into her brother first thing is the closest I'll get to a past that's way behind me now.

"It's good to see you, Colt. This your place now?" It's a rhetorical question. Colton used to work here, but he's clearly the owner now, judging by the name painted on the facade. Funny how things change.

The garage I'm looking at is nothing like I remember. Gone is the junk in the front. In its place, a vintage baby blue Chevy. The gas pumps are still old as dirt, but they seem in good working order. They're clean, and there's rags and stuff to clean the windshields. Hell, the small office even has potted flowers that someone seems to water.

"Nice bay you got there." The main improvement is in the garage, and Colton straightens proudly at my words.

"Thanks, man." Colton was never a talker.

My tank full, I place the pump back and pocket my credit card. "Business is good?"

"Doin' good. How 'bout you? Where'd you live now?"

"Right now, the back of my bike. Next up, hoping for somewhere warm."

Colton doesn't ask questions. Just lifts his chin and pats my bike. "Two thousand eighteen?" He crouches to take a look at the exhaust.

I nod. "Been giving me a little rattle, but other'n that, she runs smooth."

"Bet she does. Drop her off whenever, I'll take a look at that rattle."

"Careful, might take you up on that."

He unfolds his frame and lays an unsettling gaze on me. "Yeah. Hope you do." He takes a step back, and I straddle my bike, grab my helmet. "Never took you as a bike guy," he drops.

"Never thought I'd be one. Just wanna make sure I don't settle in a place with six months of winter," I say with a grin. "No offense."

He gives me a full smile. "None taken. I get it, man. No risk of that with a ride like this."

Yeah, that's partly why I bought it.

We're saved from the awkward moment between us by a teenage girl wearing blue coveralls, her hair in a bun on top of her head, calling from the mouth of the bay. "Yo, Colt! I'm all done here. What next?"

"Just a sec," Colton calls back to her.

She walks to us, wiping her hands in a greasy rag, and eyes me top to bottom, a frown on her face, like she's trying to place me. She does look vaguely familiar. "Hey."

"Hey," I answer.

Colton tips his chin at me. "You know who this is?"

She tilts her head. "Maybe?"

"Surprised a hockey girl doesn't know her legends."

The girl's mouth gapes. "Hold on. *Ethan King*?" she asks tentatively.

Colton nods. "Taught me blocking like no coach ever has."

I look at him in surprise, but he's still looking at her. "No way," she says, her eyes like saucers on me. "*The* Ethan King who took us to Nationals?"

"The one and only," Colton answers.

"Coach will be stoked to know you're in town. Can I tell him?"

"Coach Randall?" I can't believe he's still around. Ten years is a lifetime for me. I suppose at his age, it's nothing. "He must be what—a hundred years old?"

The girl laughs. "I won't tell him you said that."

"Yeah, I wouldn't either."

"He'd have me benched. But hey, you'll come to the Arena, right? Do some training with us? We have preseason camp soon."

Being pulled into my hometown's life is exactly what I don't want. Just as I bought a bike to prevent me from settling in the Yankee part of the country if I can help it, I gave myself a hard rule of not sticking around too long. Not getting sucked in.

"I'll probably be gone, but if I can, I'll stop by." I don't want to crush her hopes.

"Cool. I'll tell Coach," the girl says as she saunters back to the bay, pulling her phone from her pocket.

Ah shit. I guess there's no getting around saying hello to the old man. And what's wrong with that, anyway? Except that I was hoping to make my stay here painless. Absent of memories. I'm not big on nostalgic reunions.

The girl comes back running to us. "Mr. K, can I get a selfie?" She nudges herself against me, holding her phone at arm's length.

Colton frowns. "You don't have to, man."

I smile toward the phone while the girl takes several pictures. I'm not used to fake-smiling—or smiling—and my cheeks kinda hurt.

"Thanks!" The girl runs back to the bay and shouts out to Colton. "Boss, gonna start on the Bronco?"

"Not without me you're not. Be just a sec."

"I should go," I say.

"It's okay. She's just messing with me. Funny girl."

"She looks familiar. Do I know her?"

Colton shrugs. "I doubt it—she's barely fifteen. Tracy Prescott. Big family. They live above Chandler's Knoll. Dad's with Fish and Game."

I suppose I know the family. That's what life in a small town is like. Everyone's linked one way or another. You can't step foot anywhere without meeting someone you know.

The feeling sits uncomfortably in the pit of my stomach. On base, people come and go all the time. You quickly learn to make new friends or risk having no friends at all. You're also free to feed them whatever backstory you make up for your own sorry life, and no one cares if you're pretending to be who you're not, as long as you do an honest job and buy a round of beers every once in a while.

Here, there's no escaping who you are. Your past. Your present actions. People's opinions on what your future should look like. Who you're with, who you should be with, and especially—*especially*—who you *shouldn't* be with.

I roll out of Colton's garage on an empty promise of a beer together, feeling a little bit like a jerk. Why did I need to tell him about not wanting to settle here? And why did I agree to a beer at my brother's pub, when I know darn well I'm going to find an excuse to get out of it? The last thing I want is to hear about his sister, and she's bound to come up in conversation if we share a drink.

I take the long way alongside the river, down Deweys' Hollow. I thought this would be a fun bike ride—and it is—but *fuck*. So many memories suddenly resurfacing.

Heading back into the village through the covered bridge, I notice how the downtown looks busier than I expected. There's a banner across main street announcing the town fair this Saturday, and another one congratulating Christopher Wright for being New England's Best Baker. *Shit, Chris won New England's Best Baker? That's huge. Colton must be proud of his cousin.*

Main street is crawling with stop-and-go traffic and jaywalkers. A car pulls out of a parking spot in front of a flower shop where the video store used to be.

I slide in and minutes later, I'm walking out with a gorgeous bouquet that set me back... a lot. But hey. I've missed so many of Mom's birthdays, I can splurge a little.

"Well if it isn't Ethan King in the flesh!"

I look down to the petite woman in a modest flowery dress. "Ms. Angela!" I bend down to hug her, the instinct strong, then hesitate. Is it appropriate to hug your third-grade teacher?

"Come here, you big goof!" She takes me in a strong hug that surprises me. "Are these for me? Why, you shouldn't have," she says, laughing.

I laugh with her. "They're for Ma."

She frowns. "She didn't mention you were coming."

"It's a surprise," I confirm.

She rolls her eyes and looks around, at the line in front of the ice cream place—now expanded to cover the corner of the block— at the patrons going in and out of the general store—looking spiffy with fresh paint and overflowing window boxes—at the people sifting through boxes of books on sale in front of the bookshop. "Well, if you want to keep this a surprise, you should get there before she hears it from someone else." She gives me a friendly tap on the arm. "I'll see you later!"

By the time I get to the farm, I've seen a new coffee shop, a sign for the hotel I didn't even know we had, the bookshop with a new, weird name, my brother Justin's pub packed with patrons at their outdoor seating, and a restaurant right next to it that I don't remember. There are signs for a hot dog shack, the local history museum, an art exhibit, a summer fair, numerous kids' camps.

The town is hopping and nothing like I remember it. It makes me happy and vaguely unsettled at the same time. Like there's something important that I'm missing.

After the covered bridge, it's a familiar ride up to the farm on a winding road that's fucking fun on a bike. King Knoll's Farm soon spreads ahead, and a gentle hum takes ahold of me.

It's about time I'm able to come back here and visit.

Even if I'll never live here, it'll be nice to feel normal when I come.

Although I never wanted to work on the farm, even if I've been gone too long, I still want to be part of the family again. I'm done being a loner. I have three brothers and a sister who all but idolize me. A mom and dad who adore me.

I have no business staying away any longer.

Case in point. I hear Mom's shrieks of pure happiness the minute I take my helmet off. She runs to me and lunges into my arms, and I twirl her around.

You'd think I'd gone to war or something.

"Awww..." she says, at a loss for words, pinching my cheeks. She searches my eyes, and I know she's wondering. She's wondering if I'm here by accident, or if I remembered her birthday.

She still thinks I'm disconnected from the family. From her.

I grab the flowers from the saddle pocket and shove them into her hands. "Happy Birthday, Mom." Then I set back, prepared to memorize her look of disbelief and bliss and gratefulness all mixed together as she goes through the different stages a mother, I suppose, experiences at the return of the prodigal son.

"Bir...?" She looks at the flowers. At me. Squints. Tucks her nose in the flowers. "Mmm. They smell good. Why, thank you!" Then she tucks her arm under mine and takes us up the front porch. "Craig, guess who's here!" she says, shoving the flowers in a dark corner of the kitchen.

"Well, looks who's here," Dad echoes, taking me into a brief hug and slapping my back. "Why didn't you call? What brings you here?" His eyes are dancing. At least he's happy.

"Ma's birthday," I proudly announce.

"Who wants lemonade?" Ma butts in.

"Your Ma's birthday, huh? Which one?"

Oh fuck. This isn't good. Maybe it's a test? "Her...big one?" I'm pretty sure Mom is turning fifty this year. Does she not want to celebrate? Shit.

Dad chuckles, crosses his arms, and bounces on his heels. "You missed it."

"Oh f—darn." I glance at Mom, who's arranging the flowers in a vase now. "Sorry—was it last week?"

Dad is having a field day. "It was last *winter. January.* But since you're here, you could stay 'til her next birthday."

Mom looks up, hopeful.

"Next January?" I ask stupidly.

"That's typically how birthdays work. Come back like clockwork on the same day every year."

Mom sets the vase on the dining table, then hugs me. "I don't care, honey. Long's your here, I'm happy." She tilts her head back, her eyes brimming with true joy.

I hug her tighter. "Well, Happy Wednesday," I say and feel her laugh against my chest.

Her voice returns muffled. "Happiest Wednesday ever."

Minutes later, we're seated on the front porch, sipping lemonade in stem glasses—"because it's my birthday," Mom said. "Now, tell us all about what you been up to," she adds.

And I do. I catch them up from our last long phone call, up to now, when I'm between assignments.

"So what's next?" Dad asks.

"I requested orders for a billet at Hulbert Field." I don't tell them that's my second choice. My first choice, I don't get to request it. I'd be tapped on the shoulder. I'd be fucking great at it, but the brass will think I'm too young.

Mom frowns. "Hulbert Field?"

I nod. "Florida."

"Florida?!" she beams. "Why that's closer than Germany! Still the crypto thingy?"

"Yep. Cryptoanalysis and SINGINT."

"I bet you're great at it."

I nod. "I am." I'm fucking great at it. No reason not to say it.

I'm proud of what I'm doing. I've always wanted to do the right thing. To have an impact. That's why I joined the Air Force.

"No way you could do that with the Green Mountain Boys, huh?' she asks, referring to the Air National Guard in Burlington.

Dad does the chin lift.

"Nah, they specialize in combat. Look, end of the day, I'll go where I'm needed. I can tell you as much, I won't be needed here." My last words ring awkwardly, at least to me. I don't know if Mom and Dad ever fully understood why I left, back in the day. How I felt I had let my family down, messed up so spectacularly I had no other option than to leave and enroll in order to finally do something fucking useful. I've come around since then.

Mom stands and gathers our empty glasses. "Well, Hulbert would be stupid not to hire you," she says before going back inside.

The landline trills, then Mom's voice distant voice reaches us.

Dad crosses his arms and squints at me. "Proud of ya. Even if Florida is... kinda far."

"Same time zone. And I'd have a guest room."

"Yeah, that'd be nice. Florida. For your mother's birthday."

I tilt my head and smile. "Florida in January. You gotta admit. Better'n Vermont."

"Warmer," Dad concedes.

That afternoon, I join my siblings—Justin, Haley, Logan, and Hunter—at Clark's Meadow, where the town fair is being held this upcoming weekend. Everyone who can is helping to set up tents. My brothers and sister throw themselves at me, and before I can get too emotional, I ask them what to do.

We end up erecting tents for hours, setting up a base for bleachers that haven't been delivered yet, and lining up porta-potties.

I make it sound like it was a pain in the neck, but honestly? Best fun I've had in years.

We get home just in time for my brothers to take care of a few chores while Mom makes a fuss about settling me in the new guest room they arranged in the finished basement.

My childhood bedroom has been turned into an office. The pine shelf running across the small end of the room where I had my trophies and my favorite books is now stacked with accounting binders. With the way I left, I'm not going to ask where my stuff is.

When I get out of the shower, the waft of pot roast hits a tender spot. I surprise Mom in the kitchen, grab her from behind and give her a quick hug. "You remembered that's my favorite dish, or is that your Wednesday night special?"

"It is *not* a Wednesday night special." She turns to face me, her eyes misty. She opens her mouth to say something, then closes it.

"I'll set the table," I say to clear the moment. I need to occupy myself or else stuff is going to start choking me. Stuff like missing books and pot roast and how some things change—like people—and others never do—like feelings.

Haley joins us, followed by Justin. His huge dog, Moose, sprawls with a sigh on the porch as we take our seats around the farmhouse table. The whole King family is around the table for the first time in a very long time.

"So," Justin says once we start digging in our heaping plates, "How long you here for this time?"

I finish my mouth, wipe my lips, rinse the pot roast with beer. "It's kinda open right now. Don't have a timeline yet."

Mom gasps, Haley freezes with her glass of wine midair, and my three brothers stop their chewing.

Dad rubs his nose. "You can stay here as long as you like. I'll keep you busy."

I know what he means. He's disappointed I never considered working on the farm, but I think—I hope—deep down he understands where I'm coming from. The need to be useful in a grand way.

Mom shrieks and drops her fork. "Ohmygod, my baby is staying!" she says and for some reason, everyone laughs.

"Mom—I just said, I didn't know how long I was staying."

Mom waves my comment away. "That's a good start. A very good start."

Seeing the need to redirect the general conversation, Dad turns to Haley to discuss some wine making production of some sort that she wants to start on the farm. Turns out, she has a whole business plan, with projections and market research. She also works on the farm and at my brother Justin's pub in town. I'm impressed by her drive.

Once dinner is over, I stand to clear dishes alongside my siblings. "Thanks for dinner, Ma."

Mom and Dad follow us into the kitchen. With seven of us, we're done cleaning in no time. "That was fast. You finally got everyone trained," I joke, my memory pulling up endless arguments over who was supposed to do what, ended by Dad's threats that whoever didn't help wouldn't get fed the next meal. My joke falls flat, my siblings clearly having no idea what I'm talking about. Or choosing to ignore it entirely.

"I forgot how the days were so long here in the summer," I say to change the conversation but really end up pointing out how much I've forgotten about my hometown. And I'm sorry if it hurts their feelings, I didn't mean it that way, but I still stand by my choice of living my life on different terms.

Dad stores the broom away. "Makes up for the short season. More hours in the day to fit in the work."

"Let's go to the Growler," Logan declares, maybe to change the conversation, but more probably because he does have an itch to go out. He and Hunter are men now. They were the babies in the family, but now they're almost as tall as me and just as strong, if not stronger, judging by the work they did on the fairgrounds today. At dinner, they asked me a dozen questions about my job, life on base, and my next steps, before giving Mom and Dad a full recap of everything that should be done differently for the fair and could Mom just talk to the Events Committee about having axe throwing next year?

"I'm out," Haley says. "You guys have fun."

"Aww come on, Haley," Hunter insists. "Let's go and find you a *decent* boyfriend."

"With you as my sidekicks? No thank you."

I follow up with Dad's last comment before chiming in. "Need me to do something?"

"Nah. Workday's over. You go have a beer with your brothers. It's not like they see you that often." He doesn't mean it like it's a bad thing. He just says it as it is. And he's right.

"Where's that place you wanted to go?" I ask Logan.

"The Growler. It's up in the hills. We can take Justin's truck."

"Why don't we go to Lazy's?" I'm anxious to see my brother's pub, but I'd understand if that's the last place he wants to go tonight. He took the night off, after all. Still, I add, "I wanna check it out."

"Sure," Justin says, holding in a smile, while Hunter and Logan shrug their okays.

"You okay, man?" I ask as we climb into his truck. Justin is the closest to me in age—four years younger. He's also been mostly quiet all evening, except for a couple of questions for me.

He looks at me with a quick smile and shrugs. "Course. Why?"

I wonder if Dad's insinuations about working on the farm got to him too. After all, he also bailed out of the family business to open the only pub in town, the Lazy Salamander. But I don't want to get into that conversation with him. It seems useless. "Nothin'," I answer, and he leaves it at that.

We park on The Green and push the large doors open when we get to the pub. The clatter of dozens of patrons eating and chatting mixed with background music pulls us in. Moose follows us and trots right to the office beyond the bar while Justin guides us to a booth.

Lazy's is busy for a Wednesday night in small town America, but nothing that Justin's staff can't handle. His place is large, with high ceilings and dark wood paneling, yet it feels comfortable and homey. It could be the black-and-white photos of locals on the walls, or maybe the dim lighting from the small lamps next to each table. More probably, because of the easy banter that greets us when we walk in.

As soon as we're seated, a round of beers appears on our table, and our server leaves immediately. We sprawl on the comfortable seats, just happy to be together.

"Wow, that's a rare sight." I look up to the soft-spoken man about my age standing at the top of our table.

Shit! "Noah, man!" I stand and we back slap each other. He tilts his chin at my brothers. Memories of AP Math and cramming together in high school mingle with earlier ones of sharing candy in the back of his family's general store.

"Saw you roll into town earlier, and I couldn't believe it. Figured I'd come here to find out." He pushes his glasses up his nose, and warmth spreads through me at the familiar gesture. Noah was the self-assured nerd among us, but being in Emerald Creek, he was outdoorsy, too, and from the looks of him, he still is. "I'll let you catch up with your brothers, but before you leave, you better come in to the store and tell me all about your life, yeah?"

I nod. "I will."

"Cryptoanalysis," he adds with a huge smile. "Damn you."

I laugh. "I'll catch up with you, promise."

The rest of the evening goes by quickly, with people stopping by to greet me and comment about the four King brothers being together.

We get back to the farm around midnight. Hunter and Logan crash right away. Justin lingers, not leaving yet. I take two bottles of beer out of the fridge, making a mental note to go to the store tomorrow and stock up. I'll have to borrow a car.

Didn't think about that when I bought the bike.

We sit on the porch, his big-ass dog at our feet. "So fucking proud of you," I finally tell him after a long silence.

He turns his head to me, bottle midair. "Proud of what?"

I state the obvious. "The way you rebuilt your life. The way you created something for this whole town."

He stares at me. "Anybody did something good with his life, it's you, man. I just sell beer."

He takes a long pull on his beer, then looks away to the dark fields. "Aren't you tired of running away?" he asks softly. With compassion, not accusation. I know what he's talking about. That night that changed everything. When he almost died because of something I did, and the next morning I still left.

But I've learned to forgive myself. And I know Justin carries guilt for that night too. He was wounded, but someone died. "What about you?" I ask him. It was hard not to notice, even from a distance, the electricity coursing between him and a pretty brunette on the fairgrounds. Yet he didn't introduce her to me, and no one brought her up at dinner.

"What about me?"

Maybe I shouldn't broach that topic now. I don't know where he is, mentally. I just got back. "You ever think of settling down?"

"Settling down?"

"Yeah. Having what Mom and Dad have. That sounds pretty awesome to me. You?"

"I—I can't do that. Not after what happened. Not after what I did to you. It's just not gonna happen."

I reel back in shock. "Fuck man, what are you talking about?" I look at him, not sure where to even start. "I ran away like a fucking coward when you were in the hospital. I barely knew if you were gonna make it. I can't believe you never said anything about that. *I* failed *you*." Moose sets his big head on my lap. "But you know what? I forgave myself. I was just a kid. I was scared. I messed up. People mess up, bro. The only thing to do is pick up the pieces and keep going."

"Yeah, except not everyone got to do that."

He's talking about the girl who died in the car crash. The one I pushed away, and he picked up. I was selfishly focusing on other stuff, and I did feel guilty, at the time. All the what-ifs. But not anymore. "It wasn't your fault. You almost died to save her. You did everything you could, and more."

"It doesn't matter. I shouldn't have... driven her home."

Fuck. I barely got here, and I have to talk about that night again. And of course I do. It was the night Justin almost died, *and the next morning I still left.*

Mom and Dad made it clear that I shouldn't thwart my own plans because of the accident. I was scheduled to start Officer Training at Maxwell Air Force Base in the next few days. It was enough they had one son whose life was on hold; they didn't want me to give up on my dream career. And so after some negotiating, I left once we knew for sure Justin was out of the woods and it was all about a long, painful recovery for him. *"It's so unfair to him,"* I'd told Mom.

"That's why I need you to go and have the life he won't have. You owe it to him."

And fuck, but my mother telling me these words to help me cope, nearly killed me with guilt. And anger. And powerlessness. All these emotions fighting to bring me down. The guilt was the strongest, and in my young mind, it felt as if my mother couldn't stand the sight of me. As if she knew that if I'd acted differently, Justin wouldn't be lying in a hospital bed. As if it was painted all over my face.

I tried to tell her, tell them—Mom and Dad—I said, *"I should've—"* but Dad cut me off. *"Don't go there, son,"* he'd simply stated, and he never elaborated, so I drew my own conclusions.

Don't go there, or your mother won't stand the sight of you.

Don't go there, or you'll carry the burden of your brother's injuries.

Don't go there, it's too late to do anything now.

Don't go there, but don't stay here either.

Just go. Leave.

Leave us.

They never said any of that, of course, and possibly they didn't think this way either. But in my young mind, that's how it went.

It didn't help that it was also the night the only girl I ever loved broke my heart. In a way, it made it easier to leave Emerald Creek. I could hide my guilt and forget my pain.

I'd make myself as scarce as possible to my family so they didn't have to stare in the eye the person who could have, should have, prevented Justin's accident. And I was never going to see her again.

I never talked about my breakup to anyone, in the years that followed, because it would seem so petty compared to the drama they've all endured. But tonight, even that pain, as petty as it is, digs acutely in my chest. It *is* so petty, and I *am* over it, but reliving that night makes the pain raw again, these two wounds of unequal importance hurting me almost equally.

But I'm here with my brother, and I can do something for him. "We were kids, Justin. You were a baby. But if you want to go down that road, then—you... you did right by her. She came to the party to find me. I should have been looking out for her." The truth is, she came to the party to cause trouble. I took care of it. Who could predict the chain of events that would unfold?

"What do you mean? She was your girlfriend. I hit on your girlfriend. I took her home to get lucky and—"

"She wasn't my girlfriend. I didn't even know where she lived. We'd hooked up once before, and I'd called it off. Then she came onto me a little strong at the party, and I told her off a little strong too. There was nothing between us."

Justin seems lost. "I thought... I thought... I thought that's why you never came back."

"Nah, she wasn't the one," I feel necessary to say, handing him another beer. Trying not to think about the girl who broke my heart. We sit for a while, talking about the girl who died in the crash—who he almost gave his life for, trying to save her. We talk about her parents too. And about the guy who crashed his car into theirs.

I try to dole out a little bit of wisdom without acting like an older brother know-it-all, which I definitely am not. I might feel like I'm in an okay place right now, but I could be wrong. But hey, I'll do anything for my brother. For the little time that I'm here, the least I can do is fix some of the stuff I broke.

We talk a little longer about the accident, and then we call it a night, Justin sleeping on the couch on account of too many beers.

The next couple of days, I stay at the farm, helping Dad fix fences and adjust a wobbly barn door.

Then Saturday, I go to the fair, thinking it's going to be just another day in small town America. Which, in a way, it is.

And in another way, it rocks me to my core.

Read Ethan's story in Return To You.(Scan the QR code below)

Acknowledgements

Much as for Never Let You Go, I owe this book to the support of the amazing indie writing community. I mentioned previously the precious knowledge that established writers generously share in various online groups. Here I'd like to tip my hat to the creators of virtual sprint or co-working rooms in which friendships are created across countries and continents, and where the writing process is a less solitary experience.

Thank you as always to my Redbirds tribe of writers: Teresa Beeman, Ariana Clark, Diana Divine, Michele Ingrid, and Kenna Rey. This book wouldn't be here without your weekly cheer, our constructive discussions, and the friendships of fellow writers who understand each other's struggles and insecurities. Teresa, I am so grateful in particular for your sense of logic and eagle eye in re-reading The Promise Of You days before release and catching persistent inconsistencies and hilarious typos!

Just as for Never Let You Go, this book would not be what it is without the stellar feedback and guidance of my truly amazing developmental editor, Angela James. Thank you so much for the tough love! Writing a book with you in my corner is like jumping off a bridge with a tight bungee rope—now how's that for a cringy metaphor?

Thank you also to Grace Wynter for the wonderful copyedits. You seem to know Emerald Creek better than I do!

Grace and Angela are like fairy godmothers looking over the baby book and fixing everything the mom is doing wrong, with Teresa sweeping in at the last minute to wipe off its snotty nose (the baby book's snotty nose, not the mom's. See, this is why I need editors.)

And for this book in particular, a special thanks to E for her feedback on the restaurant industry, including the fact that there is no such thing as polite language in a professional kitchen.

About the author

Bella Rivers writes steamy small town romances with a guaranteed happily ever after, and themes of found family and forgiveness. Expect hot scenes, fierce love, and strong language!

A hopeless romantic, Bella is living her own second chance romance in the rolling hills of Vermont. When she's not telling the stories of the characters populating her dreams, you can find her baking, hiking, skiing, or just hanging around her small town to soak in the happiness.

Her newsletter is where Bella shares progress on her writing as well as sneak peeks into upcoming books, the occasional recipe from her characters, and books from other writers she thinks her readers might like. You can also find her and interact with her on social media. To subscribe, browse her books, follow along on social, or get in touch, visit www.bellarivers.com

Printed in Dunstable, United Kingdom

WJEC/Eduqas

Religious Studies
for A Level Year 2 & A2

Christianity

Gregory A. Barker

Edited by Richard Gray

Illuminate Publishing

Published in 2017 by Illuminate Publishing Ltd, P.O Box 1160, Cheltenham, Gloucestershire GL50 9RW

Orders: Please visit www.illuminatepublishing.com
or email sales@illuminatepublishing.com

British Library Cataloguing-in-Publication Data

A catalogue record for this book is available from the British Library

ISBN 978-1-911208-36-5

Printed by Barley Print, Cuffley, Herts

06.18

The publisher's policy is to use papers that are natural, renewable and recyclable products made from wood grown in sustainable forests. The logging and manufacturing processes are expected to conform to the environmental regulations of the country of origin.

Every effort has been made to contact copyright holders of material reproduced in this book. If notified, the publishers will be pleased to rectify any errors or omissions at the earliest opportunity.

This material has been endorsed by WJEC/Eduqas and offers high quality support for the delivery of WJEC/Eduqas qualifications. While this material has been through a WJEC/Eduqas quality assurance process, all responsibility for the content remains with the publisher.

WJEC/Eduqas examination questions are reproduced by permission from WJEC/Eduqas

Series editor: Richard Gray
Editor: Geoff Tuttle
Design and Layout: EMC Design Ltd, Bedford

Acknowledgements

Cover Image: © DarrylBrooks / Shutterstock

Image credits:

p. 1 © DarrylBrooks / Shutterstock; p. 7 VenturaStock; p. 8 Freedom Studio / Shutterstock.com; p. 12 © The British Library Board; p. 16 Public domain; p. 17 Andrea Izzotti; p. 25 (top) © National Portrait Gallery, London; p. 25 (bottom) Public domain; p. 27 (top) German Federal Archive; p. 27 (bottom) MamabaB; p. 29 (top) Everett - Art; p. 29 (bottom) ailhumnoi; p. 37 Fotokon; p. 39 Courtesy Carole Raddato; p. 41 Creative commons; p. 43 (left) Morphart Creation; p. 43 (right) Jacob Lund; p. 50 Ritu Manjo Jethani; p. 51 Public domain; p. 53 mangostock; p. 54 Pkpix; p. 55 (top) Senderistas; p. 55 (bottom) juliasudnitskaya; p. 63 (top) Ms Jane Campbell; p. 63 (bottom) Renata Sedmakova; p. 65 Jesus House; p. 66 (top) FCI; p. 66 (bottom) Courtesy Instant Apostle, photo by David Salmon; p. 68 The Church of England; p. 75 Creative commons; p. 76 wjarek; p. 77 (top) steaheap; p. 77 (bottom) Everett Historical; p. 78 remore; p. 79 Creative commons; p. 81 Creative commons; p. 82 Creative commons; p. 83 Mark Waugh / Alamy Stock Photo; p. 90 Alastair Wallace; p. 91 (top) AF archive / Alamy Stock Photo; p. 91 (bottom) CURAphotography; p. 92 (top) ONS; p. 92 (bottom) Courtesy British Humanist Association; p. 93 World Religious Photo Library / Alamy Stock Photo; p. 94 Courtesy British Humanist Association; p. 95 Public domain; p. 97 (top) Ms Jane Campbell / Shutterstock.com; p. 97 (bottom) Philippe Hays / Alamy Stock Photo; p. 104 (left) Albert H. Teich; p. 104 (middle) Creative commons; p. 104 (right) Courtesy Joanna Collicutt McGrath; p. 105 Andrey Khachatryari; p. 106 (top) Nando Machado; p. 106 (bottom) Juergen Faelchie; p. 108 OFC Pictures; p. 110 Maximillian Laschon; p. 118 (top) Keystone-France / Contributor; p. 118 (bottom) Public domain; p. 120 http://w2.vatican.va/content/vatican/en.html; p. 121 Universal Images Group North America LLC / DeAgostini / Alamy Stock Image; p. 122 (top) dmitry_islentev; p. 122 (bottom) Mmaxer; p. 123 Georgetown University; p. 124 Solarisys; p. 132 Courtesy World Council of Churches; p. 133 Public domain; p. 134 Courtesy World Council of Churches; p. 136 Courtesy World Council of Churches; p. 137 Renata Sedmakova / Shutterstock.com; p. 138 Courtesy World Council of Churches; p. 139 Public domain; p. 146 tom carter / Alamy Stock Photo; p. 147 By permission from the Apostolic Faith Church of Portland, Oregon; p. 149 (left) Courtesy of Dr Rita Bennett; p. 149 (right) *Nine O'Clock In The Morning* by Dennis Bennett, ISBN 978-0-88270-629-0, used with permission by Bridge Logos Inc. www.bridgelogos.com; p. 149 (bottom) Everett Collection, Inc. / Alamy Stock Photo; p. 150 Courtesy of Patti Gallagher Mansfield, author of *As By A New Pentecost: The Dramatic Beginning of the Catholic Charismatic Renewal*: Golden Jubilee Edition, New Life Publishing, order online at: www.goodnewsbooks.co.uk; by phone: 01582 571011, by post at: Goodnews Books, 296 Sundon Park Road, Luton, Bedfordshire LU3 3AL; p. 151 Dreamstime.com; p. 152 Wordpress; p. 153 Creative commons; p. 154 ZUMA Press, Inc. / Alamy Stock Photo; p. 154 CountrySideCollection – Homer Sykes / Alamy Stock Photo; p. 155 Intervarsity.org; p. 164 (bottom) Catholic News Agency; p. 164 (top) Courtesy of www.DiegoRivera.org; p. 165 Rodolfo Arellano; p. 166 (top) viastas; p. 166 (middle) Fritz Eichenberg; p. 166 (bottom) Courtesy Church Ads; p. 168 Creative commons; p. 169 Creative commons; p. 172 Public domain; p. 179 Margie Politzer

Contents*

*   The contents listed correspond to the Eduqas Full A Level
    Specification which matches the equivalent WJEC A2 Specification as follows:
    Eduqas Theme 1: D,E,F = WJEC Theme 1: A,B,C
    Eduqas Theme 3: A,B,C = WJEC Theme 3: A,B,C
    Eduqas Theme 3: D,E,F = WJEC Theme 2: A,B,C
    Eduqas Theme 4: D,E,F = WJEC Theme 4: A,B,C

About this book

With the new A Level in Religious Studies, there is a lot to cover and a lot to do in preparation for the examinations at A Level. The aim of these books is to provide enough support for you to achieve success at A Level, whether as a teacher or a learner, and build upon the success of the Year 1 and AS series.

Once again, the Year 2 and A2 series of books is skills-based in its approach to learning, which means it aims to continue combining coverage of the Specification content with examination preparation. In other words, it aims to help you get through the second half of the course whilst at the same time developing some more advanced skills needed for the examinations.

To help you study, there are clearly defined sections for each of the AO1 and AO2 areas of the Specification. These are arranged according to the Specification Themes and use, as far as is possible, Specification headings to help you see that the content has been covered for A Level.

The AO1 content is detailed but precise, with the benefit of providing you with references to both religious/philosophical works and to the views of scholars. The AO2 responds to the issues raised in the Specification and provides you with ideas for further debate, to help you develop your own critical analysis and evaluation skills.

Ways to use this book

In considering the different ways in which you may teach or learn, it was decided that the books needed to have an inbuilt flexibility to adapt. As a result, they can be used for classroom learning, for independent work by individuals, as homework, and they are even suitable for the purposes of 'flipped learning' if your school or college does this.

You may be well aware that learning time is so valuable at A Level and so we have also taken this into consideration by creating flexible features and activities, again to save you the time of painstaking research and preparation, either as teacher or learner.

Features of the books

The books all contain the following features that appear in the margins, or are highlighted in the main body of the text, in order to support teaching and learning.

Key terms of technical, religious and philosophical words or phrases

> ### Key terms
> **Canon:** 'measuring rod', 'rule' or 'standard'

Quickfire questions simple, straightforward questions to help consolidate key facts about what is being digested in reading through the information

quickfire

> **1.1** What are the three parts of the Hebrew canon?

Key quotes either from religious and philosophical works and/or the works of scholars

> ### Key quote
> The main burden of the kerygma is that the unprecedented has happened: God has visited and redeemed His people. (C. H. Dodd)

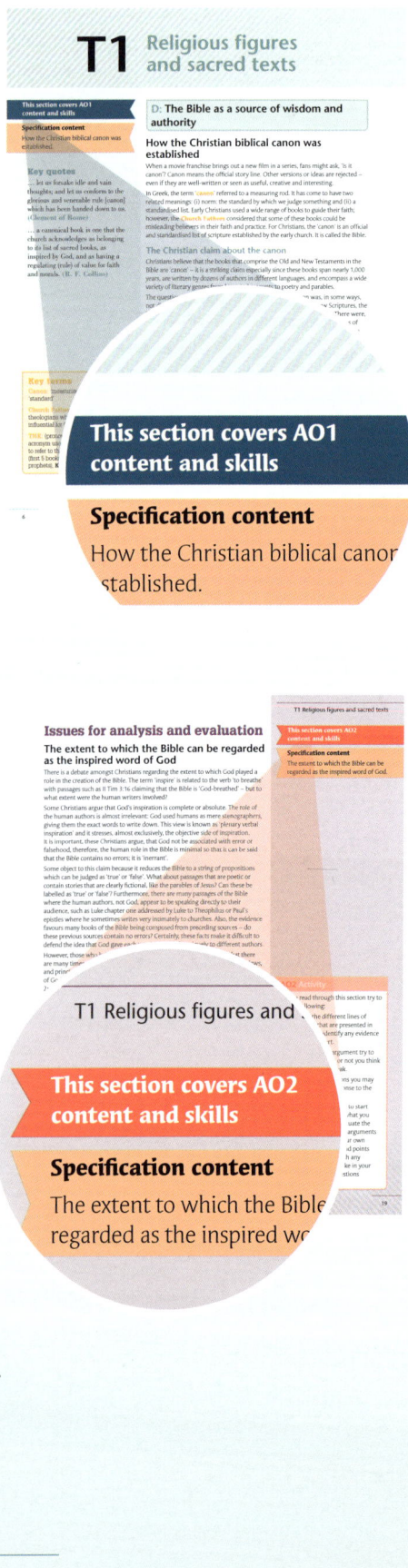

T1 Religious figures and sacred texts

D: The Bible as a source of wisdom and authority

How the Christian biblical canon was established

This section covers AO1 content and skills

Specification content
How the Christian biblical canon was established.

This section covers AO2 content and skills

Specification content
The extent to which the Bible regarded as the inspired word of God.

Study tips advice on how to study, prepare for the examination and answer questions

Study tip

When you are discussing the Jewish canon from the point of view of Judaism, avoid the mistake of referring to the Jewish or Hebrew Bible as the 'Old Testament'; it is the 'Old Testament' for Christians, but not for Jews.

AO1 Activities that serve the purpose of focusing on identification, presentation and explanation, and developing the skills of knowledge and understanding required for the examination

AO1 Activity

Get some cards and label each with a different section of the Bible: Torah, Prophets, Writings, Gospels, Letters and Deutero-canonical/Apocrypha. Then write down a brief explanation of what each of these parts of the Bible contain, as well as a brief summary of when scholars think these parts may have become 'canon'.

AO2 Activities that serve the purpose of focusing on conclusions, as a basis for thinking about the issues, developing critical analysis and the evaluation skills required for the examination

AO2 Activity

As you read through this section try to do the following:

1. Pick out the different lines of argument that are presented in the text and identify any evidence given in support.

Glossary of all the key terms for quick reference.

Specific feature: Developing skills

This section is very much a focus on 'what to do' with the content and the issues that are raised. They occur at the end of each section, giving 12 AO1 and 12 AO2 activities that aim to develop particular skills that are required for more advanced study at Year 2 and A2 stage.

The Developing skills for Year 2 and A2 are grouped so that each Theme has a specific focus to develop and perfect gradually throughout that Theme.

AO1 and AO2 answers and commentaries

The final section has a selection of answers and commentaries as a framework for judging what an effective and ineffective response may be. The comments highlight some common mistakes and also examples of good practice so that all involved in teaching and learning can reflect upon how to approach examination answers.

Richard Gray
Series Editor
2017

AO1 Developing skills

It is now important to consider section; however, the informati be processed in order to meet be done by practising more 'hat run throughout this ' ination. For a⸱⸱

T1 Religious figures and sacred texts

Specification content

How the Christian biblical canon was established.

Key quotes

… let us forsake idle and vain thoughts; and let us conform to the glorious and venerable rule [canon] which has been handed down to us. **(Clement of Rome)**

… a canonical book is one that the church acknowledges as belonging to its list of sacred books, as inspired by God, and as having a regulating (rule) of value for faith and morals. **(R. F. Collins)**

Key terms

Canon: 'measuring rod', 'rule' or 'standard'

Church Fathers: ancient Christian theologians whose writings have been influential for Christians

TNK: (pronounced Tanak) – an acronym used by Jewish believers to refer to the Hebrew Bible: **T**orah (first 5 books of the Law), **N**evi'im (the prophets), **K**ethuvim (the writings)

D: The Bible as a source of wisdom and authority

How the Christian biblical canon was established

When a movie franchise brings out a new film in a series, fans might ask, 'Is it canon?' Canon means the official story line. Other versions or ideas are rejected – even if they are well-written or seen as useful, creative and interesting.

In Greek, the term '**canon**' referred to a measuring rod. It has come to have two related meanings: (i) norm: the standard by which we judge something and (ii) a standardised list. Early Christians used a wide range of books to guide their faith; however, the **Church Fathers** considered that some of these books could be misleading believers in their faith and practice. For Christians, the 'canon' is an official and standardised list of scripture established by the early church. It is called the Bible.

The Christian claim about the canon

Christians believe that the books that comprise the Old and New Testaments in the Bible are 'canon' – it is a striking claim especially since these books span nearly 1,000 years, are written by dozens of authors in different languages, and encompass a wide variety of literary genres from historical accounts to poetry and parables.

The question of which books should be included in the canon was, in some ways, not difficult since most early Christians came to see that the Hebrew Scriptures, the letters of Paul and the four Gospels were invaluable for their churches. There were, however, disagreements about some books and there were different versions of the Hebrew Bible in circulation at the birth of Christianity. There were also some books that claimed to be written by figures important to believers, but which were falsely using these names to gain authority.

Study tip

When answering questions on the canon, make sure you refer to both the Jewish and Christian canons. In addition to knowing books that were included in these canons, it is good to know of examples of books that were rejected; you will see some of these below.

The Jewish canon

The Jewish Bible is not exactly the same as the Christian 'Old Testament'. Firstly, Jewish believers do not consider it to be 'old' – it is seen as God's revelation to Israel. Secondly, not all Christian 'Old Testaments' are the same; all Jews agree on the books in the Hebrew Scriptures. These books are presented in a three-fold division: (i) the Law (Torah), the 5 books traditionally thought to be written by Moses; (ii) the Prophets (Nevi'im), these include the 'former prophets', the 'latter prophets' and the 12 'Minor Prophets'; and (iii) a diverse set of Writings (Kethuvim) which includes poetical books, prophecy and history. Many Jews refer to the Hebrew Bible by the acronym of **TNK** (pronounced *Tanak*), from the first letters of Torah, Nevi'im and Kethuvim.

When did the Hebrew Bible become canon?

We do not know the exact date when any of these books were first considered canonical by Jewish believers. Many scholars believe that these three parts represent three successive stages in the formation of the canon, with the Torah as the earliest part to be recognised, shared orally for perhaps centuries and then written down just prior to or during the Exile of Judah to Babylon in the 6th century BCE (although this would be disputed by conservative Jews and conservative Christians who would give a much earlier date). This was a time when Jews lost the Temple as the centre of their faith and practice and would have needed written accounts to help to remember and teach their religion in a distant land. The writings of the prophets, those who spoke in the name of God, likely occurred soon after this. The collection of 'Writings' (Kethuvim) were not recognised as authoritative by Jews until the first centuries of the Common Era. In fact, Luke 24:44 gives us an interesting glimpse into a time when the canon was not considered to have been completed. Jesus, reflecting Jewish belief, refers to the scriptures as the 'Law of Moses, the Prophets and the Psalms'. In other words, only one of the 'Writings' is mentioned as Scripture in this passage. Other places in the Gospels refer only to 'the Law and the Prophets'. The great first-century Jewish historian Josephus mentions the Law, the Prophets and 'four books' which he describes as 'hymns to God and precepts for the conduct of human life'. These four books are thought to have been the Psalms, Song of Solomon, Proverbs and Ecclesiastes. Clearly, the final part of the canon was in process, although not yet fixed.

Study tip

When you are discussing the Jewish canon from the point of view of Judaism, avoid the mistake of referring to the Jewish or Hebrew Bible as the 'Old Testament'; it is the 'Old Testament' for Christians, but not for Jews.

How were the decisions made?

On what basis did Jews accept or reject books that did make it into the canon? There were several factors at work: (i) First, of course, the books had to survive! There are references in the Hebrew Bible to books that we have no knowledge of today (for instance 'The Book of Jashar' referred to in Joshua 10:13). (ii) Books must be seen as supporting the Torah (sometimes referred to as the '**canon within the canon**'. (iii) Perhaps the most important fact is that the books that form today's Jewish Bible were recognised by a wide variety of Jews in diverse locations as supporting their faith and practice.

Different Christian Old Testaments

If you pick up a Catholic Bible and compare its Old Testament list of books to those found in a Protestant Bible, you will discover a slightly different list! This is because the Jewish canon was not closed at the time of the New Testament. Furthermore, the New Testament writers used the Greek version of the Hebrew Bible (the **Septuagint**) which included some Jewish writings written only in Greek which were later excluded from the Jewish canon. Though some Church Fathers such as Jerome also rejected these books as canonical, following the Hebrew canon, other Church Fathers such as Augustine accepted these works. The opinion of Augustine and others prevailed and the following books were included in the Old Testament

quickfire

1.1 What are the three parts of the Hebrew canon?

Reading the Torah

Key terms

Canon within the canon: the idea that within the canon there are central ideas or themes that strongly influenced the basis on which writings were chosen

Septuagint: the Greek translation of the Hebrew Bible in the 3rd to 2nd centuries BCE, also referred to as the LXX in reference to a legend of 70 Jewish scholars translating the Torah

Key terms

Apocrypha: from the Greek word meaning, 'hidden', applied positively to books that were thought of as containing hidden wisdom, or negatively to books of unknown origin and considered to be of questionable value

Deutero-canonical: from a secondary canon, later than the first, but of equal authority

Intertestamental literature: works written between the date of the final book of the Hebrew Bible and the beginning of the New Testament

Key quote

Anglicans do not consider the Apocrypha to be canonical:

The books commonly called the Apocrypha, not being of divine inspiration, are not part of the canon of Scripture; and therefore of no authority to the Church of God, not to be otherwise approved, or made use of than any other human writings. **(The Westminster Confession of Faith)**

quickfire

1.2 Why do Catholic Bibles and Protestant Bibles have different Old Testaments?

(but were ultimately excluded by Jews from their canon): Tobit, Judith, 1 and 2 Maccabees, Wisdom, Sirach, Baruch – as well as additions to Daniel and Esther. Catholic Christians included these in the Latin translation of the Bible, the Vulgate – which was the main translation for the Church through the centuries. They refer to these books as **Deutero-canonical**, simply because they come after the proto-canonical works of the rest of the Old Testament. Catholics believe that all books of the Bible (both Proto- and Deutero-canonical) are fully and equally inspired.

Study tip

It is important to know that there was both a Hebrew version of the Jewish scriptures/Old Testament as well as a Greek version (the Septuagint). The Greek version contained some Jewish books written only in Greek, which ended up not being accepted as canonical for Jewish and Protestant Bibles.

Protestant Bibles

However, Protestants use the term **Apocrypha** to refer to this collection, a word meaning 'hidden', and was first applied in the context of a book giving hidden meaning to believers; however, the term came to take on the meaning of 'false, heretical' for many Christians. Martin Luther raised doubts about their inclusion. He viewed 2 Maccabees 12.46 as giving support to the doctrine of purgatory. This doctrine, in turn, undermined the theme that was most important for Luther: justification by faith, as a gift of God – not something to be earned through purgatory. Protestant Bibles soon began to place the Apocrypha into a separate section – or omitted these altogether from the Bible. In some Protestant Bibles today you will see these books in their own section along with other Jewish works that circulated at the beginning of the Common Era, but these are not held by Protestants to be canonical. This collection is also called **Intertestamental literature** since these books were written between the closing of the Hebrew canon and the beginning of the New Testament literature.

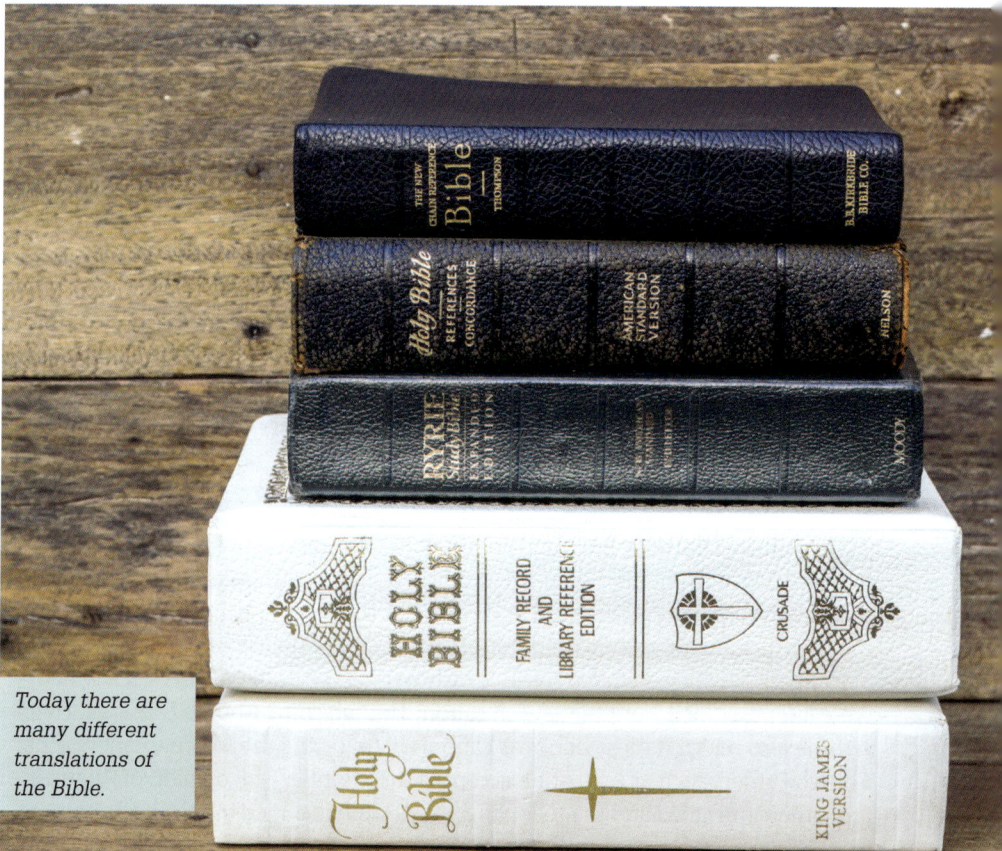

Today there are many different translations of the Bible.

Books of the Hebrew Bible in order (24 books; this is the same as the 39 books in Protestant Bibles; many of the books have not been divided into first and second parts)	Books in Old Testament of Catholic Bibles in order (46 Books), Deutero-canonical/Apopcryphal books are in bold	Books of the Protestant Old Testament Bible In Order (39 books, excluding the Apocrypha)
Genesis (Torah) ↓	Genesis	Genesis
Exodus	Exodus	Exodus
Leviticus	Leviticus	Leviticus
Numbers	Numbers	Numbers
Deuteronomy	Deuteronomy	Deuteronomy
Joshua (Nevi'im) ↓	Joshua	Joshua
Judges	Judges	Judges
Samuel	Ruth	Ruth
Kings	I Samuel	I Samuel
Isaiah	II Samuel	II Samuel
Jeremiah	I Kings	I Kings
Ezekiel	II Kings	II Kings
The Twelve (Minor Prophets)	I Chronicles	I Chronicles
Psalms (Kethuvim) ↓	II Chronicles	II Chronicles
Proverbs	Ezra	Ezra
Job	Nehemiah	Nehemiah
Song of Solomon	**Tobit**	
Ruth	**Judith**	
Lamentations	Esther **(note: longer than Hebrew/ Protestant Esther)**	Esther
Ecclesiastes	Job	Job
Esther	Psalms	Psalms
Daniel	Proverbs	Proverbs
Ezra/Nehemiah	Ecclesiastes	Ecclesiastes
Chronicles	Song of Solomon	Song of Solomon
	The Wisdom of Solomon	
	Sirach	
	Isaiah	Isaiah
	Jeremiah	Jeremiah
	Lamentations	Lamentations
	Baruch	
	Ezekiel	Ezekiel
	Daniel **(note: longer than Hebrew/ Protestant Daniel)**	Daniel
	Hosea	Hosea
	Joel	Joel
	Amos	Amos
	Obadiah	Obadiah
	Jonah	Jonah
	Micah	Micah
	Nahum	Nahum
	Habakkuk	Habakkuk
	Zephaniah	Zephaniah
	Haggai	Haggai
	Zechariah	Zechariah
	Malachi	Malachi
	I Maccabees	
	II Maccabees	

The Apocrypha is included in some Protestant Bibles in a separate section (sometimes between the the Old and New Testaments); it is not considered to be canonical. It usually includes these books (note: the book in bold is not in Catholic Bibles) I Esdras, II Esdras, Tobit, Judith, Additions to Esther, Wisdom, Sirach, Baruch, Song of the Three Children (part of the additions to Daniel), Susanna (Daniel 13), Bel and the Dragon (Daniel 14), **Prayer of Manasseh** (Daniel), 1 Maccabees, and 2 Maccabees.

*Note: there is no disagreement about the number or order of New Testament books amongst Christian churches.

The New Testament canon

There was a short period in early Christianity when the only scriptures that Christians possessed were the Jewish writings. In this early phase, distinctly Christian messages were conveyed orally by the teaching of the Apostles, sayings of Jesus and through prophets who would share truths they believed to have come directly from God. The next phase in the development of the Christian canon came with the letters of Paul to various churches beginning in the 6th decade of the Common Era. These letters were prized by the churches that received them; they were eventually copied and circulated. These letters were followed by the Gospels, (70–100 CE) as well as other letters and one book of prophecy: Revelation.

In the 2nd century there were many collections of Christian writings, most of these contained the four Gospels as well as many letters of Paul. There was a growing recognition that these writings were 'scriptures', just as important as the Hebrew Bible (see II Peter 3:16). Many churches in Syria and elsewhere used a harmony of all four Gospels created in the 2nd century for several centuries. This was called the **Diatessaron**, meaning 'made of four'.

The **Muratorian Canon** is perhaps the oldest known list of books in the New Testament, with some scholars dating this list at about 170 CE. It contains 22 of the 27 books in today's New Testament. It also mentions books that should not be included since they are forgeries. This shows us that early Christians were careful about the selection process.

How New Testament books were chosen

As with the Hebrew Bible, there are no written criteria to guide the selection of books to the canon; however, there are three factors that clearly guided the early church: (i) books considered 'scripture' had to have a connection to the Apostles, either being written by them or by someone in direct contact with them; (ii) the writings had to have a connection with churches, recognised as supporting faith and practice by Christians in diverse places; and (iii) the books had to conform to the faith of Christianity. Christians have always been clear that the coming of Jesus, his life, death and resurrection are of utmost importance for the relationship between humanity and God. Any books not seen to support this central belief were rejected.

Key terms

Diatessaron: a harmony of the four Gospels written in the 2nd century, popular in some Syrian churches for up to two centuries

Muratorian Canon: perhaps the oldest known list of books of the New Testament, possibly dating to about 170 CE

quickfire

1.3   Before Paul wrote his epistles, what were the first books considered by Christians to be a part of their canon?

Key quote

There is current also [an epistle] to the Laodiceans, [and] another to the Alexandrians, [both] forged in Paul's name to [further] the heresy of Marcion, and several others which cannot be received into the Catholic Church – for it is not fitting that gall be mixed with honey.
(The Muratorian Canon)

quickfire

1.4   What are the main parts of the New Testament canon?

AO1 Activity

Get some cards and label each with a different section of the Bible: Torah, Prophets, Writings, Gospels, Letters and Deutero-canonical/Apocrypha. Then write down a brief explanation of what each of these parts of the Bible contain, as well as a brief summary of when scholars think these parts may have become 'canon'.

Disagreements about the New Testament

Even though there was wide consensus on the books that came to be in the New Testament, there were disagreements. In the 2nd century, a church leader named Marcion created a Bible composed only of the Gospel of Luke (without the birth narratives) and the letters of Paul. He believed that the God of Jesus Christ was completely different (and superior to) from the God of the Hebrew Bible, so he attempted to remove all references to Judaism from his version of the Bible. The **Apostolic Fathers** (early Christian theologians who knew some of the of the Apostles or were significantly influenced by them) rejected Marcion's Bible. They believed strongly that the Christian Bible should contain the Old Testament as well as Christian writings since the same God that was at work in Israel was also active in the life of Jesus.

By looking at the writings of the Apostolic Fathers in the late 1st and 2nd centuries CE we have a very good idea which books in the New Testament were universally accepted as well as which ones were debated. There was some debate about both the book of Hebrews and the book of Revelation, for example, because of a lack of clarity about apostolic authorship. Furthermore, the fact that some Christian groups considered heretical favoured these two books cast doubt as to their status. Eventually the Church came to believe that these books had apostolic origins and affirmed the Christian faith. There are also other books that the Church found helpful written by the second generation of church leaders. These include books such as the **Didache** and the **Shepherd of Hermas** – these were part of some New Testaments but were ultimately rejected, not because they were wrong but simply because they were written later than Apostolic writings.

AO1 Activity

Do some further research on the canonical status of certain books – this might include books that eventually were included in the canon such as Hebrews and Revelation as well as those that were not, such as *Didache*, *Shepherd of Hermas* and *I Clement*.

Aside from a few debates, there emerged a wide consensus about the 27 books found in today's New Testament. However, an actual official decision that these books were 'canon' did not come until the end of the 4th century and the beginning of the 5th century by leaders in the eastern and western churches.

AO1 Activity

Imagine that you are an early 5th-century reporter covering an announcement of the Christian New Testament canon. Prepare a news flash in which you quickly present several factors that guided the Church to declare some books to be canonical and others non-canonical. You can also make your presentation especially journalistic by including references to books which caused controversy.

Study tip

It is popular to think that the canon was determined by political pressures or an imperial decree. Make sure that you understand that there was a great deal of consensus amongst most believers about the inclusion of most books – and that this consensus grew over centuries.

Key terms

Apostolic Fathers: Christian theologians of the first two centuries CE who were taught by the twelve Apostles, or at least were significantly influenced by their writings

Didache: an ancient Christian book of instruction (*didache* is Greek for 'teaching'), from the first century CE; some early versions of the New Testament were included this book

Shepherd of Hermas: an early Christian book containing visions and parables dated from the 1st and 2nd centuries CE; some early versions of the New Testament included this book

Why is order important?

At first glance, one might think that the Bible follows a chronological order from the creation of the world in the book of Genesis to the announcement of the coming of a new heaven and new earth in the book of Revelation. However, this is not always the case. In the Hebrew Bible, the book of Ruth follows the Song of Solomon even though it refers to events far earlier. In the New Testament, the first book that was written (Thessalonians in the early 50s) has been placed after the Gospels which were composed decades later. Clearly more is going on in the order of biblical books than at first appears.

The order of the Hebrew Bible/Old Testament

How we order things often reflects their importance. The Bible begins with the Torah, which includes the history leading up to God establishing a covenant with Israel through the Law given to Moses as well as the explanation and extension of those laws. The prophets can be seen as describing the 'highs and lows' of Israel living with that covenant. Finally, the writings give various insights on living faithfully in different situations. So, at the heart of the Hebrew Bible is the Torah (the 'canon within the canon'), supported by three types of literature: legal, prophetic and poetic.

One difference you will see from comparing the list of books in the Hebrew Bible to those in the Christian Old Testament is that whereas the Christian Old Testament ends with the Minor Prophets, the Hebrew Bible ends with Ezra/Nehemiah and Chronicles. The reason for this is that Christian Bibles follow the order of the Septuagint (LXX) whereas the Hebrew Bible places the writings last (it is also true that Ezra/Nehemiah and Chronicles were written after the Minor Prophets). Some theologians also note that the ending of the Hebrew Bible places the focus on the Jews having returned from exile and rebuilding their nation, whereas the Minor Prophets, in part, look ahead to the return of Elijah which the New Testament interprets as John the Baptist.

The order of the New Testament

In the New Testament the life, death and resurrection of Jesus is the 'canon within the canon'; it is therefore placed first. This is followed by the narrative of the birth of the Church (Acts), and the letters of Paul, first those to the churches (generally, the longer letters are first) and those to individuals (the Pastoral Epistles). These are followed by letters not attributed to Paul (again with the longest ones first). The New Testament ends with the only piece of apocalyptic literature in the New Testament: the book of Revelation.

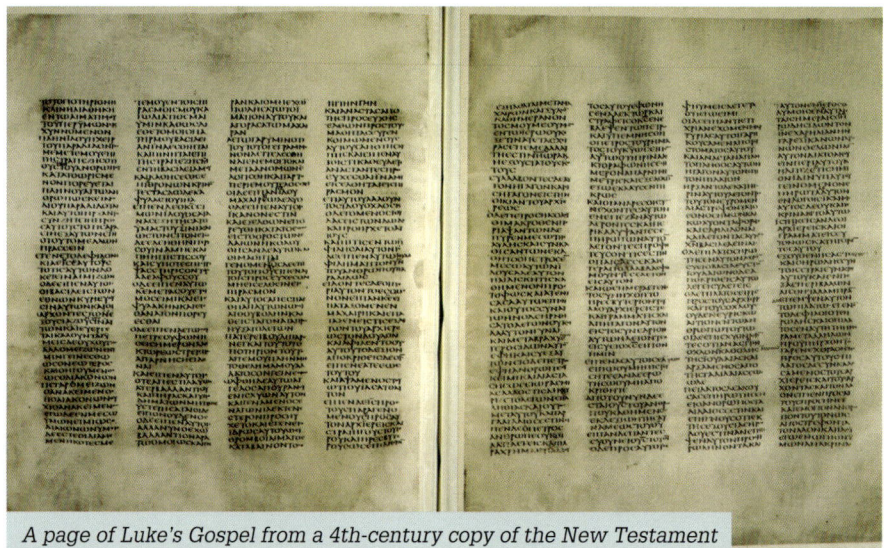

A page of Luke's Gospel from a 4th-century copy of the New Testament

Key quotes

… the Bible is … a chaotically cobbled-together anthology of disjointed documents, composed, revised, translated, distorted and 'improved' by hundreds of anonymous authors, editors and copyists, unknown to us and mostly unknown to each other, spanning nine centuries. (Dawkins)

AO1 Activity

As you read through the next few pages write down some responses that could be used to challenge Dawkins (in the quote above) by summarising the views of different Christian understandings about how the Bible is 'inspired'.

Other factors on the ordering of biblical books

But there is more to the ordering of biblical books than chronology and importance. When books have been thought to be by the same author they may be placed together. This is the case with Jeremiah-Lamentations in the Septuagint and with Luke-Acts in the New Testament. Story-line thread is also a factor: for instance, Joshua through to Kings tells one successive account. Books are sometimes also organised according to their type of literature, such as the Prophetic books or wisdom books of the Old Testament/Hebrew Bible and 'The Gospels' in the New Testament.

Diverse views on the Bible as the word of God

Specification content
Diverse views on the Bible as the word of God.

Have you ever felt inspired? Perhaps you've had an unusual and important idea, written something with unique quality, or played a sport or a musical instrument with incredible skill. Sometimes we have an experience that leaves us feeling inspired, a film or concert that moves us deeply – and, as a result, makes us want to think and act differently.

Christians believe that the Bible is 'inspired' because when they read it they often want to think and act differently. Furthermore, they believe that the Bible is not merely a result of human inspiration, but that it has been inspired by God.

The word 'inspire' comes from a Greek verb meaning 'to breathe on or in'. The exact word used in the New Testament to describe this process is *theopneustos*, literally 'God-breathed' (see II Tim 3:16 and II Peter 1:21). Christians are united in believing that the Bible is the 'word of God' because they see that, in some sense, God is the author of the Bible. But this claim raises a number of questions: What was the human role in this book? Is the Bible partly human and partly divine? Did the human authors have access to ideas that were not their own or were they simply an unconscious tool in the 'hands' of God? What about passages in the Bible that we now see as historically or scientifically incorrect? Can something be called 'God-breathed' if it contains errors?

> **Key term**
> *Theopneustos:* the Greek term used in II Tim. 3:16 meaning 'God-breathed'

Different understandings of inspiration

Specification content
Different understandings of inspiration.

Christians have a variety of answers to these questions. Broadly speaking, these answers move between two poles: either emphasising the objective, 'God-side' of inspiration or the subjective, 'human-side' of inspiration. At the extreme end of the objective pole is the view that the biblical writers were nothing more than mere stenographers (a person whose job is to transcribe speech into shorthand), dutifully writing down only the words verbally spoken to them by God.

However, most theologians have recognised that there is a clear subjective, or human side to inspiration since each of the books of the Bible have their own character, tone and 'feel' based on the personality and unique expressions of their author. At the extreme end of the subjective pole is the view that it actually isn't the words of the Bible that are inspired, but the human authors themselves through the influence of Jesus and the Church. In other words, God did not act in a special way to write the Bible; God acted in human history and experience. According to this view, the Bible is inspired because it was written by inspired people. Between these extremes of subjective and objective views are a variety of viewpoints of expressing how the Bible is the word of God.

Study tip

When answering a question on inspiration, make sure that you include a wide range of views. Not all Christians believe that the Bible was dictated word for word by the Holy Spirit. There are a many different views that include a significant role for the human author.

Specification content
The objective view of inspiration.

Objective views of inspiration

Many of the early Church Fathers emphasised the objective side of inspiration: God directly moved the biblical writers to write certain texts. Indeed, there are many passages in the Bible that present God as speaking directly to or through a prophet. Some of these early theologians took the view that the biblical writers were possessed in a special way by God's spirit, led into some kind of ecstasy so that their complete utterance could be seen as coming directly from God. The 2nd-century theologian Athenagorus described God using the prophets 'as a flautist might blow into a flute'. In other words, inspiration is a kind of divine dictation. This point of view is echoed by medieval Christian writers who used Aristotelian categories of efficient and instrumental causes: An efficient cause is responsible for initiating an event whereas an instrumental cause is used by the efficient cause to bring the event about. One way to understand this is with a carpenter using a saw to create lumber – the carpenter is the efficient cause and the saw is the instrumental cause. These images of inspiration emphasise the objective side of this process.

However, other early Church Fathers disagreed with assigning merely a passive role to the human authors. The 2nd–3rd CE thinker Origen believed that the authors of the Bible were fully conscious of the process of inspiration and were able to express their own views. Later on, Thomas Aquinas shows how even instrumental causes could play a part in influencing and shaping divine revelation. Though many church leaders viewed God as the author of the Bible, or referred to the Bible as 'dictated by the Holy Spirit', they had a different notion than we do today when we say the words 'author' or 'dictation'. For example, we associate an author only with literary works, but in Latin the term 'auctor' can also be applied to things like bridges or buildings; it can mean 'producer'.

Furthermore, in the ancient world dictation of letters could go beyond a word-for-word approach with those dictating giving their scribes the general idea of what to write rather than the exact words. When it comes to the biblical writers receiving divine dictation, this could be seen as something rigidly done (emphasising the objective pole of inspiration) or a process that gave them relative freedom to say things the way they thought best – giving a larger role to the subjective mode of inspiration.

Key quotes

It is wicked to doubt that they [the writings of the Apostles and Prophets] are free from all error. (Augustine)

Catholic authors tended to prefer images that allow a real place to the human mind. Even the idea of divine 'dictation' (first in Irenaeus) was designed for this purpose. The ancient amanuensis was not a slavish copyist but often played an active role in giving final form to a composition. (R. D. Williams)

quickfire

1.5 Is the idea of a flautist blowing into a flute used to support an objective or subjective view of inspiration?

Specification content
The subjective view of inspiration.

Subjective views of inspiration

The European enlightenment put an emphasis on human knowledge and understanding; traditional belief in God, miracles, and the Bible as God's word were questioned.

Some thinkers of this period, who were sympathetic to Christianity, viewed inspiration as a human rather than a divine activity. They believed that the Bible could still have meaning for Christians as the witness of writers inspired by God's work in the world and the life of Jesus. In other words, there is a link between the Bible and God, not through the words of the Bible but in the inspired experience of the writers. Some Christians objected to this approach since it left the door open to other books being equally inspired as the Bible.

Inerrancy and plenary verbal inspiration

In the late 19th and early 20th centuries there was a reaction to the enlightenment focus on human wisdom and knowledge in the form of Christian **fundamentalism.** Fundamentalists asserted that scientific advancements would never be at the cost of key Christian doctrines (fundamentals) such as the creation of the world in seven 24-hour days, belief in miracles as reported in the Bible and the need to believe in the substitutionary atonement of Christ. At the heart of fundamentalism was an objective view of revelation: God gave each word of the Bible to the human writers, so that there would be no error, contradiction or falsehood. In other words, the Bible is not merely a testimony to an experience of God by inspired writers, its very words are inspired. The technical phrase used to describe this view is 'inerrancy' or **plenary verbal inspiration**. Plenary means complete, entire, or absolute: God spoke verbally to the authors so that every single word in the Bible is true – much like stenographic dictation. The logic behind this position is simple:

a. God is not associated with falsehood or error

b. God has inspired the Bible

c. Therefore, there are no falsehoods, contradictions, or errors in the Bible (some fundamentalist thinkers distinguish between the original text of the Bible which is perfect and without error and later copies into which some errors may have crept).

Christian thinkers and leaders through the ages have proclaimed the Bible to be free of error, but what makes fundamentalism unique is a rigid theory that turns all parts of the Bible into propositional truths which can be labelled 'true' or 'false'.

Many Christians have questioned this kind of objective view of inspiration: is a poem or a story 'true' or 'false'? Did the writers of the Bible each receive a verbal message? Some passages of the Bible suggest that this was the case (i.e. messages of God spoken by the prophets), but most biblical writers make no mention of this process and appear to write personally as if this is not the case (i.e. the pastoral epistles of Paul, e.g. 1 Corinthians 7:12). It appears, therefore, that the Bible contains both propositional and non-propositional language. Furthermore, certain biblical books (such as the Gospels) make use of multiple sources and even refer personally to their efforts in producing the written text (Acts 1:1) – does this not contradict the view that each author received verbal dictation? For these and other reasons, many Christian theologians have rejected verbal plenary inspiration.

> ### AO1 Activity
>
> What key words would you use if you were going to write your own essay on the topic of biblical inspiration? Choose four to six terms and write a few sentences justifying why each of these terms are critical for this discussion.

More subjective theories of inspiration

Other subjective theories of inspiration include Karl Barth's view that Jesus (and not the Bible) is the 'word of God'. However, if one listens to the Bible with humility and a spirit of obedience, then certain passages can become transformed into the word of God in a reader's experience. In other words, inspiration is not the quality of the text but of a reader's experience with the text under certain conditions. Other theologians have said that divine inspiration is much more complex than a text being produced by one individual. This insight has led to 'social theories of inspiration' which view the Bible as the product not of an individual working with God but as an entire faith community being impacted by God and, passing that impact on to an author.

> ### Key terms
>
> **Fundamentalism:** the movement from the late 19th/early 20th century dedicated to defending key biblical doctrines and later becoming associated with a literal approach to the Bible
>
> **Plenary verbal inspiration:** the belief that the words of the Bible were given directly by God to the human authors and therefore the Bible is fully (plenary) inspired

Balancing subjective and objective views

Many Anglican and Catholic theologians seek to balance objective and subjective viewpoints: on the one hand, they affirm that God is the author of the Bible, but on the other hand, that God has worked through unique human authors each with their own style, personality and historical situations. What is important for these theologians is not that the Bible conforms to some view of perfection that can be defined in logical or scientific terms, but that it is 'true' when it comes to matters of salvation, faith and morality. As II Timothy 3:16 says, the Bible is 'useful for teaching ... and training in righteousness'.

Key quote

These [books of the Christian canon] the Church holds to be sacred and canonical, not because, having been carefully composed by mere human industry, they were afterwards approved by her authority, nor merely because they contain revelation without errors, but because, having been written by the inspiration of the Holy Spirit, they have God for their author and have been delivered as such to the Church herself. **(Vatican II)**

Accommodation

One way that some theologians have explained how God's authorship of the Bible can co-exist with historical or scientific errors is by using the concept of **accommodation**. Think of the verb 'to accommodate' – if you purchase a pet, you have to make changes to your home in order to accommodate your pet: food and water placed at an accessible level, a special cage or living space, a bed of the right size, etc. Just as there is a gap between us and our pets, so too is there a gap between God's reality and our reality. One could say that expressions about history or science in the Bible were God's way of accommodating those who were writing and reading the Bible long ago, they were made a level at which they could be understood.

John Calvin's use of accommodation

This idea comes from the great reformation theologian John Calvin who, through his early work as a humanist scholar, was aware of the possibilities and limits of language. 'We must never forget', said Calvin, 'that God is above and beyond our language'. The transcendent God chooses to lower himself to become intelligible in our experience. Calvin used the analogy of a nurse making 'baby talk' to a young toddler – the nurse can make far more sophisticated expressions but chooses to communicate in a way that encourages interaction. For Calvin, the fact that God has decided to accommodate his 'language' to us in a book is a cause for thanksgiving.

Calvin also speaks about the human authors of the Bible choosing to speak in a language that would be easily intelligible

Portrait of John Calvin (1509–1564) attributed to Hans Holbein (1497–1543)

Specification content

John Calvin's doctrine of accommodation.

Key term

Accommodation: to adapt, fit, suit or adjust (as in God accommodating herself/himself to speak to humans)

Key quote

The ancient doctrine of the inspiration and inerrancy of the Bible not only is impossible for intelligent people today, but represents a deviation in Christian doctrine, whatever salutary uses may have been made of it in the past by the Holy Spirit, who often turns human error to good ends. (A. T. Hanson and R. P. C. Hanson)

Key person

John Calvin: 16th-century French theologian and reformer who established Protestantism in Geneva. Calvin was a prolific writer who wrote *The Institutes of the Christian Faith* and commentaries on almost every book of the Bible; he insisted that his theology was entirely based on the Bible. Today, many Congregational, Reformed and Presbyterian churches across the world consider him to be their main theologian and sometimes call themselves 'Calvinist'.

to most of their readers. For instance, Genesis 1:16 says, 'God made two great lights – the greater light to rule the day and the lesser light to rule the night – and the stars.' This is a reference, of course, to the sun and the moon. However, Calvin is aware of the discovery of other planets such as Saturn that are, technically, a greater light in the sky than the moon. Was Moses (who Calvin believed to be the author of this passage) in error? Not at all: it is technically true that Saturn is also a lesser light than the sun but Moses was simply adapting truth to the common person. Moses could have given a long discourse about the nature of heavenly spheres and the relative sizes of planetary bodies but this would detract from communicating the essential message of the passage.

Calvin believed the Bible to be without error. In this case he said that Genesis 1:16 is actually true: the moon is the light that rules the night sky, *from the point of view from someone on earth*. So, even when biblical writers are accommodating their language to the common reader, the scriptures are wholly true.

The idea of accommodation is also used by some contemporary theologians who do believe that there are errors in the Bible. These theologians believe that the biblical writers had scientific, cultural and historical assumptions that are, by today's standards, simply incorrect. These errors are part of God's overall calculations when accommodating to human language. However, the Bible's main message for our lives is still relevant since it is not mainly about these scientific, cultural and historical assumptions. These errors detract little or nothing from the theological message of God's sovereignty and provision of salvation through faith in Jesus.

quickfire

1.6 Did John Calvin believe there were errors of science and history in the Bible?

Study tip

John Calvin did not believe that the Bible had errors, but his views on accommodation have been adapted by others to account for biblical errors in science and history.

Scribes had a very important role in ensuring the accurate writing down and later translation of biblical texts.

Key skills Theme 1

The first theme has tasks that deal with the basics of AO1 in terms of prioritising and selecting the key relevant information, presenting this and then using evidence and examples to support and expand upon this.

Key skills

Knowledge involves:

Selection of a range of (thorough) accurate and relevant information that is directly related to the specific demands of the question.

This means:

- Selecting relevant material for the question set

- Being focused in explaining and examining the material selected.

Understanding involves:

Explanation that is extensive, demonstrating depth and/or breadth with excellent use of evidence and examples including (where appropriate) thorough and accurate supporting use of sacred texts, sources of wisdom and specialist language.

This means:

- Effective use of examples and supporting evidence to establish the quality of your understanding

- Ownership of your explanation that expresses personal knowledge and understanding and NOT just reproducing a chunk of text from a book that you have rehearsed and memorised.

As you work through each section of the book, the focus will be on a variety of different aspects associated with AO1 so that you can comprehensively perfect the overall skills associated with AO1.

AO1 Developing skills

It is now important to consider the information that has been covered in this section; however, the information in its raw form is too extensive and so has to be processed in order to meet the requirements of the examination. This can be done by practising more advanced skills associated with AO1. The exercises that run throughout this book will help you to do this and prepare you for the examination. For assessment objective 1 (AO1), which involves demonstrating 'knowledge' and 'understanding' skills, we are going to focus on different ways in which the skills can be demonstrated effectively, and also refer to how the performance of these skills is measured (see generic band descriptors for A2 [WJEC] AO1 or A Level [Eduqas] AO1).

▶ **Your task is this:** Below is a summary of **the formation of the New Testament canon**. It is about 200 words long. You need to use this for an answer but could not repeat all of this in an essay under examination conditions so you will have to condense the material. Discuss which points you think are the most important and then re-draft into your own summary of 100 words.

The New Testament was not written at the same time, nor was it formally recognised as canonical until centuries after its writing. Some of the epistles of Paul were the earliest books to be written (50s and 60s CE) and shared between churches; the Gospels were written later (70–100 CE), followed by other epistles and the book of Revelation. Though there was wide agreement on most books (as testified to by the Muratorian Canon), there were disagreements; for instance, Marcion's Bible, Hebrews and Revelation. Also, some churches used books that were later rejected as canonical, not because they were considered heretical, but because they were not written by Apostles (The Shepherd of Hermas; Didache). There were no universally agreed upon criteria for the books that came to be a part of the New Testament, but there are clearly some common factors such as apostolic origins, recognition by a wide number of churches and conformity to the 'rule of faith' as taught by the Apostles who were impacted by the life, teachings and resurrection of Jesus. The New Testament canon was officially declared at the end of the 4th century/ beginning of the 5th century – even though there was already a wide consensus about most books.

When you have completed the task, refer to the band descriptors for A2 (WJEC) or A Level (Eduqas) and, in particular, have a look at the demands described in the higher band descriptors towards which you should be aspiring. Ask yourself:

- Does my work demonstrate thorough, accurate and relevant knowledge and understanding of religion and belief?

- Is my work coherent (consistent or make logical sense), clear and well organised? ***(WJEC band descriptor only but still important to consider for Eduqas)***

- Will my work, when developed, be an extensive and relevant response which is specific to the focus of the task?

- Does my work have extensive depth and/or suitable breadth and have excellent use of evidence and examples?

- If appropriate to the task, does my response have thorough and accurate reference to sacred texts and sources of wisdom?

- Are there any insightful connections to be made with other elements of my course?

- Will my answer, when developed and extended to match what is expected in an examination answer, have an extensive range of views of scholars/schools of thought?

- When used, is specialist language and vocabulary both thorough and accurate?

Issues for analysis and evaluation

The extent to which the Bible can be regarded as the inspired word of God

There is a debate amongst Christians regarding the extent to which God played a role in the creation of the Bible. The term 'inspire' is related to the verb 'to breathe' with passages such as II Tim 3:16 claiming that the Bible is 'God-breathed' – but to what extent were the human writers involved?

Some Christians argue that God's inspiration is complete or absolute. The role of the human authors is almost irrelevant: God used humans as mere stenographers, giving them the exact words to write down. This view is known as 'plenary verbal inspiration' and it stresses, almost exclusively, the objective side of inspiration. It is important, these Christians argue, that God not be associated with error or falsehood, therefore, the human role in the Bible is minimal so that it can be said that the Bible contains no errors; it is 'inerrant'.

Some object to this claim because it reduces the Bible to a string of propositions which can be judged as 'true' or 'false'. What about passages that are poetic or contain stories that are clearly fictional, like the parables of Jesus? Can these be labelled as 'true' or 'false'? Furthermore, there are many passages of the Bible where the human authors, not God, appear to be speaking directly to their audience, such as Luke chapter one addressed by Luke to Theophilus or Paul's epistles where he sometimes writes very intimately to churches. Also, the evidence favours many books of the Bible being composed from preceding sources – do these previous sources contain no errors? Certainly, these facts make it difficult to defend the idea that God gave each word of the Bible uniquely to different authors.

However, those who believe in verbal plenary inspiration might argue that there are many times when God speaks directly: though prophets, the giving of the laws, and principles through the words of Jesus. They might also stress that their view of God's authorship of the Bible goes back to the early Church Fathers, citing the 2nd-century view of Athenagoras that God wrote the Bible as 'a flautist blows into a flute'.

However, not all of the early Church Fathers believed that God worked in that way. For example, Origen believed that the human authors were conscious of inspiration and could express their own views. Furthermore, it is a fact that each book of the Bible has its own 'character' or 'tone' which reflects the author, their unique grammar and vocabulary and their historical circumstances. For example, one need only consider the differences between Luke and Matthew in their birth narratives, where it is clear that each author has a different audience in mind and communicates in different ways. How could this be the case if the authors were merely the 'flutes' played by the 'flautist'?

Supporting a more subjective approach to inspiration is the idea that the term 'author', in the Greco-Roman world, could have a wider meaning than simply being applied to literary works; it was also used to refer to building bridges or buildings. Therefore, it can take on the meaning of 'producer'. Thus, one could say that God 'produced' the Bible in some sort of cooperation with human writers. Supporting this view is the fact that sometimes scribes were expected to be much more than stenographers – to fill out key ideas of those 'dictating' to them in their own way. For these reasons, many Anglican and Catholic theologians reject plenary verbal inspiration and believe that God worked through human authors, and their individual personalities, in creating the Bible. There is a balance, they say, between objective and subjective views of inspiration.

This section covers AO2 content and skills

Specification content
The extent to which the Bible can be regarded as the inspired word of God.

AO2 Activity

As you read through this section try to do the following:

1. Pick out the different lines of argument that are presented in the text and identify any evidence given in support.
2. For each line of argument try to evaluate whether or not you think this is strong or weak.
3. Think of any questions you may wish to raise in response to the arguments.

This activity will help you to start thinking critically about what you read, and help you to evaluate the effectiveness of different arguments and from this develop your own observations, opinions and points of view that will help with any conclusions that you make in your answers to the AO2 questions that arise.

Of course, there are some thinkers who believe that the Bible is not the inspired word of God – some of these are Christians! The theologian Karl Barth believed that Jesus is the inspired word of God, not the Bible. The Bible is a testimony to Jesus; it can become God's work at a particular moment when it is read with a humble heart – but it is not automatically God's word as that would mean it was more important than Jesus.

Friedrich Schleiermacher also did not believe the Bible to be inspired; he viewed it as having been written by inspired writers, so it is like any inspired work. What makes the Bible special is that it is the first book written by inspired writers in the Christian Church. This view does not rule out other books being equally inspired. This approach to inspiration might be seen by some Christians as too subjective, reducing inspiration to human creativity and putting the Bible on the same level as other books as a creative human endeavour.

While Schleiermacher's views could fit in an era that was questioning belief in miracles and the authority of the Church, it does not fit for many Christians who feel that God must be involved in the creation of the Bible in some sort of objective way. But what about limitations in the Bible in terms of science and history? Can a modern person believe that God was involved in the Bible when there may be errors? Are the only alternatives to choose between plenary verbal inspiration and purely human creativity?

Some Christians believe that it is possible to see God as the author of the Bible but at the same time allow for a human role in the process that could lead to scientific or historical limitations. These Christians use the idea of 'accommodation' – God is beyond human language and abilities but chose to lower herself/himself to the human level to give a message – like an adult who chooses simple language to speak to a toddler, even if that language is not spoken with grammatical perfection or scientific precision.

Those who want to believe in a wholly objective view of God's inspiration might point out that this idea comes from John Calvin, who believed that the Bible was without error and any supposed error in science or history is only because the biblical author is trying to communicate things at the level of their audience. Furthermore, Calvin believed that there are actually no scientific or historical errors in the Bible – when these are looked at closely they are always true from the point of view of the reader at the time, though there are levels of understanding which the biblical authors chose to not explain since this would detract from the primary message.

In conclusion, views on the extent to which the Bible is the inspired word of God can be seen as a continuum with those on one pole insisting on only the most minimal human input and those on the extreme other end believing that the Bible is a human book, inspired by those who have had experiences with God. In between these viewpoints are those who believe that there is a kind of partnership between God and the human writers. It is not likely that these many theoretical differences will ever be resolved. On a practical level, perhaps it can be argued that despite all of these different views, there is unity amongst Christians that the Bible has a great deal of utility when it comes to offering, as II Timothy 3:16 says, 'usefulness for teaching and training in a godly life'.

AO2 Activity

List some conclusions that could be drawn from the AO2 reasoning from the above text; try to aim for at least three different possible conclusions. Consider each of the conclusions and collect brief evidence to support each conclusion from the AO1 and AO2 material for this topic. Select the conclusion that you think is most convincing and explain why it is so. Try to contrast this with the weakest conclusion in the list, justifying your argument with clear reasoning and evidence.

Whether the Christian biblical canonical orders are inspired, as opposed to just the texts they contain

Specification content
Whether the Christian biblical canonical orders are inspired, as opposed to just the texts they contain.

Christians believe, in different ways, that God inspired the authors of individual books – this issue asks about a broader question: do Christians believe that the contours of the Bible itself are inspired by God? In other words, did God work to establish the flow of the Bible from Genesis to Revelation, or is this ordering purely a human phenomenon?

To say that there is an order might suggest that some books in the Bible are more important, or more foundational than other books – it is to say that one should prioritise some books more than others. Some Christians might disagree with this, believing that God's Spirit inspired the very words the authors used in every part of the Bible (plenary verbal inspiration). In fact, there are many examples of Christian theologians and leaders finding inspiration from books across the entire Bible. Also, if there is a divine order to the books of the Bible, does this mean that some are 'more inspired' than others?

However, it could be said that order by no means reflects importance: the first chapter of a book is not necessarily more important than the last chapter. Furthermore, any teacher (in this case, God) has a plan for their students which includes learning some things before other things. Those who argue in this way can note that there is clearly a 'canon within a canon'. In the Hebrew Bible this is the Torah, the first five books attributed to Moses which focus on the Law of God. The books of the prophets (Nevi'im) and the writings (Ketuvim) reference God's Law, challenge interpretations of it or apply it to daily living. For Christians, the 'canon within the canon' is the life and teaching of Jesus in the Gospels, giving primary place as the first four books of the New Testament. Christians reflect their importance in some churches by rising out of their seats when the Gospels are read (whereas they remain seated for other parts of the Bible).

Yet, if the biblical canonical orders are inspired – then why are there different orders between Bibles? For example, there are different orders between the Jewish and Christian Bibles with the Hebrew Scriptures ending with the books of Ezra/Nehemiah and Chronicles (from the Writings/Kethuvim), which seem to indicate that God has fulfilled his promises to Israel after the exile with a new start in Judea. However, Christian Bibles end their Old Testament with the Minor Prophets – which suggests something entirely different – the sense of anticipation for deliverance. Did God change her/his mind about the ordering in the period between the two Testaments? Or are these differences better accounted for by human interpretation?

Furthermore, Catholic Bibles contain a group of writings accepted by neither Protestants nor Jews – Jewish literature written in Greek in the few hundred years before the opening of the New Testament (i.e. Tobit, Judith, 1 and 2 Maccabees, Wisdom, Sirach, Baruch – as well as additions to Daniel and Esther). These were books considered inspired by some Jews as well as many early Christians but which were ultimately rejected as canonical by Jewish believers after the first century. The fact that Christians disagree on the status of these books makes the ordering of the canon look like a human rather than a divine process.

Yet, if one believes that Jesus is the word of God, then we have a very clear piece of evidence that God was at work ordering the shape of his revelation: Jesus' announcement that he was bringing a 'New Covenant'.

AO2 Activity
As you read through this section try to do the following:

1. Pick out the different lines of argument that are presented in the text and identify any evidence given in support.
2. For each line of argument try to evaluate whether or not you think this is strong or weak.
3. Think of any questions you may wish to raise in response to the arguments.

This activity will help you to start thinking critically about what you read, and help you to evaluate the effectiveness of different arguments and from this develop your own observations, opinions and points of view that will help with any conclusions that you make in your answers to the AO2 questions that arise.

This new covenant meant that the understanding of 'covenant' given in the Hebrew Bible had been superseded – or made secondary. This accounts for Christians placing the New Testament at the end of their Bibles and, therefore, could be seen as God giving direction to the shape of the Bible.

However, the order of the Bible was not fully determined until the end of the 4th/ early 5th century CE. Certainly, if God was at work inspiring the process of canon-formation she/he would not have taken so long to do so?

In response, some Christians could argue that it took some time simply because there was no urgency: the prophets and apostles alive after the resurrection knew which books were inspired and their relative importance. Then, after they died, their followers were actively teaching the same things. God's timing was perfect, bringing together the canon in its present order when there was no longer access to those who were involved in writing them and their immediate followers.

Yet, if God was involved in establishing the order of the canon, then why were there so many disputes about whether individual books should be included or not? For example, Marcion suggested a Bible that did not contain the Hebrew Scriptures, only one Gospel (edited) and some letters of Paul. Other disputes were had about Hebrew revelation, the Didache, the Shepherd of Hermas – to name a few. Certainly, it does not appear that God was very successful in creating agreement, much less order.

Those defending God's ordering of the Bible can point to widespread agreement on books to be included. Even by the 2nd century, most New Testament books were widely recognised – as shown by the Muratorian fragment. Those books that were disputed were not, for the most part, disputed because of their content, but merely because of questions about their authorship.

In conclusion, one can make both a strong case for specific historical circumstances and human disagreements lying behind the present order of the Bible and for a sense of underlying unity and flow which makes sense from a believer's point of view. One issue that can be further explored is whether or not one believes that God works through the Church and its decisions. In the response to the reformation emphasis on Sola Scriptura, we saw that the Council of Trent proclaimed God's work through both Scripture and tradition – thus the decisions by councils affirming the inclusion and ordering of biblical books could be seen to reflect God's will. One who does not take this point of view may be more likely to emphasise the human role in the ordering of biblical books.

AO2 Activity

List some conclusions that could be drawn from the AO2 reasoning from the above text; try to aim for at least three different possible conclusions. Consider each of the conclusions and collect brief evidence to support each conclusion from the AO1 and AO2 material for this topic. Select the conclusion that you think is most convincing and explain why it is so. Try to contrast this with the weakest conclusion in the list, justifying your argument with clear reasoning and evidence.

AO2 Developing skills

It is now important to consider the information that has been covered in this section; however, the information in its raw form is too extensive and so has to be processed in order to meet the requirements of the examination. This can be done by practising more advanced skills associated with AO2. The exercises that run throughout this book will help you to do this and prepare you for the examination. For assessment objective 2 (AO2), which involves 'critical analysis' and 'evaluation' skills, we are going to focus on different ways in which the skills can be demonstrated effectively, and also refer to how the performance of these skills is measured (see generic band descriptors for A2 [WJEC] AO2 or A Level [Eduqas] AO2).

▶ **Your task is this:** Below is a summary of two different points of view concerning **the formation of the Bible**. It is 150 words long. You want to use these two views and lines of argument for an evaluation; however, to just list them is not really evaluating them. Present these two views in a more evaluative style by firstly condensing each argument and then, secondly, commenting on how effective each one is (weak or strong are good terms to start with). Allow about 200 words in total.

The formation of the Bible can be seen as a haphazard process which makes it easy for it to be seen as a purely human book. Alternatively, one can see evidence of a widely held consensus that these are inspired books that come from God. In favour of the former point of view is the fact that there are lost books of the Bible and that the canon was in constant development. Furthermore, there were many books of the Bible that were debated as to their divine status. It took, literally, centuries for believers to agree on the canon. On the other hand, it appears the most believers have agreed on the 'canon within the canon' that have guided the choices made of most books. There actually has not been significant disagreement on most books that compose the Bible. Furthermore, these books have inspired the faith of believers through the centuries.

When you have completed the task, refer to the band descriptors for A2 (WJEC) or A Level (Eduqas) and, in particular, have a look at the demands described in the higher band descriptors towards which you should be aspiring. Ask yourself:

- Is my answer a confident critical analysis and perceptive evaluation of the issue?
- Is my answer a response that successfully identifies and thoroughly addresses the issues raised by the question set.
- Does my work show an excellent standard of coherence, clarity and organisation? **(WJEC band descriptor only but still important to consider for Eduqas)**
- Will my work, when developed, contain thorough, sustained and clear views that are supported by extensive, detailed reasoning and/or evidence?
- Are the views of scholars/schools of thought used extensively, appropriately and in context?
- Does my answer convey a confident and perceptive analysis of the nature of any possible connections with other elements of my course?
- When used, is specialist language and vocabulary both thorough and accurate?

Key skills Theme 1

The first theme has tasks that deal with the basics of AO2 in terms of developing an evaluative style, building arguments and raising critical questions.

Key skills

Analysis involves:

Identifying issues raised by the materials in the AO1, together with those identified in the AO2 section, and presents sustained and clear views, either of scholars or from a personal perspective ready for evaluation.

This means:

- That your answers are able to identify key areas of debate in relation to a particular issue
- That you can identify, and comment upon, the different lines of argument presented by others
- That your response comments on the overall effectiveness of each of these areas or arguments.

Evaluation involves:

Considering the various implications of the issues raised based upon the evidence gleaned from analysis and provides an extensive detailed argument with a clear conclusion.

This means:

- That your answer weighs up the consequences of accepting or rejecting the various and different lines of argument analysed
- That your answer arrives at a conclusion through a clear process of reasoning.

As you work through each section of the book, the focus will be on a variety of different aspects associated with AO2 so that you can comprehensively perfect the overall skills associated with AO2.

Specification content

The early church: Its message and
format: the kerygmata.

Key terms

Jewish apocalypticism: belief in
the sudden and cataclysmic coming of
God to rule the world in justice

Kerygma: a proclamation or
declaration of an event

Key person

Hermann Samuel Reimarus:
(1694–1768) a German philosopher
who denied the supernatural origins of
Christianity.

E: The early church (in Acts of the Apostles)

Its message and format: the kerygmata

Did the early church 'get Jesus right'?

Have you heard the statement, 'everyone is a saint at their own funeral'? It refers
to the truth that when a group gathers to remember someone's life, they tend
to remember only the accomplishments, breakthroughs, successes and happy
memories. Is what is said at a funeral historically accurate? Does it present the real
picture of who someone was?

Scholars have been asking this same question of the Christian Church in the way
it remembers Jesus. Did the early Christian Church 'get Jesus right'? Did they
represent his teaching in the way he wanted it to be represented? Or, when they
proclaimed their message about Jesus, did they twist and distort his message to
suit their purposes?

Criticism of the early church

Hermann Samuel Reimarus was the first enlightenment thinker to accuse the
disciples of changing the views of Jesus. Reimarus said that Jesus accepted a Jewish
viewpoint popular in his time that the world was about to end – this is known as
Jewish apocalypticism. The noun 'apocalypse' means 'a revelation' or 'disclosure'
and has come to be associated with the sudden end of the world by God in an
act of judgment. Reimarus believed that the disciples removed the apocalyptic
viewpoint of Jesus, changing his message into timeless and spiritual truths.
They did this because the world didn't end and they faked Jesus' resurrection
and founded a new religion. In other words, they did not want to return to their
occupations as fishermen. This is a devastating critique! Many scholars disagree
with Reimarus but there are others, as we shall see, who think he was on to
something.

Kerygma

At the heart of the debate is the **kerygma** of the Apostles in Acts 2 and 3. Kerygma
is the Greek term for 'preaching' or 'proclamation' and is related to *keryx*, meaning
herald, or one who makes a bold declaration. In other words, a kerygma is an
announcement rather than a set of teachings or doctrines. The term is used
many times in the New Testament; for example, it is used by Luke to describe the
ministry of Jesus: 'He has sent me to *proclaim* release to the captives and recovery
of sight to the blind' (Luke 4:18) and by Paul: 'And how can they hear without
someone *preaching* to them' (Romans 10:14). When the disciples presented their
message about Jesus publicly, they did not deliver a lecture, but 'heralded' an
event. Note: a plural form of kerygma, 'kerygmata', is used by the specification
because you are asked to study two passages in the book of Acts. However, the
term kerygma will be used in this book as it is the standard term to refer to the
proclamation of the Apostles in the New Testament.

quickfire

1.7 What is the difference between
kerygma and 'teaching'?

C. H. Dodd on kerygma

The British New Testament scholar C. H. Dodd said that we should be careful not to confuse kerygma with teaching or with historical facts – though it can include both of these. We should also, he said, not think of the New Testament as a 'memoir' because at its heart it is a bold set of claims that confront its readers with a decision. Finally, he warned about seeing the New Testament as merely a call to moral improvement. The speeches in Acts are about being confronted with truths and experiencing a joyful transformation of our lives.

Acts 2:14–39 and 3:12–26

The book of Acts shows the progression of the Christian message from Jerusalem, throughout the Roman Empire and then ends with the Gospel coming to Rome itself. In Acts 2 and 3 we are confronted by the first of many speeches by the Apostles in the books of Acts. These speeches share the main idea that God's plan for salvation, unfolding through the Jewish scriptures, has reached fulfilment in the life, death and resurrection of Jesus. This plan continues, say the Apostles, by the power of the Holy Spirit in the life of the Church.

What makes the speeches in Acts 2 and 3 especially interesting is that these are presented as the first public messages of a tiny group of Jewish Christians in Jerusalem. Even sceptics of traditional Christian belief find it noteworthy that this small movement prevailed and became a major world religion when there were so many other small movements which died out after the first generation.

The main elements of the kerygma

C. H. Dodd says that there are six main elements of the kerygma in these messages; they are announcements that:

1. The age of fulfilment has dawned. The words of the Hebrew prophets about the coming of the new age are used by the Apostles to explain the miracles that the crowds have witnessed.

2. This new age has come about through the ministry, death and resurrection of Jesus. That the power of Jesus is behind these events is confirmed by: (a) his Davidic descent, (b) the works of power during his ministry, (c) God using his unfair death at the hands of men, and (d) the raising of Jesus from the dead.

3. Jesus has ascended to the right hand of God; this confirms that he is the Messianic head of the new Israel.

4. God's Holy Spirit has been poured out on the Church so that it is now the sign of Christ's power and glory.

5. Christ will soon return to bring the messianic age to its full consummation.

6. Everyone should repent so that their sins can be forgiven and they can receive the Holy Spirit to participate in the special, new life of the Church.

Contemporary depiction of St Peter announcing the kerygma on the Day of Pentecost.

Specification content

The kerygmata as presented by C. H. Dodd, with reference to Acts 2:14–39; 3:12–26.

C. H. Dodd (1884–1973)

Study tip

Read the passages in Acts 2:14–39 and 3:12–26 for yourself. See if you can find the elements listed by Dodd in each of the speeches.

quickfire

1.8 What are the main elements of the speeches in Acts 2 and 3?

Key quotes

The main burden of the kerygma is that the unprecedented has happened: God has visited and redeemed His people. (C. H. Dodd)

Let us recall the general scheme of the kerygma. It begins by proclaiming that 'this is that which was spoken by the prophets'; the age of fulfillment has dawned, and Christ is its Lord; it then proceeds to recall the historical facts, leading up to the resurrection and exaltation of Christ and the promise of His coming in glory; and it ends with the call to repentance and the offer of forgiveness. (C. H. Dodd)

Specification content

The challenges to the kerygmata
(with reference to the historical value
of the speeches in Acts and the work
of Rudolf Bultmann). The adapting
of the Christian message to suit the
audience.

The challenges to the kerygmata

Is the book of Acts a trustworthy historical document?

Some scholars have viewed Acts as more a literary product rather than a historical account, with its speeches not having been delivered by Peter, Stephen or Paul, but representing summaries of the author's point of view. The main arguments for this point of view are:

- Luke (if this is indeed the author) is a Gentile, not a Jewish Christian. Therefore, he was not present at some or any of the events he is reporting – certainly not for the events of Acts 2 and 3.

- Luke-Acts was probably written in the 80s CE, up to 40–50 years after the events reported.

- It seems that the book of Acts is a highly organised work, which may be evidence that its material has changed from the original form in which it existed. For instance, there are eleven speeches in the book (the Apostolic kerygma); each of these have similar elements and are the centrepiece of a scene described by the authors.

- The language used by the author is more characteristic of Luke-Acts than of what we know of Paul's theology expressed elsewhere in the New Testament. In other words, the 'voice' of Paul in the later speeches of Acts really sounds more like the voice of Luke-Acts than it does the 'Paul' of the early letters scholars agree were written by him.

- Furthering the previous point, many of Paul's most important themes from his letters (faith vs. works, spiritual gifts in the Church, issues on keeping the law) are absent when Acts reports on his preaching.

- The events portrayed in the book of Acts contain reports of miraculous events and sudden, dramatic reversals of points of view such as we associate with ancient literature and legends and not with a modern, scientific age.

Study tip

It's easy to dismiss an ancient document that includes miraculous events as not having historical value, but make sure that you dig into the specific reasons for accepting or rejecting the speeches in Acts as having actually occurred.

Many scholars strongly disagree with the assumption that there is no historical value in Acts. First, this book was never seriously questioned as a key document by the early church. Since the book reports on public events known to many, one would think that if these were seriously misrepresented, there would have been an outcry from others who knew of different traditions. The opposite is the case. Luke's reporting is not questioned; the book is affirmed by the Muratorian Canon, Tertullian, Clement, Origen and others.

Even though Acts was written long after the events it describes, there is a clear tradition that Luke accompanied Paul on his missionary journeys in Colossians 4:14, Philemon 24 and II Timothy 4:11. Thus, he would have had access to first-hand accounts of the events he describes. Furthermore, the amount and kind of detail conveyed in the narrative is such that it would be difficult to imagine that it was completely made up.

In terms of the style and language used by Luke, it is common for any writer to arrange material in a certain order – this does not mean that the material does not have historical roots. In addition to this, it is also to be expected that an author will bring his own vocabulary and language into her/his writing. More importantly, Luke's purpose is to convey how the good news of Jesus spread through the work and message of the disciples; how would it serve his purpose to completely ignore history?

quickfire

1.9 When do most scholars think that the book of Acts was written?

The differences between the presentation of Paul in Acts and of Paul's own writings can simply be accounted for by the fact that Paul had different aims in his speeches to the public in Acts than he did for his letters, which were more pastoral in nature.

C. H. Dodd has examined the letters of Paul to see if they contain the main elements of the kerygma as they are presented in Acts (see the six points above). His answer is a resounding 'yes'. For Paul, there is no doubt that Jesus is the fulfilment of prophecy, and that his life, death, resurrection and future coming are all key elements of the Christian faith, just as they are also presented in the book of Acts.

In addition to this, Dodd does not doubt that the author of Acts is a careful historian. For example, Acts includes differing accounts of the conversion of Paul – one would think that someone determined to create a unified literary work would have re-worked this into one consistent account.

These points lead many to the conclusion that Luke was personally acquainted with the Apostles and witnessed their preaching; he had no need to make anything up because he had direct access to the messages of the early church. He had spent time with Paul and he knew those who had witnessed the birth of the church in Jerusalem.

AO1 Activity

Get a stack of blank index cards and on the front of each card write one reason to trust or to not trust the author of Acts as a reliable historian. On the back of each card write a key term to remind you of that reason. Mix these cards up and see if you can remember the reason from the key word that you chose.

Is the kerygma irrelevant?

Some have argued that both the kerygma of the Apostles and Jesus are irrelevant since the historical Jesus believed that world would end in his lifetime with the sudden and cataclysmic coming of God. In other words, Jesus should be viewed as an apocalyptic or 'eschatological figure' (**eschatology** refers the study of the 'end times').

According to this view, Jesus' aim was to bring his own generation to God before the coming judgement – he never envisioned that he was founding an ongoing movement, a church that would endure for centuries. Jesus himself said, 'There are some standing here who will not taste death before they see the Son of Man coming in his kingdom' (Matthew 16:28). There is also evidence that the early church also believed this: '... for the coming of the Lord is near' (James 5:8) and '... the dead in Christ will rise first. Then we who are alive, who are left, will be caught up in the clouds together with them to meet the Lord in the air...' (I Thessalonians 4:16–17). So, perhaps in the book of Acts the early church was still in the grip of this apocalyptic view and, even though Luke wrote several decades after the crucifixion, they still believed the world was about to end. In the early 20th century **Albert Schweitzer** declared that the one thing that could be known about the historical Jesus was the very thing that made him irrelevant for today: his belief in the imminent end of the world. Thus, the Apostles were awaiting his return and perhaps were beginning to lose hope as time passed.

Key quote

The Kingdom of God is conceived as coming in the events of the life, death, and resurrection of Jesus, and to proclaim these facts, in their proper setting, is to preach the Gospel of the Kingdom of God. (C. H. Dodd)

quickfire

1.10 Why did Dodd think that the author of Acts was a good historian?

Key term

Eschatology: the study of the end things; in biblical theology this encompasses the soul, death, resurrection, the final judgement, immortality, heaven, and hell

Key person

Albert Schweitzer: (1875–1965) theologian and medical missionary whose book, *The Quest for the Historical Jesus* viewed Jesus as mistakenly believing in the imminent end of the world.

Many scholars see Jesus as having believed that the end of the world was about to occur.

Key quotes

The more we try to penetrate in imagination to the state of mind of the first Christians in the earliest days, the more are we driven to think of resurrection, exaltation, and second advent as being, in their belief, inseparable parts of a single divine event. It was not an *early* advent that they proclaimed, but an *immediate* advent. They proclaimed it not so much as a future event for which men should prepare by repentance, but rather as the impending corroboration of a present fact: the new age is already here, and because it is here men should repent. **(C. H. Dodd)**

The possibility of eschatological fanaticism was no doubt present in the outlook of the primitive church, but it was restrained by the essential character of the Gospel as apprehended in experience. **(C. H. Dodd)**

We must ask whether the eschatological preaching and the mythological sayings as a whole contain a still deeper meaning which is concealed under the cover of mythology. **(R. Bultmann)**

Key terms

Myth: a story containing divine beings or supernatural themes used to understand natural events, or social and political concerns

Realised eschatology: the idea that the quality of life normally associated with a relationship with God after death can be experienced now

C. H. Dodd: the relevance of the kerygma

C. H. Dodd said that there was much more going on than Jewish apocalypticism (a focus on the imminent end of the world) in the preaching of Jesus and the life of the early church. In fact, if you examine the elements of the kerygma, he said, very little has to do with the imminent return of Jesus – most of it is concerned with the experience of forgiveness and living in the power of the Holy Spirit in the present rather than in the future. Early Christians were focused more on the joy they had in their experience of the risen Jesus and in the community of the Church than they were on the life to come – even though they probably did expect that the world would soon end. This explains why the Church did not fall apart as time went on.

Dodd said that Jesus himself believed not only in the coming of God at the end of the world, but that God had already broken into the world through his own life and ministry. Dodd calls this '**realised eschatology**'. In other words, one does not have to wait to the end of the world to experience the fullness of God – this can be 'realised' now, in the present. The focus of the early church was on the power that God brings with forgiveness, community and renewed hope much more than on the theme of the world's sudden demise. The fact that Jesus hadn't returned was simply not significant for most Christians as they could go on enjoying the full power of Christian living for the rest of their lives.

However, what are we to make of the dark, apocalyptic passages which seem to so clearly speak about the coming end of the world, such as Mark 13, Matthew 24 and the book of Revelation? Dodd said that some of these passages should be viewed not as pictures of a final judgment but as an interpretation of the challenges that come to all people when they are faced with the power of the kerygma. Some passages do indeed present an apocalyptic point of view, but this should be viewed as an 'eschatological fanaticism' which has always been on the fringe of the Christian Church. However, at the heart of Christian belief is the saving power of Jesus, which can be experienced in this life. This kerygma is what Jesus himself announced in Mark 1:15: 'The time is fulfilled [or, 'realised'], and the kingdom of God has come near; repent, and believe the good news.' Jesus and the Apostles, Dodd said, were united by the same kerygma, a message relevant whether or not the end of the world was about to occur.

Rudolf Bultmann on the kerygma

The New Testament scholar Rudolf Bultmann, like Dodd, believed that the kerygma was an announcement rather than a doctrine or a teaching. However, Dodd had put a great deal of energy into showing how the kerygma and its various elements were unified across the New Testament. Bultmann did not care about proving the unity of the New Testament or its historical value. This is because he saw the New Testament as full of myths that are irrelevant to people living in a modern age. What is important is to distinguish the kerygma from the **myth** so that it becomes relevant to our lives. Bultmann is convinced that when we do this, we will each be individually confronted with an existential decision about our faith.

Study tip

Make sure you understand the difference between Dodd's realised eschatology and Jewish apocalypticism.

Bultmann: hearing kerygma in the myth

A myth, for Bultmann is a primitive science which explains events in terms of supernatural causes (i.e. describing the eclipse of the sun as happening because God is punishing us for our sins). Bultmann argued that the mythological views of biblical writers make it difficult for people today to read the Bible. In fact, there are three options we can take with the biblical message:

1. Believe the myths of the Bible literally; this can be done by retreating from the modern world and joining certain religious communities where everyone accepts the mythological viewpoint as real. However, this option may not appeal to modern people who believe that the world can largely be understood through the scientific principle of cause and effect.

2. You can 'cut out' the mythological sections from the Bible and build a religion on what remains – the ethical admonitions of Jesus (such as the readiness to love others). Many rationalistic 19th-century theologians did this, however, it reduces Christianity to a set of moral admonitions and seems to lose the sense of power and joy that religious believers derive from their faith.

3. Try to find the underlying truth (the kerygma) that is a part of the myth. This path means exploring the myth to try to discover the truths about humanity and existence they are expressing through its mythological language. Bultmann took this third path, which begins by trying to grasp the mythological beliefs behind the New Testament.

Two mythologies in the New Testament

Bultmann saw two main mythologies at work in the New Testament. The first mythology, as we have seen, is Jewish apocalyptic belief in the sudden and cataclysmic end of the world, brought about by the miraculous power of God. Of course, says Bultmann, history triumphed over this myth. However, there was another myth at work: **Gnosticism**. This was a widespread set of beliefs in the ancient world which pictured all the created world in a spiritual battle. Each person is, essentially, a 'spark of light' which has become trapped in the world through demonic forces. A being of light has been sent down from the highest God to bring people special knowledge (*gnosis* is the Greek word for knowledge) so that our 'sparks' can be liberated. Bultmann believed that Christians adapted this mythology to their own beliefs in Jesus and this led them to believing in Jesus as a pre-exiting being, born of the Virgin Mary, a heavenly being who descended to earth to redeem humanity. In other words, the gnostic myth emphasises the high status of Jesus.

Each of these myths about the imminent end of the world or of the heavenly origin of Jesus are difficult to believe today. However, Bultmann said that when the disciples encountered Jesus they had something new awakened in them – not beliefs in doctrines about Jesus, but an experience of God. This is because the kerygma itself expresses some basic truths about humanity:

- We are not masters of the world
- Our plans and powers are finite
- There is a transcendent power in the universe
- There is forgiveness
- It is false to think that we can and should control life
- It is possible to find a spirit of openness to the future.

18th-century depiction by Benjamin West of Adam and Eve being cast out from the Garden of Eden. Bultmann would view this as a mythological portrayal of the reality that the world we live in is not ideal.

Key quote

This method of interpretation of the New Testament which tries to recover the deeper meaning behind the mythological conceptions, I call *de-mythologising* – an unsatisfactory word, to be sure. Its aim is not to eliminate the mythological statements but to interpret them. It is a method of hermeneutics [or interpretation].
(R. Bultmann)

Key term

Gnosticism: from the Greek for 'having knowledge'; a movement which taught that we are trapped in an evil, material world. We must find special knowledge in order to be redeemed

Bultmann believed that early Christians were influenced by gnostic beliefs as well as by apocalypticism.

AO1 Activity

Dodd and Bultmann each have a different way of dealing with the challenge of reducing Jesus and the message of the Apostles to end-time fanaticism. Close the book and see if you can write down the main thrust of each of their arguments in two minutes.

1.11 What are the two myths at work
in the early church according to
Bultmann?

Key quote

This then, is the deeper meaning
of the mythological preaching of
Jesus: to be open to God's future
which is really imminent for every
one of us; to be prepared for this
future which can come as a thief in
the night when we do not expect it;
to be prepared, because this future
will be a judgment on all men who
have bound themselves to this world
and are not free, not open to God's
future. (R. Bultmann)

1.12 What does it mean for Bultmann to
de-mythologise?

Key quote

That the kerygma never appears
without already having been given
some theological interpretation rests
upon the fact that it can never be
spoken except in a human language
and formed by human thought.
(R. Bultmann)

Bultmann: the kerygma involves a personal decision

Since ideas can never be expressed without words, there is never a 'pure kerygma'
that exists apart from cultural beliefs and ideas. However, when the Apostles
proclaimed their message, individuals felt a power behind their words, a power
we can still hear today. The most important aspect of Acts chapters 2 and 3 for
Bultmann is expressed in 2:37: 'Now when they heard this, they were cut to the
heart and said to Peter and to the other Apostles, "Brothers, what should we do?"'
This verse indicates that there was a deep personal confrontation for those that
heard the words of the Apostles. They did not want to analyse the truths they
heard, study them, or explore their historical foundations – but, instead, they made
a decision. For Bultmann, the kerygma is a personal message that proclaims truth
and elicits a response:

- It is not about the exact elements that compose it
- It is not perceived by scientific explanation
- It is never complete – it will be expressed in new ways in each generation
- It is not about doctrine
- It cannot be proven to be true through historical means
- It is not a myth, but can be heard through the myth.

Criticisms of Bultmann

Some have said that Bultmann too easily 'wrote off' Christian doctrine as
mythological, and that there are good reasons to believe that Christian claims
about Jesus are historically true. Or, at least, there is an historical foundation to
Christianity. Thus, the kerygma should be interpreted as having a basis in historical
events.

Others have accused Bultmann of creating a new myth for 'modern people'. That
is, he has replaced one set of myths (apocalyptic and gnostic views) with another
(his ideas about meaning). Related to this is the question: what makes Bultmann's
essential message distinctively Christian? Can't one get at these truths about the
meaning of our existence in the kerygma in other ways (such as existentialist
thought)? Finally, whereas the book of Acts is about a public declaration of
the good news as well as public response leading to the formation of a new
community, Bultmann has distorted the setting by turning the kerygma into a
personal and individualistic message.

AO1 Activity

What might a Christian who believed in a literal interpretation of the Bible
dislike about Bultmann's point of view? What might someone who was
attracted to spirituality but not to Christianity like about Bultmann's point of
view? Make a list for each imaginary person. Finally, is there any area about
Bultmann where they might find agreement? Why or why not?

AO1 Developing skills

It is now important to consider the information that has been covered in this section; however, the information in its raw form is too extensive and so has to be processed in order to meet the requirements of the examination. This can be done by practising more advanced skills associated with AO1. The exercises that run throughout this book will help you to do this and prepare you for the examination. For assessment objective 1 (AO1), which involves demonstrating 'knowledge' and 'understanding' skills, we are going to focus on different ways in which the skills can be demonstrated effectively, and also refer to how the performance of these skills is measured (see generic band descriptors for A2 [WJEC] AO1 or A Level [Eduqas] AO1).

▶ **Your task is this:** Below is a summary of **Rudolf Bultmann's approach to the kerygma**. It is about 200 words long. You are needed to use this for an answer but could not repeat all of this in an essay under examination conditions so you will have to condense the material. Discuss which points you think are the most important and then re-draft into your own summary of 100 words.

The challenge in understanding the New Testament kerygma, for Bultmann, is that it is embedded in a mythological worldview that is foreign for people today. A myth, for Bultmann expresses human truths using supernatural beings and events. Specifically, the New Testament reflects two mythologies: (i) Jewish apocalypticism – the belief that God will bring on a sudden and dramatic end to the world and (ii) Gnosticism, a belief that secret knowledge is needed to escape our entrapment in this world. This knowledge has come from a being of light. Christians adapted this theme and created doctrines such as the virgin birth. What we need to do, said Bultmann, is not believe any of these myths literally, nor to cut them out of the Bible and retain only the non-mythological aspects. Instead, we must try to find the truth about human life that they are expressing. When Bultmann examined the kerygma in the book of Acts he saw that it reflected the fact that the disciples had a deep, existential encounter with Jesus. This encounter raised many truths, such as it is a mistake to think that we and our plans are all-powerful, but that we can have hope, forgiveness and a new life. For Bultmann, the most important aspect of the kerygma was that the listeners were 'cut to the heart' and made a change in their lives; this shows its power to change lives both then and today.

When you have completed the task, refer to the band descriptors for A2 (WJEC) or A Level (Eduqas) and, in particular, have a look at the demands described in the higher band descriptors towards which you should be aspiring. Ask yourself:

- Does my work demonstrate a thorough, accurate and relevant knowledge and understanding of religion and belief?

- Is my work coherent (consistent or make logical sense), clear and well organised? **(WJEC band descriptor only but still important to consider for Eduqas)**

- Will my work, when developed, be an extensive and relevant response which is specific to the focus of the task?

- Does my work have extensive depth and/or suitable breadth and have excellent use of evidence and examples?

- If appropriate to the task, does my response have thorough and accurate reference to sacred texts and sources of wisdom?

- Are there any insightful connections to be made with other elements of my course?

- Will my answer, when developed and extended to match what is expected in an examination answer, have an extensive range of views of scholars/schools of thought?

- When used, is specialist language and vocabulary both thorough and accurate?

Key skills

Knowledge involves:

Selection of a range of (thorough) accurate and relevant information that is directly related to the specific demands of the question.

This means:

- Selecting relevant material for the question set

- Being focused in explaining and examining the material selected.

Understanding involves:

Explanation that is extensive, demonstrating depth and/or breadth with excellent use of evidence and examples including (where appropriate) thorough and accurate supporting use of sacred texts, sources of wisdom and specialist language.

This means:

- Effective use of examples and supporting evidence to establish the quality of your understanding

- Ownership of your explanation that expresses personal knowledge and understanding and NOT just reproducing a chunk of text from a book that you have rehearsed and memorised.

Specification content

The extent to which the kerygmata (within the areas of Acts studied) are of any value for Christians today.

Issues for analysis and evaluation

The extent to which the kerygmata (within the areas of Acts studied) are of any value for Christians today

The kerygma in Acts 2 and 3 are, according to the Bible, the first public speeches of the Church. They can be seen as giving the first glimpse into the theology of early Christians. It is for this reason that Acts 2 is featured in churches on the Day of Pentecost, a special day for many churches around the world to remember the birth of the Church.

However, the kerygma is not only a historical relic for Christians – many today see this as a model for the Church's message. First, the kerygma brings together, in several short elements, significant aspects of theology: prophecy in the Hebrew Bible about a coming age, events from the life of Jesus and belief in the future return of Jesus. The kerygma expresses how a longing for a better world found fulfilment in Jesus. These speeches in Acts also provide a concise statement of faith in Jesus and the power of the Christian life which can be seen to unify Christians across denominations in various parts of the world.

Not only do these passages have theological or creedal value, they also express the power and energy of the early church – qualities that many Christians long for today. The Apostles had courage to take a stand for their beliefs, performed miracles in public and gave a reasoned defence for their faith to those who did not share their beliefs. Their message moved the crowd to repentance and a decision to join their movement. These are qualities many Christians would like to see more present in their churches. In fact, some churches call themselves 'Pentecostal' since they seek to emulate the energy and sense of purpose that the early church displayed on the day of Pentecost.

Some Christians, however, might object to placing such importance on these speeches; after all, if every scripture is inspired by God (II Timothy 3:16) then God's message can be found everywhere in the Bible. Therefore, suggesting that some passages in the Bible are more important than others seems to lessen the value of other passages.

Furthermore, some might ask if we can really expect to recreate this unique situation (such as performing miracles in public) in the Church today? Some churches believe that the age of miracles has passed; they believe that Acts represents an era where God was especially involved in the creation of the Church but that this period and its need for miracles has ended. It could be argued that, as inspiring as these accounts are, the Church is in an entirely different situation today. In countries where the Church is firmly established, it needs to work with the government, build coalitions on moral issues, reach out to other religions, and work with those who have no religion to build a just society. In other words, the mission of the Church is not to preoccupy itself with the ancient kerygma, but to evolve into ever new situations.

There are also historical issues which might cause some Christians to question the value of these passages for today. For instance, some scholars have suggested that Jesus and his disciples believed in an apocalyptic worldview. The term apocalyptic (from 'apocalypse' – to reveal or disclose, and used in relation to heavenly secrets) has come to be associated with the sudden and cataclysmic end of the world. According to this view, Jesus founded his movement and delivered all his teaching in the expectation that the Kingdom of God was to arrive in his lifetime. He was mistaken. The disciples, in turn, then expected Jesus to return soon after the resurrection and, by the time that the book of Acts was written, may have been wavering in their faith.

As you read through this section try to do the following:

1. Pick out the different lines of argument that are presented in the text and identify any evidence given in support.

2. For each line of argument try to evaluate whether or not you think this is strong or weak.

3. Think of any questions you may wish to raise in response to the arguments.

This activity will help you to start thinking critically about what you read, and help you to evaluate the effectiveness of different arguments and from this develop your own observations, opinions and points of view that will help with any conclusions that you make in your answers to the AO2 questions that arise.

Thus, the kerygma in the book of Acts is bound up with a worldview (the imminent coming of Jesus) – and in the wake of that not happening, the kerygma is of little value and Christians are better off basing their faith on other themes from the Bible.

Rudolf Bultmann believed, too, that the kerygma was bound up with myths irrelevant to modern people; however, he thought it could still have value today. He defined myth as a kind of crude science that uses supernatural beings and occurrences to explain what are, essentially, human truths. Bultmann found value in the kerygma not by believing in its literal truth, or by ignoring it but by asking, 'what is the deeper meaning behind these beliefs?'.

Bultmann's answer is that the kerygma expresses truths that were awakened in the Apostles through their encounter with Jesus: there is hope, forgiveness and a new future with God that overcomes preoccupations with ourselves and our own plans. In other words, it is the experience of the Apostles and their witnesses conveyed in the kerygma rather than the actual words themselves that is of value. This kind of experience is most clearly heard when the crowds were 'cut to the heart' and made a commitment to the Church.

However, C. H. Dodd would find this view overly critical. Why assume that Jesus and his followers were bound up in an outmoded worldview? Dodd argued that there was much more going on in the ministry of Jesus and his followers than Jewish apocalypticism. Jesus not only believed in God's imminent return, but that God had already broken into the world through his ministry – the great things happening in the present prevented them from being too preoccupied with the future. Dodd calls this 'realised eschatology' to signify that the end times (eschaton) was not merely in the future but could be experienced (or realised) in the present.

When Dodd analysed the kerygma he saw that very little of it had to do with Jesus' imminent return. Most of it had to do with the power of God experienced by the disciples which, in turn, attracted the crowds. For example, in the six elements that characterise the kerygma, only one has to do with future expectation. Dodd would therefore agree with those who place a high value on the kerygma as relevant for today's Church.

In conclusion, one determining factor in whether one places a high or low value on these speeches of Acts is the judgement that one makes about the worldview of Jesus and his followers. That is, if Jesus' teachings are seen to represent an outdated worldview, then the kerygma might be considered to have little value for today; Christians will be advised to find other themes in the Bible on which to base their faith, perhaps turning to the Christian existentialism of Rudolf Bultmann. However, if Dodd is correct, then the Church is right to examine itself when it does not follow the example of the energy and courage of the early church.

Key quotes

The Kingdom of God had made its appearance with the coming of the Messiah; His works of power and his 'new teaching with authority' had provided evidence of the presence of God among men; His death 'according to the determinate counsel and foreknowledge of God' had marked the end of the old order, and his resurrection and exaltation had definitely inaugurated the new age, characterised, as the prophets had foretold, by the outpouring of the Holy Spirit upon the people of God. It remained only for the new order to be consummated by the return of Christ in glory to judge the quick and the dead and to save his own from the wrath to come. (C. H. Dodd)

The proclamation is not about '…a doctrine or a dogma, but the opening up, through God's act, of the possibility of having faith.' (R. Bultmann)

AO2 Activity

List some conclusions that could be drawn from the AO2 reasoning from the above text; try to aim for at least three different possible conclusions. Consider each of the conclusions and collect brief evidence to support each conclusion from the AO1 and AO2 material for this topic. Select the conclusion that you think is most convincing and explain why it is so. Try to contrast this with the weakest conclusion in the list, justifying your argument with clear reasoning and evidence.

Specification Content

Whether the speeches in Acts have
any historical value.

Whether the speeches in Acts have any historical value

The kerygma in Acts are a part of an ancient document that reports miraculous events and dramatic changes in people's lives. For example, Acts 2:14–39 takes place just after the account of the speaking in tongues and Peter delivers his speech in Acts 3, right after the healing of the lame man. Belief in ancient books filled with accounts of the supernatural strains against the modern spirit, especially if we believe in a scientific understanding of the world based on the law of cause and effect.

Looking past this general scepticism, there is more specific ground to question the historical value of these speeches. Scholars who have studied the biblical documents in detail raise several issues that prevent them from taking this author's testimony at face value.

Firstly, there are questions about the identity of the author and the time at which he wrote. Even if one follows the traditional view that the book of Acts was written by Luke the physician, this would mean that the author is a Gentile and not a Jewish Christian and therefore did not have direct access to the occurrences in Jerusalem at the birth of the Church. Furthermore, if the book was written, as most scholars agree, in the 80s CE, then this means that the author is removed from some of the events being reported by as much as 50 years. If we truly value first-hand accounts of events, then we are robbed of this possibility from the outset.

Then, there are other clues having to do with grammar, style and structure which make Acts appear to be much more a literary creation than a straightforward historical account. For instance, the book has clearly been organised so that a series of dramatic events are described, most of which feature a speech by an Apostle. Furthermore, each of these speeches follows a similar format, including key elements. This has led many to suggest that Luke is presenting his own theology, using the Apostles merely as his mouthpiece.

This insight is strengthened by the observation that when the Paul of the letters (that are nearly universally agreed were written by him) is compared to the Paul in the book of Acts, there are vast differences in word choice and subject matter. For instance, many of the key concerns of Paul expressed in his letters (faith vs. works of the law and spiritual gifts in the Church) are simply absent from Paul in the book of Acts.

Thus, the case for Acts having little historical value can be seen to be strong. However, other scholars warn of exchanging historical suspicion with historical paranoia – too quickly dismissing Luke as a source of historical information.

Firstly, it is no small matter that we have a book from the ancient world written little more than a generation from the events reported. Furthermore, the speeches of the book of Acts were public events, well known to so many in the early church. If these were fabricated, then one would expect there to be an outcry against the historicity of this book. However, this is not the case; Acts was recognised as canonical by the earliest documents and Church Fathers discussing such issues: The Muratorian Canon, Tertullian, Origen, Clement and others.

These facts raise a larger question: If the purpose of the book of Acts was to describe the progression of God's good news in Jesus from Jerusalem outward through the Roman Empire and even to Rome itself, what purpose would it have served the author to have made all this up? Certainly, to do so would be self-defeating.

As to the question of how the author of the book of Acts could have accessed historical data, there are many arguments to be made. First is the fact that he may have very well been a companion of Paul on some of Paul's journeys. In fact, the New Testament identifies Luke with Paul on several occasions (Colossians 4:14, Philemon 24 and II Timothy 4:11) – even if these references do not derive from Paul himself, they may be displaying a commonly held belief that a companion of Paul wrote the book of Acts. Any companion of Paul would likely have had occasion to meet with those who had been present in Jerusalem and could have given the author first-hand testimony of the events in Acts 2 and 3.

Perhaps the easiest scepticism to deal with are the issues of language, structure and style. After all, we expect an author's language and forms of expression to be a part of how they report on events. Furthermore, why is adding a structure to reporting events seen as taking away from their historical value? Every report we read in the newspaper is told in relation to selected events. History textbooks are formulated into chapters which are imposed by the author. In other words, all reports of historical events are found within a created structure – why should the book of Acts be any different? Finally, the fact that there is a difference between the theology of Paul as expressed in his letters and in the book of Acts can simply be accounted for by a difference in focus: Acts is about Paul's theology presented in the public square whereas the letters are internal, pastoral messages directed at believers – we would expect to see a difference.

C. H. Dodd has directly challenged the claim that the author of Acts has created a different Paul from his letters (in the later kerygmatic speeches). He has done this by comparing the main elements of the kerygma (such as viewing Jesus as a fulfilment of Hebrew prophesy, the importance of the crucifixion, resurrection and future return of Jesus) with the letters of Paul. He has found that the main elements of the kerygma are found in Paul's letters. Furthermore, Dodd sees much evidence of the author of Acts doing careful historical work. For instance, there are two accounts of Paul's conversion, each with some differences from the other. Someone who was more concerned with literary rather than historical themes would certainly have harmonised this into one account.

In conclusion, there are many good arguments for accepting or rejecting the historical value of these speeches. However, even if we could identify that behind the speeches in Acts is a solid historical core, of what meaning would that be? Can faith rest completely on history? What about the meaning that the author gives to these events – does that have historical value?

Rudolf Bultmann believes that the writings of the Bible are permeated with a worldview or mythological viewpoint that modern people can no longer accept. In particular, he sees that the New Testament reflects an apocalyptic (end-of-the-world) mythology and a Gnostic mythology which views Jesus as a divine redeemer with a virgin birth – though Gnosticism has been adapted to Christian themes.

If one tries to 'strip away' the mythology to try to find a historical core, one will miss the incredible energy and power of the early church. The most important aspect for Bultmann in these accounts is not the mythological lens of the author, but that the disciples had an encounter with Jesus which led them to renewed hope and vision – and that this can be experienced today, whether or not the speeches have historical value.

Key quote

There is no way of going behind the preaching to a saving fact separable from the preaching – whether to a 'historical Jesus' or to a cosmic drama. Access to Jesus Christ exists only in the preaching. (R. Bultmann)

AO2 Activity

List some conclusions that could be drawn from the AO2 reasoning from the above text; try to aim for at least three different possible conclusions. Consider each of the conclusions and collect brief evidence to support each conclusion from the AO1 and AO2 material for this topic. Select the conclusion that you think is most convincing and explain why it is so. Try to contrast this with the weakest conclusion in the list, justifying your argument with clear reasoning and evidence.

Key skills

Analysis involves:

Identifying issues raised by the materials in the AO1, together with those identified in the AO2 section, and presents sustained and clear views, either of scholars or from a personal perspective ready for evaluation.

This means:

- That your answers are able to identify key areas of debate in relation to a particular issue
- That you can identify, and comment upon, the different lines of argument presented by others
- That your response comments on the overall effectiveness of each of these areas or arguments.

Evaluation involves:

Considering the various implications of the issues raised based upon the evidence gleaned from analysis and provides an extensive detailed argument with a clear conclusion.

This means:

- That your answer weighs up the consequences of accepting or rejecting the various and different lines of argument analysed
- That your answer arrives at a conclusion through a clear process of reasoning.

AO2 Developing skills

It is now important to consider the information that has been covered in this section; however, the information in its raw form is too extensive and so has to be processed in order to meet the requirements of the examination. This can be done by practising more advanced skills associated with AO2. For assessment objective 2 (AO2), which involves 'critical analysis' and 'evaluation' skills, we are going to focus on different ways in which the skills can be demonstrated effectively, and also refer to how the performance of these skills is measured (see generic band descriptors for A2 [WJEC] AO2 or A Level [Eduqas] AO2).

▶ **Your next task is this:** Below is a brief summary of two different points of view concerning **the historical value of the speeches in Acts**. You want to use these two views and lines of argument for an evaluation; however, they need further reasons and evidence for support to fully develop the argument. Re-present these two views in a fully evaluative style by adding further reasons and evidence that link to their arguments. Aim for a further 100 words.

There are many reasons to accept the speeches in Acts 2 and 3 as having a historical basis. First, all the early Church Fathers accept the reports in Acts as true. Furthermore, if Luke had fabricated these speeches there would have been many in the early church who could have refuted this. In fact, it would not have served Luke's purposes to invent these stories as he was attempting to write a history of the early church. Luke would have had access to eyewitnesses of these events. On the other hand, most scholars believe that Acts was not written until many decades after the events it describes. Luke is a Gentile and not a Jewish Christian, so therefore represents a different part of the Church than the one described. There is a similarity between the speeches in Acts that betrays the influence of an editor. Finally, the presence of the miraculous is something that we do not accept today as pointing to a historically accurate document.

When you have completed the task, refer to the band descriptors for A2 (WJEC) or A Level (Eduqas) and, in particular, have a look at the demands described in the higher band descriptors towards which you should be aspiring. Ask yourself:

- Is my answer a confident critical analysis and perceptive evaluation of the issue?
- Is my answer a response that successfully identifies and thoroughly addresses the issues raised by the question set.
- Does my work show an excellent standard of coherence, clarity and organisation?
- Will my work, when developed, contain thorough, sustained and clear views that are supported by extensive, detailed reasoning and/or evidence?
- Are the views of scholars/schools of thought used extensively, appropriately and in context?
- Does my answer convey a confident and perceptive analysis of the nature of any possible connections with other elements of my course?
- When used, is specialist language and vocabulary both thorough and accurate?

F: Two views of Jesus

N. T. Wright: worldviews make a difference

A **worldview** is a set of assumptions that uses story and symbols to answer basic questions such as who are we? When are we? What's wrong with the world? What's the solution? In other words, it is the lens through which an entire culture looks at the world. We may find it easy to dismiss worldviews of the past as being superstitious or unenlightened – but could our dismissal itself be a part of a worldview?

N. T. Wright believes that we have all been affected by an **enlightenment** worldview. According to this story, only sense perceptions give us sure and certain knowledge about the world; any statement that cannot be verified by sense perception is nonsense. In this context, history and faith are split off from each other, with history as a part of a public discussion about evidence; faith is considered only as a private realm of personal, spiritual beliefs. One of the unfortunate things about this story, for Wright, is that it forces people to either live in the 'attic' of a faith that is divorced from history (faith becomes highly personal and less attached to public life) or the 'dungeon' of history (history is a sterile activity in which we find no meaning or importance). Too many Christians accept an enlightenment worldview and thus keep their faith to themselves.

AO1 Activity

Make a list of symbols and key messages from culture that have always been a part of your life. Then make a list of ideas and themes that N. T. Wright says are important in the worldview of the New Testament. How different are these lists? Where are they the most different? The least different?

The worldview behind the New Testament

An enlightenment worldview is completely different from the worldview we find at work in the New Testament, says Wright. There, we find belief in a God who cares passionately about the world in general and Israel in particular. God establishes a **covenant** with God's people and thinks that it is important that people live out their faith. It is a worldview where history, faith, politics and spirituality are not separated from one another. Jesus was born into that worldview and speaks from it. This means that when Christians turn Jesus into a spiritual, inspirational figure who speaks only privately to human hearts, they will be distorting his message.

Key quotes

History, then, prevents faith becoming fantasy. Faith prevents history becoming mere antiquarianism. **(N. T. Wright)**

Humans tell stories because this is how we perceive, and indeed relate to, the world. **(N. T. Wright)**

AO1 Activity

Make a list of symbols and key messages from culture that have been a part of your life. Then make a list of ideas and themes that N. T. Wright says are important in the worldview of the New Testament. How different are these lists? What key questions about life do these lists answer? Where are they the most different from each other? The least different?

This section covers AO1 content and skills

Specification content

A comparison of the work of two key scholars, including their views of Jesus with reference to their different methods of studying Jesus: John Dominic Crossan and N. T. Wright.

Wright: Jesus the true Messiah; critical realism; texts as 'the articulation of worldviews'; seeks to find the best explanation for the traditions found in the Gospels.

quickfire

1.13 What's wrong, for N. T. Wright, with our modern worldview?

N. T. Wright says we are all born into a worldview.

Key terms

Covenant: an agreement between two or more parties based on obedience and involving promises

Enlightenment: a European intellectual movement emphasising reason over religious revelation and superstition as the basis of knowledge

Worldview: the way in which a culture looks at the world; this involves stories, symbols and answers to key questions about existence

Key quotes

We cannot find a neutral place on which to stand, a theory of knowledge, or a theory of knowledge about Jesus, which can be established independently of its object. History and faith (taking *faith* in the broadest sense, as whatever worldview, commitment or metaphysical assumption one may make) need each other at every step, and never more so than here. (N. T. Wright)

[It is] wrong to imagine that perception is prior to the grasping of larger realities. On the contrary, detailed sense-perceptions not only occur within stories; they are verified (if they are) within it. (N. T. Wright)

Critical realism

In an enlightenment worldview, we think that facts or sense perception comes before a worldview. N. T. Wright questions this assumption. He believes that the worldview precedes everything; it is the lens through which we make sense of data. How do we know, then, if our worldview, or cultural story, is 'true' or 'right'?

To answer this question, Wright explores the enlightenment worldview more deeply. We have already seen how our **modern** story includes the view that only statements that can be verified by sense perception can be seen as conveying truth. This is known as **positivism**, the view that you can have positive knowledge of the world as long as any claims for knowledge can be verified through the senses. This can also be called **naïve realism**, the optimistic view that you can make judgments on 'raw data' and sense experience. There is a second pessimistic side to the modern narrative about knowledge, says Wright. This is **phenomenalism**, the insight anything we think we know in the external world is only knowledge of our sense data – we only know that we have certain types of knowledge. In other words, we only really know the knower! One of the important insights of our era is that what we took for 'certain knowledge' has been coloured by our biases. In this view, it is not certain that I can know anything outside of myself. Some thinkers refer to this as **postmodernism.** So, the enlightenment, says Wright, has given us both an optimistic and a pessimistic view of human knowledge. Positivism is the optimistic view and phenomenalism is the pessimistic view.

Study tip

N. T. Wright has shared his views freely on YouTube. You can search him there, using 'N. T. Wright worldviews', 'N. T. Wright history' and 'N. T. Wright atheism'. Spend a few minutes listening to him for yourself.

Wright combines insights from each of these views. **Critical realism** (i) accepts that things can be known as something different from ourselves (realism) but (ii) recognises that the only way we can know something is from our own point of view. We bring our own biases to anything we know, the conditioning of our psychological, historical, sociological, and political context. We therefore need to be critical about the objectivity of our point of view.

Key quotes

This is a way of describing the process of 'knowing' that acknowledges the reality of the thing known, as something other than the knower (hence 'realism'), while also fully acknowledging that the only access we have to this reality lies along the spiraling path of appropriate dialogue or conversation between the knower and the thing known (hence 'critical'). (N. T. Wright)

Knowledge, in other words, although in principle concerning realities independent of the knower, is never itself independent of the knower. (N. T. Wright)

How do we know the truth?

The first step to finding the truth is recognising this fundamental insight that a worldview precedes facts. We have to come clean that we bring biases, even biases about science, to the table. Instead of 'writing off' other points of view (for instance those we find in the New Testament), we must accept that there might be truth beyond our own viewpoint. There is no such thing as a completely neutral, detached observer.

The next step is to be willing to enter into a dialogue between our point of view and the object we are encountering. In this dialogue, we may become aware of our own biases and of truth in a new story. Three things can happen to our worldview:

(i) My story might be confirmed,

(ii) My story might need to be modified or

(iii) My story might need to be abandoned.

History involves groups of people with their stories, meeting other groups with their stories and entering into a kind of hypothesis-verification process where, over time, stories are confirmed, modified or abandoned. We need to be willing to enter this process, says Wright, as we study the life and teachings of Jesus.

Wright's view of Jesus: the true Messiah

Entering into this process of dialogue means, on the one hand, that one's faith in Jesus must meet the facts of history. Christians cannot build images of Jesus that are divorced from information gleaned from historical sources. On the other hand, Wright says, we must not assume that history will disprove Christian claims. In other words, we must not turn historical scepticism into a paranoia that rules out the possibility that events have happened in history that can be of meaning and value for our lives today. When Wright enters into a historical study of Jesus he finds these points significant:

- *Jesus was a Jewish prophet* announcing the Kingdom of God. This should be the starting point for any historical study of Jesus: his Jewish context, the perception of those around him that he was a prophet, and the political declaration of the coming Kingdom of God. This means, for Wright, that Jesus should not be seen so much as a 'wandering preacher giving sermons' or a 'philosopher offering maxims', but as someone who was initiating a movement.

- *Eschatological expectation.* The Jewish world in which Jesus lived was 'on tiptoe with expectation'. Jesus shared the view that the Jews were the chosen people of God and that history was going somewhere. He believed the kingdom was breaking into history. Some call Jesus a 'social prophet', but it is important to recognise that his agenda for society comes out of his sense of what time it is: the kingdom is about to come.

- *Messiah* There were other Jewish figures at the turn of the first millennium announcing the Kingdom of God (Judas the Galilean and Simeon ben Kosiba). These figures were considered by many to be messiahs; Jesus acted and spoke in ways that showed he believed that he was the Messiah, the one in whom God would accomplish his decisive purpose.

- *A Messiah who gave his life.* The Jewish Messiah was popularly thought of as being a victorious figure. His defeat was therefore the sign that he was not the Messiah. However, there are at least two important facts about Jesus' life that reveal he was re-interpreting the meaning of Messiah: (i) he rejected violent revolutionary behaviour and (ii) he drew upon Jewish traditions about God using the suffering of his people to bring about **redemption**. Wright believes that Jesus began to think of his own death as a part of his messianic task.

Bronze statue 'Bar Kokhba' (1905) by Henrik Hanoch Glitzenstein

Key quote
The reason why stories come into conflict with each other is that worldviews, and the stories that characterise them, are in principle *normative*: that is, they claim to make sense of the whole of reality. (N. T. Wright)

quickfire
1.14 What is the starting point for Wright's historical study of Jesus?

Key terms
Messiah: (literally, 'anointed one') a figure who is expected to unite the Jews and save them from their oppressors, ushering in an era of peace

Redemption: to be saved from sin, or to regain something through an exchange of money or goods

Key quote
… we actually know more securely that Jesus of Nazareth was a Jewish prophet announcing the Kingdom of God than we know anything about the history of the traditions that led up to the production of the Gospels as we have them. (N. T. Wright)

Key Person
Simeon ben Kosiba: The leader of a revolt in 132–135 CE against the Roman occupation of Jerusalem. His followers referred to him as bar Kokhba (son of the star). Leading rabbis declared that he was the Messiah, and an independent Jewish state was established for a short period of time. Severe Jewish persecution followed the end of the revolt and later Jewish leaders referred to him as 'bar Koseva', 'son of lies', and considered the rabbis that followed Kosibah to have been in error.

Key quotes

… to say 'Jesus acted and spoke in ways consistent with his launching a veiled claim to be messiah, and inconsistent with his having no intention of making such a claim' is a historical hypothesis that, I believe, can be powerfully sustained. **(N. T. Wright)**

…the categories that Jesus' own world offered to describe someone doing and saying the sort of things Jesus was doing and saying were: prophet, messiah, martyr. Jesus could and, I have argued, did believe that in filling these roles, was doing something for Israel that Israel could not do for itself, something that in its scriptures only its God YHWH, could and would do. **(N. T. Wright)**

The really interesting thing about Christianity, says Wright, is that there is actually a Christianity! All of the other movements around 'messiahs' of Jesus' era ended with that figure's death. Not so with Jesus. This means that the reinterpretation of messiahship to include the idea of dying for sins was an idea that caught on. Jesus' resurrection confirmed for his followers that he was the true Messiah. Furthermore, the writers of the Gospels were convinced that these events were historical events: Israel's God was acting in history through the life, death, and resurrection of Jesus. Due to the intention of writers to present history in a public context, and because of the compelling nature of the claims themselves, we should take the Gospels seriously.

Key quotes

I see why some people find themselves driven to distinguish the Jesus of history and the Christ of faith, but I do not think the early Christians made such a distinction, and I do not find the need to do so myself. **(N. T. Wright)**

… the Gospels are what they are precisely because their authors thought the events they were recording – all of them, not just some – actually happened. Of course, we may as historians judge that in some cases they were mistaken; but, if this is so, they were to that extent failing to convey the most important meaning they had in mind, which was precisely that in these events *as historical events*, Israel's God, the world's creator, had acted decisively and climactically within creation, within Israel's history. These stories were never designed to express or embody a dehistoricised spirituality… **(N. T. Wright)**

Crossan's method

John Dominic Crossan is a historian and New Testament scholar who has come to different views than N. T. Wright. Crossan attempts to find this historical Jesus by pursuing three areas:

(i) Cross cultural anthropology – what can we know about the ancient Mediterranean culture, agrarian society, gender relations, colonialisms, ethnicity class, taxes, etc., at the time of Jesus? Certainly, any insights that can be gained from this area might help one to understand Jesus and his world.

(ii) Jewish and Greco Roman history. The land where Jesus lived was a colony of the Roman Empire and there are many sources that can be used to understand what Jewish life under Roman rule might have been like. The challenge of this kind of study is that historical sources are largely written by elite, wealthy and powerful males. Therefore, one has to think critically to attempt to understand what life might have been like for lower classes or peasants.

(iii) Literary and textual study of the New Testament and books outside of the New Testament that might also inform us about Jesus' life.

---

quickfire

1.15 What is the main difference, for Wright, between Jesus' movement and other messianic movements?

Specification content

Crossan: Jesus the social revolutionary; using apocryphal Gospels; seeing Jesus as a product of his time; what the words of Jesus would have meant in Jesus' time.

Jesus is a Mediterranean Jewish peasant

After looking at these three areas, Crossan sees Jesus as a 'Mediterranean Jewish peasant' – each of these three terms is very important, reflecting each of his areas of study. For one not only has to know what it means for Jesus to be Jewish (literary and textual study), but that his status as a peasant gives insight on his life and teaching (Jewish and Greco Roman history) and understanding social and psychological relationships in the Mediterranean context at that time sheds more valuable light on Jesus' life and times (cross-cultural anthropology).

Should we rely only on the four Gospels?

When it comes to working with texts that appear to report directly on Jesus' life, Crossan has two main strategies: (i) to only use materials that he dates between 30 and 60 CE and (ii) to never base any insight on Jesus' life that has only a single independent **attestation**. In other words, there needs to be more than one early source for the same saying or event before Crossan will consider it as possible evidence for Jesus' life. The four Gospels reached their final form after 60 CE, so one has to be careful to discern between earlier and later layers in the Gospels.

Using apocryphal Gospels

Crossan believes there are other texts that may provide sources for the life of Jesus independent of the New Testament: the **apocryphal Gospels**. This is the term given to non-canonical Gospels rejected by the Christian Church because they are considered heretical, legendary or of only secondary importance. Many of these Gospels are also called **pseudepigrapha** ('falsely inscribed') because they are written by an anonymous author who gave the name of an Apostle to their writing. These Gospels, *in their present form*, are from the 2nd to 4th centuries CE, dating much later than the majority of the New Testament writings. Some, such as the *Gospel of Thomas* and the *Apocryphon of James*, are found in the Nag Hammadi library, a collection discovered in the Nag Hammadi valley in Egypt in 1945. This collection dates from the 4th century and reflects a view called 'gnosticism', that truth from the universe is known through secret knowledge. Other apocryphal Gospels, such as The *Gospel of the Hebrews*, are preserved in the quotations of Church Fathers; others, such as *Oxyrhynchus 1224* exist only in fragments, separated from larger works. The Church and many New Testament scholars believe that these Gospels neither give reliable information on the life of Jesus nor independent sayings from Jesus. In the words of John P Meier, what we see in these later documents are 'imaginative Christians reflecting popular piety and legend, and gnostic Christians developing a mystical speculative system'. Crossan disagrees.

Key quote

If Jesus was a carpenter, therefore, he belonged to the Artisan class, that group pushed into the dangerous space between Peasants and Degraded or Expendables. **(J. D. Crossan)**

Study tip

Look into these Apocryphal Gospels for yourself; there are English versions for many of these online. For instance, you can easily find the *Gospel of Thomas*, read it and see if you can identify the qualities in it that attract Crossan.

quickfire

1.16 What are the three overlapping areas of study on which Crossan builds his picture of the historical Jesus?

John Dominic Crossan

Key quote

[there is a] 'Lexicon of Snobbery' filled with terms used by literate and therefore upper-class Greco Roman authors to indicate their prejudice against illiterate and therefore lower-class individuals. Among those terms is *tekton*, or 'carpenter', the same term used for Jesus in Mark 6:3 and for Joseph in Matthew 13:55. **(J. D. Crossan)**

Key terms

Apocryphal Gospels: writings about Jesus not accepted by the Church; some exist as complete documents, others as fragments or as quotations in early Christian writings

Attestation: a piece of evidence presented in support of a claim

Gospel of Thomas: a book of 114 sayings of Jesus in the 4th century CE gnostic library discovered near Nag Hammadi, Egypt in 1945

Pseudepigrapha: literally, 'false writings', books written by unknown authors who claimed to be from a well-known figure in order to gain a readership

quickfire

1.17 Where was the Gospel of Thomas
found and what era is it from?

Key quotes

I understand the virginal conception
of Jesus to be a confessional
statement about Jesus' status and
not a biological statement about
Mary's body. **(J. D. Crossan)**

Jesus, finding his own voice, began
to speak of God not as imminent
apocalypse but as present healing.
To those first followers from the
peasant villages of Lower Galilee
who asked how to repay his
exorcisms and cures, he gave a
simple answer – simple, that is,
to understand, but hard as death
itself to undertake. You are healed
healers, he said, so take the
Kingdom to others, for I am not its
patron and you are not its brokers.
(J. D. Crossan)

His [Jesus'] ideal group is, contrary
to Mediterranean and indeed most
human familial reality, an open one
equally accessible to all under God.
It is the Kingdom of God, and it
negates that terrible abuse of power
that is power's dark spectre and
lethal shadow. **(J. D. Crossan)**

quickfire

1.18 According to Crossan what activities
of Jesus challenged his society?

Crossan: Q and the Gospel of Thomas

Crossan believes that even though many of these sources are later than the
New Testament, they may contain traditions that are independent of the New
Testament. In addition to this, he believes there may be early layers within some
of these books that predate the four Gospels. Crossan believes that there are
two Gospels that should especially concern everyone that wants to know about
the historical Jesus. The first of these isn't actually an apocryphal Gospel; it is
'hidden' in Matthew and Luke. It is called '**Q**' (based on the German word *Quelle*,
'source'). Scholars have long thought that behind the shared sayings in Matthew
and Luke is a source that they both used, a simple collection of sayings from Jesus.
Crossan believes that this source should be privileged for giving information on
the historical Jesus not only because it predates the Gospels but also because it
does not contain birth narratives, resurrection narratives or other material which
Crossan feels may have been added later by Christians but does not stem from
the historical Jesus. In addition to this, Crossan draws heavily from the Gospel
of Thomas. This Gospel, like Q, is a collection of sayings by Jesus without a birth
or resurrection narrative. Many scholars, like Crossan, believe that the Gospel
of Thomas dates from a much earlier period not only because a list of sayings is
what we might expect from an early attempt to remember Jesus, but also because
of the discovery of several fragments from the Gospel of Thomas from a much
earlier period.

Crossan's picture of Jesus

Crossan does not see the birth and resurrection narratives as having happened in
history. Rather, they are later additions that express the importance of Jesus for his
followers and, in the case of the resurrection, establish community leadership after
the crucifixion. The reason that Jesus' movement continued after his death has
nothing to do with the miraculous 'bookends' of his life, but with other facts that
you can see in the earliest layers of the tradition:

- **He intended a social revolution.** It appears that Jesus may have begun as
  an apocalyptic preacher, following John's example, but that he did not stay this
  way. Instead of staying in the desert and living as an **ascetic**, calling for God's
  judgment on the world, Jesus became known for sharing meals with others –
  even the gossip about him reflects this: 'look at him, a glutton and a drunkard, a
  friend of tax collectors and sinners'. (Matthew 11:19)

- **He advocated a kingdom lifestyle.** Crossan believes that Jesus turned from
  an apocalyptic future to the idea that the Kingdom of God can be experienced
  now through a wise lifestyle that even peasants could live out. This will lead to
  an open community without distinction of gender status. Jesus had a dream of a
  just and equal world.

- **He served at an open table.** A study of the ancient Mediterranean world (or
  almost any culture) reveals that sharing food involves a complex set of rules that
  have do to with maintaining and reinforcing social boundaries. Jesus' pattern
  was to disrupt those boundaries by eating with people regardless of gender, rank
  or social acceptability; this is preserved in his teaching about inviting those off
  the street to the table.

- **He performed miracles of social healing.** Rather than seeing Jesus' miracles
  of healing as having to do with medical cures, we should understand that the
  people Jesus healed were viewed as impure and were socially ostracised. Jesus
  healed illnesses without curing the disease by welcoming outcasts back into
  society and encouraging his followers to do the same. In this way, he challenged
  traditions both within his religion and wider society – and awakened criticism
  and fear about this 'Kingdom of God'.

- **He practised an itinerant lifestyle.** Jesus kept on the move to prevent individuals and villages from profiting from his activity (by becoming **brokers** between himself and the people that he taught and healed). In fact, Jesus wanted others to become **itinerant** teacher-healers as well, encouraging them to stay on the move and introduce others to the Kingdom lifestyle.
- **He can be compared to the Cynics.** **Cynicism** was a Greek philosophical movement pre-dating Jesus that flouted basic human social codes and ordinary cultural values. Cynics went out of their way to reject a materialistic orientation, were often itinerant, carrying as few possessions as possible. However, Cynics operated in urban centres and were largely individualistic. Jesus, by contrast, was active in rural areas and was dedicated to growing a community with like-minded values.

AO1 Activity

Make a list of the most important things that stand out from the life of Jesus for N. T. Wright. Then make a second list for John Dominic Crossan. Here comes the interesting part: where could you say there is agreement for these two thinkers?

Key quotes

What Jesus should have done, as any Mediterranean family knew, was settle down at his home in Nazareth and establish there a healing cult. He would be its *patron*, the family would be its *brokers*, and as his reputation went out along the peasant grapevine, the sick would come as *clients* to be healed. That would have made sense to everyone … But instead Jesus kept to the road, brought healing to those who needed it, and had, as it were, to start off anew every day. (J. D. Crossan)

Here is the heart of the original Jesus movement, a shared egalitarianism of spiritual (healing) and material (eating) resources. I emphasise this as strongly as possible, and I maintain that its materiality and spirituality, its facticity and symbolism, cannot be separated. (J. D. Crossan)

What does Constantinian Christianity have to do with the original Jesus movement?

When Jesus was put to death, these ideas lived on in many of his followers – they experienced the continuing 'power' of Jesus as they lived his lifestyle, without the need to experience the physical resurrection of Jesus. Yet, at the same time, some of his followers were changing his ideas to modes of power and authority more familiar in a Greco-Roman world. This included having clear leaders in the Church and changing the open meal to a closed Eucharist ruled over by an 'approved' authority. Later on, Constantine became a 'Christian' Emperor and presided over an all-male clergy who, in turn, helped him unite a Christian Kingdom. For Crossan, nothing could be more opposed to Jesus' lifestyle of radical equality.

19th-century depiction of Diogenes, the 4th to 3rd-century BCE Cynic philosopher

Key quotes

The Kingdom of God as a process of open commensality, of a non-discriminating table depicting in miniature a non-discriminating society, clashes fundamentally with honour and shame, those basic values of ancient Mediterranean culture and society. (J. D. Crossan)

I presume that Jesus, who did not and could not cure that disease or any other one, healed the poor man's illness by refusing to accept the disease's ritual uncleanness and social ostracisation … By healing the illness without curing the disease, Jesus acted as an alternate boundary keeper in a way subversive to the established procedures of his society. (J. D. Crossan)

Pagan Cynicism involved practice and not just theory, lifestyle and not just mindset, in opposition to the cultural heart of Mediterranean civilisation – a way of looking and dressing, of eating, living, and relating that announced its contempt for honour and shame, for patronage and clientage. Jesus and his first followers fit very well against *that* background; they were hippies in a world of Augustan yuppies. (J. D. Crossan)

Key terms

Brokers: those who buy or sell goods on behalf of others

Cynicism: a school of Greek philosophers who rejected social convention to live a simple life in tune with nature and reason

Itinerant: on the move, travelling from place to place

In Crossan's interpretation, Jesus was the leader of an egalitarian movement.

43

Key skills

Knowledge involves:

Selection of a range of (thorough) accurate and relevant information that is directly related to the specific demands of the question.

This means:

- Selecting relevant material for the question set

- Being focused in explaining and examining the material selected.

Understanding involves:

Explanation that is extensive, demonstrating depth and/or breadth with excellent use of evidence and examples including (where appropriate) thorough and accurate supporting use of sacred texts, sources of wisdom and specialist language.

This means:

- Effective use of examples and supporting evidence to establish the quality of your understanding

- Ownership of your explanation that expresses personal knowledge and understanding and NOT just reproducing a chunk of text from a book that you have rehearsed and memorised.

AO1 Developing skills

It is now important to consider the information that has been covered in this section; however, the information in its raw form is too extensive and so has to be processed in order to meet the requirements of the examination. This can be done by practising more advanced skills associated with AO1. The exercises that run throughout this book will help you to do this and prepare you for the examination. For assessment objective 1 (AO1), which involves demonstrating 'knowledge' and 'understanding' skills, we are going to focus on different ways in which the skills can be demonstrated effectively, and also refer to how the performance of these skills is measured (see generic band descriptors for A2 [WJEC] AO1 or A Level [Eduqas] AO1).

▶ **Your task is this:** Below is a summary of **Crossan's view of Jesus**. It is about 200 words long. You need to use this for an answer but could not repeat all of this in an essay under examination conditions so you will have to condense the material. Discuss which points you think are the most important and then re-draft into your own summary of 100 words.

John Dominic Crossan describes Jesus as a 'Mediterranean Jewish peasant'. Each of these words is significant for Crossan: Jesus is a part of a Mediterranean culture which is based on traditions of honour and shame, with strict divisions. As a Jew, Jesus would have been familiar with the covenant, and the desire of God for a community that was living justly. As a peasant in a colony of the Roman Empire, Jesus would have experienced oppression; his role as a carpenter meant that, economically, he barely had enough. What makes Jesus truly a remarkable person is not the miraculous events attributed to him but how he transformed these challenges. Looking at the earliest layers of the Gospels (such as Q) and some other sources (such as the Gospel of Thomas), it appears that Jesus was an itinerant preacher committed to radical equality. He invited people to dine at an open table where there were no social divisions. His healings challenged the idea that ill people needed to be separated from society. Jesus can be compared to the Greco Roman Cynic philosophers. Like them, he was radically committed to an itinerant lifestyle with few possessions that challenged traditions. Unlike them, he was not an individualist, but tried to create a community committed to these ideals.

When you have completed the task, refer to the band descriptors for A2 (WJEC) or A Level (Eduqas) and, in particular, have a look at the demands described in the higher band descriptors towards which you should be aspiring. Ask yourself:

- Does my work demonstrate thorough, accurate and relevant knowledge and understanding of religion and belief?

- Is my work coherent (consistent or make logical sense), clear and well organised? ***(WJEC band descriptor only but still important to consider for Eduqas)***

- Will my work, when developed, be an extensive and relevant response which is specific to the focus of the task?

- Does my work have extensive depth and/or suitable breadth and have excellent use of evidence and examples?

- If appropriate to the task, does my response have thorough and accurate reference to sacred texts and sources of wisdom?

- Are there any insightful connections to be made with other elements of my course?

- Will my answer, when developed and extended to match what is expected in an examination answer, have an extensive range of views of scholars/schools of thought?

- When used, is specialist language and vocabulary both thorough and accurate?

Issues for analysis and evaluation

The validity of using critical realism to understand Jesus

Critical realism combines two ideas: (i) that there really are objects that exist beyond ourselves which we can understand through sense experience (realism), but (ii) we can distort our understanding through our own standpoint and biases (therefore we need to be critical of 'realism'). N. T. Wright applies this concept to the attempt to understand the historical Jesus. On the one hand, we should use historical study with its focus on achieving knowledge via the senses but, on the other hand, we must be critical of the assumptions that it really gives us the entire truth. When it comes to Jesus, Christians shouldn't have to accept that Jesus is merely an object of historical study representing a superstitious age, but that we can find him relevant to challenging our own assumptions.

Many would challenge Wright, saying that one simply must choose the side of science and the testimony of sense experience. After all, this is how we know that there are not ghosts, goblins, angels and demons determining the course of our lives. The focus on science from the time of the enlightenment put power back into the hands of humanity and can be seen as responsible for technological achievements that make our lives much more bearable today – from reading glasses to cures for cancer. Jesus represents a bygone era where disease was seen as caused by demons, and healing from disease the province of miracle workers. Should we return to those days?

N. T. Wright speaks of the worldview of the New Testament as different than our own. This is most certainly true. He goes on to say that worldviews precede scientifically determined facts and that therefore we should be sceptical about the claims of our own modern worldview. His method for establishing the truth is to enter into a dialogue between worldviews – but has this not already been done? In the hundreds of years since the first stirrings of scientific critiques against the Church, there has been such a dialogue between science and religion. The result is that religion has been removed from the 'throne'; it is no longer the queen of the sciences. It is now widely recognised that human knowledge about psychology, society and technological progress can evolve without the worldview of the New Testament. It seems that the rejection of the supernatural world of the New Testament has happened in just the way that Wright has prescribed. The story that Jesus has told about God and the universe has met the story of the enlightenment and it has been rejected after a long period of challenge.

However, Wright notes that a challenge to scientific certainty has emerged apart from Christianity, from secular thinkers who are sceptical of views proclaimed by the positivists. If we can only trust our sense experience, what is to prevent us from saying that all we can be certain of is our sense experience and nothing beyond it? Against this, N. T. Wright appears to be saying something quite reasonable: we should accept that there is a reality beyond our senses, but acknowledge that we only understand this reality through our own lenses, our own point of view. However, how does such a position lead one to accept the validity of the realities Jesus spoke of? Wright would say that 'scientific certainty' itself is a 'point of view' and that we should not see the world as a closed system, but that other points of view, like Jesus', may make a contribution to our view of things. However, it seems that it is quite a leap from 'accepting other points of view' to 'accepting their metaphysical views'.

This section covers AO2 content and skills

Specification content

The validity of using critical realism to understand Jesus.

Key quote

… instead of working from particulars of observation, or 'sense-data', to confident statements about external reality, provisionally conceived, critical realism (as I am proposing it) sees knowledge of particulars as taking place within the larger framework of the story or worldview which forms the basis of the observer's way of being in relation to the world. (N. T. Wright)

AO2 Activity

As you read through this section try to do the following:

1. Pick out the different lines of argument that are presented in the text and identify any evidence given in support.

2. For each line of argument try to evaluate whether or not you think this is strong or weak.

3. Think of any questions you may wish to raise in response to the arguments.

This activity will help you to start thinking critically about what you read, and help you to evaluate the effectiveness of different arguments and from this develop your own observations, opinions and points of view that will help with any conclusions that you make in your answers to the AO2 questions that arise.

Key quotes

… the differences as well as similarities between the Jesus and the Cynic preachers are instructive even if not derivative. Both are populist, appealing to the ordinary people, both are life-style preachers, advocating their position not only by word but deed, not only in theory but in practice; both use dress and equipment to symbolise dramatically their message. But he is rural, they are urban; he is organising a communal movement, they are following an individual philosophy; and their symbolism demands a knapsack and staff, his no-knapsack and no staff. Maybe Jesus is what peasant *Jewish* Cynicism looked like. **(J. D. Crossan)**

That ecstatic vision and social program set out to rebuild a society upward from its grass roots, but on principles of religious and economic egalitarianism, with free healing brought directly to the peasant homes and free sharing of whatever they had in return. **(J. D. Crossan)**

AO2 Activity

List some conclusions that could be drawn from the AO2 reasoning from the above text; try to aim for at least three different possible conclusions. Consider each of the conclusions and collect brief evidence to support each conclusion from the AO1 and AO2 material for this topic. Select the conclusion that you think is most convincing and explain why it is so. Try to contrast this with the weakest conclusion in the list, justifying your argument with clear reasoning and evidence.

In fact, it is possible to understand and appreciate the New Testament apart from Wright's critical realism. The work of John Dominic Crossan draws on historical, anthropological and textual studies that focus on the time of Jesus. Using a careful system which attempts to date the layers of traditions in the Gospels, Crossan concludes that the birth and resurrection narratives were never a part of the original Jesus tradition. Furthermore, the power that Jesus demonstrated through his 'miracles' can be explained in sociological and psychological terms. Jesus changed people's hearts by creating a truly inclusive movement – even people who were on the fringes of society were invited in. Therefore, the healings attributed to him can be seen as 'social miracles'. Crossan's method leads him to a full appreciation of Jesus in a way that reflects our modern worldview and its rejection of miracles and supernatural claims.

However, N. T. Wright questions this kind of scepticism about the New Testament point of view – he suggests that this is actually paranoia about accepting biblical claims that comes from clinging to our enlightenment story. Is it very open minded to rule out the worldview given to us in the New Testament?

Wright argues that we must take seriously the postmodern insight that there is no neutral point of view; even the view that only certain knowledge of the world can come through verifiable sense experience is a part of a story, a way of seeing the world. If this 'positivist' view is right, then why hasn't the world come to agreement? Why has there continued to be so much untruth and unrest in the countries from which this 'truth' has been announced? We must also not fall into a completely relativist mindset (phenomenalism) because common sense shows us that there is a reality outside of ourselves. Critical realism is the best way to balance our approach to reality – to accept that there can be a truth beyond ourselves but remain humble about our claims about that truth since we look at things through the lenses of our culture and experience.

We must not forget that the Gospel writers were, after all, plain individuals who were recording what they believed really happened. They may have got some of the details wrong here and there, but their claims are strong and bold about God acting in Jesus. Shouldn't we give them a hearing before writing them off? Furthermore, Wright raises questions about the so-called historical method of Crossan: why assume that a single attestation isn't of historical worth? Why assume that oral traditions couldn't have survived intact after 60 CE? Why assume that the Gospel writers did not make careful use of the first-hand testimonies they possessed? The truth is that we are not historically certain that isolated fragments about the teaching of Jesus even circulated and developed apart from the narrative frameworks that are a part of the New Testament.

After all, the really surprising fact of history, says Wright, is that the Christian Church was born and has thrived. From an era of so many failed messiahs and religious movements, the survival of Christianity is noteworthy. Furthermore, if Jesus was merely a 'social healer' or a wandering philosopher, as Crossan suggests, would his movement have really survived?

No one can build a life on 'dry facts' – we must find meaning in history. On the other hand, having a faith that is divorced from historical study is also problematic – we can end up living in a spiritual fantasy. The best way to proceed is to determine what meaning we can gain from history and what ways our faith needs to be modified by historical and scientific insight. Both faith and history are important; critical realism is the path to find this balance.

In conclusion, it could be said that N. T. Wright starts from a position of faith, having been raised in the Christian 'story'. He sees critical realism as a way to give Christian faith validity in a post-enlightenment world. But how much can he expect that his approach is likely to convince someone who has grown up in a different story, one which so long ago rejected the beliefs of the early church?

The validity of using apocryphal Gospels to understand Jesus

The Church has based its understanding of the life of Jesus on the four Gospels as well as the witness of the Apostles as recorded in Acts and the epistles of the New Testament. However, are there other documents that have been forgotten, ignored or intentionally suppressed that could provide information about the historical Jesus? John Dominic Crossan says, 'Yes': the apocryphal Gospels.

One of the challenges to using the apocryphal Gospels as sources has to do with their date. All of them are dated from the 2nd to the 4th centuries, much later than the books of the New Testament – this should caution historians from the outset. Furthermore, many of these 'Gospels' are merely fragments, or quotations in the later writings of the Church Fathers; why would we turn to them as sources for Jesus' life rather than to the earlier and more complete work of the four Gospels?

On the subject of dating, Crossan raises several points. Even though these Gospels are dated after the writings of the New Testament, they may contain traditions that are independent of the New Testament. Therefore, they shouldn't be overlooked simply because of their date.

Furthermore, not all of these sources are fragments. The Gospel of Thomas is a complete document of 114 sayings attributed to Jesus. Even though the Gospel of Thomas is from the 4th century, there is direct evidence that it existed in earlier versions. The discovery of fragments (some from the early second century) of portions of the Gospel of Thomas, suggest that this Gospel circulated widely. If this is the case, then it is conceivable that it existed earlier than the 2nd century – this could take us back to the 1st century, the time of the canonical Gospels themselves.

There are several features of the Gospel of Thomas in favour of an early date. First, it is the kind of document we might expect early Christians to have composed – simply a list of sayings of Jesus. In fact, many of these sayings are like those found in the Gospels, but in a shorter form – again, this is what one would expect from an early source.

What is also significant for Crossan is that the Gospel of Thomas doesn't have birth or resurrection narratives. This fits for our contemporary study of history, which is guided by the notion that supernatural events do not occur. The image of Jesus as a wise teacher rather than a miracle worker is much more believable than the view of Jesus given in the Gospels.

However, isn't Crossan simply assuming that the supernatural cannot occur and then finding a source that affirms that basic view? N. T. Wright warns against a scientific worldview which rules out positions without taking their claims seriously. Is this not what Crossan is doing? Crossan challenges the Church to accept that its central figure is not an irrelevant supernatural figure, but an 'earthly' teacher with radical wisdom that can apply in our day – by listening to the Gospel of Thomas we have access to this teacher.

Also, why would the writing down of sayings of Jesus entail the accompanying belief that the Christians who used Q (if it did indeed exist independently of the Gospels) did not believe in Jesus as a supernatural figure? Couldn't it simply be that these early Christians wanted to remember the exact words of Jesus and were more concerned about this aspect than the miraculous deeds that were part of his life and that would always be remembered?

Specification content

The validity of using apocryphal Gospels to understand Jesus.

Key quote

The Jesus I know in prayer, in the sacraments, in the faces of those in need, is the Jesus I meet in the historical evidence – including the New Testament, of course, but the New Testament read not so much as the church taught me to read it but as I read it with my historical consciousness fully operative. (N. T. Wright).

AO2 Activity

As you read through this section try to do the following:

1. Pick out the different lines of argument that are presented in the text and identify any evidence given in support.

2. For each line of argument try to evaluate whether or not you think this is strong or weak.

3. Think of any questions you may wish to raise in response to the arguments.

This activity will help you to start thinking critically about what you read, and help you to evaluate the effectiveness of different arguments and from this develop your own observations, opinions and points of view that will help with any conclusions that you make in your answers to the AO2 questions that arise.

Key quotes

He was not so much like a wandering preacher giving sermons or a wandering philosopher offering maxims as like a radical politician gathering support for a new and highly risky movement. (N. T. Wright)

He was, in short, announcing the kingdom of God: not the simple revolutionary message of the hard-liners, but the doubly revolutionary message of a kingdom that would overturn all other agendas, including the revolutionary one. (N. T. Wright)

Jesus as a first-century Jewish prophet announcing and inaugurating the Kingdom of God, summoning others to join him, warning of the consequences if they did not, doing all this in symbolic actions, and in cryptic and coded sayings, that he believed he was Israel's Messiah, the one through whom the true God would accomplish his decisive purpose. (N. T. Wright)

Furthermore, there is simply is no direct evidence for the Gospel of Thomas before the 2nd century. We are on much more certain historical ground accepting the Gospels, keeping in mind that the formation of the Bible was not a 'top-down' affair but that Christian communities from many geographical areas reached consensus on most of the books of the New Testament – there is no mention of the Gospel of Thomas in the earliest discussions of the canon – this is evidence that it simply didn't exist at that time.

However, Crossan would question if it is indeed true that we are on certain ground with the Gospels. Weren't they written long after Jesus' life? Aren't there enough differences between them to question if they provide a straightforward account of Jesus life? For instance, only two of the Gospels contain a birth narrative and the others have wide differences in how the resurrection is reported, to name only a few of the differences. Clearly, the authors of the Gospels were influencing the material they selected in order to support their views of Jesus.

In other words, Crossan says, we really need to go behind the Gospels to get a true picture of Jesus. Fortunately, this is possible since there are *four* Gospels and we can therefore detect differences and make educated guesses as to the existence of earlier layers in the tradition. One of the most significant sources is 'Q' (from the German word 'Quelle' for 'source'). Q is the shared sayings of Matthew and Luke which many scholars think existed apart from these Gospels. Crossan believes it is reasonable to think that Q was actually a Gospel in its own right that was later absorbed into the New Testament. If we look at Q in this way, we see many of the same elements as we do in the Gospel of Thomas: short sayings of Jesus with no narrative portions, including no birth or resurrection narratives. Q could therefore be seen as an apocryphal Gospel, a hidden work, behind the layers of the New Testament. Is this not more compelling evidence for approaching Jesus in a different way than the New Testament?

However, N. T. Wright might say that Crossan has moved from historical scepticism to historical paranoia. We do indeed have four different Gospels and their differences are precisely what we would expect of people looking at the same event from their own points of view. The early church recognised that these accounts stem from eyewitnesses and were trustworthy. No historical doubts are expressed about the four Gospels in the earliest discussions about the canon. Furthermore, it is clear that the writers were bearing witness to what they really believed happened – including the resurrection.

In conclusion, the debate about the sources of Jesus is a debate not only about the dating of texts but also involves our own biases surrounding the nature of history. Scholars like Crossan, who do not accept the supernatural Jesus of the Church, can find textual evidence for their views. On the other hand, scholars like N. T. Wright, who believe that the Jesus of faith *is* the Jesus of history, find it much easier to trust the New Testament as a historical record for the life and teachings of Jesus.

Key quotes

If all he had done was talk about the Kingdom, Lower Galilee would probably have greeted him with a great big pleasant yawn. But you cannot ignore the healings and the exorcisms, especially in their socially subversive function. You cannot ignore the pointedly political overtones of the very term *Kingdom of God* itself. (J. D. Crossan)

… for Jesus, the Kingdom of God is a community of radical and unbrokered equality in which individuals are in direct contact with one another and with God, unmediated by any established brokers or fixed locations. (J. D. Crossan)

AO2 Developing skills

It is now important to consider the information that has been covered in this section; however, the information in its raw form is too extensive and so has to be processed in order to meet the requirements of the examination. This can be done by practising more advanced skills associated with AO2. For assessment objective 2 (AO2), which involves 'critical analysis' and 'evaluation' skills, we are going to focus on different ways in which the skills can be demonstrated effectively, and also refer to how the performance of these skills is measured (see generic band descriptors for A2 [WJEC] AO2 or A Level [Eduqas] AO2).

▶ **Your next task is this:** Below is an argument concerning **traditional views of Jesus as mistaken**. You need to respond to this argument by thinking of three key questions you could ask the writer that would challenge their view and force them to defend their argument.

Traditional Christian doctrine concerning Jesus is completely misguided. This is because attributing a miraculous birth, life and resurrection to Jesus obscures the most interesting historical facts about his life – that he was a peasant living in an unpleasant backwater of the Roman Empire who somehow, in spite of this, founded a social movement that challenged others to transcend their social limitations. By placing the emphasis on the miraculous nature of his life, we miss the astounding fact that Jesus presided at an 'open table', had a radically inclusive movement, brought those who were condemned as impure back into the community ('healing'), and challenged those who aspired merely to have riches and an easy life. Too bad that all of this was forgotten and Jesus was turned into a 'King' by a state church that was eventually run by powerful elites. If only the Church would now consider sources for Jesus' life that do not focus on the miraculous aspects, then there might be hope that Christianity could return to its roots. We must not simply accept that the New Testament reflects the only view of Jesus, but must examine the life of Jesus using other sources (like the Gospel of Thomas) as well as determining the earliest layers in the New Testament.

When you have completed the task, refer to the band descriptors for A2 (WJEC) or A Level (Eduqas) and, in particular, have a look at the demands described in the higher band descriptors towards which you should be aspiring. Ask yourself:

- Is my answer a confident critical analysis and perceptive evaluation of the issue?
- Is my answer a response that successfully identifies and thoroughly addresses the issues raised by the question set.
- Does my work show an excellent standard of coherence, clarity and organisation?
- Will my work, when developed, contain thorough, sustained and clear views that are supported by extensive, detailed reasoning and/or evidence?
- Are the views of scholars/schools of thought used extensively, appropriately and in context?
- Does my answer convey a confident and perceptive analysis of the nature of any possible connections with other elements of my course?
- When used, is specialist language and vocabulary both thorough and accurate?

Key skills

Analysis involves:

Identifying issues raised by the materials in the AO1, together with those identified in the AO2 section, and presents sustained and clear views, either of scholars or from a personal perspective ready for evaluation.

This means:

- That your answers are able to identify key areas of debate in relation to a particular issue
- That you can identify, and comment upon, the different lines of argument presented by others
- That your response comments on the overall effectiveness of each of these areas or arguments.

Evaluation involves:

Considering the various implications of the issues raised based upon the evidence gleaned from analysis and provides an extensive detailed argument with a clear conclusion.

This means:

- That your answer weighs up the consequences of accepting or rejecting the various and different lines of argument analysed
- That your answer arrives at a conclusion through a clear process of reasoning.

Specification content

Attitudes toward wealth.

Specification content

The dangers of wealth
(with reference to Mark 10: 17–25, Matthew 6: 25–34, Luke 12: 33–34, 1 Timothy 6:10).

What would Jesus think of today's ornate cathedrals?

A: Attitudes toward wealth

Years ago, a saying became very popular: 'He who dies with the most toys wins', referring to the race for material prosperity. But there are losers, too: poor working conditions, oppressive poverty in countries that produce goods for the wealthy and a devastating impact on the environment. Believers across all religions also wonder about the effect of money and wealth on one's soul. The quest for riches stands in stark contrast to the words of Jesus, 'life does not consist in the abundance of possessions' (Luke 12:15).

So, how are Christians to view money, wealth and possessions? Does the Bible prescribe how much one is supposed to make, give and keep? There are a variety of answers to this question, each claiming biblical support. These range from voluntary poverty to the belief that God wants to bless his followers with wealth. In between these two positions Christians have various convictions about how to live responsibly with money and possessions.

The dangers of wealth

We now look at four biblical passages which issue warnings about wealth. After each passage, you will see a brief description of its context, its main message, some scholarly insights, and an interesting fact.

Mark 10:17–25

[17] As he was setting out on a journey, a man ran up and knelt before him, and asked him, "Good Teacher, what must I do to inherit eternal life?" [18] Jesus said to him, "Why do you call me good? No one is good but God alone. [19] You know the commandments: 'You shall not murder; You shall not commit adultery; You shall not steal; You shall not bear false witness; You shall not defraud; Honour your father and mother.'" [20] He said to him, "Teacher, I have kept all these since my youth." [21] Jesus, looking at him, loved him and said, "You lack one thing; go, sell what you own, and give the money to the poor, and you will have treasure in heaven; then come, follow me." [22] When he heard this, he was shocked and went away grieving, for he had many possessions. [23] Then Jesus looked around and said to his disciples, "How hard it will be for those who have wealth to enter the kingdom of God!" [24] And the disciples were perplexed at these words. But Jesus said to them again, "Children, how hard it is to enter the kingdom of God! [25] It is easier for a camel to go through the eye of a needle than for someone who is rich to enter the Kingdom of God."

- **Context:** This passage comes in a section of Mark (8:21–10:52) where Jesus is teaching the meaning of discipleship. Jesus was Jewish, so his answer to the question of how to obtain eternal life is also Jewish: keep the Mosaic Law. The man asking him the question is also Jewish – he has been raised in the Law his entire life, but this has not led him to the answer he seeks. Traditional Jewish teaching on wealth sees it as a sign of divine favour and urges those with wealth to be generous, but Jesus provides an answer that is out of step with the traditional approach: give up all possessions and join the Jesus-movement. The idea of dispossessing oneself of all possessions wouldn't have been unheard of in Jesus' time (you can read about the Qumran community), but it might not have been an expected answer from a respected Rabbi.

- **Main message:** This passage is clearly about money and material possessions. Jesus is teaching that it is impossible to enter the Kingdom of God if one is wealthy. He uses the striking and grotesque image of a camel going through the eye of a needle. Did Jesus mean to apply this insight to all who wanted to follow him – or just to this man? This has been debated through the centuries. What is clear is that for Jesus the Kingdom of God is of infinitely more importance than money and wealth.

- **Scholarly detail:** The laws that Jesus lists are mostly from the second half of the 10 commandments, having to do with one's relationships to others. The commandment to 'not defraud' is not, however, a part of the 10 commandments, but is a variation on the theme of theft. To defraud is to gain money though illegal means; for example, holding back wages. Some scholars see including 'defraud' as an example of Jesus going beyond the letter of the law to insights about its spirit (see his teaching on adultery) and perhaps even an awareness that the man before him had not stolen in the sense spoken about in the 10 commandments but was guilty of other financial sins.

- **Interesting fact:** Some early manuscripts use the word *kamilon* (rope) instead of *kamelon* (camel). Also, a story circulated that here was a passage into Jerusalem open only at night called 'The Needle Gate'; if one had a camel, it would have to be divested of its luggage in order to crouch down and make it through the entry. However, this is likely a fanciful medieval legend meant to impress pious tourists to Jerusalem rather than a historical fact. Both of these suggestions (rope and needle gate) make actual words of Jesus appear more 'palatable' or 'sensible'; the plain sense (the camel going through the eye of the needle) is so striking and grotesque that may scholars believe it is likely the earliest.

Matthew 6:25–34

25 "Therefore I tell you, do not worry about your life, what you will eat or what you will drink, or about your body, what you will wear. Is not life more than food, and the body more than clothing? 26 Look at the birds of the air; they neither sow nor reap nor gather into barns, and yet your heavenly Father feeds them. Are you not of more value than they? 27 And can any of you by worrying add a single hour to your span of life? 28 And why do you worry about clothing? Consider the lilies of the field, how they grow; they neither toil nor spin, 29 yet I tell you, even Solomon in all his glory was not clothed like one of these. 30 But if God so clothes the grass of the field, which is alive today and tomorrow is thrown into the oven, will he not much more clothe you—you of little faith? 31 Therefore do not worry, saying, 'What will we eat?' or 'What will we drink?' or 'What will we wear?' 32 For it is the Gentiles who strive for all these things; and indeed your heavenly Father knows that you need all these things. 33 But strive first for the Kingdom of God and his righteousness, and all these things will be given to you as well. 34 So do not worry about tomorrow, for tomorrow will bring worries of its own. Today's trouble is enough for today."

- **Context:** This passage is a part of the Sermon on the Mount, where Jesus outlines what it means to live in the presence of God. One of the main themes of this sermon is that righteousness must be defined in a new way, going beyond the letter of the law to an all-embracing lifestyle of love and commitment.

Depiction of the Jesus and the rich young ruler by Heinrich Hofmann (1889)

Key quote

The difference between ourselves and the rich young man is that he was not allowed to solace his regrets by saying: "Never mind what Jesus says, I can still hold on to my riches, but in a spirit of inner detachment. Despite my inadequacy I can take comfort in the thought that God has forgiven me my sins and can have fellowship with Christ in faith." But no, he went away sorrowful. Because he would not obey, he could not believe. In this the young man was quite honest. **(D. Bonhoeffer)**

quickfire

3.1 What does Jesus say that believers should put first in their life?

Key quotes

The passage does not mean, however, that food, drink, clothing, and other such necessities will come to the disciple automatically without work or foresight. It addresses only problems of anxiety about these things. The answer to this anxiety and all such debilitating anxiety is to be found in an absolute allegiance to the kingdom …
(D. Hagner)

Idolatry is the heart of rebellion against God (Rom, 1:18–32), and no other rival to God than Mammon appears more often or centrally in Scripture. (C. Blomberg)

- **Main message:** Jesus urges his followers to have the right priorities, with the climax of this passage being verse 33, putting the Kingdom of God and righteous living first. The enemy of any priority is anxiety; in this case, it is anxiety about food or clothing. Jesus' audience are not especially rich or powerful, in fact they were likely living a hand-to-mouth existence. Yet, he still insists that the priority is not food and clothing, but spiritual things. How can he demand this? Because he has faith in the provision of God, as reflected by God's goodness in the natural world.

- **Scholarly insight**: The term anxiety is used in this passage more than in any other place in the New Testament. It has to do with being afraid in such a way as to cause distress. Some passages that might have been known to the Gospel writers include Sirach 30:24: 'Jealousy and anger shorten life, and anxiety brings on premature old age'; in I Maccabees 6:10 and Sirach 42:9 the term is used in relation to losing sleep.

Study tip

When it comes to describing Jesus' view on money and wealth, you will want to refer to his view of the Kingdom of God and the issue of priorities.

- **Interesting fact:** Jesus' audience would have been very familiar with the wealth of Solomon (I Kings 3:13, 10:14–17), perhaps even longing for God to restore their nation to that former glory. So, it might have been quite surprising to have Jesus point out that they were already surrounded by a beauty greater than Solomon's.

Luke 12:33–34

[33] Sell your possessions, and give alms. Make purses for yourselves that do not wear out, an unfailing treasure in heaven, where no thief comes near and no moth destroys. [34] For where your treasure is, there your heart will be also.

- **Context:** Earlier in this same chapter (Luke 12: 16–21) is the parable of the rich fool: a wealthy man celebrates the fact that he has hoarded enough material wealth to secure his future. The problem is that death now comes to him and he has made the mistake of not providing for his spiritual life. This passage now recommends exactly the opposite lifestyle.

- **Main meaning:** The striking aspect about these verses is the requirement that Jesus' followers sell their possessions and give the proceeds to the poor. In fact, this is the test that reveals whether one is living for God's Kingdom. For, when faced with this demand, the decision one makes reveals that they are either on the path of the rich fool (see Luke 12: 16–21) or on the path of eternal life. Jesus reinforces this teaching with the imagery of a kind a spiritual bank account that is free of the anxieties and inevitable corruption of earthly bank accounts.

- **Scholarly insight:** Most of the material in this passage is also in Matthew – except the first sentence: 'Sell your possessions and give alms'. In fact, the book of Acts (widely held to be written by the same author as Luke) shows the followers of Jesus living out this instruction to sell their possessions (see Acts 2:44–5; 4:32–5). Giving to the poor is very important in Jewish thought at the time of the New Testament (see Tobit 4:8–9, I Enoch 38:2 and 2 Enoch 50:5–6). Did Jesus expect all of his followers to live this way? This passage seems to suggest this, though Jesus commands Zacchaeus to give away only half of his wealth in Luke 19:1–10.

- **Interesting fact** – Some Greco-Roman thinkers would have agreed with the sentiment of this passage. Dio Chrysostom (CE 40–115) wrote that wealth can lead to self-indulgence and should be put to use for human need: 'But greed is not only the greatest evil to a man himself, but it injures his neighbours as well.'

quickfire

3.2 Does the New Testament present Jesus as consistently teaching that all Christians should sell all of their possessions?

Write down the biblical reference to each verse on a separate card. Then, jot down a short description in your own words of what is *actually* condemned, prohibited or discouraged in each passage. Is it wealth itself?

1 Timothy 6:10

[10] For the love of money is a root of all kinds of evil, and in their eagerness to be rich some have wandered away from the faith and pierced themselves with many pains.

- **Context:** The Pastoral Epistles (of which I Timothy is a part) are concerned with heretical teachings and lax morality entering the Church. The author wants the Church to keep to the true faith, avoiding obscure beliefs and developing a strong moral centre: 'But the goal of our instruction is love from a pure heart and a good conscience and a sincere faith' (I Timothy 1:5). I Timothy 6:10 is the final sentence in a section describing the conduct of true Christians (5:1– 6:10).

- **Main meaning:** Money is not evil or 'dirty' in itself. The real danger is the 'love of money,' or, in other words, greed. This greed has motivated false teachers to ignore the plain truth and drift from the faith. Does this passage take a negative view to wealth itself? Strictly speaking, no. However, wealth and faith appear to be awkward partners! Material prosperity comes with a warning label, though it is the eagerness to be rich rather than riches itself that is the real danger.

- **Scholarly insight:** The phrase, 'the love of money is the root of all kinds of evil' was a common saying in the ancient world. Several centuries earlier, the Cynic philosopher Diogenes of Sinope said, 'the love of money is the mother-city of all evils'.

- **Interesting fact:** It was common for ancient philosophers to charge their opponents with teaching for pay and therefore seeking to please rather than to present the whole truth.

Biblical teaching on stewardship

Stewardship means administration or management; it comes from the role of a steward in ancient times, one who managed various aspects of a house. The theological concept of stewardship views humans as having the God-given position of managing all their resources well. The concept of stewardship involves several key principles for Christians:

- God has created the earth; it belongs, therefore, not to us but to God. Humans have been given charge over it (Genesis 1:26–28; Genesis 2:15; Psalm 8).

- The material world is good. Genesis speaks of God's creation as 'good'; this goodness remains even though there is sin in the world (Romans 1:20). Therefore we should not flee from the management of the material world.

- The Bible assumes that there is private ownership (the 8th commandment; see also Leviticus 19:35 and Numbers 27:1–11). Therefore, stewardship applies not only to nations and groups but also to individuals.

- Because God is the defender of the poor and the oppressed (Psalm 68:4–5 Proverbs 14:31), stewardship always includes generous giving to those in need.

- Some Christians see the concept of a tithe from the Hebrew scriptures (the giving of 10% of one's income) as an aspect of stewardship.

Key quote

Because the opponents [of Paul in the Church] had fallen in love with money, they had, as it were, stabbed themselves with the sword of greed and bore the intense pain and grief of self-inflicted wounds. It can refer to the pangs of guilt, conscience, remorse, and the actual pains incurred by the sin itself. (W. Mounce)

Key terms

The Pastoral Epistles: the New Testament letters (I and II Timothy and Titus) written to Christian ministers on the theme of guiding the Church

Stewardship: management, administration

Tithe: the giving of 10% of one's produce or earnings in support of a religious organisation

Specification content

Apparent contradiction between biblical teaching on stewardship and the ascetic ideal.

Do Christians expect this kind of answer to prayer?

3.3 List three or more principles underlying the concept of stewardship.

Key quotes

Religion that is pure and undefiled before God, the Father, is this: to care for orphans and widows in their distress, and to keep oneself unstained by the world. **(James 1:27)**

Those who oppress the poor insult their Maker, but those who are kind to the needy honour him. **(Proverbs 14.31)**

Generous giving, especially to the materially neediest people of our world, proves so pervasive in Scripture, and is so often either commanded or commended, that it is hard to envision anyone seriously studying the Bible in detail and not concluding that stewardship must play a central role in any truly Christian lifestyle. **(C. Blomberg)**

Key terms

Asceticism: discipline or training, such as avoiding various indulgences for religious reasons

Fasting: abstaining from food, drink or other activities for religious reasons

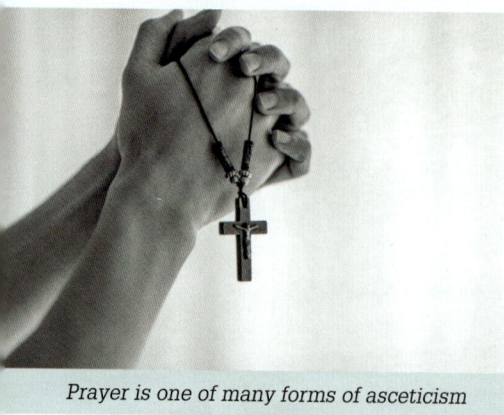

Prayer is one of many forms of asceticism

The opposite of stewardship is greed and covetousness, each of which are consistently condemned in the Old and New Testaments (see, for example, Psalm 10). In fact, the Hebrew prophets are remembered for their searing rebukes over economic sins even to the point of declaring that participating in religious activities such as sacrifices and festivals is meaningless if one is involved in oppressing the poor (see Isaiah 1:10–20 and Amos 5:11–27). The unbridled quest for wealth is never approved; in fact, even Kings are told that there are limits to their wealth (Deuteronomy 17:16–17).

Those who see their role in life as stewards do not necessarily embrace a communistic view of Christian community (i.e. the monastic ideal) or voluntary poverty; instead, they view their role as managing wisely the resources God has given them. In a sermon that reflected on Jesus' parables about stewards, the great Methodist preacher John Wesley (1703–1791) shared a message that has been summarised as, 'Make all you can, save all you can, give all you can.'

The ascetic ideal

Asceticism comes from the Greek term *askeo* which means 'exercise' or 'training'. In Greek philosophy, it referred to refraining from available pleasures in order to achieve a moral or intellectual goal. The word is only used once in the New Testament, in Acts 24:16 where Paul refers to 'striving' to live in such a way that he has a clear conscience toward God and others. Yet, the idea of undertaking a special discipline or lifestyle as a part of the Christian path permeates the New Testament.

Key quote

[Asceticism] … springs from the love of God and aims at overcoming all the obstacles to this love in the soul. It is thus not an end in itself but essentially a preparation for the life of union with God, since, in its positive aspect, it seeks to foster the interior tendencies that serve to develop the life of charity. **(The Oxford Dictionary of the Christian Church)**

Study tip

Be sure to note the many different forms asceticism can take as well as the fact that more extreme forms appear to conflict with the way Jesus lived. Does the biblical teaching on the goodness of the material world conflict with strict asceticism?

Jesus declared, 'If any want to become my followers, let them deny themselves and take up their cross and follow me (Mark 8:34). What does it mean to deny oneself? For Jesus, it involved **fasting**, devotion to prayer, turning away from possessions and living an itinerant lifestyle (constant travel, relying upon the support and hospitality of others). It seems to have entailed abstaining from sexual relationships – though this was not commanded. Jesus refers to this area in Matthew 19:12 and Paul discusses the appropriateness of the celibate life in light of God's return in I Corinthians 7. At the same time, the Gospels show Jesus as less ascetic than John the Baptist and enjoying hospitality. Jesus quoted gossip about himself (Luke 7:34) to the effect that he was a drunkard and a glutton in comparison with John!

Asceticism in the history of the Church

Ascetic practices became widespread amongst early Christians, with some renouncing marriage, home, property and turning to extreme forms of fasting and self-deprivation. The theologian and spiritual writer Origen (185–254), dedicated himself to an ascetic lifestyle of voluntary poverty, fasting and vigils so that his soul could be purified from passion in order to secure true knowledge of God in this life. The **Desert Fathers** renounced an increasingly worldly church to focus on a simple lifestyle of prayer and devotion in remote locations. They viewed Jesus' 40 days in the wilderness and the lifestyle of John the Baptist as examples to follow.

In the Middle Ages monasteries attempted, in different ways, to build Christian character though a disciplined life. Some Christians focused on the suffering of Christ and more violent forms of asceticism became a part of the Christian tradition – the wearing of hair shirts and chains as well as **self-flagellation**. Other Christians developed spiritual disciplines such as prayer, penitence, reading spiritual works, pilgrimage and reflecting on the meaning of the sacraments. The rise of humanism and Protestantism brought questions about the value of asceticism, though fasting, prayer and concerns about 'worldly pleasures' have also been a part of Protestant **piety**. Asceticism can therefore refer to different practices depending on the type and branch of Christianity to which one is referring.

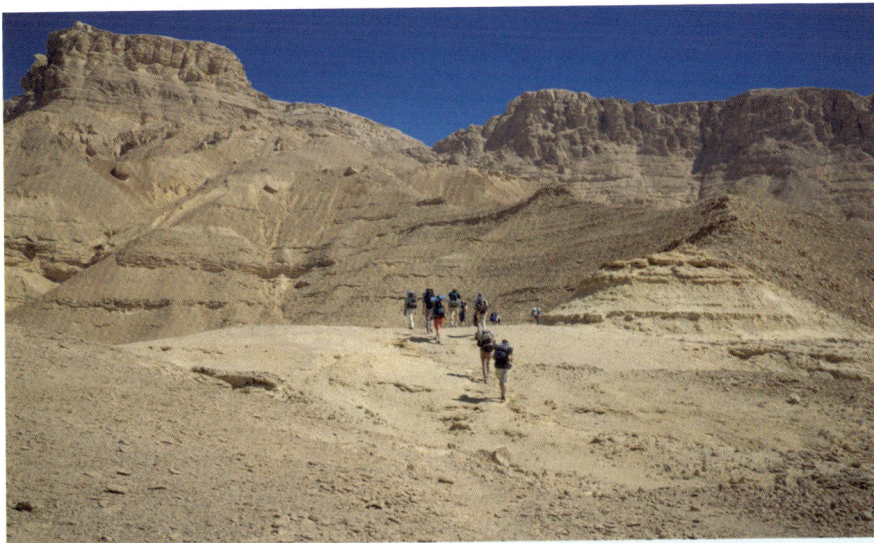

Pilgrims walk in the area of the monastery founded by St Antony's followers.

AO1 Activity

Look up 'Desert Fathers', 'Antony of Egypt' or 'Simeon Stylites' (an early hermit who lived on top of a 60' tower for 36 years). Try to notice what they were trying to achieve through their ascetic practices.

Asceticism raises the question of the attitude a Christian is to take towards the world. This might sound like a strange question in light of our cultural focus on the pursuit of happiness and increasing material prosperity. Yet, Christians view the world as in some way separated from God; therefore, care needs to be taken as to how to rightly participate in this world. On the one hand, Hebrew religion is known for embracing the world, celebrating the bounty of nature, enjoying festivals and even requiring its religious leaders to be married. At the other extreme, movements such as **Manichaeism** and **Montanism** considered the world to be evil and advocated extreme forms of discipline. Though these movements were judged to be heretical, most Christian churches believe that some training and discipline is essential to live a God-oriented life, though there is disagreement as to which types of discipline and how much.

quickfire

3.4 At the time of Jesus, who was popularly considered to be more of an ascetic than Jesus?

Key quote

You should fast on Wednesdays and Fridays. (the Didache, a 1st-century manual of Christian instruction)

Key terms

Desert Fathers: early Christian hermits who lived an ascetic life in the Egyptian desert

Manichaeism: a religious movement that viewed the world as a conflict between good and evil, with the soul's release found through asceticism

Montanism: an early Christian movement which believed in the imminent end of the world, asceticism and continuing revelation of God in prophecy

Piety: dutiful and devout reverence to God

Self-flagellation: striking oneself with a whip

Key person

Antony of Egypt: (c.251–356) gave away all his possessions and moved to the desert to live a life of solitude as a hermit. Despite his intention to live alone, he attracted many followers and he organised them into a community of hermits living under a set of rules. The formation of communities around hermits such as Antony is considered by many to be the earliest form of Christian monasticism.

Digital device detox: a modern form of fasting?

Specification content

The prosperity Gospel of the
Word-Faith movement.

Key terms

Charismatic churches: individual churches that may differ from their denomination in that they emphasise ecstatic religious experiences and miracles of healing

Pentecostal churches: independent churches and denominations that emphasise the working of the Spirit in the Church, especially through prophesy, speaking in tongues, healing and exorcism

Prosperity Gospel: the teaching that faith and giving to the Church will bring health and financial blessings

quickfire

3.5 According to the prosperity Gospel, what is required to receive health and financial blessings from God?

Key quotes

When people do not receive what they have confessed, it is usually because of a negative confession, unbelief, or a failure to observe the divine laws. Some faith teachers reject the use of medicine as evidence of weak faith, and overlook the role of suffering, persecution and poverty in the purposes of God. The Word of Faith has been one of the most popular movements in Pentecostalism. **(A. H. Anderson)**

In the Old Testament it is clear that the multiplication of resources was viewed as the blessing of God. … in the New Testament, however, this enrichment is reinterpreted as spiritual fruitfulness and caring support in the family of Christians. … What Paul promises to the generous giver is not wealth-in-return but *all that you need* and also sufficient for *every good work* [2 Cor 9:8]. **(P. Barnett)**

The prosperity Gospel

The **prosperity Gospel** is the teaching that Christians have the right to expect wealth and good health. They can achieve this by making a positive confession of faith as well as 'sowing seeds' through the payment of tithes and offerings to religious causes. This approach became popular through prominent television evangelists at the end of the 20th century and now has a following among some in traditional Protestant churches, as well as in many **Pentecostal** denominations and **charismatic churches**. It is also known as the 'Word–Faith' movement, because of the teaching that it is not good enough to merely believe what the Bible says about well-being; one must proclaim or confess out loud that one has health and wealth. For example, if one is ill or disabled, one must say out loud that the healing has occurred, even though the symptoms may still be present. This positive confession demonstrates faith and initiates God's healing powers.

Those who preach this message take their starting point in a variety of biblical passages which emphasise the importance of faith, such as, 'You do not have, because you do not ask' (James 4:3) and 'If you have faith the size of a mustard seed, you will say to this mountain, "Move from here to there," and it will move; and nothing will be impossible for you' (Matthew 17:20). The theme of faith is combined with the view that the covenant that God made with Israel included a promise of material blessing.

Does God want his followers to be wealthy?

The patriarchs in the Hebrew scriptures did experience, at times, enormous wealth. In addition to this, God's instructions for the tabernacle include costly materials. There are powerful images of the people of God inheriting a land that is 'flowing with milk and honey'. These insights seem to portray a God who is not an ascetic, nor prescribing an ascetic ideal. Of course, there are many more insights on wealth in the Hebrew Bible than these, such as the hypocrisy of participating in worship whilst ignoring the needs of the hungry, the fatherless, the widow and other suffering people.

The prosperity Gospel is popular in economically deprived places, offering Christians a sense of hope for upward mobility. It is popular, too, in more affluent areas as can be seen through the success of the book *The Prayer of Jabez* which centres on a prayer for material blessing (I Chronicles 4:10). This book topped the *New York Times Bestseller List* soon after its publication.

Problems with prosperity

Biblical scholar Craig L. Blomberg makes three critical observations on using the Bible to establish a Gospel of prosperity:

1. God never promised prosperity to all individual Israelites based on their personal levels of faithfulness or obedience to Torah. This promise was given to the nation as a whole. It was clear that godly Israelites could remain poor, in part, through oppression by others.

2. God never made similar arrangements with any of the other countries surrounding Israel; therefore, it is a mistake to apply promises in the Old Testament to modern-day nations.

3. No New Testament text ever makes the promise of peace and prosperity contingent on faith or obedience to the Church of Jesus Christ or to individual believers.

In fact, Blomberg notes, the blessing that believers receive for their faith is often not wealth but the spiritual qualities of hope and love to achieve more good works in the world (2 Corinthians 9:8). The Bible does not say that we should aspire to extravagant luxury; in fact, throughout the Old and New Testaments the message is about being aware of its corrupting influence. Finally, Blomberg notes that there are many passages that speak about God's power being perfected in weakness and suffering. The hardships Jesus endured in his life and his manner of death do not seem to confirm the prosperity Gospel.

AO1 Developing skills

It is now important to consider the information that has been covered in this section; however, the information in its raw form is too extensive and so has to be processed in order to meet the requirements of the examination. This can be achieved by practising more advanced skills associated with AO1. The exercises that run throughout this book will help you to do this and prepare you for the examination. For assessment objective 1 (AO1), which involves demonstrating 'knowledge' and 'understanding' skills, we are going to focus on different ways in which the skills can be demonstrated effectively, and also refer to how the performance of these skills is measured (see generic band descriptors for A2 [WJEC] AO1 or A Level [Eduqas] AO1).

▶ **Your next task is this:** Below is an outline of **Christian views of asceticism**. At present it has no quotations at all to back up the points made. Underneath the outline are two quotations that could be used in the outline in order to improve it. Your task is to rewrite the outline but make use of the quotations. Such phrases as 'according to …', 'the scholar … argues', or, 'it has been suggested by …' may help.

Christian views of asceticism:

- Asceticism is the idea that the world and its pleasures can distract us from God's path; discipline is needed.
- Forms of discipline can include prayer, worship, reading, fasting, celibacy, giving up possessions and an itinerant lifestyle.
- The Bible can be seen as endorsing asceticism.
- The Bible also celebrates the goodness of creation; many examples of faith were *not* known for their asceticism.
- The early church took a variety of approaches from the Desert Fathers and their extreme forms of deprivation to a variety of monastic disciplines.
- Many Christians today practise some form of spiritual discipline.
- Some Christians reject asceticism and embrace the prosperity Gospel.

Luke 7:33–34 [33] For John the Baptist came neither eating bread nor drinking wine, and you say, 'He has a demon'. [34] The Son of Man has come eating and drinking, and you say, 'Look, a glutton and a winebibber, a friend of tax collectors and sinners!'

Lest asceticism be dismissed … it bears mentioning that one of the greatest of all the heroes of the Tanakh was the mighty Samson, whom it describes as a 'Nazarite', the adherent of 'a special vow' of asceticism laid down in the Torah forbidding use of the fruit of the vine in any form and any cutting of the hair. … Even when I myself am too busy with the important business of life and the life of business to take time off for 'prayer and fasting', there are these athletes of asceticism who actually live as though the biblical command to 'pray continually' means what it says. (Jaroslav Pelikan)

When you have completed the task, try to find another quotation that you could use and further extend your answer.

Key skills Theme 3ABC

The second theme has tasks that concentrate on a particular aspect of AO1 in terms of using quotations from sources of authority and in the use of references.

Key skills

Knowledge involves:

Selection of a range of (thorough) accurate and relevant information that is directly related to the specific demands of the question.

This means:

- Selecting relevant material for the question set
- Be focused in explaining and examining the material selected.

Understanding involves:

Explanation that is extensive, demonstrating depth and/or breadth with excellent use of evidence and examples including (where appropriate) thorough and accurate supporting use of sacred texts, sources of wisdom and specialist language.

This means:

- Effective use of examples and supporting evidence to establish the quality of your understanding
- Ownership of your explanation that expresses personal knowledge and understanding and NOT just a chunk of text from a book that you have rehearsed and memorised.

Specification content

The extent to which wealth is a sign
of God's blessing.

Issues for analysis and evaluation

The extent to which wealth is a sign of God's blessing

Christianity is a diverse religion, so it is not surprising that there are a variety of attitudes found on money and material goods in relation to a Christian lifestyle.

Some Christians are very clear that having an abundance of material possessions and/or money is not only the sign of having been blessed by God, but is actually what Christians should expect to have in their lives. This is expressed by advocates of the 'prosperity Gospel' with their teaching that if one is walking in faith and giving generously to religious causes, God will give wealth. What is the source of this confidence?

These Christians argue that the Patriarchs, who responded to God's call in faith, were often blessed with wealth – just think of Abraham's large flocks and wealth in silver and gold (Genesis 13:2). God himself wanted the finest materials to be used for the tabernacle and, later, Solomon built an ornate temple and palace so much so that his wealth became renowned through Jewish history. These biblical facts do not at all suggest that God is an ascetic, but wants people to enjoy the material world. But, perhaps the most important argument for wealth as a blessing is that God made this a part of the covenant agreement with Israel – if they were obedient, God would make them 'abound in prosperity' in terms of children, livestock and food (Deuteronomy 28:11). A part of Israel's obedience was to give a tithe for the maintenance of religious festivals – so this is part of the human side of the equation, in order to receive wealth.

This clear promise of God is seen by those who advocate the 'prosperity Gospel' as being developed by the New Testament's emphasis on faith: 'you do not have because you do not ask' (James 2:3) and the idea that one can move mountains if they only have enough faith (Matthew 17:20) Thus, walking in faith and obedience should guarantee that one receives wealth – the precise message that can be found in many charismatic and Pentecostal churches. However, this view that God can be counted on to automatically dispense wealth in return for faith and obedience has been challenged by many churches and theologians.

First, just a glance at the Hebrew scriptures indicates that not everyone who walked in faith was consistently given health and wealth. Craig Blomberg notes that this blessing is never promised to individual Israelites, but is a promise made to the nation of Israel. We actually find the opposite situation for some individuals in the Old Testament. Job, for example, had faith in God but suffered incredible pain and the loss of all his wealth despite this fact. Some interpretations suggest that this book offers no rationale for his suffering other than that God's ways are mysterious.

Furthermore, asks Blomberg, is it right to apply a promise made to a nation under the conditions of the Old Covenant to other nations in this era? Certainly, we must not assume that Christians are under the same agreement as Jews, since Jesus announced a 'new covenant'. Furthermore, in the New Testament, there is simply no promise of health and wealth in return for faith and obedience. In fact, there is the principle that faith and one's spiritual life can be strengthened through suffering. This is quite the opposite of prosperity Gospel teaching.

AO2 Activity

As you read through this section try to do the following:

1. Pick out the different lines of argument that are presented in the text and identify any evidence given in support.

2. For each line of argument try to evaluate whether or not you think this is strong or weak.

3. Think of any questions you may wish to raise in response to the arguments.

This activity will help you to start thinking critically about what you read, and help you to evaluate the effectiveness of different arguments and from this develop your own observations, opinions and points of view that will help with any conclusions that you make in your answers to the AO2 questions that arise.

In addition to this observation, it must be noted that the statement above says wealth is 'a blessing', or, one of many types of blessing that a believer receives. In fact, the same New Testament passages that are used to prove that believers will receive wealth do not indicate exactly what those blessings will be. The book of James, which says, 'You do not have because you do not ask', follows this by saying that we do not know what to ask for and are often taken from spiritual goals by wanting pleasure. The passage about faith in Matthew 17 is in the context of healing someone with a physical illness – not about wealth. In 2 Corinthians 9:8 where Paul speaks of God blessing those who give, he does not define what those blessings will be. He only says that those who give will be able to continue to do good works. Presumably, then, the blessings that one could receive might be of a spiritual nature.

Perhaps the strongest argument against viewing wealth as a sign of God's blessing is the life and death of Jesus. Christians believe that Jesus is God's beloved Son, someone who exemplifies a close relationship with God. Yet Jesus possessed no wealth at all; he was born to a poor family and lived a life as an itinerant preacher, having to rely on the hospitality of others. Furthermore, he died a violent death after physical abuse which included being beaten, whipped, forced to wear a crown of thorns and to carry a cross through the city streets. He then died a violent death on the cross. How, therefore, could God be taught to automatically confer health and wealth in return for obedience when this did not happen to God's own Son?

In conclusion, the Bible does show that some followers of God have received the blessing of wealth, and that some followers of God have received the very opposite – suffering and poverty. Is there anything that unites these diverse viewpoints?

A message that is consistent across the Bible is that wealth as a goal in itself is never viewed as a good thing. In many Old Testament passages God is portrayed as the defender of the poor and oppressed, and those with wealth are urged to give generously. In the New Testament, there are repeated warnings about wealth, not that it is bad or 'dirty' in itself, but that a focus on it can lead people away from God's priorities. Even to ask if wealth can be an aspect of God's blessing could be a sign that one is not focused on living a godly life.

AO2 Activity

List some conclusions that could be drawn from the AO2 reasoning from the above text; try to aim for at least three different possible conclusions. Consider each of the conclusions and collect brief evidence to support each conclusion from the AO1 and AO2 material for this topic. Select the conclusion that you think is most convincing and explain why it is so. Try to contrast this with the weakest conclusion in the list, justifying your argument with clear reasoning and evidence.

Specification content

Whether the ascetic ideal is
compatible with Christianity.

Whether the ascetic ideal is compatible with Christianity

Jesus is viewed by Christians not only as a member of the Trinity, the God they worship, but also as an example of how to live a godly life. If one focusses on trying to live the way in which Jesus lived, then this could be argued to involve some form of asceticism, the denial of earthly pleasures in order to follow God's path.

Just consider many striking aspects of Jesus' life: the beginning of his ministry with 40 days of prayer and fasting in the desert, his poverty, his teaching about giving away one's possessions and his extreme dedication to an itinerant lifestyle as he spread his message about the Kingdom of God. Many early Christians were also impressed by John the Baptist, his strict diet, his life removed from society, his poverty and simple lifestyle. In the early centuries of Christianity many lived as hermits in the Egyptian desert, devoting their lives to prayer and reflection in the context of a simple life. These early movements developed into monasticism, communal Christian living centring around rules of poverty, chastity and obedience. There were a variety of monastic movements, with varying interpretations of asceticism, but with the shared emphasis that Christian living requires some sort of denial of worldly pleasures and comfort.

In support of the ascetic ideal are the many passages in the New Testament about the dangers of wealth. In Mark 10, for example, Jesus recognises that the man who had kept the Mosaic Law was restless, so Jesus invited him to give up his possessions and join his movement. When the man refused to do this, Jesus warned how wealth made it impossible to follow God's path. Jesus' appeal to the natural world in Matthew 6 seems to indicate that we spend far too much time devoted to the quest for clothing and food and too little time on spiritual matters. In Luke 12 Jesus simply tells his followers to 'sell your possessions' and give the money to the poor – an action that we are told was lived out in the early church (Acts 2). Those who argue for an ascetic ideal, then, can appeal to both the lifestyle and the teachings of Jesus.

Yet, if we look at Jesus' teaching a little more closely, we can see that there are problems with turning it into a law for all Christians. First, Jesus only offered the teaching to the rich man when the latter made it clear that keeping the commandments was not enough for his soul. This suggests that Jesus was not presenting a universal teaching but a prescription meant for one individual. In fact, Jesus approves of Zacchaeus giving up only half of his wealth; he does not refer to this theme at all in relation to others who are mentioned in the Gospels – some he invited to join his movement, others are sent away to live a spiritual life in their own community.

In Matthew, Jesus makes it clear that it is not money or wealth itself that is the problem, but one's priorities. In other words, one needs to be dedicated to the Kingdom of God; anything that gets in the way of this is to be sacrificed. I Timothy, with its teaching that the *love of* money is the root of all kinds of evil reinforces this point. In Jesus' pursuit of the kingdom he received food and hospitality by those who had these possessions to share. Could it not therefore be that different people have different ways to live out the Christian life rather than having to embrace a single ascetic ideal? The teaching to give up one's possessions was lived out by the early Christians, but there is no clear indication that everyone in the early church gave up everything. Instead of a thoroughly communistic society in Acts 2 we seem to have voluntary acts of generosity.

AO2 Activity

As you read through this section try to do the following:

1. Pick out the different lines of argument that are presented in the text and identify any evidence given in support.

2. For each line of argument try to evaluate whether or not you think this is strong or weak.

3. Think of any questions you may wish to raise in response to the arguments.

This activity will help you to start thinking critically about what you read, and help you to evaluate the effectiveness of different arguments and from this develop your own observations, opinions and points of view that will help with any conclusions that you make in your answers to the AO2 questions that arise.

It may be that Jesus did not always live in an ascetic manner. He is known to have received hospitality from those who were well off, eating and drinking in ways that may not have reflected an ascetic lifestyle. In fact, popular opinion noticed a difference between John the Baptist's strict lifestyle and Jesus' relatively lax one: 'For John the Baptist has come eating no bread and drinking no wine, and you say, "He has a demon"; the Son of Man has come eating and drinking, and you say, "Look, a glutton and a drunkard, a friend of tax collectors and sinners!"' (Luke 7:33–34).

Also, did Jesus live in an ascetic manner because it was an ideal or a necessity? In other words, be may have adopted a certain lifestyle because he believed the world was about to end and that, therefore, there was a heightened urgency to get out his message to as many people as possible (eschatological expectation). Some of Jesus' disciplines may have come from his ideal; Jesus was a rabbi, and a rabbi typically lived with his disciples to teach in deeds as well as words. However, it is widely thought that Jesus believed that the world was about to end and that this belief drove him to adopt an itinerant lifestyle. It might have simply made more sense for Jesus to receive hospitality rather than to live a settled life given the fact that he wanted to spread his movement across Israel. Furthermore, if one views Jesus as an eschatological figure, then he might have prescribed more extreme forms of living, thinking that they would not need to be endured long term.

Sexual abstinence is a common form of asceticism. It appears that Jesus was celibate, but this could have been because of his eschatological expectations – it was normal for Rabbis to be married in Jesus' day. Paul discusses his own choice to be celibate but explains how married Christians can live a spiritual life. He even urges some Christians to get married so that they will not be constantly distracted by the 'flames of passion'.

It might even be argued that an ascetic ideal detracts from what is more clearly central in the Bible: the positive action of helping those who are poor and oppressed and supporting God's work in the world through the ministry of the Church. To carry out this work, it may be more effective to consider oneself as a 'steward' rather than an 'ascetic'. Stewardship involves a positive affirmation of the material world, a dedication to the wise use of one's resources and a generous heart to those who need help. Stewardship seems to presuppose private ownership. Rather than retreating from the world in asceticism, one might better live out God's plan through the advice of John Wesley, 'Make all you can, save all you can, give all you can.'

In conclusion, a major difficulty for the position that Christians should live by an ascetic ideal is that there appears to be no single ideal in Christianity. For example, it is not clear how often Jesus fasted and prayed. As Christianity developed, there were different degrees and forms of asceticism. In the medieval era, some Christians believed they should identify with the suffering of Jesus by physically punishing their bodies by wearing hair shirts or engaging in self-flagellation. Other ascetic practices were more 'spiritual' in nature: the regular reading of theological books, various forms of meditation, and reflection on the meaning of the sacraments. If Christians cannot agree on an ascetic ideal, may this be because there is no ascetic ideal in the Bible?

Key quotes

For most of Christian history, the battle about asceticism has been not whether Christian piety should be associated with it, but about the type, intensity of expression, and meaning of the ascetic that is appropriate or required. (V. L. Wimbush)

The Bible does not promote asceticism, except in small, temporary ways. [There are] … an abundance of texts that speak of wealth and material possessions as good and wholesome, when used and kept in proper perspective. (C. Blomberg)

AO2 Activity

List some conclusions that could be drawn from the AO2 reasoning from the above text; try to aim for at least three different possible conclusions. Consider each of the conclusions and collect brief evidence to support each conclusion from the AO1 and AO2 material for this topic. Select the conclusion that you think is most convincing and explain why it is so. Try to contrast this with the weakest conclusion in the list, justifying your argument with clear reasoning and evidence.

Key skills Theme 3ABC

The second theme has tasks that concentrate on a particular aspect of AO2 in terms of using quotations from sources of authority and in the use of references in supporting arguments and evaluations.

Key skills

Analysis involves:

Identifying issues raised by the materials in the AO1, together with those identified in the AO2 section, and presents sustained and clear views, either of scholars or from a personal perspective ready for evaluation.

This means:

- That your answers are able to identify key areas of debate in relation to a particular issue

- That you can identify, and comment upon, the different lines of argument presented by others

- That your response comments on the overall effectiveness of each of these areas or arguments.

Evaluation involves:

Considering the various implications of the issues raised based upon the evidence gleaned from analysis and provides an extensive detailed argument with a clear conclusion.

This means:

- That your answer weighs up the consequences of accepting or rejecting the various and different lines of argument analysed

- That your answer arrives at a conclusion through a clear process of reasoning.

AO2 Developing skills

It is now important to consider the information that has been covered in this section; however, the information in its raw form is too extensive and so has to be processed in order to meet the requirements of the examination. This can be achieved by practising more advanced skills associated with AO2. The exercises that run throughout this book will help you to do this and prepare you for the examination. For assessment objective 2 (AO2), which involves 'critical analysis' and 'evaluation' skills, we are going to focus on different ways in which the skills can be demonstrated effectively, and also refer to how the performance of these skills is measured (see generic band descriptors for A2 [WJEC] AO2 or A Level [Eduqas] AO2).

▶ **Your next task is this:** Below is an evaluation of **the claim that the prosperity Gospel represents biblical teaching on wealth and stewardship.** At present it has no quotations at all to support the argument presented. Underneath the evaluation are two quotations that could be used in the outline in order to improve it. Your task is to rewrite the outline but make use of the quotations. Such phrases as 'according to ...', 'the scholar ... argues', or, 'it has been suggested by ...' may help.

The claim that God wants all believers to experience wealth and health is questionable on several grounds. First, in the Hebrew scriptures not all of those who followed God were given these gifts (i.e. Job); they sometimes went through long periods of time of deprivation, suffering or hardship (i.e. Abraham's wandering). Clearly the focus of the Hebrew scriptures is not one should aspire to wealth, but that one should be compassionate with wealth, use it to help others and take care of those experiencing social oppression. Turning to the New Testament, there are clear teachings on the danger of wealth. Jesus himself lived an itinerant existence, relying on the welfare of others. In fact, the suffering at the end of his life seems to be the opposite to what is prescribed by the prosperity Gospel – does this mean that he had no faith? The early church, as described in Acts 2, focuses on generously sharing with those in need so that all can have a degree of comfort – this is not the same as wealth.

... we reject the unbiblical notion that spiritual welfare can be measured in terms of material welfare, or that wealth is always a sign of God's blessing (since it can be obtained by oppression, deceit or corruption), or that poverty or illness or early death, is always a sign of God's curse, or lack of faith, or human curses (since the Bible explicitly denies that it is always so). (The Lausanne Theology Working Group)

If some measure of material comfort is inherently desirable, then all people should have the chance to gain it. If too much unnecessary wealth leads so often to sin, then those with excess amounts should divest themselves of it. These two truisms, amply demonstrated from all portions of Scripture ... lead inexorably to a third: God's people should give generously from their surplus (and be ruthlessly honest about how much is surplus). (Craig L. Blomberg)

When you have completed the task, try to find another quotation that you could use and further extend your evaluation.

B: Migration and Christianity in the UK

Migration and immigration

Open any newspaper or news site and you are likely to see a story that involves immigration. The United Nations has declared that the number of people currently displaced by conflict is higher than ever recorded. Here in the UK we are aware of the needs of many from Syria, Afghanistan, Iraq, Kosovo and other countries who are seeking refuge and asylum. The desperate efforts to reach a safer land involve fatalities on a weekly basis.

Forced migration due to humanitarian crises, however, is only one aspect of immigration. There are many who come to Great Britain from the European Union, Commonwealth countries and elsewhere seeking economic opportunities. Others arrive from countries which are not at war but which they find oppressive for a variety of reasons from religious discrimination to a lack of educational opportunity.

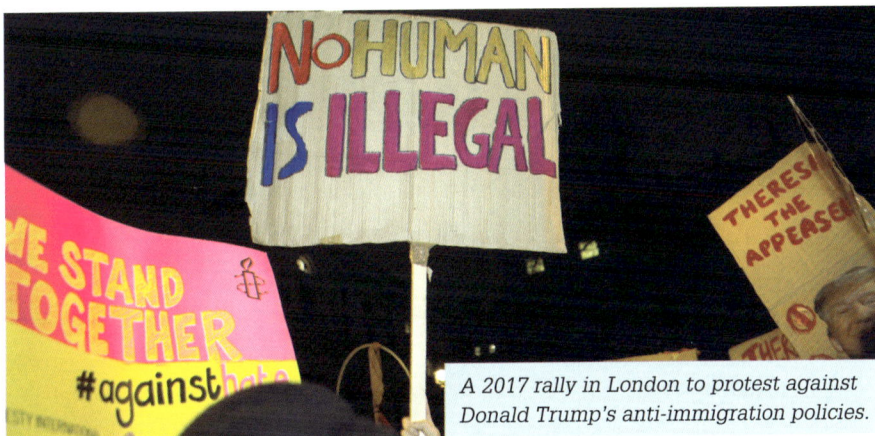

A 2017 rally in London to protest against Donald Trump's anti-immigration policies.

Immigration is a complex phenomenon which can benefit a host country, provide opportunities to enrich a population as well as raise fears about security, economic stability and social cohesion. It appears that news stories about immigration will continue to be on the front page for some time to come.

Christianity: a story of migration?

Christians involved in welcoming migrants to their country and their churches believe that many biblical passages support their work. The story of Israel's faith begins with the call to Abraham and Sarah to leave their land and make a journey to Canaan. Later, Jewish tribes suffered an oppressive regime in Egypt and then wandered for decades without a home. It was during this period that the Bible says they received a command to treat those from other places with equality: 'The alien who resides with you shall be to you as the citizen among you; you shall love the alien as yourself, for you were aliens in the land of Egypt: I am the LORD your God.' (Leviticus 19:34). The Gospels relate that Mary and Joseph were uprooted from their community three times: from Nazareth to Bethlehem, from Bethlehem to Egypt and from Egypt to Galilee. Jesus told a story of a man who was robbed, abused and left to die – and ignored by 'upright' citizens (religious leaders). Then, a stranger, moved with compassion, performed first-aid, took him to a shelter, cared for him and provided money for further care. The irony of this story is that the stranger who acted compassionately was from a group despised by many of Jesus' contemporaries (Luke 10:30–37). These passages inform the conviction of many Christians as they offer humanitarian aid to refugees and extend a welcome to those migrants who are looking for a church home no matter what culture they are from. The importance of Christian outreach to migrants is reflected, for example, by the fact that the Catholic Church celebrates, annually, The World Day of Migrants and Refugees.

Specification content

The challenges of Christian migration to the UK, with reference to assimilation, provision of worship, style of worship and issues of culture. The reverse mission movement to the UK.

Key quote

The story of humanity is a story of mobility: the creation and revision of borders, of communities, the rules governing who can move and who can't, the social and political practices that shape who is accepted within what kinds of spaces. (Centre of Migration, Policy and Society – COMPAS)

quickfire

3.6 What are some reasons for immigration?

Modern mosaic of the parable of the Good Samaritan

Key terms

Congregation: an assembly of
people for worship, usually in a church
building

Denomination: an autonomous
religious organisation composed of
many congregations

Independent churches: a
congregation that does not belong to a
denomination

Pentecostalism: a worldwide
Christian movement composed of
many denominations and independent
churches that focus on the experience
of the worshipper and the miraculous
gifts of the Spirit of God

quickfire

3.7 What is the difference between a
denominational congregation and an
independent congregation?

The challenges of Christian migration to the UK

Christianity is the religion with the largest representation amongst immigrants
to the UK who have a religious affiliation. This means that tens of thousands of
'new' Christians are joining churches each year; some of these will attend churches
that have long been in Britain and that are also in their country of origin – such as
Anglican, Catholic or Methodist churches. Others will join new **denominations** or
independent churches with a significant immigrant population. This large influx
of Christians has caused traditional churches to reflect on how effectively they
welcome and integrate newcomers into their communities.

Some Christians who are new to Britain will be familiar with many aspects of
worship and church life in their new church; however, this does not mean that
it will be easy to integrate into the worshipping community. For example, the
Catholic Church in Britain has had an influx of believers from EU countries such as
Poland and Lithuania. This has raised several cultural issues on which the Church
actively seeks to help **congregations**.

AO1 Activity

Imagine that a large group of non-English speakers have suddenly begun
attending your 6th form classes. Make a list of issues that would need to be
addressed so that they – and you – could continue to learn. Then compare your
list to the issues noted in the text that congregations need to face to assimilate
worshippers from diverse backgrounds.

- A large influx of worshippers who may just be learning English can make pastoral
care a challenge – how can a vicar or priest respond in a situation of personal
crises when there is a language barrier? This has led, in some places, to the
appointment of an 'immigrant chaplain' or an 'episcopal vicar' who can take
responsibility for a migrant community within a church.

- Language barriers can also hinder the teaching of the catechism, confirmation
classes and preparation for the sacraments. Older migrants or others with
relevant language skills are seen as an invaluable church resource in this
situation; leaflets in the language of the migrant population can be used in
worship services to increase understanding.

- There can be significant differences in worship styles – even when an immigrant
is attending the same denomination in Britain as in their country of origin.
Churches attempt to respect diversity and are encouraged to incorporate
different forms of worship.

The overall challenge is to maintain both a sense of community cohesion as well
as an openness to the traditions and preferences of those who are new to the
worshipping community.

Pentecostalism in the UK

The largest influx of Christians in Britain has come from the Caribbean and West
African countries where Pentecostal Christianity is pervasive. This has led to
thousands of new churches in Britain, the reversal of overall church decline in some
regions and even to active outreach from migrant communities to what is viewed
as secular, atheist Britain.

Pentecostalism is a movement in Christianity that emphasises the experience of
the worshipper. It makes constant reference to the powerful experiences of the
early church in Acts chapter 2, when it is reported that the Spirit of God came upon
the followers of Jesus, enabling them to speak in other languages and perform

acts of healing. Pentecostal worship services do not follow a written liturgy and can have many of these components: exuberant singing, dancing, clapping, spontaneous prayer, sermons punctuated by impromptu responses ('Yes!', 'Amen!'), faith healing and speaking in tongues.

Study tip

Make sure you understand the difference between a denominational congregation and an independent congregation. Migrants who are Christians may join either of these kinds of churches; you should be able to give examples of each type.

Pentecostal forms of Christianity have experienced dramatic growth in Africa, Asia and Latin America in recent years. A conservative estimate is that there are just less than 300 million Pentecostal Christians in the world, though it could be as high as half a billion. Most of these are in the southern hemisphere. This means that, for the first time in history, there are probably more Christians in the southern hemisphere than in the northern hemisphere. Thus, the geographical centre of Christianity has shifted. In the UK, there are now 500,000 Christians who attend Black majority churches – whereas 60 years ago there were hardly any.

Britain has many indigenous Pentecostal churches that were established at the beginning of the twentieth century. However, immigration in the past few decades has introduced new Pentecostal denominations and independent churches planted by African and Caribbean church leaders. For example, the Redeemed Christian Church of God (RCCG) is a Nigerian denomination founded in 1952 which has experienced dramatic growth and has a vision for global expansion. There are now almost 800 RCCG congregations in Britain with hundreds having opened in the past few years. This outnumbers indigenous Pentecostal church bodies such as the Assemblies of God and Elim Pentecostal Church.

The RCCG's largest church in Britain is Jesus House which has over two thousand people in attendance on a Sunday morning. There are also several independent Pentecostal churches such as Freedom Centre International in Welling, which meets in a refurbished bingo hall. The interior of the church displays the words 'Free to Prosper' and the church states that their mission is to 'set people free to pursue their God-given life'. Kingsway International Christian Church is another example of a large, independent church with a predominately West African membership. It claims to be the largest church in Europe and seeks to 'share the Good News of Jesus Christ with the 1.5 million people resident in Kent and the 64.1 million in the UK at large'.

AO1 Activity

To learn about evangelical Christianity in denominations with a historical presence in the UK and in new denominations planted from church bodies in the southern hemisphere, examine the websites of Holy Trinity Brompton, the Redeemed Christian Church of God and Kingsway International Christian Church. Take special note of their 'mission' or 'vision' statements as well as the pages which describe their history.

Key quote

Pentecostalism is revolutionary because it offers alternatives to 'literary' theology and defrosts the 'frozen thinking' within literary forms of worship and committee debate. It gives the same chance to all, including the 'oral' people. (W. Hollenweger)

quickfire

3.8 Why are there so many new Pentecostal denominations and congregations in the UK?

Key quotes

The 'Pentecostalisation' of African Christianity can be called the African Reformation of the twentieth century which has fundamentally altered the character of African Christianity, including that of the older mission churches. (A. H. Anderson)

The declining fortunes of Christianity in the public space in Britain have been assuaged by the proliferation of Black Majority Churches [BMCs]. The involvement and influence of BMCs in various cities seem to position them as a source of religious hope in Britain. (Daniel Akhazemea of the Reformed Christian Church of God)

Theresa May visits Jesus House in North London in 2017

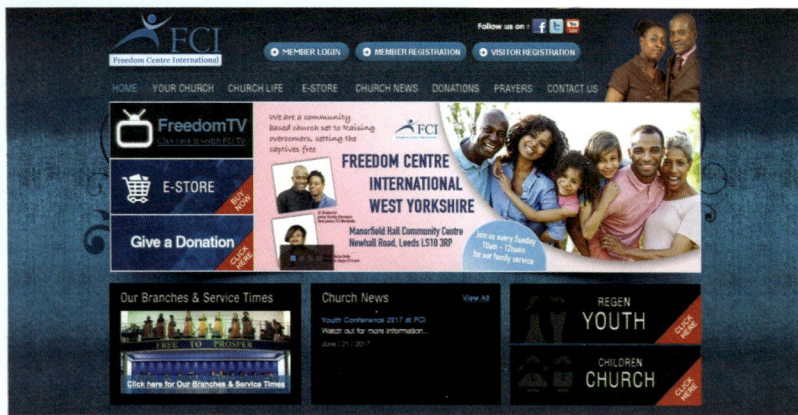

Freedom Centre International is a new Pentecostal denomination.

Key terms

Evangelise: from the Greek term for 'good news', to share the Christian message with the hope of bringing about conversions

Liturgical: relating to formal worship prescribed by a church body; for example, the Book of Common Prayer contains liturgies

Reverse mission: countries that once sent missionaries become themselves the target for missionary work from the countries they once evangelised

Key quote

… most of these churches function as a hub for restructuring and transforming the self-worth and economic worth of their members through dissemination of information about job opportunities, advisory services and free immigration advice to assuage the challenges of acculturation into Britain. **(Daniel Akhazemea of the Reformed Christian Church of God)**

quickfire

3.9 List three reasons why more traditional churches have not assimilated people who have immigrated to the UK.

Why aren't more congregations integrated?

There are many examples of British congregations which once had a majority white-British membership which have become multi-ethnic, having assimilated new members from diverse cultures. At the same time, many of the new churches and denominations appearing in Britain have a majority immigrant membership. Why is it the case that traditional British churches have not assimilated more foreign-born worshippers? There may be several reasons:

- Worship differences. There are clear differences between the experiential style of Pentecostal worship and the more literary and **liturgical** approaches of many traditional churches. However, this need not necessarily lead to a lack of assimilation since (i) there are many churches from long-standing denominations that have embraced a Pentecostal style of worship (these are often called 'charismatic churches') and (ii) there are indigenous Pentecostal denominations in Britain.

- Social support. Migrant groups have their own needs, related to the pressures of establishing a new home, a source of income and a social network. Churches that have a significant proportion of membership from migrant backgrounds can offer understanding and support for these challenges. In fact, many black and ethnic minority churches offer counselling on legal aspects of the immigration process and classes on career development, educational issues and financial management.

- The uneven spread of immigration. The Office of National Statistics reports that nearly 75% of all migrants go to London and an additional 10% to the south west. This may reflect the fact that there are strong social and economic reasons for immigrants to settle in cities. This means that there are large regions across the UK that do not have a significant number of immigrants; thus, there are no opportunities for some churches to assimilate those from different cultures.

The reverse mission movement to the UK

The UK has had a long history of sending missionaries to spread the Christian message throughout the world. As a result, one can find, for example, Anglican and Methodist churches in almost every place that was once a part of the British Empire: from India to the far north of Canada. Journalists, church leaders and scholars have noticed a recent phenomenon: missionaries are coming to the UK from some of these very countries. This is called **reverse mission**: countries that once sent missionaries become themselves the target for missionary work from the countries they once **evangelised.**

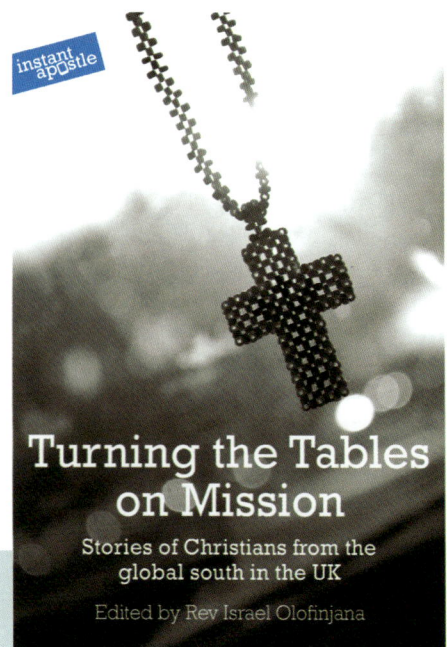

Recent books, documentaries and studies document the experience of reverse mission.

AO1 Activity

Type 'Reverse Missionaries BBC' into your YouTube search bar and you will find documentaries that have been made on this subject. Watch one of these and take note of the reasons that these missionaries give for wanting to spread their faith in the UK.

One reason for reverse mission has do with the global shift of Christianity to the southern hemisphere; this shift is bound up with the growing rise of Pentecostal Christianity. Brazil, Korea and Nigeria lead in sending the most Protestant missionaries across the world; these are also countries where Pentecostal Christianity has experienced dramatic growth. Another impetus for reverse mission is the fact of dramatic church decline in the UK and the perception of those from majority Christian countries that Britain is increasingly atheistic and secular.

There are many different activities that could be labelled 'reverse mission':

- Short-term visits of a group of non-British Christians, perhaps sponsored by a host church in the UK. For example, a church group from an African country comes to share music, drama and dance in churches and in public spaces with the intention of spreading their faith.
- Church workers who come to the UK with the intention to 'evangelise' and bring about conversions to Christianity from British citizens; this may be in conjunction with the need to work or study. These individuals may be hosted by a church body (here or abroad) or may be wholly independent.
- Churches, church bodies or theological colleges intentionally appointing a leader from a migrant background as a pastor, priest, tutor or church leader as a part of a plan to reinvigorate the British church.
- A church in Britain that has a significant migrant population and views outreach to white-British nationals as a part of its God-given mission.

These different activities are united by the perception of Britain as increasingly hostile to Christianity and the desire to see Christianity thrive here once again.

Has reverse mission met with success in the UK? One scholar, Rebecca Catto, says that many reverse missionaries report facing cultural challenges including the resistance of secular British nationals to the Christian message and difficulties in adjusting to a new country with cold, cloudy weather and bland food. Thus far, 'reverse mission' has not appeared to have stemmed the tide of Church decline. Additionally, some reverse missionaries have shifted their focus to their fellow nationals, establishing churches that support the unique needs of migrant communities. Reverse mission has caused long-standing British church bodies to reflect more intensely on the quality of their own outreach.

Does Christianity in the UK need the support of missionaries?

Many scholars of sociology and religion have supported the 'secularisation thesis', the view that modern societies such as Britain are becoming secular in at least one of three ways: (i) a decline in Church attendance, (ii) a decreasing role for the Church in public life and (iii) a loss of personal faith in God and other Christian beliefs. Advocates of this thesis predict that Britain faces a future of steady Christian decline.

Supporting this thesis is the dramatic increase of those citing 'no religion' in response to a question on religious belonging from the Census for England and Wales (from 15% in 2001 to 25% in 2011). This number is much higher in other surveys which ask the question somewhat differently. There has also been a

Key quotes

There is an increase in numbers of committed, often young, people willing and able to travel, wishing to evangelise the 'dark continent of Europe' and give 'back', combined with an increased desire among British churches and organisations to learn from examples of growth and success. (R. Catto)

A Melanesian bishop now leading a parish in Devon sounded a warning note in our interview. He critiqued the concept of 'reverse mission' for implying a proud mentality – pride on the part of the West in the former dominance of colonial missions and pride on the part of non-Westerners believing that they have the better situation and solution. (R. Catto)

It seems that the growth of Christianity in the 'global south' and of immigrant congregations has made mainline churches in Britain take notice and realise that they also have something to learn in what is a period of transition for them and for wider society. (R. Catto)

quickfire

3.10 Why do reverse missionaries want to come to the UK?

Key quotes

During the last 30 years we have all become familiar with shrinking congregations and churches closing. But few people realise that the same period has seen the opening of several thousand new churches across the UK. And while larger denominations have all lost members, other small denominations, as well as many independent congregations have grown. (H. McLeod)

… elite culture in Britain may well be secularising, whilst other parts of British life are seeing church growth. A survey of the religious views of, for instance, BBC executives and those who clean the BBC Television Centre in London might well indicate both secularisation and resacralisation. (D. Goodhew)

Key term

Evangelicals: Christians from across many denominations who emphasise the importance of conversion and personal faith; evangelicals have a high regard for the Bible and can believe that faith should influence public life

quickfire

3.11 Name one fact that could be seen to contradict the secularisation thesis.

corresponding decrease in the Census for those associating with Christianity – from 72% to 59% in the same ten-year period. Additionally, Christianity has the oldest age profile of all religious groups. There is also evidence that more people believe in life after death than believe in God (the British Cohort Survey). Anecdotal evidence also points to decline: The Church of England reports about 20 church closures a year, with many of these church buildings becoming available for lease or sale.

Will the sale of church buildings continue to increase?

However, there are also statistics which challenge the secularisation thesis. Though only 47% of 18–34 year olds declare themselves to have a religious affiliation, 67% say that they pray occasionally or regularly. There is also evidence of growth in some areas of the Church. The number of **evangelicals** in the Church of England has risen from 26% to 34% between 1989 and 2005 and there are several churches such as Holy Trinity Brompton (HTB) which are known for their vibrancy and their relatively young membership. HTB's popular 'Alpha Course' has been implemented in churches across the UK – and the world. Church membership in some locations is on the increase: the London Diocese of the Church of England has grown by 70% since 1990.

Study tip

No one questions the fact that attendance at Christian churches has declined in recent decades. However, there is serious disagreement between scholars on the inevitability of continued religious decline in Britain. Make sure that you can list reasons that support each side of this debate, including the role that immigration plays in the religious life of the UK.

Though it is difficult to make a prediction on what may happen in the future, it is true that much Church growth that has occurred in recent decades in the UK has been a result of immigration. A study of churches in north-east England shows that 125 churches opened between 1980 and 2015. Several of these have been new denominations or independent churches with a primarily migrant make up. Of the 125 churches, 47 have a majority of attendees from black and ethnic minority backgrounds and a further 37 churches have a significant minority of members from black and minority ethnic communities. Only 18 of the 125 are historical denominations – none are Catholic and only one is Church of England. However, this picture of Church 'growth' is not as positive as it might sound: between 1989 and 2010 there were about 148 church closures in the same area.

AO1 Developing skills

It is now important to consider the information that has been covered in this section; however, the information in its raw form is too extensive and so has to be processed in order to meet the requirements of the examination. This can be achieved by practising more advanced skills associated with AO1. For assessment objective 1 (AO1), which involves demonstrating 'knowledge' and 'understanding' skills, we are going to focus on different ways in which the skills can be demonstrated effectively, and also refer to how the performance of these skills is measured (see generic band descriptors for A2 [WJEC] AO1 or A Level [Eduqas] AO1).

▶ **Your next task is this:** Below is a summary of **challenges and opportunities for churches assimilating migrants into their communities**. At present, it has no references at all to support the points made. Underneath the summary are two references to the works of scholars, and/or religious writings, that could be used in the outline in order to improve the summary. Your task is to rewrite the summary but make use of the references. Such phrases as 'according to …', 'the scholar … argues', or, 'it has been suggested by …' may help. Usually a reference includes a footnote but for an answer in an A Level essay under examination conditions this is not expected, although an awareness of which book your evidence refers to is useful (although not always necessary).

- It is not always easy for churches to assimilate migrants into their communities.
- Christians have many biblical reasons for making the attempt to create strong, integrated worship communities.
- Pastoral care can be challenging with those who are not yet proficient in English.
- Language barriers can prevent Christian instruction from happening.
- Styles in worship between cultures can cause confusion and misunderstandings.
- Some churches work with their denomination headquarters to solve the problems.
- Some churches identify volunteers who can help teach and support the migrant community.
- Some churches create resources and implement changes to complement their approach to worship with new ideas.

People who are so desperate to flee that they will entrust their entire future to a leaking boat are examples of the man fallen among thieves [Luke 19: 30–37]. Jesus asks us today: who is their neighbour? Who will bind their wounds and carry them to a place of safety and pay for their rehabilitation? The man fallen among thieves did not recover overnight. (The Church of England)

One culture may use music more than another; others will use dancing, poetry or storytelling. Likewise, styles and patterns of prayer may differ … Dancing, for example, is an essential part of prayer and praise in Africa. In Asia, there is a deep awareness of the sacred place or space, so altars, shrines and statues become an important focus of prayer. In Orthodox traditions, icons have a special place in Christian spirituality. In Spain, Portugal and South America, processions are a very important part of communal prayer and popular faith. Add to this the fact that the deeper the sentiment, the more difficult it is to express it in another language, we see how creating a community of prayer poses huge challenges. (The Catholic Bishops' Conference of England and Wales)

When you have completed the task, try to write another reference that you could use and further extend your answer.

Key skills

Knowledge involves:

Selection of a range of (thorough) accurate and relevant information that is directly related to the specific demands of the question.

This means:

- Selecting relevant material for the question set
- Being focused in explaining and examining the material selected.

Understanding involves:

Explanation that is extensive, demonstrating depth and/or breadth with excellent use of evidence and examples including (where appropriate) thorough and accurate supporting use of sacred texts, sources of wisdom and specialist language.

This means:

- Effective use of examples and supporting evidence to establish the quality of your understanding
- Ownership of your explanation that expresses personal knowledge and understanding and NOT just reproducing a chunk of text from a book that you have rehearsed and memorised.

This section covers AO2
content and skills

Specification content

The extent to which the UK is a
modern mission field.

Issues for analysis and evaluation

The extent to which the UK is a modern mission field

Matthew 28 describes the mission that Jesus gave his disciples: to make disciples of all nations, baptising and teaching them to obey the commandments of Jesus. The countries that now make up the UK were, at one time, leaders in sending missionaries out to the rest of the world, especially those places ruled by the British Empire. Should the UK continue to be regarded as a 'Christian nation' or should it be viewed as a 'post-Christian,' secular or even atheist nation in need of receiving (or resisting) them?

From a Christian point of view, any place where there are people who do not yet follow the way of Jesus is a mission field. Thus, the UK has always been and will always be a mission field. Evangelical Christians, especially, would embrace this point of view – they see having and sharing a faith experience in the atoning work of Jesus on the cross as central to their Christian lives. There are many evangelical Christians in long-standing traditional churches in the UK. An example is Holy Trinity Brompton which declares their 'vision to play our part in the evangelisation of the nations, the revitalisation of the Church and the transformation of society'. It has attempted to fulfil its mission to the UK through the popular Alpha Course, which teaches the Christian path to non-Christians.

Whilst there have long been 'indigenous' evangelical Christians in the UK, what is new are unprecedented numbers of Pentecostal Christians from the Caribbean and West African countries. These Christians are also evangelical, viewing the UK as mission field. New denominations such as the Redeemed Christian Church of God and Independent churches such as Kingsway Christian Centre see evangelising (sharing the good news about Jesus) as a central activity – the RCCG church proclaims that its goal is 'To make heaven. To take as many people with us.' And Kingsway church declares its intent to reach the entire population of Kent with the message of Jesus.

One of the factors that make Britain appear to be a significant mission field to these Christians is the sharp decline of Christianity in recent decades. This decline can be seen in the sharp decrease of those who identify with Christianity (a drop from 72% to 59% in the ten years between 2001 and 2011 according to the Census for England and Wales); it can also be seen in the increase of those who say they belong to 'no religion', a 10% increase in the same period. At the same time, there has been the popularity of new atheist thinkers and the lease or sale of empty church buildings. All of these facts support the view that Britain has moved from a Christian nation to a secular one. Thus, it could be interpreted that Britain is not only a mission field in the sense that all countries are mission fields – it is an especially needy one in light of Christian decline.

Stepping back from the Christian perspective, one could argue that the UK is a mission field simply because that is how it is viewed and treated by those nations who now have a predominately Christian population. This is underscored by the fact of 'reverse mission' – where the countries once targeted by British missionaries are now sending missionaries to the UK. Reverse missionaries are sometimes invited by a host church in the UK to revitalise worship services and share the good news in public spaces. Other reverse missionaries are sponsored by churches outside of the UK, or come as independent agents, feeling the call to this 'non-Christian' land. Therefore, both from the point of view of an evangelical outlook as well as a sociological one, the UK is a mission field.

However, not all Christians are of the evangelical variety; thus, they may not see the purpose of their faith as the conversion of others. They may interpret 'mission' in terms of offering humanitarian aid and they may be comfortable with the idea of theological pluralism (that there are many paths to God). Thus, the fact of the decline of the Church may not be seen as a critical issue and therefore the question of Britain as a mission field is not relevant.

Alongside this approach to Christianity may exist the notion that the conversion of souls is an activity that God performs, not humans – therefore it is arrogant and presumptuous to treat any country (including the UK) as a mission field (unless 'mission' is interpreted in terms of humanitarian aid). Instead, what is needed is interfaith dialogue, an appreciation of other faiths and cultures and a joining together over projects which promote morality and well-being. Christians who take these approaches may reflect the theology of John Hick who elevated religious experience over religious doctrine and who viewed each religion as having an ethical mandate in which there were more similarities than differences.

One might also resist the notion of the UK as a 'mission field' based upon the view that Christianity remains an integral part of each of the lands that make up the UK – despite reports of decline. The Church offers pastoral acts such as weddings, funerals and baptisms and is also active in each community in a variety of ways. Furthermore, it leads the nation in times of crisis, mourning and celebration. For example, the Archbishop of Canterbury regularly speaks for the Church in reaction to political direction perceived to be unjust to the poor and needy; church leaders conduct public services such as on Remembrance Day.

Furthermore, the Royal Monarch is the head of the Church in England and 26 Bishops sit in the House of Lords, a political body that complements the work of the elected Parliament. In addition to this, because of religious freedom, many Christian denominations (as well as other religions) and Christian organisations flourish – so that there are churches of many types in every region of the UK. In fact, new churches are formed each year. Thus, if people want to hear the Gospel, it is all around them – there is no need for missionaries to spread the message. Surely these facts of how Christianity is embedded in the UK mean that it cannot be seen as a mission field in the same way that a country with a different religious background might be?

One could also argue that the notion that the UK should be the target of reverse missionaries is misguided. The secularisation thesis predicts the future decline of Christianity in terms of its presence in public life, attendance at churches and individual acceptance of its doctrines. Those who embrace the secularisation thesis might see the drift from Christianity as a part of human evolution, increasing our survival value since beliefs and morals derived from religious authority are, ultimately, inferior to those that can be established by the various fields of science. In this view, it is important for this culture to resist the work of missionaries and attempt to view the UK not as a mission field but as a secular society.

Those who resist the secularisation thesis might point to the fact that the future decline of the Church is by no means inevitable and that there are many signs of life in the Church. In fact, they may argue that instead of Christianity dying it is in a 'dormant phase'; that is, it continues to be a part of the national consciousness and influences the lives of individuals even if they are not conscious of this fact. One example of this are the explicitly Christian themes in Harry Potter and the Deathly Hallows where the Gospel story is integral to a plot.

In conclusion, the extent to which the UK is a mission field depends on the kind of Christianity one embraces. Or, if one is not a Christian, it depends on one's view of the 'inevitability' of secularisation and on how deeply Christianity is embedded in the lives of those who makes up the UK.

Key quotes

In Britain the Christian churches have shrunk to a point where reproduction is threatened, the major non-Christian religions brought to Britain by migrants since 1945 have not recruited beyond their original ethnic bases, and 1970s NRMs [New Religious Movements] have failed to make any headway. We now have a society that is very largely secular, not just in the formal operations of major social institutions but also in popular culture. We are in a historically novel position. (S. Bruce)

The across-the-board claim – that both religion and 'alternative spirituality' are in decline – is clearly wrong. A great deal of evidence might show that regular church attendance is falling in many countries … but virtually all indices show that New Age spiritualities of life are growing, most especially the activities of the holistic milieu, activities and beliefs within mainstream institutions, and personal beliefs. (P. Heelas)

AO2 Activity

List some conclusions that could be drawn from the AO2 reasoning from the above text; try to aim for at least three different possible conclusions. Consider each of the conclusions and collect brief evidence to support each conclusion from the AO1 and AO2 material for this topic. Select the conclusion that you think is most convincing and explain why it is so. Try to contrast this with the weakest conclusion in the list, justifying your argument with clear reasoning and evidence.

Specification content

The relative ease of assimilation of
Christian migrants into Christian
churches in the UK.

The relative ease of assimilation of Christian migrants into Christian churches in the UK

One would think that church congregations would exert a tremendous effort to make it easy for Christian migrants to assimilate into their communities – especially since the story of biblical faith involves themes of migration (Abraham's call from Ur, the wandering of the Israelites in the desert and Mary and Joseph's three migrations) – as well as the specific command in the Hebrew Bible to help 'aliens' and of Jesus' redefinition of 'neighbour' in the parable of the Good Samaritan. These imperatives of faith are especially relevant given that Christianity is the largest religion represented of all migrants coming to the UK.

To some degree existing historic congregations have assimilated Christian migrants into their churches. This is especially true for Catholic churches with migration from the EU. Migrants who attended Catholic churches in their countries of origin will find many familiar features in their UK counterparts including the liturgy, the roles of the priest and laity, and the celebration of the sacraments.

However, assimilation into churches even within the same denomination is challenged by issues related to language, culture and worship styles. For example, advice from the Catholic Bishops' Conference of England and Wales notes several areas that must be addressed: offering pastoral care when English is not spoken by those in need, offering Christian instruction (i.e. confirmation classes) when those wishing to learn are not proficient in English, and differences in worship style (i.e. the emphasis on certain forms of music, dance and poetry in the migrants' countries of origin). Considering these issues, the ease of assimilation depends on how well the congregation does in recruiting leaders who know the language of their immigrant community and how willing the Church is to diversify its worship experience.

However, many existing traditional churches are not assimilating migrants who come to their communities. One reason for this is the proliferation of new denominations and independent churches from outside of the UK.

It is much easier for migrants to assimilate into these churches than to attempt to join a denomination indigenous to the UK. One example of this is the Redeemed Christian Church of God, a West African based denomination. There are also independent churches that have grown out of these new denominations. These churches are especially attuned to the challenges of migration. For example, they offer classes on immigration, financial management and educational issues. They are also well placed to meet the social needs of new immigrants. So, in these settings many migrants would find that that assimilation is easy – but this may be integration into a minority subculture in the UK rather than into an ethnically diverse community that includes a significant proportion of white-British worshippers (though these churches exist as well).

There is evidence that many traditional churches are not assimilating those born outside of the UK. Each year a number of new churches open that serve primarily migrant communities – many of these are not denominations that have had a historic presence in the UK. For example, a study of 125 new churches that opened in north-east England between 1980 and 2015 shows that 47 of these have a primarily migrant make-up and a further 37 have a significant minority of members from black and ethnic minority backgrounds. None of these new churches are Catholic and there is only one new Anglican congregation in the area studied.

Key quote

… what is happening is that the energy of Christians in particular coming to a wearied, western secularised culture is giving it new hope and, certainly in the

AO2 Activity

As you read through this section try to do the following:

1. Pick out the different lines of argument that are presented in the text and identify any evidence given in support.

2. For each line of argument try to evaluate whether or not you think this is strong or weak.

3. Think of any questions you may wish to raise in response to the arguments.

This activity will help you to start thinking critically about what you read, and help you to evaluate the effectiveness of different arguments and from this develop your own observations, opinions and points of view that will help with any conclusions that you make in your answers to the AO2 questions that arise.

life of the Christian faith, new resilience and enthusiasm. And I think it rubs off on us weary westerners and we should take great heart from the fact that we are discovering again, under that impetus, some of our own wellsprings of faith. (Vincent Gerard Nichols, Cardinal and Archbishop of Westminster)

A further reason that may make it difficult for some congregations to assimilate new members of migrant background is where there are differences of theological orientation and worship style. An example of this are Christians arriving from Africa from countries where Pentecostal Christianity is a majority form of religion. These Christians will have an evangelical orientation and a worship style that focuses on the experience of the worshipper, including spontaneous expressions of prayer as well as faith healing and speaking in tongues. This form of 'oral liturgy' bears little resemblance to the highly formal literary forms of worship that take place in many churches across the UK.

This theological and practical divide between many indigenous Christians and Christian migrants may be reflected in the observations of reverse missionaries who note the difference between what they perceive to be vibrant forms of Christianity in their home countries compared to the aging and more 'routine' forms of worship found in many UK churches. There are, however, indigenous evangelical and Pentecostal churches in the UK. When these haven't assimilated those with a migrant background this may be because they cannot rival the support some migrants can receive from new, non-indigenous denominations and independent churches.

However, it may not be entirely fair to accuse traditional churches of failing to assimilate more migrants of Christian backgrounds into their ranks. This is partly because studies show that up to 75% of migrants settle in London and a further 10% in the South East – there are, thus, vast areas of the UK without a significant migrant population.

David Goodhew notes that Church decline is most pronounced in parts of Scotland, Wales and England that are distant from 'economic and demographic dynamism'. This means that immigrants are less likely to consider moving to areas where there is (i) less economic opportunity and (ii) less chance of meeting others from a similar social and ethnic background. As a result, Christian immigrants have a much stronger presence in London and along the 'trade routes' of Britain and Northern Ireland.

In conclusion, there are many factors helping or hindering the assimilation of Christian immigrants into congregations in the UK – these include theological, geographical and sociological reasons. Where a migrant Christian has access to a congregation that has a significant proportion of worshippers with the same ethnic background, located in a place where there is economic opportunity, and offering support for challenges specifically faced by those establishing a new home, one will find ethnically diverse and dynamic congregations. In places where there is less economic and cultural dynamism and where there are gaps between the religious expression and theology of indigenous Christians and Christian migrants one should not be surprised to find that churches are less ethnically diverse.

Key quote

It is a crude, but correct, generalisation to say that Church growth diminishes the further away you get from London. Thus, the best data to support the secularisation thesis is to be found in parts of the north of England, Wales and Scotland. (D. Goodhew)

Key quotes

The old assumption that the city is the incubator of all things secular, is no longer true – and, arguably, was never as true as has been sometimes assumed. The evidence suggests that in twenty-first century Britain the reverse is often true – with religiosity most vibrant in cities and often more fragile in remote rural communities. (D. Goodhew)

In recent times the Catholic Church has been further strengthened with the arrival of migrants from the new Members States of the EU. They have increased both the membership of the local Church and challenged it to new forms of solidarity and communion. Catholic migrants new and old have brought to Britain symbols, practices and devotions that add visible substance to the Church's catholicity. (The Catholic Bishops' Conference of England and Wales)

AO2 Activity

List some conclusions that could be drawn from the AO2 reasoning from the above text; try to aim for at least three different possible conclusions. Consider each of the conclusions and collect brief evidence to support each conclusion from the AO1 and AO2 material for this topic. Select the conclusion that you think is most convincing and explain why it is so. Try to contrast this with the weakest conclusion in the list, justifying your argument with clear reasoning and evidence.

Key skills

Analysis involves:

*Identifying issues raised by the
materials in the AO1, together with
those identified in the AO2 section, and
presents sustained and clear views,
either of scholars or from a personal
perspective ready for evaluation.*

This means:

- That your answers are able to
identify key areas of debate in
relation to a particular issue
- That you can identify, and comment
upon, the different lines of argument
presented by others
- That your response comments on
the overall effectiveness of each of
these areas or arguments.

Evaluation involves:

*Considering the various implications
of the issues raised based upon
the evidence gleaned from analysis
and provides an extensive detailed
argument with a clear conclusion.*

This means:

- That your answer weighs up the
consequences of accepting or
rejecting the various and different
lines of argument analysed
- That your answer arrives at a
conclusion through a clear process of
reasoning.

AO2 Developing skills

It is now important to consider the information that has been covered in this
section; however, the information in its raw form is too extensive and so has
to be processed in order to meet the requirements of the examination. This
can be achieved by practising more advanced skills associated with AO2. For
assessment objective 2 (AO2), which involves 'critical analysis' and 'evaluation'
skills, we are going to focus on different ways in which the skills can be
demonstrated effectively, and also refer to how the performance of these
skills is measured (see generic band descriptors for A2 [WJEC] AO2 or A Level
[Eduqas] AO2).

▶ **Your next task is this:** Below is an evaluation of **the UK as a modern
mission field**. At present, it has no references at all to support the arguments
presented. Underneath the evaluation are two references made to the works
of scholars, and/or religious writings, that could be used in the evaluation in
order to improve it. Your task is to rewrite the evaluation but make use of the
references. Such phrases as 'in his/her book ... (scholar) argues that ...', 'an
interesting argument in support of this is made by ... who suggests that ...', or,
'the work of (scholar) has made a major contribution to the debate by pointing
out ... ' may help. Usually a reference included a footnote but for an answer in
an A Level essay under examination conditions this is not expected, although an
awareness of which book your evidence refers to is useful (although not always
necessary).

Does the UK need missionaries from outside it if Christianity is to grow? There are
several reasons that this idea can be refuted – whether or not one is a Christian. It
can be argued that nothing yet has significantly stemmed the tide of secularism.
Fewer people attend Church and even new churches are not making up for
the emptying and closure of old churches. Religion is increasingly irrelevant to
contemporary society. There have been 'reverse missionaries' but no one claims
that these have made a significant impact on the UK. From a different point of
view, yet still refuting the idea that Britain needs missionaries from the outside,
it can also be argued that Christianity has an indigenous presence that is strong
underneath the surface. That is, there is quite a bit of 'Christian life' and influence
already present in Britain that has the potential to grow and spread. If this already
strong Christian presence isn't enough for Christianity to grow, then nothing else
will be.

We may want to explain the secularity of some elite groups (such as professional
scientists) by the impact of science and rationalism, but to understand the
mass of the population it is not self-conscious irreligion that is important. It
is indifference. [And] the primary cause of indifference is the lack of religious
socialisation. (Steve Bruce).

A Christian nation can sound like a nation of committed believers, and we are
not that. Equally, we are not a nation of dedicated secularists. I think we're
a lot less secular than the most optimistic members of the British Humanist
Association would think. (Rowan Williams)

When you have completed the task, try to write another reference that you could
use and further extend your evaluation.

C: Feminist theology and the changing role of men and women

This section covers AO1 content and skills

Specification content

The contribution of Rosemary Radford Ruether to feminist theology.

What is feminist theology?

Feminist theology is an examination of theology, religious history and religious communities which takes seriously the experience of women. At the heart of feminist theology is the recognition that religion has played a part in this historic and continuing oppression of women, an oppression that is pervasive and frequently violent.

Both Rosemary Radford Ruether and Mary Daly share the view that **sexism** plays a large role in the Bible, Christian theology and in the rituals and practices of the Christian Church. Ruether believes that there is something more authentic in Christianity than sexism; she examines aspects of the Christian tradition, including marginalised forms of Christianity, that do not entail a male God, a male saviour and an exclusively male Church leadership. She would like to see a reformation of the language, rituals and theology of Christianity. This reformation would include a greater commitment to the well-being of women. By contrast, Mary Daly believes that sexism is far too embedded in Christianity for there to be such a reformation. She encourages women to separate from the Church and to define 'God' in ways that are affirming to the journey of becoming a whole person.

The contribution of Rosemary Radford Ruether to feminist theology

When churches, theologians or preachers use 'she' to refer to God, says Ruether, there is sometimes a negative or even hostile reaction amongst Christians. Why is this – especially since Christian theology understands God as a being beyond gender? The reason is that biblical and theological traditions have reflected the cultural view that men are more authentically human than women. This is called '**androcentrism**' and it has been widespread not only in biblical myths and teachings but also in the intellectual tradition of the West from the Greek philosophers to the present day.

The story of Adam and Eve has been interpreted to suggest that sin entered the world through Eve – and therefore women are more responsible than men for the 'fall'. Male pronouns have been used in relation to the term 'God', and the Bible has declared in both the Old and New Testaments that women are to be 'subject' to men (Genesis 3:16 and Ephesians 5:24). Many medieval theologians were inspired by the writings of Greek philosophers who viewed women as representing the emotional, instinctive and sensual side of humanity – inferior to the more rationalistic nature of men. Aristotle characterised women as 'misbegotten males', naturally servile people who should be ruled by those who are dedicated to reason (men). Augustine adopted Aristotle's view and Aquinas believed that the male-female hierarchy is not just a result of sin but is a part of the natural order created by God. Androcentrism is not restricted to just these theologians but has been found throughout Christian theology to the present day. So, when the Bible has declared that humans are created in the image of God and need to be saved by Christ, the association is that a male God created us and a male God saves us – and that males, therefore, are somehow closer to God than females. This is nothing less, says Ruether, than the sin of idolatry.

Key quotes

… no part of the Church, no part of the world, is liberated until we are all liberated. (R. Ruether)

…sexism is gender privilege of males over females. It is males *primarily* who have originated this form of oppression, benefitted from it, and perpetuated it, legally and ideologically. (R. Ruether)

Among the primary distortions of the self-other relationship has been the distortion of humanity as male and female into a dualism of superiority and inferiority. This is fundamentally a male ideology and has served two purposes: the support for male identity as normative humanity and the justification of servile roles for women. (R. Ruether)

Key terms

Androcentrism: focused or centred on men; placing of the male sex or gender associations at the centre of history and culture

Sexism: prejudice, discrimination or stereotyping based on sex or gender

Rosemary Radford Ruether

Notice how the snake is over Eve's head rather than Adam's in this contemporary mosaic. Adam is passive – is he portrayed as more innocent?

quicKfire

3.12 How did Aristotle describe women?

Key quotes

Recognising sexism as sin has nothing to do with any notion that males are 'by nature' evil or that women are incapable of any sin other than the sin of cooperating in their own victimisation. Both males and females, as human persons, have the capacity to do evil. Historically, however, women as well as subjugated men, have not had the same *opportunities* to do so. (R. Ruether)

We need to go beyond the idea of a 'feminine side' of God, whether to be identified with the Spirit or even with the *Sophia*-Spirit together, and question the assumption that the highest symbol of divine sovereignty still remains exclusively male. (R. Ruether)

Key term

Androgynous: having a combination of both female and male characteristics

quicKfire

3.13 Do feminist theologians believe that the true nature of women is feminine, masculine or androgynous?

Study tip

Feminist theologians believe that ideas on how men and women differ apart from their reproductive roles are often oppressive and limiting creations of society. Make sure you can summarise their viewpoint by using the following terms correctly: androcentrism, androgyny, feminine, gender, sex, masculine and patriarchy. You may find it helpful to create your own short list of terms and definitions.

AO1 Activity

Give yourself one minute to make a list of as many names as you can from the Bible from memory. After you have written down the names, ask yourself, how many of these were male? How many were female? Do you have any positive or negative associations with these names? What might be the significance of the proportion of male names to female names?

What is a male? What is a female?

Ruether believes that how society defines 'maleness' and 'femaleness' has no real biological connection. That is, the only real difference between men and women has to do with reproductive roles and that men and women can each manifest any number of traits that culture declares are 'male' or female'. In other words, our nature is **androgynous**, the idea that notions of masculinity and femininity come from culture and socialisation but are not a part of our inner nature. What we know, says Ruether, is that there are two sides to our brain and that the cultural tendency is for men to identify their ego with the left-brain characteristics and women to identify themselves with their right-brain characteristics. However, each of us has both a left brain and a right brain.

Mary vs. Eve

In the Church, however, women have been restricted to some characteristics (associated with cultural ideas of femininity) rather than others. They have been urged, for instance, to follow the example of Mary who exhibits qualities of passivity, gentleness, meekness and obedience. Mary has been extolled as a perpetual virgin (though Matthew seems to indicate that Mary did have children with Joseph). The implication is that for a woman to be truly spiritual she must not be 'sexual'- and even then she cannot attain to the rationalistic prowess of males. The only other alternative is to be associated with Eve, who is viewed as the temptress and bringer of sin into the world!

Is the idea of Mary as a role model for women fair? Ruether says that it is no wonder that women have been persecuted when they have manifested leadership tendencies or expressed views at odds with men. She suggests that the persecution and murder of women labelled as 'witches' stems from religious gender stereotyping and she cites a 15th-century Dominican manual that states, 'Since women are feebler both in mind and body, it is not surprising that they should come under the spell of witchcraft. For as regards intellect, or the understanding of spiritual things, they seem to be of a different nature from men … But the natural reason is that she is more carnal than a man, as is clear from her many carnal abominations.'

Given that gender stereotyping has long been a part of the Church, it is no wonder, says Ruether, that women have been excluded from ordination. Women can't be priests, because they are considered by male clergy and theologians to be inferior in mind and in soul to men. She cites the 1976 Vatican declaration against women's ordination which stated '... there must be a physical resemblance between the priest and Christ'. In other words, possessing male genitalia is the essential pre-requisite for representing Christ, who is the disclosure of the male God.

Mary is usually portrayed as passive, modest, obedient and prayerful. Does this role model suit the purposes of men more than women?

Marginalised forms of Christianity

Ruether points to several movements in Christianity which have not followed the dominant tradition in the role accorded to women in the Church. Montanism, for example, believed in the continuing inspiration of the Holy Spirit in prophecy given to men and women. There is evidence that women were given equal status to men in the ministry of Montanist churches. Some **Gnostic** writings viewed women as Apostles and describe the nature of God as having female and male principles. Both Montanism and Gnosticism came to be viewed as heretical by the Church 'Fathers'. Later, **Quakers** and some Baptist movements included women in leadership. One group known as the '**Shakers**' (because of their trembling when having spiritual experiences) promoted a view of God as bisexual or androgynous. This stems from the notion that since male and female humans were created in the image of God, then God must be, in some sense, both male and female.

Ruether does not believe that these marginalised forms of Christianity are perfect: these groups often had a negative view of sexual activity and marriage. Shakers were celibate and Gnostics advocated an unworldly asceticism. Furthermore, Ruether notes that none of these groups fought for women's rights outside of their gatherings. Yet, they are indications that not all Christians have seen sexism as a necessary part of Christianity.

The prophetic tradition

Ruether sees feminist theology as a part of the prophetic tradition in the Bible. The prophets of Israel fought against the oppression of the poor and dispossessed by powerful individuals and groups – even when that oppression came from the religious establishment (see Isaiah 10:1–2 and Luke 4:18–19). Even though these prophets did not specifically fight against sexism, they manifested principles which extended to all forms of oppression. There are four themes in the prophetic-liberating traditions: (i) God's defence and vindication of the oppressed; (ii) a critique of dominant systems of power and their powerholders; (iii) a vision of a new age where injustice ends under the reign of God; and (iv) a critique of the religious ideology maintaining injustice.

Key quote

It is said that … To become eternal and everlasting we must flee the body, the woman, and the world. She is the icon of the corrupted nature, seduced by the serpent in the beginning. Through her, death entered the world. Even now she collaborates with devils to hold men in fast fetters to the ground. A million women twisted on the rack, smoldered in burning fagots pay homage to this lie. **(R. Ruether)**

Key terms

Gnostic: relating to an ancient spiritual movement focussed on attaining spiritual knowledge

Quakers: 17th-century movement promoting the belief in one's direct apprehension of God without the need for clergy, creeds or other ecclesiastical forms

Shakers: 18th-century Protestant Christian movement dedicated to celibacy and belief in the imminent return of God; called 'Shakers' because of their ecstatic movement in worship

Lucretia Mott (née Coffin; 1793–1880) an American Quaker, abolitionist, a women's rights activist and social reformer

Key quote

The Church is where the good news of liberation from sexism is preached, where the Spirit is present to empower us to renounce patriarchy, where a community committed to the new life of mutuality is gathered together and nurtured, and where the community is spreading this vision and struggle to others. **(R. Ruether)**

Was Jesus a God-Man or a human who believed in liberation for all?

Key terms

Liberalism: in politics, the focus on the protection and freedom of the individual

Marxism: the political and economic theories of Karl Marx and Friedrich Engels that developed into communism and aimed at a classless society

Patriarchal: usually refers to male control over society or religion

Romanticism: 18th–19th-century intellectual and artistic movement focussed on emotion and the imagination; critical of the rationalism of the enlightenment

Suffragettes: from the Latin term for 'vote'; women who fought for the right of women to vote in the late 19th to 20th centuries

quickfire

3.14 Instead of Jesus primarily being identified as the 'Son' of God, a pre-existing being incarnated as a man, Ruether believes that he should be identified primarily as belonging to what tradition?

It is more accurate to see Jesus as a part of this prophetic tradition than it is to view him as the imperialistic Davidic Messiah-King and Son of God as he became known in Christian theology. This is because the Jesus-movement had a counter-cultural character; like the prophets, he rejected the use of religion to establish oppressive hierarchy and stood up for the poor and oppressed. In fact, his movement appeared to place women on equal footing to men. His naming of God as 'Abba,' (a familial and emotional term for a father) could be him distancing himself from **patriarchal** views of God and it can be argued that he did not see himself as a political Messiah. Instead he viewed himself as a servant determined to help liberate those who were suffering. Ruether says that Feminist theology must reclaim this view of Jesus in which his 'maleness' is of no importance.

Problems and solutions

The 20th century, says Ruether, has seen several attempts to liberate women from sexism. **Romanticism**, a movement from the late 18th century, viewed emerging industrialism and the violence of war as stemming from male traits and that social salvation would come through embracing female qualities: intuition, emotional sensitivity and moral purity. Because women have been forbidden to entire political realms, they retain more purity and goodness and are less prone to the sins of egoism. The weakness of this approach is that it leaves women trapped in romantic notions of what a female should be (cultural definitions of femininity) and can elevate the role of women in the home as the only way to maintain purity.

AO1 Activity

Examine popular religious perceptions of Mary and of Eve in art, literature, sermons and religious writings simply by 'Googling' 'Eve – Bible' and 'Mary – Bible'. Do the qualities you see attributed to these women reinforce the insights of Rosemary Radford Ruether and Mary Daly when they describe the 'boxes' these two figures have been put into by the Church?

Liberalism rejects traditional role models and attempts to fight for social reform – including the right to vote, obtain divorce, birth control and have equal pay. One of the main thrusts of liberalism is to give women the opportunity to enter into education so that they can develop the qualities needed to wield power in the spheres that have been dominated by men. In liberalism, the reform of church structures is a part of a larger fight for women in society. Liberalism has succeeded in many ways from the time of the **suffragettes** in the late 19th century. Ruether notes, however, that liberalism is a largely middle/upper class phenomenon that has at least two weaknesses: (i) in its concern to see women represented in traditionally male spheres, it does not critique the way power in those spheres functions and (ii) middle- and upper-class women, after winning freedom for themselves may hire lower-class women to take care of the work that they no longer do, thus perpetuating sexism in lower classes.

Marxism believes that both men and women should be viewed as equally able to contribute to society. Women, therefore, should be freed from the patriarchy that has bound them to the home and enter fully into the world of work, alongside men. Ruether notes two issues with the Marxist solution for women: (i) many women in communist countries are still expected to work more in the home than men. In other words, communism has not decreased patriarchal expectations and (ii) women are viewed as subservient to their productivity on behalf of the communist state rather than as valued for themselves.

What does a liberating church look like?

Ruether hopes that a reformed theology and Church can provide a setting that will be truly liberating for women. However, she is aware that many women will be required to find the support they need outside of the Church in female '**base communities**' since patriarchy and sexism continues in the Church. Her ideal is of the Church as a community that manifests the prophetic-liberation strand found in the Bible. This Church becomes free of patriarchy and institutes changes in language that is used for God and is committed to fighting against the oppression of women (i.e. sponsoring projects such as a battered women's shelter and rape hotline). The Church also has an inclusive approach to leadership. However, this is about more than women's ordination. She questions **clericalism** itself, noting that a powerful clergy that sees the laity as passive, is just another form of patriarchy – whether or not there are female priests. A new understanding of leadership accompanied by new rituals will be a part of making the Church a liberating community.

The contribution of Mary Daly to feminist theology

The goal of human life, says Mary Daly, is for all people to be free to engage in a journey of growth, becoming creative and fulfilled individuals, freely participating in communities that are healthy and liberating. But the opposite has been the case – especially for women. Instead of the freedom to be on a journey of growth, women have been trapped into oppressive roles. They have been told that their biology is their destiny, reduced to objects of men's desires and tools to accomplish male goals. Daly sees society has having created a 'sexual **caste system**', a rigid hierarchy which places the female gender beneath the male gender. The Church has played a large role in helping culture maintain this caste system. It is time for women to overcome this system and the structures which force women into 'non-being'.

God is not a noun

Daly's description of the goal of life uses verbs: being, acting, changing, moving, actualising, etc. However, the problem is that women are treated as objects – as nouns. One of the themes in theology that has helped to turn women into objects is a static view of God. God has been defined as a noun rather than a verb. Traditional theology views God as a changeless, static being, a creator, and a ruler. Patriarchal images of God reinforce the notion of God as a noun: a white bearded man in the sky. This God, says Daly, must be dethroned. There are three versions of this noun-God:

(i)   God as a stop-gap (God being used as an explanation of the unknown)

(ii) God as otherworldliness (God gives rewards and punishments after death)

(iii) God as a judge of sin (God insists on rules and establishes roles for men and women).

These images of God are static, doing nothing to inspire creativity, dynamism and growth.

Jesus has also been turned into a noun by the Church: the otherworldly God-Man who is the model for all Christians to follow. Women can and should follow Jesus, though they can never hope to be as spiritual as men, since they are the 'wrong' gender. However, Daly asks, why should there just be one model for human living?

Key terms

Base communities: small, self-governing religious groups mentioned by Latin American liberation theologians

Caste system: usually associated with Hindu culture but also referring to a rigid social hierarchy based on hereditary status

Clericalism: a focus on increasing the power and influence of the clergy or church hierarchy

Specification content

The contribution of Mary Daly to feminist theology.

Key quote

Real liberation is not merely unrestricted genital activity (the 'sexual revolution'), but free and defiant thinking, willing, imagining, speaking, creating, acting. It is be-ing. (M. Daly)

Mary Daly (1928–2010)

Key quote

The widespread conception of the 'Supreme Being' as an entity distinct from this world but controlling it according to plan and keeping human beings in a state of infantile subjection has been a not too subtle mask of the divine patriarch. (M. Daly)

Key terms

Bibliolatry: from 'idolatry': the worship of the Bible instead of God; associated with a literalistic approach

Christolatry: from 'idolatry': a term used by some feminist theologians to refer to the worship of the 'Son' of God according to patriarchal categories rather than to a God who is beyond gender and sex

Key quote

Obscene is not the picture of a naked woman who exposes her pubic hair but that of a fully clad general who exposes his medals rewarded in a war of aggression; obscene is not the ritual of the Hippies but the declaration of a high dignitary of the church that war is necessary for peace. **(M. Daly)**

quickfire

3.15 According to Mary Daly, what was the real sin committed in pre-history and what sins do Christians commit today?

God is a verb

What we must do, says Daly, is to consider God as a verb, to see God in a process of becoming with the universe as the force that helps us to become the people we are meant to be. Simply changing from male language to female language for God will not address the root issue but simply perpetuate the idea of God as a noun, now a female rather than a male noun. We must think of God as a transforming power, the power of being for all persons. When we do this, we come to see that:

- Original sin is not disobedience, but turning women into objects who are forbidden to develop outside of their biological destiny.
- Salvation is not passive acceptance of doctrine or worship of a God-Man, but participating in being and becoming.
- Worshipping the God of patriarchy, which includes the God-Man Jesus, is a form of idolatry. Christians commit '**Christolatry**' and '**Bibliolatry**' when they insist that biblical forms of patriarchy are the final truth.
- Our goal is to struggle to be free human beings, staying open to the future.
- If there is no fall, no frowning judge, and no punishment, there is no need of a saviour.
- To believe in the power of God is to believe in the power of being and becoming in all people.

A matter of life and death

Treating women as objects, says Daly, is at the heart of all human violence. She investigates the 'unholy trinity' of rape, genocide and war. Her argument is that violence becomes permissible in society when we no longer see human beings as on a valuable journey of being and becoming, but turn them into objects which are a means to increase our pleasure or decrease our pain. Rape involves just such an objectification of women. Furthermore, a patriarchal society has a vested interest in rape continuing since the fact of rape reinforces the need for males to protect all women. Could this be one reason that police and other authorities have often disbelieved women who report rape?, Daly asks.

Genocide is another form of objectification: the 'enemy' is viewed as an object or possession of a conquering army who can be dealt with in any way deemed satisfying in the moment – including wholesale murder. The link between rape and genocide can be seen in biblical commands to Israel to engage in both activities: 'Now therefore, kill every male among the little ones, and kill every woman who has known a man by sleeping with him. But all the young girls who have not known a man by sleeping with him, keep alive for yourselves.' (Numbers 31:17–18) In other words, these humans are merely objects rather than human beings. War itself is about masculine dominance and the promotion of certain virtues which are associated with 'manliness'. Men are encouraged to be adventurous in violent ways, 'clobber the bad guy' and treat the enemy as an object.

Study tip

Feminist theologians are critical of Christians associating God with the male gender and the male sex. Be prepared to discuss their views on God: Ruether's God beyond gender and Mary Daly's God as a verb rather than a noun.

Society also contains different values, of passivity, gentleness, self-sacrifice but it associates these with females – the very people who are treated as objects by men. Daly believes that this assigning of values by gender is a strategy to ensure that women do not change the social order, that they do not interrupt the work of this unholy trinity. In fact, women who have these 'feminine' qualities are rarely permitted into leadership positions because these are not the values that most influence society. This fact underscores the need for women to strive not for feminine values but for an androgynous form of life in which they make their own decisions and build their own ethics apart from gender.

The need for sisterhood

Daly believes that the Church is too bound to patriarchy to ever become a place where women can find the transformation they seek. She calls herself a 'post Christian' and calls upon women to be 'antichurch' and leave this patriarchal structure. However, in a patriarchal world, nearly all organisations are to some degree patriarchal, so that women who want to enter into a journey of growth will need to live on the boundaries of society. To do this, they will need to seek the support of other women.

The term 'sisterhood', for Daly, speaks to finding relationships with other women in order to oppose the lovelessness of a sexually hierarchical society. She warns women that as they attempt to change their lives, they will be criticised by men, being called names like 'castrating female', 'man-hater' and 'unfeminine'. Women will also confront criticism from women who have not recognised the true oppression of a patriarchal culture. The sisterhood, however, will offer support. It will have no hierarchy, no dogmas and will assist in bringing women out of patriarchal spaces and onto a path where they can develop into an androgynous form of living.

The issue of the ordination of women priests and bishops; the impact on the lives of believers and communities within Christianity today

Ordination is a rite that sets apart certain individuals for specific roles in the Church. The Latin term for this rite, *ordinatio*, comes from the word 'ordo', meaning order or rank. It comes from an earlier Greek word (*cheriotonia*) originally meaning 'to raise the hand in order to elect'. The New Testament does not describe a rite of ordination and considers all Christians to be '**ministers**' (those who serve). However, it is clear in the New Testament that there were some who were set apart for certain tasks and there are references to **bishops**, **presbyters** and **deacons**. Today, ordination services in many denominations involve the Church gathering together and offering prayer, the laying on of hands and the invocation of the Spirit in the lives of those it is setting aside for specific roles.

AO1 Activity

Examine the Internet for articles on the 1992 vote to ordain women in the Church of England and the subsequent qualification of that decision in 1993 and the reactions to the first ordinations in 1994. Then write your own short news story of these events.

Elizabeth Canham

Key terms

Bishop: a rank above a pastor who presides at ordinations and oversees the work of pastors/priests and congregations

Deacon: an ordained minister ranking below a pastor/priest/presbyter

Minister: usually means an ordained Christian, though the term simply means 'servant' and can be applied to all Christians

Ordination: the ritual of recognising church leaders through the laying on of hands, prayer and the invocation of the Spirit of God

Presbyter: from the Greek word for 'elder'; usually a minister between a deacon and a bishop in rank

Specification content

The changing role of men and women with reference to the issue of the ordination of women priests and bishops; the impact on the lives of believers and communities within Christianity today.

Key person

Elizabeth Canham: (1939–) was the first British woman to be ordained to the episcopal priesthood (1981). She left England to be ordained in the United States as at that time the Church of England did not ordain women. She writes, 'Some saw me as a hopeful sign of freedom for women; others as a confrontational challenge to the Church. Mary Kenny writing in the *Daily Mail* December 1981, considered that my hairstyle and lipstick rendered me an unsuitable candidate for the priesthood! (Others are 'put off' by women priests who do not look 'feminine' enough.)'

Historical scholars note that there were many women in leadership positions in the early church. One female apostle is mentioned in the New Testament: Junia; she is described by Paul as being 'prominent among the apostles' (Romans 16:7). Other women in the New Testament were considered Apostles by some traditions in the early church and the early Middle Ages including Mary Magdalen and the Samaritan woman at the well. In addition to this, there are stories told about holy women (such as Thecla and Nino) who are also described as apostles. Some descriptions of these figures maintain that their ministry was restricted to other women, but other traditions indicate they ministered to men as well. There are also possible references to female deacons (I Timothy 3:11) and prophetesses (Acts 21:9).

In contrast to these observations is the fact that it was rare to find women in publicly recognised leadership positions in the Church until the last few decades. In fact, many early translations of the Bible altered the name Junia to the male form Junias as it was supposed that a female apostle must have been a mistranslation of Paul's words! The concept of apostleship as described by Luke-Acts (later than Paul's letters) limited them to twelve – all men. Most theologians through the centuries have argued that women's ministry should be restricted in line with admonitions in the New Testament. Common arguments against women in ministry included:

- God chose to incarnate 'himself' in the form of a male.
- Christ appointed only men as the Apostles.
- Ordaining women would destroy the unity and **catholicity** of the Church which has, for centuries ordained only men.
- Scripture forbids the leadership of women.

However, in the 19th century, when movements for the liberation of women began intensifying, counterarguments were raised:

- Jesus did not seem to restrict his message and teaching to men.
- Many passages in the Bible refer to ministry in inclusive terms.
- Women were ordained to the diaconate in the early church.
- Not ordaining women has been a part of the historical suppression of women.

On rare occasions, some women were ordained or given public leadership positions in the Church since the time of the Reformation. However, it was not until the 1970s that women's ordination became standard practice in established denominations. In the Church of England, for instance, the vote to ordain women passed by a narrow margin in 1992. However, in 1993 the Church voted to allow individual congregations to opt out of accepting women priests. In 1994 nearly 1,500 women were ordained in the Church of England but over 470 male clergy protested by leaving the Church (many of these joined the Roman Catholic Church, which allowed them to function as married priests).

Key term

Catholicity: the quality of being catholic, having a universal doctrine

Key quote

… the speedy success of our cause depends upon the zealous and untiring efforts of both men and women for the overthrow of the monopoly of the pulpit, and for the securing to women of equal participation with men in various trades, professions and commerce. (Lucretia Mott, Quaker minister, 1848)

A 20th-anniversary celebration in Coventry of the ordination of women in the Church of England.

Current issues with the ordination of women

Most Christians in the world today belong to churches which do not ordain women. For example, women cannot be ordained as deacons, priests or bishops in the Roman Catholic Church. In 2014 Pope Francis affirmed the centuries-long tradition of refusing to ordain women to the priesthood, though he has indicated a willingness to study the issue of women becoming deacons (a role which, for men, includes leading services and conducting baptisms but not celebrating Mass). In 2016 the Roman Catholic Church commissioned a study to look into this issue. It is only since the late 1960s that women were ordained as deacons and priests in parts of the worldwide Anglican Communion and only since the 1990s that they have been ordained as Bishops (2015, Church of England; 2017, Church in Wales) – though this is only in a minority of the member churches that compose the Anglican Church.

In churches that ordain women, there are continuing issues that impact the freedom of women to become fully equal to their male counterparts:

- The proportion of unpaid women clergy has increased in many church bodies that ordain women.

- Ordained women have had to fight for maternity rights in some denominations.

- Interview committees have been challenged to produce guidelines on appropriate or inappropriate questions for women candidates (i.e. 'are you planning to have children?' is an inappropriate question).

- Many congregations who belong to church bodies that do ordain women are reluctant to accept a female minister.

- Women find it difficult to access 'senior pastorates' or the role of Bishop – with lack of experience used as an excuse.

quickfire

3.16 What are the three types of ordained ministry in the Roman Catholic, Anglican and other traditional denominations? Which one of these has Pope Francis indicated a willingness to consider women for as candidates?

Libby Lane was the first female bishop in the Church of England. She was consecrated on 26 January 2015 by the Archbishop of York.

Key skills

Knowledge involves:

Selection of a range of (thorough) accurate and relevant information that is directly related to the specific demands of the question.

This means:

- Selecting relevant material for the question set

- Being focused in explaining and examining the material selected.

Understanding involves:

Explanation that is extensive, demonstrating depth and/or breadth with excellent use of evidence and examples including (where appropriate) thorough and accurate supporting use of sacred texts, sources of wisdom and specialist language.

This means:

- Effective use of examples and supporting evidence to establish the quality of your understanding

- Ownership of your explanation that expresses personal knowledge and understanding and NOT just reproducing a chunk of text from a book that you have rehearsed and memorised.

Key quote

Women and slave, the old Roman Hellenistic household code had it, are possessions of males, and therefore they are subject to them and less than them 'in all things'. Against the basic tendency of the earliest Christian inspiration, Christianity took over this pagan house code, brought it within the Church and, moreover, gave it theological legitimation.
(E. Schillebeeckx)

AO1 Developing skills

It is now important to consider the information that has been covered in this section; however, the information in its raw form is too extensive and so has to be processed in order to meet the requirements of the examination. This can be achieved by practising more advanced skills associated with AO1. For assessment objective 1 (AO1), which involves demonstrating 'knowledge' and 'understanding' skills, we are going to focus on different ways in which the skills can be demonstrated effectively, and also refer to how the performance of these skills is measured (see generic band descriptors for A2 [WJEC] AO1 or A Level [Eduqas] AO1).

▶ **Your task for this theme:** Below is a summary of **Rosemary Radford Ruether's contribution to feminist theology**. You want to use this in an essay but as it stands it is undeveloped and has no quotations or references in it at all. This time you have to find your own quotations (about 3) and use your own references (about 3) to develop the answer. Sometimes a quotation can follow from a reference but they can also be used individually as separate points.

Rosemary Radford Ruether is a feminist theologian who believes that sexism has played too large a role in Christianity. She sees sexism in both the Old and New Testaments. In Christian theology, she notes that the androcentrism of Greek philosophers has been taken up by major theologians. All of this is tragic because the real goal is for all humans to be androgynous, with both male and female characteristics.

There are some Christian groups in which women have had leadership positions and in which God was not conceived as male. Though many of these groups have been branded as heretical, they point to the fact that God does not need to be defined as male by Christians. There are many aspects of the historical Jesus which indicate that he did not view 'maleness' as important; however, Church doctrine has turned him into a male saviour. A reformation is needed in the Church. This reformation needs to go far beyond the ordination of women as priests.

The result will be a fairly lengthy answer and so you could then check it against the band descriptors for A2 (WJEC) or A Level (Eduqas) and in particular have a look at the demands described in the higher band descriptors towards which you should be aspiring. Ask yourself:

- Does my work demonstrate a thorough, accurate and relevant knowledge and understanding of religion and belief?

- Is my work coherent (consistent or make logical sense), clear and well organised?

- Will my work, when developed, be an extensive and relevant response which is specific to the focus of the task?

- Does my work have extensive depth and/or suitable breadth and have excellent use of evidence and examples?

- If appropriate to the task, does my response have thorough and accurate references to sacred texts and sources of wisdom?

- Are there any insightful connections to be made with other elements of my course?

- Will my answer, when developed and extended to match what is expected in an examination answer, have an extensive range of views of scholars/schools of thought?

- When used, is specialist language and vocabulary both thorough and accurate?

Issues for analysis and evaluation

Whether men and women are equal in Christianity

Christianity can be seen, at times, as articulating the ideal of full equality of men and women such as in Paul's statement, '... there is no longer male and female; for all of you are one in Christ Jesus' (Galatians 3:28). At the same time, Christianity has been deeply embedded in culture and society which is marked by patriarchal views. The question is: is there an 'essence' of Christianity which stands against patriarchal or androcentric views of gender – or has Christianity merely served to reinforce cultural stereotypes in service of an agenda which has reinforced the power of men at the expense of women?

It is clear that Christianity inherited an androcentric orientation from both the religious and philosophical contexts which have shaped its development. For instance, there is a clear exaltation of men over women in some key texts of the Hebrew scriptures. For example, Numbers declares that, in the context of war, women can be treated as objects to be killed (if they are not virgins) or raped (if they are). Greek philosophers such as Aristotle viewed women as 'misbegotten males'. This meant that women were imperfect forms of males both physically and psychologically. Males, by contrast were seen to be more rational so that it was justified that women be subservient to men. Aristotle's views have influenced Christian theology (through Thomas Aquinas and others) and reflect widely held attitudes inside and outside of the Church which stereotype women as inferior to men.

In line with these views of gender have been interpretations of two women in the Bible: Eve and Mary. Eve has been viewed as more responsible for sin than Adam from her 'fleshly' nature and tendency to lust and pride. In contrast to this the passive, gentle and obedient attitude of Mary is held out to be an example to all women. This reinforces that women are passive and subservient. Mary Daly sees these attitudes as merely serving male interests for power. They also make it easier to view women as objects, the main factor behind the violence of rape, war and genocide. For, as soon as we see humans as objects, then we can justify treating them as we wish. Therefore, Mary Daly sees the original 'fall' in Genesis as not the eating of the fruit, but the dominance of one gender over another.

Jesus may not have been androcentric, however. He had an inclusive ministry in which women appear to be treated equally to men. Jesus announced his intention to bring liberation to those who have been oppressed (Luke 4); Ruether believes that Jesus embodies the prophetic spirit of the Hebrew scriptures. The prophets are known for fighting for those on the fringes of society even when that fight pits them against the religious establishment. Jesus, too, criticises the religious leaders of his day when they use God to justify the mistreatment of others. Though the Hebrew prophets did not include sexism in their struggle against injustice, Jesus seems to have moved towards this theme. If the Church pays attention to the style of Jesus' ministry, says Ruether, it will see that it must view androcentrism as a sin that God opposes.

However, both Ruether and Daly note that Christian beliefs about Jesus moved quickly away from Jesus as a prophet fighting for justice to Jesus as the God-Man who brings salvation to the world. Patriarchal views of the superiority of men over women appear to now become associated with Jesus: he is the 'logos' (the rational principle behind the universe), the 'Son' of God and the only one through whom salvation comes to the world. It is no surprise, say these feminist theologians, that the Church came to believe that only men should become priests since God chose to incarnate 'himself' in a man.

The same ambiguity about equality can also be seen in the early church. On the one hand, Paul declares that 'in Christ' gender is not important'. Furthermore,

This section covers AO2 content and skills

Specification content
Whether men and women are equal in Christianity.

AO2 Activity

As you read through this section try to do the following:

1. Pick out the different lines of argument that are presented in the text and identify any evidence given in support.

2. For each line of argument try to evaluate whether or not you think this is strong or weak.

3. Think of any questions you may wish to raise in response to the arguments.

This activity will help you to start thinking critically about what you read, and help you to evaluate the effectiveness of different arguments and from this develop your own observations, opinions and points of view that will help with any conclusions that you make in your answers to the AO2 questions that arise.

Key quotes

Philosophers minimize her contribution to the acts of conception and birth. Aristotle proclaims through two thousand years of teachers that woman is a misbegotten male, that the male seed alone provides the form of the child, the women is only the passive receptacle for man's active power. **(R. Ruether)**

…the woman, together with her own husband, is the image of God, so that the whole substance may be one image, but when she is referred to separately in her quality as a helpmeet, which regards the woman alone, then she is not the image of God, but as regards the male alone, he is the image of God as fully and completely as when the woman too is joined with him in one. **(Augustine)**

AO2 Activity

List some conclusions that could be drawn from the AO2 reasoning from the above text; try to aim for at least three different possible conclusions. Consider each of the conclusions and collect brief evidence to support each conclusion from the AO1 and AO2 material for this topic. Select the conclusion that you think is most convincing and explain why it is so. Try to contrast this with the weakest conclusion in the list, justifying your argument with clear reasoning and evidence.

Paul mentions that there is a highly respected female apostle (Junia) as well as women deacons and prophetesses. It appears that there are many women in key public leadership positions in the Church. Yet Paul also urges women to 'be silent in the Church' and to defer to their husbands – commands that reflect the wider culture. Pauline writings such as I Timothy command women to be silent and Ephesians declares that women are to be submissive to their husbands. Luke-Acts, written many decades after Paul's early letters, maintains that there are only 12 Apostles and that all of these are male.

Ruether notes that there have been some Christian movements that did not adopt androcentric views. Montanists, who believed in continuing prophecy, accepted women as leaders and some Gnostic writings refer to female apostles and appear to have had women in leadership. After the Reformation, Quakers recognised women as leaders and Shakers had an androcentric view of God. However, none of these groups fought for the equality of women outside of their religious community. Furthermore, many of them had a low view of sexuality and intercourse, seeing these as non-spiritual (especially true of Gnosticism and Shakerism). Most significantly, these groups were all branded as heretical by the wider Church! It is simply rare for a woman to have been a publicly recognised Church leader prior to the 19th century. In fact, many biblical manuscripts mistranslated Junia to the male form Junias since it was thought inconceivable that there should have been a female apostle!

Mary Daly examines these facts and concludes that there has been nothing less than a 'sexual caste system' at work in the entire history of the Christian Church. She sees this caste system continuing with the contemporary refusal of the Catholic Church to ordain women. She says that the only way for women to grow into the full psychic potential as androgynous beings is to be 'antichurch', to leave the Church and find support in a 'sisterhood' which lives outside all patriarchal organisations.

Is Daly right? The fact that there are many women who enjoy participating in church might be seen to contradict this fact, unless these women are perceived as being ignorant and misguided, supporting sexist notions which leave men with more power than women. Ruether and Daly recognise that some women choose to accommodate cultural stereotypes because they are uncomfortable with personal change. Yet, Ruether believes that there is an essence in Christianity which rises beyond this: the prophetic spirit of Jesus which does not pay attention to gender but to love and justice.

In conclusion, it appears that, at times, gender equality has been realised in Christianity. However, it is difficult to resist the conclusion that women have been systematically disempowered in the Church, their experience ignored and their contributions minimised. Whether or not this conclusion defines the heart of Christianity has to do with what one defines as the heart: the prophetic spirit of Jesus (Ruether) or the creation of inequality in the earliest layers of Judeo-Christian traditions (Daly).

Key quotes

Even in the 20th century, major Protestant theologians like Karl Barth and Dietrich Bonhoeffer continued to insist upon God-given differences between the sexes that make male leadership appropriate. Though they often speak in terms of a complementarity between the sexes, they retain a typically Protestant insistence that the family is the proper context for human living, and that women's task is the maintenance of this institution. **(L. Woodhead)**

… the wife should stay at home and look after the affairs of the household as one who has been deprived of the ability of administering those affairs that are outside and concern the state … In this way Eve is punished. **(M. Luther)**

The extent to which feminist theology impacts modern Christian practice

When Christianity is examined from the point of view of the experience of women, its history is one that has systematically suppressed (or, to use a biblical term: 'subjugated') women. However, in the last decades of the 20th century feminist theology has rigorously criticised theology and Church history and has called for reform in the Church. One area that can offer evidence as to the progress feminist theology has made in the life of the Church is the practice of Christian ordination, the dedication of Christian leaders, though prayer and the laying on of hands to positions of leadership in the Church.

Since the 1970s many Protestant denominations have ordained women. This could be interpreted as an impact of feminist theology, since it coincides with the work of female theologians such as Rosemary Radford Ruether who have highlighted the patriarchal nature of this ancient practice. Ruether, Mary Daly and other feminist theologians have influenced women studying for the ministry as their textbooks have been a part of the seminary curriculum. Now most parts of the worldwide Anglican communion ordain women as priests; some parts of this communion also ordain women as Bishops (England in 2015 and Wales in 2017); it would appear, then, that a dramatic reversal has been made in the history of the Church.

Furthermore, in 2014 Pope Francis indicated his willingness to consider women as deacons. 'Deacon' is a term meaning 'servant' and is one of three Church leadership positions (alongside presbyter and bishop) mentioned in the New Testament. In the Catholic Church, a deacon can lead worship services and perform a variety of acts such as baptism, witnessing marriages and conducting funeral services – but cannot preside at Mass. Currently the Catholic Church ordains married men over the age of 35 as deacons. The step of even studying the issue of women as deacons represents a significant change for the Catholic Church.

However, these signs of change should not obscure the fact that most Christians in the world belong to churches where women are not ordained. Pope Francis has also recently stated that women will not be admitted to the priesthood. The justification of this position by the Catholic Church is related to God choosing a male (Jesus) in the incarnation; this has led to Rosemary Radford Ruether to observe that the criterion for full leadership in the Church is the possession of male genitalia. Both Rosemary Radford Ruether and Mary Daly have shared their frustration that whereas Vatican II promised equality in the life of the Church, this was not realised in relation to women. In fact, women, who compose more than half of the Catholic Church, were not even an official part of any of the decision of Vatican II. Mary Daly has concluded that patriarchal attitudes run too deeply in the Church for women to have any hope of meaningful change.

Feminist theology appears to have had no impact on conservative or evangelical Protestant churches. Not only are women not ordained in many of these churches, these churches take a literal approach to the Bible, viewing it as reflecting the will of God. This includes statements in the Hebrew scriptures such as women being subject to men because of Eve's sin in the Garden of Eden (Genesis 3:16) to Paul commanding women to be submissive to their husbands (Ephesians 5:24). Though these churches are in many ways different from the Catholic Church in terms of authority and structure, they share the use of patriarchal language for God; the creator of the world is a male and this male God sent a male saviour to establish a church where only males can be leaders. Rosemary Radford Ruether believes this patriarchy is a sin and Mary Daly labels the use of the Bible to establish gender superiority 'Bibliolatry'.

AO2 Activity

As you read through this section try to do the following:

1. Pick out the different lines of argument that are presented in the text and identify any evidence given in support.

2. For each line of argument try to evaluate whether or not you think this is strong or weak.

3. Think of any questions you may wish to raise in response to the arguments.

This activity will help you to start thinking critically about what you read, and help you to evaluate the effectiveness of different arguments and from this develop your own observations, opinions and points of view that will help with any conclusions that you make in your answers to the AO2 questions that arise.

Key quotes

Women play the ministerial role by endlessly proving that they can think, feel and act like one of the boys. The 'boys,' in turn, accept them only in token numbers that do not threaten their monopoly on ecclesiastical power (anything above five percent is perceived as a threat to this monopoly). (R. Ruether)

With respect to the fundamental rights of the person, every type of discrimination, whether social or cultural, whether based on sex, race, colour, social condition, language or religion, is to be overcome and eradicated as contrary to God's intent. Such is the case of a woman who is denied the right to choose a husband freely, to embrace a state of life or to acquire an education or cultural benefits equal to those recognised for men. (The Roman Catholic Church: Gaudium Et Spes, Vatican II, 1965)

AO2 Activity

List some conclusions that could be drawn from the AO2 reasoning from the above text; try to aim for at least three different possible conclusions. Consider each of the conclusions and collect brief evidence to support each conclusion from the AO1 and AO2 material for this topic. Select the conclusion that you think is most convincing and explain why it is so. Try to contrast this with the weakest conclusion in the list, justifying your argument with clear reasoning and evidence.

Key quotes

Christian theology widely asserted that women were inferior, weak, depraved and vicious. The logical consequences of this opinion were worked out in a brutal set of social arrangements that shortened and crushed the lives of women. (M. Daly)

… churches which display least concern for women's ministry often show a corresponding lack of concern for other marginalised groups. (from 'Women and Ordination in the Christian Churches: International Perspectives')

Even in churches that ordain women, there are several issues that prevent their full equality with male priests and pastors. For instance, the Church of England has made it optional for congregations to 'opt-out' of considering a female priest. Accordingly, the proportion of unpaid women clergy has increased in many Church bodies that ordain women. Ordained women have also had to fight for maternity rights in some denominations. Interview committees have sometimes asked inappropriate questions to women candidates (i.e. are you planning to have children?). So, it seems that the struggle for women's rights is far from over in the Church.

Both Rosemary Radford Ruether and Mary Daly say that it is not enough to simply have equal numbers of men and women in leadership if the model of leadership is itself patriarchal and in need of reform. Ruether says that one of the problems of clericalism is that it treats the laity as a passive group that needs the leadership and guidance of a small group of officially sanctioned leaders. Does this model really lead to the liberation of the Church – or does it serve to simply strengthen the egos of clergy? Mary Daly actually urges her readers to be 'antichurch', to leave the Church altogether and to support one another in a sisterhood which is non-hierarchical, inclusive and non-dogmatic. She has reached this conclusion because of her perception that feminist theology has not impacted the Church very deeply at all.

Rosemary Radford Ruether is more hopeful than Daly about reform, but she too recognises that women will need to find support in female 'base communities' as they struggle for a less patriarchal church.

In conclusion, when it comes to the issue of ordination a case can be made both that there are significant signs of movement *and* that the Church continues to be deeply mired in patriarchal views. It may be that one can only answer this question by looking at specific churches and asking women in those churches, 'do you feel that you can become a full human being in this community, not limited by your reproductive biology? '

In judging whether individual Church communities have been impacted by feminist theology, one could look at three areas that feminist theologians consider will change because of their message being taken seriously: (i) language – do these churches speak of God using terminology from both genders as well as terms that are beyond gender altogether? Do examples of the life of faith include women who are not conceived of as 'feminine' in stereotypical ways? (ii) rituals – does the Church have rituals that imagine women as well as men progressing on a path of growth and healing – and do women as well as men lead these rituals? (iii) social commitments – are these churches committed to causes that directly help oppressed women such as women's shelters and rape hotlines? Only when there are positive answers in all three of these areas will feminist theologians themselves be prepared to say that their work has had an impact.

AO2 Developing skills

It is now important to consider the information that has been covered in this section; however, the information in its raw form is too extensive and so has to be processed in order to meet the requirements of the examination. This can be achieved by practising more advanced skills associated with AO2. For assessment objective 2 (AO2), which involves 'critical analysis' and 'evaluation' skills, we are going to focus on different ways in which the skills can be demonstrated effectively, and also refer to how the performance of these skills is measured (see generic band descriptors for A2 [WJEC] AO2 or A Level [Eduqas] AO2).

▶ **Your final task for this theme:** Below is an evaluation of **the continuing inequality of women in the Church**. You want to use this in an essay but as it stands it is a weak argument because it has no quotations or references in it at all as support. This time you have to find your own quotations (about 3) and use your own references (about 3) to strengthen the evaluation. Remember, sometimes a quotation can follow from a reference but they can also be used individually as separate points.

Although many denominations have now ordained women as priests for several decades, it is not true to say that women have achieved equality with men when considering the worldwide context of Christianity. The starkest fact is that most Christians continue to worship in churches where women are not ordained. Even many churches that ordain women as priests do not ordain them as bishops. There are examples of churches in denominations that ordain women who avoid calling a women priest. Or, if they do call women priests, of not being fair in the way they ask interview questions. Though the Roman Catholic Church has very recently decided to study the issue of women as deacons, this is at the level of 'study' only; no decision has been reached. Furthermore, the Pope has made it clear that there are areas of ministry where women will not be permitted to go.

The result will be a fairly lengthy answer and so you could then check it against the band descriptors for A2 (WJEC) or A Level (Eduqas) and in particular have a look at the demands described in the higher band descriptors towards which you should be aspiring. Ask yourself:

- Is my answer a confident critical analysis and perceptive evaluation of the issue?
- Is my answer a response that successfully identifies and thoroughly addresses the issues raised by the question set.
- Does my work show an excellent standard of coherence, clarity and organisation?
- Will my work, when developed, contain thorough, sustained and clear views that are supported by extensive, detailed reasoning and/or evidence?
- Are the views of scholars/schools of thought used extensively, appropriately and in context?
- Does my answer convey a confident and perceptive analysis of the nature of any possible connections with other elements of my course?
- When used, is specialist language and vocabulary both thorough and accurate?

Key skills

Analysis involves:

Identifying issues raised by the materials in the AO1, together with those identified in the AO2 section, and presents sustained and clear views, either of scholars or from a personal perspective ready for evaluation.

This means:

- That your answers are able to identify key areas of debate in relation to a particular issue
- That you can identify, and comment upon, the different lines of argument presented by others
- That your response comments on the overall effectiveness of each of these areas or arguments.

Evaluation involves:

Considering the various implications of the issues raised based upon the evidence gleaned from analysis and provides an extensive detailed argument with a clear conclusion.

This means:

- That your answer weighs up the consequences of accepting or rejecting the various and different lines of argument analysed
- That your answer arrives at a conclusion through a clear process of reasoning.

Significant historical developments in religious thought

Specification content

The conflicting religious and non-religious views on Christianity in the UK: whether the UK can be called a 'Christian country'.

Key quotes

For centuries, the parish determined the parameters of life for the great majority of British people from the cradle to the grave. Its significance has diminished over time, but the residues still resonate, sometimes in unexpected ways. **(G. Davie)**

Britain is now regularly spoken of as a secular country with a secular state, yet it still has an established church, and the majority of Britons still call themselves 'Christian'. **(L. Woodhead)**

Key terms

Anglican communion: a worldwide association of episcopal (having a bishop) churches

Church of England: a Church body that is a part of the Anglican communion and is the state (or 'established') Church in England

---

D: Challenges from secularisation

Whether the UK can be called a 'Christian country'

Imagine a tourist visiting the UK. Prior to her visit, she's watched some royal weddings on television, enjoyed performances of Shakespeare and read the *Narnia Chronicles* to her children. Now she is going to see what things are 'really like'. What might she conclude about the importance of Christianity in Britain?

Like many tourists, she visits great cathedrals, some of which have seen continuous worship for almost a thousand years. Then, driving though the countryside, our tourist notices the prominence of church buildings in nearly every town and village. Not only are there the expected churches of the **Anglican communion** (the **Church of England**, the Church in Wales and the Scottish Episcopal Church), but Roman Catholic Churches and a variety of other non-conformist churches such as Baptist, Methodist, Quaker and Unitarian – many Christian movements that began in Britain and spread to the rest of the world. Furthermore, she discovers that the entire geography of Britain is divided up into parishes in which the Church played a central role in governance. As she travels she realises that even the English language itself has been shaped by the *King James Bible* and the *Book of Common Prayer*!

Study tip

Make sure that you are accurate when you report on statistical examples. There are several good sources for this area that can be found online: The Office for National Statistics, the British Social Attitudes Survey (BSA) and British Religion in Numbers (BRIN). Spending some time searching for Religion and/or Christianity data on each of these sites will strengthen your grasp of this material.

If our tourist really keeps a close eye on her surroundings, she might notice that up to 30% of all primary and secondary schools in some regions have a Christian affiliation and that 26 Bishops sit in the House of Lords, one of the main decision-making bodies in the UK.

When she turns on the TV, there are re-runs of *The Vicar of Dibley* and new episodes of *Songs of Praise*. She remembers that *The Narnia Chronicles* were written by C.S. Lewis, an evangelical Anglican, and *The Lord of the Rings* by J. R. R. Tolkien, a Catholic Christian. J. K. Rowling has shared that her plot from the final book in the Harry Potter series draws on the Christian Gospels. When she turns on BBC Radio 4, she listens to *Thought for the Day* which regularly features a Christian minister of religion sharing on the intersection between life and faith. Considering these experiences, she concludes that the UK continues to be a thoroughly Christian country.

Durham Cathedral, England. The foundations were laid in 1093; each year there are 700,000 visitors and 1,700 services.

What is underneath the 'Christian surface'?

But would she be justified in this conclusion? Many would argue that this tourist has formed a false impression. First: how many people are inside those churches? The 2011 Census indicated that 54% of the population affiliated with Christianity. But that does not mean that 54% of the population actively participates in Church. The British Social Attitudes Survey shows that less than 15% report attending religious services on a weekly basis. This number includes all religions and may be inflated since people tend to think they attend more than they do. Some estimate that Christian attendance in churches is less than 5%; attendance in the Church of England has recently fallen to under 2%.

Though it is true that over half of the population say they believe in God, studies indicate that these beliefs do not affirm anything like traditional Christian notions found in the creeds or embodied in the doctrine of the Trinity. In the year 2000 an ORB survey commissioned by the BBC discovered it might be accurate to say that the population is less Christian but more 'spiritual' with the following percentages responding to the question, 'which of these would you say you are?':

- A spiritual person – 31%
- A religious person – 27%
- An agnostic person – 10%
- Not a spiritual person – 7%
- Not a religious person – 21%
- A convinced atheist – 8%
- Don't know – 5%

> ### AO1 Activity
>
> Make a list of all the features of your village, town or city that provide evidence for the public side of Christianity. Of course, specific church buildings will be on your list – but can you find anything more?

The decline of Christianity

The decline of Christianity can be seen dramatically in terms of those participating in rites such as baptism, marriage, and funerals. Before the beginning of the twentieth century it would have been normal to have undergone each of these life passages in the Church; now it is increasingly rare. In the Church of England, for example, 67% of the population were baptised in 1950 but only 12% in 2011. In 1957 72% of all marriages in England and Wales were conducted in churches; by the year 2000 this had dropped to 36.3%. Whilst religious funerals remain quite common, many families now choose to have a 'celebration of life' perhaps conducted by a representative from the British Humanist Association.

The decline in Church attendance has been accompanied by a decline in participation in Christian rites such as baptism and marriage.

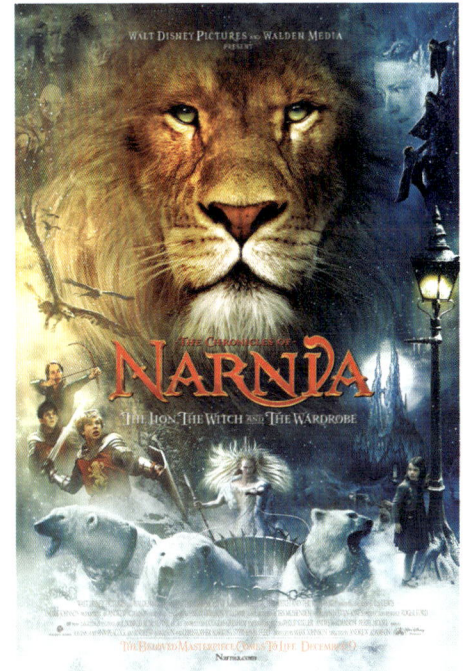

The popular film, 'The Lion, the Witch and the Wardrobe' is based on the fantasy novel of evangelical Anglican, C. S. Lewis.

Key quotes

The centre of British society is gradually shifting away from Christianity, but remains deeply coloured by it. (G. Davie)

… we have some evidence that for those people who do not go to church yet say they are religious and pray often, religious belief has moved quite far from the orthodox church position and is really much closer to what would normally be called superstition. (N. Abercrombie)

quickfire

3.17 True or false: surveys indicate that more than half of the population of the UK are atheists?

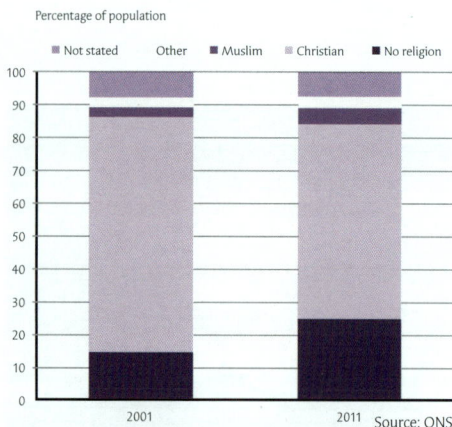

Percentage of population

■ Not stated   Other   ■ Muslim   ■ Christian   ■ No religion

Religious belonging in England and Wales between 2001 and 2011. Where has the shift in belonging taken place?

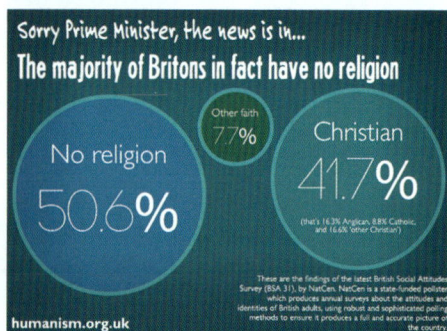

A response of the British Humanist Association to David Cameron's assertion that Britain is a 'Christian country'. Note the higher rate of 'no religion' on the British Social Attitudes survey of 2013 than on the Census for England and Wales.

Key quote

Between half and two-thirds of British people assent to 'belief in God' in more general terms, and roughly similar proportions touch base with the institutional churches at some point in their lives, often at times of crisis. (G. Davie)

There may be Bishops in the House of Lords but former Deputy Prime Minister Nick Clegg has been clear that he is 'not a man of faith' and does not practise religion. British politicians are often silent about matters of religion. When it comes to popular culture there is at least as much evidence (if not more) of criticism as there is of acceptance of religion. Just think of the disapproval of Christianity in shows such as *Monty Python* and *Dave Allen* (popular in the 70s and 80s) as well as *Father Ted* (1990s). *The God Delusion* (2006), a book advancing atheism and science over religion was a national bestseller and on the New York Times bestseller list for 51 consecutive weeks and BBC Radio 4's *Thought for the Day* has an increasing number of presenters from other religions.

There are additional points that can be explored and debated in relation to the UK as a Christian country.

Seeming to support the notion of the UK as a Christian country:

- Some studies have shown that numbers are growing at cathedrals amongst worshippers, pilgrims, tourists and visitors.
- It is relatively rare for someone to die without some form of religious ceremony.
- There is a Christian presence through chaplains in many areas of our social life: health care, the prison service, the armed services and higher education.
- A study by the AHRC/ESRC in 2010/11 showed that just over 50% of undergraduate students self-identified as Christians (55.7 % think of themselves as religious or spiritual; 33.1 % are neither and 11.2 percent don't know).
- There are many popular Christian festivals such as Greenbelt, Spring Harvest, New Wine and Soul Survivor.
- 77% of British believe that 'there are things in life we simply cannot explain through science or any other means' (only 18% disagree).

Seeming to challenge the notion of the UK as a Christian country:

- According to the Census for England and Wales, between 2001 and 2011 there has been a decline in those saying they belong to Christianity from 72% to 59% and an increase in those professing 'no religion' from 15% to 25%.
- There is a continuing shift away from those who believe in a personal God towards those who prefer a less specific formulation.
- Over the last several decades, there has been a dramatic shift from what one cannot do to what one can do on Sundays, with increasing participation in sports, shopping and work.
- Churches are being turned into commercial spaces, dwellings, temples and mosques.
- Atheism and humanism are now presented more widely in British schools (including in this text book).
- Data from the British Social Attitudes survey reveals that for every single convert, the Church of England currently loses twelve people, mainly through death.

What does it mean to have 'no religion' in the UK?

One of the most striking results from the recent census was the growth in the 'no religion' category. Many believe that the census figure of 25% underestimates the true number. This is because the question used on the census led people in the direction of giving a positive answer: 'what is your religion?' (seeming to assume that people had one). However, the British Social Attitudes Survey asked, more straightforwardly, 'Do you regard yourself as belonging to any particular religion?' In 2013 this led to over half of those surveyed answering 'no' (50.6% – up from 31.4% in 1983). The dramatic shift to 'no religion' in, perhaps, over half of the population may provide some insights into whether the UK can be called a Christian country.

Sociologist Linda Woodhead has conducted further research into this category and shows that 18 to 24 year olds make up 60% of those stating, 'no religion'; only 27% adhere to Christianity in this age group. This contrasts with 34% of those who are 60 and older declaring 'no religion', with 60% of this age group stating that they adhere to Christianity. It appears, therefore, that 'no religion' is expanding as Christianity is diminishing.

But what are the beliefs and attitudes toward religion for those in the 'no religion' category? Woodhead shows that less than half in this category are atheist (41.5%); the largest group is composed of those who doubt the existence of God or think that 'maybe' God exists. Only 13.5% are hostile to public forms of religion (such as faith schools) and religious belief. Many in this category have a positive opinion for religious leaders such as the Dalai Lama, Desmond Tutu and Pope Francis. About a quarter of those in this category even report taking part in some sort of religious or spiritual practice at least monthly (such as praying). What binds this group together is not, therefore, hostility to Christianity or religion but, simply, not being a part of a religious community.

Study tip

Expose yourself directly to some of the organisations covered in this theme. Go to the websites of the *British Humanist Association* and the *National Secular Society* to discover views on Christianity and secularism. Then, go to the *Church of England* site and to *Theos Think Tank* and try to find opposing viewpoints. Search also for *Living with Differences: Report on the Commission on Religion and Belief in British Public Life* for a point of view relevant to all of the ideas presented in these sections.

The value of Christian faith schools

The UK has many '**faith schools**'; these are primary and secondary schools affiliated with a religious tradition. In England and Wales these are called 'schools with a religious character' and in Scotland and Northern Ireland these are known as 'denominational schools'. Most faith schools are affiliated with Christianity and, in some regions of the UK, account for over 30% of all schools.

These schools receive some of their funding from a religious organisation, which may own the school buildings and the land. A certain number of the school's governors are appointed by the school to represent its religious ethos. Often it is the governors, rather than the Local Authority, that are responsible for the school's admission policy and appointing staff. This means that there can be a preference for hiring teachers and support staff who adhere to the school's religion.

In terms of admission, some Christian faith schools might prioritise students who are affiliated with the school's faith. They may ask for a baptismal certificate and/or a letter from a religious leader certifying their family's attendance at worship to strengthen their application.

This has led to some families attending church to simply get a place at the school to the detriment of those who live nearer to the school but do not have a religious affiliation. However, many faith schools have removed any faith criteria from their admissions policy to avoid this issue.

A significant percentage of children in the UK attend faith schools.

Key quotes

Almost three-quarters of Britons may describe themselves as Christian, but very few of them can put any religious content to that term. Opinion polls and attitude surveys show large numbers willing to say they believe in a wide variety of supernatural entities and experiences but very little of this is Christian. **(S. Bruce)**

Britain is no longer the 'Christian country' Mr. Cameron and the *Daily Mail* imagine, but neither is it 'no religion'. It exists somewhere in-between – between Christian, multi-faith and 'none'. **(L. Woodhead)**

quickfire

3.18 Why is there such a big difference between the 'no-religion' category in the 2011 Census (approximately 25%) and in BSA data (approximately 50%)?

Specification content

The conflicting religious and non-religious views on Christianity in the UK (the value of Christian faith schools).

Key term

Faith school: a school that is associated with a religious tradition, many of these schools are state funded, though many independent schools also have an association with religion

quickfire

3.19 True or false: state-funded faith schools do not teach the National Curriculum?

Faith schools must follow the National Curriculum in all subjects; however, in RE these schools can focus on their religious tradition, though many do present other religions. Faith schools are inspected regularly by Ofsted.

Those who support faith schools point to several advantages:

- Parents who want their children to have a religious grounding in their education can have this need met.
- Faith schools tend to be amongst the best-performing state schools.
- They add an element of diversity and choice to the educational landscape.
- The values and ethics of the religious tradition these schools represent fosters inclusivity, tolerance, love and justice.

Objections to faith schools

The British Humanist Association, however, actively campaigns against faith schools, invites the public to petition the government against the creation of new faith schools and urges that existing faith schools be made more inclusive. They believe that faith schools, by their very nature, contradict the principle of a fully inclusive and integrated education system that does not exclude staff, students or governors based on belief. In other words, they believe that faith schools create a segregated future and public funds should not be used to promote religion.

The BHA has raised the following objections in relation to the curriculum at faith schools:

- The teaching of religious education in faith schools is not specifically inspected by Ofsted.
- Religious education aims to instruct children in the doctrine and practices of a particular religion rather than taking a more objective approach.
- Religious education in faith schools does not have to cover other religions and 'almost certainly fails to give a fair account of non-religious views'.
- Ethical issues such as abortion or assisted dying might be approached from an explicitly religious perspective.
- Personal, Social, Health and Economic Education (PSHE) might teach the sex and relationship components in a way that is homophobic or gender discriminatory.
- Some faith schools have taught creationism and intelligent design as scientific theories.

How important is 'faith' to those who send their children to a faith school? Many say that their main motivations to sending their children to these schools have little to do with the religious element. According to a study conducted by Linda Woodhead, it was discovered that the reasons parents choose (or hypothetically would choose) a faith school are: (i) academic standards 77%, (ii) location 58%, (iii) discipline 41%, (iv) ethical values 23%, (v) prestige 19%, (vi) exposure to a faith tradition 5%, and (vii) transmission of belief about God (3%).

A pin-badge of the British Humanist Association

Beliefs conflicting with laws of the country and perceived challenges to Christianity: the declining role and impact of Christianity and restricted religious liberty

Ban on the Lord's Prayer at Star Wars

In 2015 the Church of England produced an advertisement to be shown in cinemas at the beginning of Star Wars, the Force Awakens. The ad shows several people in different settings saying the Lord's Prayer – including weightlifters at a gym, refugees, a sheep farmer, a Gospel choir and the Archbishop of Canterbury, Justin Welby.

The company that administrates media ads in cinemas, Digital Cinema Media, banned the advert because it transgressed its policy of not promoting ads with political or religious messages. It was thought that the film could offend people of 'differing faiths or no faith'. This caused an outcry from several leaders and personalities including Sadiq Khan, Stephen Fry and the Prime Minister at the time, David Cameron. The Equality and Human Rights Commission (EHRC) spoke in favour of the ad saying, 'There is nothing in law that prevents Christian organisations promoting their faith through adverts'. However, many commentators disagreed saying that the public did not want religions 'preaching' to them: 'The C of E is perfectly entitled to make its views known, but it should do so from the pulpit. But of course, they can't get many people to go to church so they want to take their message to the cinemas.' (John Hegarty, advertising executive.) The ad was not shown in the cinemas but was released, instead, on YouTube. Does the decision to ban an advert of the established Church of England reflect the decreasing influence of Christianity in Britain or does the outcry against its banning show widespread support for Christianity?

Illegal to wear a crucifix?

In 2006, British Airways suspended Nadia Eweida because she refused to cover up a crucifix whilst at work. This contravened BA's uniform policy for jewellery, though the company allows hijabs and turbans to be worn. In 2007 BA changed their rules to allow Ms Eweida to wear a symbol of faith, but it refused to pay her for her period of suspension.

She and three other Christians brought cases against the UK government for not protecting their rights; in her case the UK argued that wearing a crucifix is not a requirement of Christianity and that therefore this reflected only the personal belief rather than disadvantaging a group. She then took her case to the European Court of Human Rights (ECHR) which heard her case at the same time as three other cases:

- Shirley Chaplin, 57 a nurse – her employer stopped her wearing necklaces with a cross because this could be unsafe around patients and possibly spread disease.

- Gary McFarlane, 51, a marriage counsellor for the group Relate was dismissed for saying he might object to giving sex therapy advice to gay couples.

- Lillian Ladele, a registrar for a Local Authority, was disciplined after she refused to conduct same-sex civil partnership ceremonies.

Ms Eweida won her case. The ECHR declared: 'in these circumstances where there is no evidence of any real encroachment on the interests of others, the domestic authorities failed sufficiently to protect the applicant's right to manifest her religion'. According to the BBC, the Prime Minister at the time, David Cameron, said he was 'delighted' that the 'principle of wearing religious symbols at work has been upheld', adding that people 'shouldn't suffer discrimination due to religious beliefs'.

Specification content

The conflicting religious and non-religious views on Christianity in the UK: beliefs conflicting with laws of the country; perceived challenges to Christianity (decline of role and status of Christianity; reduced impact in public life; restricted religious liberty).

Key quote

This is a prayer that is 2,000 years old and informs our whole culture. (Sadiq Khan, Mayor of London)

#justpray
our Father in heaven

The Lord's Prayer advertisement banned from cinemas in 2015.

quickfire

3.20 Why was the Lord's Prayer advertisement banned from cinemas?

Key quote

Christians and those of other faiths should be free to wear the symbols of their own religion without discrimination. (John Sentamu, Archbishop of York)

However, Ms Eweida's case hinged on the fact that, her cross was discrete and was judged to not adversely affect BA's corporate image. Significantly, the three other cases were *not* successful.

'Ordinary Christians' and same-sex civil partnerships

Hazelmary and Peter Bull own a hotel in Cornwall; in 2008 they refused to let civil partners Steven Preddy and Martyn Hall stay in a room. They based their decision on their Christian beliefs: 'We are just ordinary Christians who believe in the importance of marriage as the union of one man and one woman. Our B&B is not just our business, it's our home. All we have ever tried to do is live according to our own values, under our own roof.' Their court case was based on their right to 'manifest their religion' under the European Court of Human Rights.

The Bristol court found that they had acted unlawfully and were ordered to pay damages. The Supreme Court upheld this decision after an appeal, affirming the rights of all people to have relationships with others regardless of sexual orientation. The homosexual rights group Stonewall suggested that it might have been more 'Christian' for the Bulls to have fought the evils of poverty and disease worldwide than to have pursued this case. In fact, many Christians in Great Britain have reinterpreted the Bible in such a way to support acceptance of homosexual relationships. Surveys show that whereas in 1989 most Christians disagreed with same-sex marriage (70–80%), by 2014 this had fallen to less than 30%. This dramatic change in belief means that the Bulls now represent a minority position amongst those who call themselves Christians in Britain.

To be or not to be … secular

The word secular means to not be connected to the Church or religion. **Secularisation** is the process of a society once dominated by religious institutions becoming non-religious. Few people would deny that there has been a process of secularisation at work in the UK – this is shown, as we have seen, by decline in several areas: attendance, the performance of rituals and influence in government and society. However, there is disagreement as to whether secularisation is a good thing.

> ### AO1 Activity
>
> Do your friends and family reflect the statistics you have read in this theme? Make a list of people that you know – try to get this list to over 25 people (100 would be fantastic!). Then beside each name write a comment about their attitudes and practices toward Christianity. You might note how many attend church regularly, irregularly? How many believe in the Christian God, have more 'fuzzy' forms of belief, are adherents of other religions, or are opposed to Christian belief? You may have to guess in several cases. Compare the results you come up with to figures you have learned in this section.

There are many who are committed to an ideology of **secularism**, the belief that religion is 'otherworldly' and that less of a religious focus entails a more humane society. Those who embrace secularism believe that it is both natural and good that society should become secular. It is not uncommon to see that 'Christianity' and 'religion' are associated with 'superstition', 'violence', 'authority', 'monarchy', 'control', 'repression', 'intolerance' and that 'science' is associated with 'progress', 'peace', 'humanity', 'tolerance' and 'democracy'. The assumption that some secularists make is that the more 'modern' society becomes, the less religious it will be. In other words, one cannot be both religious and modern.

Is Christianity merely a relic from the past?

There are some reasons for questioning this viewpoint. First, many people are disillusioned with 'modern science': prosperity and health care have not been delivered for all, famine persists, there is global warming and the threat of nuclear warfare.

Furthermore, there are not always strong boundaries between 'science' and 'religion'. For instance, the Occupy movement (protesting the excesses of global capitalism) moved from Fleet Street to the grounds of St Paul's Cathedral, hoping that the Church would be an ally with their cause. Some of the protestors asked, 'What would Jesus do?'. The Campaign for Nuclear Disarmament is just another example of a social cause that brings together both believers and those with no religion.

Some have suggested that rather than the decline of the Church what we are seeing is a movement from religion as duty and obligation to religion as a choice. Even though this may mean fewer numbers in church, it may also mean that those who believe and practise their faith may find it more meaningful.

There are several Christian initiatives which might be seen as progressive, positive, 'modern' and yet as reflecting the time-honoured values of religion. One example is the 'Street Pastor' movement, a church response to urban needs. Volunteers are trained in providing a positive and helpful presence on the streets of UK cities on a Friday and Saturday night, offering a helping hand, a listening ear and practical help. Their 'mission' is 'listening, caring and helping'. At present 'Street Pastors' work in over 300 towns and cities across the UK. Over 20,000 volunteers are associated with this initiative.

Of course, these points could be interpreted as the 'last gasps' of a dying religion. However, sociologists Elisabeth Arweck and James A. Beckford name six factors that committed secularists may want to consider before they reach this conclusion:

- Religious vitality – religion continues to be popular for many in different forms including, but not limited to, charismatic expressions, Cathedral worship and various forms of spirituality.

- The nature of modernity – there are different ways of being 'modern'; many 'modern' people see religion as a resource for modern living when science does not provide all the solutions.

- De-privatisation – rather than seeing religion only as a private personal belief, some observe that religion has helped to bring about positive social change.

- Globalisation – there are transnational religious movements which focus on faith or human rights across the world. This can give Christianity a boost in some locations.

- Gender: Christianity has a wide range of views on women's roles in leadership and the Christian community which might explain the success or failure of various individual denominations and churches and forms of spirituality.

- Rational choice – some suggest that religion is a 'market' that thrives when state regulation (in the form of the established Church) is lower. This suggests that the decline of the state church is not the same as the decline of Christianity.

Street Pastors work to strengthen community and create safer streets.

Key term

Privatisation: the movement from public to private; in terms of religion, belief and practice becoming a matter of inner disposition rather than outer practice

Church for sale in England

97

Key skills Theme 3

The first Theme has tasks that deal
with the basics of AO1 in terms of
prioritising and selecting the key
relevant information, presenting this
in a personalised way (as in Theme 1)
and then using evidence and examples
to support and expand upon this (as in
the previous Theme).

Key skills

Knowledge involves:

*Selection of a range of (thorough)
accurate and relevant information
that is directly related to the specific
demands of the question.*

This means:

- Selecting relevant material for the
  question set

- Being focused in explaining and
  examining the material selected.

Understanding involves:

*Explanation that is extensive,
demonstrating depth and/or breadth
with excellent use of evidence and
examples including (where appropriate)
thorough and accurate supporting use
of sacred texts, sources of wisdom and
specialist language.*

This means:

- Effective use of examples and
  supporting evidence to establish the
  quality of your understanding

- Ownership of your explanation
  that expresses personal knowledge
  and understanding and NOT just
  reproducing a chunk of text from a
  book that you have rehearsed and
  memorised.

AO1 Developing skills

It is now important to consider the information that has been covered in this
section; however, the information in its raw form is too extensive and so has to
be processed in order to meet the requirements of the examination. This can be
achieved by practising more advanced skills associated with AO1. The exercises
that run throughout this book will help you to do this and prepare you for the
examination. For assessment objective 1 (AO1), which involves demonstrating
'knowledge' and 'understanding' skills, we are going to focus on different ways
in which the skills can be demonstrated effectively, and also refer to how the
performance of these skills is measured (see generic band descriptors for A2
[WJEC] AO1 or A Level [Eduqas] AO1).

▶ **Your task is this:** Below is a summary of **the value of Christian faith
schools**. It is 150 words long. There are three points highlighted that are key
points to learn from this extract. Discuss which two further points you think are
the most important to highlight and write up all five points.

Christian faith schools are primary and secondary schools affiliated with
a religious tradition; sometimes they are called 'schools with a religious
character'. There are many of these across the UK, with some regions having
more than 30% of students attending these schools. They receive their funding
both from the religious organisation and, in many cases the state (if they are
not fee-paying schools). Many see that they have value in terms of their high
academic attainment and the fact that they are open to all potential students.
Others are concerned that these schools are exempt from teaching the National
Curriculum in regards to religious education. Furthermore, the admissions
policies at some of these schools sometimes favour children from a religious
background. A recent study on parents and faith schools revealed that very few
children are sent to faith schools in order to deepen their faith; they attend
for the quality of education. This suggests that the value of faith schools lies in
their educational rather than religious ethos.

Now make the five points into your own summary (as in Theme 1 Developing
skills) trying to make the summary more personal to your style of writing.

1 ....

2 ....

3 ....

4 ....

5 ....

Issues for analysis and evaluation

The effectiveness of the Christian response to the challenge of secularism

Specification content
The effectiveness of the Christian response to the challenge of secularism.

Secularism is a fact in the sense of the decline of the Church in terms of attendance, social influence and political power. However, secularism is also an ideology – there are those who feel strongly that the decline of the Church is necessary if society is going to progress into a more just and modern state. This section will evaluate some Christian responses to both the fact and the ideology of secularism.

One might conclude that Christian responses to secularism have not been effective given the fact of Church decline. Most significant is the increase of the 'no religion' category which, according to the British Social Attitudes Survey of 2013, could be more than half of the population. Accompanying the growth of this group is a corresponding decline of those who believe in and practise Christianity. However, Christians might argue that this is not the whole story – there are many signs of vitality in the Christian Church. These signs include the growth of charismatic churches and Cathedral worship – each of these types of Christianity offers different experiences that are attractive to those new to Christianity. Nonetheless, Christian vitality is not limited to worship; there are a number of social initiatives that seek to address issues of poverty, welfare and well-being. These include efforts of churches to relieve human suffering through programmes such as Christian Aid and to provide a positive presence in society through a programme such as 'Street Pastors' which includes more than 20,000 volunteers 'listening, caring and helping' on the streets of over 300 cities on Friday and Saturday nights. So, there is evidence both in worship and practice that complete secularisation is not a certain outcome.

However, a secularist could respond that these activities may not prove that the Church is actually being strengthened. Immigration has been behind the creation of new charismatic congregations, for example. Cathedral worship includes pilgrims from other countries, tourists and those who may simply be curious about a historic form of Christian gathering. In fact, in a large Cathedral one can easily remain anonymous, and stay uninvolved in the Church. The social initiatives may simply be a 'stop-gap' and will disappear as society introduces more changes. The British Humanist Association stresses that religious programmes tend to discriminate based on religion (for instance, 'Street Pastors' can only be Christians) whereas solutions created by the state can be more inclusive.

The results of several recent court cases also seem to reinforce the idea of Christian weakness in the face of secularism. Whilst Ms Eweida did gain the right to wear a crucifix at work, this took several years to achieve; others have not gained this right. Hazelmary and Peter Bull lost the right to prevent those in same-sex civil partnerships from staying at their hotel even though doing so would transgress an aspect of their faith. Of course, it might be argued that these rights (to wear a crucifix and to not allow homosexual customers) have little to do with Christianity and are not essential aspects of the faith of most UK Christians.

Looking at those aspects of the Christian tradition that are in decline, Christians might argue that traditional church structures and rituals continue to be a resource to society – not only in high profile rituals that are a part of royal weddings or national ceremonies (such as Remembrance Day) but also for the services that are provided in every town and village in the UK from baptisms and marriages to funerals. To be sure, not all people use the Church as a public utility but the Church provides a presence that many make use of in times of life change and crisis. Furthermore, it is interesting that even in the face of the decline of the Church, the media gives so much attention to the views of Christian leaders such as the Archbishop of Canterbury (Anglican) and the Archbishop of Westminster (Catholic). The former Archbishop of Canterbury, Rowan Williams, has observed that the Church is a place where unsolved issues in society are debated and discussed.

AO2 Activity

As you read through this section try to do the following:

1. Pick out the different lines of argument that are presented in the text and identify any evidence given in support.
2. For each line of argument try to evaluate whether or not you think this is strong or weak.
3. Think of any questions you may wish to raise in response to the arguments.

This activity will help you to start thinking critically about what you read, and help you to evaluate the effectiveness of different arguments and from this develop your own observations, opinions and points of view that will help with any conclusions that you make in your answers to the AO2 questions that arise.

Key quotes

Old habits die hard in the sense that there are still large sections of the population who expect their parish church, just like the NHS, to be there at the point of need for those who want it. Among the latter are many who do not have the luxury of choice. (G. Davie)

… the Church of England is still used by British society as a stage on which to conduct by proxy the arguments that society itself does not know how to handle. It certainly helps explain the obsessional interest in what the Church has to say about issues of sex and gender. (R. D. Williams)

[Modernity involves] … the rediscovery of religion as a cultural resource for re-instilling human values into work, politics and family life and for holding off the bleakness and moral vacuity for the secularised world. (E. Arweck and J. Beckford)

AO2 Activity

List some conclusions that could be drawn from the AO2 reasoning from the above text; try to aim for at least three different possible conclusions. Consider each of the conclusions and collect brief evidence to support each conclusion from the AO1 and AO2 material for this topic. Select the conclusion that you think is most convincing and explain why it is so. Try to contrast this with the weakest conclusion in the list, justifying your argument with clear reasoning and evidence.

One way that the established Church has attempted to respond to secularism is to promote itself in public venues. One example of this is the recent attempt of the Church of England to promote a one minute film of the Lord's Prayer in cinemas that were showing Star Wars Episode 7: The Force Awakens. When the Church was prevented from doing so, several high-profile leaders attempted to defend its rights. David Cameron spoke in favour of the Church's right to promote itself and Sadiq Khan, a Muslim, expressed his dissatisfaction with the decision saying, 'This is a prayer that is 2,000 years old and informs our whole culture'. Furthermore, it is interesting that Star Wars promotes a form of spirituality ('the Force') which appears to be accepted in our culture. It might be argued that the Church can make an effective connection between popular forms of spirituality and its own traditions.

However, just how valid are these arguments for the Church as a public utility? After all, utilities come and go based on their usefulness to society. Years ago, the provision of a water fountain in the centre of a town or village was considered a valuable public utility. However, with the rise of technology and social progress, we now have fresh water in every home – the water fountain is no longer seen as a public utility, and remains only as a relic of the past. The same could be said of the established Church: society is creating new ways for people to access the kind of support that the Church used to offer. This includes everything from humanist weddings to social apps that bring people together in meaningful communities. The fact is that more people are choosing to be married and buried outside of the Church. As we continue to create technological and scientific solutions to human problems, the Church will continue to decline.

Is this simple equation of 'science' with 'progress' and Christianity with 'backwardness' really true? Some Christians might argue that 'science' and 'technology' actually have not delivered solutions to some of our most pressing social problems. Has 'science' stopped pollution, global warming, poverty, personal health, depression and other issues that we all know need to be solved? One could make a case that 'science' and 'technology' have been used as tools to simply increase the amount of waste, unhealthy consumption, and inequality of wealth in the world. The truth may be that life is more complicated than seeing 'science' and 'religion' as two forces facing off against each other. It may be argued that humans need the resources of both.

Christians as well as those with no religious commitments join together in several movements in an attempt to build a more just society. For example, some in the Occupy movement sought the sponsorship of the Church and appealed to the example of Jesus; the Campaign for Nuclear Disarmament (and many other movements) include both Christians and those who have no religious commitments. One might argue that Christians bring time-honoured values such as compassion to these movements, and that the scripture and traditions that inspire them are a positive element in social change. Of course, this argument could be insensitive to those who do not have a religious belief or commitment – do you need to be a Christian to be compassionate?

In conclusion, some Christian responses to secularism do reflect vitality and gain support even from those who are not Christians. However, all of this is in the context of the decline of Christianity – including legal resistance and challenges from groups that believe that Christianity is a force of inequality in society. What is clear is that a completely secular society is not a foregone conclusion as long as so many pockets of Christian activity remain.

The extent to which the UK can be called a Christian country

Specification content

The extent to which the UK can be called a Christian country.

It could be argued that the UK is so thoroughly Christian that is it surprising that the question even needs to be asked. Those who take this viewpoint can point to the historic presence of Christianity which has shaped UK culture, language, architecture – even the calendars that we live by (the first day of the week is Sunday on many calendars). Even those that do not profess to be Christian have had their attitudes and values shaped by Christian traditions. In this regard one thinks of the popularity of the *Narnia Chronicles*, *The Lord of the Rings* and the *Harry Potter* series, each one influenced by Christian ideas and values. For example, in *Harry Potter and the Deathly Hallows*, Harry Potter decides to give his life as a sacrifice so that others might live; he appears to die, to have a resurrection-like experience and then to have victory over the evil one (Voldemort). J. K. Rowling has shared that she was inspired by the Gospels in creating this plot.

The pervasive influence of Christianity in Britain's past is undeniable, reflected in the prominent role of the Church in the monarchy and the division of all of Britain into administrative parishes in which all inhabitants had to give a portion of their produce and income to support the Church. Alternative religious viewpoints were also Christian with the emergence of Quakers, Methodists, Unitarians and other groups which began in Britain and spread to the rest of the world. Significantly, prior to the twentieth century it would have been normal for most people in Britain to have been baptised, married and buried through the Church.

It isn't only in the past that Christianity has influenced national life. Contemporary life in the UK continues to permeate UK society. Twenty-six Bishops of the Church of England sit in the House of Lords, one of the main decision-making bodies. In some regions, over 30% of all schools are faith schools, partly funded by the state. Most of these schools have a relationship with a Christian denomination and offer religious instruction that is specific to the faith tradition partly funding the school. The UK has an 'established church' which is highly visible during national events such as royal weddings, Remembrance Day ceremonies and in celebrations of nationally recognised festivals such as Christmas and Easter. Furthermore, popular radio and TV programming reflects the influence of Christianity through shows such as The Vicar of Dibley, Songs of Praise and BBC Radio 4's Thought for the Day which features a reflection from, usually, a Christian minister of religion.

Whilst few would disagree that Christianity has shaped culture in the UK, many would argue that this influence is declining to the extent that it is no longer correct to call the UK a 'Christian country'. This decline can be seen in the dramatic fall in numbers of those who undergo Christian rituals. For example, in England 67% of the population was baptised in the Church of England in 1950. By the year 2000, this had fallen to only 10%. Those married in the Church in England and Wales has halved in roughly this same time (from 72% to 36%) and there is an increase in the number of humanist funerals conducted.

Key quotes

So, for younger people in Britain today being religious is very much the exception rather than the norm, whereas for older people it is the other way round. (L. Woodhead)

British people are both attached to this inheritance and suspicious of it: the physical and cultural presence of these historic churches may be one thing; a hands-on role in the everyday lives of British people quite another. (G. Davie)

In Britain 'believers' outnumber 'belongers' though for how much longer is harder to say; the reverse is true in the Nordic countries. (G. Davie)

Britain emerges as religious and secular. (L. Woodhead)

Key quote

There is not enough to support
the idea that religion has been
inexorably or catastrophically
declining in post-war Britain at
the level of personal adherence or
public life. Britain has not become a
secular country. (L. Woodhead)

It can be argued that the presence of other religions in Britain and the many people who say they do not belong to a religion means that Britain is a pluralist country rather than a Christian one. In fact, the teaching of many of the world's religions is a part of the National Curriculum and the British Humanist Association (BHA) has been successful in the inclusion of humanist and non-religious points of view in Religious Education. In fact, a recent study has shown that whilst many students in the UK attend faith schools, only 3% of parents send their children there to learn about God; the main reason for choosing these schools has to do with academic standards rather than religious faith. BBC Radio 4's Thought for the Day includes a growing number of representatives from other religions and the BHA and other groups have called for the inclusion of non-religious viewpoints so that this programme can be seen not as religious in nature but as a more general reflection.

Perhaps the biggest indicator of the decline of Christianity in Britain has to do with the rise of those claiming 'no-religion'. This category dramatically increased between the 2001 and 2011 Censuses (from 15 to 25%); however, the British Social Attitudes survey suggests that this may actually account for half of the population, depending on how the question is worded. This does not mean that Britain is filled with atheists opposed to the Church (atheism, for example, is a position that marks less than half in this category), but it is clear that there is a drift from attendance and traditional beliefs.

Given that a majority of those claiming no-religion are young (60% are 18–24 year olds) and a majority of those saying that they adhere to Christianity are over 60 (60%), it seems clear that the Christian Church is in decline and that the 'no-religion' category will continue to rise. This means that describing the UK as Christian is simply out of step with how most people live their lives.

However, does the rise of those who identify with no-religion mean that the UK is not a Christian country?

One argument in favour of the UK as a Christian country in spite of decline is the fact that even though there has been a steep decline in participation in Christian churches, the number of those who say they believe in God is still quite high. This has led sociologist Grace Davie to suggest that religion is strongly present in the UK in terms of believing rather than belonging. Supporting this position is the fact that firm atheism is relatively small (likely under 10%) and the fact many people report believing in God – including over 50% of undergraduates surveyed who say they believe in God. Furthermore, about a quarter of those in the 'no-religion' category engage in a 'spiritual' activity on at least a monthly basis (such as prayer). However, one has to ask how 'Christian' these beliefs and practices really are. Many surveys suggest that these beliefs in 'God' are quite 'fuzzy', nothing at all like traditional Christian belief in the Trinity and the tenets of the historic creeds. Those who might argue from this data that Christianity could make a dramatic come-back in the UK may not be facing up to the changing nature of spiritual beliefs.

AO2 Activity

List some conclusions that could be
drawn from the AO2 reasoning from
the above text; try to aim for at least
three different possible conclusions.
Consider each of the conclusions
and collect brief evidence to support
each conclusion from the AO1 and
AO2 material for this topic. Select
the conclusion that you think is most
convincing and explain why it is so.
Try to contrast this with the weakest
conclusion in the list, justifying
your argument with clear reasoning
and evidence.

It is by no means certain that Christianity is on the road to extinction. Davie also suggests that what has happened in the UK is the end of Christianity as a duty and a stronger focus on Christianity as a voluntary activity. The result of this transition would be as we have observed: a dramatic decrease in belief and participation in the established Church. However, it may be that this decrease in numbers is leading to a stronger 'core' – it really means something to be a Christian in an environment where it is normal to profess no religion. This might explain growth and vitality in some forms of Christianity. Furthermore, many people may continue to want Christianity to be available to them as a 'utility' at times of transition or crisis. It is by no means clear, therefore, that Christianity will continue to decline. Decline may end and the resulting smaller community of Christians may develop a strong presence in the UK.

In conclusion, even if Christianity continues with an active voluntary core of believing, this would be a minority presence. Given this, it would be inaccurate to describe the UK as a 'Christian country'; the real question is if it is better to describe the UK as a pluralistic or multi-faith country, or as an increasingly secular country.

AO2 Developing skills

It is now important to consider the information that has been covered in this section; however, the information in its raw form is too extensive and so has to be processed in order to meet the requirements of the examination. This can be achieved by practising more advanced skills associated with AO2. The exercises that run throughout this book will help you to do this and prepare you for the examination. For assessment objective 2 (AO2), which involves 'critical analysis' and 'evaluation' skills, we are going to focus on different ways in which the skills can be demonstrated effectively, and also refer to how the performance of these skills is measured (see generic band descriptors for A2 [WJEC] AO2 or A Level [Eduqas] AO2).

▶ **Your task is this:** Below is a one-sided view concerning **the UK as a secular nation**. It is 160 words long. You need to include this view for an evaluation; however, to just present one side of an argument or one line of reasoning is not really evaluation. Using the paragraph below, add a counter-argument or alternative line of reasoning to make the evaluation more balanced. Allow about 100 words for your counter-argument or alternative line of reasoning.

There are many reasons to support the view that the UK is a secular nation. By secular it is meant that there is a marked decline in religious belief, religious attendance and in the presence of Christianity in cultural and political 'spaces'. We have solid statistics concerning the dramatic decrease in participation and interest in religion. It seems that the UK is less Christian than it ever was and it is only a matter of time before even Christians who want to support a state church admit that this has become a truly secular nation in all three senses of the word. Since all this is compelling evidence, we can agree with Steve Bruce who writes: 'the voluntary association type of religion continues to engage perhaps 10 to 12 per cent of the population. With around 80% of the population showing no interest in any form of religion, it seems entirely sensible to describe the UK as a largely secular country'.

Theos Think Tank argue that for all that formalised religious belief and institutionalised religious belonging have declined over recent decades, the British have not become a nation of atheists or materialists. On the contrary, a spiritual current runs, as, if not more, powerfully through the nation than it once did.

Next, think of another line of argument or reasoning that may support either argument or it may even be completely different and add this to your answer.

Then ask yourself:

- Will my work, when developed, contain thorough, sustained and clear views that are supported by extensive, detailed reasoning and/or evidence?

Specification content

Richard Dawkins' and Alister McGrath's contrasting views on the relationship between religion and science, and the nature of proof; the limits of science; the 'God of the gaps' argument.

E: Challenges from science

Contrasting views

At the heart of the scientific enterprise is the basing of beliefs on evidence: making observations, testing those observations and arriving at a theory – and then subjecting that theory to further tests. Richard Dawkins, the renowned scientist and proponent of atheism, declares that he is passionate about the scientific method. Alister McGrath and Joanna Collicutt McGrath say that they too are passionate about the evidence and maintain that their Christian faith is compatible with the discoveries of science.

Dawkins says the evidence suggests that religion offers no real answers to the questions we ask. In fact, it is prone to anti-intellectualism and violence. Science, on the other hand, is actively unlocking the mysteries of life: 'I am thrilled to be alive at a time when humanity is pushing against the limits of understanding. We may eventually discover that there are no limits.' McGrath disagrees with Dawkins' description of religion and believes that there are questions that science simply cannot answer. In fact, he says, science and religion need each other.

Richard Dawkins, the Charles Simonyi Professor of the Public Understanding of Science at Oxford University (1995–2008)

Alister McGrath, the Andreas Idreos Professor of Science and Religion at the University of Oxford

Joanna Collicutt McGrath, Karl Jaspers Lecturer, Psychology and Spirituality, Ripon College

AO1 Activity

Give yourself two minutes to make a list of things that you believe science can explain. Then give yourself another two minutes to make a list of things that science cannot explain. As you look at your lists, ask yourself, how confident are you that science will eventually explain the things that you have noted on your second list? What areas outside of science – if any – do you feel make a valuable contribution to the areas you have noted on your second list?

The relationship between religion and science

One of the most interesting facts about life is the incredible complexity of the natural world. Just consider almost any element, for example an eye or a wing. Each of these is composed of a myriad of processes that work together to accomplish the functions of sight or flight. How did these come to be?

Dawkins says that when faced with something that is incredibly complex, humans have tended to turn to a religious answer – God created these. For the idea that an eye or a wing could have somehow come about by chance seems impossible. **William Paley** attempted to justify this kind of religious answer. He spoke about someone on a hike and finding a watch. To come across something in nature that is incredibly complicated, that displays intricate design is surely different from coming across a rock or a blade of grass. We think, says Paley, that there must have been a designer. Dawkins refers to a contemporary example of this

Key person

William Paley: British priest and philosopher who believed that God's existence could be proved from the design of the natural world.

religious argument: to consider that a tornado could blow through a scrapyard and somehow randomly throw together a fully functioning Boeing 747 aircraft would be absurd according to this way of arguing.

Problems with religious answers

Dawkins says that there are two problems with the 'God hypothesis' of design in the natural world:

1. We are not faced with a choice between chance and God. Natural selection actually explains how there can be the appearance of complex, seemingly improbable things from small and relatively simple causes. Natural selection is the process whereby an organism that is better adapted to the environment tends to survive and produce more offspring. Those traits that helped the organism survive are passed down to the next generations so that over long periods of time there can be huge and complex developments. In other words, natural selection breaks down the problem of improbability into small pieces. Looking at the development of the eye or a wing doesn't seem that improbable from the evolutionary point of view.

2. Saying that God designed complex things is no answer at all because God would have to be at least as complex as the thing 'he' designed. Religious believers explain a highly improbable thing in terms of a more highly improbable thing. This means that God is the 'ultimate Boeing 747'! It does no good insisting, as some theologians do, that God is 'simple', because a God who could know everything that was happening, listen to everyone's prayers, sustain the world and design complex biological forms of life would have to be very complicated. To say that God designed the world just begs the question – who designed God? Natural selection is the alternative we must embrace to avoid these religious dilemmas.

Key quotes

…I shall define the God hypothesis more defensibly: there exists a superhuman, supernatural intelligence who deliberately designed and created the universe and everything in it, including us. This book will advocate an alternative view: any creative intelligence, of sufficient complexity to design anything, comes into existence only as the end product of an extended process of gradual evolution. (R. Dawkins)

I started out as an atheist, who went on to become a Christian – precisely the reverse of Dawkins' intellectual journey. (A. McGrath)

… the designer himself, in order to be capable of designing, would have to be another complex entity of the kind that, in his turn, needs the same kind of explanation. It's an evasion of responsibility because it involves the very thing it is supposed to be explaining. (R. Dawkins)

Study tip

Make sure that you know the difference between (i) the argument from design which would say that a Boeing 747 created by a tornado in a scrapyard is as ridiculous as believing that the natural world was created by chance and (ii) Dawkins' view that the design argument itself is ridiculous because it posits an 'ultimate Boeing 747' as the creator – invoking an even more complicated and improbable thing (God) as the reason for the existence of a complicated and improbable thing (the natural world).

quickfire

3.22 True or false: Richard Dawkins is impressed with the design argument as a proof for the existence of God?

What are the chances of a Boeing 747 being created as a tornado blows through a scrapyard?

Key terms

God hypothesis: Dawkins' phrase to describe the claim that there is an interventionist God in the universe; this should be treated like any other scientific hypothesis

Natural selection: the process that results in the survival of organisms best suited to their environment; their traits are passed on to subsequent generations

quickfire

3.23 Some religious believers say that the world was either designed by God or created by chance. What does Dawkins say is a third alternative?

Charles Darwin (1809–1882) His book, The
Origin of the Species *explains the process
of natural selection (statue at Natural
History Museum, London).*

Key quotes

Darwin is a role model to inspire
all who follow the logical and
courageous compulsion to
explain complex things in the
only legitimate way, which is in
terms of simpler things and their
interactions. (R. Dawkins)

The general theory of religion as an
accidental by-product – a misfiring
of something useful – is the one I
wish to advocate. (R. Dawkins)

I have often wondered how Dawkins
and I could draw such totally
different conclusions on the basis
of reflecting long and hard on
substantially the same world. One
possibility might be that, because
I believe in God, I am deranged,
deluded, deceived and deceiving,
my intellectual capacity having
been warped through having been
hijacked by an infectious, malignant
God virus. (A. McGrath and
J. Collicutt McGrath)

Key terms

Anthropic principle: the universe
must contain the properties that allow
the observer to exist

Meme: a term coined by Richard
Dawkins meaning an element of
culture that is passed from one person
to another by imitation or other non-
genetic means

Multiverse: the hypothesis that there
are multitudes of universes of which
ours is only one

How did life originate?

Natural selection explains our complex world. It does not, says Dawkins, explain
why there is life in the universe and how life came to be on the planet earth.
Instead of turning to a God-hypothesis (we don't understand, so it must be God's
doing), natural selection should inspire us to find an explanation which makes
sense of the improbable existence of life.

Dawkins proposes the 'anthropic approach': since we exist, the earth is the kind of
place that is 'life-friendly'. When one considers that there are billions of billions
of planets where life could have developed, is it unreasonable to think that the
conditions friendly to life could occur on at least one of these? 'The **anthropic
principle** states that, since we are alive, eukaryotic [having the kind of cells with
features not present in bacteria], and conscious, our planet has to be one of the
intensely rare planets that has bridged all three gaps.' Why is the universe able to
support life? Instead of invoking God, we might consider **multiverse** theory, the
idea that there are an endless number of universes each with different variations;
ours happens to be one with the variations to support life. Dawkins says that
there is a 'Darwinian' feel to this kind of thinking – explaining life in terms of
developments and variations rather than just positing a God.

Religion is an aberration

An artistic rendering of the
multiverse concept

Religion does not offer reasonable answers
to questions about life, says Dawkins,
because it has been flawed from its very
beginning. His theory is that religion
(defined as belief in God) originated as
a misfiring in the brain of an otherwise
useful activity. There are many things that
give creatures survival value – however, in
some situations those things can lead to
destruction. Dawkins gives the example
of the moth's navigation system that is
oriented to celestial bodies and guides it to
warmth and light; however, it can also guide it to death in a flame. Religion (death
in the flame) is a by-product of at least two qualities that often provide survival
value:

(i) The human tendency to obey elders. This is a very good trait that saves lives and
increases our safety – except when the elders are mistaken.

(ii) The biologically programmed tendency to assign meaning and purpose to
animals and objects. If a lion is snarling at you, it is a good idea to assign to that
lion the purpose of wanting to eat you, says Dawkins. This activity of assigning
purpose and value will save your life. However, humans assign value to all kinds
of things: 'that rock exists to help that creature scratch its back' and 'the being
that made this universe loves me'.

These traits explain why people have a psychological disposition that can favour
religious belief. In terms of how we came up with the actual details of religious
belief, Dawkins uses the concept of '**memes**', an element of culture that is passed
on from one person to another by imitation or non-genetic means. There are many
elements of culture (memes) that include God and have added appeal because they
are associated with other memes. These memes can be manipulated by religious
leaders in ways that give rise to varieties of religious belief. Therefore, we inherit
culturally all kinds of beliefs and values that include belief in God.

The wall between religion and science

Because religion provides only unreasonable answers to our deepest questions and science only proceeds on evidence, Dawkins finds it hard to imagine that any real scientist can be a religious believer. He thinks that many scientists who speak positively of Christianity aren't really Christians. Either they are afraid of sharing their real beliefs or they confuse Christianity with cultural values about beauty and goodness. Dawkins, for example, does not believe that Einstein was a theist and he accuses many contemporary scientists of accepting prizes from religiously based bodies by passing themselves off as 'faith-friendly' when they do not really believe in a being who creates and sustains life.

AO2 Activity

Both Dawkins and McGrath are well represented on YouTube; by typing in 'Alister McGrath Science' and 'Richard Dawkins Religion' into the YouTube search bar you can select clips that cover much of the material on this specification and use these to understand and further explore key points.

Alister McGrath and Joanna Collicutt McGrath, authors of *The Dawkins Delusion*, couldn't disagree more. They note that there are a number of scientists who are quite clear about their Christian belief. In fact, they point to a survey in the United States conducted both in 1916 and again in 1997 that shows that the number of scientists who believe in a 'God who actively communicates with humanity' has held steady at about 40%. Can Dawkins, then, really speak for the entire scientific community? In order for Dawkins to maintain his view, he would have to declare that almost half of all scientists are mentally deficient.

Some arguments against Dawkins

It is significant, say the McGraths, that so many thoughtful human beings become Christians in their adult years. This is not what we would expect if belief in God were like belief in Santa Claus or the Tooth Fairy. They note the change of thinking of Anthony Flew, who wrote *There is a God: How the World's Most Notorious Atheist Changed his Mind* when he was in his 80s. In fact, one of the greatest weaknesses of atheism is the 'persistence of belief in God, when there is supposedly no God in which to believe'.

If religion really were a 'virus of the mind', with a biological foundation, then one would expect that there would be some scientific evidence to back up this theory. The McGraths note that Dawkins has provided no evidence. Furthermore, the idea that religious belief reflects a deficient psychology which makes faulty assumptions about the natural world and tends to irrational and violent behaviour is yet another assertion that is presented without evidence. Is it wrong to expect an eminent scientist such as Dawkins to present evidence for his ideas? This lack of evidence is an indication to the McGraths that *The God Delusion* is a work of **polemic** that is 'more designed to reassure atheists whose faith is faltering than to engage fairly or rigorously with religious believers and others seeking for truth'.

Study tip

Make your own list, based on this chapter, of all of the reasons why Richard Dawkins views religion as having no scientific value. Then make a list of all of the reasons that the McGraths have for questioning Dawkins' views. This will help make you more clear on the central disagreements.

Key quotes

Science without religion is lame. Religion without science is blind. (A. Einstein)

It was, of course, a lie what you read about my religious convictions, a lie which is being systematically repeated. I do not believe in a personal God and I have never denied this but have expressed it clearly. If something is in me which can be called religious then it is the unbounded admiration for the structure of the world so far as our science can reveal it. (A. Einstein)

Key term

Polemic: an aggressive verbal or written attack, from the Greek for 'warlike' or 'hostile'

quickfire

3.24 Does Dawkins believe that belief in God has given the human race survival value?

Key quote

The God Delusion is a work of theatre, rather than scholarship – a fierce, rhetorical assault on religion, and passionate plea for it to be banished to the lunatic fringes of society, where it can do no harm. (A. McGrath and J. Collicutt McGrath)

quickfire

3.25 What do the McGraths say is one of the greatest weaknesses of atheism?

Key quotes

There can be no question of scientific 'proof' of ultimate questions. Either we cannot answer them, or we must answer them on grounds other than the sciences. … Scientific theories cannot be said to 'explain the world' – only to explain the *phenomena* which are observed within the world. **(A. McGrath and J. Collicutt McGrath)**

Either half my colleagues are enormously stupid, or else the science of Darwinism is fully compatible with conventional religious belief – and equally compatible with atheism. **(S. J. Gould)**

quickfire

3.26 What is the difference between NOMA and POMA?

God of the GAPS

Some religious believers explain gaps in our knowledge by appealing to God.

The limits of science

The McGraths find evidence lacking for many of Dawkins' views in *The God Delusion*. Not only has Dawkins re-invented religious belief according to his own negative views, but he has artificially constructed a wall between religion and science when, for many scientists, there is no wall.

The McGraths point to the writings of the evolutionary biologist Stephen Jay Gould. Gould, himself a sceptic of religious belief, said that science and religion represent '**non-overlapping magisteria**' (NOMA). The term magisterium means 'domain of competency'; Gould was referring to the domain of science as the empirical realm and the domain of religion as questions of ultimate meaning. These two realms do not overlap – they each focus on their separate realms of enquiry. The McGraths find this approach widespread amongst scientists. For instance, the astrophysicist Martin Rees says that ultimate questions lie beyond science and that there is never enough evidence to actually prove answers to these questions. The biologist Sir Peter Medawar says that there are three questions that science cannot answer: (i) how did everything begin? (ii) what are we here for? and (iii) what is the point of living? The McGraths actually prefer the concept of POMA (partially overlapping magisterial) to NOMA. This means that science and faith can interpenetrate each other, helping each other to become more informed.

When it comes to natural selection, the McGraths' view is that this is a fact which can be interpreted atheistically, theistically or in any number of other ways. We bring our worldviews to the facts. He accuses Dawkins of confusing the worldview of atheism with the fact of natural selection.

The God of the gaps argument

As we have seen, Dawkins questions the God hypothesis, the idea that God can be invoked to explain a gap in our knowledge. He notes that theologians have often explained gaps by invoking God. One contemporary example he gives is of those who describe themselves as '**Intelligent Design**' theorists. These theorists point to complex features of biology which they think cannot be argued to be a part of the process of natural selection. For instance, how an underdeveloped wing offers survival value to an organism. These theorists propose, as William Paley did, that the only answer is God. Yet Dawkins shows how each of their proposals has failed. For instance, half a wing can be of enormous survival value, increasing the height an animal can jump to escape death, or glide to find food. The Intelligent Design theorists have to retreat to yet another complex aspect of life that does not yet have a natural explanation.

The problem with this strategy is that as the gaps in our knowledge decrease, God becomes increasingly irrelevant, retreating further and further away from daily life. Dawkins notes that since Darwinian evolution explains the complexity of the natural world, gap theologians now pin their remaining hopes on the origin of life. However, as soon as science discovers evidence that points to a theory, then God will have disappeared.

Another way to fill the gap

There is a gap in our lives in the sense that we need to find inspiration and meaning. Dawkins believes that science can fill that gap. In fact, science can fill the four main roles that religion has traditionally filled:

(i)   **Explanation.** By understanding natural selection and scientific ideas that can explain the existence of life in the universe, we no longer need religion to explain life.

(ii)   **Exhortation.** Religion used to exhort us to live moral lives, so much so that people think that religion is the only source of morality. However, it is easy to prove that religious people do not lead more moral lives than non-religious people – you can be good without God. In fact, religion leads, for Dawkins, to violence and segregation (as anecdotal evidence he cites the violent hate mail he has received from Christians).

(iii) **Consolation.** Whilst it is true that religion offers consolation, this does not make it true. One can find many examples of atheists who are consoled not by religion but by discovering new ways of thinking about the world.

(iv) **Inspiration.** One does not need religion to be inspired. Gazing at the sheer grandeur and complexity of life all around us is an endless source of inspiration: 'The fact that we live at the bottom of a deep gravity well, on the surface of a gas-covered planet going around a nuclear fireball ninety million miles away and think this to be *normal* is obviously some indication of how skewed our perspective tends to be.'

Interestingly, Dawkins notes that the theologian Dietrich Bonhoeffer rejected the 'God of the gaps' approach. The McGraths do as well, pointing out that this approach only represents a small portion of Christians and stems from the 18th and 19th centuries. The majority of theologians, according to the McGraths, have viewed the reality of God as intimately and actively involved in all of life.

In fact, say the McGraths, it is not the gaps in our knowledge that require an explanation but the notion that we live in an intelligible and explainable universe. Why do we take the idea that we live in such a universe for granted? They point to the philosopher Richard Swinburne who argues that the best explanation for the fact of the intelligibility of the universe is that it has been created by an intelligent being.

Is religion the axis of evil?

The McGraths share their surprise and disappointment that a fine scientist such as Dawkins could so easily mischaracterise religion as an evil and violent reality. They think that this must be because Dawkins cares more for the eradication of religion than he does about the truth. For the McGraths, there are several facts about religion that Dawkins ignores:

- **The prophetic critique of religion.** Religion is capable of self-critique; this is proved by the prophets of Israel who criticised religious practices when they involved social oppression and transgressed the spirit of the law.

- **The inclusive ministry of Jesus.** Dawkins characterises Jesus as having an in-group mentality, but this ignores the admonition to love one's enemy, the anti-nationalistic tone of the parable of the Good Samaritan, including tax collectors and prostitutes (who had been rejected by the religion of his day) in his movement, and having open dialogue with Gentiles.

- **The capacity of religion to transcend and transform human conflicts.** Some of the biblical passages that Dawkins condemns appear alongside passages that encourage compassion, welcoming the stranger, hospitality, forgiving debt, prohibiting slavery and forbidding infant sacrifice.

- **The danger of an absence of religion.** Without religion, society can turn ideas into idols and commit violence against people who reject those ideas. The McGraths cite the excessive violence that accompanied the French Revolution.

- **The fact that religion is more than belief.** Dawkins reduces religion to dogmatic beliefs and ignores the fact that religion has many dimensions. The faith of believers often goes beyond intellectual assent to the kinds of propositions that Dawkins attacks.

Why, ask the McGraths, does Dawkins ignore the fact that institutionalised atheism, such as practised by the Soviet authorities from 1918 to 1941 led to incredible violence? Furthermore, millions were killed by Pol Pot in the name of

But could it be that God clutters up a gap that we'd be better off filling with something else? Science, perhaps? Art? Human friendship? Humanism? Love of this life in the real world, giving no credence to other lives beyond the grave? A love of nature, or what the great entomologist E. O. Wilson called *Biophilia*? (R. Dawkins)

I write as a Christian, who holds that the face, will and character of God are fully disclosed in Jesus of Nazareth. And as Dawkins knows, Jesus of Nazareth did no violence to anyone. (A. McGrath and J. Collicutt McGrath)

To give a brief summary of his [John Hartung's] thesis, Jesus was a devotee of the same in-group morality – coupled with out-group hostility – that was taken for granted in the Old Testament. Jesus was a loyal Jew. It was Paul who invented the idea of taking the Jewish God to the Gentiles. (R. Dawkins)

socialism. Even when it seems that religion is directly behind violent acts such as the destruction of the Twin Towers on 9/11, there are studies that show that religious belief is not sufficient to alone cause these acts. Social oppression, foreign occupation, and other psychological and material factors are hugely contributing factors. Perhaps, then, religion does not have a 'corner on the market' of violence as Dawkins suggests. Furthermore, there are many studies which indicate that religious belief and commitment had a positive effect on human well-being and longevity. This does not mean that religion is true, but it does mean that assertions of the 'badness' of religion can be proven to be non-scientific in nature.

Scientism or science?

The McGraths accuse Dawkins of confusing **scientism** with science. Scientism is the faith that scientific knowledge and techniques will find answers to everything – this might even include areas currently investigated by philosophy, the social sciences, and the humanities. They base their accusation on the lack of evidence provided for key assertions in *The God Delusion*, the mischaracterisation of religion as violent and the claim that science will provide answers to everything. Dawkins, however, is adamant that he is committed to the evidence – wherever it leads. Thus far it has led away, he says, from a religious point of view on the world. Even though there are questions that science cannot answer at the moment, there is no reason to declare that it has limits. Furthermore, if there is no metaphysical reality beyond the created world, it is quite right to focus on scientific rather than religious answers.

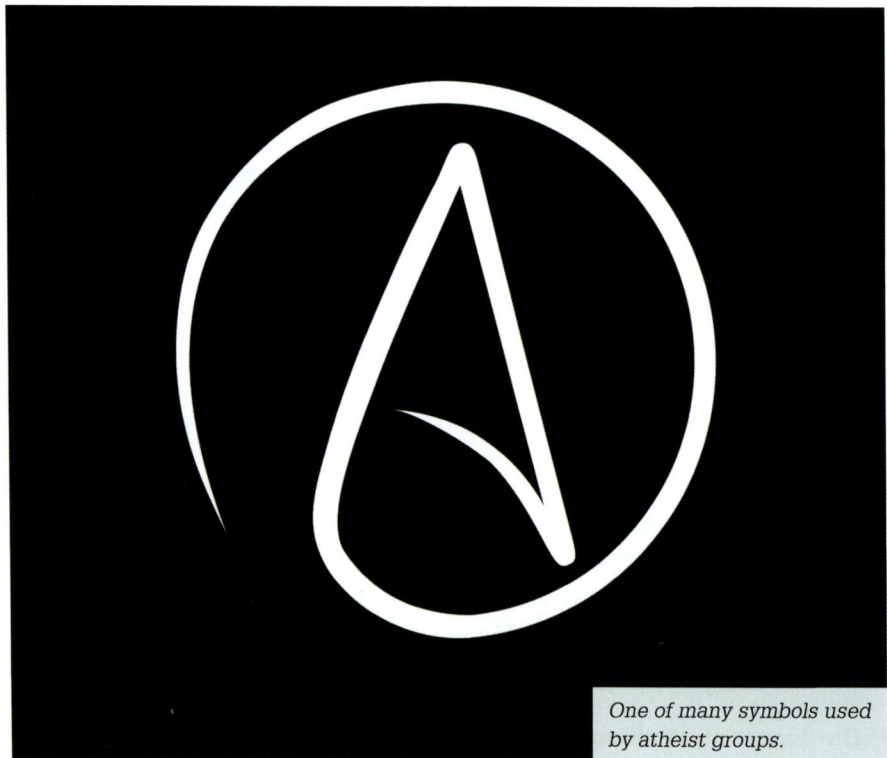

One of many symbols used by atheist groups.

quickfire

3.27 What is one reason that could be cited against the view that religion is necessarily violent?

Key term

Scientism: belief in the universal applicability of scientific knowledge and techniques

AO1 Developing skills

It is now important to consider the information that has been covered in this section; however, the information in its raw form is too extensive and so has to be processed in order to meet the requirements of the examination. This can be achieved by practising more advanced skills associated with AO1. For assessment objective 1 (AO1), which involves demonstrating 'knowledge' and 'understanding' skills, we are going to focus on different ways in which the skills can be demonstrated effectively, and also refer to how the performance of these skills is measured (see generic band descriptors for A2 [WJEC] AO1 or A Level [Eduqas] AO1).

▶ **Your next task is this:** Below is a summary of **the relationship between religion and science according to Richard Dawkins**. It is about 150 words long. This time there are no highlighted points to indicate the key points to learn from this extract. Discuss which five points you think are the most important to highlight and write them down in a list.

Richard Dawkins believes that the assertion that an interventionist God is responsible for the complexity of the natural world is a 'God hypothesis' that should be treated like any other theory. When it is investigated it is found 'wanting' because all it does is to propose a more complicated and improbable solution than the question it seeks to answer. Natural selection, is a better alternative because it explains phenomena by breaking them down into parts. When these scientific facts are combined with observations about the origins of religion (as a misfiring of the brain) and the current reality of religion as inciting violence, hatred and exclusion, then it is clear that religion has no place alongside science. Many scientists, after all, are not religious believers once one sees past their 'faith-friendly' language. Not only does it appear that there are no limits to the questions that science will one day answer, science can provide meaning, inspiration and direction for our lives – roles formerly assumed by religion.

Now make the five points into your own summary (as in Theme 1 Developing skills) trying to make the summary more personal to your style of writing. This may also involve re-ordering the points if you wish to do so.

1 ....
2 ....
3 ....
4 ....
5 ....

Key skills

Knowledge involves:

Selection of a range of (thorough) accurate and relevant information that is directly related to the specific demands of the question.

This means:

- Selecting relevant material for the question set
- Being focused in explaining and examining the material selected.

Understanding involves:

Explanation that is extensive, demonstrating depth and/or breadth with excellent use of evidence and examples including (where appropriate) thorough and accurate supporting use of sacred texts, sources of wisdom and specialist language.

This means:

- Effective use of examples and supporting evidence to establish the quality of your understanding
- Ownership of your explanation that expresses personal knowledge and understanding and NOT just reproducing a chunk of text from a book that you have rehearsed and memorised.

This section covers AO2
content and skills

Specification content

The extent to which a scientist must
be an atheist.

Issues for analysis and evaluation

The extent to which a scientist must be an atheist

Some scientists, such as Richard Dawkins, believe that scientific discovery puts one on a path to atheism. He states that this is the case for many scientists, though we have to be careful to sort out the truth from the rhetoric since many scientists use faith-friendly language. When you look at the statements of Einstein carefully, for example, it becomes clear that his 'religious feeling' has little or nothing to do with traditional belief in God. Dawkins accuses other scientists of making positive statements about religion in order to receive awards from religious bodies or because they genuinely confuse culturally Christian attitudes and traditional Christian belief. If these scientists were to sit down and think about their position, very few would say anything to affirm belief in a supernatural creator.

Yet, even if all scientists were atheists, would this prove that a scientist *must* be an atheist? The McGraths note that many scientists are sceptical of religious belief but see science and religion as two separate spheres of study. The evolutionary biologist Stephen Jay Gould described this with the acronym NOMA (non overlapping magisteria). The astrophysicist Martin Rees says that ultimate questions lie beyond science, and the biologist Sir Peter Medawar points to three questions that science cannot answer: (i) How did everything begin? (ii) What are we here for? And (iii) What is the point of living? Of course, Dawkins could respond that NOMA is merely a strategy to avoid conflict, be polite or that these scientists have not looked closely enough at their scientific point of view.

If atheism and science are fully compatible, then why is it that so many mature, thinking and intelligent human beings come to believe in God as adults or persist in believing despite their having given up other beliefs from childhood such as Santa Claus and the Tooth Fairy? In particular, it is noteworthy that so many scientists believe in God, not in a vague cultural sense but in a specifically Christian sense. Furthermore, a survey conducted twice over an 80-year period show that there was no decrease amongst scientists who believe in a personal God – about 40%.

However, it could be argued that this survey does not give strong evidence that many scientists are believers since it was conducted in the United States where there are cultural pressures to support the prominence of religion. This survey does not, therefore, represent all cultures in all places. It could be that a similar survey conducted in Europe would have shown results not as friendly to religious belief.

Perhaps the strongest claim that can be made against the incompatibility of science and theism is that religious belief is a biological and psychological aberration (irregularity). Therefore, it has no value in our quest for knowledge and can even act to deter us from the quest for truth. This is the view of Dawkins who describes religion as a 'misfiring of the brain', like a moth who, despite a functioning navigation system, flies into the flames. In other words, religion represents undesirable traits that are associated with qualities that give us survival value: the tendency to obey elders and the tendency to ascribe meaning and purpose to the natural world. These tendencies 'work' most of the time, keeping us from danger and death. However, elders can make mistakes and we can be mistaken ourselves when we ascribe meaning to inanimate objects. Viewed in this way, religion is neither vital nor helpful to life, much less the scientific quest for truth.

Key quote

Every worldview, whether religious or not, has its point of vulnerability; there is a tension between theory and experience, raising questions over the coherence and trustworthiness of the worldview itself. In the case of Christianity, many locate that point of weakness in the existence of suffering within the world. In the case of atheism, it is the persistence of belief in God, when there is supposedly no God in which to believe. (A. McGrath and J. Collicutt McGrath)

AO2 Activity

As you read through this section try to do the following:

1. Pick out the different lines of argument that are presented in the text and identify any evidence given in support.

2. For each line of argument try to evaluate whether or not you think this is strong or weak.

3. Think of any questions you may wish to raise in response to the arguments.

This activity will help you to start thinking critically about what you read, and help you to evaluate the effectiveness of different arguments and from this develop your own observations, opinions and points of view that will help with any conclusions that you make in your answers to the AO2 questions that arise.

But where is the evidence for this explanatory theory of religion? The McGraths view these theories as representing the opposite of what science is about: the quest for evidence. Dawkins would say that the evidence is all around us: the events of 9/11, the extreme beliefs of terrorists, the long history of religiously motivated wars, the segregation and dehumanisation of people based on their religious beliefs (or lack of them), the suppression of scientific truth by the Church and other religious bodies. Does not the bloodshed, violence and repression in the name of religion provide more than enough evidence of the incompatibility of religion and science?

However, this characterisation of religion is not based on a scientific and rational assessment of the role religion plays on the planet. For, it does not take into account the many aspects of religion which have actually been a part of transcending conflicts in the world – one could cite Desmond Tutu's Truth and Reconciliation Commission which drew upon Christian values of compassion in the healing of South Africa after Apartheid, the many humanitarian efforts sponsored in the name of religion, and the many sacrificial acts of kindness and love by religiously motivated individuals. Simply considering the Judeo-Christian tradition, we see the power of religion to critique itself when it loses a humanitarian focus (the prophets). Furthermore, the ministry of Jesus was fully inclusive, reaching past barriers of cultural impurity and ethnicity (the parable of the Good Samaritan and the inclusion of tax collectors and prostitutes in the Jesus movement). Of course, the admonition to love one's enemies does not seem likely to promote violence!

Furthermore, one has to ask what happens in places where religion is eradicated or suppressed? Does this entail less violence and scientific progress? The McGraths point to the violence of institutionalised atheism in Soviet Russian from 1918 to 1941 and the murder of millions in the name of socialism by Pol Pot in Cambodia. Moreover, the tendency to deify ideals when religion is absent – and persecute people who do not agree with these ideas (such as in the French Revolution), suggests that the tendency to violence and intolerance is deeper than religion.

There are studies that show that religious belief is related to a sense of well-being and longevity. This does not mean that religion is true but that more science might get accomplished with these factors in place!

In conclusion, it is true that religion can get in the way of science. This can happen on both collective and individual levels. There are times when communities have hindered progress in the name of religious truth. It is also possible that individual scientists may not think through their observations to an anti-religious conclusion because of social or family pressures. But these facts are not true in all times and in all places; there are many scientists who conduct research and push forward the frontiers of science whilst holding religious beliefs. The proposal that scientists who are also believers in God are a variation of the 'scientific species' that will inevitably 'die out' is a matter of faith rather than of certainty – at least until more evidence can be found.

Key quotes

I think we should all wince when we hear a small child being labelled as belonging to some particular religion or another. Small children are too young to decide their views on the origins of the cosmos, life and morals. The very sound of the phrase, 'Christian child' or 'Muslim child' should grate like fingernails on a blackboard. (R. Dawkins)

Dawkins is forced to contend with the highly awkward fact that his views that the natural sciences are an intellectual superhighway to atheism are rejected by most scientists, irrespective of their religious views. (A. McGrath and J. Collicutt McGrath)

Key quotes

… the knowledge that we have only one life should make it all the more precious. The atheist view is correspondingly life-affirming and life-enhancing, while at the same time never being tainted by self-delusion, wishful thinking, or the whingeing self-pity of those who feel that life owes them something. (R. Dawkins)

When I read *The God Delusion* I was both saddened and troubled. How, I wondered, could such a gifted populariser of the natural sciences, who once had such a passionate concern for the objective analysis of the evidence, turn into such an aggressive anti-religious propagandist, with an apparent disregard for evidence that was not favourable to his case? (A. McGrath and J. Collicutt McGrath)

AO2 Activity

List some conclusions that could be drawn from the AO2 reasoning from the above text; try to aim for at least three different possible conclusions. Consider each of the conclusions and collect brief evidence to support each conclusion from the AO1 and AO2 material for this topic. Select the conclusion that you think is most convincing and explain why it is so. Try to contrast this with the weakest conclusion in the list, justifying your argument with clear reasoning and evidence.

Specification content

Whether science has reduced the role
of God in Christianity.

Whether science has reduced the role of God in Christianity

We are all familiar with certain beliefs fading from our lives such as childhood notions of Santa Claus, the Tooth Fairy and other fictional beings. Belief in these 'entities' might have been encouraged by our family and we might have even had evidence to support these beliefs (the appearance of money in place of our tooth or the sound of footsteps on the roof on Christmas Eve). Yet, as we grew up and saw that there were other explanations for these phenomena, they faded into quaint remnants of our childhood memories. Is belief in God like these beliefs – destined to fade only to be remembered as a quaint aspect of human life?

It can be argued that science has already replaced the role of God in Christianity in one significant area: by providing an answer to the appearance of complex design in the natural world. Many religious believers have posited God as the explanation for the wonders of the natural world. However, with the discovery by Darwin of the processes of natural selection, a much more believable approach has been found. We no longer need to posit a highly improbable complicated being as the solution to the existence of a highly improbable and complicated natural world (a solution which really raises more questions than it solves). Instead, natural selection provides a simple and elegant explanation to the rise of complex life forms.

However, this does not mean that science has an explanation for all mysteries. The largest mystery of all is why there is something and not nothing. In other words, natural selection cannot explain why there is life on our planet and why the universe is such that it can give rise to life. Don't we need to posit God to explain these areas?

Why keep turning to a 'God hypothesis?' asks Richard Dawkins. If natural selection has proven anything, it has shown us that it is possible to find solutions to life's biggest questions without invoking God. If we focus on just the existence of life on our one planet, it certainly seems improbable that this should be the case. Dawkins asks us to consider the fact that there are billions and billions of planets and that we have the good fortune to exist on the one planet which had the right conditions for life. This is known as the 'anthropic principle' because it asks us to begin not with God but with the fact that we humans exist. If we exist, then the earth must be a life-friendly place. Instead of asking how God made this so, we ask what considerations were in place on the earth for this to be the case – this is the scientific quest. On the question of why the universe is fine-tuned for the emergence of life, Dawkins suggests that one scientific approach would be to consider multiverse theory: our universe just happens to be the one of billions of universes with the necessary variations to produce life.

Yet these are just theories without the kind of evidence to support them that natural selection has achieved. In light of this, does it not make sense to posit God as the creator of life? Dawkins is convinced that this is really just another 'gaps' argument – we invoke God when we do not have an explanation. However, when we do have an explanation, God retreats until 'he' finally becomes irrelevant.

In addition, do all Christians take a 'God of the gaps' approach? The McGraths say, 'no'. The 'gaps' approach is associated with William Paley and was popular in the 18th and 19th centuries. Many Christian thinkers reject this approach altogether, instead seeing God as actively sustaining all of life. In fact, McGrath points out that evolution through natural selection is a fact that is fully compatible with theistic belief. This is because we can bring different interpretations (theistic, atheistic, polytheistic, etc.) to different facts that we come across.

Furthermore, it can be argued that the assumption that God is retreating is not at all a fact but a 'worldview', a bias that Dawkins brings to the facts. Instead of

AO2 Activity

As you read through this section try to do the following:

1. Pick out the different lines of argument that are presented in the text and identify any evidence given in support.

2. For each line of argument try to evaluate whether or not you think this is strong or weak.

3. Think of any questions you may wish to raise in response to the arguments.

This activity will help you to start thinking critically about what you read, and help you to evaluate the effectiveness of different arguments and from this develop your own observations, opinions and points of view that will help with any conclusions that you make in your answers to the AO2 questions that arise.

Christians having to justify their 'fading' beliefs in front of 'advancing' science, it can be said that science has not offered an explanation for one of the most important facts of all: that we live in an intelligible world. Richard Swinburne says that the most convincing explanation for this fact is that there is an intelligent being behind all that we see and know. It is this compelling idea that may be the reason that many scientists persist in their faith in God, despite the many claims of atheism. Furthermore, the fact that belief in God is so prevalent in the world is not what we would expect if belief in God were really the same as belief in Santa Claus or the Tooth Fairy.

Of course, it could be argued that Swinburne's view simply returns us to the main problem of suggesting God as a solution: it is not convincing to suggest a highly improbable and complicated solution for a highly improbable and complex fact. Science attempts to show how complex problems can be explained in terms of smaller and less complex interactions – exactly what the theory of natural selection achieves.

Furthermore, belief in God could be said to persist because people are afraid that they will not be able to fill the gap in their need for meaning, purpose and direction without belief in God. Dawkins believes that science is able to fill this gap. We can find consolation through finding new ways of observing the world around us, inspiration through grasping the wonders of the natural world, explanations for our deepest questions from new scientific theories and moral guidance from a humanistic basis which does not lead us to the segregation and violence that is so often a part of the religious scene.

In conclusion, it has to be admitted that there are scientific explanations for many phenomena that have been attributed to God. Natural selection is but one theory that has accomplished this and it would be silly to think that there will not be more theories to cover other areas for which we still have questions. However, there are phenomena that science has not yet explained. The idea that science will one day explain everything could be called scientism, a new kind of faith. On the other hand, if there is no metaphysical basis for life, science may one day replace the God that religious believers worship.

Key quotes

It is astonishing, moreover, how many people are unable to understand that 'X is comforting' does not imply 'X is true'. (R. Dawkins)

Dawkins' criticism of those who 'worship the gaps', despite its overstatements, is clearly appropriate and valid. So we must thank him for helping us kill off this outdated false turn in the history of Christian apologetics. It is a good example of how a dialogue between science and Christian theology can lead to some useful outcomes. (A. McGrath and J. Collicutt McGrath)

Obviously, there are exceptions, but I suspect that for many people the main reason they cling to religion is not that it is consoling, but that they have been let down by our educational system and don't realise that non-belief is even an option. This is certainly true of most people who think they are creationists. (R. Dawkins)

AO2 Activity

List some conclusions that could be drawn from the AO2 reasoning from the above text; try to aim for at least three different possible conclusions. Consider each of the conclusions and collect brief evidence to support each conclusion from the AO1 and AO2 material for this topic. Select the conclusion that you think is most convincing and explain why it is so. Try to contrast this with the weakest conclusion in the list, justifying your argument with clear reasoning and evidence.

Key skills

Analysis involves:

Identifying issues raised by the materials in the AO1, together with those identified in the AO2 section, and presents sustained and clear views, either of scholars or from a personal perspective ready for evaluation.

This means:

- That your answers are able to identify key areas of debate in relation to a particular issue
- That you can identify, and comment upon, the different lines of argument presented by others
- That your response comments on the overall effectiveness of each of these areas or arguments.

Evaluation involves:

Considering the various implications of the issues raised based upon the evidence gleaned from analysis and providing an extensive detailed argument with a clear conclusion.

This means:

- That your answer weighs up the consequences of accepting or rejecting the various and different lines of argument analysed
- That your answer arrives at a conclusion through a clear process of reasoning.

AO2 Developing skills

It is now important to consider the information that has been covered in this section; however, the information in its raw form is too extensive and so has to be processed in order to meet the requirements of the examination. This can be achieved by practising more advanced skills associated with AO2. For assessment objective 2 (AO2), which involves 'critical analysis' and 'evaluation' skills, we are going to focus on different ways in which the skills can be demonstrated effectively, and also refer to how the performance of these skills is measured (see generic band descriptors for A2 [WJEC] AO2 or A Level [Eduqas] AO2).

▶ **Your next task is this:** Below is an evaluation concerning **religion as a destructive and violent force in the world, antithetical to science**. It is 150 words long. After the first paragraph, there is an intermediate conclusion highlighted for you in yellow. As a group try to identify where you could add more intermediate conclusions to the rest of the passage. Have a go at doing this.

Alister McGrath and Joanna Collicutt McGrath raise a number of arguments against Dawkins' portrayal of religion. First, where is the evidence for the assertion that religion is a misfiring of the brain? We would expect that an assertion involving biology would be backed up with observations. Furthermore, the assertion that religion is the dark side of the traits of obeying elders and attributing intention to the environment appears to be merely a suggestion. It seems then, that the Dawkins' view of the origin of religion is based on opinion rather than fact.

When one examines religion, one finds many positive aspects. Studies indicate that it contributes positively to health and longevity. Furthermore, the ethics of the prophets and of Jesus seem to lead in an opposite direction to violence: critique of inhumanity amongst religious leaders, the admonition to love one's enemy, teaching on compassion, etc. Furthermore, there are times in history when religion has acted as a force for healing and reconciliation. None of these observations mean that religion is true, of course, but they help to provide a more complete picture of religion.

When you have done this, you will see clearly that in AO2 it is helpful to include a brief summary of the arguments presented as you go through an answer and not just leave it until the end to draw a final conclusion. This way you are demonstrating that you are sustaining evaluation throughout an answer and not just repeating information learned.

This section covers AO1 content and skills

F: Challenges from pluralism and diversity within a tradition

The exclusivist and inclusivist views expressed in the Christian Bible (Deut. 6:5; Joshua 23:16; John 14:6; Acts 4:12)

What do Christians believe about people in other religions? Do they think they are morally, ethically and spiritually depraved – and going to hell? Or, do they believe that there is wisdom and truth in other religions? If Christians think there is truth in other religions, what does that mean for the status of their own beliefs? Are all religions of equal value?

Broadly speaking, theologians have taken three views on the potential for salvation for those who are not Christians. The first of these is **exclusivism**: salvation exclusively belongs to Christianity – there are no other paths. Some exclusivists, though not all, have thought that everyone who is not a Christian will be damned. However, this position has been considered too harsh by many. This is because there are many people who have never known Christianity, will never know it, or are in societies where it is unlikely that Christianity will ever be a serious option. This has led to **inclusivism**; Christ's work somehow 'includes' all people – though the fullest expression of salvation is found in explicitly knowing Christ and belonging to his Church. More recently a third option has appeared, though it is seen as too radical to be accepted by any major Christian denomination: **religious pluralism**. Religious pluralism views Christianity as the way to God for Christians only; other religions have equally valid paths to divine reality. In a broader sense the term pluralism extends to the idea of different communities and cultures fostering tolerance and living side by side.

AO1 Activity

Go online and find the popular evangelical Protestant Christian statement '4 Spiritual Laws'. Read it and then consider if it is an example of exclusivism, inclusivism or pluralism.

Exclusivism

There are passages in the Bible that seem to reflect the exclusivist viewpoint. In the Hebrew scriptures, God called out a group of people to follow him and commanded that they dedicate themselves to exclusive worship: 'You shall love the Lord your God with all your heart, and with all your soul, and with all your might.' (Deuteronomy 6:5) Furthermore, to turn away from this exclusive worship of God had negative consequences: 'If you transgress the covenant of the Lord your God, which he enjoined on you, and go and serve other gods and bow down to them, then the anger of the Lord will be kindled against you, and you shall perish quickly from the good land that he has given to you.' (Joshua 23:16).

In the New Testament, Jesus appears to echo these exclusivist views: 'Jesus said to him, "I am the way, and the truth, and the life. No one comes to the Father except through me."' (John 14:6). The early church is quite clear that salvation is only to be found in Jesus: 'There is salvation in no one else, for there is no other name under heaven given among mortals by which we must be saved.' (Acts 4:12). Clearly the plain sense of these passages is that Christianity provides the only path to God. These are far from the only exclusivist passages in the Bible – there are a number of verses which speak of condemnation for unbelief and eternal punishment (for instance, see: Matthew 13:50, John 3:18, Revelation 21:8).

Specification content

Difference between religious pluralism and tolerance of religious diversity; the exclusivist and inclusivist views expressed in the Christian Bible (Deut. 6:5; Joshua 23:16; John 14:6; Acts 4:12).

Key terms

Exclusivism: the view that one's own religion is the only way to salvation/liberation

Inclusivism: the view that one's religion is the 'final' way to salvation/liberation; there may be other religions which have partial or incomplete truth

Religious pluralism: the view that all religions, in different ways, reflect divine truth, or Ultimate Reality

quickfire

3.28 Which of the three views of salvation is least found as the official teaching of Christian churches?

Theological statements developed that were exclusive in nature such as the dogma *extra ecclesiam nulla salus* ('outside of the Church, no salvation'). This phrase comes from the 3rd-century Christian theologian Cyprian of Carthage and continues to be a part of Catholic teaching. Many Protestants have a similar approach, but, because of a different view of the Church, express their exclusivism as 'no salvation outside of faith in Christ'. The message is essentially the same: if one wants to be saved by God and live the way God wants us to live, one had better become a Christian.

The contribution of Karl Rahner

Karl Rahner (1904–1984) was one of the most important Roman Catholic theologians of the twentieth century; his views were a major influence on the documents produced by Vatican II, the assembly of Roman Catholic leaders who reconsidered Church practice and theology in the 1960s.

Rahner thought it was possible to make a positive use of modern philosophy while, at the same time, holding true to Catholic doctrine. One of his central ideas was that all human beings have an awareness of something beyond the finite realm. All things, persons and events are a part of a larger horizon, an infinite reality – God. When we think about particular, finite things, we are, whether we know it or not, reaching out beyond these things to an infinite reality which is God. Thus, it is possible for people to have an implicit awareness of God without explicitly knowing that this is the case. Furthermore, Rahner believed that God is actively offering grace to all people, wherever they are, in whatever religion (or non-religion) they may be involved.

Key quotes

Rahner's rather daring claim then, is that everyone is in some sense aware of God whether they realise it or not, and that all our most pedestrian dealings with the world would in fact be impossible without this awareness. (K. Kilby)

… grace … always surrounds man, even the sinner and the unbeliever, as the inescapable setting of his existence. (K. Rahner)

Study tip

This section explores Christian inclusivism from Rahner's Catholic point of view. Do your own research to find Protestant Christian expressions of inclusivism. You can search 'inclusivism vs. exclusivism' on Google to find these.

Specification content

The contribution of John Hick and Karl Rahner to Christian inclusivism (and the difference between their positions).

A session of the second Vatican council in St Peter's Basilica, 1962

Key terms

Extra ecclesiam nulla salus: Latin for 'outside the Church, no salvation'

Vatican II: the council of Roman Catholic leaders that met in 1962–1965 to consider the relationship between the Church and the modern world

Key quote

… every human being is really and truly exposed to the influence of the divine, supernatural grace which offers an interior union with God and by means of which God communicates himself whether the individual takes up an attitude of acceptance or of refusal towards this grace. (K. Rahner)

Karl Rahner, 1904–1984

Anonymous Christianity

Because God is active everywhere in all experiences, offering grace and the opportunity to respond to 'his' presence, Rahner felt that the Church should not view those outside of it as merely 'non-Christians' but as **anonymous Christians**. An anonymous Christian is one who responds to God's presence but may not be explicitly aware of God, and is certainly not aware of God's full expression in Christ and the Church. In one of his most famous essays, 'Christianity and the Non-Christian Religions', Rahner develops this idea in four theses:

1st Thesis: *'... Christianity understands itself as the absolute religion, intended for all men, which cannot recognise any other religion beside itself as of equal right.'* For Rahner, this thesis is necessary since the Church believes that God has chosen to relate to the world though 'his' incarnation as Christ. However, Christianity has a starting point in time and space and, prior to this, God did not demand explicit assent to Christianity – there were other ways to come to God, even though from God's point of view these ways were all through a single plan. The question that Rahner raises is whether there can be other ways to come to God in the present. Does God really expect for people to know Christ if Christianity has not become a real factor in their personal history and society?

2nd Thesis: *'... a non-Christian religion can be recognised as a lawful religion (although only in different degrees) without thereby denying the error and depravity contained in it.'* By **'lawful religion'** Rahner means a religion that provides a way for people to find a right relationship with God. Christians normally associate 'lawful religion'; with Christianity – but Rahner introduces the idea that there may be other lawful religions to a greater or lesser degree. For instance, in the Old Testament there were people who pleased God but were outside of God's 'lawful religion' of Judaism. Rahner calls this the theme of the 'God-pleasing pagan'. These people surely must have been involved in other religions – yet they pleased God. Furthermore, Paul in Acts 17 refers positively to pagan religion. God wants to reach out to all human beings with salvation; this means that every single person must have the possibility of a genuine saving relationship to God. Yet, there are many places where the message of Christianity cannot be heard (or not be *truly* heard by individuals who are immersed in their own culture and traditions). Therefore, we must be open, says Rahner, to the idea that God uses other religions to reach people. This does not mean that everything in these religions is true and right, but merely that God is using it as a part of his plan of salvation.

3rd Thesis: *'If the second thesis is correct, then Christianity does not simply confront the member of an extra-Christian religion as a mere non-Christian but as someone who can and must already be regarded in this or that respect as an anonymous Christian.'* Rahner wants the Church to recognise that even before missionaries arrive to proclaim their message, God has already been at work. This does not mean, however, that Christianity is not needed. For, becoming a Christian is the final step of a process that begins with anonymous Christianity. Those who are anonymous Christians might, at some point, recognise that God intends them to experience the 'higher stage of development' of their faith through belief in Christ and participation in the Church. In the meantime, the Church should have an attitude of respect for those it is trying to reach with its message.

4th Thesis: *'... the Church will not so much regard herself today as the exclusive community of those who have a claim to salvation but rather as the historically tangible vanguard and the historically and socially constituted explicit expression of what the Christian hopes is present as a hidden reality even outside the visible Church.'* Here, Rahner is trying to change the attitude of the Church. The Church should not see itself as the sole possessor of truth and goodness opposed to all who are outside of it. Instead, it should remember that God is greater than the Church, working beyond its walls through the reality of religious pluralism. At the same time it

Key quotes

... the actual religions of 'pre-Christian' humanity too must not be regarded as simply illegitimate from the very start, but must be seen as quite capable of having a positive significance. **(K. Rahner)**

If, however, man can always have a positive, saving relationship to God, and if he always had to have it, then he has always had it within *that* religion which in practice was at his disposal by being a factor in his sphere of existence. **(K. Rahner)**

... the Church is not the communion of those who possess God's grace as opposed to those who lack it, but is the communion of those who can explicitly confess what they *and* the others hope to be. **(K. Rahner)**

Theology has been too long and too often bedevilled by the unavowed supposition that grace would be no longer grace if it were too generously distributed by the love of God! **(K. Rahner)**

quickfire

3.29 Which New Testament passage does Rahner think reinforces his idea that God works in religions other than Christianity?

Key terms

Anonymous Christian: Karl Rahner's description of a person who attains salvation outside of knowing and accepting Christ and the Church

Lawful religion: a religion that contains God's grace. Rahner believed that all religions could be lawful, though to different degrees

Read the statements below and then give yourself two minutes to create a summary of their contents in your own words. Also: Imagine that someone from another religion were reading these statements. What are some passages they might like? What are some things they might object to?

should be thankful that it is knows the full expression of God. Rahner ends his essay by urging the Church to have the attitude of St Paul when he said to the Greeks, 'What therefore you do now know and yet worship (and yet worship! [Rahner's emphasis]) that I proclaim to you.' (Acts 17:23)

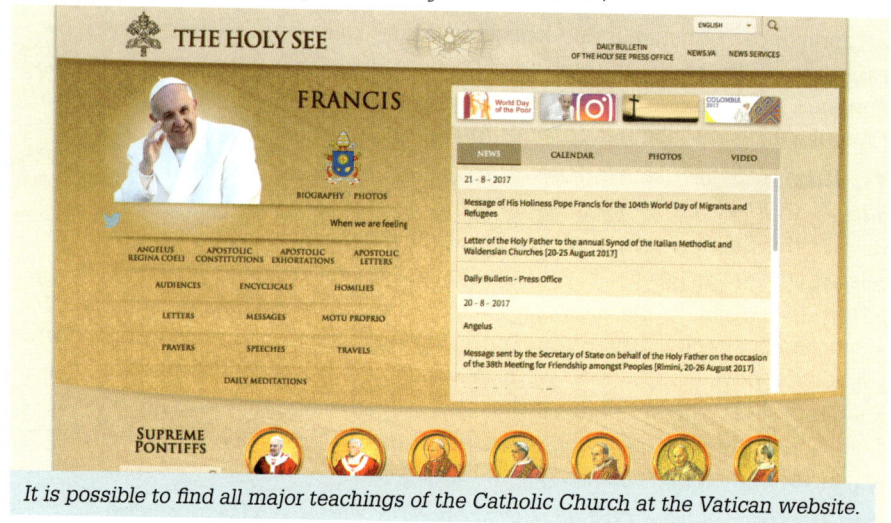

It is possible to find all major teachings of the Catholic Church at the Vatican website.

Inclusivism as Church doctrine

Rahner's stress on God's work outside of the Church was one of many contributing factors to statements by the Catholic Church at Vatican II. Here are some short excerpts from key texts in which you might see some of his ideas reflected:

Nostra Aetate ('In Our Time')

In our time, when day by day mankind is being drawn closer together, and the ties between different peoples are becoming stronger, the Church examines more closely her relationship to non-Christian religions. In her task of promoting unity and love among men, indeed among nations, she considers above all in this declaration what men have in common and what draws them to fellowship.

... From ancient times down to the present, there is found among various peoples a certain perception of that hidden power which hovers over the course of things and over the events of human history; at times some indeed have come to the recognition of a Supreme Being, or even of a Father. This perception and recognition penetrates their lives with a profound religious sense. ... The Catholic Church rejects nothing that is true and holy in these religions. She regards with sincere reverence those ways of conduct and of life, those precepts and teachings which, though differing in many aspects from the ones she holds and sets forth, nonetheless often reflect a ray of that Truth which enlightens all men. Indeed, she proclaims, and ever must proclaim Christ 'the way, the truth, and the life' (John 14:6), in whom men may find the fullness of religious life, in whom God has reconciled all things to Himself. The Church, therefore, exhorts her sons, that through dialogue and collaboration with the followers of other religions, carried out with prudence and love and in witness to the Christian faith and life, they recognise, preserve and promote the good things, spiritual and moral, as well as the socio-cultural values found among these men. ... (Vatican II)

Lumen Gentium ('Light for the Nations')

... Nor is God far distant from those who in shadows and images seek the unknown God, for it is He who gives to all men life and breath and all things, and as Saviour wills that all men be saved. Those also can attain to salvation who through no fault of their own do not know the Gospel of Christ or His Church, yet sincerely seek God and moved by grace strive by their deeds to do His will as it is known to them through the dictates of conscience. Nor does Divine Providence deny the helps necessary for salvation to those who, without blame on their part, have not yet arrived at an explicit knowledge of God and with His grace strive to live a good life. Whatever good or truth is found amongst them is looked upon by the Church as a preparation for the Gospel. She knows that it is given by Him who enlightens all men so that they may finally have life. But often men, deceived by the Evil One, have become vain in their reasonings and have exchanged the truth of God for a lie, serving the creature rather than the Creator. Or some there are who, living and dying in this world without God, are exposed to final despair. Wherefore to promote the glory of God and procure the salvation of all of these, and mindful of the command of the Lord, 'Preach the Gospel to every creature', the Church fosters the missions with care and attention. ... (Vatican II)

The contribution of John Hick

John Hick notes that for many centuries we used to think that the earth was the centre of the universe. Ptolemy was the Greek mathematician and astronomer who conceived of the sun, planets and the stars as rotating around the earth. However, as astronomers noticed more details about how the planets actually moved, it became difficult to maintain this theory. Rather than to abandon the notion of the earth at the centre of the universe, astronomers conceived that the planets moved in a series of smaller circles within their orbit, called epicycles. Thinking in this complicated way enabled these thinkers to maintain their belief that the earth really was the centre of the universe.

Then came the Copernican revolution: it is the sun and not the earth that is the centre of universe. The earth is just one of several planets that circle the sun. Suddenly, the complicated theory of epicycles was no longer needed and the science of astronomy took a large leap forward.

A Copernican revolution for theology

John Hick believes that a Copernican revolution is needed today in theology. For centuries, Christian theologians have believed that Christ was the centre of the religious universe, that all of the world's religions, whether they knew it or not, were circling Christianity. However, this was, according to Hick, a 'Ptolemaic' way of thinking. What is needed is the realisation that Christianity is, like other religions, circling something else, which Hick calls 'Ultimate Reality'. We need to move from a Christocentric or ecclesio-centric universe (the Church or Christianity at the centre) to a theocentric one (God/Ultimate Reality at the centre).

Key quotes

… the Copernican revolution … involves a shift from the dogma that Christianity is at the centre to the realisation that it is *God* who is at the centre, and that all the religions of mankind, including our own, serve and revolve around him. (J. Hick)

Let us begin with the recognition, which is made in all the main religious traditions, that the ultimate divine reality is infinite and as such transcends the grasp of the human mind. God, to use our Christian term, is infinite. (J. Hick)

A depiction of the Ptolemaic universe – note the Earth at the centre.

Key quotes

Can we then accept the conclusion that the God of love who seeks to save all mankind has nevertheless ordained that men must be saved in such a way that only a small minority can in fact receive this salvation? It is the weight of this moral contradiction that has driven Christian thinkers in modern times to explore other ways of understanding the human religious situation. (J. Hick)

Rahner's is a brave attempt to attain an inclusivist position which is in principle universal but which does not thereby renounce the old exclusivist dogma. But the question is whether in this new context the old dogma has not been so emptied of content as no longer to be worth affirming. (J. Hick)

Key terms

Christocentric: Christ as the centre of the experience of salvation/liberation

Ecclesio-centric: the Church as the centre of the experience of salvation/liberation

Theocentric: God as the centre of the experience of salvation/liberation

Ultimate Reality: Hick's term to describe the object of religious belief for the world's religions

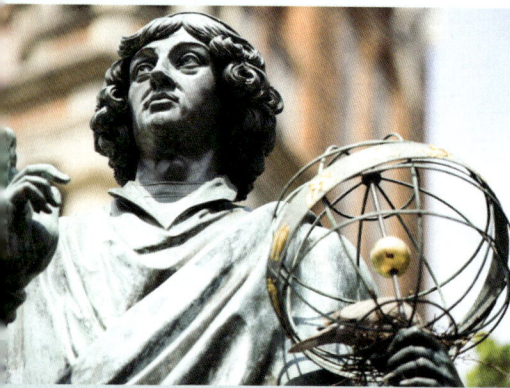

Monument to Nicolaus Copernicus, famed for his model of the solar system with the sun at the centre.

One of John Hick's many books, The Rainbow of Faiths argues that behind all of the religions is a single, ultimate reality, like 'white', un-refracted light. The religions, like the colour spectrum, reflect this single reality each in their own way.

quickfire

3.31 What kind of revolution does Hick want to see in theology?

Hick: Inclusivism is an awkward epicycle

Theologians through the centuries realised that there were spiritual people and profound truths to be found outside of Christianity – how could they account for these whilst holding to the Church/Christ as centre of the theological universe? Like astronomers of old, they created their own version of 'epicycles', adjustments to the theory so it could still work. This entailed viewing God as forgiving to those in other religions who did not have a chance to know Christ. Furthermore, those outside of Christianity could be viewed as having 'implicit faith' – they would accept Christ if they had the opportunity to. Without this opportunity, they could be seen as possessing the 'baptism of desire' (that is, their desire to live in a right way could be counted as baptism). Hick sees Rahner's theory of anonymous Christians as well as Vatican II statements about truth in other religions as further epicycles.

In fact, Hick attacks inclusivist theology for failing to recognise one central fact: that Ptolemaic theology often depends on where a believer happens to be born. We now know enough about the world to say that most people born in India, who study within certain traditions will form a Hindu inclusivism. Other people elsewhere in the world might form a Muslim, Buddhist, Sikh, or Jewish inclusivism – seeing their religion as the centre of the universe with the other religions as distant planets, perhaps having some truth but always less than the planet at the centre. Why, asks Hick, do we not see this thinking for what it is: an outdated and perhaps imperialistic way of looking at the world.

Further criticisms of inclusivism

The inclusive approach does not give up the exclusivist message that one cannot be saved outside the Church (exclusivist Catholic Christianity) or outside of Christ (exclusivist Protestant Christianity). At the same time, it reaches to a new understanding of the world where many people seem to live spiritually rich lives who will never hear the Christian message. So, it sees that salvation is taking place for some people who have no conscious connection with Christ, the Christian Church or the Christian message. For Hick, this seems like sticking a 'Christian label' on people and predicting that they will one day (perhaps at the end of time) become a part of the Christian Church. However, the question that must be asked, says Hick, is if the old exclusivist message has been emptied of content, is it still worth affirming? That is, once people in other religions are viewed as having access to truth in ways that lead to fulfilling lives in God's eyes, is there really any meaningful tie to traditional theology? Would it not be better to move to a position which affirms that all people can potentially be on different paths leading to one Ultimate Reality?

Study tip

To firm up your understanding of some of the key issues, find an example online of criticisms against pluralism by more conservative or traditional Christian believers – there are many! Reading their criticisms will reinforce many of the main issues covered in this section.

One further question has to do with the inclusivist claim that though all people can come to a partial truth in their own religion, the full truth is only to be found in Christianity. This would presumably include the fact that though one could attain a changed and elevated moral life in one's own religion, one could reach even greater spiritual heights by being a Christian. If this were true, then one would expect to find more 'saintliness' in Christianity compared to other religions. This does not appear to be the case, says Hick, though it is hard to tell how this could ever be measured!

Pluralistic universalism

John Hick argues for a philosophy of religious pluralism, the belief that there is a common experiential basis underlying all the major world religions. This common basis moves us from self-centredness to 'Reality-centredness'. In developing this idea, Hick was influenced by both his philosophical reflections as well as his experience of attending worship services of different religious communities.

In the field of Philosophy, Hick, following Kant, came to the view that though there is a reality that is beyond our sense perceptions (the 'noumenal' realm), we are strongly empirical creatures; we interpret reality through our senses in our historical, social and cultural contexts. This means that we never have direct access to the noumenal realm; we can only know something through our interpretation of it. The noumenon (that which is beyond the senses) is always a phenomenon (something we grasp through our interpretation).

Even statements about religion and God are 'phenomenal' – coloured by our own unique language, history, culture, geography, etc. However, when you study many religions in all their differences, there appears, for Hick, to be a common core, a 'noumenal' reality behind them. The analogy that Hick uses to explain this is the refracted light from the sun. The earth's atmosphere refracts the light from the sun into different colours of the rainbow: 'Perhaps the ultimate light of the universal divine presence is refracted by our different human religious cultures into the spectrum of the different world faiths. Or, in the words of the medieval Sufi thinker, Jalaluldin Rumi, 'The lamps are different but the Light is the same: it comes from Beyond.'

In 1967, when Hick arrived in Birmingham to teach theology, he became interested in the ethnic diversity in the city and wanted to play a part in reducing interracial tensions through an appreciation of the many religions represented. So, he began visiting the many religious communities and attending religious services. When he did this, he noticed many differences between them in the concepts, the scriptures and the many ways of worship. However, he also noticed one element common to them all: when women and men came together in their religious place of worship, their hearts and minds could be opened to a higher reality which called them to live an ethical life. Hick viewed this as reflecting his views of the phenomenal and noumenal realms: these religions had many different human phenomena, but seemed to bear witness to one noumenal reality.

Key quote

Pluralism, then, is the view that the transformation of human existence from self-centredness to Reality-centredness is taking place in different ways within the contexts of all the great religious traditions. There is not merely one way but a plurality of ways of salvation or liberation. (J. Hick)

Hick's theory of religious experience

These philosophical insights and observations about religious communities led Hick to form a theory of religious experience. At the heart of religion is an experience of the divine world that raises us beyond our mundane life in the material world. In this experience we are called away from a self-centred life and opened up to a new world. When we attempt to communicate these experiences, we have to use culturally conditioned language, and express our experience through stories or myths that make use of cultural concepts. Over time, religious traditions harden this language into doctrine. These doctrines develop and are viewed as absolute by believers in that religious tradition. This absolutism, in turn, breeds intolerance and feeds into violence, war and inhumanity. However, the problem isn't religion itself but the turning away from religious experience. Hick believes strongly that the heart of religion is not scripture or tradition but experience. In fact, religious

Specification content

The differences between Christian universalism and pluralistic universalism.

Key quotes

If … salvation is understood as the actual transformation of human life from self-centredness to Reality centredness, this is not necessarily restricted within the boundaries of any one historical tradition. (J. Hick)

But if we look for the transcendence of egoism and a recentring in God or in the transcendent Real, then I venture the proposition that, so far as human observation and historical memory can tell, this occurs to about the same extent within each of the great world religions. (J. Hick)

quickfire

3.32 What is the difference between a noumenon and a phenomenon?

Key terms

Noumenon: a thing in itself, as distinct from our senses

Phenomenon: a thing as we perceive it through our senses and context

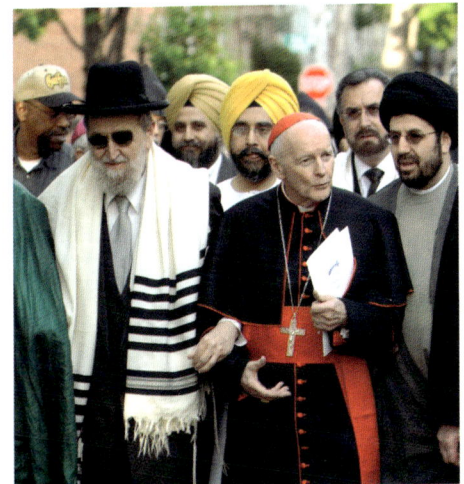

Interfaith gathering, Berkley Centre for Religion, Peace, and World Affairs, 2012

experience is a force for good in the world, and an antidote for religion that becomes harsh and inhumane through the tendency to cling absolutely and exclusively to one's own doctrine, creeds, scriptures and traditions.

If one experience, why so many religions?

Hick uses the parable, attributed to the Buddha, of the blind men and the elephant. In this story, an elephant is brought to a group of blind men who had never encountered the animal before. Each of the men felt a different part of the elephant and mistook their experience for the entire creature: one man felt the leg and concluded that the elephant was a giant pillar, another felt the trunk and reported that the elephant was a great snake – and so on. Hick compares this to different accounts of God or the Ultimate Reality. Every major religion, he says, believes that the divine is beyond its grasp, so we can only witness to the partial understanding that we have. However, Hick says that there are two qualifications to using the story in this way: (i) not all religious experience is equally valid. Religion is a human phenomenon and can be motivated by fear or attempts to control the spiritual world for personal gain. Hick is speaking of what he calls the 'great revelatory experiences' of the main world religions. These experiences have been tested through a long tradition of worship and have sustained and inspired millions of lives over many centuries. (ii) The parable should not be used to make the point that there are different 'parts' of the divine. There is, says Hick, one Ultimate Reality. The differences arise as we come to religious experience with different historical and cultural viewpoints.

The biggest roadblock to Christian pluralism

Hick says that the most difficult part of the Pluralistic hypothesis for Christians is the doctrine of the incarnation. This is traditionally expressed in the **Chalcedonian creed** (451 CE) that Jesus was fully God and fully man. This means that Christians have viewed Jesus as God incarnate, the second member of the Trinity living a human life. This uniqueness would seem to demand exclusivism. For Christians would be correct in holding that all people must come to Christ if there was but one unique incarnation of God in the world.

However, Hick notes that there are many issues with viewing Jesus in the traditional way. Not the least of these issues is the fact that no one has ever satisfactorily explained how the two natures ascribed to Jesus work together. Furthermore, Hick accepts contemporary research that questions the historicity of supernatural reports of the Bible. He sees the infancy narratives as a reflection of the importance of Jesus to the disciples rather than as historical fact, and the resurrection as having been a spiritual rather than a physical event. What is crucial for Hick is that there is another way of having a Christology than that prescribed by Chalcedon. Instead of viewing Jesus as 'God-Man', one can see him as a human being on a spiritual journey where he reached a high 'degree' of God-consciousness. Hick calls this a '**degree Christology**' and it enables Christians to see Jesus as an example they can follow, one who opens the reality of God for them – but to also be open to other figures in other religions who also reached a high degree of God (or, 'Reality') consciousness.

Pluralism on exclusive claims in the Bible

We've already seen that the Bible contains many passages which seem to clearly promote an exclusive view of salvation. How does a Christian pluralist explain these? The Catholic theologian and pluralist thinker Paul Knitter believes there are several factors which should be kept in mind when reading these passages:

1. **Absolutist language is a result of historical factors.** The disciples had a lack of historical consciousness of other religions, other teachings and other ways. Furthermore, they represented a minority under threat of religious

Key terms

Chalcedonian creed: the creed adopted at Chalcedon in 451 CE that declared Jesus to have had two natures

Degree Christology: Hick's phrase for seeing Jesus as a human being with a high degree of God consciousness rather than a divine being having two natures

quickfire

3.33 What are the two illustrations that Hick uses to teach religious pluralism?

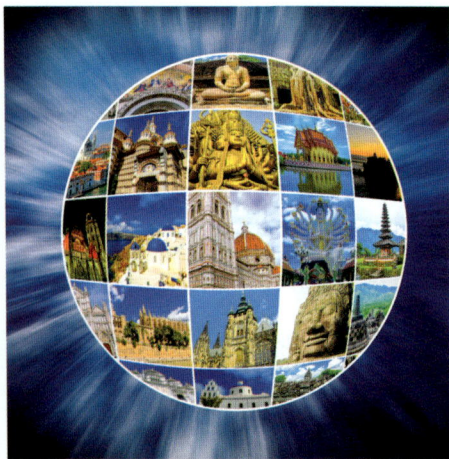

According to John Hick, all major world religions can be a path to the Ultimate Reality.

persecution – when this happens hard and absolute positions develop in order to maintain a sense of identity. They also had an 'apocalyptic mentality'; their beliefs in the coming end of the world enabled 'all-or-nothing' thinking. Without these factors, the disciples might have said 'God *really* acted in Jesus'. What they ended up saying was 'God *only* acted in Jesus'.

2. **Titles given to Jesus are not propositional truths but literary or symbolic expressions of experience.** In other words, the disciples had experiences of Jesus which led them to have their own experiences of God. They expressed their admiration and awe for Jesus' role in this – but these expressions were never meant to be 'hardened' into absolute dogma.

3. **'Christ' is more than 'Jesus'.** John chapter one talks about a divine 'Logos' that permeates the universe, that reveals God. It is therefore possible to say that God is in the 'revealing business' and that Jesus is but one of many expressions of this 'logos' or 'Christ'.

AO1 Activity

Give yourself 5 minutes to read through the views of Christian pluralism above. Now, close the book and write a list of all of the items that an exclusivist would object to. See if you can identify more than five points.

Knitter believes that there is a strong biblical reason to accept pluralism: Jesus' teaching to, 'Love your neighbour as yourself'. To love someone includes seriously considering their views, not assuming – before you have even spoken to them – that they have less wisdom than you. They might even have more wisdom.

Universalistic pluralism and Christian universalism

Hick's pluralism is 'universal' in the sense that it sees salvation and liberation as offered in all the major world religions. It makes the radical step of declaring that the universe contains many religions that can each be a path to salvation in their own right without one of them being 'more true' than another. Hick, however, is quick to say that this is not relativistic, because religions can be judged by how effectively they help people to become less self-centred and more Reality-centred.

Hick's pluralism is different from Christian universalism. Christian universalism is simply the belief that God, though Christ, will save everyone – in the end. This position is founded on scriptural principles:

- God wills that everyone be saved (I Timothy 2:4)

- Jesus died for the sins of the entire world (I John 2:2)

- The Bible speaks of a universal restoration (Acts 3:21, I Corinthians 15:22)

- God's love is incompatible with eternally damning people to hell (Ezekiel 18:23).

Universalism appeals to the simple logic that God cannot fail. If God wills that everyone be saved and has enabled this through the sacrifice of Jesus, then, surely, God will accomplish this. Many early theologians raised this possibility including Clement of Alexandria, Origen and Gregory of Nyssa. In fact, Origen even taught that the devil, after a time of punishment, would be purified for heaven.

Universalism was condemned in 543 CE at Constantinople; however, it has emerged in the writings of many mystics and theologians through the centuries. Near the end of the 18th century the Universalist Church was founded in the United States which distinguished itself from other denominations with its denial of the final reality of hell and its declaration of salvation for all. Opponents of universalism say that it denies free will and contradicts clear biblical teaching about eternal punishment. Some denominations, such as the Church of England allow universalist belief.

Key quotes

By defining Jesus Christ in absolute terms, by announcing him as the one and only saviour, the early Christians cut out for themselves an identity different from that of all their opponents or competitors. Such language also evoked a total commitment that would steel them in the fate of persecution or ridicule. **(P. Knitter)**

[the devil and his angels] …after having undergone heavier and severer punishments … improved by this stern method of training, and [are] restored … and thus advancing through each stage to a better condition, reach even to that which is invisible and eternal… **(Origen)**

quickfire

3.34 Which of these systems says that all people are saved through the work of Jesus Christ: pluralistic universalism or Christian universalism?

Key skills

Knowledge involves:

Selection of a range of (thorough) accurate and relevant information that is directly related to the specific demands of the question.

This means:

- Selecting relevant material for the question set

- Being focused in explaining and examining the material selected.

Understanding involves:

Explanation that is extensive, demonstrating depth and/or breadth with excellent use of evidence and examples including (where appropriate) thorough and accurate supporting use of sacred texts, sources of wisdom and specialist language.

This means:

- Effective use of examples and supporting evidence to establish the quality of your understanding

- Ownership of your explanation that expresses personal knowledge and understanding and NOT just reproducing a chunk of text from a book that you have rehearsed and memorised.

AO1 Developing skills

It is now important to consider the information that has been covered in this section; however, the information in its raw form is too extensive and so has to be processed in order to meet the requirements of the examination. This can be achieved by practising more advanced skills associated with AO1. For assessment objective 1 (AO1), which involves demonstrating 'knowledge' and 'understanding' skills, we are going to focus on different ways in which the skills can be demonstrated effectively, and also refer to how the performance of these skills is measured (see generic band descriptors for A2 [WJEC] AO1 or A Level [Eduqas] AO1).

▶ **Your final task for this theme is:** Below is a summary of **inclusivism as true Christian teaching**. It is 150 words long. Again there are no highlighted points to indicate the key points to learn from this extract. Discuss which five points you think are the most important to highlight and write them down in a list.

It can be argued that Christian inclusivism offers the best summary of biblical and theological teaching on salvation. In favour of this idea is the fact that there are passages in the Bible which clearly do not condemn those outside of the Christian faith. Furthermore, those passages which appear exclusivist are focussed on people who do have a clear choice to make as they have been fairly confronted with the Christian message; they do not deal with those who have not considered the Christian message in a serious way. Inclusivism also takes serious the historic Christian approach to the uniqueness of Jesus and the biblical teaching that Christ and the cross are at the centre of salvation for all people. In addition to this, major theologians of the Church embrace inclusivism and key Church documents reflect this view. It can also be seen as a compromise position between exclusivism on the one hand and pluralism on the other.

Now make the five points into your own summary (as in Theme 1 Developing skills) trying to make the summary more personal to your style of writing. This may also involve re-ordering the points if you wish to do so. In addition to this, try to add some quotations and references to develop your summary (as in Theme 2 Developing skills).

The result will be a fairly lengthy answer and so you could then check it against the band descriptors for A2 (WJEC) or A Level (Eduqas) and in particular have a look at the demands described in the higher band descriptors towards which you should be aspiring. Ask yourself:

- Does my work demonstrate thorough, accurate and relevant knowledge and understanding of religion and belief?

- Is my work coherent (consistent or make logical sense), clear and well organised?

- Will my work, when developed, be an extensive and relevant response which is specific to the focus of the task?

- Does my work have extensive depth and/or suitable breadth and have excellent use of evidence and examples?

- If appropriate to the task, does my response have thorough and accurate reference to sacred texts and sources of wisdom?

- Are there any insightful connections to be made with other elements of my course?

- Will my answer, when developed and extended to match what is expected in an examination answer, have an extensive range of views of scholars/schools of thought?

- When used, is specialist language and vocabulary both thorough and accurate?

This section covers AO2 content and skills

Issues for analysis and evaluation

The extent to which it is possible to be both a committed Christian and a religious pluralist

Specification content

The extent to which it is possible to be both a committed Christian and a religious pluralist.

Since a religious pluralist believes that Christianity is but one path of salvation among many, is it really possible to accept that the two words 'Christian' and 'pluralist' can go together? Or, can pluralists who call themselves Christian be seen as having left the historic Christian faith in favour of a new form of spiritualty which has nothing to do with the Bible, the creeds and the views of the Church?

It could be argued that pluralism has nothing to do with Christianity because all of the major denominations of the Church agree on the doctrine of Council of Chalcedon in 451CE that Christ is unique among all humans – *and all religions* – for being the incarnation of God, one person with two natures, human and divine. Furthermore, Jesus Christ came to offer salvation through his death on the cross to *all* human beings. Therefore, to say that other religions offer a path of salvation is to deny Jesus' universal status and thus, to deny the most important doctrine of Christianity. This is, in fact, heresy and explains why pluralism has been officially condemned by the Roman Catholic Church as well as by the majority of Protestant Church bodies.

However, the 'Christian pluralist' could make the case that many people were considered to have been Christians prior to 451CE! The Bible contains no clear statement of the 'two natures' and therefore it may be wrong to make this doctrine the standard for all Christians to believe. In addition to this, the doctrine of the two natures has never been explained – it is merely an assertion of the Church, a compromise in a larger and complicated philosophical discussion that may have surprised the historical Jesus. John Hick says that there is an alternative way to think of Jesus than the 'two-natures' approach. Jesus could be considered someone who achieved a very high degree of God-consciousness, so much so that he became an example and inspiration for others. This means that a Christian can be led to God through Jesus without having to believe, literally, in the creeds. A Christian can therefore be open to the idea that figures in other religions could have achieved God/Reality consciousness. What makes them a Christian rather than, for example, a Buddhist, is not the uniqueness of their doctrine, but the fact that they came to a deeper understanding of life through Jesus rather than through the Buddha.

Of course, Christians who believe in the historic creeds could reply that while Chalcedon's views may not be explicit in the Gospels, they are implicit – these ideas grew out of the real experience of the disciples with the miraculous life of Jesus. Therefore, it is no mere accident that it became a central doctrine of Christianity. Furthermore, the fact that Hick uses terms like 'Ultimate Reality', 'divine reality', and 'transcendent reality' alongside the term 'God' means that he has really departed from Christianity and its more definite view of a Trinitarian God.

John Hick, himself a Christian pluralist, raises several challenges to these viewpoints. First, there are issues with the miraculous beliefs about Jesus' life according to modern historical research. However, to focus only on these questions is to miss the fact that belief in the miraculous nature of Jesus is an expression of how important Jesus was to the disciples. Jesus opened up for them an experience of reality that was new, a less self-centred way of life that utterly changed them, gave them purpose and a sense of mission about sharing the love of God. Surely it is this experience that is at the heart of Christianity? In terms of having a more vague view of God, isn't it true that God is a mystery? So, to define the word 'God' precisely would mean that we are turning God into an object of human enquiry.

AO2 Activity

As you read through this section try to do the following:

1. Pick out the different lines of argument that are presented in the text and identify any evidence given in support.
2. For each line of argument try to evaluate whether or not you think this is strong or weak.
3. Think of any questions you may wish to raise in response to the arguments.

This activity will help you to start thinking critically about what you read, and help you to evaluate the effectiveness of different arguments and from this develop your own observations, opinions and points of view that will help with any conclusions that you make in your answers to the AO2 questions that arise.

Key quotes

AO2 Activity

List some conclusions that could be drawn from the AO2 reasoning from the above text; try to aim for at least three different possible conclusions. Consider each of the conclusions and collect brief evidence to support each conclusion from the AO1 and AO2 material for this topic. Select the conclusion that you think is most convincing and explain why it is so. Try to contrast this with the weakest conclusion in the list, justifying your argument with clear reasoning and evidence.

Furthermore, if we say that an experience is at the heart of Christianity, then Christianity is more about having an authentic experience rather than believing in the 'right things'. In fact, Christianity should be thought of in this way: individuals who are inspired by Jesus to have less of a self-centred life and more of a God-centred life. This person comes to know Jesus through their encounter with scripture, tradition and the Christian community – but it is not these things, but their experience, that should remain central.

After all, isn't so much discord in the world the result of experience being hardened into teaching which then becomes further hardened into absolute doctrines? This then leads to people feeling 'right' and seeing others as 'wrong' which, in turn, fuels hatred, segregation and violence. We would all be better off, says Hick, by basing Christianity on our experience of Jesus and being open to the idea that those in other religions can have equally valid experiences which can also lead to less self-centred lives.

Of course, it may be objected that this way of thinking can lead to an 'anything goes' philosophy. For instance, does this mean that all religions are automatically 'good'? What about a religion that worships the devil and engages in all sorts of anti-humanitarian practices? Furthermore, the religious pluralist ignores that there are other Christian paths that can recognise goodness and wisdom in other religions – as well as hope that non-Christians will also make it to heaven. These paths do not require that Christians surrender what is truly unique about their religions, the incarnation of the God-Man Jesus.

One of these paths is Christian inclusivism which recognises that God is working in other religions to make, as Rahner says, 'anonymous Christians'. Therefore, Christians can hold to their historical doctrines and, at the same time, appreciate truth and wisdom in other religions. In addition to this, Christian universalists believe that no one is going to hell; everyone will be saved by Christ since the determined and loving nature of God cannot be stopped. Thus, God will work tirelessly until each person is saved, even, according to Origen, the devil. Additionally, universalism retains Jesus' work on the cross at the centre, thus staying true to historic Christianity.

However, there are a number of assumptions in these points that the pluralist could take issue with. First, Hick does not believe that his views are relativistic: you can judge a religion, but not on its doctrines. Rather, they can be judged on how well they enable people to be less egocentric. Therefore, a religion which has anti-humanitarian practices can be judged as less God/Reality centred than other religions. Furthermore, an inclusivist approach can be seen as patronising: 'you have some truth, but I have more and better truth'. Is that really an attitude that is in line with the biblical mandate to love our neighbours? Christian universalism has been deemed heretical by most churches – which again reinforces the need to focus less on doctrine and more on experience.

In conclusion, most churches simply do not consider it possible to be a Christian and a religious pluralist. However, this does not mean that there are not religious pluralists sitting on the pews in those churches. Therefore, the reality 'on the ground' may be different than official Church views. The degree to which this is true and how this may or may not change Church views in the future would need further study.

Key quote

The extent to which the Christian Bible promotes exclusivism

Christian exclusivism is the belief that only Christians can find God's path in the present and God's salvation in eternity. It can be argued that this position is firmly supported by the Bible. For there are many passages in the Hebrew scriptures and the New Testament which appear to indicate that there is only one way to eternal truth and salvation. For example, we find passages in the Old Testament which urge Israel to worship only God, with punishments if they do otherwise (see Deuteronomy 6:5 and Joshua 23:16). In the New Testament, it is made clear that Jesus is 'the way' (John 14:6) and the 'only name' given to humanity that has saving power (Acts 4:12).

Furthermore, there are many passages in the Bible that emphasise punishment and damnation for those who do not follow God's path. For example, one of these condemnations appears in the same passage that declares the love of God. John 3:16 says that 'God so loved the world that he gave his son...' and this is immediately followed by a pronouncement that those who do not believe this are 'condemned already because they do not believe in the name of the only son of God'.

It is because of these clear declarations in the Bible that Christians through the centuries have formulated exclusive doctrines such as *extra ecclesiam nulla salus* ('outside the Church, no salvation) and 'we must individually receive Jesus Christ as our saviour ...' (from the evangelical Protestant leaflet, '4 Spiritual Laws'). It seems then, that the Bible presents an 'open and shut case' for exclusivism.

However, the great Roman Catholic theologian Karl Rahner disagrees. He believed that God makes his presence known throughout the world – even outside of Israel and the Church. His biblical evidence for this is the fact that the Old Testament refers several times to people who are 'God pleasing pagans'. These are individuals outside of Israel who were recognised as being righteous. Rahner notes that they must have attained this through their religion. This, then, is the opposite of the condemnation that is found in exclusive viewpoints.

Rahner also gives an example from the New Testament. In Acts 17 Paul is in Athens preaching to a Greek audience who hold various beliefs. Rather than condemn their beliefs, Paul quotes a poet who is familiar to them: 'In him we live and move and have our being'. Paul holds this verse up as an example of the truth he is trying to convey. This, for Rahner, is a further example that God is at work throughout the world and therefore it is incorrect to conclude that the Bible teaches only a narrow exclusive viewpoint. Rahner does believe that the fullest expression of truth is found in the life of Jesus and the community of the Church, but that these passages show that it is not *only* found in those places.

In response, the exclusivist might ask, 'Why is the Bible so clear about the "only way" and damnation for those who are not on that way?' One reason for this, could be that the most exclusive passages in the Bible are addressed to those who already possess clear knowledge of the truth – so that they are fully responsible for making a choice for Jesus and the Church. However, Rahner notes, there are many places in the world where the message of Christianity is never heard, or if it is known, is not a part of society in any way that could invite serious engagement. In these situations, God works through other religions – God is greater than the Church, says Rahner. Thus, the Bible can be said to teach inclusivism rather than exclusivism.

The extent to which the Christian Bible promotes exclusivism.

Key quote

Thus the great religious traditions are to be regarded as alternative soteriological 'spaces' within which, or 'ways' along which, men and women can find salvation/liberation/enlightenment/fulfillment. (J. Hick)

AO2 Activity

As you read through this section try to do the following:

1. Pick out the different lines of argument that are presented in the text and identify any evidence given in support.
2. For each line of argument try to evaluate whether or not you think this is strong or weak.
3. Think of any questions you may wish to raise in response to the arguments.

This activity will help you to start thinking critically about what you read, and help you to evaluate the effectiveness of different arguments and from this develop your own observations, opinions and points of view that will help with any conclusions that you make in your answers to the AO2 questions that arise.

However, this view does not grasp deeper themes in the Bible, say the pluralists. These deeper themes include the loving mystery of God who is beyond all particular religions. When the Bible says, 'Love your neighbour as yourself,' can one be loving with an exclusivist or an inclusivist attitude? For, the exclusivist would say or think, 'I love you, but if you are not a Christian you are on the wrong path and will be damned'. The inclusivist would say or think, 'I love you but I know more truth than you – even before I find out what you think'. Is this really what loving one's neighbour entails? No. The only way to love our neighbour is to be open to the fact that they may have truth or wisdom that we do not have. This, according to the pluralists, is the deeper message of the Bible, one that we discover when we consider its teaching on love.

Of course, this view flies in the face of the plain meaning of all the Bible passages we have already considered. How do pluralists deal with those passages? One way is to see these passages as historically conditioned: when a minority group is under threat it strengthens its identity by making their beliefs firmer and absolute. We know that the early Christians were a minority and that they faced a great deal of persecution, so it is no wonder that they expressed their beliefs in an exclusive way. Of course, this approach would not appeal to a Christian who believes that God inspired the Bible in a special way compared to other books, but it would appeal to those who admire some of the teachings in the Bible but find it difficult to take it all literally.

Pluralists also find other reasons, based on the Bible, to support their views such as viewing the titles given to Jesus ('Lord', 'Saviour') as poetic expressions of experience rather than as dogmatic statements. Also, the idea of the 'Logos' in John chapter 1 can be interpreted to mean that 'Christ' is but one aspect of the revelation of God in the world.

In conclusion, there are exclusivist messages in the Bible – whether or not these are just one aspect of a wider inclusivist message has to do with how seriously one takes the biblical passages that Rahner refers to. Pluralists are able to use the Bible to illustrate and support their approach, but it is not clear that they can actually point positively to as many passages as exclusivists and inclusivists can. Rather, their position seems to require that one takes a lower view of the Bible, less as a revelation and more as a human document. This is not a welcome point of view among many Christians.

AO2 Activity

List some conclusions that could be drawn from the AO2 reasoning from the above text; try to aim for at least three different possible conclusions. Consider each of the conclusions and collect brief evidence to support each conclusion from the AO1 and AO2 material for this topic. Select the conclusion that you think is most convincing and explain why it is so. Try to contrast this with the weakest conclusion in the list, justifying your argument with clear reasoning and evidence.

AO2 Developing skills

It is now important to consider the information that has been covered in this section; however, the information in its raw form is too extensive and so has to be processed in order to meet the requirements of the examination. This can be achieved by practising more advanced skills associated with AO2. For assessment objective 2 (AO2), which involves 'critical analysis' and 'evaluation' skills, we are going to focus on different ways in which the skills can be demonstrated effectively, and also refer to how the performance of these skills is measured (see generic band descriptors for A2 [WJEC] AO2 or A Level [Eduqas] AO2).

▶ **Your final task for this theme is:** Below are listed three basic conclusions drawn from an evaluation of **Christian exclusivism**. Your task is to develop each of these conclusions by identifying briefly the strengths (referring briefly to some reasons underlying it) but also an awareness of challenges made to it (these may be weaknesses depending upon your view).

1. Christian exclusivism has the strength of not being overly complicated; the Bible makes it clear in many places that there is only one way to salvation.
2. Christian exclusivism takes seriously beliefs about Christ that the Church has held for hundreds of years.
3. Christian exclusivism avoids relativism: there is a clear path to find salvation and clear ways that one can go wrong (other religions).

The result should be three very competent paragraphs that could form a final conclusion of any evaluation.

When you have completed the task, refer to the band descriptors for A2 (WJEC) or A Level (Eduqas) and in particular have a look at the demands described in the higher band descriptors towards which you should be aspiring. Ask yourself:

- Is my answer a confident critical analysis and perceptive evaluation of the issue?
- Is my answer a response that successfully identifies and thoroughly addresses the issues raised by the question set?

Key skills

Analysis involves:

Identifying issues raised by the materials in the AO1, together with those identified in the AO2 section, and presents sustained and clear views, either of scholars or from a personal perspective ready for evaluation.

This means:

- That your answers are able to identify key areas of debate in relation to a particular issue
- That you can identify, and comment upon, the different lines of argument presented by others
- That your response comments on the overall effectiveness of each of these areas or arguments.

Evaluation involves:

Considering the various implications of the issues raised based upon the evidence gleaned from analysis and provides an extensive detailed argument with a clear conclusion.

This means:

- That your answer weighs up the consequences of accepting or rejecting the various and different lines of argument analysed
- That your answer arrives at a conclusion through a clear process of reasoning.

T4 Religious practices that shape religious identity

This section covers AO1 content and skills

Specification content

The development of the Ecumenical Movement since 1910 (World Missionary Conference); the World Council of Churches, its rationale, its mission and its work in three main areas: Unity, Mission, and Ecumenical Relations; Public Witness and Diakonia; and Ecumenical Formation.

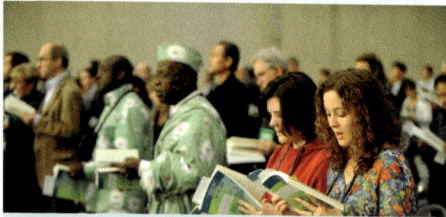

Millions of Christians worldwide annually celebrate the week of prayer for Christian unity from 18 to 25 January.

Key quotes

This other thing also is to be ranked among the chief evils of our time, viz., that the Churches are so divided that human fellowship is scarcely now of any repute among us, far less that Christian intercourse which all profess but few sincerely practise. **(J. Calvin, 1509–1564)**

Ecumenism is the quest for unity among Christians now divided by denomination. **(S. Harmon)**

Tonight we can be as one …
The real battle just begun,
To claim the victory Jesus won
(U2, 'Sunday Bloody Sunday')

Key term

Ecumenical: the entire, inhabited world, from the Greek term *oikoumene*. Used to describe efforts at Christian unity

---

D: Religious identity through unification

The development of the Ecumenical Movement since 1910 (World Missionary Conference)

One criticism of Christianity that you might hear is, 'Since they believe in a loving and forgiving God, but can't get along with each other, why should I listen to their message?!' One of the sad facts of Christianity are the many divisions and conflicts that have persisted from the early centuries of the movement to the present day. There are many Christians who feel the force of this criticism, and want to see Christianity known more for what Christians share with one another than by what they don't. The Ecumenical Movement is this quest for unity. The term '**ecumenical**' comes from the Greek word *oikumene*, meaning the entire, inhabited world.

Several passages in the Bible are considered especially important by those involved in the Ecumenical Movement. The most cited of these is the prayer of Jesus in John 17: 20–22: 'I ask not only on behalf of these, but also on behalf of those who will believe in me through their word, that they may all be one. As you, Father, are in me and I am in you, may they also be in us, so that the world may believe that you have sent me.' In this prayer, Jesus recognises that the success of the mission of the Church is tied to Christian unity. The Apostle Paul lamented the arguments and division in the early church, and urged that Christians be united (see I Corinthians 1:10 and 2 Corinthians 5:19). From the very beginning, the Church came together to overcome differences (Acts 15) and to feel the spiritual power of being united in worship (Matthew 18:19–20). Underlying these passages is the conviction that all Christians are called to a deep fellowship with God and therefore can and should live in deep fellowship with one another.

AO1 Activity

From memory, write down as many different types of churches that you have come across. Rather than the actual names of the individual churches (i.e. St Mark's) this activity is asking you to identify the denomination (Anglican, Catholic, Reformed, etc.) – how many of these can you think of? Now, do some quick online research to discover if any of these denominations are a part of the World Council of Churches.

Does unity mean uniformity? The Church has always valued different perspectives, cultures and languages. There are, after all, four Gospels, each with different perspectives on the life and teaching of Jesus. In fact, one popular attempt to harmonise the Gospels, The Diatessaron, for inclusion in the Christian canon was rejected in favour of the four Gospels. However, the question of what churches need to agree on and what they can surrender as 'non-essential' is perhaps the most important challenge that faces the Ecumenical Movement.

The Edinburgh Missionary Conference

Many scholars trace the beginning of the modern Ecumenical Movement to the **Edinburgh World Missionary Conference** of 1910. Of course, this should not obscure the fact that, prior to this, Christians had been gathering formally and informally over the centuries for common worship and common causes. In fact, the first use of the term 'ecumenical' in Christian discussions was in 381CE when the Council of Constantinople applied this to the council of Nicea of 325CE. The Nicene creed is known as an 'ecumenical creed', one to which the entire Christian world at the time gave assent.

What makes the Edinburgh Missionary Conference so outstanding is that it brought together an unprecedented number of Christian groups and, in its wake, led to the formation of Church organisations which have evolved into today's World Council of Churches.

Over 1200 missionaries from about 160 missionary boards gathered for ten days to consider reports on various aspects of missionary work. The goal that united these missionaries was the bringing into being a self-governing, self-supporting church in 'each non-Christian nation' which would reflect the undivided Church of Christ. However, the reality on the ground was often different: the divisions and arguments that marked the churches in the West were manifesting themselves in new churches in Africa and Asia. This is why the conference adopted the slogan, 'Doctrine Divides but Service Unites'. It was felt that the way to make progress was not to engage in disputed theological questions but to focus on the need felt by all churches to spread the Christian message. The only resolution of the conference – which passed unanimously – was that a committee should carry on coordinating missionary activity.

On the one hand, this event was a breakthrough for the cause of ecumenism since there was an acceptance of one another despite different denominational labels, a willingness to work together and a commitment to further gatherings. On the other hand, this was solely an evangelical Protestant gathering attended by mostly Anglo-American missionaries. Neither the Roman Catholic Church nor the Orthodox Churches were invited – though some Anglican speakers at the conference urged that they be included in future gatherings. Furthermore, some at the conference viewed avoiding Church doctrine as a limitation. Surely, if there were to be greater unity between the churches, differences in beliefs would need to be explored and agreement reached?

After the conference

There were several developments after the Edinburgh conference that furthered the cause of ecumenism. In 1920 the Orthodox Patriarch of Constantinople, inspired by the proposal of a 'League of Nations' proposed a 'league' of churches as a response to God's desire for Church unity. The **International Missionary Conference** was founded 1921. This Conference extended the work of 1910 by bringing together Church leaders from around the world to consider issues such as the Christian message in a secular world and the relevance of the Gospel in response to issues such as war and slavery. The **Life and Work Movement** met in 1925 and focused on the responsibility of Christians in the social and economic

quickfire

4.1 What is the most cited Bible passage on the subject of Church unity?

World Missionary Conference, Edinburgh, 1910

Key quote

Most mainstream ecumenism assumes that a purely inward or spiritual unity among Christians is not enough. (J. Mangina)

quickfire

4.2 Was the Edinburgh Missionary Conference a Protestant, Catholic or Orthodox event?

Key terms

Edinburgh World Missionary Conference: the 1910 conference of mostly Anglo-American Protestant missionaries to promote unity in mission work

International Missionary Conference: A group founded in 1921 to carry on the work of the Edinburgh Missionary Conference; merged with the WCC in 1961

Life and Work Movement: A group founded in 1925, dedicated to the promotion of social responsibility amongst Christians

Key term

The Faith and Order Movement:
a group founded in 1927 dedicated
to examination of doctrinal issues
separating churches. Came together
with Life and Work in 1948 to form the
World Council of Churches

Specification content

The World Council of Churches: its
rationale and its mission.

The 10th Assembly of the World Council
of Churches at Busan, Republic of Korea
in 2013

quickfire

4.3   Which two groups combined to form
the World Council of Churches?

problems in the aftermath of World War I. **The Faith and Order Movement**
met in 1927 to consider matters of doctrinal divisions between churches. There
were also a number of dialogues and mergers; the most comprehensive was the
formation of the Church of South India in 1947 that brought together Anglican,
Methodist, Presbyterian, Congregational, Lutheran and Reformed churches
into one denomination. (In 1971 the Church of North India formed as a merger
between Anglican, Congregational, Presbyterian, Methodist, Baptist, and Disciples
of Christ.) In 1937 leaders from the Life and Work and Faith and Order Movements
met together and proposed that they merge into a 'World Council of Churches'.
World War II delayed their plans.

The World Council of Churches: rationale and mission

The first assembly of the World Council of Churches was held in Amsterdam in
1948 with Willem A. Visser 't Hooft as its first General Secretary: 351 delegates
gathered, representing 147 Church bodies. The WCC defined itself as '…
a fellowship of churches which accept our Lord Jesus Christ as God and Saviour'.
The WCC has sometimes been called an 'ecclesiastical United Nations'. Like the
United Nations, it was born shortly after a period of war and international conflict.
Church bodies, like countries in the United Nations, send representatives to general
assemblies. Also, like the United Nations, not all churches are yet members and
some churches are observers rather than full members.

Study tip

Make use of the World Council of Churches' website. It is clear to understand.
Reading about its history, programmes and aims will strengthen your
knowledge of this area – https://www.oikoumene.org

Hint: try finding current areas of disagreement between churches on the site,
doing so will begin to prepare you for the evaluative section.

AO1 Activity

Make a simple flow chart of the main movements that merged into the World
Council of Churches. Include dates and brief descriptions of each of the
movements on your chart.

What it is and what it is not: from the 1950 Toronto Statement

[What the WCC is not:]

1. *The World Council of Churches is not and must never become a superchurch.*

2. *The WCC does not negotiate unions between churches … but to bring the churches into living contact with each other and to promote the
study and discussion of the issues of Church unity.*

3. *The World Council cannot and should not be based on any one particular conception of the Church.*

4. *Membership in the World Council of Churches does not imply that a church treats its own conception of the Church as merely relative.*

5. *Membership in the World Council does not imply the acceptance of a specific doctrine concerning the nature of Church unity.*

[What the WCC is:]

*The member churches of the Council believe that conversation, cooperation and common witness of the churches must be based on the
common recognition that Christ is the Divine Head of the Body … The member churches enter into spiritual relationships through which they
seek to learn from each other and to give help to each other in order that the Body of Christ may be built up and that the life of the churches
may be renewed.*

The WCC has a General Assembly about every seven years; between these assemblies a central committee meets regularly and programmes run continuously. In 1961 there was a particularly significant assembly in the history of the WCC:

- The WCC revised and expanded its definition to include a reference to the Christian scriptures and to the Trinity: 'The World Council of Churches is a fellowship of Churches which confess the Lord Jesus Christ as God and Saviour according to the scriptures and therefore seek to fulfil together their common calling to the glory of the one God; Father, Son and Holy Spirit.'
- The International Missionary Council, which had been associated with the WCC since 1948, became fully integrated.
- The first Roman Catholics attended as official observers.
- The Russian Orthodox Church and other Eastern Orthodox Churches became members (the Ecumenical Patriarchate of the Eastern Orthodox Church was one of the founding members).
- The first Pentecostal Christian Church bodies joined the WCC; these were from Latin America.

The WCC describes its intentions in this way: 'The aim of the WCC is to pursue the goal of the visible unity of the Church. This involves a process of renewal and change in which member churches pray, worship, discuss and work together.' This visible unity of the Church includes these elements:

- A common confession of the apostolic faith
- A common sacramental life
- Mutual recognition of all members and their ministries
- A common mission in spreading the Gospel
- Participation of all churches locally and internationally in agreed structures
- Common service to the world so that all might believe.

Of course, these elements are a final destination at which the WCC has not arrived; it is on a journey toward this goal through its various programmes.

The Work of the World Council of Churches in three areas

There are three programme areas of the WCC: 1. Unity, Mission and Ecumenical Relations, 2. Public Witness and **Diakonia**, and 3. Ecumenical Formation. Each of these areas includes specific projects, activities, conferences, networks and think tanks that aim at advocating issues within the member churches and wider society.

1. Unity, Mission and Ecumenical Relations

Unity, Mission and Ecumenical Relations is devoted to the pursuit of visible Christian unity. The fact that the term 'unity' comes first reflects Jesus' prayer in John for believers to be united so that the world might believe. Thus, this area also includes 'mission', the reaching out of the Christian message, as well as 'ecumenical relations,' the strengthening of relationships between Christian churches. There are at least two main challenges that the WCC faces in these areas:

- The WCC defines mission as witnessing to the Christian Gospel but it also says that mission is 'increasingly seen too as fostering solidarity and respect for people's dignity' – thus, the WCC is involved in a number of projects aimed at social justice such as advocating for those with disabilities, indigenous people and migrants. This has sometimes drawn criticism from member churches that it is 'watering down' the focus on evangelism. The fact that the WCC also engages in interfaith relations has added to these tensions.

Key quotes

The goal of the search for full communion is realised when all the churches are able to recognise in one another the one, holy, catholic and apostolic church in its fullness. (The World Council of Churches)

… the lives of churches in relationship to other churches and the lives of individual believers in relationship to other believers ought to be as inseparably intertwined as the three interlocking circles that symbolise the Trinity. (S. Harmon)

Specification content

The World Council of Churches, its work in three main areas: Unity, Mission, and Ecumenical Relations; Public Witness and Diakonia; and Ecumenical Formation

Key term

Diakonia: the Greek word for service; in the WCC it is used in the context of activities aimed at justice and peace for the poor and oppressed

Key terms

Baptism, Eucharist & Ministry: a key ecumenical document prepared by the Faith and Order Commission of the World Council of Churches

Ecumenical Formation: giving shape to ecumenical themes for individuals and churches through study, reflection and participation

- Not all churches are members of the WCC; most notably, the Roman Catholic Church and a number of evangelical and Pentecostal churches. This is why there are special working groups at the WCC tasked with building relationships with these churches.

Finally, this programme area includes the Commission of Faith and Order, one of the two main movements that merged to form the WCC. This commission is responsible for producing perhaps the most widely studied ecumenical document of recent history, *Baptism, Eucharist & Ministry* (1982) which explores the growing agreement and remaining disagreements between Christian churches in these areas.

2. Public Witness and Diakonia

Public Witness and Diakonia recognises that Christians share many areas of social responsibility. This area is the legacy of the Life and Work movement which formed the WCC in 1948 and was dissolved into the various programmes that now make up this area. The programmes in this area seek to accomplish two main goals:

- Offer a highly public 'prophetic voice' which calls awareness to areas where churches and the world need to pay especial attention. This includes peace building in 'priority countries': the Korean Peninsula, Syria, South Sudan, Democratic Republic of Congo and Nigeria as well as supporting churches who find themselves in situations of conflict. This area includes the sending of observers to Israel and Palestine and seeking to influence key activities at the United Nations.

- Bring Christians together to tirelessly and persistently live out Christian values of social responsibility. The WCC uses the Greek term 'diakonia' which means 'service' and refers to the to the care of the poor and the oppressed. This area includes activities around climate change, global health, water rights, a just economy, women's rights, stateless people, and HIV and AIDS work.

3. Ecumenical Formation

Key quote

The eye of faith discerns the embodiment of a God who out-suffers, out-loves and out-lives the worst that worldly powers can do. **(The World Council of Churches)**

Ecumenical Formation is the area of study, training and education so that the knowledge and convictions of ecumenism can take shape in the lives of individuals and churches. The WCC has its own institute at Bossey, near Geneva, Switzerland. The Ecumenical Institute at Bossey has its own

The Ecumenical Institute at Bossey of the World Council of Churches

teaching faculty, facilities for residential study, and grants diplomas through the University of Geneva. But the WCC also provides training and education opportunities throughout the world, through member churches in cooperation with the WCC. Examples of recent seminars include training for youth in justice and peace issues in Indonesia and a seminar entitled 'Sharing the Faith in a Multi-cultural and Multi-faith World' at Bossey. One of the reasons that the WCC sponsors seminars such as these is to try to counteract the tendency of an inward orientation in Church bodies: 'The particular mandate of ecumenical theological education is to sustain the vibrancy of the ecumenical vision – that all may be one – manifested in faith, communion, witness and service.' (The WCC)

Reactions of the Catholic Church

The Catholic Church did not react positively to the growing Ecumenical Movement of the 1920s. In 1928 Pope Pius XI published a letter in which he declared that the only way to realise the will of Christ for Church unity was for all Christians to simply return to the Church of Rome. The 'Apostolic See has never allowed its subjects to take part in the assemblies of non-Catholics: for the union of Christians can only be promoted by promoting the return to the one true Church of Christ of those who are separated from it ...' Pius XI feared that agreements between churches would lead to watered down doctrine and, eventually, to irreligion. Not only did the Roman Catholic Church refuse to join the World Council of Churches in 1948, it forbade its members from even attending as observers.

Study tip

Read for yourself some of the key documents referred to in this chapter. You can find *Unitatis Redintegratio*, for example, on the Vatican website: http://www.vatican.va/ . You might find it interesting to visit the new resource site for Anglican-Roman Catholic Dialogue: https://iarccum.org/

With the election of Pope John XXIII in 1958, a new approach to ecumenism was taken. In 1960 the Pope met with the **Archbishop of Canterbury**, Geoffrey Fisher – the first time an Archbishop of Canterbury had visited the Vatican in 600 years! That same year the Pope appointed a 'Secretariat for Promoting Christian Unity' with the purpose of developing an ecumenical spirit in the Catholic Church and developing dialogues and collaborations with other churches. Shortly thereafter, the Vatican approved Catholic observers for the WCC's assembly in Delhi in 1961. Not only this, but the Pope invited non-Catholics to be observers at Vatican II.

This new approach to ecumenism found expression in the Vatican II documents *Unitatis Redintegratio* ('restoration of unity'):

Excerpts from Vatican II's *Unitatis Redintegratio*

In recent times more than ever before, He has been rousing divided Christians to remorse over their divisions and to a longing for unity. Everywhere large numbers have felt the impulse of this grace, and among our separated brethren also there increases from day to day the movement, fostered by the grace of the Holy Spirit, for the restoration of unity among all Christians. This movement toward unity is called 'ecumenical'. Those belong to it who invoke the Triune God and confess Jesus as Lord and Saviour, doing this not merely as individuals but also as corporate bodies. For almost everyone regards the body in which he has heard the Gospel as his Church and indeed, God's Church. All, however, though in different ways, long for the one visible Church of God, a Church truly universal and set forth into the world that the world may be converted to the Gospel and so be saved, to the glory of God.

The Sacred Council gladly notes all this. It has already declared its teaching on the Church, and now, moved by a desire for the restoration of unity among all the followers of Christ, it wishes to set before all Catholics the ways and means by which they too can respond to this grace and to this divine call.

Catholics must gladly acknowledge and esteem the truly Christian endowments from our common heritage which are to be found among our separated brethren. It is right and salutary to recognise the riches of Christ and virtuous works in the lives of others who are bearing witness to Christ, sometimes even to the shedding of their blood. For God is always wonderful in His works and worthy of all praise.

... when the obstacles to perfect ecclesiastical communion have been gradually overcome, all Christians will at last, in a common celebration of the Eucharist, be gathered into the one and only Church in that unity which Christ bestowed on His Church from the beginning. We believe that this unity subsists in the Catholic Church as something she can never lose, and we hope that it will continue to increase until the end of time.

Key quote

... it is clear that the Apostolic See cannot on any terms take part in their assemblies, nor is it anyway lawful for Catholics either to support or to work for such enterprises; for if they do so they will be giving countenance to a false Christianity, quite alien to the one Church of Christ. **(Pope Pius XI)**

Pope John XXIII 1881–1963 (Pope from 1958–1963); he is remembered for calling together the Second Vatican Council.

Key terms

Archbishop of Canterbury: the senior bishop and principal leader of the Church of England; also the symbolic head of the worldwide Anglican Communion

Unitatis Redintegratio: A Vatican II Document that signalled a new attitude to ecumenical relations

This text is significant for many reasons:

- It describes Christians outside of the Roman Catholic Church as 'separated brethren' rather than as 'heretics' or 'dissidents'.

- It accepts that both sides share a responsibility for divisions in the Church.

- It demonstrates an appreciation for the contributions non-Catholic Christians make to the spirituality and practice of Christianity.

- It moves away from the simple identification of the one true Church with the current form of the Roman Catholic Church.

This last point is very significant. Instead of saying, simply, that the true Church of Christ *is* the Roman Catholic Church, this document states that the true church *subsists* in the Catholic Church. The exact meaning of the term 'subsist' in this document has been debated. However, as Pope Benedict XVI has said, 'the Council Fathers meant to say that the being of the Church as such is a broader entity than the Roman Catholic Church, but within the latter it acquires, in an incomparable way, the character of a true and proper subject'. In other words, the positive message to the Ecumenical Movement is that the Catholic Church recognises that there are Christian activities outside of it, but at the same time it insists that the Church of Christ is in the Roman Catholic Church in a way that is incomparable to other churches. For, *Unitatis Redintegratio* also says, 'For it is only through Christ's Catholic Church, which is "the all-embracing means of salvation," that they can benefit fully from the means of salvation. We believe that Our Lord entrusted all the blessings of the New Covenant to the apostolic college alone, of which Peter is the head, in order to establish the one Body of Christ on earth to which all should be fully incorporated who belong in any way to the people of God.'

This positive attitude to the Ecumenical Movement continued with the Catholic Church becoming full members of the Faith and Order commission of the World Council of Churches (1968; though not full membership of the WCC itself). In 1965 Pope John Paul VI and the Patriarch of Constantinople Athenagoras issued a joint statement which retracted the mutual excommunications and condemnations between their two churches of 1054. The Pope famously gave the Archbishop of Canterbury, Michael Ramsey an episcopal ring in 1966 and, the following year, they established the Anglican-Roman-Catholic International Committee (**ARCIC**) dedicated to the ecumenical progress between these two churches. Over the years there have also been numerous dialogues between the Church of Rome and other churches throughout the world.

Tensions in the Ecumenical Movement

There are currently 348 church bodies in the World Council of Churches; one can well imagine that they do not always agree! In fact, there have been some serious disagreements in the past few decades. One of these concerns the Orthodox churches. The Orthodox see themselves as identified with the universal Church. Their belief is that other churches need to find consensus with the Orthodox Church if unity is to be achieved. This position conflicts with the tendency in the WCC to seek consensus between churches rather than to favour one church. Even though there are only about 20 Orthodox Church bodies as a part of the WCC, the baptised orthodox members worldwide number nearly one-half of all church members represented by the WCC. This had led to the Orthodox representatives feeling a tension about being treated as a small minority within the World Council of Churches when they represent nearly a majority in terms of their overall size. Other sources of tension include:

- The fall of communism has resulted in a strengthening of the Orthodox Church. One side of this development has been a rise in nationalism and xenophobia in countries where the Orthodox Church is strong. This, in turn, has led to suspicions about the Ecumenical Movement.

Key term

ARCIC: The acronym for the Anglican Roman Catholic International Committee established in 1967

quickfire

4.4 What is one reason why *Unitatis Redintegratio* is important for the Ecumenical Movement?

Key quotes

… there are also many true Christians and much that is truly Christian outside the church.
(J. Ratzinger, Pope Benedict XVI)

Today I see with satisfaction that the already vast network of ecumenical cooperation is constantly growing. Thanks also to the influence of the World Council of Churches, much is being accomplished in this field.
(Pope John Paul II)

World Council of Churches

The logo of the World Council of Churches

- Some Orthodox members of the WCC feel uncomfortable with the worship style adopted at WCC gatherings.
- There are difficulties with what is perceived by the Orthodox as a 'liberal' attitude to other religions and issues of social justice such as homosexual rights.

In 1991, a critical statement was issued by Orthodox participants to the WCC: '… we miss from many WCC documents the affirmation that Jesus Christ is the world's Saviour. We perceive a growing departure from biblically based understandings of: (a) the Trinitarian God; (b) salvation; (c) the "good news" of the Gospel itself; (d) human beings as created in the image and likeness of God; and (e) the Church.' In 1997, the Georgian Orthodox Church quit the WCC. Evangelical and Pentecostal Church bodies both inside and outside of the WCC have raised similar concerns. Given the fact that traditional Protestant bodies are declining in membership and that Pentecostalism is the fastest growing movement in Christianity, this could mean future tensions in the WCC in the areas of understanding interfaith dialogue, and the role of sexuality and gender in ministry and social justice.

Anglican-Roman Catholic tensions

In 1981 the ARCIC released a report which noted many areas of agreement, especially in understandings of the Eucharist and ordained ministry. It offered the view that the only really significant difference between the Anglican Church and the Roman Catholic Church was that the former was not in visible unity with the latter. The report even suggested that Anglicans might welcome a merging with the Catholic Church if the Papacy were seen more as a practical route to Church unity rather than a theological necessity. This would also deal with the criticisms many Anglicans have about Catholic doctrines of Mary (Immaculate Conception and The Assumption of Mary) which originated as pronouncements by 'infallible' papal teachings.

The Catholic Church, however, was quick to respond, noting that the Papal office is indeed a theological necessity, rooted in Scripture; it 'belongs to the divine structure of the Church'. It is therefore not willing to surrender any doctrines that have been introduced by Papal authority. Thus, at the heart of division between these two churches is the nature of authority.

The ARCIC has been threatened by several events:

- The ordination of women by churches in the Anglican Communion has been perceived by the Catholic Church as damaging to hopes of future unity.
- The ordination of an openly homosexual man (Gene Robinson) as an episcopal bishop in the United States caused Pope John Paul II in 2003 to suspend participation in the ARCIC.
- The ordination of women as bishops has been called an 'obstacle for reconciliation between the Catholic Church and the Church of England' by Walter Kasper, the President of the Pontifical Council for Promoting Christian Unity.
- On the Catholic side, the setting up of a structure in 2009 to facilitate Anglican Clergy becoming ordained in the Catholic Church deepened tensions for Anglicans.

Despite these tensions, the ARCIC continues to meet and to encourage unity between Anglicans and Catholics. This initiative has been given new energy through the warm mutual relationship between Pope Francis and the Archbishop of Canterbury Justin Welby.

Key quote

Conflicts *within* denominations over biblical authority, gender, and sexuality have greatly complicated efforts to secure unity *between* denominations. (S. Harmon)

Given the practical difficulties posed by issues of gender and sexuality, it is hard to see what unity between Catholics and Anglicans might look like – certainly not uniformity. But if the intellectual difficulties are greater now than 50 years ago, emotionally the two churches are closer than at any time since the reign of Henry VIII. (P. Vallely)

quickfire

4.5 Name two different Christian groups who believe that the World Council of Churches is 'watering down' Christian beliefs.

Pope Francis and Archbishop of Canterbury Justin Welby have met several times and produced a joint statement on the importance of Christian unity.

Key skills Theme 4

The fourth theme has tasks that consolidate your AO1 skills and focus these skills for examination preparation.

Key skills

Knowledge involves:

Selection of a range of (thorough) accurate and relevant information that is directly related to the specific demands of the question.

This means:

- Selecting relevant material for the question set
- Being focused in explaining and examining the material selected.

Understanding involves:

Explanation that is extensive, demonstrating depth and/or breadth with excellent use of evidence and examples including (where appropriate) thorough and accurate supporting use of sacred texts, sources of wisdom and specialist language.

This means:

- Effective use of examples and supporting evidence to establish the quality of your understanding
- Ownership of your explanation that expresses personal knowledge and understanding and NOT just reproducing a chunk of text from a book that you have rehearsed and memorised.

AO1 Developing skills

It is now important to consider the information that has been covered in this section; however, the information in its raw form is too extensive and so has to be processed in order to meet the requirements of the examination. This can be achieved by practising more advanced skills associated with AO1. The exercises that run throughout this book will help you to do this and prepare you for the examination. For assessment objective 1 (AO1), which involves demonstrating 'knowledge' and 'understanding' skills, we are going to focus on different ways in which the skills can be demonstrated effectively, and also refer to how the performance of these skills is measured (see generic band descriptors for A2 [WJEC] AO1 or A Level [Eduqas] AO1).

▶ **Your new task is this:** You will have to write a response under timed conditions to a question requiring an examination or explanation of **the groups that evolved into the World Council of Churches**. This exercise is best done as a small group at first.

1. Begin with a list of indicative content, as you may have done in the previous textbook in the series. It does not need to be in any particular order at first, although as you practise this, you will see more order in your lists that reflects your understanding.

2. Develop the list by using one or two relevant quotations. Now add some references to scholars and/or religious writings.

3. Then write out your plan, under timed conditions, remembering the principles of explaining with evidence and/or examples.

When you have completed the task, refer to the band descriptors for A2 (WJEC) or A Level (Eduqas) and in particular have a look at the demands described in the higher band descriptors towards which you should be aspiring. Ask yourself:

- Does my work demonstrate thorough, accurate and relevant knowledge and understanding of religion and belief?
- Is my work coherent (consistent or make logical sense), clear and well organised?
- Will my work, when developed, be an extensive and relevant response which is specific to the focus of the task?
- Does my work have extensive depth and/or suitable breadth and have excellent use of evidence and examples?
- If appropriate to the task, does my response have thorough and accurate reference to sacred texts and sources of wisdom?
- Are there any insightful connections to be made with other elements of my course?
- Will my answer, when developed and extended to match what is expected in an examination answer, have an extensive range of views of scholars/schools of thought?
- When used, is specialist language and vocabulary both thorough and accurate?

Issues for analysis and evaluation

Whether the work of the World Council of Churches can be viewed as a success or a failure

This section covers AO2 content and skills

Specification content

Whether the work of the World Council of Churches can be viewed as a success or a failure.

By sheer numbers alone the World Council of Churches (WCC) has achieved an impressive amount of participation. There are now 348 church bodies involved that represent more than half a billion Christians around the world. This is an achievement that is unprecedented since the divisions that came into being from the time of the Reformation. Furthermore, these member churches are not only Protestant; most Eastern Orthodox Churches are involved. Though the Roman Catholic Church is not a member of the WCC, it does participate fully in certain programme areas.

However, are these numbers really as impressive as they seem? For almost half of the 'half a billion' Christians represented by the WCC are in just 22 of the member churches (Orthodox), which means that any tensions experienced by the Orthodox as a result of their participation could have wide-ranging effects on the success of the WCC. Furthermore, the fastest growing movements in Christianity are Pentecostal and Evangelical forms. There are only a few of these that participate in the WCC; most Pentecostal Churches look upon the WCC with suspicion and feel that participation would 'water down' their doctrines and commitment to Christ. In addition to this, perhaps the elephant in the living room is that the largest Christian Church, the Roman Catholic Church (numbered by the Vatican as 1.2 billion Christians) is not a member of the WCC.

So, clearly the WCC would have a long way to go in order to be viewed as a success in its mission to bring all churches together. Alternatively, it could be argued that it has come a long way in a very short time. For it only came into being in 1948 and, prior to this, many of the Protestant and Orthodox Churches did not work together. The Roman Catholic Church forbade any involvement in the Ecumenical Movement prior to the 1960s, and has since become fully involved in several programme areas of the WCC.

Looking past the issue of numbers, the WCC can be said to be a success because of the sheer number of dialogues and Church mergers that have come into being at the same time as its birth and development. For instance, the Church of South India formed in 1947 as a result of six denominations coming together and the Church of North India in 1971 as a result of six denominations merging. Though the WCC did not play a direct role in these mergers, it did add positively to the ecumenical climate and has given all of those member churches an experience of ecumenical involvement. Furthermore, the breadth and vitality of the WCC's many programmes also speak of its success. These cover everything from mission and ecumenical relations to political activism and a wide variety of social justice issues in Church and wider society. These programmes not only take place in Geneva, the Headquarters of the WCC, but all over the world in mutual sponsorship between the WCC and its member churches.

However, there are fractures developing in these programmes. One of the main divisions has to do with how 'mission' is conceived. The WCC can be traced back to the World Missionary Conference in Edinburgh in 1910 where it was very clear that mission was conceived of as evangelism with the goal of conversions to Christianity and the establishment of new Christian churches. The WCC, however, has been perceived by some to have moved from this 'evangelical fervour' to a greater emphasis on interfaith 'dialogue' and the pursuit of social causes including issues of gender in leadership and sexuality.

AO2 Activity

As you read through this section try to do the following:

1. Pick out the different lines of argument that are presented in the text and identify any evidence given in support.
2. For each line of argument try to evaluate whether or not you think this is strong or weak.
3. Think of any questions you may wish to raise in response to the arguments.

This activity will help you to start thinking critically about what you read, and help you to evaluate the effectiveness of different arguments and from this develop your own observations, opinions and points of view that will help with any conclusions that you make in your answers to the AO2 questions that arise.

Key quotes

Neither isolation nor relativism characterises Christian identity.
(W. Keeler)

The Bedrock theological principle of ecumenism is that the Church is already one in Christ, for we are one body, the body of Christ.
(S. Harmon)

This perceived shift of focus has caused, for example, the WCC members of Orthodox Churches to issue a statement critical of the WCC. In this statement, they say that the WCC has moved away from a clear understanding of Jesus as the Saviour of the world as well as from straightforward biblical views on key Christian doctrines. It has been for similar reasons that many Evangelical and Pentecostal Churches do not participate in the WCC. Since Pentecostalism is the fastest growing movement in Christianity, it could be that the WCC will meet with future failure if it does not respond positively to the Orthodox critique. However, to respond positively would be to possibly alienate more 'liberal' churches who interpret mission in more humanitarian ways. It appears, then, that the WCC has reached a significant impasse. In 1997 the Georgian Orthodox Church left the WCC – is this a sign of things to come?

It is no small achievement, however, to have brought together most Orthodox Church bodies (collectively, the second largest Christian group in the world), with hundreds of Protestant denominations. In addition, the Roman Catholic Church, though not a full member, participates fully as members in two programmes (Faith and Order and a Joint Working Group). Certainly, all of this is a breakthrough for the Ecumenical Movement. However, it should be noted that many of the Orthodox Churches are increasingly tense about belonging to the WCC – not only for the theological reasons noted above, but because of the rise of nationalism and xenophobia in some of the countries in which they represent the majority of Christians.

Perhaps the deepest issue of all that imperils the mission of the WCC is the tendency of member churches to insist that they alone are the 'true Church'. An example of this is the Eastern Orthodox Churches who identify themselves with the Universal Church so that other churches need to move towards it rather than they towards other churches if unity is to be found. This is not merely an issue for Eastern Orthodox Churches; all Church bodies have been formed through time, hardship, persecution, study and reflection so may be uneasy about having to 'give up' aspects of their identity in order to engage in dialogue and joint projects with other churches. This type of tension makes any claim to ecumenical success seem premature.

Those involved in the Ecumenical Movement would say that, ultimately, it does not matter if the WCC is a failure or a success – for, it is Jesus who longs for Christian unity (John 17:20–22) and therefore Christian unity is a value that should be striven for regardless of how difficult or impossible it is to achieve. Furthermore, this Bible passage makes it clear that it is God's work to create unity. Therefore, it could be argued that the success or failure of the WCC is God's business rather than human business. Christians are called to faithfulness not success.

In conclusion, perhaps the question of the success or failure of the WCC is similar to the question of the success or failure of the United Nations. Clearly the fact that each of these bodies exist is of importance, though, at times many lament their ineffectiveness.

AO2 Activity

List some conclusions that could be drawn from the AO2 reasoning from the above text; try to aim for at least three different possible conclusions. Consider each of the conclusions and collect brief evidence to support each conclusion from the AO1 and AO2 material for this topic. Select the conclusion that you think is most convincing and explain why it is so. Try to contrast this with the weakest conclusion in the list, justifying your argument with clear reasoning and evidence.

The extent to which the non-membership of the Roman Catholic Church affects the aims of the World Council of Churches

Specification content

The extent to which the non-membership of the Roman Catholic Church affects the aims of the World Council of Churches.

One of the aims of the World Council of Churches, articulated clearly in the 1950 Toronto statement is that the WCC is not to be a 'superchurch' but is to encourage spiritual sharing between churches so that the Church can be strengthened and renewed.

It can be argued that even though the Roman Catholic Church is not a full member of the WCC, this spiritual sharing has happened. For, prior to the 1960s, the Roman Catholic Church refused to participate in the Ecumenical Movement. It insisted that if Christians wanted to find Church unity, they had simply better join the Catholic Church. However, with the election of Pope John in 1958, there was a movement to spiritual dialogue. This was directly stated in the Vatican II document *Unitatis Redintegratio* which recognises expressions of genuine Christianity outside of the Catholic Church and encourages the Church to participate in dialogue and cooperation. Accordingly, the Roman Catholic Church sent observers to the WCC Assembly in 1961, initiated dialogues with many individual Protest churches and has since become full members of two programme areas of the World Council of Churches.

However, it could be argued that there are limits to this sharing since the WCC thinks of itself as a group of 'traditions' in dialogue with one another and the Roman Catholic Church sees itself as the 'Tradition' ordained by God to be the universal Church through a divinely ordered papacy. How, then, can full spiritual sharing take place if one of the dialogue partners feels that it is more centred in the truth than the other? How deep can a relationship become if one person continually feels that the other should adopt their viewpoint?

However, spiritual sharing has to start somewhere and no relationship is perfect. If one considers that the dialogue between the Roman Catholic Church and the churches of the WCC is only just over 50 years old in comparison to centuries of strife and division then any sharing, however limited, is a cause for celebration. Furthermore, the Roman Catholic Church is not alone in feeling that it possesses the truth in a special way. For example, the Edinburgh World Missionary Conference in 1910 is widely regarded as the beginning of the modern Ecumenical Movement which evolved into the WCC. At the 1910 conference Roman Catholics and the Orthodox were not even invited.

However, the WCC has aims other than spiritual sharing. They state that the ultimate goal is 'visible unity of the Church' – this includes common worship, common sacraments, a common creed and participation in unified governing bodies. Judged by this aim, the non-membership of the Roman Catholic Church is indeed an impediment! Furthermore, despite the positive attitude towards dialogue in *Unitatis Redintegratio* (UR) there is also an assumption about the place of the Roman Catholic Church in God's plan that would seem to rule out 'visible unity' with the churches that make up the WCC. For, UR is clear that the Roman Catholic Church is the full expression of the Church and that all Christians must eventually belong to it in order to experience a full Christian life. This approach is at odds to the approach of the WCC which does not endorse a particular doctrine about the Church or a particular path to Church unity.

AO2 Activity

As you read through this section try to do the following:

1. Pick out the different lines of argument that are presented in the text and identify any evidence given in support.
2. For each line of argument try to evaluate whether or not you think this is strong or weak.
3. Think of any questions you may wish to raise in response to the arguments.

This activity will help you to start thinking critically about what you read, and help you to evaluate the effectiveness of different arguments and from this develop your own observations, opinions and points of view that will help with any conclusions that you make in your answers to the AO2 questions that arise.

Key quotes

… there was a millennium of Christianity from the end of the New Testament era to the early Middle Ages that preceded the current divisions of the Church. … Catholic, Orthodox and Protestant Christians of all stripes have this Great Tradition as their common heritage. (S. Harmon)

The dogmatic definition of the First Vatican Council declares that the primacy of the Bishop of Rome belongs to the divine structure of the Church; the Bishop of Rome inherits the primacy of Peter who received it 'immediately and directly' from Christ. (Catholic response to ARCIC I)

However, if the aim of full visible communion is viewed more as a journey than a destination then there are grounds for optimism despite the non-membership of the Roman Catholic Church. For, it can be argued that the Roman Catholic Church itself is on a journey which has led it closer to the WCC. This journey has deepened over the years with the full membership of the Roman Catholic Church on the Faith and Order Commission and on a Joint Working Group. In these areas, there have been solid achievements such as participation in numerous dialogues, one of which has given rise to one of the most studied ecumenical documents of recent history, 'Baptism, Eucharist and Ministry' (1982).

This journey, however, is fragile since changes in denominations that belong to the WCC are viewed by the Roman Catholic Church as threatening even their minimal level of participation. For instance, the ordination of women as priests and bishops in the Anglican communion has been singled out as an 'obstacle of reconciliation' and the appointment of an openly homosexual Episcopal bishop caused Pope John Paul II to suspend the dialogue with the Anglican Communion in 2003. Since there are several other Church bodies travelling in a similar direction as the Anglican Communion, this could create an unbridgeable gulf between the Roman Catholic Church and the WCC.

In conclusion, the extent to which the non-membership of the Roman Catholic Church affects the aims of the WCC may depend on the expectations one has about the timing of 'visible union'. If one expects that this should happen in one's lifetime then there are many reasons for scepticism. For, there are deep divisions, as we have seen, between the Roman Catholic Church and the many churches that belong to the WCC. A significant and seemingly insurmountable difference has to do with the issue of authority and the claim of the Roman Catholic Church to be, ultimately, the divinely appointed Church for all Christians.

Alternatively, if one adopts a more historical perspective there are grounds for optimism. For, prior to the 1960s there was little or no relationship between the Roman Catholic Church and the church bodies that make up the WCC. Now, there is not only participation, but active dialogues between the Roman Catholic Church and many individual Church bodies. These relationships may not always operate smoothly, but after centuries of Church division they could be viewed as a movement toward the aim of the WCC for visible unity.

AO2 Activity

List some conclusions that could be drawn from the AO2 reasoning from the above text; try to aim for at least three different possible conclusions. Consider each of the conclusions and collect brief evidence to support each conclusion from the AO1 and AO2 material for this topic. Select the conclusion that you think is most convincing and explain why it is so. Try to contrast this with the weakest conclusion in the list, justifying your argument with clear reasoning and evidence.

AO2 Developing skills

It is now important to consider the information that has been covered in this section; however, the information in its raw form is too extensive and so has to be processed in order to meet the requirements of the examination. This can be achieved by practising more advanced skills associated with AO2. The exercises that run throughout this book will help you to do this and prepare you for the examination. For assessment objective 2 (AO2), which involves 'critical analysis' and 'evaluation' skills, we are going to focus on different ways in which the skills can be demonstrated effectively, and also refer to how the performance of these skills is measured (see generic band descriptors for A2 [WJEC] AO2 or A Level [Eduqas] AO2).

▶ **Your new task is this:** you will have to write a response under timed conditions to a question requiring an evaluation of **the degree to which tensions in the World Council of Churches threaten to tear it apart**. This exercise is best done as a small group at first.

1. Begin with a list of indicative arguments or lines of reasoning, as you may have done in the previous textbook in the series. It does not need to be in any particular order at first, although as you practise this you will see more order in your lists, in particular by way of links and connections between arguments.

2. Develop the list by using one or two relevant quotations. Now add some references to scholars and/or religious writings.

3. Then write out your plan, under timed conditions, remembering the principles of evaluating with support from extensive, detailed reasoning and/or evidence.

When you have completed the task, refer to the band descriptors for A2 (WJEC) or A Level (Eduqas) and in particular have a look at the demands described in the higher band descriptors towards which you should be aspiring. Ask yourself:

- Is my answer a confident critical analysis and perceptive evaluation of the issue?
- Is my answer a response that successfully identifies and thoroughly addresses the issues raised by the question set.
- Does my work show an excellent standard of coherence, clarity and organisation?
- Will my work, when developed, contain thorough, sustained and clear views that are supported by extensive, detailed reasoning and/or evidence?
- Are the views of scholars/schools of thought used extensively, appropriately and in context?
- Does my answer convey a confident and perceptive analysis of the nature of any possible connections with other elements of my course?
- When used, is specialist language and vocabulary both thorough and accurate?

Key skills Theme 4
The fourth theme has tasks that consolidate your AO2 skills and focus these skills for examination preparation.

Key skills
Analysis involves:

Identifying issues raised by the materials in the AO1, together with those identified in the AO2 section, and presenting sustained and clear views, either of scholars or from a personal perspective ready for evaluation.

This means:

- That your answers are able to identify key areas of debate in relation to a particular issue
- That you can identify, and comment upon, the different lines of argument presented by others
- That your response comments on the overall effectiveness of each of these areas or arguments.

Evaluation involves:

Considering the various implications of the issues raised based upon the evidence gleaned from analysis and providing an extensive detailed argument with a clear conclusion.

This means:

- That your answer weighs up the consequences of accepting or rejecting the various and different lines of argument analysed
- That your answer arrives at a conclusion through a clear process of reasoning.

Specification content

The Charismatic Movement.

Charismatic worship in a Roman
Catholic congregation

Key quote

… at the heart of Christianity there
is and should be an *encounter with
the Holy Spirit*. This encounter
is free, spontaneous, dynamic,
transformative and should be
an ongoing experiential reality
within the purposes of God.
(M. Cartledge)

Key terms

Charismatic: from the Greek word
charismata, 'gifts of grace'; special
qualities Christians believe they
receive through the Holy Spirit

Charismatic Movement: the
experience of gifts of the Spirit in
churches other than Pentecostal
denominations from the 1960s to today

E: Religious identity through religious experience

Introduction to the Charismatic Movement

Imagine that someone who has never attended Church before has been invited to a Sunday morning service at an Anglican or Catholic church. What might they expect it to be like? If they have watched royal weddings, or papal visits on television, they might imagine that the service will be formal in nature: robed processions, organ music, chanting, singing hymns, and kneeling to recite written prayers.

However, the reality in some traditional churches is the opposite of all of this. In these churches people spontaneously lift their hands in the air and sway as soft-rock music is played by a worship band at the front of the church. At the end of songs some people engage in a kind of gentle 'babbling', a language which makes no sense but which is called 'tongues'. During the Eucharist, the priest might encourage people who want healing to come forward for 'laying on of hands' and prayers that ask the Spirit of God to bring about healing immediately. After the service, there may be an invitation to attend a prayer meeting focused on learning about the 'power of the Spirit' in the believer's life. If someone attended a church with a service like this, they have just discovered the **Charismatic Movement**.

What does 'charismatic' mean?

Charismatic comes from the Greek word *charismata* means 'gifts of grace'. This is the word the Apostle Paul uses to refer to special qualities that Christians receive through the Holy Spirit. There are several lists of these 'spiritual gifts' in the New Testament. As you can see in the table below, these lists don't agree with each other; it does not seem that Paul and others were trying to present a standardised list but drawing attention to the many different ways that Christian believers could express God's grace.

It is also interesting that in passages scholars believe were written later (Ephesians and I Peter), many of the 'miraculous' gifts are missing. Was the Church quickly moving toward a more formal and regulated order? We simply do not know the answer to this question. However, it is true that in the early centuries of the Church there was the development of formal leadership and very little evidence of the more miraculous gifts in regular practice in Christian worship services.

New Testament passages that mention spiritual gifts	
Romans 12:6–8	**I Corinthians 12:8–11**
prophecy	word of wisdom
serving	word of knowledge
teaching	faith
exhorting	healing
giving	miracles
leadership	prophecy
compassion	discernment of spirits
	tongues
	interpretation of tongues

New Testament passages that mention spiritual gifts		
I Corinthians 12:28	Ephesians 4:11	I Peter 4:11
Apostles	Apostles	speaking for God
prophets	prophets	serving
teachers	evangelists	
deeds of power	pastors	
healing	teachers	
serving		
leadership		
tongues		

Key term

Tongues: from the Greek term glossalia (gloss = speak, laleo = tongue or language); using a language unknown to the speaker. In the Bible this can be either a foreign language or a special, heavenly language

The most extensive discussion of spiritual gifts is in I Corinthians 12–14. Paul is concerned that the Church becomes aware of the true purpose of spiritual gifts: to strengthen the body of Christ. The gifts, then, are not for attaining an individualistic spiritual 'high'; they are to be shared with others so that everyone in the Church can have a deeper relationship with God. For this reason, Paul discouraged a chaotic practice of the gifts where there were multiple and simultaneous displays of **tongues** or prophecies so that all an observer would hear is a confusing babble of noise. For instance, he preferred that if one was going to speak in tongues, then this was more fitting for one's private worship unless the experience was interpreted in an orderly fashion so that everyone could understand what has being communicated. What was most important for Paul was that people would seek spiritual gifts in an attitude of love and helpfulness for those around them.

AO1 Activity

Read I Corinthians chapters 12–14 and write your own answers to these questions: What were the problems Paul was trying to address at this church? What were the solutions he proposed? In your opinion what are the appealing qualities of the church he describes? What are the unappealing qualities?

quickfire

4.6 True or false: Paul believed that those who were not leaders in the Church could experience spiritual gifts.

Pentecostalism

Pentecostalism is the early twentieth-century movement that believed the miraculous events in the book of Acts, with its outpouring of the Spirit on the Apostles, mass conversions and miracles of healing should not be seen as part of a past age but should be a present reality for the Christian Church. Many scholars trace the beginnings of this movement to a temporary Bible school set up by preacher Charles Fox Parham in Topeka Kansas. Parham believed that the Holy Spirit was going descend in special way on the Church. He asked his students to read the book of Acts and to pray that they would receive the Spirit. On the first of January 1901, one of these students, Agnes N. Ozman, is reported to have spoken in tongues and soon after many of the students experienced what they believed to be the gifts of the Spirit.

Key quote

Pentecostals have turned to the narrative of Luke-Acts as the main source for their theology. (M. Cartledge)

An itinerant African-American preacher, William James Seymour, also followed Parham's ministry. In 1906 Seymour moved to Los Angeles and led a small prayer group which rapidly grew as a result of having similar experiences. In 1906 this group moved to an unused building at 312 Azusa Street; this quickly became the

The Azusa Street Mission, Los Angeles, California

largest church in Los Angeles. What was especially striking about this church was that Seymour, as an African American, worked with an interracial congregation of African Americans, Mexican-Americans, and European-Americans.

In the first few decades of the last century the various churches that focused on these experiences gradually formed denominations including The Assemblies of God, the Foursquare Gospel Church, Elim Pentecostal Church (the United Kingdom) and The Apostolic Church (Wales). Pentecostal denominations are known for being evangelical in nature. Alistair McGrath notes four qualities of evangelicalism: (i) scripture is the ultimate authority, (ii) the saving death of Jesus on the cross is the only source of redemption, (iii) all people need to have a conversion experience, and (iv) the Christian faith should be shared through evangelism. However Pentecostal denominations also manifest the following qualities which distinguish them from other Evangelical Churches:

- Pentecostal Churches believe that there is a second baptism, that of the Holy Spirit – this takes place after conversion.
- Many Pentecostals believe that speaking in tongues is the confirmation that one has received this second baptism.
- There is a focus on spontaneous worship and healing, and a belief that these are the 'end times'.
- Pentecostal Churches in the first decades of the 20th century were anti-ecumenical, rarely having anything to do with 'mainstream' traditional churches.
- This anti-ecumenical tendency can be seen in Pentecostal attitudes to the Roman Catholic Church which has been viewed by many Pentecostal Christians as outside of Christianity altogether because of its formalism, hierarchy and worldliness.

The development of the Charismatic Movement post-1960

The Charismatic Movement refers to the experience of the gifts of the Spirit in churches outside of Pentecostal denominations. From the mid twentieth century onwards many members of traditional churches experienced speaking in tongues, healing and other gifts described in the New Testament, but chose to remain in their denominations rather than leave them. They saw their experiences as ways to bring renewal to their denominations. At the same time, the Roman Catholic Church, the Anglican Communion and many other denominations chose to study and observe this phenomenon rather than to reject it. There were questions about whether this movement was anti-intellectual and could breed an indifference to the classic doctrines of the Christian faith by indulging in emotional experiences. At the same time, it was recognised that the Bible advocated spiritual gifts and that the testimony of those in the movement was that it strengthened their faith and their commitment to their churches.

Study tip

Make sure that you understand the difference between Pentecostalism, a movement that began at the beginning of the 20th century and formed Pentecostal denominations; and the Charismatic Movement, which shares similar emphases to Pentecostalism, which became an aspect of many traditional denominations from the 1960s.

The Charismatic Movement spread very quickly from the 1960s, finding acceptance in both the Roman Catholic Church as well as many Protestant denominations. It can be described as a 'renewal movement' within churches and is sometimes referred to as 'neo-Pentecostalism' because it shares many traits with Pentecostal

quickfire

4.7 In Pentecostalism what is usually considered the sign that you have been 'baptised in the Holy Spirit'?

Specification content

The development of the Charismatic Movement post-1960.

denominations. As in Pentecostal Churches there is the conviction that the gifts of grace described by Paul in I Corinthians 12 are just as valid today as they were in the early church. However, there are some different emphases:

- Speaking in tongues is generally not tied as tightly to one's first experience of the Holy Spirit as it might be in Pentecostal denominations. There has been a tendency especially in early Pentecostalism to see speaking in tongues as the initial proof of Spirit baptism. In the Charismatic Movement tongues are viewed as a gift to all believers, but not one that necessarily confirms their spiritual experience.

- There is generally less reference to the baptism of the Holy Spirit as the second part of a two-stage initiation. Churches in the Charismatic Movement prefer to speak of 'being filled by the Spirit' or 'released by the Spirit'. This is to emphasise the biblical teaching that there is only one Baptism and that all Christians have the Spirit of God in their lives, but that Christians can have a fuller experience of the Spirit later in their journey.

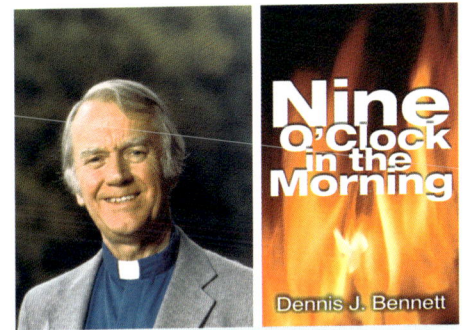

Dennis Bennett and his book which inspired many in the Charismatic Movement.

The beginning of the Charismatic Movement

The Charismatic Movement came to world attention in 1960 when an Episcopalian minister in California, Dennis Bennett, had a charismatic experience and introduced it to his congregation. A small group in the church voiced their opposition and rather than cause a split in the congregation, Bennett resigned; the Bishop of Los Angeles banned speaking in tongues. *Time* and *Newsweek* magazines picked up this story. A Bishop in Washington State, more open to these experiences, placed Bennett in a dying church in Seattle. Under Bennett's leadership this church soon became the largest in the diocese and hosted conferences on the Charismatic Movement for leaders across the country.

However, ministers and lay people in traditional churches were becoming increasingly aware of spiritual gifts apart from Bennett's experience:

- David du Plessis, an Assemblies of God minister, felt called to witness to Pentecostalism in ecumenical circles. He was involved with the World Council of Churches and had audiences with three different popes. He was known widely as 'Mr Pentecost' by those in traditional churches.

- Oral Roberts, a Methodist Minister, brought Pentecostalism to a large audience as a pioneer of televangelism, though his fundraising techniques earned him much criticism.

- The Full Gospel Businessman's Fellowship began in 1953. This was a popular movement that brought together businessmen (women and ministers were excluded) with Pentecostal speakers in informal settings. Many from traditional denominations attended.

- Popular books began to bring Pentecostal themes to wider audiences. One of these was *The Cross and the Switchblade (1963)*, the true story of a Pentecostal minister who left his comfortable suburban denomination to work with violent street gangs in New York City.

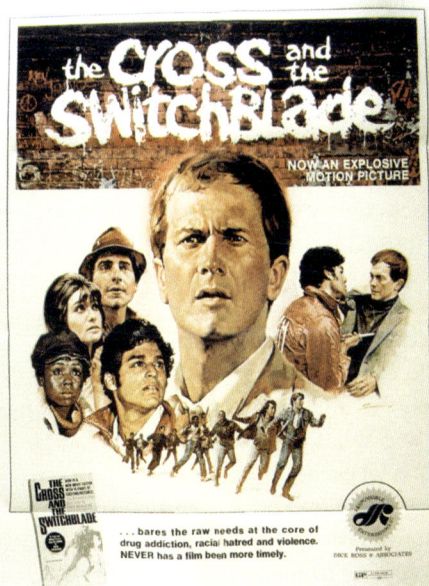

The Cross and the Switchblade was made into a widely seen film in 1970.

Key quotes

Is it possible that an institutionalised, intellectualised, formalised (and even fossilised) practice of Christianity has left a thirst in the inner being which only the springs of charismatic renewal could satisfy? (Church of England Report, 1981)

… the charismatic movement gentrified Pentecostalism. (A. Mason)

quickfire

4.8 What is usually considered the beginning of the Charismatic Movement in traditional Protestant Churches and what is usually considered to be the beginning of the Charismatic Movement in the Catholic Church?

The students and teachers at Duquesne University that gathered in February 1967.

The first Church of England congregation to declare itself as charismatic was in 1963. Soon after, a national network, The Fountain Trust, was founded to encourage charismatic worship across denominations in the United Kingdom. Here is a description of charismatic renewal in one Church of England congregation:

> The Renewal started at St Hugh's soon after a new Vicar came in 1970. He himself was experiencing a new opening out of his faith at the time and shared this with the church. A number of people were fairly quickly influenced and as they opened up their lives through confession and absolution and prayer for the gift of the Holy Spirit, began to know a much closer relationship with the Lord and to experience his activity in their lives. Gifts of the Spirit were manifested; tongues, prophecy, healing, etc., the movement spread, more and more people were affected and there was a growing sense of blessing and expectancy and a measure of excitement in the life of the Church. … Prayer groups sprang up. Worship was enlivened and became to be freed from too much formalism. (Church of England Report, 1970)

The Charismatic Movement in the Roman Catholic Church

Prior to the rise of the Charismatic Movement in the Catholic Church, Vatican II (1962–1965) had focused on the need for renewal. Pope John XXIII began Vatican II with a prayer, 'Divine Spirit, renew your wonders in this our age, as in a new Pentecost'. This openness to renewal is expressed clearly in one of the key documents of Vatican II, *Lumen Gentium* [Light to the Gentiles]. This document asserts both the authority of the Church and the need to be open to new spiritual expressions.

from *Lumen Gentium*

It is not only through the sacraments and the ministries of the Church that the Holy Spirit sanctifies and leads the people of God and enriches it with virtues, but, 'allotting his gifts to everyone according as He wills, He distributes special graces among the faithful of every rank. By these gifts He makes them fit and ready to undertake the various tasks and offices which contribute toward the renewal and building up of the Church', according to the words of the Apostle: 'The manifestation of the Spirit is given to everyone for profit'. These charisms, whether they be the more outstanding or the more simple and widely diffused, are to be received with thanksgiving and consolation for they are perfectly suited to and useful for the needs of the Church. Extraordinary gifts are not to be sought after, nor are the fruits of apostolic labour to be presumptuously expected from their use; but judgment as to their genuine and proper use belongs to those who are appointed leaders in the Church, to whose special competence it belongs, not indeed to extinguish the Spirit, but to test all things and hold fast to that which is good.

Scholars often cite February 1967 as the beginning of Charismatic Renewal in the Catholic Church. At Duquesne University, a Catholic University in Pittsburgh Pennsylvania, two lecturers had been praying for renewal in the Church. They then asked about twenty students to read *The Cross and the Switchblade* and to gather for a weekend conference. The group then had dramatic experiences of speaking in tongues and other spiritual gifts. The movement spread to the University of Notre Dame which began to host annual conferences with thousands of Catholics attending from around the world. Soon the Charismatic Movement could be found in Catholic Churches on every continent.

Cardinal Leo Joseph Suenens, a leading voice at Vatican II, was sympathetic to the Charismatic Movement and represented this movement to the Pope. He said, 'We should not see in this renewal just one more movement to be set alongside many others in the Church today. Rather than a movement, charismatic renewal is a moving of the Holy Spirit which can reach all Christians, lay or cleric. It is comparable to a high voltage current of grace which is coursing through the Church.'

The movement has been recognised in many significant ways by the Church:

- In 1975 Pope Paul VI welcomed 10,000 charismatic Christians attending a conference on the Charismatic Movement.
- In 1980 Pope John Paul II appointed the charismatic priest Raniero Cantalamessa as a preacher to the papal household (he remains in this role for Pope Francis).
- In 1993 the Vatican officially recognised the International Charismatic Renewal Services (ICCRS), an organisation that promotes charismatic renewal amongst Catholics across the world.

Today, some estimates place the number of Catholics involved in charismatic renewal between 10 and 15% of all Catholics worldwide – this could mean that there are as many as 150 million charismatic Catholics. It is difficult to provide accurate numbers because the Charismatic Movement in the Catholic Church does not have a single founder and does not occur in a just one single area. According to the International Catholic Charismatic Renewal Services it is, '... a highly diverse collection of individuals, groups and activities – covenant communities, prayer groups, schools, small faith-sharing groups, renewed parishes, conferences, retreats, and even involvement in various apostolates and ministries – often quite independent of one another ... that nevertheless share the same fundamental experience and espouse the same general goals.'

AO1 Activity

Find a charismatic church that belongs to a traditional denomination on the Internet and make a list of its activities and beliefs that, according to this theme, reflect their being in the Charismatic Movement. You may wish to research Mother of God sanctuary in São Paolo Brazil. This is one of the largest church buildings in the world, accommodating up to 100,000 worshippers on its grounds. The priest is Father Marcelo Rossi. Known as the 'Pop Star Priest' for his use of music in Mass, his numerous album sales and other media productions.

Other expressions of the Charismatic Movement

In the 1980s and 90s many who had been involved in non-charismatic Evangelical Churches began to join the Charismatic Movement. The fastest growing Christian movement in Britain in the 1980s was the House Church movement also known as **Restorationism** for its belief that, through it, God was restoring his Kingdom in the last days. The movement was composed of both Christians who had left established denominations (such as the Brethren, Baptists and those from classical Pentecostal denominations) as well as new Christians. They renounced denominations, had charismatic experiences, met in homes and also formed larger assemblies under those who saw themselves as Apostles. There has been a strong eschatological emphasis in the movement, with adherents believing that they were living in the end times when demonic powers would be overcome. Dr Andrew Walker describes the attitudes of those in the Restoration movement: 'The legalism of clericalism, church order, standardised liturgies, denominational certainties and dogmatic doctrines were seen to be swept aside by the coming of the Spirit.'

Key quotes

One description of the Catholic Charismatic Renewal is: *A personal experience of the presence and power of the Holy Spirit, who brings alive in new ways the graces of our baptism. The Holy Spirit not only sets on fire all that we have already received, but comes again in power to equip us with his gifts for service and mission.* (From the Catholic Charismatic Renewal Website www.ccr.org.uk)

The Catholic charismatics are undoubtedly the strongest and by far the most numerous in the Charismatic Renewal in older churches today. (A. H. Anderson)

By and large, the Pentecostal churches had been deeply hostile to Catholicism, which in their eyes was the epitome of that formalism and organisation which suffocates the Spirit. It was axiomatic among them that a Catholic would have to leave his church in order to receive the Spirit. On the other hand, most Catholics either had not taken the Pentecostals seriously, or had recoiled from the emotionalism and fanaticism associated with them. (E. O'Connor)

Worship at Mother of God Roman Catholic Church, São Paolo, Brazil

Key term

Restorationism: an anti-denominational Christian movement in Britain emphasising the gifts of the Spirit and seeking to 'restore' the beliefs and practices of the early church

quickfire

4.9 Name one example of the Charismatic Movement from non-denominational groups.

Specification content

Main beliefs; implications for Christian practice in the experience of believers and Christian communities; philosophical challenges to charismatic experience (verification and natural explanation).

The church, now named 'Catch the Fire', where the 'Toronto Blessing' takes place.

Key terms

Prophecy: direct speech from God

Spring Harvest: an organisation which hosts non-denominational charismatic festivals across Britain

Toronto Blessing: an especially ecstatic set of experiences at a Vineyard Church near the Toronto airport that has attracted worldwide attention from the 1990s to the present day

Vineyard churches: an association of over 1500 charismatic churches led by John Wimber in the 1980s and 1990s

Xenolalia: a type of speaking in tongues in which the speaker uses a foreign language that they have not consciously learned

Key quote

Many have found that tension, depression, fear and temptations which could not be gotten rid of in any other way are promptly banished when they pray in tongues. (E. O'Connor)

There have also been a number of movements, festivals and leaders who have been influential in spreading the Charismatic Movement amongst evangelical Christians. This includes the **Toronto Blessing**, the **Vineyard** association of churches founded by John Wimber and the Spring Harvest ministries. **Spring Harvest** is a non-denominational gathering of Christians of all ages in a festival setting at several locations across the UK. It is known for its charismatic worship and inspiring speakers.

Main beliefs and implications for Christian practice in the experience of believers and Christian communities

Those in the Charismatic Movement believe that Christians outside of their movement can have a much fuller experience of the Holy Spirit. This can happen in several ways:

1. *Speaking in tongues.* Glossalia (glossa = speaking, laleo = language, tongue) is the Greek term used to refer to the miracle made possible by the Holy Spirit of speaking in a language (either human or divine) unknown to the speaker. There is a debate about the relationship of this word in the contexts of Acts chapter 2 and I Corinthians 12–14. In Acts chapter 2 it appears that the disciples were speaking in human languages that they did not know themselves – but were recognised by various members of the international Jewish community that had gathered in Jerusalem. This is known as **xenolalia**: speaking in a known language that one has not consciously learned. This seems to be different from the experiences described in I Corinthians 12–14 where Paul speaks of a kind of heavenly language that cannot be understood by anyone without the spiritual gift of interpretation. In I Corinthians 14 Paul makes it clear that the language is meant for a divine rather than a human audience; its primary function is in private prayer. It is permissible in public worship if there is someone who can interpret the message. Early in Pentecostalism there were frequent claims of xenolalia, though these were never proven. Most Pentecostal Christians and those in the Charismatic Movement see tongues as a divine prayer language that leads one to making an incomprehensible babbling kind of noise whilst simultaneously feeling close to God. In an effort to reconcile Acts and Corinthians, some theologians have said that what is happening in Acts is not xenolalia; rather, the Apostles were speaking in a heavenly language and the Spirit of God was simultaneously giving listeners a miracle of interpretation. This is a minority position; most theologians believe that these passages are about two different phenomena.

Study tip

Know the difference between xenolalia and the type of glossalia that is referred to as a 'heavenly' language by some charismatic Christians. You should be able to explain why xenolalia, potentially, could be a source of scientific verification of religious experiences whereas speaking in a 'heavenly language' could not be.

2. **Prophecy**. We normally associate the term prophecy with someone foretelling the future. However, in the Bible, a prophet is someone who conveys the word of God in a direct way. Sometimes this has to do with foretelling future events, but more often it has to do with speaking a message that will bring about greater loyalty to God, increased morality, or a more worshipful attitude. This is the same case in the Charismatic Movement. A prophecy is a type of exhortation known for its directness – it claims to come directly from God. In the context of charismatic worship someone may say, 'I the Lord say unto you...' or 'God wants us to know that...'. The message that follows inspires confidence

and obedience amongst believers. Examples of prophecy are 'This is the year you will reclaim your confidence as a believer, for I am with you and will not leave you. Do not let the enemy subvert you.' Or 'God says to not worry about your decision about your job, for he will guide you and lead you.' In I Corinthians 14:29 Paul says that prophecies need to be tested. For this reason, churches have criteria to discern true from false prophecy. These criteria usually include that the prophecy does not contradict the teaching of the Bible, is accepted by Church leaders, clearly recognises that Jesus is God, and inspires love, joy, peace and other 'fruits of the spirit' (see Galatians 5:22–23).

A worship service at Holy Trinity Brompton, a charismatic Church of England congregation

3. *Healing.* In Mark chapter 16 (although seen by some scholars as added later to Mark's Gospel), when Jesus gave the command to the disciples to spread the Gospel across the world, he said that a number of signs would accompany their work. One of these was healing: 'they will lay their hands on the sick, and they will recover'. (Mark 16:18) Thus, when charismatic Christians are gathered they fully expect that the Spirit of God can move to heal believers. They think this can happen through the prayers of elders (James 5:14) but also through those that have the spiritual gift of healing. Prayers for healing often involve the laying on of hands by several people. Sometimes there are healing prayers offered during the administration of the Eucharist. Healing is conceived of not just in physical terms but also as having psychological or emotional dimensions – the healing of relationships, buried memories or of one's conscience.

4. *Inspiration in worship.* Charismatic services are marked by a mood of joyful expectation as to what the Spirit of God might do. Worshippers generally feel free to move their bodies, swaying with the music, raising hands in the air, clapping, dancing and linking arms. Usually the style of music is contemporary with a 'worship band' using a variety of instruments such as guitars, drums, bass, keyboards and having singers using microphones. Many charismatic churches will project lyrics on screens in the sanctuary so that worshippers are free from using books (a practice common amongst Evangelical Churches). Music is also used in informal ways in charismatic churches: times of prayer can be punctuated with spontaneous singing of familiar songs or choruses, there can be gentle singing during the Eucharist and songs can conclude with worshippers transitioning into speaking/singing in tongues.

Philosophical challenges to charismatic experience

One of the appeals of the Charismatic Movement is that it offers an experience of God to Christians who may have only possessed an intellectual relationship with Christianity. In contrast to mere 'knowledge about' God, charismatic believers claim to have direct 'experience of' God's presence through a variety of experiences. The fact that many people have become believers after observing and experiencing the 'gifts of the Spirit' seems to confirm this belief that God can be known through experience.

However, Christian churches do not accept every claim of a charismatic experience as true. Churches have a set of criteria to judge experiences. These vary from denomination to denomination but usually include the following factors: (i) Do the messages that come from charismatic experiences (such as prophecy) conform to the teaching of the Bible? (ii) Does the experience produce spiritual fruits such as love, joy and peace? (iii) Is the message or experience supportive of the direction set by the leaders of the congregation? And (iv) Do the experiences affirm that Jesus is Lord, to be esteemed as God and followed?

Key quote

In meetings where the Holy Spirit's power is strongly manifest, some people seem a little drunk … They may describe a heaviness that is on them. Their speech may be slightly slurred, their movements uncoordinated. They may need support to walk. (D. White)

quickfire

4.10 List at least five qualities that can be found in charismatic worship.

The fact that churches have tests for charismatic experiences suggests that at least sometimes they see these experiences as not coming from God at all, but perhaps from other spiritual forces or generated by one's own ego. However, a much wider question can be asked: is it possible that none of these experiences come from God?

The verification of charismatic experiences

It is the most human thing in the world to want to have proof before we believe something. At a surface level, charismatic experiences seem to provide proof. Instead of offering complicated arguments for the existence of God which can be refuted by complicated counter arguments, the Charismatic Movement seems to point to empirical evidence: tens of millions of people who have seemingly miraculous experiences with God resulting in healings, speaking in languages previously unknown to believers, and offering inspired insights in the context of deeply inspirational worship. Certainly, all of this must count as evidence for the existence of God?

The philosopher A. J. Ayer said that all knowledge outside of formally true statements (2 + 2 = 4) must be able to be verified through sense experience. If we apply this criterion to claims for God based on charismatic experience, are we able to verify them as evidence of a transcendent realm? Acts chapter two seems to provide such a verifiable experience: the disciples spoke in languages they had not learned (xenolalia), and this was interpreted by making sense to those who knew those languages. However, though this is the kind of evidence that could lead to verification, this account comes to us in one ancient religious document without outside confirmation. The Charismatic Movement has sometimes included claims for xenolalia, but this has never been confirmed by any scientific studies.

Furthermore, most current accounts of speaking in tongues are of heavenly languages, known only to God. In this experience, the speaker uses what sounds like nonsense syllables. Often this form of tongues is not interpreted but when an interpretation is given, there is absolutely no way to verify a relationship between the interpretation and the language it was supposedly based on. So, though there are physical signs to work with (speech), there is no physical way to prove that these experiences come from God.

Claims for healing

Claims for healing present another difficult case to verify by A. J. Ayer's standards. In charismatic worship services and prayer meetings, Christians will often lay their hands on someone who is ill and ask God for healing. When someone experiences a dramatic improvement in their health, some Christians might be tempted to credit the prayer for healing. However, there are several difficulties with doing so:

- Some diseases, such as multiple sclerosis, are known to have symptoms come and go erratically.
- There are reports of healing which, when followed up, find patients just as ill or worse off.
- Claims for miraculous cures of cancer through prayer have been made when cancer was a merely a medical hypothesis rather than proven by biopsy. Thus, the one 'cured' may not have had cancer in the first place.
- Spontaneous remission of disease is rare, but does sometimes happen outside of prayers for healing.
- No scientifically conducted study has yet proven a correlation between prayers for healing and actual healing.

Sometimes those in the Charismatic Movement will make the claim that if someone isn't physically healed that there has been still been an emotional or

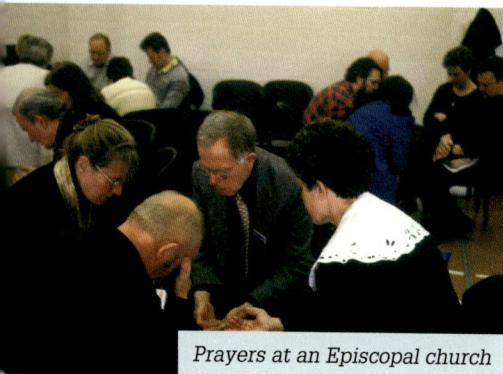
Prayers at an Episcopal church

psychological kind of healing. In other words, a miracle has taken place whether or not there has been physical healing. The philosopher Antony Flew said that what makes assertions meaningful is that they can be falsifiable. In order for any statement to be taken as meaningful there must be conditions which, if said to exist, would make the assertion false. Without the ability to falsify claims, science cannot proceed. When those in the Charismatic Movement claim that God has healed in response to prayer but then claim that the healing may not be physical, this sounds like a claim that can never be falsifiable and is therefore meaningless according to Flew.

Perhaps the strongest scientific claim that has been made about religious experience is a correlation between religious participation and physical and emotional health. There have been many scientifically conducted studies which can demonstrate benefits to religious belonging. However, these studies aren't limited to charismatic forms of Christianity. Furthermore, their results can be questioned because only people already in fairly good health can attend Church and some religious groups forbid certain behaviours with known negative health effects. However, even if this claim were to be proven true, this would not entail the existence of God. Thus, it could be true that people are emotionally strengthened after receiving prayers for healing, experiencing tongues or other charismatic gifts, but this fact alone does not verify the existence of God.

Natural explanations for charismatic experiences

Those who have charismatic experiences are convinced that these are caused by the Holy Spirit, but are there alternative explanations? One such explanation is to see these experiences as a cultural phenomenon. We know that one's cultural context plays a role in religious experiences. For example, someone raised in a geographical area that has been influenced by Christianity is more likely to have an experience of Jesus than of Krishna – but the opposite would be true in India. Cross-cultural studies have shown that traditions other than Christianity have experiences which may be the same or close to the Christian practice of tongues. In cultures where Christianity has been prevalent, speaking in tongues is viewed as a sign of the Holy Spirit, but in in other cultures there would be a different understanding of the 'power' behind these experiences. Of course, this does not rule out the existence of a transcendent realm, but it might challenge claims that see the origin of these experiences in a specifically Christian way.

Psychology and sociology can also offer naturalistic explanations for charismatic gifts. In terms of psychology we live in a world full of anxiety and neediness. This means that some of us may be especially open to experiences which ease our anxiety and meet our emotional needs – no matter how questionable the beliefs associated with those experiences are. For example, Sigmund Freud viewed religion as an illusion based on our primal need for a father figure. Could the absence of relational support in one's life make one especially prone to a charismatic experience?

Sociologists have noted how both nature and society are chaotic so that humans have needed rules in order to survive. However, society needs to give as much force to its rules as possible, so it uses religion to do this – 'you must live this way because God says so'. Religion has been society's way of stating how important these rules are. The founder of modern sociology, Emile Durkheim, equated God with society. 'God wants us to live this way' can be translated as 'Society wants us to live this way'.

Key quotes

The sense of knowing is never on its own a sufficient sign of knowledge. (P. Donovan)

There is no question that it is possible for people to have profoundly transformative experiences. And there is no question that it is possible for them to misinterpret those experiences, and to further delude themselves about the nature of reality. (S. Harris)

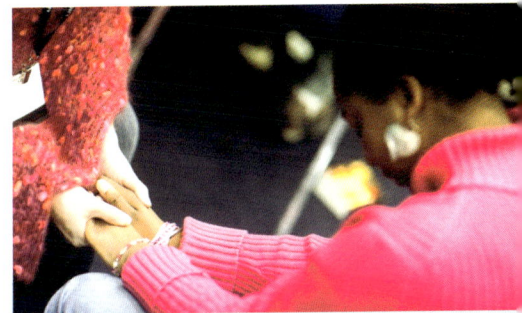

Some studies show that there is a correlation between religious attendance and well-being.

Key quotes

As every enquiry which regards
religion is of the utmost importance,
there are two questions in particular
which challenge our attention, to
wit, that concerning its foundation
in reason, and that concerning its
origin in human nature. (D. Hume)

Even if religious and spiritual
experience do not reliably yield
cognitive information that can
be translated into doctrinal
propositions – and at this point
I have made no judgement on
that question – they perform an
invaluable function by engaging
people with the ultimate mysteries
to which they are drawn.
(W. Wildman)

According to these views, the experiences of those in the Charismatic Movement are projections onto the universe of our human needs, problems and longings. In other words, people have religious experiences because they need to have them regardless of their ultimate truth-value. This conclusion takes on an especially negative tone when those who are especially weak and needy are seen as being more in need of these experiences than others. According to this view those with charismatic experiences are 'weaker' human beings with more psychological and social needs than the average human being.

Justifying charismatic experiences?

A number of arguments could be put forth to defend against the reduction of charismatic experiences to psychological or sociological factors:

- *These people are not all lunatics.* The sheer numbers of people who have charismatic experiences mean that a broad cross-section of society is involved: from those who are emotionally instable and socially awkward to mature, healthy individuals with high intellectual capacities. Claiming that all people who have these experiences are especially needy or psychologically deficient doesn't fit the fact of diversity in the movement and certainly has not been proven scientifically.

- *You can say the brain is involved without saying it originates in the brain.* There is a difference between saying that the brain is providing the experience of God and the brain is 'mediating' an experience of God. Those with charismatic experiences could say that though the brain plays a role in interpreting the experience, the experience is caused outside of one's brain. The fact that these experiences happen in different cultures could be seen as supporting John Hick's view that there is one divine reality that is 'refracted' by different cultures.

- *These experiences are a part of a cumulative case for God.* Whilst it is true that there is no scientifically proven evidence of the miraculous in the Charismatic Movement, isn't there some weight to the fact that tens of millions of people have unusual experiences that bring them joy, happiness, a positive social experience and renewed confidence to live their lives? The philosopher Richard Swinburne says that there is a compelling case for God's existence to be made from the 'cumulative evidence': the sheer numbers of people who believe in God, the sheer number of ways that God's existence can be argued intellectually, and the sheer number of people who have religious experiences. Taken separately, powerful arguments can be made against any one of these areas, but, taken together, do they not have evidential force?

AO1 Developing skills

It is now important to consider the information that has been covered in this section; however, the information in its raw form is too extensive and so has to be processed in order to meet the requirements of the examination. This can be achieved by practising more advanced skills associated with AO1. For assessment objective 1 (AO1), which involves demonstrating 'knowledge' and 'understanding' skills, we are going to focus on different ways in which the skills can be demonstrated effectively, and also refer to how the performance of these skills is measured (see generic band descriptors for A2 [WJEC] AO1 or A Level [Eduqas] AO1).

▶ **Your new task is this:** you will have to write a response under timed conditions to a question requiring an examination or explanation of **the main practices of the Charismatic Movement**. This exercise can either be done as a group or independently.

1. Begin with a list of indicative content, as you may have done in the previous textbook in the series. This may be discussed as a group or done independently. It does not need to be in any particular order at first, although as you practise this you will see more order in your lists that reflects your understanding.

2. Develop the list by using one or two relevant quotations. Now add some references to scholars and/or religious writings.

3. Then write out your plan, under timed conditions, remembering the principles of explaining with evidence and/or examples. Then ask someone else to read your answer and see if they can then help you improve it in any way.

4. Collaborative marking helps a learner appreciate alternative perspectives and possibly things that may have been missed. It also helps highlight the strengths of another that one can learn from. With this in mind, it is good to swap and compare answers in order to improve your own.

When you have completed the task, refer to the band descriptors for A2 (WJEC) or A Level (Eduqas) and in particular have a look at the demands described in the higher band descriptors towards which you should be aspiring. Ask yourself:

- Does my work demonstrate thorough, accurate and relevant knowledge and understanding of religion and belief?
- Is my work coherent (consistent or make logical sense), clear and well organised?
- Will my work, when developed, be an extensive and relevant response which is specific to the focus of the task?
- Does my work have extensive depth and/or suitable breadth and have excellent use of evidence and examples?
- If appropriate to the task, does my response have thorough and accurate reference to sacred texts and sources of wisdom?
- Are there any insightful connections to be made with other elements of my course?
- Will my answer, when developed and extended to match what is expected in an examination answer, have an extensive range of views of scholars/schools of thought?
- When used, is specialist language and vocabulary both thorough and accurate?

Key skills
Knowledge involves:

Selection of a range of (thorough) accurate and relevant information that is directly related to the specific demands of the question.

This means:

- Selecting relevant material for the question set
- Be focused in explaining and examining the material selected.

Understanding involves:

Explanation that is extensive, demonstrating depth and/or breadth with excellent use of evidence and examples including (where appropriate) thorough and accurate supporting use of sacred texts, sources of wisdom and specialist language.

This means:

- Effective use of examples and supporting evidence to establish the quality of your understanding
- Ownership of your explanation that expresses personal knowledge and understanding and NOT just a chunk of text from a book that you have rehearsed and memorised.

This section covers AO2
content and skills

Specification content

The strengths and weaknesses of the
Charismatic Movement.

Issues for analysis and evaluation

The strengths and weaknesses of the Charismatic Movement

The Charismatic Movement has grown to encompass a significant portion of the Christian Church across the world. Yet, the fact that far from all Christians embrace this movement underscores the fact that it has weaknesses as well as strengths for Christians.

Perhaps one of the most compelling aspects of the Charismatic Movement is that it presents a form of Christianity that has not succumbed to dry intellectualism and passive participation. Popular characterisations of traditional Christian worship are portrayed as exceptionally dull: services that are devoid of emotional content, have intricate liturgies, long sermons and the use of multiple books to guide one through the service. After the service people line up to shake the minister's hand and may go home without having greeted anyone else. This formalism may have an appeal for some in the context of a funeral service or a wedding ceremony where we may want tradition, but it seems out of step with our needs for emotion, warmth, joy and excitement. The liberal theologian Rudolph Otto warned of European Christianity losing its real power by denying the experiential dimension of the numinous that is found throughout the Bible.

The Charismatic Movement promotes this experiential dimension; it recognises that each Christian has been given a spiritual gift that can be shared with the 'body of Christ'. Furthermore, it expects that the Holy Spirit will move in special ways in each and every worship service so that all congregation members experience these gifts. The Charismatic Movement seems to reflect the New Testament situation of fluidity in worship and in Church leadership. For, not only were there teachers and Apostles, but also prophets, miracle workers, healers and a variety of people who participated with words inspired by the Holy Spirit. The idea that a variety of gifts both from and outside of the established leadership of the Church can contribute to worship is recognised by Church bodies such as the Catholic Church. 'It is not only through the sacraments and the ministries of the Church that the Holy Spirit sanctifies and leads the people of God and enriches it with virtues, but, allotting his gifts to everyone according as He wills, He distributes special graces among the faithful of every rank.' (*Lumen Gentium*)

Perhaps it is the active engagement of the laity in worship and the lack of formalism that has led to dramatic increases in numbers of charismatics worldwide as well as dramatic growth of individual churches such as David Bennett's episcopal congregation in Seattle and the Holy Mother Sanctuary in San Paolo Brazil which can accommodate up to 100,000 worshippers.

However, it can be argued that the characterisation above of non-charismatic church services as overly intellectual and passive is unfair and inaccurate. First, who is to say that one cannot experience active emotions in a traditional worship setting? Cannot one be moved by an organist playing Bach or by an ornate and stately procession with banners and robes? Furthermore, can it not be said that worshippers in traditional settings can be engaged physically through a variety of liturgical actions such as making the sign of the cross, kneeling for prayer, going forward for communion and standing and sitting through various parts of the service? Does the Charismatic Movement simply have a judgmental attitude towards other forms of worship? If so, this would certainly be a weakness since the New Testament encourages church unity.

AO2 Activity

As you read through this section try to do the following:

1. Pick out the different lines of argument that are presented in the text and identify any evidence given in support.

2. For each line of argument try to evaluate whether or not you think this is strong or weak.

3. Think of any questions you may wish to raise in response to the arguments.

This activity will help you to start thinking critically about what you read, and help you to evaluate the effectiveness of different arguments and from this develop your own observations, opinions and points of view that will help with any conclusions that you make in your answers to the AO2 questions that arise.

Another weakness of the Charismatic Movement has to do with its claim that all Christians should experience the gifts of the Holy Spirit. Whilst it appears to be true that charismatic Christians can be observed speaking in tongues, singing, sharing and engaged in extroverted forms of expression during the service, is this really what the New Testament describes? If one examines the lists of spiritual gifts in the New Testament, one also sees a number of gifts that are not so easily seen in charismatic services; service, teaching, giving and leadership. Could it be that some gifts have been exalted at the expense of other gifts? In other words, the focus on more extroverted gifts described in the Bible may not be achieving the kind of Church that was envisioned by Paul.

It could be seen as a strength that the Charismatic Movement focuses on the member of the Trinity that has received the least attention in Christian theology: The Holy Spirit. For, Christians have long said that the doctrine of the Trinity is central to Christian belief. However, the focus on this doctrine has mostly been to establish the relationship of Jesus to God. Hence much Christian discourse has involved God the Son and God the Father and made very little reference to God, the Holy Spirit. The Charismatic Movement seems to address this imbalance. It does so by placing importance on the book of Acts and other passages which clearly declare that the Holy Spirit has a role to play in Christian living. The New Testament describes believers having special experience of 'baptism' in the Holy Spirit and with it, special empowerment to live and act as Christians. Passages that describe the Holy Spirit as the cause of miraculous conversions, answers to prayer, healings, inspiration and wisdom are not 'glossed over' as aspects of a forgotten era by those in the Charismatic Movement, but are taken seriously.

What is a theological strength could also be seen as a serious weakness. For, the implication in the Charismatic Movement is that those who do not experience the spiritual gifts have not had a full Christian experience. Do adherents to charismatic churches believe, then, that non-charismatics are 'second-class' Christians? This seems to be the case since those in the movement proclaim that they now have a spiritual experience that they did not have before. This two-tiered approach to Christian spirituality is in contrast to a true variety of gifts that the Holy Spirit gives – which includes those of a non-miraculous nature.

The traditional argument against Pentecostalism and the Charismatic Movement is that the dramatic use of spiritual gifts is limited to a special era early in the life of the Church when it was necessary for the Church to be established. As soon as the Church was strong enough, miracles were no longer needed. Of course, this viewpoint is not spelled out as such in the New Testament, but Jesus does praise those who believe without needing miracles and Paul says that prophesies will one day end, but that love will always be of pre-eminent importance (I Corinthians 13). Therefore, does this not mean that to stress the spiritual gifts of tongues, prophecy and healing, as is often done in the Charismatic Movement, weakens the Christian focus on what is truly most important: love?

Charismatic Christians may point, however, to the many manifestations of love that can be found in worship services. They can also point to the fact that their charismatic experiences did not lead them to leave their churches but to stay and work for them to become stronger. Indeed, there was a cross-fertilisation of stories and experiences outside of denominational boundaries especially in the early Charismatic Movement. One thinks of Roman Catholic Professors reading the *Cross and the Switchblade,* a book by an Assemblies of God minister. This kind of cross-denominational sharing continues today with, for example, the charismatic preacher to the Papal Household, Ranieri Cantelamessa, preaching at the charismatic Anglican Church in London, Holy Trinity Brompton. All of this is in marked contrast to traditional Pentecostal approaches which viewed non-charismatic Christians with suspicion and even questioned if Catholics were

Key quotes

The Catholic Charismatic Renewal movement has remained unlike any other movement in the Catholic Church, for there is no inspired human founder and there are no universal programmes of initiation or formation. It is simply, powerfully and uniquely a sovereign work of God though his Holy spirit. (J. C. Whitehead)

… the central feature of the movement is an overwhelming sense of the presence and power of God not previously known in such a combination of otherness and immediacy' (Church of England Report, 1981)

…there has been a tendency to downplay the reality of the cross and to overplay the power of the resurrection in Christian life. (C. Cocksworth)

Christians at all. Many denominations in which the Charismatic Movement flourishes are a part of the World Council of Churches.

However, one has to question how truly ecumenical the Charismatic Movement is. Most in the Charismatic Movement have an evangelical theology; this means that they are destined to struggle in similar ways as the evangelicals and orthodox do with some aspects of the World Council of Churches. Furthermore, non-denominational Christian movements such as the Toronto Blessing and the Vineyard association of churches are less connected to the Ecumenical Movement than more long-standing denominations such as the Church of England. In fact, the Restorationism movement is actually anti-denominational. It is simply not clear that the Charismatic Movement is a force that will unite Christians.

In conclusion, there is no doubt that millions upon millions of Christians have reported receiving joy, insights and inspiration from the Charismatic Movement. Perhaps the issue that most determines whether the Charismatic Movement is a strength or a weakness for worldwide Christianity is not arguments about the 'fruit of the spirit' being present in the movement but whether or not those in the movement view these fruits as *only* or *most fully* present in their movement in contrast to the experience of other Christians. For, the degree to which one insists that the Charismatic Movement is more spiritual than other forms of Christianity may be the degree to which the Charismatic Movement becomes a source of division rather than a form of unity for the Christian Church.

Key quotes

From one point of view the Charismatic Movement is a form of Christian existentialism. Above all, God is alive and well, and is meeting with us, teaching us, leading us – NOW! (Church of England Report, 1981)

… the kind of emotional intensity I once experienced in charismatic services I am now most likely to experience in something like an English cathedral evensong, if there is a very good choir. (M. Higton)

One of the continuing debates of twentieth-century Christianity was whether an overemphasis on Christian experience was as much of a threat to an authentic Christianity as an overemphasis on an intellectualism that threatened to remove the essentials of the faith from the grasp of the majority of Christians. (N. Davies and M. Conway)

Some within the Catholic Church consider the Catholic Charismatic Renewal to be introspective and deeply conservative, the antithesis of liberation theology with its concerns for social justice and human rights. (A. H. Anderson)

AO2 Activity

List some conclusions that could be drawn from the AO2 reasoning from the above text; try to aim for at least three different possible conclusions. Consider each of the conclusions and collect brief evidence to support each conclusion from the AO1 and AO2 material for this topic. Select the conclusion that you think is most convincing and explain why it is so. Try to contrast this with the weakest conclusion in the list, justifying your argument with clear reasoning and evidence.

Whether a natural explanation for charismatic experiences conflicts with the religious value of the experience

Those who are involved in the Charismatic Movement are clear about the source of their experiences: The Holy Spirit. If it could be proven that there is an alternative explanation for their experiences, would this entail that there is no value to those experiences and those in the movement would have been better off never having joined?

Those in the Charismatic Movement would argue, firmly, 'no'. They see the value of their experiences as distinctly religious. For, they trace the origin of their faith to the 2nd chapter of the book of Acts and the set of extraordinary events that persuaded many non-Christians to join their movement. They have experiences which they believe come through religious activities such as prayer (individual and communal), the laying on of hands, meditation on Bible passages and the experience of vibrant Christian worship. Finally, charismatic Christians would point to the supernatural nature of their experiences: speaking in a heavenly language unknown to the speaker, giving and receiving direct messages from God that strengthens their Christian life, and dramatic changes in health and well-being as a result of the laying on of hands for healing.

However, those who are outside of the movement – both Christian and non-religious – who value the role of empirical evidence for establishing claims can see difficulties with a religious explanation of these events. First, viewing Acts chapter 2 as proof of God's work in the world is problematic given the age of the document and the lack of independent attestation from other sources. Also, the claims for a supernatural source for these experiences have simply not been proven in a scientific way.

For example, reports of xenolalia in the Charismatic Movement have not been confirmed. In the case of glossalia (heavenly tongues), there is simply no way of confirming that those interpreting tongues are actually doing so – since the speaker of the tongues is not aware of the meaning of what they are saying. In the case of prophecy, much of this is too vague ('This is the year where you will find special strength from God.') to provide verification through sense experience (i.e. how do you empirically prove that this year God gave one more strength than last year?). The fact that most denominations with a Charismatic Movement believe that prophecy must not contradict what has already been said in the Bible is further proof that it is not supernatural but derived from what Christians already believe.

Claims of healing is another area where misinterpretations could be said to abound. Some diseases have erratic symptoms so that a remission or temporary alleviation of suffering is mistaken for healing. Also, claims for miraculous cures have been made in cases where the disease has not actually been medically diagnosed but was a hypothesis. Furthermore, the medical community does know of rare cases of spontaneous remission – these can happen outside of prayer. Finally, reports of healing cannot be taken seriously since Christians claim that if God has not performed an act of physical healing, then 'He' has brought about emotional or psychological healing. This claim means that Christians can avoid testing their beliefs. Finally, if as many healings have truly happened as charismatic Christians report, one would think that there would be proof enough for the entire world to believe – but this is not the case.

One conclusion that could be reached from these objections is that charismatic Christians have misinterpreted their experiences. Thus their experiences have no value because they are based on a lie which serves to separate them from the rest of humanity who do not belong to their group. According to this view, there would be more value in abandoning these religious beliefs and exchanging them for humanistic ones.

Key quotes

In your relationship with God there are also times when you want to say things and you're trying to find the words to express them. In a human relationship, sometimes you struggle for words and you've got to do it, but in a relationship with God he can actually give you a language which enables you to communicate. (N. Gumbel)

Experts readily agree that social groups condition the way such experiences are felt and expressed, and that this embedding can magnify their political and economic effects in quite spectacular ways. (W. Wildman)

Prayer dissolving into a kind of verbal noise can be a powerful witness to the reality of God. (M. Higton)

AO2 Activity

List some conclusions that could be drawn from the AO2 reasoning from the above text; try to aim for at least three different possible conclusions. Consider each of the conclusions and collect brief evidence to support each conclusion from the AO1 and AO2 material for this topic. Select the conclusion that you think is most convincing and explain why it is so. Try to contrast this with the weakest conclusion in the list, justifying your argument with clear reasoning and evidence.

Of course, Christians could reply that the proof of religious value is in the experience itself – that millions upon millions of believers have found love, joy and peace. Supporting the claim are studies that correlated religious participation with higher levels of physical and emotional health. However, there are difficulties with this claim: only those in fairly good heath can attend religious gatherings in the first place and some religious groups ban unhealthy activity. In any case, even if this claim were true, it does not confirm the source of these experiences – though it could show that they have value outside of a religious interpretation.

These objections have led to naturalistic interpretations; namely, that charismatic experiences can be explained by cultural, sociological and psychological factors. There are, for example, studies that show speaking in tongues in traditions other than Christianity. This fact can be used to prove that it is not the 'Holy Spirit' that is the source of this phenomenon, unless 'Holy Spirit' is interpreted in a very open way (such as Hick's 'Ultimate Reality'); this would not be an acceptable interpretation for many in the Charismatic Movement who tend to be conservative and 'evangelical' in their beliefs. Sociologists have noted the power of experiences when we are in a group. Could it be that charismatic Christians mistake a group experience for a God experience? Finally, psychologists note how anxious and difficult the human experience can be; it may be that we are open to any experience that eases our tensions no matter how questionable the beliefs are that are associated with these experiences. One of the implications of these insights for some theorists is that religious believers are more needy and susceptible to religious experiences than the average human being.

So far we have viewed the question of the source and value of charismatic experiences as an 'either/or': either they are truly from God and therefore have value or they are not supernatural in nature and have no value. Is there another alternative? Could one affirm that there are, at the same time, both natural as well as religious explanations for these experiences? After all, one could believe that God uses culture, society and psychology as the avenues through which the Holy Spirit works. This means that one does not have to deny naturalistic interpretations but can say that there is still 'something more' behind the experiences. This also has the advantage of not reducing those in the Charismatic Movement to an especially needy cross-section of society – a questionable conclusion given the vast numbers and diversity of those involved in the movement.

The problem with this position is, of course, trying to prove that there is 'something more'. Richard Swinburne believes that the strongest case for God is 'cumulative'. Though arguments can be made against any particular Christian claim, there is evidential force for God to be found in the sheer numbers of intellectual arguments, personal conviction and religious experiences that millions upon millions of Christian believers have all over the world.

Of course, it is possible for those who do not believe in God to see value in charismatic experiences – though not 'religious' value. In this view, Christians have found a way to access positive experiences available to all human beings, but have done this through their religious tradition. Though it might be more intellectually developed to see the source of their experiences as non-religious, the most important thing is that people find positive ways to engage in life. If the Charismatic Movement provides this, then it can be affirmed as a source of values.

In conclusion, those in the Charismatic Movement are unlikely to be convinced either by the dismissal of their beliefs in the Holy Spirit or even by a positive but humanistic assessment of their experiences. For believers, these experiences have value because of, not in spite of, their religious interpretations.

AO2 Developing skills

It is now important to consider the information that has been covered in this section; however, the information in its raw form is too extensive and so has to be processed in order to meet the requirements of the examination. This can be achieved by practising more advanced skills associated with AO2. For assessment objective 2 (AO2), which involves 'critical analysis' and 'evaluation' skills, we are going to focus on different ways in which the skills can be demonstrated effectively, and also refer to how the performance of these skills is measured (see generic band descriptors for A2 [WJEC] AO2 or A Level [Eduqas] AO2).

▶ **Your new task is this:** you will have to write a response under timed conditions to a question requiring an evaluation of **naturalistic explanations for charismatic experiences**. This exercise can either be done as a group or independently.

1. Begin with a list of indicative arguments or lines of reasoning, as you may have done in the previous textbook in the series. It does not need to be in any particular order at first, although as you practise this you will see more order in your lists, in particular by way of links and connections between arguments.

2. Develop the list by using one or two relevant quotations. Now add some references to scholars and/or religious writings.

3. Then write out your plan, under timed conditions, remembering the principles of explaining with evidence and/or examples. Then ask someone else to read your answer and see if they can then help you improve it in any way.

4. Collaborative marking helps a learner appreciate alternative perspectives and possibly things that may have been missed. It also helps highlight the strengths of another that one can learn from. With this in mind, it is good to swap and compare answers in order to improve your own.

When you have completed the task, refer to the band descriptors for A2 (WJEC) or A Level (Eduqas) and in particular have a look at the demands described in the higher band descriptors towards which you should be aspiring. Ask yourself:

- Is my answer a confident critical analysis and perceptive evaluation of the issue?
- Is my answer a response that successfully identifies and thoroughly addresses the issues raised by the question set?
- Does my work show an excellent standard of coherence, clarity and organisation?
- Will my work, when developed, contain thorough, sustained and clear views that are supported by extensive, detailed reasoning and/or evidence?
- Are the views of scholars/schools of thought used extensively, appropriately and in context?
- Does my answer convey a confident and perceptive analysis of the nature of any possible connections with other elements of my course?
- When used, is specialist language and vocabulary both thorough and accurate?

Key skills

Analysis involves:

Identifying issues raised by the materials in the AO1, together with those identified in the AO2 section, and presenting sustained and clear views, either of scholars or from a personal perspective ready for evaluation.

This means:

- That your answers are able to identify key areas of debate in relation to a particular issue
- That you can identify, and comment upon, the different lines of argument presented by others
- That your response comments on the overall effectiveness of each of these areas or arguments.

Evaluation involves:

Considering the various implications of the issues raised based upon the evidence gleaned from analysis and providing an extensive detailed argument with a clear conclusion.

This means:

- That your answer weighs up the consequences of accepting or rejecting the various and different lines of argument analysed
- That your answer arrives at a conclusion through a clear process of reasoning.

Specification content

The basis (political, ethical and religious) of South American liberation theology with reference to Gustavo Gutiérrez and Leonardo Boff.

Key quotes

The Kingdom [of God] and social injustice are incompatible. (G. Gutiérrez)

… this theology has fought against the separatist mentality that dichotomises reality into the sacred and the profane, or into the individual and the social. (G. Gutiérrez)

The story of liberation theology is about how in less than twenty years, a quiet conversion among a few out-of-the-way Latin Americans became a worldwide theological movement. (H. Cox)

Key term

Liberation theology: a movement developed by Roman Catholic thinkers and activists in Latin America in the 1960s that viewed freedom from social oppression as a key area of Christian concern

Key person

Gustavo Gutiérrez: was born 1928 in Lima, Peru and was educated at the Universities of Louvain, Lyons and Rome. He began his priesthood by teaching at the Catholic University of Lima whilst living in the slum area of the city. He views Jesus Christ as the liberator from political as well as spiritual oppression.

Gustavo Gutiérrez

F: Religious identity through responses to poverty and injustice

Introduction to liberation theology

Is the point of Christianity to shuffle into church, listen to an uplifting message and feel reassured about one day going to heaven? When Christians leave church, they walk out into a world where there is human slavery, death by malnutrition, and sweatshops where some people never see daylight. This is the same world where people gain wealth through the commercialisation of drinking water and the control of plant pollination. Should Christians respond to this by shuffling back into church to hear another uplifting message about heaven? **Liberation theology** attacks this version of Christianity and calls all Christians to see that their salvation includes fighting for social justice.

What is liberation theology?

Liberation theology is a movement that developed in Latin America in the 1960s. Priest and theologian Gustavo Gutiérrez wrote a highly influential book *Teología de la Libercíon* (*A Theology of Liberation*, 1971) where he says that theology should start with the fact of human suffering rather than with intellectual and rational reflection. When Christians take seriously the oppression around them, they will be moved to fight for justice.

Flower Carrier by Diego Rivera, 1935 Liberation theologians say that the hope for capitalistic development has brought only suffering and poverty to Latin America.

Gutiérrez contrasts liberation theology with modern European theology. The context of European theology is a world 'come of age' with scientific and technical progress. European theology tries to make a case for God and spirituality in the face of atheism; it tends to be intellectual and rationalistic. The context of liberation theology is that of people dying. Liberation theology springs from the pastoral work of priests, observing suffering in the shadow of technical and scientific progress. It declares that salvation is a 'total gift' that must apply also to this suffering. Leonardo and Clodovis Boff say that liberation theology is the result of 'faith confronted by oppression'.

Key quote

American foreign policy must begin to counterattack (and not just react against) liberation theology. **(Advisors to US President Ronald Reagan, 1982)**

AO1 Activity

Look up the word 'salvation' in several dictionaries and/or encyclopaedias – either online or in printed texts. Write down the different definitions that you find. Do any of these refer to economics, social justice or emotional welfare? Are any of these definitions purely 'spiritual'? The meaning of this word in the Bible is a debated area between liberation theologians and some theologians who do not accept liberation theology.

Liberation theology is not about a spirituality divorced from social sinfulness. It is also not about merely attempting to reform political structures. Gutiérrez says that it is about abolishing the status quo that has led to this suffering, and replacing it with a different set of relationships which include different relationships to production and the economy. Thus, liberation theology has a political edge which has been a target of criticism by some Christians, including some in the Roman Catholic Church as well as governments opposed to socialism and communism.

Key quote

The cries of the oppressed keep rising to heaven … more and more loudly. God today goes on hearing these cries, condemning oppression and strengthening liberation. Anyone who does not grasp this has not understood a word of liberation theology. (G. Gutiérrez)

The political basis of Latin American theology

Liberation theologians say that their theology has grown out of the brutal situation facing many people in Latin America; they note that Latin America has faced economic exploitation for 500 years at the hands of colonial powers such as Spain, Portugal and Britain. During this time, the Church was frequently associated with the ruling classes, the elite and the landowners.

In the 1950s there was hope that economic development would result as Latin American countries became less dependent on imports and, instead, produced more of their own goods for national use and international export. This was a development model which hoped that by participating in the economies of richer, Western countries, all people would benefit. However, capitalism demanded that goods and labour be cheap; the result was that there was no development of a middle class in Latin America and continued impoverishment for most people.

In the wake of the failure of this development model, economic aid packages have been seen by liberation theologians to simply maintain the status quo and keep workers in poverty and passivity. Sometimes the flaws in economic 'development' became obvious, such as the 1954 CIA overthrow of the government of Guatemala which is seen by many to have been motivated only by the United States wanting to protect the US-owned United Fruit Company. All of this played into the socialist and communistic movements of Fidel Castro, Che Guevara and others. In the 1970s, some priests, inspired by liberation theology, took part in the Sandinista revolution in Nicaragua. This influenced rebellions in Mexico and Columbia where one of the main guerilla factions was led by a de-frocked priest. There have been executions and assassinations of bishops, priests and Church workers across Latin America in this violent context.

Study tip

Becoming familiar with some key figures who are not listed in the specification will help you to understand the work of Gustavo Gutiérrez and Leonardo Boff in a larger perspective. Spend a few minutes to understand some key facts about Che Guevara, Manuel Pérez, Cardinal Joseph Ratzinger, Oscar Romero and Jon Sobrino. (Hint: try entering their name along with 'liberation theology' into your search bar.)

Liberation theologians such as Gustavo Gutiérrez have not promoted violence but been sympathetic to socialist and communist movements and ideas – especially since capitalist development models have been perceived as helping only the rich. Many bishops in Latin America have been open to liberation theology, especially in Brazil. In 1968, Latin American Bishops met in Medellín and issued a statement which urged action by the Church on behalf of the poor. They denounced

quickfire

4.12 According to Boff, what is the context for liberation theology?

Key terms

Capitalism: an economic and political system of private or corporate ownership of goods rather than state ownership

Communism: an economic and political system which replaces private property and a free market with public ownership and communal control of goods

Socialism: any economic or political theory that advances collective ownership of production, distribution and exchange of goods

quickfire

4.13 Which of these does Gutiérrez favour: capitalism, economic aid, development, exploitation, socialism, Marxism?

Key quotes

Struggle for liberation alongside the oppressed has provoked persecution and martyrdoms. (L. Boff and C. Boff)

The majority of the Church has covertly or openly been an accomplice of the external and internal dependency of our peoples. It has sided with the dominant groups, and in the name of 'efficacy' has dedicated its best efforts to them. It has identified with these sectors and adopted their style of life. (G. Gutiérrez)

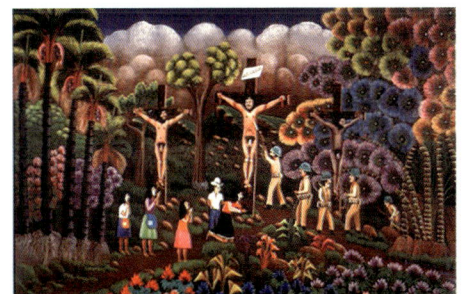

Che-Jesus Dies on the Cross by Rodolfo Arellano, 1984
Many Latin Americans see the struggle and suffering of Jesus as reflecting their own struggles and suffering.

PHARAOH was a rich JOB CREATOR, so why did GOD side with a COMMUNITY ORGANISER?

The account of the Exodus is viewed by liberation theologians as evidence that God wants social justice for oppressed people.

Christ of the Breadlines, woodcut by Fritz Eichenberg, date unknown
Christ waiting to receive bread, likely inspired by Matthew 25: 31–46.

quickfire

4.14 What was the theme of Jesus' first sermon in the Gospel of Luke?

Christ portrayed as Che Guevara. Though many liberation theologians have been careful to differentiate their thinking with violent revolutions, they have pointed out that there was a political dimension to the ministry of Jesus.

Key term

Zealots: a militant Jewish sect opposing the Roman domination of Palestine in the 1st century CE

'institutionalised injustice' and 'institutionalised violence'. These bishops believed that they were acting in accord with the principles of Vatican II of the Church becoming relevant to contemporary society and making a priority of helping the poor.

The religious basis of Latin American theology

Liberation theologians are inspired by many passages in the Bible which reveal, for them, that God desires all people to be liberated from structures that cause oppression. In fact, Gutiérrez has described liberation theology as a 'critical reflection on Christian praxis in light of the Word of God'. Several passages are popular with liberation theologians:

- Accounts of the Exodus (Exodus chapters 1–14). In this narrative, God hears the cries of his oppressed people and leads them from Egypt on a journey to a 'promised land' where they will be free to establish a society free of misery and alienation.

- Many of the prophets harshly criticise social injustice as well as religious adherents who attend worship rituals but avoid the humane treatment of others. An example is Micah 6:8: 'He has told you, O mortal, what is good; and what does the LORD require of you but to do justice, and to love kindness, and to walk humbly with your God?'

- Jesus' first sermon in Luke 4 is an announcement of liberation: '... he has anointed me to bring good news to the poor. He has sent me to proclaim release to the captives and recovery of sight to the blind, to let the oppressed go free, to proclaim the year of the Lord's favour.' (Luke 4:18–19)

- In Matthew 25:31–46, Jesus announces that the future judgement of humanity will be based on whether those in most need were helped in practical ways.

- Acts 2:43–47 shows a free and liberating Church community that practises a form of communism: 'they would sell their possessions and goods and distribute the proceeds to all, as any had need'.

- I John 4:20–21 makes it clear that it is impossible to love God without loving human beings. Liberation theologians say that social justice must not be mechanical – it springs from an experience of loving those who are oppressed.

These passages and others show that salvation is not divorced from history, says Gutiérrez. Not only is God to be found in tangible, geographical places (the tabernacle, the ark, Mount Sinai), God has worked through 'his' prophets, 'his' Son, the Apostles and others to bring freedom in their historical situations.

A Christology that liberates

Liberation theologians say that Christology (the study of the divine and human aspects of Jesus) has emphasised images of Jesus which place him outside of history and reinforce a passive attitude to human suffering: the impotence of the suffering and dying Christ, the helpless baby Jesus in the arms of Mary and the king Jesus who stands outside of the world. These images have been used by governments to support their policies. Contrary to these images, Jesus did not preach about his divine identity or the Church; he presented the Kingdom of God as an inclusive society committed to justice.

Key quote

The first and primary aspect of following Jesus is proclaiming the utopia of the kingdom as the real and complete meaning of the world that is offered to all by God. **(G. Gutiérrez)**

In fact, there are three aspects of Jesus' life that stand out: (i) his complex relationships with the **zealots**, a nationalistic Jewish group committed to violent revolt against the Romans; (ii) critical attitudes towards the religious leaders, especially when they burdened people with excessive demands; and (iii) Jesus' death at the hands of political authority. These aspects reveal that there was a political dimension to Jesus' ministry. We know that there was at least one zealot among the 12 disciples. Though Jesus was not as fiercely nationalistic as the zealots (he accepted the **Samaritans**) and he did not advocate violence, he must have been recognised by them as having some shared aims such as the liberation of humans from systems of suffering. Furthermore, Jesus' condemnation of excessive legalism in religion is reminiscent of the social justice of the prophets. Finally, Jesus was perceived as a threat to the Roman authorities – therefore, says Gutiérrez, we should not spiritualise Jesus.

It is true, however, that though Jesus fought for liberation, he did not organise his movement for the long-term application of love and justice in society. The reason for this, says Gutiérrez, is that he was affected by his culture's belief in **apocalypticism**, the sudden and dramatic coming of God to set up a new social order. Since we know that this did not happen, we should apply Jesus' attitude and teaching to the task of building a less oppressive society. Furthermore, eschatology in the Bible is never merely presented as a future reality – it is always viewed as transforming our attitude and actions in the present.

Orthodoxy and orthopraxy

In traditional theology, one starts with the Bible or with intellectual thought and seeks to determine the truth (**orthodoxy**, 'right teaching') and apply that to life. From the 12th century, says Gutiérrez, theology considered itself to be a science that presented faith in clear, rational categories. To become more religious, then, meant devoting oneself to study or withdrawing to a monastery to contemplate biblical or theological themes. In either case, one started with thought and reflection.

However, we must remember, says Gutiérrez, that for centuries the Church did nothing to help the world; it was involved in creating and reinforcing itself as 'Christendom'. What is needed now is to see the churches rather than monasteries, academies and cathedrals as the place that theology happens. For, it is in pastoral situations that the Church encounters human suffering. This encounter with suffering calls forth a response. Gutiérrez calls this '**praxis**', the practice of faith applied to life. **Orthopraxis** must come before orthodoxy.

Gutiérrez says that he has been impacted by the Marxist insight that what is most important is finding the truth in one's action. Marx said, 'The philosophers have only interpreted the world, in various ways; the point is to change it.' Likewise, theology should not begin with a 'concrete' intellectual starting point, but with a situation. We discover the truth through 'praxis'.

The ethical basis of Latin American theology

The chief concern of liberation theologians is the suffering caused by poverty and economic exploitation. This area is also of vital concern for the Vatican; Pope John XXIII declared that the Church is called to be a Church of the poor. This concern is reflected in the documents of Vatican II which urge the Church to walk in poverty, following the example of Jesus who identified with the poor.

Gustavo Gutiérrez says that it is important to distinguish between three kinds of poverty:

1. *Material poverty.* This kind of poverty is consistently condemned in the Bible as being outside of God's plan for humanity. Poverty contradicts the heart of the message in Genesis that all humans have been created in the likeness of God and given the vocation of taking care of the earth. It also transgresses the nature of Mosaic religion which sees God guiding 'his' people to a new and

quickfire

4.15 (i) Name one theme in Jesus' ministry that reveals for Gutiérrez that he had a political 'edge'.

(ii) Name one popular image of Jesus that Gutiérrez thinks reinforces passivity and inaction by the poor.

Key quotes

Before we can do theology we have to 'do' liberation. (G. Gutiérrez)

… we encounter God in the commitment to the historical process of humankind. (G. Gutiérrez)

Key quotes

The poverty of Third World countries was the price to be paid for the First World to be able to enjoy the fruits of overabundance. (G. Gutiérrez)

Love for others, and especially for the poor, is made concrete by promoting justice. (Pope John Paul II)

quickfire

4.16 Which kind of poverty is consistently condemned by the Bible according to liberation theologians?

Key person

Leonardo Boff: a native of Brazil, studied with Karl Rahner at the University of Munich. He has been a university professor, advisor to the Brazilian conference of Bishops and has worked amongst the poor in South America. Some of the views in his book, *Charisma and Power* (1981), led him to being summoned to the Vatican; subsequently, he had a year's silence imposed upon him. During this time, he was not allowed to teach.

prosperous land. Yet, some have given this poverty a romantic or paternalistic 'spin': 'the simple life'. This notion is rejected as there is a growing social consciousness across the world that poverty is wrong and that all oppressed people are called to live more full lives.

2. *Spiritual poverty.* This is the inner attitude of being completely ready and available to do God's will. One of the problems in the Church is that sometimes material poverty has been confused with 'spiritual' meaning poor people are thought to be more spiritual than other people (i.e. less distracted by material things, closer to God). This has been a popular interpretation of 'Blessed (or, 'happy') are the poor' Matthew 5:3; Luke 6:20. However, this interpretation simply serves the interests of the rich minority. The true interpretation of this phrase, according to Gutiérrez, is that since Jesus saw his task as liberation and the promotion of a community of justice, those who are poor had a reason to be happy – their poverty was about to end.

3. *Voluntary poverty.* This is the act of the Church choosing to be poor so as to identify with the poor. Especially relevant is the example of **kenosis**, the self-emptying of Christ involved in his incarnation: the second member of the Trinity chose to become 'poor' in order to relate God's love and justice to the human race. Gutiérrez also notes that something amazing happened to the Church in the book of Acts when it chose to volunteer its goods to everyone's welfare: everyone actually had enough (see Acts 4:34–35).

Religious, ethical and political dimensions of liberation theology cannot be neatly distinguished from each other since this theology, as we have seen, is more invested in practical concerns (praxis) than it is with establishing a firm rational basis for its expression.

This is clearly seen by the approach of liberation theologians to the subject of poverty. Why are people poor? Liberation theologians note that there are political explanations for this phenomenon which exist only to maintain the status quo of capitalistic exploitation: (i) People are poor because of vice; they are lazy, ignorant or wicked. Therefore, the solution is to offer them economic aid, but they cannot be trusted with more than that. (ii) Poverty is the result of economic or social backwardness. Therefore, reforms may help: adjustments to the system for more education and employment opportunities.

In contrast to these solutions, liberation theologians view the poverty in their countries as the logical outcome of cheap labour and goods required as a part of the capitalistic enterprise. Only a dramatic change in the system can lead to a better life for the poor.

The phrase '**preferential option for the poor**' began to be used by liberation theologians in the 1970s and became embraced by Catholic bishops in Latin America and then by the Vatican when Pope John Paul II and Pope Benedict XVI also used the term. It is now viewed as an integral aspect of Catholic social teaching. While the Vatican has not accepted the political and economic analysis of Gutiérrez and other liberation theologians, it has embraced the idea that the poor must be prioritised in the commitment to social justice.

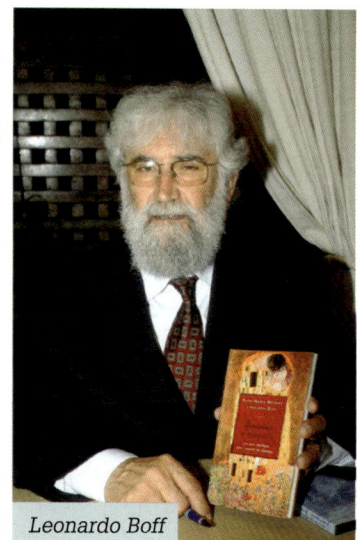

Leonardo Boff

'Preferential option for the poor' does not mean that others are excluded from concern. It means that Christians must make the free choice (option) to prioritise the needs and concerns of those who are poor. Gutiérrez notes that the poor are on the 'lowest rung' of the ladder of society but that God's wisdom is that 'the last shall be first'. This teaching represents both an ideal and a challenge to the Church since most people in the world live in poverty stricken countries.

Base communities

Base ecclesial communities are small groups of about 15–20 families who meet together to support one another, read the Bible and apply their insights to their struggles against oppression. According to Leonardo Boff, these communities bring together many of the themes important to liberation theology: praxis, the struggle against oppression, and a Christian faith informed by belief in a God who wants justice on the earth.

Base communities developed in the 1960s as a result of at least two factors:

- A movement in populist education across Latin America which brought together small communities for literacy and skill building. Some governments viewed this with suspicion as this education enabled the poor to vote and take a more active interest in their future.

- A shortage of priests, making necessary the lay leadership of Catholic Christian communities. Pentecostal and Evangelical Churches were spreading across Latin America and absorbing Roman Catholic Christians, especially in areas where there were no priests.

Leonardo Boff shares a story commonly associated with the beginning of these communities: 'It all began with the lament of one humble old woman: "Christmas Eve, all three Protestant Churches were lit up and full of people. We could hear them singing ... And the Catholic Church closed and dark! ... Because we can't get a priest." A question hung in the air. "If there are no priests, must everything grind to a halt?"' Boff shares how Latin American Bishops quickly supported the formation of small communities led by lay-leaders. The number of these communities exploded through the 60s and 70s with 1–2 million people participating by the 1980s in Brazil alone.

Liberation theologians call these communities, 'base ecclesial communities'; each word is significant. 'Base' refers to the nature of these communities as basic 'building blocks' of the Church, a small group of Christians who are exactly the people that the Church says should be prioritised: the poor. These are 'ecclesial' in that they have a link to the wider Church. When there is a priest available, they look to the Church for the celebration of the sacraments such as baptisms, weddings and the Eucharist. Finally, they are communities because there is sharing not only of faith but of all of life; there is mutual support in the quest to build a better life. Sometimes they have functioned as treatment centres for malnutrition and disease.

For the most part, these groups have been accepted by the Vatican as valid expressions of the Church if they centre on the Word of God, avoid a hyper-critical attitude toward the larger Church, maintain a link with the wider Church, and remain aware of the benefits of their link to the Church of Rome.

A base community in El Salvador

Key term

Base ecclesial communities: small Christian communities who meet without a priest for worship, study and support

Key quotes

Liberation theology and the base communities grew together out of the same impetus to reach the poor, but now one can quite generally say that the communities embody the spirit of liberation theology. **(A. McGovern)**

In some places they are the only channel for popular expression and mobilisation. They organise memorials, group projects, community activities, neighbourhood credit unions, efforts to resist land takeovers, and many other concerns of the people. **(L. Boff)**

Reaction of the Vatican to base communities by Pope Paul VI, Evangelii Nuntiandi (1975):

In some regions, they [base communities] appear and develop, almost without exception, within the Church, having solidarity with her life, being nourished by her teaching and united with her pastors. In these cases, they spring from the need to live the Church's life more intensely, or from the desire and quest for a more human dimension such as larger ecclesial communities can only offer with difficulty, especially in the big modern cities which lend themselves both to life in the mass and to anonymity.

… In other regions, on the other hand, *communautes de base* come together in a spirit of bitter criticism of the Church, which they are quick to stigmatise as 'institutional' and to which they set themselves up in opposition as charismatic communities, free from structures and inspired only by the Gospel. Thus their obvious characteristic is an attitude of fault-finding and of rejection with regard to the Church's outward manifestations: her hierarchy, her signs. They are radically opposed to the Church. By following these lines their main inspiration very quickly becomes ideological, and it rarely happens that they do not quickly fall victim to some political option or current of thought, and then to a system, even a party, with all the attendant risks of becoming its instrument.

Even though these communities have sprung from the situation of a lack of priests, Boff believes that they actually represent the most important building blocks of the Church. He asks if the entire Church should simply be transformed into base communities.

His answer is that the Church needs both small communities as well as larger structures to support and serve them, to keep them from utopian errors. The larger Church desperately needs these small communities to renew its faith. But he calls the Church to take these communities more seriously. According to Boff, there are two models of the Church: (1) the Church as a grand institution with all its services and resources concentrated in cultural centres in affluent areas of society where it enjoys social power, and (2) the Church that is centred in the network of basic communities which are composed of the poor masses on the margins of power. In this second model, the institutional Church sees its main task as serving these communities.

Criticism of the Church: religious, ethical and political

Liberation theologians go beyond merely extolling base communities, but see these as highlighting deep problems with the institutional Church. Both Gutiérrez and Boff see the Church as having been relatively open and inclusive until the 4th century when it became a part of the political establishment under Constantine.

At this point **ecclesio-centrism** emerged: to be for or against Christ was now interpreted as being for or against the Church. This started a process where the focus of Church life was placed on hierarchy, sacred powers, dogmas, rites, traditions and clericalism. In this institutional Church, Christ was transformed from a suffering servant into an Emperor – a priestly power on a throne. The Pope eventually became thought of as God on earth as the Church became a conservative force attempting to protect its power rather than seeking to bring real solutions to human liberation.

Key quotes

This situation of oppression has received the direct or indirect support of the Church's hierarchy, who since colonial times have legitimised the interests of the elites. (L. Rivera-Rodriguez)

The Church has no qualms of conscience in accepting authoritarian and even totalitarian regimes as long as its own rights are not attacked. (L. Boff)

A theology which has as its points of reference only 'truths' which have been established once and for all – and not only the Truth which is also the Way – can be only static and, in the long run, sterile. (G. Gutiérrez)

Study tip

This textbook contains several excerpts from key documents in 'text boxes'; you can deepen your understanding by reading these more extensively. Simply look these up online and find more references to 'liberation theology', 'Marxism', 'salvation' and other key ideas presented in this chapter.

Boff says that the solution to these problems is found by reflecting on the doctrine of the Trinity. The Trinity has three distinct persons which are in perfect communion with one another. The Father is the ultimate mystery, the Son communicates the truth of that mystery and the Spirit shares that mystery with the world. These three live in a perfect fellowship ('**koinonia**'), where each shares in the life of the others yet retains their uniqueness. Humans, created in the likeness of God, are also mysteries. Therefore, they should also have a koinonia which is marked by both individual uniqueness and perfect sharing.

AO1 Activity

Take a few minutes on the Internet and see if you can find out why Leonardo Boff was 'silenced' by the Vatican in 1985 – this will help you to deepen your understanding of his criticisms of the Roman Catholic Church.

However, this is not the case: the institutional church denies participation and equality to a majority of women and men who remain oppressed and permanently marginalised. In fact, the institutional Church is organised, says Boff, not along Trinitarian lines, but along a monotheistic line as there is, '... a single church body, a single head (the pope), a single Christ, a single God ... the concentration of all power in one person, the sole representative of the sole God'. The solution is for the institution to abandon its paternalistic attitude and submit all of its strength and power to the service all people. Only then will it fulfill the model of the Trinity.

Liberation theology and Marxism

Marxism is the name given to the ideas presented by Karl Marx (1818–1883) and Friedrich Engels (1820–1895). In the *Communist Manifesto*, Marx says that instead of viewing historical change as coming about by the actions of individual heroes and leaders, change has really been driven by an ongoing conflict between upper classes (the '**bourgeoisie**', property owning) and lower classes (the '**proletariat**', working class). The root of this conflict lies in economics. The upper classes are ruled by self-interest and see the lower classes only as a means to increase their wealth; they will employ even brutal means to ensure that their wealth is maintained. What is a required is a dramatic change to a classless society in which everyone works harmoniously to serve the greater good. The only way to maintain this ideal is for the tools of economic production to become common property so that every person can work to their capacity and consume according to their needs.

In Gustavo Gutiérrez' *A Theology of Liberation* Marxism is seldom mentioned. His focus is on how capitalist models of development exploit the poor in contrast to God's will for society. He observes the creation of two classes in Latin America: those dominating and those who are dominated. Gutiérrez comes to the conclusion that those who are poor will not discover a better life through capitalism; the answer lies in socialism. He appreciates Marx's understanding that exploitation is a necessary part of the capitalist model. Elsewhere, he makes a stronger statement that appears to be endorsing Marxist ideas, 'Only by overcoming a society divided into classes, only by installing a political power at the service of the great popular majorities, only by elimination the private appropriation of wealth created by human toil, can we build the foundation of a more just society.'

Leonardo Boff says that Marxism is not a '**monolithic**' reality; he points out that Pope Paul VI distinguished between four types of expression of Marxism and offers his own views on each of these levels:

Key quotes

… authority adopts a paternalistic attitude; it is imbued with goodwill and caring, but fails to recognise and appreciate the capacity of subordinates to think intelligently and creatively. **(L. Boff)**

The Trinitarian vision produces a version of a church that is more communion than hierarchy, more service than power, more circular than pyramidal, more loving embrace than bending the knee before authority. **(L. Boff)**

Key terms

Bourgeoisie: property owners who own most of society's wealth and means of production

Koinonia: fellowship or communion between Christians and God or Christians and one another

Monolithic: literally, 'a single stone', used to refer to something that is simple rather than complex

Proletariat: the working class who own little or no property

Key quotes

From each according to his abilities, to each according to his needs. **(K. Marx)**

The ruling ideas of each age have ever been the ideas of its ruling classes. **(K. Marx)**

The class struggle is a fact, and neutrality in this matter is impossible. **(G. Gutiérrez)**

Key quotes

If there is any truth in Marxism, we ought to adopt it and incorporate it into our own broader, Christian vision of reality. (L. Boff)

Marxist historical materialism is eminently valid in its criticism of capitalism and its proposition of socialism. (L. Boff)

The poverty of Third World countries was the price to be paid for the First World to be able to enjoy the fruits of overabundance. (L. Boff and C. Boff)

Capitalism has a dismal record in Latin America, even the staunchest critics of liberation theology do not attempt to defend it. (A. McGovern)

Specification content

The Roman Catholic Church's responses to South American liberation theology.

quickfire

4.18 What is one aspect of Marxism rejected by Leonardo Boff?

1. *A historical practice of class struggle.* Boff notes that both Christians and Marxists share the dream of a society where there is neither rich nor poor. They also share a strong desire to fight against the kinds of class oppression that create an unjust society – though Marxists view this as a fight to the death and Christians believe in first using non-violent means because of their conviction that the oppressors themselves are also sons and daughters of God.

2. *An economic and political practice.* The results of Marxism can be seen and assessed. Liberation theologians are critical of the Soviet form of Marxism, especially when it turns into a bureaucratic tyranny and suppresses individual liberties.

Karl Marx, left (1818–1883) and Friedrich Engels, right (1820–1895)

3. *An atheistic and materialistic viewpoint.* Boff says that Christians simply reject the atheism that accompanies the Marxist model. Engels denied a transcendent meaning to history and reduced God to an empty syllable; this is unacceptable for Christians.

4. *A form of social and material analysis.* Marxism is a branch of science which examines social reality from the viewpoint of historical materialism. Boff says that Christians can view that all truth that science reveals is God's truth. Marxism is to be valued for its criticism of capitalism and its proposal that a more socialistic society has the potential to be more humane. It is this last point that is most relevant for liberation theology and the creation of a more just society.

Overall, liberation theologians feel that the answer to the poverty they encounter is to be found in some sort of socialism. They agree that the experience of capitalism in Latin America has had disastrous results on the environment, created a class system, and generated a humanitarian crisis.

Roman Catholic Church responses to South American liberation theology

Liberation theologians claim that their views are a logical extension of the God revealed in the Bible and in church traditions, especially those articulated at Vatican II which urged that theology be made relevant for daily life and that a concern for the poor be made a priority in the Church.

In Latin America, liberation theology was strongly supported by two key conferences of Bishops, in Medellín in 1968 and at Puebla in 1979. The Bishops at Medellín said, 'Because all liberation is an anticipation of the complete redemption of Christ, the Church in Latin America is particularly in favour of all educational efforts which tend to free our people … A deafening cry pours from the throats of millions of men, asking their pastors for a liberation that reaches them from nowhere else.'

At the Vatican, liberation theology has had a mixed reception. In 1975 Pope John Paul II wrote a document on the theme of evangelisation (*Evangelii Nuntiandi*). In it he stated the importance of spreading the Gospel through preaching, teaching, and the giving of sacraments. He admitted that there is a link between evangelism and human advancement: '... how in fact can one proclaim the new commandment without promoting in justice and in peace the true, authentic advancement of man?' However, he was concerned about the potential of liberation theology to reduce evangelism to social justice and to ignore the spiritual and eschatological dimensions of salvation. In fact, he warned that without a spiritual change, new structures can themselves become inhumane. He said that the primary thrust of evangelism is spiritual and preparation for a future; these dimensions must not be lost by those in Latin America. Furthermore, he condemned the use of violence to bring about social change: 'We exhort you not to place your trust in violence and revolution: that is contrary to the Christian spirit, and it can also delay instead of advancing that social uplifting to which you lawfully aspire.'

Cardinal Joseph Ratzinger, later Pope Benedict XVI, expanded on this criticism of liberation theology. In the document *Instruction on Liberation Theology* (1984) He recognises the validity of the term 'liberation theology' since human freedom from oppression is one aspect of salvation. However, he makes several criticisms:

1. Liberation theology is deluded if it believes that a structural or economic change can bring about salvation. This is because sin is a larger issue than the challenges caused by economic structures. History teaches that those who fight for liberation, in turn, often become oppressors. This is why spiritual solutions are needed.

2. Marxism is not a science but an atheistic ideology. Getting involved in Marxism involves a Christian in 'terrible contradictions'. One of these is the loss of theology itself. The Marxist conception of 'praxis' says that the truth can only be known by being involved in class struggle against the upper classes. This denies the transcendent nature of truth that is a part of Christian theology.

3. Marxism makes everyone an enemy who is outside of the fight of the poor and the oppressed. Furthermore, Marxism encourages violence to bring about change – this is not an ethic that reflects Christian principles.

4. The Bible is given only a political interpretation. For example, interpreting the Exodus as only a political liberation misses the importance of Israel's relationship with God. In fact, the Exodus does not end suffering. God provides continuing spiritual liberation and purification. For instance, the Psalms address human suffering from the perspective of spirituality not politics.

In an essay on the subject of eschatology, Ratzinger says that it is delusional to think that an historic, golden age can be established by political means. In the Bible, the expectation for a perfect world is outside of history – it is brought about by God after the conclusion of history. One of the main reasons that utopian schemes fail is that they place their trust in a new institution and ignore the need for the management of the forces in the human soul: '... the management of forces in the soul determine the fate of the community more than the management of economic means'.

AO1 Activity

The visit of Gustavo Gutiérrez in 2015 to the Vatican was widely covered by the media. Find some news reports of this event and write down the perceptions of liberation theology in the news reports you read – are these neutral? See if you can discover different media biases in the press.

The current Pope, Francis, has spoken out strongly about greed, materialism, and the evils involved in capitalistic excesses. Interestingly, as a young priest and leader in the Jesuit order in Argentina, he was a harsh critic of liberation theology and sought to prevent priests from involvement with political organisations. Instead, he devoted himself to acts of charity and encouraged others to do the same. Later, as Assistant Bishop in Buenos Aires it is reported that his views on priests involved in social justice softened. In 2015 Pope Francis invited Gustavo Gutiérrez to the Vatican as a guest of honour. Though Pope Francis has never proclaimed himself as a liberation theologian, some of his statements appear to be influenced by a similar kind of social awareness.

quickfire

4.19 True or false: Cardinal Joseph Ratzinger (later, Pope Benedict XVI) believed that it was possible to form a perfect community on earth.

Key quotes

If one looks at the bulk of writings by liberation theologians, Marxism plays a relatively small part. (A. McGovern)

... masses of people find themselves excluded and marginalised: without work, without possibilities, without any means of escape. Human beings are themselves considered consumer goods to be used and then discarded. We have created a 'throw away' culture which is now spreading. It is no longer simply about exploitation and oppression, but something new. Exclusion ultimately has to do with what it means to be a part of the society in which we live; those excluded are no longer society's underside or its fringes or its disenfranchised – they are no longer even a part of it. The excluded are not the 'exploited' but the outcast, the 'leftovers'. In this context, some people continue to defend trickle-down theories which assume that economic growth, encouraged by a free market, will inevitably succeed in bringing about greater justice and inclusiveness in the world. This opinion, which has never been confirmed by the facts, expresses a crude and naïve trust in the goodness of those wielding economic power and in the sacralised workings of the prevailing economic system. Meanwhile, the excluded are still waiting. (Pope Francis, Evangelii Gaudium, 2013)

Key skills

Knowledge involves:

Selection of a range of (thorough) accurate and relevant information that is directly related to the specific demands of the question.

This means:

- Selecting relevant material for the question set

- Be focused in explaining and examining the material selected.

Understanding involves:

Explanation that is extensive, demonstrating depth and/or breadth with excellent use of evidence and examples including (where appropriate) thorough and accurate supporting use of sacred texts, sources of wisdom and specialist language.

This means:

- Effective use of examples and supporting evidence to establish the quality of your understanding

- Ownership of your explanation that expresses personal knowledge and understanding and NOT just a chunk of text from a book that you have rehearsed and memorised.

AO1 Developing skills

It is now important to consider the information that has been covered in this section; however, the information in its raw form is too extensive and so has to be processed in order to meet the requirements of the examination. This can be achieved by practising more advanced skills associated with AO1. For assessment objective 1 (AO1), which involves demonstrating 'knowledge' and 'understanding' skills, we are going to focus on different ways in which the skills can be demonstrated effectively, and also refer to how the performance of these skills is measured (see generic band descriptors for A2 [WJEC] AO1 or A Level [Eduqas] AO1).

▶ **Your new task is this:** It is impossible to cover all essays in the time allowed by the course; however, it is a good exercise to develop detailed plans that can be utilised under timed conditions. As a last exercise:

1. Create some ideal plans by using what we have done so far in the Theme 4 Developing skills sections.

2. This time stop at the planning stage and exchange plans with a study partner.

3. Check each other's plans carefully. Talk through any omissions or extras that could be included, not forgetting to challenge any irrelevant materials.

4. Remember, collaborative learning is very important for revision. It not only helps to consolidate understanding of the work and appreciation of the skills involved, it is also motivational and a means of providing more confidence in one's learning. Although the examination is sat alone, revising as a pair or small group is invaluable.

When you have completed each plan, as a pair or small group refer to the band descriptors for A2 (WJEC) or A Level (Eduqas) and in particular have a look at the demands described in the higher band descriptors towards which you should be aspiring. Ask yourself:

- Does my work demonstrate thorough, accurate and relevant knowledge and understanding of religion and belief?

- Is my work coherent (consistent or make logical sense), clear and well organised?

- Will my work, when developed, be an extensive and relevant response which is specific to the focus of the task?

- Does my work have extensive depth and/or suitable breadth and have excellent use of evidence and examples?

- If appropriate to the task, does my response have thorough and accurate reference to sacred texts and sources of wisdom?

- Are there any insightful connections to be made with other elements of my course?

- Will my answer, when developed and extended to match what is expected in an examination answer, have an extensive range of views of scholars/schools of thought?

- When used, is specialist language and vocabulary both thorough and accurate?

Issues for analysis and evaluation

Whether the political and ethical foundations of liberation theology are more important than any religious foundations

This section covers AO2 content and skills

Specification content
Whether the political and ethical foundations of liberation theology are more important than any religious foundations.

Liberation theology is the creation of Roman Catholic priests, trained in Catholic seminaries, committed to Church ministry, administering the sacraments and writing books heavily informed by biblical themes. Both Gustavo Gutiérrez and Leonardo Boff hold PhDs in theology and are concerned that the Church develops religious approaches to oppression and poverty that reflect the attitude of its founder, Jesus Christ. Therefore, it is unlikely that they would agree with the idea that politics and ethics are more important than religion.

Yet one aspect of their teaching that has been criticised is the notion of 'praxis'. Gutiérrez, Boff and other liberation theologians stress that it is action rather than intellectualising that must come first in their work. What they have in mind is the distinction that Karl Marx made between merely philosophising about the world and changing the world. In the face of suffering and oppression, theology should not be about finding the right intellectual truths, but about taking action to end suffering. Liberation theology's stress on praxis has been seen by some in the Catholic Church as an abdication of religion. This is because, in Marxism, one cannot know the truth apart from the fight against the upper classes in the creation of a classless society where private ownership is banned. Cardinal Joseph Ratzinger says that this clearly makes theology subservient to a political ideology. From this point of view the phrase 'liberation theology' implies an order: liberation first, theology (or religion) second.

It is true that liberation theologians speak of 'orthopraxy' as coming before 'orthodoxy'. However, once we examine their reasons for doing this, it is clear that they have no intention to reduce God and their beliefs to Marxist ideas, but to redress an imbalance in the Church. Gutiérrez says that European theology takes place in a context of technical and scientific progress where theologians are addressing a world 'come of age' with arguments and reflections of the relevance of God. These take an intellectual and rational form. On the other hand, liberation theology takes place in a context of suffering; to proceed on an intellectual basis seems to lack love. Thus the phrase 'liberation theology' doesn't reflect a decision to place God or religion in second place but a decision to put the task of rationalising and reflection in second place – one should be moved first by a living faith in the face of suffering. However, it should be noted that the original Spanish title of Gutiérrez' book puts the term 'theology' first: *Teología de la Liberción*. Boff says that liberation theology is 'faith confronted by oppression', so, clearly, religion is not divorced from the concerns of liberation theologians.

Further evidence that liberation theology is informed by religion as much as ethics or politics is found in their heavy reliance on the Bible. Gutiérrez, Boff and others take inspiration for their theology across the entire Bible, from the Exodus where God liberates 'his' people from suffering to the creation of the Church, an egalitarian community devoted to prayer, teaching, common meals and mutual support – including the distribution of goods. In between these are the prophets who fought against social injustice and Jesus whose first sermon was on the theme of liberation (Luke 4: 16–30). However, the Church has accused liberation theologians of politicising these passages. For instance, Cardinal Ratzinger (later Pope Benedict XVI) says that to see the Exodus merely as a political liberation misses several aspects of the narrative including the theological theme of God's people becoming close to God and God providing spiritual and emotional sustenance for suffering that occurs after the Exodus (such as found in the book of Psalms).

AO2 Activity

As you read through this section try to do the following:

1. Pick out the different lines of argument that are presented in the text and identify any evidence given in support.
2. For each line of argument try to evaluate whether or not you think this is strong or weak.
3. Think of any questions you may wish to raise in response to the arguments.

This activity will help you to start thinking critically about what you read, and help you to evaluate the effectiveness of different arguments and from this develop your own observations, opinions and points of view that will help with any conclusions that you make in your answers to the AO2 questions that arise.

Key quotes

The Church considers it to be undoubtedly important to build up structures which are more human, more just, more respectful of the rights of the person and less oppressive and less enslaving, but she is conscious that the best structures and the most idealised systems soon become inhuman if the inhuman inclinations of the human heart are not made wholesome, if those who live in these structures or who rule them do not undergo a conversion of heart and of outlook.
(Pope John Paul II)

Salvation is not something otherworldly, in regard to which the present life is merely a test.
(G. Gutiérrez)

AO2 Activity

List some conclusions that could be drawn from the AO2 reasoning from the above text; try to aim for at least three different possible conclusions. Consider each of the conclusions and collect brief evidence to support each conclusion from the AO1 and AO2 material for this topic. Select the conclusion that you think is most convincing and explain why it is so. Try to contrast this with the weakest conclusion in the list, justifying your argument with clear reasoning and evidence.

The Vatican is also concerned about the Marxist tone of the proposals for liberation put forward by liberation theologians. From this perspective, Marxism is synonymous with oppression and atheism. Another reason for seeing liberation theology as synonymous with politics are statements by some of its leaders, such as Gutiérrez that speak of the 'elimination' of private wealth.

In spite of this, liberation theology is clear about its appreciation for Marxist social analysis. But is this at the expense of the religious dimension? Capitalistic interests in Latin America seem to prove the Marxist principle that those in the upper classes will brutally exploit the poor in order to maintain their wealth. It is because of these reasons that many liberation theologians believe that socialism holds more promise than capitalism.

However, The Vatican has been quick to point out that Marxism is a form of utopianism that falsely promises a perfect society in history – and that this has certainly not happened. According to Cardinal Ratzinger (later Pope Benedict XVI) the Bible teaches that the fullness of the Kingdom of God only comes after history has ended; it is 'delusional' to think that there can be perfection on earth. Furthermore, Marxism involves violence in order to achieve this so-called just social order. These points reinforce the point of view, for some, that liberation theology has 'sold out' spirituality to purchase a system to replace the Kingdom of God. One of the implications of these criticisms is that not only have liberation theologians devalued the religious component of their teaching, but they have committed idolatry, worshipping a system that is completely outside of God's will.

Leonardo Boff says that this is not the case. Marxism is a complex phenomenon and as a Christian he simply adopts what is true in Marxism into his 'broader Christian vision of reality'. For instance, he distances liberation theology from the violence of Marxism, saying that it is only a last resort and Christians must view oppressors as the children of God. He also notes that liberation theology does not support the development of Marxism in 'Soviet' forms when this has meant atheism, a loss of human freedom and political and bureaucratic oppression. However, the dimension that liberation theology values is the insight into understanding the dark side of capitalism and the social analysis which predicts the kinds of experiences of oppression felt in Latin America.

So far we have seen some clear criticisms about liberation theology having denied the primacy of religion in its formulation. However, is it just as easy to find evidence that liberation theology puts religion behind politics and ethics? Arthur F. McGovern notes that 'Marxism' is seldom mentioned in books on liberation theology. Yet, it is true that the social theories advanced by liberation theologians 'dance' around Marxist ideas.

Perhaps one way to evaluate the question is to ask what is meant by the term 'religion'. Gutiérrez and others note that the classic way of doing theology was to attempt to arrive at some sort of 'truth' prior to engaging the world (if the world was ever engaged with). Sometimes this involved committing oneself to monastic life where one would reflect on the Bible and worship in intense ways. Since the 12th century, theology viewed itself as a 'science' in which one used intellect and reason to discover truth. If what is meant by 'reason' are these traditional ways of doing theology (the intellectual establishment of beliefs), then perhaps liberation theology can be said to have put politics and ethics before religion.

However, the term 'religion' can also be defined as 'faith' (in contrast to 'The Faith'), one's heartfelt response to the situation around them. These liberation theologians are certainly people of faith; they seek to apply the faith of the prophets, of Jesus and of the early church – and of the traditions of the Church to the pastoral situations that they face. In this sense, they have not put religion in second place. They might argue, if anything, that their religion is driving their theology.

The extent to which liberation theology offered a cultural challenge to the Roman Catholic Church

Specification content

The extent to which liberation theology offered a cultural challenge to the Roman Catholic Church.

Liberation theologians have sought to influence the Roman Catholic Church to embrace the poor and suffering in Latin America. Sometimes this has involved criticisms of the institutional Church such as ecclesio-centrism (placing the institution rather than the people at the centre), clericalism (viewing ordained clergy as more important than the laity), promoting an overly spiritualised theology, accommodation to unjust governments, and not offering social solutions in the face of suffering.

Have these concerns and criticisms made 'inroads' to the Church outside of Latin America? One could argue that, on the level of language, they have. For instance, 'preferential option for the poor' was a phrase used by Latin American theologians in the 70s to speak of the need to ensure that those on the lowest rungs of society were treated as of paramount importance by the Church, reflecting God's priority – 'the last shall be first'. This phrase was used subsequently by both Pope John Paul II and Pope Benedict XVI. Furthermore, Pope Benedict has written extensively about 'liberation theology' and the theme of 'liberation' which indicates that much attention has been paid to these ideas.

Yet, one can question how deeply this change in language in Vatican documents reflects the concerns and convictions at the heart of liberation theology. First, at Vatican II in 1962–1965 there was a marked emphasis on the Church prioritising its focus on those suffering from poverty apart from liberation theology. Therefore, it wasn't much of a 'leap' for the Church to embrace this terminology. Furthermore, though Pope Benedict has used the term liberation theology, he has been one of its foremost critics. In his 1984 'Instruction on Certain Aspects of Liberation Theology' he accuses liberation theology of theological confusion as it ignores the spiritual dimensions of sin and salvation and 'wrongly' thinks that Marxism provides a scientific analysis. Thus, 'liberation theology' is viewed as a dangerous influence that can lead the Church away from its true calling. In fact, the Vatican 'silenced' Leonardo Boff in 1985 for just less than a year and has formally investigated the theology of Gustavo Gutiérrez many times. Of course, the negative attention given to these theologians does indeed reveal that the challenge they have posed has been deemed of considerable importance.

The position of the Roman Catholic Church on liberation theology, however, is not merely one of resistance. Liberation theology has been warmly received by the Bishops of Latin America. Both at Medellin (1968) and Puebla (1969) statements were issued that can be seen to affirm the main concerns of liberation theologians and to 'favour all educational efforts which tend to free our people' (Medellin). Furthermore, liberation theologians themselves are recognised priests in the Church and as such, lead communities in teaching, worship and the sacraments. The fact that many of liberation theology's most prominent teachers continue to serve as priests suggests that we should see the Roman Catholic Church as having diverse views of liberation theology.

The development of base ecclesial communities in Latin America is viewed by liberation theologians as one of the biggest challenges and opportunities facing a church that says that it wants to relate itself to the contemporary world. However, reactions to the existence of these communities also illustrates resistance to some of the key themes of liberation theology.

AO2 Activity

As you read through this section try to do the following:

1. Pick out the different lines of argument that are presented in the text and identify any evidence given in support.
2. For each line of argument try to evaluate whether or not you think this is strong or weak.
3. Think of any questions you may wish to raise in response to the arguments.

This activity will help you to start thinking critically about what you read, and help you to evaluate the effectiveness of different arguments and from this develop your own observations, opinions and points of view that will help with any conclusions that you make in your answers to the AO2 questions that arise.

Key quotes

Basically we shouldn't need a pope. The Church could build a network of religious communities which communicate with each other as it had when it was founded. But during the period of the Roman Empire, Christianity turned into an institution with political duties, so that it became a centre of power. It is very characteristic of this pope [Francis] that he refused to cover his head with the golden mitre after his election. He said: 'Carnival is over. I don't want this.' (L. Boff)

The Church, which until AD 312 was more of a movement than an institution, became an heir of the empire's institutions: law, organisation by diocese and parish, bureaucratic centralisation, positions, and titles. … It began on a path of power that continues today and that we must hasten to end. (L. Boff)

Base ecclesial communities are gatherings of 15–20 families for worship, prayer and support in areas where there is no priest. These communities were formed for at least two reasons: concerns about Catholics joining Protestant and secular communities and a popular Catholic movement of literacy and education which spread across Latin America, encouraging the poor to take more control of their lives. Base communities gather for worship, education and mutual support. They are connected to the larger church though they experienced dramatic growth across Latin America in the 60s and 70s with millions of people involved.

Leonardo Boff and others see the base ecclesial communities challenging ecclesio-centrism and clericalism as they meet without priests to engage with the Bible, singing, prayers and other spiritual activities outside of the sacraments. They also challenge a Church, says Boff, that has frequently avoided helping people find practical solutions to their suffering – this is because base communities engage in education, training and mutual support. Boff believes that there is a role for the institutional Church in providing identity and continuity for base communities, but that the institutional Church should consider itself nothing less than a servant to these communities.

It is not clear that this challenge has been taken up by the Vatican. On the one hand, the Vatican recognises these communities and affirms them as a valid expression of the Church. It sees these as places where Catholics can grow in their faith and find a supportive and intimate community in an impersonal world. On the other hand, there is a concern that some of these communities are critical of the institutional Church and its hierarchy and become 'ideological' in their orientation – this likely means 'Marxist' or 'revolutionary'. In other words, these communities are considered to be either critical of the hierarchy and therefore 'ideological' or they have a solid connection to the Church and are therefore free of 'ideology'. This approach underscores different accents placed on the term 'evangelism'. The Vatican defines evangelism primarily in terms of engaging in activities that relate people to the Church: preaching, teaching and administering sacraments. Liberation theologians believe that the accent on 'salvation' should be political action for social justice. Accepting the base communities without 'ideology', as the Vatican does, appears to show that this expression of liberation theology has not made an impact amongst those with more of a 'spiritual interpretation' of the duties of the Church.

However, Boff wants the Church to see that these communities present a theological challenge – they confront rampant ecclesio-centrism since they are active, egalitarian and positive communities without the constant presence of a priest. Boff explains that these communities mirror Trinitarian theology which holds that the members of the trinity are unique but interpenetrate each other in perfect harmony. As humans are created in the likeness of God they too should manifest this harmony in the midst of uniqueness. What we find in the Church, Boff says, is the opposite: a monotheistic approach which emphasises that the Church is just one reality with one 'head', one Pope. Boff wants to see the Church return to more of a New Testament model where there was apostolic succession and a New Testament but less concentration of power in a single person or institution. It is widely believed that these criticisms are what led to Boff's temporary silencing by the Vatican in 1985.

In light of the many criticisms of liberation theology and the strong reactions by the Vatican to its most prominent leaders, it may be easy to conclude that liberation theology is largely a Latin American phenomenon that has not found wider acceptance in the Church. However, this viewpoint can be challenged in that the current Pope, Pope Francis, has made some steps in the direction of liberation theology. Though he has not called himself a liberation theologian, he invited Gustavo Gutiérrez to the Vatican in 2015 as a guest of honour. Additionally, his messages to the Church have included strongly worded criticisms of greed and some forms of capitalism. Specifically, he has questioned 'trickle-down economics' which reflect the criticisms of a capitalist 'development' model criticised by Gutiérrez in the 1970s.

Pope Francis' own journey is one from criticism of liberation theology when he was a younger priest and leader in the Jesuit order of Argentina. At that time, he was widely known for having engaged in acts of charity but also of discouraging priests from engaging in political activities. From his recent statements of denunciations of greed and his positive encounter with Gustavo Gutiérrez, could it be that the 'tide has turned' and that liberation theology is now at the heart of the very same Vatican that had criticised it decades before?

It is too early to tell. What is more certain is that the worldwide Roman Catholic Church is a broad and diverse body that allows for different viewpoints. It seems that the story of liberation theology is far from over.

Archbishop Óscar Romero was assassinated while giving mass in 1980. He is considered a hero by the people of El Salvador for speaking out against poverty, social injustice, assassinations and torture. Liberation theologians have been inspired by his life, although Romero himself was informed by traditional spirituality and had no sympathy for Marxist-inspired thought. The words in the image say, 'The structures of social injustice are those that have given our poor a slow death.'

Key quote

Nor can one localise evil principally or uniquely in bad social, political, or economic 'structures' as though all other evils came from them so that the creation of the 'new man' would depend on the establishment of different economic and socio-political structures. (The Vatican, Instruction on Liberation Theology)

AO2 Activity

List some conclusions that could be drawn from the AO2 reasoning from the above text; try to aim for at least three different possible conclusions. Consider each of the conclusions and collect brief evidence to support each conclusion from the AO1 and AO2 material for this topic. Select the conclusion that you think is most convincing and explain why it is so. Try to contrast this with the weakest conclusion in the list, justifying your argument with clear reasoning and evidence.

Key skills

Analysis involves:

Identifying issues raised by the materials in the AO1, together with those identified in the AO2 section, and presenting sustained and clear views, either of scholars or from a personal perspective ready for evaluation.

This means:

- That your answers are able to identify key areas of debate in relation to a particular issue

- That you can identify, and comment upon, the different lines of argument presented by others

- That your response comments on the overall effectiveness of each of these areas or arguments.

Evaluation involves:

Considering the various implications of the issues raised based upon the evidence gleaned from analysis and provides an extensive detailed argument with a clear conclusion.

This means:

- That your answer weighs up the consequences of accepting or rejecting the various and different lines of argument analysed

- That your answer arrives at a conclusion through a clear process of reasoning.

AO2 Developing skills

It is now important to consider the information that has been covered in this section; however, the information in its raw form is too extensive and so has to be processed in order to meet the requirements of the examination. This can be achieved by practising more advanced skills associated with AO2. For assessment objective 2 (AO2), which involves 'critical analysis' and 'evaluation' skills, we are going to focus on different ways in which the skills can be demonstrated effectively, and also refer to how the performance of these skills is measured (see generic band descriptors for A2 [WJEC] AO2 or A Level [Eduqas] AO2).

▶ **Your new task is this:** It is impossible to cover all essays in the time allowed by the course; however, it is a good exercise to develop detailed plans that can be utilised under timed conditions. As a last exercise:

1. Create some ideal plans by using what we have done so far in the Theme 4 Developing skills sections.

2. This time stop at the planning stage and exchange plans with a study partner.

3. Check each other's plans carefully. Talk through any omissions or extras that could be included, not forgetting to challenge any irrelevant materials.

4. Remember, collaborative learning is very important for revision. It not only helps to consolidate understanding of the work and appreciation of the skills involved, it is also motivational and a means of providing more confidence in one's learning. Although the examination is sat alone, revising as a pair or small group is invaluable.

When you have completed the task, refer to the band descriptors for A2 (WJEC) or A Level (Eduqas) and in particular have a look at the demands described in the higher band descriptors towards which you should be aspiring. Ask yourself:

- Is my answer a confident critical analysis and perceptive evaluation of the issue?

- Is my answer a response that successfully identifies and thoroughly addresses the issues raised by the question set.

- Does my work show an excellent standard of coherence, clarity and organisation?

- Will my work, when developed, contain thorough, sustained and clear views that are supported by extensive, detailed reasoning and/or evidence?

- Are the views of scholars/schools of thought used extensively, appropriately and in context?

- Does my answer convey a confident and perceptive analysis of the nature of any possible connections with other elements of my course?

- When used, is specialist language and vocabulary both thorough and accurate?

Questions and answers

Theme 1: DEF

AO1 answer: *An answer examining the formation of the Christian biblical canon.*

A weaker answer

There was a lot of controversy and mystery surrounding the creation of the Bible in Christianity – both with the Jewish people and their Old Testament as well as with the Christians and the New Testament. **1**

The Pentateuch came first – it was written by Moses on Mt Sinai and was given to the people who followed its laws. Then came other books, some by prophets and others by other writers such as the Psalms. By the time of Jesus, it was pretty much all together and could be read in Greek or Hebrew. There are some books referred to in the Old Testament that have been lost. **2**

The Christians used the Old Testament and started adding books – but they couldn't always agree. Churches in different places had differing collections of letters, Gospels and other books and there were arguments about certain books. In fact, the entire collection didn't even come together until the end of the 4th century. Now, there is a clear order of Gospels, letters and the book of revelation. **3**

Some Bibles have more books than other Bibles; this has to do with whether or not it is a Protestant or Catholic Bible – the Catholic Bibles use Jewish books that were written in Greek but Martin Luther didn't like this because one of those books mentions purgatory – so he threw out these Jewish books – which actually made his 'Old Testament' the same as the Jewish Bible since the Jews also did not accept that these books originally written in Greek should be included – though they find them helpful for their faith. **4**

So, after lots of fighting and decisions, Christians finally came to agree on the many books that made up their canon, even though there are other books that could have been included and that we can still see today. **5**

Commentary

1 There is an attempt at an introduction, but it is at the GCSE level with no specific themes mentioned. By using 'controversy' and 'mystery' it feels as if a point of view has already been taken and that there is not going to be the kind of detailed response expected at this level.

2 This is simplistic, superficial and vague. There are many examples of individual books that could have been mentioned. Stages in the development of the canon could have been presented in a more detailed manner. There is very little use of specialist language here and throughout the rest of the answer.

3 There are some correct facts here; however, other critical points and facts have been left out of the discussion; limited use of scholarly views.

4 This paragraph is the strongest with some understanding of a key issue between Protestant and Catholic canons. However, there is no reference to specific texts.

5 These sentences add nothing to the discussion.

Summative comment

Overall, this response is very superficial and misses many key points. There is an obvious lack of specific examples and specialist language.

AO2 answer: *An answer evaluating whether or not the Bible can be regarded as the inspired word of God.*

Excerpt from a strong answer

There are a number of reasons why it is possible to disagree with the view that the Bible is the inspired word of God. However, first we must know what it is that we are disagreeing with. In other words, what does the claim of 'inspiration' actually mean for Christians? In fact, there are different Christian claims for inspiration and each of these must be evaluated in turn. So, overall, Christians believe that the Bible is 'God-breathed' (theopneustos), but see this working in different ways. **1**

Some Christians, such as those behind the Chicago Statement on biblical inerrancy, believe in 'verbal plenary inspiration'. This is the view that God gave each and every word to each and every author so that not only is there no doubt that the Bible is from God (plenary means absolute), but there is no doubt about the truth of each statement. Those who promote this view see the Bible as a string of propositions which are true rather than false – the Bible is 'inerrant'. **2**

There are a number of difficulties with this point of view. What is most obvious is that the Bible contains different literary genres. So, not only are there direct statements of prophets which appear to be the direct words of God, there is also poetry, fiction (i.e. parables) and history – to name a few genres. In fact, sometimes you will see a 'red letter' edition of the Bible where the editors attempt to put the words of Jesus in red ink. The challenge with this is that there are some passages (especially in the Gospel of John) where it is difficult to tell where Jesus starts speaking and the narrator stops speaking! Perhaps the most difficult aspect of this position is that it is clear that different authors have not only different personalities and literary styles but also different masteries of language and grammar (just consider the differences in style and expression between the four Gospels). If God inspired every word of the Bible, one would not expect to find these variations.

However, many Christians do not express 'inspiration' in this way – many church bodies, such as the Church of England, are content by stating that God inspired the Bible but recognise that God communicated God's truth through human personalities. This certainly deals with the objections noted above. However, one has to ask, 'how can this be verified?' What is it that really distinguishes a claim for inspiration from God from simply humanistic claims for inspiration? **3**

Some Christian views claim that the writers are not themselves inspired by God but are witnesses to inspired events. This means that... **4**

Commentary

1 What makes this introduction strong is that it 'interrogates the question' – it notices that there are different approaches that could be taken and argued. This leads us to believe that there will be a perceptive analysis.

2 Now there is an engagement with one point of view rooted in a scholarly reference with use of technical language.

3 This paragraph engages with the argument in an extensive way citing not one but several objections that could be made before moving onto the next argument. Notice the frequent references to examples to support the argument.

4 If the student deals with the next argument in the same depth as the previous one and moves into a conclusion that summarises and supports their overall point of view, then this would be a very strong response.

Summative comment

This answer displays well-developed responses to specific arguments, using a number of examples to support key points. It is good to see that the response has both a clear point of view as well as an awareness of different ways counterarguments can be made.

Theme 3: ABC

AO1 answer: *An answer examining the contribution of Mary Daly to Feminist theology.*

A strong answer

Mary Daly's main concern is that women be free to develop into the people they were meant to become, regardless of their gender, background and societal expectations.

This journey, however, has been made nearly impossible through women being reduced to objects of men's desires. Considering women as less than fully human has helped men to continue to treat women in ways that serve only themselves and the power structures they have created rather than women. **1**

Daly says that theology has a great deal to do with this problem. Theology has conceived of God as a male. Not only this, it has approached God as a 'noun' – a static, unchanging being who functions to explain what we do not know, give rewards and punishments and insist on roles and rules. By extension, men are the ones to reflect these qualities, ensuring that there is a rigid system in which they can exercise power and authority at the expense of women.

In fact, Daly says that this gender inequality is the 'original sin'. For, to see women as objects is to rob them of their humanity and leads humanity to 'unholy trinity' of sin: rape, murder and genocide. There are many passages in the Bible in which 'God' is seen as promoting all three of these activities (see Numbers 31:17–18). How could this be, asks Daly? The answer is that when humans treat other humans as objects (in this case women), anything becomes possible and permissible. **2**

Part of the answer, says Daly, is to see God as a verb rather than a noun. This means more than simply using feminine terms for God. It means that we identify God with the process of becoming for every human being. When God is identified as a process, then it becomes sinful to stand in the way of that process. In order to adopt this view of God it will be necessary to abandon traditional theology, including a Christology that sees Jesus as a God-Man. To believe in the power of God is to believe in the power of being. **3**

Another part of the answer is for women to leave the Church and become involved in supportive female groups which she calls 'sisterhood'. For, patriarchy is simply too deeply embedded in the Church to change. Furthermore, culture pressurises women to conform to its image of what is 'feminine' and women will need focussed support as they struggle to find their own androgynous being – a way of life that is free from gender stereotypes. **4**

Commentary

1 This introduction is effective because it makes a clear statement of the major themes in Daly's thought.

2 These next two paragraphs move into a more detailed explanation of her thought. Notice the accurate use of key words, concepts and examples.

3 There is an effective use of an example (Jesus as God-Man) to illustrate Daly's idea of God as a noun.

4 This paragraph effectively summarises her proposals, again with accurate explanations of key terms.

This answer displays many excellent characteristics, moving from a clear overview into theoretical detail with key terms and examples.

AO2 answer: *An answer evaluating whether men and women are equal in Christianity.*

A weaker answer.

The Christian Church is filled with sexism and sexist ideas – that's the main message of feminist theologians. It is so bad that some of these, like Mary Daly, want women to simply leave the Church. [1]

There are many reasons that the Church is sexist. These have to do with the Bible itself. In the creation story, it is clear that Eve is being 'put down'; her subservience to Adam is really the 'original sin' according to feminist theologians. This subservience led to her being treated like an object and once you think it is valid to treat someone like an object, then it becomes easier to abuse them. This is why the Old Testament condones rape, murder and genocide. [2]

This inequality was added to by Greek philosophy: Aristotle viewed women as 'misbegotten males' and Christian theologians picked up on this. The idea is that women are less rational and rationality is the fundamental principle of the universe; therefore, women need men to do the thinking for them. [3]

The fact that most Christians in the world worship in churches where women cannot be priests underscores the fact that women are not equal in Christianity – though some women can be priests in other churches.

In conclusion, the Bible, Christian theology and Christian practice all prove that women are not equal in Christianity. [4]

Commentary

1 This introduction leaves the reader thinking that this will be a very one-sided response.

2 The ideas presented here are valid, though they could be developed. Also, an alternative viewpoint should be introduced. For instance, Rosemary Radford Ruether's view of the Hebrew prophets and Jesus could be considered. There are also some interesting insights on the early church that could be brought into the discussion.

3 Again some good ideas, but lacking specificity – which theologians?

4 This is true, but the opposite point of view that gains have been made could be discussed including recent developments in the Roman Catholic Church. It is good that this answer has looked at these dimensions; however, the discussion has been one-sided.

This answer suffers in two main areas: (i) crucially, opposite points of view have not been introduced and (ii) many of the points have been presented without depth. More scholars, more scriptural sources and additional detail could have been easily added to the many good points that have been made.

Theme 3: DEF

AO1 answer: *An answer examining Christian inclusivism.*

A weaker answer

Christian inclusivism is the idea that other religions have a bit of truth and salvation in them, but Christianity has the full truth. This means that you can find your way to God in other religions – though it would be much better for you to become a Christian. Karl Rahner, a Catholic, promoted this idea. [1]

He called people in other religions 'anonymous Christians' because though they might not consider themselves Christians, Christians could consider them as walking with God. This was a huge change from Christian exclusivism which thinks there can be no truth in other religions and actually condemns people in other religions as being totally depraved, ignorant, confused and immoral. [2]

Rahner bases his thinking on the idea that God is working all over the world, not only in the Church. [3]

Rahner's ideas made it into the Catholic Church in a pretty big way and now many Christians think it is possible for people outside of the Church to have truth – though it would be better if they were to become Christians. Some people, like John Hick, see inclusivism as a kind of 'half-way house' between inclusivism and pluralism. [4]

Commentary

1 There are several correct facts here that could be further developed. For instance, when did Rahner develop these ideas and is Catholic inclusivism different from Protestant inclusivism? Also, this answer does not provide any scriptural sources; there are many that could have been used.

2 Rahner's theory has only been superficially presented – what are his four theses?

3 This is a true statement, but it is presented without any development. What does Rahner think the implication of this is for the Church?

4 There is pointless repetition here. Particular documents at Vatican II could have been referred to. Providing a definition of Christian theological pluralism along with an explanation of the differences between pluralism and inclusivism would have strengthened this answer.

Summative comment

The lack of scriptural sources and vagueness about scholars, definitions and key texts are the main causes of weakness in this response.

AO2 answer: *An answer evaluating the extent to which a Christian can be a religious pluralist.*

An excerpt from a strong answer

There are many reasons why religious pluralism is not the official position of any major church bodies: it does not have solid scriptural support, it is only a recent development in the history of Christian theology and its proponents have to dilute the meaning of Christian claims to such an extent that it would lead many Christians to an identity crisis in which they would wonder if it was even worth being a Christian at all. Of course, there are counterarguments to this position, and these will be examined. **1**

Whilst there has been a significant movement from Christian exclusivism to Christian inclusivism (due, in part, to the work of Karl Rahner), there has been no similar significant movement to Christian pluralism. Of course, this does not mean that it is not popular. John Hick achieved a degree of fame through his many books on the subject and pluralism remains popular for its attitude of acceptance to the truth in other religions. **2**

Perhaps one of the reasons that Christian pluralism has been resisted is that it is not able to provide as firm a scriptural basis for its main claims as can exclusivists and inclusivists. For instance, there are exclusivist statements to be found throughout the Bible from injunctions of the Torah to not worship or serve other Gods, to the statement in Acts 4:12 that there is 'no other name' through which people can find salvation. Furthermore, even though inclusivism was not adopted as an official position of the Catholic Church until Vatican II, it appears as an attitude in many biblical passages such as references to those who were 'pleasing to God' outside of the Jewish faith in the Old Testament and Paul's speech in Acts 17 where he recognises a true statement from pagan philosophy. **3**

Pluralism, on the other hand, cannot appeal to a scriptural foundation. It can only attempt to explain away exclusivist and inclusivist passages by looking at historical and cultural factors. For example, Paul Knitter explains that it is not unusual for minority groups under threat to become exclusivist and that it is possible to interpret the high

status of Jesus as poetic expressions of faith rather than statements to be taken literally. The closest he comes to a scriptural justification for pluralism is to say that it is an implication of the command to love one's neighbour: can you love your neighbour if you prejudge him or her to be either completely wrong or only partially right even before there has been an exchange? **4**

Yet many Christians may not feel that this is a strong enough basis upon which to build a theological doctrine. An even bigger difficulty lies in the pluralist reinterpretation of the meaning of important Christian beliefs – especially those about Jesus **5**

Commentary

1 This response begins with a firm point of view to which the candidate consistently returns throughout. Furthermore, this point of view does not prevent a strong presentation of counterarguments. Also, notice that there is a summary of key arguments that will be made. This is concise and effective.

2 It is good to see key scholars are mentioned at the outset.

3 The first argument against the incompatibility of pluralism with Christian commitment is made in depth. There are numerous scriptural references within a strongly made argument about the importance of a biblical foundation for theological claims.

4 The argument is developed further with a scholarly reference along with a perceptive analysis of the weakness of the pluralist's claims.

5 This answer is on target to achieve a very high level if it shows (i) continued sophistication in its presentation of Hick's views on Christology and religious experience and (ii) provides a conclusion that reinforces the views presented in the introduction.

Summative comment

This is a clear and coherent presentation that rests key arguments solidly on scriptural and scholarly sources and ideas.

Theme 4: DEF

AO1 answer: *An answer examining the basis of, and reasons for, the development of South American liberation theology.*

A weaker answer

Liberation theology concerns third world countries after World War II. It is concerned about the suffering of poor and oppressed people. Many Roman Catholic priests felt that the Church was not doing enough and that lives needed to change for the better – this is why it came into being. **1**

Leonardo Boff is one such theologian. He says that what people really need is not just handouts or to work in factories making things for rich people, but 'liberation' – a real change in the way society works. He says that this is what the Bible is all about – especially Jesus who lived with the poor, died poor and encouraged his followers to help the poor by giving food to the hungry and drink to the thirsty (Matthew 25). There's also the story of the Exodus where God leads his people away from slavery in Egypt. **2**

Some priests in South America would leave the rich places they were living and live and help poor people. Some even became revolutionaries and used the ideas of Karl Marx – saying that the poor classes needed to fight against the richer classes. A priest named Gutiérrez even says that God wants the poor to go first. **3**

Not all Catholics agree with liberation theology – in fact some of the popes in the 70s and 80s were against it because Marxism is about atheism. **4** But liberation theologians have said that the Church needs to focus less on 'orthodoxy' and more on 'orthopraxy' meaning that there needs to be more activity to help poor people and that rich people will only find the truth if they get active in helping poor people. **5**

Commentary

1 Mainly accurate but could be more detailed – where, exactly, did it arise?

2 This is accurate – and there is use of some texts, though this could be expanded. There is some evidence of scholarly views.

3 It would be good to see more detailed specialist language here like 'preferential option for the poor' – though what has been written is accurate.

4 True, but this could be strengthened by being more precise – 'some popes'? Who? Explain more fully their reaction to Marxism.

5 Good to see more specialist terms here used in the right way, though this could be developed. What exactly do these words mean?

Summative comment

This is an example of a paper that could easily be developed to reach a higher band. The student has written accurate statements but some of this is superficial and all of it could have been explored in more depth.

AO2 answer: *An answer evaluating whether or not the responses of the Roman Catholic Church to liberation theology were mainly positive.*

A strong answer

There have been many different responses to liberation theology from Catholics across the world – some of these have been positive and some of these have even condemned liberation theology. This answer will argue that this range of responses shows that the Roman Catholic Church is broad and diverse and that there is some evidence that liberation theology is increasingly gaining acceptance despite a period of harsh criticism. **1**

Liberation theology is, after all, a movement in the Catholic Church, involving Catholic priests, like Gustavo Gutiérrez and Leonardo Boff, who have been trained and educated in some of the finest Catholic schools. Their books on the subject are about Christian theology, showing how revelation and tradition relate to extreme poverty. Liberation theology has come out of their pastoring work, to address the suffering of poor people who are mainly religious and Catholic. **2**

At the same time that liberation theology was growing, Vatican II, a major council of the Church, insisted that the Church is a 'church of the poor' and that theology should address modern issues – such as poverty and oppression. In fact, Leonardo Boff, Gustavo Gutiérrez and others have said that liberation theology should be seen as bringing these themes of Vatican II to life. **3**

Official documents of the Catholic Church (such as 'The Instruction on Certain Aspects of the Theology of Liberation') have used terms from liberation theologians such as 'liberation' and 'preferential option for the poor'. These documents make it clear that salvation is indeed more than a spiritual matter and involves the humane treatment of human beings such as fair wages and good working conditions. These documents agree with the idea of liberation theologians that God 'prefers' the poor not in the sense of loving them more than other people, but that they are a priority in the purposes of God as revealed in the Bible: 'the last shall be first'. **4**

Key councils and meetings of the Church have affirmed the many ideas of liberation theology. An example of this is the Latin American Episcopal Council that met in Columbia in 1968; they affirmed many ideas of Gustavo Gutiérrez, including the idea of base communities (church groups in remote areas fighting for justice). This conference played a part in the popularity of liberation theology in Latin America. **5**

After Vatican II and the spread of liberation theology in Latin America, the Church in Rome grew concerned about liberation theology for a number of reasons. Cardinal Ratzinger (later Pope Benedict XVI) warned that liberation theology was not taking traditional theology seriously enough. For example, it could lead people to think that an economic change alone could end sin or bring about the Kingdom of God. Sin is bigger than economics, he insisted. 6

He was also concerned about using only political interpretations of the Bible – and neglecting spiritual interpretations. An example of this is the Atonement: Jesus is viewed only as a moral example, a martyr for the cause of the oppressed. This leaves out many of the other themes of redemption on the cross that have been looked at by theologians such as Anselm, Luther, Augustine and others. 7

Many Catholic theologians have criticised the use of Marxist terms and ideas in liberation theology. For example, they have pointed out that Marxism is not a science that helps us understand society but an 'ideology' in conflict with Christianity because it is atheistic. Marxism justifies violence in the name of class struggle, but Christianity does not endorse violence, say many Catholics. At the same time that the Church in Rome was criticising liberation theologians, it was concerned about loss of freedom of religion in communist bloc countries. How can Marxism truly be helpful since it leads to religious oppression – they asked? 8

Even though there have been some very harsh responses to liberation theology, it is difficult to say that it has either been mainly positive or mainly negative – if anything the Catholic response has been becoming more positive. For example, when the current Pope (Pope Francis) was a young priest, he criticised liberation theology in many of the ways noted above. Yet, over the years he became more sympathetic with it and in 2015 he invited Gustavo Gutiérrez as a special guest of honour at the Vatican. Though he has not described himself as a liberation theologian, Pope Francis has written extensively on the dangers of capitalism in ways similar to liberation theologians. 9

Commentary

1 Brief, relevant introduction.

2 Excellent depth of response.

3 These paragraphs demonstrate an extensive range of views.

4 Accurate reference made to key sources. Thorough and accurate use of specialist language and vocabulary.

5 Extensive depth.

6 Several relevant responses are made for the opposite side of the question in this paragraph and the paragraphs below.

7 Insightful connection here made with material elsewhere in the specification.

8 An excellent range of responses.

9 An excellent conclusion that responds well to the question.

Summative comment

This paper presents a coherent point of view as well as a range of viewpoints using technical terms from key documents.

Quickfire answers

Theme 1: DEF

1.1 The Law, prophets and writings (or, Torah, Nevi'im and Kethuvim).

1.2 Because Protestants follow the Jewish canon and the Catholic Church accepts a number of Jewish books found in the Septuagint but that were later judged to be non-canonical in Judaism.

1.3 The books used by Jewish believers, the Hebrew Bible.

1.4 The Gospels, the letters (or epistles) and the Book of Revelation.

1.5 Objective.

1.6 No.

1.7 Kerygma is an announcement or declaration whereas teaching involves an organised explanation of knowledge.

1.8 C. H. Dodd says there are six: (i) fulfillment of Jewish prophesy, (ii) a new age with the coming of Jesus, (iii) the ascension of Jesus, (iv) the Holy Spirit coming to the Church, (v) the return of Christ, and (vi) the call to repentance.

1.9 In the 80s of the first century CE.

1.10 (i) Likely access to first-hand accounts, (ii) he provides a detailed account, and (iii) agreement with themes in other New Testament books (such as Paul's letters).

1.11 Apocalypticism and Gnosticism.

1.12 To find the deeper meaning behind the mythological expressions.

1.13 It splits off faith from history, confining faith to the realm of personal spirituality only and reducing history to the dry study of facts.

1.14 Jesus was a Jewish prophet announcing the Kingdom of God.

1.15 All messianic movements of Jesus' era ended with the death of their leader; the Jesus movement continued.

1.16 Cross-cultural anthropology, Jewish and Greco-Roman history and, literary and textual studies.

1.17 Near Nag Hammadi, Egypt in 1945; the manuscript dates from the 4th century CE, though fragments from the 2nd century CE have also been found.

1.18 Including all people at his table, regardless of gender, wealth or position in society. Also, his healing miracles to those cast out of society brought them back into social life.

Theme 3: ABC

3.1 The Kingdom of God.

3.2 No. Jesus certainly tells some people to sell their possessions and follow him, but others, like Zacchaeus, are given different instructions.

3.3 The goodness of the material world, the command from God to humans to take charge of the world, the principle of private ownership, God as a defender of the poor and oppressed, and, for some, the concept of the tithe.

3.4 John the Baptist.

3.5 Faith and donations to religious causes.

3.6 War, famine, religious persecution and/or discrimination, educational opportunities, economic opportunities, social opportunities, or for the purposes of mission (i.e. reverse mission).

3.7 A denominational congregation is one that belongs to a larger, autonomous church body. Independent churches do not have a strong formal association with a central organisation.

3.8 Because many countries (such as Nigeria and Ghana) are experiencing explosive growth in Pentecostal Christianity; migrants from these countries bring their religion with them.

3.9 Differences in styles of worship, the need for social support from other migrants and the uneven spread of immigration across the United Kingdom.

3.10 Because their home churches were planted by British missionaries and they now perceive that the United Kingdom is in need of hearing the Gospel since Christianity has been in decline.

3.11 The number of people who report praying regularly or irregularly, the vitality of individual congregations, the birth of new congregations and denominations and the growth of Christianity through immigration.

3.12 'Misbegotten males.'

3.13 Androgynous.

3.14 The prophetic tradition.

3.15 She believes that humanity fell into sexism; the treatment of women as objects is behind the worst violence in history. Today she accuses some Christians of Bibliolatry and Christolatry.

3.16 Bishops, presbyters (or priests, pastors) and deacons. In 2014 Pope Francis indicated that the issue of women as deacons could be studied further and in 2016 a study on the issue was commissioned.

Theme 3: DEF

3.17 False. Some surveys indicate that more than half of the population of the UK is in the 'no-religion category'; this includes atheists (a growing figure) but also those who doubt the existence of God and those who have spiritual beliefs but do not belong to a religion.

3.18 It is thought that the way in which the question was asked made the difference. The way the Census asked the question ('what is your religion?') seemed to imply that you *should* have one. The British Social Attitudes survey simply asked, 'Do you regard yourself as belonging to any particular religion?'

3.19 False. State-funded faith schools are required to teach the National Curriculum; however, they are free to teach their own syllabus for RE classes.

3.20 Because it was thought that the advert would offend those with 'differing faiths or no faith'.

3.21 Secularisation is the word used to describe the process of a society moving from religion to no-religion; secularism is the belief that this movement is desirable.

3.22 False. He believes it gives an even more complicated and improbable 'solution' to the question it seeks to answer.

3.23 Natural selection.

3.24 No. It is a nasty by-product of some traits that do give us survival value (the tendency to obey elders and attribute meaning and purpose to our environment).

3.25 The 'persistence of belief in God, when there is supposedly no God in which to believe'.

3.26 NOMA stands for 'non-overlapping magisteria', the idea that science and religion are two separate areas; and POMA for 'partially overlapping magisteria', the McGraths' view that science and religion can interpenetrate each other in helpful ways.

3.27 Any one of these: the prophetic critique of religion, the inclusive ministry of Jesus, the capacity of religion to transcend and transform human conflicts, the danger of an absence of religion, the fact that religion is more than belief, violence from movements where atheism is prominent, and the fact that violent tendencies are explained through a variety of factors, not merely religion.

3.28 Pluralism.

3.29 Acts 17, when Paul is preaching to the Greeks about their 'unknown God'.

3.30 *Nostra Aetate* and *Lumen Gentium*.

3.31 A Copernican revolution.

3.32 A noumenon is a thing in itself, apart from human experience; a phenomenon is our experience of things, which come through our senses and cultural interpretations.

3.33 The sun's light being refracted by the earth's atmosphere and the blind men and the elephant.

3.34 Christian universalism.

Theme 4: DEF

4.1 Jesus' prayer in John 17: 20–22.

4.2 Protestant (the Roman Catholics and the Orthodox were not invited).

4.3 Faith and Order AND Life and Work.

4.4 Any one of these: (i) the positive way non-Catholic Christians are referred to, (ii) the recognition that forms of Christian expression exist outside of the Roman Catholic Church, (iii) the understanding that Church divisions have involved both Roman Catholics and non-Roman Catholics, or (iv) a recognition that the Church of Christ is more than the present form of the Roman Catholic Church.

4.5 Some in the Orthodox Churches and the Pentecostal/ Evangelical Churches.

4.6 True.

4.7 Speaking in tongues.

4.8 Protestant: David Bennett sharing his experience with his Episcopal congregation in Califorina, 1960. Catholic: The 1967 weekend retreat between staff and students at Duquesne University.

4.9 The Toronto Blessing, Restorationism or Spring Harvest.

4.10 Speaking in tongues, singing in tongues, prophecy, healing, laying on of hands, contemporary music, dancing, raising hands in the air during singing, spontaneous prayers, ecstatic experiences such as falling over and 'holy laughter'.

4.11 The healing may have just happened naturally, the illness claimed to have been healed may have never existed (just a medical hypothesis rather than a fact), there have been rare cases of spontaneous healing, some illnesses have erratic symptoms, some follow-up investigations reveal that those 'healed' are worse off, no scientifically conducted study has verified reports of healing.

4.12 Suffering.

4.13 Socialism, Marxism.

4.14 Liberation.

4.15 (i) His association with the zealots, criticism of religious leaders and death at the hands of the political establishment. (ii)The helpless baby Jesus in Mary's lap, the suffering and passive Jesus on the cross and the monarchical or kingly Jesus standing outside of the world.

4.16 Material poverty.

4.17 The link of these communities to the wider Church through the priests who come to administer sacraments and offer guidance.

4.18 Atheism, the oppression of human freedom seen in the soviet regime, and not turning first to non-violent means of engagement.

4.19 False.

Glossary

Accommodation: to adapt, fit, suit or adjust (as in God accommodating herself/himself to speak to humans)

Androcentrism: focused or centred on men; placing of the male sex or gender associations at the centre of history and culture

Androgynous: having a combination of both female and male characteristics

Anglican communion: a worldwide association of episcopal (having a bishop) churches

Anonymous Christian: Karl Rahner's description of a person who attains salvation outside of knowing and accepting Christ and the Church

Anthropic principle: the universe must contain the properties that allow the observer to exist

Apocalypticism: belief in the sudden and cataclysmic coming of God to rule the world in justice

Apocrypha: from the Greek word meaning, 'hidden', applied positively to books that were thought of as containing hidden wisdom, or negatively to books of unknown origin and considered to be of questionable value

Apocryphal Gospels: writings about Jesus not accepted by the Church; some exist as complete documents, others as fragments or as quotations in early Christian writings

Apostolic Fathers: Christian theologians of the first two centuries CE who were taught by the twelve Apostles, or at least were significantly influenced by their writings

Archbishop of Canterbury: the senior bishop and principal leader of the Church of England; also the symbolic head of the worldwide Anglican Communion

ARCIC: The acronym for the Anglican Roman Catholic International Committee established in 1967

Ascetic: one who lives a sparse and disciplined lifestyle

Asceticism: discipline or training, such as avoiding various indulgences for religious reasons

Attestation: a piece of evidence presented in support of a claim

Baptism, Eucharist & Ministry: a key ecumenical document prepared by the Faith and Order Commission of the World Council of Churches

Base communities: small, self-governing religious groups mentioned by Latin American liberation theologians

Base ecclesial communities: small Christian communities who meet without a priest for worship, study and support

Bibliolatry: from 'idolatry': the worship of the Bible instead of God; associated with a literalistic approach

Bishop: a rank above a pastor who presides at ordinations and oversees the work of pastors/priests and congregations

Bourgeoisie: property owners who own most of society's wealth and means of production

Brokers: those who buy or sell goods on behalf of others

Canon within the canon: the idea that within the canon there are central ideas or themes that strongly influenced the basis on which writings were chosen

Canon: 'measuring rod', 'rule' or 'standard'

Capitalism: an economic and political system of private or corporate ownership of goods rather than state ownership

Caste system: usually associated with Hindu culture but also referring to a rigid social hierarchy based on hereditary status

Catholicity: the quality of being catholic, having a universal doctrine

Chalcedonian creed: the creed adopted at Chalcedon in 451 CE that declared Jesus to have had two natures

Charismatic: from the Greek word *charismata*, 'gifts of grace'; special qualities Christians believe they receive through the Holy Spirit

Charismatic churches: individual churches that may differ from their denomination in that they emphasise ecstatic religious experiences and miracles of healing

Charismatic Movement: the experience of gifts of the Spirit in churches other than Pentecostal denominations from the 1960s to today

Christocentric: Christ as the centre of the experience of salvation/liberation

Christolatry: from 'idolatry': a term used by some feminist theologians to refer to the worship of the 'Son' of God according to patriarchal categories rather than to a God who is beyond gender and sex

Church Fathers: ancient Christian theologians whose writings have been influential for Christians

Church of England: a church body that is a part of the Anglican communion and is the state (or 'established') church in England

Clericalism: a focus on increasing the power and influence of the clergy or Church hierarchy

Communism: an economic and political system which replaces private property and a free market with public ownership and communal control of goods

Congregation: an assembly of people for worship, usually in a church building

Conversion: a gradual or sudden change in one's religion or beliefs

Covenant: an agreement between two or more parties based on obedience and involving promises

Critical realism: the idea that there are real objects beyond ourselves but that we know these objects through our own point of view or standpoint which biases our experience of them

Cynicism: a school of Greek philosophers who rejected social convention to live a simple life more in tune with nature and reason

Deacon: an ordained minister ranking below a pastor/priest/presbyter

Degree Christology: Hick's phrase for seeing Jesus as a human being with a high degree of God consciousness rather than a divine being having two natures

Denomination: an autonomous religious organisation composed of many congregations

Desert Fathers: early Christian hermits who lived an ascetic life in the Egyptian desert

Deutero-canonical: from a secondary canon, later than the first, but of equal authority

Diakonia: the Greek word for service; in the WCC it is used in the context of activities aimed at justice and peace for the poor and oppressed

Diatessaron: a harmony of the four Gospels written in the 2nd century, popular in some Syrian churches for up to two centuries

Didache: an ancient Christian book of instruction (*didache* is Greek for 'teaching'), from the first century CE; some early versions of the New Testament were included this book

Ecclesio-centric: the Church as the centre of the experience of salvation/liberation

Ecclesio-centrism: literally, 'centred on the Church'

Ecumenical: the entire, inhabited world, from the Greek term *oikoumene*. Used to describe efforts at Christian unity

Ecumenical Formation: giving shape to ecumenical themes for individuals and churches through study, reflection and participation

Edinburgh World Missionary Conference: the 1910 conference of mostly Anglo-American Protestant missionaries to promote unity in mission work

Enlightenment: a European intellectual movement emphasising reason over both religious revelation and superstition as the basis of knowledge

Eschatology: the study of the end things; in biblical theology this encompasses the soul, death, resurrection, the final judgement, immortality, heaven, and hell

Evangelicals: Christians from across many denominations who emphasise the importance of conversion and personal faith; evangelicals have a high regard for the Bible and can believe that faith should influence public life

Evangelise: from the Greek term for 'good news', to share the Christian message with the hope of bringing about conversions

Exclusivism: the view that one's own religion is the only way to salvation/liberation

Extra ecclesiam nulla salus: Latin for 'outside the Church, no salvation'

Faith school: a school that is associated with a religious tradition, many of these schools are state funded, though many independent schools also have an association with religion

Fasting: abstaining from food, drink or other activities for religious reasons

Fundamentalism: the movement from the late 19th/early 20th century dedicated to a literal approach to biblical doctrines

Gnostic: relating to an ancient spiritual movement focussed on attaining spiritual knowledge

Gnosticism: from the Greek for 'having knowledge'; a movement which taught that we are trapped in an evil, material world. We must find special knowledge in order to be redeemed

God hypothesis: Dawkins' phrase to describe the claim that there is an interventionist God in the universe; this should be treated like any other scientific hypothesis

Gospel of Thomas: a book of 114 sayings of Jesus in the 4th century CE Gnostic library discovered near Nag Hammadi, Egypt in 1945

Inclusivism: the view that one's religion is the 'final' way to salvation/liberation; other religions may have partial or incomplete truth

Independent churches: a congregation that does not belong to a denomination

Intelligent Design (ID): the view of some contemporary creationists that biological forms of life are irreducibly complex and so therefore point to a designer

International Missionary Conference: A group founded in 1921 to carry on the work of the Edinburgh Missionary Conference; merged with the WCC in 1961

Intertestamental literature: works written between the date of the final book of the Hebrew Bible and the beginning of the New Testament

Itinerant: on the move, travelling from place to place

Jewish apocalypticism: belief in the sudden and cataclysmic coming of God to rule the world in justice

Kenosis: from the Greek for 'empty', the emptying or giving up by Christ of some of his divine attributes at the incarnation (from Philippians 2:7)

Kerygma: a proclamation or declaration of an event

Koinonia: fellowship or communion between Christians and God or Christians and one another

Lawful religion: a religion that contains God's grace. Rahner believed that all religions could be lawful, though to different degrees

Liberalism: in politics, the focus on the protection and freedom of the individual

Liberation theology: a movement that developed by Roman Catholic thinkers and activists in Latin America in the 1960s viewed freedom from social oppression as a key area of Christian concern

Life and Work Movement: A group founded in 1925, dedicated to the promotion of social responsibility amongst Christians

Liturgical: relating to formal worship prescribed by a church body; for example, the Book of Common Prayer contains liturgies

Manichaeism: a religious movement that viewed the world as a conflict between good and evil, with the soul's release found through asceticism

Marxism: the political and economic theories of Karl Marx and Friedrich Engels that developed into communism and aimed at a classless society

Meme: a term coined by Richard Dawkins meaning an element of culture that is passed from one person to another by imitation or other non-genetic means

Messiah: (literally, 'anointed one') a figure who is expected to unite the Jews and save them from their oppressors, ushering in an era of peace

Minister: usually means an ordained Christian, though the term simply means 'servant' and can be applied to all Christians

Modern: a loose concept to differentiate scientific and technical progress from ancient and more traditional periods

Monolithic: literally, 'a single stone', used to refer to something that is simple rather than complex

Montanism: an early Christian movement which believed in the imminent end of the world, asceticism and continuing revelation of God in prophecy

Multiverse: the hypothesis that there are multitudes of universes of which ours is only one

Muratorian Canon: perhaps the oldest known list of books of the New Testament, possibly dating to about 170 CE

Myth: a story containing divine beings or supernatural themes used to understand natural events, or social and political concerns

Naïve realism: the belief that one can have direct knowledge of reality through sense experience

Natural selection: the process that results in the survival of organisms best suited to their environment; their traits are passed on to subsequent generations

Non-overlapping magisteria (NOMA): the view advocated by Stephen Jay Gould that science and religion are two different areas of inquiry

Noumenon: a thing in itself, as distinct from our senses

Ordination: the ritual of recognising Church leaders through the laying on of hands, prayer and the invocation of the Spirit of God

Orthodoxy: literally, 'right thinking'; authorised theory or doctrine

Orthopraxis: literally, 'right practice'; correct ethical conduct

Patriarchal: usually refers to male control over society or religion

Pentecostal churches: independent churches and denominations that emphasise the working of the Spirit in the Church, especially through prophesy, speaking in tongues, healing and exorcism

Pentecostalism: a worldwide Christian movement composed of many denominations and independent churches that focus on the experience of the worshipper and the miraculous gifts of the Spirit of God

Phenomenalism: the view that what we think are material objects are really only our perceptions of sense data

Phenomenon: a thing as we perceive it through our senses and context

Piety: dutiful and devout reverence to God

Plenary verbal inspiration: the belief that the words of the Bible were given directly by God to the human authors and therefore the Bible is fully (plenary) inspired

Pluralism: the view that all religions, in different ways, reflect divine truth, or Ultimate Reality

Polemic: an aggressive verbal or written attack, from the Greek for 'warlike' or 'hostile'

Positivism: knowledge is only positively recognised when it is based on sense perception, not religion or metaphysics

Postmodernism: a range of movements in the late 20th century marked by scepticism and a suspicion of reason

Praxis: practice, as distinguished from theory

Preferential option for the poor: the choice to give preference to the well-being of the poorest in society

Presbyter: from the Greek word for 'elder'; usually a minister between a deacon and a bishop in rank

Privatisation: the movement from public to private; in terms of religion, belief and practice becoming a matter of inner disposition rather than outer practice

Proletariat: the working class who own little or no property

Prophecy: direct speech from God

Prosperity gospel: the teaching that faith and giving to the Church will bring health and financial blessings

Pseudepigrapha: literally, 'false writings', books written by unknown authors who claimed to be from a well-known figure in order to gain a readership

Q: from the German *Quelle* (source), the name given to the sayings in common between Matthew and Luke which some scholars believe was a source these Gospel writers used

Quakers: 17th-century movement promoting the belief in one's direct apprehension of God without the need for clergy, creeds or other ecclesiastical forms

Realised eschatology: the idea that the quality of life normally associated with a relationship with God after death can be experienced now

Redemption: to be saved from sin, or to regain something through an exchange of money or goods

Restorationism: an anti-denominational Christian movement in Britain emphasising the gifts of the Spirit and seeking to 'restore' the beliefs and practices of the early church

Reverse mission: countries that once sent missionaries become themselves the target for missionary work from the countries they once evangelised

Romanticism: 18th to 19th-century intellectual and artistic movement focused on emotion and the imagination; critical of the rationalism of the enlightenment

Samaritans: a Jewish group not considered orthodox by most Jews of Jesus' time

Scientism: belief in the universal applicability of scientific knowledge and techniques

Secular: not connected to the Church or religion

Secularisation: the process of society moving away from religion; this can refer to movement from official/public forms such as rituals and ceremonies and/or private forms such as attitudes, beliefs and values

Secularisation thesis: the belief that as societies modernise, religion will decline

Secularism: the belief that secularisation is a benefit to society

Self-flagellation: striking oneself with a whip

Septuagint: the Greek translation of the Hebrew Bible in the 3rd–2nd centuries BCE, also referred to as the LXX in reference to a legend of 70 Jewish scholars translating the Torah

Sexism: prejudice, discrimination or stereotyping based on sex or gender

Shakers: 18th-century Protestant Christian movement dedicated to celibacy and belief in the imminent return of God; called 'Shakers' because of their ecstatic movement in worship

Shepherd of Hermas: an early Christian book containing visions and parables dated from the 1st–2nd centuries CE; some early versions of the New Testament included this book

Socialism: any economic or political theory that advances collective ownership of production, distribution and exchange of goods

Spring Harvest: an organisation which hosts non-denominational charismatic festivals across Britain

Stewardship: management, administration

Suffragettes: from the Latin term for 'vote'; women who fought for the right of women to vote in the late 19th to 20th centuries

The Faith and Order Movement: A group founded in 1927 dedicated to examination of doctrinal issues separating churches. Came together with Life and Work in 1948 to form the World Council of Churches

The Pastoral Epistles: the New Testament letters (I and II Timothy and Titus) written to Christian ministers on the theme of guiding the Church

Theocentric: God as the centre of the experience of salvation/liberation

Theopneustos: the Greek term used in II Tim. 3:16 meaning 'God-breathed'

Tithe: the giving of 10% of one's produce or earnings in support of a religious organisation

TNK: (pronounced Tanak) – an acronym used by Jewish believers to refer to the Hebrew Bible: **T**orah (first 5 books of the Law), **N**evi'im (the prophets), **K**ethuvim (the writings)

Tongues: from the Greek term glossalia (gloss = speak, laleo = tongue or language); using a language unknown to the speaker. In the Bible this can be either a foreign language or a special, heavenly language

Toronto Blessing: an especially ecstatic set of experiences at a Vineyard church near the Toronto airport that has attracted worldwide attention from the 1990s to the present day

Ultimate Reality: Hick's term to describe the object of religious belief for the world's religions

Unitatis Redintegratio: A Vatican II Document that signalled a new attitude to ecumenical relations

Vatican II: the council of Roman Catholic leaders that met in 1962–1965 to consider the relationship between the Church and the modern world

Vineyard churches: an association of over 1500 charismatic churches led by John Wimber in the 1980s and 1990s

Worldview: the way in which a culture looks at the world; this involves stories, symbols and answers to key questions about existence

Xenolalia: a type of speaking in tongues in which the speaker uses a foreign language that they have not consciously learned

Zealots: a militant Jewish sect opposing the Roman domination of Palestine in the 1st century CE

Index